W9-CCJ-504

THE GOLDEN HAND

Das Herz ist mir beklemmt, und sehnlich
   Gedenke ich der alten Zeit.
Die Welt war damals noch so wöhnlich,
   Und ruhig lebten hin die Leut':
Und jetzt ist Alles wie verschoben,
   Es gibt ein Drängen, eine Not;
Gestorben ist der Herrgott oben,
   Und unten ist der Teufel tot.

—Heinrich Heine

THE GOLDEN HAND

by Edith Simon

G. P. Putnam's Sons

New York

COPYRIGHT, 1952, BY EDITH SIMON

*All rights reserved. This book, or parts thereof, must
not be reproduced in any form without permission.*

Library of Congress Catalog Card Number: 52-5272

Manufactured in the United States of America

TO JOAN

Contents

Part One
Edwin Widowson
(1347-1348)

THE FINDING

It WAS NIGHT in the great cathedral, the spare candles like glowworms in a spectral forest. The stranger hesitated tardily; but the two whom at first he had not seen were already helping each other rise from their knees. They were two old, old men, common lay folk by their dress. Slowly they came toward him, hand in hand. They were quite willing to stay and talk.

You cannot sleep, Pilgrim?

We? We were praying for the first founders of St. Hand's. No, not Bishop Jerome de Rocquefeuilles. In the beginning none had heard of him—just as you will not have heard tell of Edwin Widowson and others besides. Ay, we will tell you. The night is young, the night is long. But you must humor our great age in its own fashion of remembering.

The beginning was that Edwin must have Jeanne Oxerd for his wife. To you this may sound strange; to us it seems far stranger to think that, at the time of which we are speaking, where now rears the Hand of Anglemere, there was nothing but naked wasteland.

It was the nature of the Widowsons to be their own worst enemies—which perhaps in part accounted for it that everyone else was their friend. (For folk that are their own best friends often have no other, we have marked.) But only in part: they were great craftsmen, and loved as such.

All the Widowsons were woodworkers, from the time of their forebear Richard, nicknamed Duckleg, who made the great chest that took four men to move it and stood in the old parish church. Richard's two

sons, Edwin and Geoffrey, built the tithe barn which stands to this day
near the south bank of the River Tew. Soon after it was finished, with
clusters of hops and vine finely carved over the lintel, Geoffrey was
slain saving the Cinqmort lord from the bear in the forest. Two of his
sons grew up to manhood. The eldest, another Richard, was killed by a
felled tree falling too soon. The story is still told in Anglemere, how
Richard lay pinned on his broken back and reproved his brother who
in vindictive grief hacked at the tree. Richard said not to spoil a good
piece of timber, and that he would rather have got his death of a tree
than of anything else in the world. The brother lived to die in his bed;
and all his sons likewise wrought in wood: Thomas, Geoffrey, Richard,
Alfred, and Edwin—our Edwin.

They were a brown tribe, brown of hair, skin, and eye. Edwin was
small and thin, as the last-born out of ten or twelve children is apt to
be, and he was the most gifted of them all. Before Jeanne's time, the
person he loved best in all the world was his brother Alfred, nearest
him in birth; the eldest, Thomas, was old enough to have been his
father, and after their parents' death became stepfather to Edwin in
more sense than one.

All the brothers, with four wives and innumerable children, lived
together in one homestead belonging to church land. Great was Widowson anxiety over each new son born among them, before it could be
ascertained whether he had inherited their hand. They recognized no
other cause for anxiety—even to the neglect of their welfare.

They need not have been so poor. They had neither heart nor patience
for any work save woodwrithy; their field strips, wool, and small beer
were a byword; and they were content to dissipate their earnings in paying over to the church steward any amount the parish priest saw fit to
demand against releasing them from legal labor services. Though the
Widowson wives had spools carved to resemble fishes, and lifelike birds
topping their spindles, there was but one church-going gown between
the four of them. They saved rushes and straw, the floor being covered
deep in wood shavings; they did not miss flesh meat, for beef and oats
tasted alike with the all-pervading smell of resin. Yet was there more
than one woman desirous of joining Edwin the woodworkers' homestead on the southern Tew bank.

He was offered Janet Fowler, a childless widow with goods and gear
of her own, and youth and comeliness besides; and as he could not refuse her without giving a good reason, his dealings with Jeanne were
first revealed.

Jeanne belonged to the manor and was byre maid at Lord Gervase Cinqmort's new barn across the river. She was not fifteen years old, a notable worker, and fair after the manner of images, although no one else had as yet marked that. For her this was lucky, since thus her loveliness had eluded the kite's eyes of Hugh—who had no taste for pregnant women: Edwin got her with child forthwith.

It was little wonder that a craftsman was the first to discern in her what thereupon everybody learned to see. God had given her features such as the image makers loved to impart to statues, and which fine ladies attain with almost equal labor and certainly a deal more pain. She had a very high, domed forehead and arched eyebrows so thin they were almost invisible; large eyes of a clear gray, shaded by long, foldless lids with thick black lashes; and a small, pursed-looking mouth. She was no taller than Edwin, and prettily made, with long neck and hands and small, narrow feet, yet strong, and ample of hips.

Little wonder, also, that they kept their understanding secret as long as they might. They could not but know what all Bedesford town was bound to think of it. Whomsoever he wed, Edwin was obliged to pay his marriage fine to the parish priest; whosoever wed Jeanne must pay the lord the same: so if they two were to come together, the fine would be doubled. In addition, since he was to take her away from the Cinqmort demesne and into church lands, he must recompense my lord against the loss of her body and its future brood.

At any time such proceedings would have been deemed rash; at that particular time it was worse than folly.

The last few years had been lean for the whole of Anglemere, and so much the leaner for such careless husbandmen as were the Widowsons, who moreover had lost in quick succession three providers. First Richard had died, then Geoffrey, and then Alfred, leaving Thomas and Edwin to furnish the necessities of life for their sisters-in-law, nephews, and nieces, and to pay the death fines. They were behindhand in their payments. Edwin had no right to think of marriage for years to come, unless it were with such a one as Janet Fowler.

Lord Gervase was a kind master (how he could have begotten that fiend in human shape, Hugh, we never ceased to marvel at), but much recent ill fortune had placed him, too, in grave straits. Jeanne being with child already, he would have been within his rights to ask double. Yet, because it was Edwin, he agreed at last to set a time of grace, during which Jeanne's suitor might try and bring together her price.

And now Thomas Widowson threw away his life—we could not call it otherwise, though he did do it for the good of us all, as he saw it. Ever since a big forest fire in the Easterwoods, there had been no keeping the fallow deer out of Bedesford's fields and orchards. Nothing could induce Lord Gervase to relax the law, and so in grievous necessity all and sundry had taken to poaching. Having been elected hayward for that year, Thomas Widowson took it upon himself to kill a hart and carry the carcass straight up to Cinqmort Manor, putting the townsfolk's plight by way of sole defense. It did not save him. He died hung in chains from a tree in the Bad Place by the Marsh, with both his craftsman's hands cut off and tied round his neck.

Still Edwin would not hear of giving up Jeanne. From the parish priest downward (and my lord, who said it publicly that he would not hold Thomas' end against Edwin) everyone reasoned with him, in vain. Only one man commended and upheld him. This was one of the Franciscan friars, named Laurentius, who had shown Edwin great kindness ever since he first came into the parish, when Edwin was only a lad. He was Edwin's confessor; many of us used to go to the friars for that; our priest had too much farming work on his hands to forbid it outright.

The Little Gray Brethren had not always been so plentiful in Bedesford. Now and again a pair of them would pass through, to and from Ovisham harbor, where they had a stone monastery just outside the town. But some winters before the fall of Calais in France, the pirates from the Isle of Gannets made a raid on Ovisham strand, despoiling and wrecking the Gray Friars' House. The brethren had long wished to have a house in Bedesford, being the chief town of Anglemere. So they came, though, for years they had no more settled abode amongst us than the kilns and barns of the pious and a few flimsy huts at the edge of the common. For years Lord Gervase held out against their petitions to lease them a building site. But at length, early in that same year 1348, he yielded, and in addition arranged to place labor at their disposal against a large sum of ready money.

So one night, shortly before the clod-breaking time, Martin Bailiff went the rounds of the townsfolk, giving us notice to assemble at the Waste the following morning and burn off the scrub under the friars' direction.

Would that we commanded some blameless magic to make you see it all as it was then. Pavement and tiles would vanish from under your feet, to be replaced by heather, broom, and reed. Across low hills like bolsters, you would have a view of the town and a glimmering of Tew with a piece of Bede's New Bridge, and a haze of fields and meadows beyond. No, you cannot see any of it nowadays for houses. Then the Wode, which is a tributary of the Tew, meeting it north of the manor park, did not bring the foot of Cloudsway Ridge as it does today, flowing where the churchyard is, and the suburb of Lemington with its tileries.

The friars were at the Waste before us, and so, to everyone's surprise, was Jacob Tewsing, a free man and Bedesford's foremost building master, sprung from a long line of Friggsby masons, and veteran engineer of the French war.

"Have they called you in, Jacob?" We crowded around as soon as he came away from the friars. "What sort of building have they in mind? Tell us all you know."

Jacob snorted—we can hear him now. "Don't ask me," he says, says Jacob, "they know better than I in everything. The Lord God knows I do not stint reverence to Prior Haakon, but in this matter he is bearing himself as a fool. He has never even seen building done with rubble—where he comes from, they just stack unstripped logs, whether it be church or dwelling they want to make, so I have heard. See you the great book he has under his arms? It was saved from the flames at Ovisham, and I will grant it a marvelous treasure. In it are drawings and notes of buildings, made by wandering brothers of the past all over the world. But all of it, as far as I could see, is freestone work, and it would seem the good Prior wants to use all the patterns at once! Yet they talk of having but the simplest hospital for the time being."

We made murmur that, after all, Brother Laurentius used to work freestone in his youth, wandering in the southern lands beyond the sea; and had not the brothers helped build Jerusalem Yard at Ovisham for the Knights of St. Lazarus?

"Ay, and none could blame me were I to leave them to their own devices! But—but—I have not the heart, God help me. They are so blithe and jubilant. They see advantages in every disadvantage: what matter if the Wode bogs foul both earth and air, for cannot timber and stone be floated hither most usefully upon the river's bank? What matter if the ground is all hard and unwieldy, caked through and through with stones, for it will yield up more than enough rubble and flint for our needs. Listening to them, one does not know whether to laugh or cry."

Fortunately, there could be no disagreement as to the general plan of the hospital: the usual square of buildings round an inner court. It was a long way to the site for most of us, and Plow Monday was approaching; delay was counter to the interests of all concerned. Cutting the outline trenches could be put in hand before anything further was settled. Edwin was there with spade and mattock, stamping blue-mottled bare legs and kneading his arms, like the rest of us.

"Is the world coming to an end, Edwin, that the priest sends you to aid the friars?"

"Nay, I have come of my own accord," Edwin laughed a little shamefacedly. "I am off to the coast tomorrow. It is like to be a month before I am back. And in friendship I want to give them a hand at the start."

"It will be on carriage service for the parson that you're going?"

"Ay, as far as Ovisham and Ellasea. Have any of you a message for Dick Toolmaker? I shall go round by the Marsh first to place the friars' orders."

"You cannot like going away at this of all times."

"No. Yet I am not sorry, either. I have other, pleasant errands. The brethren still have some timber standing where they used to live, and I am to see the woodward of Ovisham for them and choose the trees. And then at Ellasea I am to see over John Trefeller's new ship that he is having built, and take measurements in the hold for Juliana's bed shutters."

"Is she still set on going with him? Perhaps it is not true that she is with child?"

"It is true enough—I hope," Edwin said, oddly. "Doubtless she thinks if not this year, she can fare with John the next. Else," he laughed again, "what would become of my commission?"

By then the friars had finished pacing out the square, and every man had to take his place, waiting only the benediction to begin digging. Soon singing, the thud of metal into earth, and its sharp clang against rock crumbs filled the cold, mist-gray air.

Nowhere about the Waste was the ground absolutely level, knobs and mounds alternating with abrupt hollows. Edwin, the only one to be here of his own free will, was the lustiest worker, and had himself chosen a stretch of trench arduously humped across a hillock.

Suddenly a cry was heard, and the men nearest him threw aside their tools and ran up to where Edwin struggled, with one leg out of sight below ground. Before they could drag him clear, the surrounding soil collapsed. Sneezing and spitting earth, he floundered, seeking purchase, but stopped with a gasp of pain.

"There is something down here, I know not what, but it has ripped my arm. Clear away cautiously, friends—"

The rest of us and all the friars had meanwhile collected round him, with shouts of advice, wonder, and encouragement.

The first thing unearthed, to one side of Edwin, was a portion of masonry, strange and thus alarming: clean white it was, and smooth as lard, with joins so fine they might have been mere hairs stretched taut across unbroken surface. We recoiled and appealed to the friars: "—unnatural—witchery—not a trace of dirt or lichen—," and gladly made way for Brother Laurentius and the Prior.

"See, it does not vanish under the sign of the cross," Brother Laurentius said cheerfully. "I have come across the like of this before, if not in English lands. Shore it up, then, good people, that it may not crush Edwin. Let us see what else there may be."

At last Edwin was helped out of the hole. Except for a long gash up his right forearm he was unhurt.

You know what we found. First of all, there emerged the fallen column (now prone at the foot of the shrine, below), of the same outlandish, unsullied stone, and then the fragment of picture pavement which it had protected from disintegration, and which you have doubtless made sure of viewing through the grille. Only, it cannot possibly strike you as marvelously as it did us that day with the suddenness of its perfect appearance: depicting a knight (as we then thought) on horseback, and the arm of a second figure, holding out a kind of cup.

And then—and then was uncovered that which you will never see. Edwin saw its first gleam and dived forward to pluck it whole from its black hiding place, and with a shout he raised it high for all to behold: the hand like a man's, but fashioned of brightest gold, life sized. It terminated behind a fold of drapery at the wrist, as if broken off, with jagged edges, one of which bore traces of Edwin's blood. Yet most of them were blunted by globules, as of melting congealed. It was the fairest, gladdest sight, and, although many a man crossed himself and whispered a prayer, not one was afraid this time.

CHAPTER 2

THE COFFER

ON HIS WAY to collect the packages and letters the priest's wife had ready for him, Edwin called at his home, next door to the churchyard and church farm. If he made haste he might be able to slip across to Lord Gervase's bawn later and take a second farewell of Jeanne, perchance with good news, from Trefeller Court, where he had been bidden to spend the night.

Trefeller Court, like the bawn, stood on the opposite side of the Tew; one of the largest and finest buildings in the town, and certainly the busiest. At this time of year they were in the midst of the preparations for John Trefeller's annual quest after wool through Anglemere and Danesborough. Cold, dank, mud-colored day though it was, both the big yards, front and back, resounded with people and employment. At Edwin's arrival, everyone left what he was doing. John himself and his steward Arthur Tewsing came running out of the countinghouse. Here they had only had the barest morsel of the tidings and demanded a full feast of Edwin. The mistress had to send maid after maid before Edwin was allowed to enter the hall. All who could pressed in behind.

"Set down your pack by the door, Edwin, and come and sit right close to me," Juliana Trefeller's wagon-wheel voice shrilled. "Put your feet up on the hearth bank. Do not stand there gaping, you women. Give Edwin to eat and drink. Doubtless you have already had all his story out of him before me. Mind you leave out nothing now you tell it to me, Edwin."

This proved no easy task, for the young wife herself kept on breaking into Edwin's narrative, not only to put additional questions, but finding fault with the friars' every arrangement, suggesting improvements, and offering advice. Neither did she wait to hear all about the find before expressing her views concerning it, so that the housefolk could scarce contain their impatience.

"If I were Prior Haakon, I should not touch it," she said with decision, "I should have it all covered up again and dig somewhere else. If I were you, Edwin, I should go to the parish priest with that wound—it being your right arm, too. It would not be the first time that the Evil One has baited his trap with seeming treasure. Burning it would be better than burying it again, now that I come to think of it. For, as it was found on my father's land, I have no doubt the treasure must be accounted his. And placed as he is, what with Hugh's spendthrift ways and the lawsuit, Father may well be tempted to make use of it."

There was nobody liked the sound of that, excepting John Trefeller, who stood leaning with crossed arms on the back of his wife's big foreign chair, shaking with suppressed laughter at her every utterance. A full year after their marriage, folk still wondered at it.

Juliana was my lord's youngest daughter, and she was a hunchback. Her body was slight as a child's, yet with a face far older than her sixteen years, pallid of hue as watered milk. There was an ancient curse upon the Cinqmort race, which blighted at least one of their daughters in every generation. Thus, one of Lord Gervase's sisters had been brought to bed in her father's house of a bastard; another ailed from birth and lingered into feeble, virgin middle age; a third had been ejected from Thirchester nunnery—what it was she had done no one knew, but some of us thought she and none other was our hermit woman, immured in a tiny stone box built against the wall of the parish church.

Of Lord Gervase's daughters two were cursed: this youngest, and the eldest, Isabella, who was thrice widowed in the space of three years, after which no fourth man dared marry her. Juliana had been destined for Thirchester from infancy, but before she reached the right age, her sister Anne found herself called to the religious life. So it was Anne Addertongue who went away to be a nun, dowered as became her birth. There was no money left for Juliana. No one in his senses expected her to be married—least of all to the greatest wool merchant in Anglemere. Before that Juliana had been meek; and now it was said that Sister Philippa, that had been Anne Addertongue, was by God's mercy turned into the gentlest of ladies.

"What is that you keep holding on your lap there, Edwin, wrapped in sacking?" Julia suddenly broke off to ask.

"This?" Edwin shifted slightly in his seat before answering. "Would you like to see it, Juliana?" he said, flushing. "Well—to tell the truth, I brought it along on purpose to show you and John. Look. It is a coffer, such as women use to store baby clothes in."

All the company exclaimed and craned forward as he undid the wrappings. The deformed little mistress in her voluminous headdress jumped up and down among the cushions. "I want to see. Here, let me look. He brought it for me to see! Master John, make room. I can see nothing for your fat shadow. Ah! Oh, Edwin!"

The coffer lid was divided into four squares, each depicting one season of the year. The first showed a little husbandman harnessed to his plow, with crows flying behind and hills and bare boughs bordering a fleecy sky. In the second the man and his wife were sowing the seed, with distant sheep, instead of clouds, clinging to the hilltops. The third was full of harvest, alive with scythes and sickles, and sheaves of great-eared corn; and the fourth contained a merry threshers' crew. Light and shadow, cavity and upward rounding were so sweetly balanced, liveliness and unlifelike repose of aspect so neatly blended—even Edwin had never achieved the like before.

"This is how it is, John and Juliana," Edwin said, as soon as he could make himself heard. "You said you could not pay me in advance for the bed panels since I might not live to finish them, and I see the reason of that. But now there is this coffer, more than a year's work. I thought I would offer it you for nothing—provided you pay me for the panels as soon as I come back from Ellasea. So even if anything were to happen to me before the panels are done, you would still have this coffer, which is worth at least as much."

"It is fit for the king's own hall," cried the steward.

"No wonder John incurred grave loss last year when you went bartering for him at Thirchester Fair, Arthur Tewsing!" Juliana cried. "But Arthur is right, Edwin: that coffer is too fine by far for a humble hall like ours. Besides, how can you say its value equals that of two great heavy shutters?"

More than one voice answered her impulsively: "—a deal more difficult to make, Mistress!"

"It has no lock," Juliana returned, at the same moment as her husband said, "The bargain is done, Edwin."

The mistress rallied quickly, "Now you are not to think you got the better of John, Edwin. It is only to help you make good your sin and Jeanne's that we are willing to take your coffer on these unheard-of terms, you must remember—"

John was laughing so hard he could only nod when Arthur asked him whether he might now take Edwin to look at a girder beam in the warehouse which had shrunk out of position, before it was too dark to see.

"If anyone ought to have the gold hand, it is you, Edwin," Arthur said angrily, once they were in the yard. "Finding is keeping—and you have paid good blood for it. The Cinqmorts lay no claim to the rusted bits of spear and ax and arrow we are forever finding in the ground about the Waste—why, then, should it be different when the find is gold? And if it is a question of who owns the land—why, all of it belonged to us, the Tewsings, long ages before the first Rogue Cinqmort came over along with the rest of the thieves from Normandy."

"I know," Edwin said, and indeed we were all of us well used to hearing the Tewsings' boast and grievance.

In the warehouse, he declined the offer of a ladder and a light, saying, as he swung himself aloft among the thickening brown shadows of the roof, "It is more a matter of touch and smell than of sight." Below, Arthur could see him but dimly and piecemeal through the gaps between shrouded hams and yellow-glistening flitches of beef and mutton, and salt-crusted codfish threaded by their gaping jaws on lines of pack-thread, and bundles of flax, and ropes hanging dense and straight. Edwin crept out of sight along the rafters, his progress marked by tapping.

"Edwin!" Arthur called softly.

"Yes?" Edwin's voice came flat and muted. "I should say you can save more than a third of it, with careful patching. I will just make sure once more." A little shower of dry dust fell into Arthur's upturned face.

"There is something I would ask you, Edwin. You are the head of your family now. I have been widowed these five years. I am thinking of Martha, your sister-in-law that was Alfred's wife, God rest him."

"Ay, I thought her sorrow had somewhat abated, lately," Edwin laughed a little. "And I wondered, my Arthur, what made you so very anxious for my rights to the treasure—nay, you will not take a little joke amiss? If so be you two are agreed, I can see nothing against it. You will be a good stepfather to Alfred's children."

"That I will, Edwin! I know you loved Alfred best of all your brothers."

"Yet now that they are all gone, it is Thomas I miss and mourn the most," Edwin said out of his invisibility. "Thomas, that stepped into my father's shoes, teaching me, that ensured for me a good place in our home before his very own children, all older than I. Hard and moody as he was by nature, he never changed toward me, even when everybody started praising my hand above his. Yet all I did was profit from *his* experience. Every night I lie repenting me that I did not show him more thanks and friendship while he was alive."

Arthur was silent. Edwin slid round so that only his hands grasped the warped oak, his legs dangling. With a laugh disclaiming his own doleful words, he let himself fall upon his feet beside the other.

"Now I'll tell you what you can do for me, kinsman-to-be! I want to slip out and see Jeanne after curfew. If I am missed, do you say I am looking about the timber staple to find the right piece for this beam before I go east. In fact, you can do that as well as I. You will find I marked the place where the joggles are to go."

Any stranger coming into John Trefeller's hall that night would have thought there was a feast—until he noted folks' workaday clothing—so many people were there assembled. Bedesford parish church was not big enough for all who had a voice in deciding the manifold matters that must be settled by Plow Monday. The weather was too unfriendly for them to come together in the churchyard or the market place; and it suited John Trefeller to be host at informal meetings of this kind.

There were the past year's officials (with the exception of Dick Toolmaker, who held the woodward's post for life) and those whom they wished to recommend as their successors. The church steward was there, to gather in the dues for the upkeep of the votary lamps, without which no blessing would animate our plowshares. Others had come to draw lots for field strips, and to hear what ditch and dike inspectors had to say. Further, John had again taken on several new bondmen. A pair of trappers had been asked to stay and sup. And, most rare and welcome visitor, there was John's shipmaster, Captain Lamb.

John's ship, the *Elizabeth,* had been struck by lightning in Antwerp port the autumn before last, so that John had had to return in a fellow merchant's vessel. Captain Lamb had remained to oversee the repairs, until the plague, with which God was smiting the wicked French, began to make inroad into Flanders also.

After Christmas and so early in the new year, storehouses were almost empty, spices running low. Even at Trefeller Court the last and worst of everything had now to be eaten, flavored with rot and mold and rancidness. But at least there was plenty, and though the ale be watered, it was hot, and kindled happy inward warmth. Noise spread and mounted; there was talk of the find, of our feud with Danesborough, and Master Lamb's adventures. Edwin stole out before the arguments and breakages began.

Turning his back on the river and its mists, he struck out swiftly across the fields. Here and there a throb of rabbits' drumming answered his footfall, and screech owls swooped by. The ferocious bawn dogs knew his voice, and he called to them softly from afar. He ripped his wound afresh against the thorn hurdles that flanked the wicket through which he sought to edge quietly. Not a single cow stamped. Everything was still.

The maids slept one to each byre. On the chance of his visit, Jeanne was taking the risk of leaving her door unbarred at night. The door moaned and swept some straw and refuse with it. Edwin waited, but nobody had heard. He had not even wakened Jeanne. He groped through straw and muck, with soothing murmurs at the cows. Now he could hear them stir. Every moment the concert of their gusty breathing seemed louder, the rich rankness of their odor more overpowering.

He could not discover Jeanne at first. Usually she would bed her in a crib, but this night she had huddled up close to one of the cows. He bent down to kiss her head, pressed tightly against the beast's palpitating side, its powerful heartbeat pounding in her ear: no wonder nothing else had wakened her! She was so warm, and he so cold; tenderly he caressed her and cleared wisps and stalks out of her face and hair. The hair was the sole part of her cool to the touch—two long, thick plaits, black as eels they were, when one could see them.

She moved, she wispered drowsily, spoke his name, and came into his arms.

"It might not have been me!" said Edwin; she only chuckled. "Remember to bolt the door every night after I am gone. When I come back, with God's help we shall be married—that is a thought to cheer us while we are apart! I cannot stay long tonight, Arthur is waiting up for me, so listen while I tell you about my coffer. I never showed it you as I showed it to no one, for fear it would all come to nothing—excepting only Brother Laurentius. I had to ask his advice—"

This was the point to which Jeanne returned as soon as he had done. "If you showed it to that friar," he could tell she was pouting in the dark, "you might have shown it to me, Edwin!" But then gladness overcame her again and she made as though to hug the life out of him. "Oh, Edwin—and it is a son; I made the test, and it said so thrice over!"

The remainder of their time together they vented their great joy in planning what was going to be, recklessly, without thinking of the powers of the night that surely listened overhead. Only when he had covered some distance of the way back did it strike Edwin that they had not talked of the find at all.

The air was piercing raw, but scented full of freshness. Arthur had come out to meet him as far as the bleaching meadow, to ensure that the dogs would be silent, he explained. Otherwise, he hardly said a word, and Edwin felt that he had put the other out. But as they went up to the storehouse loft where Edwin was to share the steward's bed, Arthur suddenly burst out.

"Oh, but that woman, Edwin, that evil-natured sprite whose heart is as ugly inside her as her face. She would tell me my business again, and before all the company. I know not how I kept from striking her dead!"

Edwin did not know what to say. Arthur had stepped out on to the balcony and stood clutching the rail as if it were Juliana's neck. Edwin shivered. His old blue kirtle was full of holes and possessed neither sleeves nor fur edging as did Arthur's weekday coat.

"I don't know why I have gone on serving John since his marriage," Arthur continued raging, "for you know I could go off tomorrow. Not being a free man, you do not know what it is like for me. Were I John's bondman and in peril of losing ears or life, I would have run away long ago nonetheless. But as it is, honor and affection force me to abide—for how would John fare without me on a sudden?"

Edwin saw there was no persuading Arthur to bed just yet. "For sure she would tell a winged angel how to fly," he commiserated, idly. "Heaven alone knows why John married her."

"*I* can tell you about that," Arthur said, immediately somewhat calmer. "John has a great love for her. It is singular but true. You have surely heard that kings and princes keep dwarfs and fools, and cosset and dress them up in cloth of gold. Even so does John Trefeller love Juliana Cinqmort. Nothing so cheers his heart as to watch that little cripple, whom he could break in two by merely blowing upon her, act as if she was master in his house, and queen of all creation."

"Yet what a price to pay for such amusement—if he must have her in his bed with him—"

Thus Arthur was restored to peaceable humor. They crept in between straw and fells, and said their prayers lying down.

Edwin was ready to depart before daybreak, and crossed the icy stone flags of the inner court to get a hot drink at the kitchen, where the fires were already raked and cleanly blazing. Janet Fowler, his bride-that-would-have-been, was not among the women. But just when he was about to ask for his bundles, she looked in and said she had them for him outside. He followed her reluctantly, and sure enough she took his arm in both her warm hands and pressed close against him before he had time to take up his burden.

"Will you not leave me with a better farewell, Edwin, than you gave

to the others? Anyone would think you had a horror of me, who wish
you nothing but well."

"I wish *you* nothing but well, Janet—but you know I am as good as
a married man."

"If only you were as bad as some—!" She let go of him, then pointed
at his waiting pack. "But you are wrong. I have a message for you from
the Mistress. There is your coffer; she says to tell you the bargain is off.
'Tell Edwin,' says Juliana, 'that I have heard how he spoke of me behind
my back. Tell him we have no need of him or his coffer, nor even of
his shutter panels. Plain wood knocked together by a friend is better
than a secret foe's fine carving.' Arthur Tewsing, also, she says, will find
out how mistaken he is in thinking John cannot get along without him."

"How—?" Edwin asked, as soon as he could trust his voice.

"Oh, Edwin!" Janet answered, near to tears, although for her own
sake she might have rejoiced. "Next time you have anything to say to
set a person against you, do make quite sure and have it rung from the
belfry! I was out with her last night, when you and Arthur had your
say about her on the balcony. Poor thing, her bowels are not strong, and
the green griping was upon her—and there she was, in the damp and
the cold, groaning for her manor home—where it seems they have little
rooms up in the top story, where you sit in comfort, and no stench
either. Surely it is the first time anyone has seen Juliana shed tears of
homesickness! And then to hear herself thus talked about! I pitied her
from my heart. God help me, I don't know which of you to pity first!"

"You have a kind heart, Janet," said Edwin, smiling at her sadly.

"Ay, remember that, Edwin, when you are gone. Remember there
will be one at Trefeller Court praying God to keep you from wolves,
bad men, and sickness. Here, let me help you strap these to your back.
You had best be off, if you want to be among Christians again before
nightfall."

CHAPTER 3

IN THE FOREST

Do You Know those mornings hereabouts, when it is neither spring nor winter, when green is the saddest color on earth, the very sky a mildew, the grasses spiteful with rime, every willow wand a whipstock, every stone a cruelty, when the fields are swamps, the hillocks mountains, and the constant rain more like infant devils' slaver than the tears of angels? With naked feet and a leaden heart, have you ever braved the woods on such a day, where you must wade through the old leaves that are dead, dead as your hopes?

On such a morning Edwin went from Bedesford.

Dick Toolmaker's croft lay between the Marsh and the Easterwoods. He had neither wife nor child nor servant; his twin brother, White Hugh, was all in one to him. To look at the two, you would not have believed that the difference in their ages was half an hour. Dick was a seasoned tree stump of a man. White Hugh's cheeks were smooth, fat, and shiny; his nose all nostrils; eyes mere slits behind which glittered indeterminable color; and his skin was as white as his lusterless hair. He was not quite right in the head. It was thought that Dick lived withdrawn in the wild solitude on his childish twin's account.

Had Dick taken up his abode in a town, he would soon have been well to do. William Tewsing, brother to Jacob (Arthur was their cousin), made tools in Bedesford; there were several following the same trade at Ovisham; and the shipwrights of Ellasea mostly made their own. But whenever anyone in the eastern half of Anglemere wanted anything out of the ordinary or especially durable, he went all the way to Dick's. Yet the woodland path was so little trodden, that if it had not been for a thicket of nettles pointing the way to human habitation, it might easily be missed.

Surrounded by the snapping of twigs and the resistant swish of brambles, Edwin was much startled when all at once the Toolmaker rose before him from out of the underbrush. "Dick!"

"Ay," said Dick in no overwelcoming tone of voice, "whom else did you look to find this way, Edwin Widowson of Bedesford? Quiet, you," he growled aside at his dog.

"I thought of you as working in the smithy."

"I am not yet so poor I cannot leave off working when the fancy takes

me. What brings you? What ails you?" Dick's querulous defiance
melted at the look on Edwin's face.

"Business brings me." Edwin lowered his pack to the ground. "But
first I must talk to you, Dick. I am glad to have met you out here. This
is for no other ears, not even Hughie's. Dick, you were Thomas'
friend—"

At the mention of Thomas, Dick's manner changed. He looked over
his shoulder, then stepped close to Edwin and put one sooty hand com-
passionately on his back. "He has not—appeared to you?" he whispered.

"On the contrary," Edwin said, with a shaky laugh. "I went out of
my way this morning. I did not come straight here. I went to the Bad
Place, Dick. It was in my mind to bury my brother—law or no law. You
will not betray me—though there is nothing to betray: for he was gone,
Dick. His poor corpse was gone."

For a long moment Dick said nothing. "You are surely mistaken,
Edwin."

"No."

"Birds and beasts, maybe—"

"No. They would have left rope and chains—ay, and bones. They
would have left their tracks."

"Were you not afraid to stay and look so closely?"

"Ay. I was afraid. Yet would it have been worse, I thought, had his
rotting corpse hung right there where I expected it. Dick, it would not
have been you took pity on your friend and gave him a grave to rest in?"

"Who, I? No. No."

"I thought, perhaps—you were so strange—"

"You took me by surprise, just as I did you. A lonely life breeds its
own darkling moods."

"If you had buried Thomas, I should want to be your servant forever-
more. I would do whatever you asked of me. I should never cease from
blessing you all my days. I would give anything to know where he lies,
to go pray there—"

Dick shook his head. They stood in silence for a while. Dick took a
deep breath. "Well, come up to the house, Edwin. You can tell me your
errand by the fire. And maybe Hughie will find you something to warm
your belly, too. Though I must tell you we have had some friends with
us these two days, and there will not be much left for you in the larder."

Edwin made a deprecating gesture, and hoisted his load back upon
his shoulder. "Friends?" he said, with a poor show of pleasure. "Is it
anyone I know?"

"No," said Dick shortly. He whistled a tune as they approached the croft.

To any that had not seen it before, it came as a surprise, having stone walls and a slate roof. Dick and his brother had thus rebuilt the place by themselves soon after it became theirs, for it was workshop as well as dwelling. Inside, beams and joists were covered with rubble and plaster so as not to catch fire, but everything was pitch black with the smoke.

Some dogs began to bay with chesty menace. Dick broke off his loud whistling and shouted, "Calm yourselves, curs! Dick is coming with a friend!"

White Hugh came out on the threshold and clapped his hands.

"Come in, come in, Edwin," he pranced backward hospitably. "There are two stranger hounds within, but they will not bite you, for they are tied up. I am not afraid of them. They made their own masters jump just now, but not White Hugh! Sit you down, Edwin. If you want, I will let you work Dick's bellows for a little, later!"

"Hughie likes you," Dick said gratefully. "That is an offer he has never made before."

There were three men lounging, half asleep it seemed, on the earth bank nearest the door, the two hounds being leashed to the jamb. Dick told them Edwin's name. They scarcely troubled to look at the new-comer, scarcely nodded.

Their somnolent indifference contrasted with the fact that they sat here fully armed; only one of them had an empty scabbard at his belt, and a large, old-fashioned sword lay cooling athwart the anvil. Dick went over to it, hammer in hand, and White Hugh nearly dropped the horn cup of honey and crust of bacon he had fetched for Edwin in his eagerness to resume the bellows.

Edwin hesitated where to take his seat, whether by the hearth bank or near the strangers, for politeness. One was heavily bearded, with hair falling to his shoulders, except where a bald white scar ran along the top of his skull. The second was round, but not genial of countenance; the face of the third, no more stubbled than Edwin's own on a Thursday, had very high cheekbones from which long folds of flesh drooped down to a chin like a yellow wedge of cheese. Their belts were heavy with pouches and daggers, their feet shod, though not spurred.

"Well, Edwin?" Dick prompted, between preliminary blows of his hammer. "What are your tidings? What do you want me to make for you?"

"It is not for me this time." Edwin decided to ignore the strangers as they did him. "And there are great tidings. The Gray Brethren have been granted building rights at last, on the Wode wasteland, in sight of Cloudsway Ridge. It is not far from where they were allowed to put up some shelters before. I am to pray you in their name to make them certain tools. Now that they have got their hearts' desire, they want everything of their best. The digging is already begun." Without looking, he could tell that the strangers also were listening.

"And?" said Dick.

"And what do you think? A great treasure was found. I was there and saw it all." And he told the whole story over again.

Before he had finished, White Hugh marched up to where his iron-tipped staff and Dick's long-shafted ax were hung up, and said urgently they must journey to Cloudsway Waste forthwith to view the treasure. It took Dick a deal of cajolery to dissuade him.

Meanwhile, the stranger with the wedge chin turned to Edwin and said in a pleasant tone, "All gold, did you say, Master Edwin? And you would know gold from brass? Is it hollow inside, or solid right through? How many ounces would you guess it to weigh—or would it be pounds?" and he laughed, to show that he was jesting. "To whom, think you, will it be adjudged?"

"The friars ought to have it," Edwin said staunchly. The stranger went on asking all manner of questions, which Edwin answered with growing displeasure.

Dick must have realized what went on in his mind, for at the first pause he asked, "And is this all your news, Edwin? When first I saw you, I thought you were coming to bid us to the wedding feast."

"More like you will be asked to a christening—of sorts." While Edwin had not been sorry to cease from thinking of his own troubles, now he was not sorry, either, to relieve his full heart somewhat. "And now I know not what to do or where to turn. Just when we thought, my Jeanne and I, that everything was settled! I had not the heart to go to her and unsay the good news again."

"God will perhaps punish that overtouchy mistress," the strangers' spokesman suggested.

"That would not help me either," Edwin answered, somewhat sharply. "And I cannot find it in me to blame her, since she overheard our unkind mockery."

"Wise and forbearing are you beyond your years, Master Edwin," said the stranger handsomely. "But tell me, had you thought of asking those good friends of yours, the friars, to lend you the money? Why should they not? They are so rich, they that are pledged to poverty. They might well have made you a little present since it was you unearthed the find for them. No? You know best, of course. Now I wonder, Dick, I wonder whether you could prevail upon your friend Edwin of Bedesford to favor us with a show of the coffer he spoke of? I and my friends would much like to see it."

"So would I too," Dick said cordially, and wiped his hands on his fell apron. White Hugh sprang up openmouthed.

Edwin's face shone with sudden hope, and he jumped to get the coffer and unwrap it, noticing with a beating heart that in the meantime Dick and the strangers held a hasty, whispered conversation. To give them more time, he deliberately made slow work of it.

"I thought," he said timidly as he brought the coffer into the light. "I hoped I might perhaps find a buyer for it even yet, at Ovisham, perhaps. It would be useful for a woman to store trinkets in, or medicines and suchlike. It took a long time to make—though I must admit I had only the evening hours to make it in. The wood is true silver birch, of full eight years' seasoning—"

"Oh, you clever Edwin," cried White Hugh, "I would pay you right handsomely for this fair, fair coffer!"

Edwin thanked him, but continued looking expectantly at Dick, whose judgment he valued, and who squinted closely into the hollow places of the carving, and shifted it to and fro to get the full play of light and shadow upon it from every angle. "Yes, Edwin," he then said, shaking his head, "it is very fine work. Pity that your father did not live to see you make it. Pity it is so long until fair time at Ovisham. As it is I'm thinking there will be none rich enough to pay what you need."

Striving to conceal his disappointment, Edwin turned from one to the other of the strangers, whose delight in his handiwork seemed manifest. The fluent speech of their leader and the fact that they possessed hounds and arms and such strong shoes had seemed so promisingly to belie their travel-begrimed appearance.

"Alas, look not at us. We are more needy even than you—and like you we are in desperate search of gold, Edwin of Bedesford," the one with the chin sighed heavily.

"Then I hope you may be luckier then I," Edwin said courteously.

The stranger drank to him. "No, Edwin—may your luck turn, and ours as well!"

Edwin accepted the jug after him, and they all sat chatting for a while; Dick went back to his loud work. By and by the strangers led the talk back to the subject of the find.

"So I suppose they have put a crowd of watchmen over the pit where it lies, until they decide whose it is to be?"

"No thief, surely, dare touch it," Edwin replied innocently, smiling to himself. "It might be holy. Or it might be devilry."

The other inclined his head. "Well, as you say—all this is great and marvelous news indeed. And we the first outside Bedesford town to hear of it, brothers! Tell us more, Edwin. We like hearing of the building plan also. How many men did you say are ensconced at the site?"

"I did not say," Edwin said boldly, ceasing to smile. "Strange questions do these visitors of yours ask, Dick. You told them my name and where I come from; you did not tell me about them?"

"No more I did." Dick joined them, the finished sword lightning in his hand.

The spokesman reached out and took it from him, pacifically thrusting it home at his side. "Let me make good the omission, friend Dick," he said—but it was into Edwin's eyes that he gazed. "Sir Cut-throat, Sir Snatch-purse, and Sir Lurk-in-the-woods at your service, of Cliffedge Castle, at the Beak."

The Easterwoods forest extends for many leagues, part of it thrust into Norfolk. North of Ellasea its wilderness grows up to the cliff edge; the Beak is a sheer headland (our closest coastal point to the Isle of Gannets), and was in those days well known for the lair of robbers and fugitives without the law. You must not imagine that these were greatly hated among the people. Unless so happened that we had the misfortune of meeting any of them face to face to our cost and lasting injury, we were inclined to pity them; and there were songs about them.

"Ay, outlaws such as any man can slay. So you see how right you are to distrust us, Edwin, a decent young law-abiding fellow like you. Quite right are you to rebuff the inquisitive advances of such caitiffs as we are. Shall I tell him, Dick, what caused our peculiar interest?"

"You can trust him, I think." Dick also gazed steadily at Edwin. "If what he said to me outside is true, he will be thankful to hear it."

"*You* took my brother down! *You* buried him! To you, then, I am everlastingly indebted! What made you do it? Oh, how can I thank you?"

"You would thank us best," the outlaw spokesman said a little sadly, "by not letting us see it so plainly that you think we must have done it for some dark advantage of our own. Credit us with a little Christian kindness. An unlucky man is not necessarily a bad one—as you should know, Thomas Widowson's fond brother." Resignedly smiling, he waved aside Edwin's stammered protests. "I am a priest, you see. 'Priest' is the only name by which even my comrades know me. I do not hold myself deprived of priestly power because I was falsely accused, unjustly condemned, punished, and cast out from the ranks of God's ordained servants. It may please you to hear this: your brother was not only buried, but buried with full rites. I used to know Dick ere I fell into misfortune. Perhaps his friendship will stand surety for me in your eyes, good Edwin."

"Now you see why I stood guard by the path while these my poor friends took their rest, and why I did not shout for joy to see a visitor!" Dick put in.

"You will show me my brother's grave? You will let me say a prayer where he lies?"

"Every hour we linger, Edwin, places us in greater peril. Surely you understand that."

Edwin hung his head.

"Dear Edwin, do not look so sad!" White Hugh coaxed, his own face puckering. "Look, here are the bellows. You work them, do! Edwin smile again! I know. Come out with me behind the back yard, and I will show you my new stoat that Dick got me!"

"On second thought—it *would* be cruel to deny him," the outlaw priest said to his fellows. "Cruel and craven. And since the Lord God has protected us thus far—"

"Leave Edwin be," Dick said, with unwonted sternness to his twin, who was tugging at Edwin's skirt.

"*I* will come outside with you, White Hugh," said the bearded outlaw, winking at Dick, who nodded and appeared relieved. Edwin was thanking the other two, and had no eyes for what else might be going on.

What happened next we cannot relate with absolute certainty. Edwin and the outlaws left Dick's croft together, they promising to guide him to Ellasea by a short cut through the forest, afterward.

Ay, and thus they got him out into the eerie dusk with them, beneath crowns so interlaced that no foliage is needed to shut out the light. There are monster trees crusted in deeply fissured bark, with looped hangings of pale lichens and pads of black moss, and with rearing roots the thickness of a man's thigh; and the places where sorcery seeks infernal plants amid the tough ivy, young shoots, and dead boughs crumbling into a blood-colored tinder, and the fruits of the lynx's impure cohabitation with the earth: some shaped like hats, some like batter-dripping pestles, some like an ulcerous rash, and some dainty as elfs in a moonbeam.

And there is a great stillness made up of rustlings. In that prospect-bewildering twilight, that rustling stillness, they played on Edwin's heart most cunningly, appearing by and by to yield to *his* importuning.

It was to be a night of fearsome gales; the herald gusts began to rush through the woods at the approach of darkness.

"Gold, gold, gold. That is what we all want, what is wanted every-where, in hut and mansion, in the Lord God's churches, in very Heaven. But for gold our gallant chief will die; but for gold, Edwin Widowson, your wife will belong to another, and your own true son eat the leavings of a stepfather's swine. For gold, the Cinqmorts will dismiss all thought of their souls' health and rob your kind friends the Little Gray Brethren. A little gold will buy masses for Thomas in all eternity. A little, little gold will buy pardon for all our sins. It is so easy to talk of gratitude, so hard to act upon it. See! We are nearly out of the wood."

"But this—this does not look like Ellasea boundary? Were it not for the darkness, I might almost say—"

"You would be right. We are at the edge of Cloudsway. Let us rest our weariness for a spell, brothers. Unleash the dogs, for their supper. It may well be that we, too, shall catch us sustenance this night."

CHAPTER 4

THE MIRACLE

EDWIN WAS AWAY from Bedesford until the end of lambing time. In the period of his absence, God bestowed upon the country of Anglemere its very great glory.

The golden hand and the piece of picture pavement were found on a Wednesday. On Thursday digging was resumed, while several friars left, some for the quarries at Friggsby, some for Damesbury, the Bish-op's seat. The remainder appointed among themselves relays of night-watchmen to guard the treasure pit. They had managed to beg two lengths of sailcloth from the wagonbuilder's yard, which were placed over the cavity and weighted with stones round the edges against rain, wind, and magpies. Against wolves the watchers had axes, staffs, and a fire.

As we made to go home, we saw them settle for the night, on a knoll with flattened summit: their chins resting on updrawn knees which their arms encircled; one only standing upright, a forked branch in his hand, with which he tried to goad the flinching fire to resist the onslaughts of the wind.

The winds waxed; all through the night the gale howled and blew, so that we thought our roofs would all be lifted, and snug in our beds, belike thought also of the friars out in the cold. On Friday morning there was calm.

Returning to the building site we found the watchmen gathered by the pit, and made haste to join them. All the world knows what the sight was we were granted. You that have made pilgrimage to see the Hand lifted high and distant on the reliquary bridge—for all your eyes can tell it might be all gold still as it was before that blessed Friday: for pious gifts have gloved it in gems and precious metals. But we were privileged to behold the naked miracle: the bare, poor, withered hand of mortal fabric. We saw gold turned to flesh.

In color it was yellow still, not golden, but rather like smoked bacon. It had no odor, and no other traces of decay, save that it was so very wrinkled. In which respect it minded one of some forms of leprosy. At the wrist, where it had used to be hollow, a little piece of dark bone now protruded. The drapery had become, not silk, not velvet, but that nettlecloth rag which to this day is displayed in a shrine of its own.

Supported in the other watchmen's arms, there reclined a young friar, Nicholas by name. As you know, it was he whom God had selected to explain to the world the meaning of the wonder.

Once again, then, let his vision be recounted.

The storm had soon scattered the fire. The brothers themselves trod out the embers for safety's sake, and hurried down to screen behind their hillock, that they might not also be blown away. When the stars, fitfully uncovered between racing, blue-black clouds, told Brother Nicholas that it was time to say night office, as in a dream he found himself unable to move. As in a dream, he likewise saw the others form a petrified heap against which the storm beat in vain. He could not move, and he could not pray, his whole being spellbound. All he had left was the capacity of helpless understanding.

Out of the pit, which his frozen eyes were compelled to watch, crept a something which at first he deemed to be a strange, many-limbed beast. Then he realized that it was in fact composed of two bodies, a horseman and his mount. The reason why they looked so queer was that they had come to life out of the pavement picture, unaltered—and what is right and fair in a picture must be monstrous in nature. Yet was that not the only reason; what more could there be?

The stunted little horse, its elbows knees, and knees elbows, was a human being. The little horse was Brother Nicholas' dead mother, ridden by the Evil One, in the guise of a proud straight knight clad in crimson from his heels to his head, which latter was masked in a huge helmet, like a beehive, with the visor down. Brother Nicholas thought his heart must burst with grief as his mother's gaze fixed him who was as stone, and she neighed: Thou shalt not! Thou shalt not! The most frightful thing it was to hear, said Brother Nicholas: his mother's desolate neigh commingled with the Evil Rider's laughter. And he understood the import of the hideous apparition.

The Devil was tormenting the son, showing him his mother's punishment for having done all in her power to prevent her only child from obeying St. Francis' call and forsaking the world. Evidently she had never truly repented of her fault—for whomsoever repenteth, the Devil cannot ride.

His anguish grew with the mystic knowledge that in some way the rider was also himself: the son's persistent impurities piled on the foolish mother's back. So that her Thou shalt not! besides commemorating her old opposition, reiterated at the same time God's commandments. No sooner had he grasped this—that is, directly he acknowledged his own share in her damnation (ceasing to preen himself because he had withstood her maternal wiles), one of the other friars came to his aid.

But no, it was a friar whom he had never seen before; gaunt, youthful, with a smile of inexpressible sweetness. "For I am my brother's keeper," said this friar in a clear and tranquil voice; and he raised his right hand, which was walnutlike with leprosy, but had a red mark in the center of the palm; and with this hand he made the sign of the cross. It was St. Francis himself, whose mother had sought to restrain him in the same way as Brother Nicholas.

At this the Devil's beehive head burst into a thousand pieces, and a holy relief slackened Brother Nicholas' limbs as a thick swarm of silver doves fell out of the blue night about the mouth of the pit, whither his mother sank, smiling, peacefully, to rest.

And St. Francis took the leprosy off his right hand with the left, and the leprosy came off like a glove, which he held out toward his disciple, nodding and smiling.

And the storm was stilled, the darkness faded; Brother Nicholas fell weeping upon his face. Thus he had stayed until his companions came and shook him. Then someone noticed that the covering had been wrenched off the pit. They went to replace it; and they saw.

They had seen and heard nothing in the night. Even the memory of their petrifaction was erased from their minds.

Now it was clear to all that the mosaic picture of the horseman confronted with the fragment of another holding out a bowl did in fact delineate St. Francis when, a rich young worldling, he met the leprous beggar through whom God first called him to poverty, service, and sanctity. The noisome hand, which St. Francis had once kissed, had thereupon been rendered incorruptible. How it had come to be here the scholars might in time elucidate. Probably its owner, whose name was never known, had been a pilgrim of English birth, and returned to die on native soil.

If there had been excitement on Wednesday, how is Friday's turmoil to be described? Only a small number of friars remained in Bedesford; the rest scattered to spread report of the miracle everywhere: in Thirchester, Clowes, Clavis Green, Ovisham, and Cloudesley-St.-Veron's; in Norwich and Canterbury, and across the sea; and to amend Thursday's messages to Friggsby and Damesbury Palace and London. For Bishop Jerome, then but newly come into his diocese of Danesborough and Anglemere, had not long stayed there after his arrival from France but repaired to London, where he was still.

There were monasteries at Cloudesley, Friggsby, Clavis Green; Benedictines, Dominicans, Cistercians, and Carthusians at Ovisham. Bedesford was the only sizable place where we had no monks. At one time the chapel of Bedesford Manor had been in use, but that was long ago. The friars had gained such a foothold amongst us partly because there was only the small parish church and one parish priest. This priest had a wife, a good little woman yet lonely, as was mostly the lot of priests' wives, whose wedlock could be sundered by anyone who had a mind to drag the pair before an ecclesiastical court. None would have dreamed of this injuring Parson's Joan—yet did she and her children serve to prove that there is reason why the clergy should not marry? Her husband neglected his duties in the effort to provide for his family.

Therefore did we grow much annoyed when of all people this parish priest alone sought to quibble over the miracle. He was forever hanging round Brother Nicholas to question him again and again in regard to his vision. (In any case Brother Nicholas was pestered with the most careful inquisitioning, to which Prior Haakon must needs subject him, that every single circumstance might be written down for the perusal of the Bishop and the Holy Consistory away in France.)

It was not human patience alone which the priest frayed.

In the night of the second Sunday after the miracle, we were called from our beds by the noise which all men dread, the fire alarm. Out we rushed, to find that our parish church was burning. It had stood stalwart by the south bank of the Tew before the Cinqmorts and the Normans came. None ever learned how the fire had started. We were too late, the flames far too high and the heat too fierce. All we could do was stand and watch the burning from afar. We had to watch the doors burst, with a sound as of taut linen tearing; we had to hear the belfry crash with a long-drawn last sob of the bell; we wept as the walls fell in. Ay, then he too could weep, that parish priest, who had brought this upon us.

Nothing was saved, not the rood and vessels, not Richard Duckleg Widowson's renowned chest—and not our hermit either, poor sainted woman. That was another thing we had to stand and hear. We heard her sing, in her lean-to cell turned furnace, but not for long, thanks be to God.

So the parson and his family kept out of folk's way for a while, until he found new sprightliness, being called time and again to confer with Lord Gervase about reconsecrating the manor chapel; and we deducted the fees would be high. But he quite ceased to be meddlesome, and indeed undertook to convey to Prior Haakon Lord Gervase's gift, a famous casket brought back from the Orient by some Cinqmort ancestor, for temporary storage of the Hand.

The friars did not wait to hear from Pope and Bishop ere they began to talk of an abbey church instead of the simple hospital previous envisaged. Plans were laid to borrow villeins from the neighboring shires, and to scour the roads for vagrants who might be pressed into the building work. Hitherto Jacob Tewsing had merely counseled the Prior, privately and free of charge. Now he came into his own as Bedesford's guild master, and was commissioned to put forward new designs.

By this time the first pilgrims were arriving, on foot and on horseback; singly, in pairs, and in droves. Gifts and votary endowments multiplied, and soon further miraculous happenings were recorded. Will Shearer, who had moved the pillar on his back, and Alison, his wife, were to have the child they had despaired of after eighteen years of marriage. Then a laborer working on the foundations was buried under a pile of elm trunks, accidentally disturbed. He called loudly on St. Francis, and although he languished half a day under the heavy crisscross tangle, not a hair of his head was hurt. But the third and greatest of these prodigies occurred the day that Edwin Widowson returned home from the coast.

CHAPTER 5

THE RETURN

It Was the fairest spring day imaginable. Edwin must have rubbed his eyes to see such radiance. He rubbed his eyes also at what he did not see: namely, the familiar landmark of the old church steeple.

At the building site they had carefully cut out the mosaic pavement with a thick earth base. Placed in a wicker cradle, it reposed next to the pillar some distance from the excavations, that folk might get a good view without disturbing the work. The friars began to collect round their Prior; but those of us who were digging were wont to go on until the last moment. Others stood waiting, chatting, mingling with the pilgrim strangers. We noticed Edwin, pushing through the crowd as if he knew nobody, yet craning and looking this way and that. Unseeing he made as to pass by John Trefeller, who stood with his arm linked in Arthur's and stretched out his free hand to arrest Edwin by a fold of his kirtle. Edwin was pulled up so that he stumbled; yet it was not until *after* he had turned round that he gave a start.

"Ho, Edwin," John boomed, "you look as if you'd seen a ghost."

Edwin but said, "Arthur!" under his breath.

The smile left Arthur's face. "What is it, Edwin? Why does it startle you to see me? It is not that you have had—some intimation of mischance to me?" He crossed himself.

"No, no. I merely did not look to see you with *John*."

"And why not?" said John.

"I thought you had dismissed him. The morning I left—"

John's brow cleared and he chuckled again. "Nay, Edwin, foolish was it of you to take my wife's word for that, and foolish likewise on your own behalf—going off as you did, without asking me. Master Lamb was to try and catch you on the way back from Ovisham."

"I spent this last week at Ellasea. I changed my mind and went to Ovisham first. Why? What was it they were to tell me?"

"Nothing to cause you to blench and shake, Edwin. Whatever is the matter with you today? One would think you were not glad to be back!"

"You must remember, John, that I have not been back above an hour. The first news I got was of the church, and the hermit. I cannot stop thinking of her."

"We cannot doubt she went straight up to Heaven. Cheer up, Edwin, cheer up, man! Think of other things—such as your wedding. The money is all ready for you. Juliana cried her eyes out thinking she had done herself out of your casket, till I sent Captain Lamb to let you know at Trefeller Court it is *I* that make and break bargains!"

"I have not got the casket now."

"Oh! You sold it? Well, all I hope is that you got as good a price— well, well, so long as you are satisfied and can marry your wife on it."

For the first time something like a smile quivered round Edwin's lips. He shifted his feet and looked at the ground, "I did go to see your ship at Ellasea, John. I could not keep away. I even took some measurements in the hold. You see, in my mind I had done so much work on your shutter panels already, I could not root them out of my thoughts, so soon. I had to go and see what they *might* have been like in their proper place."

John roared and slapped him on the back. "With God's help, then, can you have them ready before autumn?"

Edwin's face went all stiff again. "With God's help, perhaps!" he said in a tone that made the other two look wonderingly at each other. "Ay, if my hand does not fail me—if I keep the use of my hand."

Unconsciously he had raised his right arm, and Arthur and John pressed close to look at it. "Is this what ails you? Why, it is festering! Is that the gash you got at the Finding? Has Brother Laurentius seen it?"

"No," Edwin had gone red in the face. "I was looking for him."

"You will not find him here. He is over at the huts where some are lying sick with the marsh fever. Let the Hand that made the wound make it whole!" Arthur cried excitedly, "John, let us take Edwin where the pilgrims are lining up."

"Of course! He would not know. Have you heard about all our miracles, Edwin?"

"Ay, Edwin, every single day almost there is something new."

"Have you ever seen so many people in Bedesford? Nearly every house has strangers to lodge. We have the Flemish drainage men sleeping in the kiln at Trefeller Court, and—come away lest they overhear, though they know scarcely any English. Do you see that couple with the servingman? Ay, those. They are Flemings too. They were visiting the shrine at Friggsby, when they heard. They have a son for whom they seek healing. There, they are moving on. Time you went too, Edwin. You don't want to be right at the tail end and spend all day out here."

But Edwin resisted so vigorously that at last they had to leave him be. "It looks as if you did not want to be made well, Edwin! A fine figure will you cut at your wedding: a bridegroom that can't hug his wife!"

"It is but a scratch, and not worth a—a miracle. I will go to Brother Laurentius with it, I told you."

"Oh, but you cannot go now, when service is about to begin. Look, everyone is kneeling. Do you stay by me, and I'll tell you the rest of the news," Arthur urged, holding him fast. "Bedesford is to have an abbey now, with the sanctuary over the Finding Place. Did you know that the Cinqmort mines near Thirchester are both in pawn? So at last we know why my lord has been granting the friars everything they want, since they will pay. Poor Lord Gervase! what do you think Hugh has done now? When the messengers came from France with the ransom for the French knight, Hugh sent them all the way back and begged his captive to stay on awhile as his dear friend. Pity they are not here today, the two of them. You should see the clothes they had sent from London. Hats, like unto snail shells that three children could ride on, all colors, and trains thrice their own length trailing from their gowns. Oh, look! now you can see the Fleming child, he was hid between his parents' skirts before. He cannot move his arms and hands. They had made pilgrimage to almost every sacred place there is, barring the Holy Land. God struck the boy with a fever that left him so. Most cruel used he to be in his sport, plucking helpless little beasts in pieces his chief joy. Is it not edifying? Now it is their hope that St. Francis, friend of all beasts and fowl, may forgive the little boy on their behalf and intercede with the Lord God. But now we must stop talking."

All the workmen had dropped their tools and bowed low wherever they happened to stand about the excavations, whose sloping sides displayed riband-layers of variegated earth. By the great, bluish mounds of flint, men, women, and children knelt amid their crates and baskets. A fine sight it was, the mass of people, in holiday dress and pilgrim's garb, all kneeling down together in the grass, as far as the hillside and the river, in the clear, tender air, under the bare blue sky.

When the service was ended, the long chain of people began to file past the Hand in Its casket.

Twice the hush was broken by loud cries, followed by sobbing of women and renewed incantation. First a man flung wide the crutches on which he had hobbled up to where the Prior stood with the relic, and gave piercing thanks. And then, as everybody knows (for in the crypt there is painted a picture of it) the repentant little sinner from Flanders was made whole. No sooner had the holy Hand touched him than the child stretched forth his skinny arms, bending and straightening them and wriggling his waxen fingers, while his parents, at once laughing and crying, sought to kiss the revived members.

Those of us who had nothing wrong with them felt refreshed of body, furnished with new, better souls. Who could marvel that health was wrought in those that wanted it?

Edwin Widowson alone did not rejoice nor press forward. He was so pale his face shone like silver, and its ingrown little smile looked only wild and strange. He wretched away at last from Arthur's restraint, elbowed himself out of the throng, and ran away toward the hospital sheds.

They were made after a pattern laid down by Prior Haakon, of logs stacked on top of each other, crossing at the four corners, turf rooted so that gay gardens were their nodding crests, and without other opening than the doors, so low that even one of Edwin's stature had to stoop on entering.

Midges and early flies buzzed, shifting jerkily, about the bunches of herbs hung up to draw them off the fever-stricken men—one friar and two quarrymen from Friggsby—who lay with their gnarled foot soles facing the entrance. Brother Laurentius was wiping their foreheads with a damp rag smelling of vinegar.

"Who is it?" he asked, as Edwin stood against the light. "What is it now? I heard the cries and shouting—"

"Two cripples have been healed," said Edwin, adding with something like a laugh. "You were expecting no good, my father? I have come to pray you will let me talk to you. Here, let me do this, and do you sit and rest."

"No good, you say." The friar straightened, but did not yield up rag and basin, gazing past Edwin. "Ay, it would seem you people have had your fill of miracles already—since you will scarcely spare the breath to mention them—"

"Is that why you have kept yourself withdrawn, my father," Edwin asked eagerly, "because you do not hold with all these miracles?"

The friar looked at him and slowly sat down. "What sort of language is this? *Not hold with* the miracles!"

"I only thought that mayhap you had doubted—My father, I beg and implore your counsel in my great distress and uncertainty—"

But Brother Laurentius was too intent on unburdening his own heavy heart. "I have not withdrawn myself, Edwin. I am forbidden to leave these huts for the time being. I forgot my vows of obedience and humility, and I am undergoing punishment. I presumed to set myself against my superiors, and fell into most grievous error. I spoke against this new plan of an abbey church. I took it upon myself to say it would be defrauding the poor, in whose name we Gray Brethren have collected all we own. How the Devil must have laughed, to watch me revel in a sense of selfless virtue, holding myself better than the rest!"

"Then it is true and you are not glad of the miracles!"

"I am glad right enough, cruel sinner that I am no less than my fellow mortals—children, all of us, and must have our toys and sweetmeats, bleating out for wonders. I only wish that in all sincerity I might shame rather than joy in the miracle. Yet there is this comfort: by His forbearance and helpful mercy our childish, unholy joy is sanctified so that it will make better men and women of us all."

"Do you think so? Do you truly think so, Brother Laurentius?"

"Who can doubt it? Thousands who would have remained blind, deaf, and uncomprehending will be guided to salvation by the Hand, while if there were to be saved but one single man, we know God's purpose would be served. Have we not seen some of the results already? Has not Lord Gervase's heart been softened toward all? Has not even his son shown a measure of Christian spirit? Are not the monks of Friggsby bearing themselves as very brothers toward us poor friars whom they used to despise and persecute? Hold. Do not say it. Do you think I cannot guess what is on your tongue? The next time you would charge a brother with ill-intending hypocrisy, remember that thereby you betray the evil in yourself and the hypocrisy with which *you* guard it. For whence cometh the knowledge of evil to any of us, but from within ourselves?"

Edwin bowed his head.

"Bring me that bowl over in the corner," Brother Laurentius said, less sternly. "I think Brother Mark might take a spoonful of gruel now—our poor brother. We have had to bleed him white, nearly." After a while he asked how Edwin had fared all these weeks.

Edwin told him of Dick's consent to make all the special tools that were wanted, and of Dick's intention to come into Bedesford one day soon, to show White Hugh the treasure ("For a treasure was all I knew of when I saw him. He has not been meanwhile?") and personally discuss with Prior Haakon the question of fees and delivery.

"And what about your own fortunes, Edwin?"

Edwin guessed that the story of his quarrel with Juliana had not remained confined within Trefeller Court. He repeated what he had told John and Arthur. But the friar was more inquisitive, and more surprised that Edwin should have found a buyer at the most unseasonable time.

"I suppose one or the other convent bought it? No? A stranger, you say? A merchant knight? Oh, a sea captain. What was he doing in Ovisham this time of year? Oh, he was only passing through, was he, his ship in dock at Yarmouth. Whither, then, was he bound? You asked no questions? Ay, I can understand that, now I think of it. You must have been afraid to divert him in any wise, lest he repent him of the unpremeditated bargain! Did he pay what you asked? How much *did* you get? Is it enough?"

"Enough to spare some for the peace of Thomas' soul." Edwin winced, having wrung his hands and jarred his right arm.

Brother Laurentius drew the air through his teeth in a pitying hiss. "What have you there, Edwin? No, you must let me look. Your right arm, Edwin! How dare you risk its power and skill? But it is myself I ought to reproach. You came to show it me, did you not, and I made use of you for my own relief."

Edwin snatched his arm away and hid it behind his back. "Pray listen to me first, Brother Laurentius. I have done nothing for it purposely. If such be His intention, God could heal it without aid of man. But what if He wants to deprive me of my hand? I mean to take it as a sign. The hermit—I can think of nothing else, my father. She brought blessing on Bedesford. Now she is gone, will not Bedesford suffer for it? I have been thinking and thinking. Mind you how first she came, treading with her bare feet upon nettles and thorns with which she herself bestrewed her path—parson and chaplain escorted her, with candles, singing? Nay, it was before your time; I was an infant, and my father held me up in his arms, that I might profit from the holy sight. But it affrighted me. And even when I grew to be a man, I never could bring myself to bear the sight of her in her cell. That you know. Never did I hear her chant, even from afar, without the icy horror fell into my heart. I did not see—I did not hear her, when she burned. Therefore my ears are full of it. Incessantly I hear her. She is like a good housewife, I have thought, that dreads to see her household go to ruin, unguarded. If I have myself walled up, her steward, she may give me peace."

"I have heard you out without interruption, now must you do the same by me, my Edwin. Whenever God makes manifest His power to us mortal men in some earthly occurrence that we call a miracle, some folk are moved to a frenzy of self-mortification. It springs from a goodly sense of unworthiness, to begin with. But then the Devil seizes upon the limpid fount and muddies and deflects it. The Devil whispers into our ear that stark bodily suffering is an easier way than the slow uphill struggle of a lifetime to be better."

"A hermit's living death may last long enough."

"Ay, and all the world knows you have taken it upon yourself, and praise you almost as a saint the while you suffer in full public view!"

"Would you call our poor hermit a vainglorious woman?"

"No. *Her* confessor, whoever he was, commended her decision, else could she not have carried it out. What is good and right for one may be wrong for everybody else. Her way is wrong for you. That I know."

"How can you be so sure?" Edwin cried out.

"Hush. Remember these poor sick men. You see? Full anxious are you to suffer for all Bedesford, so you say. But you cannot even check your voice for the sake of the slumber of a mere three. You see? Harder by far is it to lead a godly life in the simple, ordinary way, than cut off from all assailments of the flesh. We read of men that gelded themselves in their piety—but how highly was their chastity accounted them afterward, I have often wondered?"

"Mayhap they did this to atone for some great sin."

"Mayhap they did, and, arrogantly measuring their own sin, mayhap they magnified it in their vanity."

"Can I not deal with myself as I like?"

"No; for you belong not to yourself. God owns you; and Jeanne Oxerd owns you. Dare you deny the claim of the child in her womb? I remember, if you do not, how you used to talk, when there did not seem to be much hope of this marriage. It was not just to make good your sin that you were willing to stake everything on bringing it about. Jeanne, weak of soul in her simplicity, needed your protection on her earthly journey."

Edwin hid his face in his hands. "If *that* was not vanity!"

"To be sure it was; but its ambition pales beside that which would now prompt you to abandon it. Oh, Edwin, Edwin! But I will not be too harsh with you. Today's miracle has turned your head. You were unprepared, having been away. Now cease from being foolish and let me tend your arm. Jeanne and the child have need of your hand. Ah, Edwin, would that you were a stonecutter! Father Haakon knows not where to find a tenth of the masons we shall now need at the Waste."

CHAPTER 6

THE FOUNDATION

THE MASS for Thomas Widowson's soul was held in the Manor chapel, where also Edwin and Jeanne were wedded. Edwin not only paid my lord in full, but made special offering to God for his sin and Jeanne's, desirous of contributing toward a new parish church. Nevertheless bride and bridegroom had to do penance at the chapel door, barefoot and in their shifts, with lighted tapers weeping shaggy tears, before the parson united them in wedlock. But all the couple's friends stood behind and heartened them with cheery jest and song. Afterward Edwin carried off his wife to the riverside homestead.

Words cannot do justice to the sweetness of Jeanne in her new, secure dignity, the softly blending forms of her tulip visage stressed by the married woman's headdress which took away the hair. The burgeoning child did not mar her. So far her figure only conformed all the more to the artificer's pattern of feminine beauty and, by reason of her slow, erecter gait, attained a wooden grace appropriate to a carving come to life. None who observed her could help loving her then. Had she been ugly, it would have been the same: for she was so very happy. The four woodworkers' widows, who had hardly looked forward to her coming, took the bride to their hearts at once.

When the household settled down to everyday life, this happy state of affairs continued. The only discord arose out of Jeanne's zest for work and the wish of her sisters-in-law and nieces to spare her, as at length she grew so big, poor child, that she could hardly stir without sweating and losing her breath.

Edwin for a spell was as happy and therefore as pleasant to be with as Jeanne. His arm healed up well and he began work on the shutters for John Trefeller immediately after the wedding. He had selected the wood for the panels before his journey east, and thoroughly explored in rendering it fit for carving. He held that in any piece of timber offered up to the craftsman the shapes which knife, gouge, and ax shall set free are already latent. There had been plenty of time for the oak panels' nature and demands to influence Edwin's design, and for them in turn to be coaxed into readiness to conform with it, so that he was not plagued with searching hesitations now, but went to work as if the primal surface were transparent, he having but to pare it off what lay beneath.

As usual, people came to watch him whenever they could find the time. But after the first few weeks they ceased to derive the same satisfaction from it as of old. Edwin had used to sing at his toil or else be entranced to silence. Now he began to complain. Once or twice he uttered curses. When we remonstrated, it was clear he had not known what he was saying, and he never did it again—not as long as he lived, to our knowledge. He did not stop the work, nor could we see that it was going anything but well. Yet was he forever muttering and groaning that the wood was insidiously forcing his hand in a perversion of his will. He even went to Brother Laurentius—he did this secretly, but of course everyone came to hear of it—and asked him for an exorcism upon the refractory timber. The friar looked at the work, snorted, and went off without a word, angrier than anyone had ever seen him with Edwin.

Some wondered at first whether this disturbing fretfulness betokened regret of bachelor freedom. But toward his Jeanne Edwin bore himself more lovingly, if possible, even than before.

She was brought to bed in July and, as everybody had predicted, gave birth to twins. Both were sons, but the elder was born dead, throttled by a ligament that, like a vine, had also wound itself round the arm of the younger. The parents had long agreed that the first son they had should be called Thomas; but now Edwin would not let the second twin bear this name, and instead had him christened Alfred in memory of that brother whom once he had loved best. The babe throve, in its cradle lined with sweet-smelling wood shavings.

Mistress Trefeller bore her child about the same time, in three days and three nights which none thought she could survive. Yet she was up and about a week after, and the stronger and fatter for it, to boot. She must have committed some error when making the same test as Jeanne: although it had promised her a son also, the child was a daughter. Her names were to be Isabella and Elizabeth, after thrice-widowed Isabella Cinqmort and John Trefeller's long-dead mother.

Brother Laurentius baptized Edwin's son the day of his birth, because they were all afraid to wait lest he follow his twin. Isabella Elizabeth, however, was exposed to grave risk by her mother's desire to let her remain heathen until the Bishop himself could make a Christian of her. The Bishop was due to arrive in Bedesford in time for the harvest boon feasts to lay the foundation stone of St. Francis' abbey church.

Lord Jerome de Rocquefeuilles was young for his office, not yet forty years of age. His home was in France. An uncle of his was a cardinal at Avignon and stood high in the Holy Father's favor. More than that none of us knew about him; and we were curious to see what he would be like, residing for some days at Bedesford Manor.

He pleased everybody. He put on high boots and tucked up his swallow-blue velvet gown to follow Lord Gervase over the new bawn, where unprompted he praised the dun bull calf which it had taken my lord nearly ten years to achieve. The French knight conceded the Bishop's lineage to be all but equal with his own; and Hugh was proud to be seen by the side of so nobly attired, so well-seated, and so wholehearted a huntsman at the chase. The Bishop's hawks and hounds bore comparison with the Cinqmorts', yet without putting these to shame. He played chess with Mistress Isabella. He laughed with John Trefeller and complimented Juliana on her running so great a house so well at her age. He remarked favorably on the parson's vineyard, and overlooked his wife. He purchased two costly harness buckles from the goldsmith and placed an order with the armorer; discussed with Jacob Tewsing the trigonometrical problem of which the west tower at Rheims was the solution; and treated Prior Haakon almost as a fellow churchman.

A heavily built, well setup man he was, proud of neck and general carriage, with a healthy complexion, large, powerful features, and clever, expressive dark eyes. He wore rich clothes and ornaments with a manner that repudiated pure love of finery, eloquent of faultless judgment as to what became his position. Clad in shimmering vestments as the central figure of the ceremony at the building site, he made a wonderfully fine showing.

Foremost among the lay congregation was the flock of fair young children ready to be confirmed, with rosy cheeks and lively round limbs and shining eyes, decked out so bravely—yes, here, on this very spot. You would not have recognized it, yet to us the visible advance seemed already very great. The foundations for the whole hexagonal area of the crypt were in place. At a depth of thirty-six feet the ground was serrated by narrow channels between which the floor rose slightly domed: a contour which it was thought would of itself serve constantly to drain off moisture. To the west stretched in shallower outline the rest of the cruciform ground plan, in one place scooped to the level where the rock bed was to be piled and sustain five layers of whole logs.

Oh, for such feasting as there was after, and went on for nigh a week! Oh, for the bygone days when such things were! We mind our fathers spoke of feasts that left us gasping for breath just to hear of. Now it is our turn to fill you up to dizziness with our memories. We shall not trouble the peace of your gorge with what there was consumed at the manor in threefold cause: in honor of the clerical guests, by way of boon feasts, and to celebrate the christening of my lord's youngest granddaughter. We will content ourselves with a tale of the fare at Trefeller Court for one night only.

It goes without saying that there was an ox roasted whole and stuffed with geese and ducklings. There were two whole sheep, besides two dozen fat sheep's tails. There was fresh pork. But then there were eaten utterly one hundred doves wrapped in bacon and crammed with honeyed herbs and a stew of hares bedded in berries and mushrooms and seethed in whey. Then fish were brought in. Ah, but what fish! The fish, too, have grown punier since our day. Sea fish there was and freshwater fish, crayfish, shellfish, broiled fish, smoked, pickled, minced. Sixty white loaves disappeared alongside these. Of such size were the two caldrons of beans and barley, that the friars were able to take away two large leather jugs of it for the poor. For that matter, twenty poor men and women dining in John's kiln that same night could eat as many boiled eggs and curd relish as they liked, and there was some left over. There was a barrel of apples and baskets of plums, and bowls of cherries preserved in syrup wine. Wine! There was Greek wine, Italian and Spanish, and a casket of parson's wine for the poor. There was thick, best pudding ale, warmed ale with spice and crab apples swimming in it, and—but you reel. It is enough. Was it not worth going without flesh meat most of the year, and going hungry every so often? And do you not go saying we did not have such eatings often. Once every two years at the least there would be like occasion—unless the harvest failed, to be sure.

The higher churchmen were all at the manor, but most well-to-do houses had some monks among their guests. There were both Benedictines and Franciscans at Trefeller Court.

The talk could scarcely revolve round holy matters all the time, but mostly it remained decorous. There were two newly betrothed couples to drink to—Martha Widowson and Arthur Tewsing, and Janet Fowler and Young Ned. Both brides were widows, but the jesting was restrained by the common knowledge that Janet had not accepted her suitor until Edwin's wife had risen hale from childbed and was no longer likely to fall prey to fever. She had hinted as much, both to Ned and to her fellow servants in Juliana's kitchen, and would still occasionally weep of nights.

Those for whom it was ordained that they must find at the bottom of their cups melancholy rather than beatitude and mirth could dwell on two meet and sobering topics. One was the steady, holy wasting away of Brother Nicholas, the visionary. The other was the news that Abbot Benedetto of Friggsby had generously undertaken to write a treatise on the subject of the holy Hand's origins.

Juliana had asked Jeanne to come and live at Trefeller Court with Alfred, as she herself had not milk enough to feed her baby daughter. She offered terms so good that Edwin could not refuse. That night Jeanne was dressed in a wine-colored gown Juliana had given her, of a web so fine that in spite of its ample folds her form was evident as though she had been steeped in water. Her skin was as white nearly as her coif—she had scarcely been out in the sun since her marriage—and when she blushed you wished you might watch her blush for hours on end. She blushed deeply as the young and handsome monk put his hands on her hips.

"It is a shame you should be working still! Come rest on my knee, Mistress Flowerface!"

Jeanne whispered something about "dress" and "gravy."

"Who cares for gravy now!" The monk laughed and tried to pull her down. "And has no one ever told you, pretty Mistress, that it is sinful vanity to care about your dress?"

"Then you will be glad if I tip the dish over yours," Jeanne returned, with more spirit. "Let go. Let go of me!" But the monk would not.

All round there were laughing faces, red and glistening. Some roared encouragement to Jeanne and some cheered the monk, so she lost her head and emptied the dish over him.

There he sat, looking foolish, with giblets in his curls, fat in his eyes, a big swollen raisin sticking to his nose, an icing of brown sauce all over him, and wings and legs and hooked necks of chicken tangled in his lap.

Men rolled off the bench, weeping with glee; women screeched and writhed and kicked their legs under the table, so that the dogs feeding there yelped in injured dismay. Poor Jeanne's matronly calm was not equal to this, and she burst out crying as loud as one of her own nurslings. The young monk, well scalded, cursed in so scandalously indecent wise that old Gilbert Ringbeard went purple in the face with laughter and his grandsons carried him outside for fear of an apoplexy.

Thereupon the monk laughed too and before she could evade him took tearful Jeanne in his arms and kissed her soundly, so that she also was covered with grease. Whereupon Brother Laurentius marched up to them, spluttering Latin, and gave Jeanne into Janet Fowler's charge to help her wash off the worst of the stains. It was a right memorable feast.

CHAPTER 7

THE BLACK DEATH

As EARLY as the festival week, several people saw the ghost of the hermit pacing the black ruins of the church. But the rest of us held it was the parson's goat they had seen, and laughed them to shame. When, so late in the year, our barns and houses were invaded by great hordes of ants, we consigned them to their progenitor, the Devil, and thought no more about it. When the owls nearly burst their lungs to warn us, we turned deaf ears. When the impudence and horrid increase of black rats presaged their expectations, we but shrugged our shoulders and starved our cats. Even when God locked His winds away, so that the trees retained their dead leaves, all we did was nod wisely and remark that the rowan-berries had foretold a mild winter. A mild winter!

Almonds and medlars had scarcely ripened when the first five work-men fell ill at the building site, it was thought, with the marsh fever. Before they died—with faces mottled a dark gray and protruding tongues black and rough as rasps—two of the friars tending them were struck down. Only a small portion of the grain harvest was in the kilns, and the vats for soaking the barley were hardly ready, when Young Ned collapsed in the middle of the market place. He died the next day, and so did Janet, his affianced. The day after that, Jeanne's father, John Oxerd, died after a bare half hour's sickness; at the same time a score of laborers at the site were laid low.

Within the week not one house could be found in Bedesford where someone did not lie stricken. Some fell down dead on a sudden in the street; some vomited forth their heartblood in a few hours; others lingered in agony for days. But none whom the disease touched lived.

In our hearts it seemed to those of us whom the Lord's scourge spared that we deserved it the more surely from day to day. Hatred instead of love (excepting self-love) dominated our relations with each otther. We met with suspicion, avoided one another's touch, each in fear that the other already be contaminated. All work flagged because we expected every dawn we saw to be our last.

In the second week, after the death of the parson and all his dependents, the manor shut it gates against everyone, so that those desiring to join together in prayer had not even a church to go to. But this availed nothing; in the fourth week the gates had to open—not to let anyone in, but to let out several. In the fifth week Hugh Cinqmort was lord of Bedesford.

But what was his heritage?

He was heir to a great manor which rang hollow to his solitary footfall. He presided over the largest hall in three counties—where only the fleas and the rats kept him company. He owned countless chests and coffers full of clothes, hangings, and plate—only he did not dare open a single one, for fear the sickness would jump out of it and at his throat. He had more than fifty beds of one sort and another—but in each a corpse had but lately cooled, so that he would slink out of nights to sleep in his dead sister Isabella's flower garden, where lingered the scent of roses and lavender, and other mellow vegetable putrescence. He commanded the finest collection of hawks in the land—only, when he remembered them, he found them all lying on the ground with their little hoods still on and chained feet in the air, and the boy who should have fed them decaying, equally forgotten, in a corner. He had vast grounds in which he walked uneasily—for in any shrubbery some servant might have met his death. He had a fish pond whose congested inmates terrified him with their ghoulish eyes and phosphorescent backs; a dovecot whose mournful noises threatened to drive him out of his mind; horses that neighed for thirst like demons; hounds that began to prey upon the derelict countryside—and God alone knows what they devoured besides game and sheep.

He was lord of a big town and many hamlets, hills, woods, and much arable land, salmon weirs, quarries, and mines. His possessions counted for nothing as he had none to work for him. A few surviving servingmen and women had fled into the town and were there making merry with others of a like mind before death snatched them, too. Only one aged couple stayed with the lord, and helped him carry the last body, that of his father, to the common corpse pit.

Returning from the churchyard, Hugh Cinqmort followed the deep ruts graven by the death cart into the town. Here and there figures grisly with nose bags flitted in the distance; a few revelers stumbled raucously past. Round a corner two gray shadows moved, tinkling: friars hastening from house to silent house with the last comfort.

Hugh Cinqmort walked on through the streets where even echo was dead of the unclean air. He could have shouted for joy when in the front garden plot of one house he saw a man and a woman in quiet, seemly employment. He hastened toward them, but fell back aghast.

The couple were very young, not man and woman, but lad and half-grown maiden; fearsomely thin, fearsomely pale, their hair like snakes and clothes like drift scum on the river. The boy held a rake and the girl a broom, which they plied before the threshold of the house. Their eyes were large and bright, but gazed nowhere. With expressionless faces and voices they sang a little song:

> We rake
> the dust
> so die
> you must.
> But th' rake
> not all
> will take.

> We sweep
> so weep!
> For where
> we sweep
> the broom
> leaves none
> to weep.

When they came to the end they started again, over and over and over. They were brother and sister, sole remnant of the church steward's family. The horror of their homestead had turned them mad, so that they thought themselves the pest boy and pest maiden of legend.

Thus it was that we came upon Hugh Cinqmort, all of us that were still alive and hale: at the head Prior Haakon with the borrowed rood, and two children helping to support it with the aid of ropes. Behind them came two other friars, one bearing the monstrance and the other the Hand, and two more lads with bell and thurible. Then came we, a dozen men perhaps, with tapers that were easily kept alight in the breathless air, and a slightly larger number of women. Forming the rear of the train and making up a good half of it were children, the smaller carried by the elder.

In the market place we halted. It was a littered shambles of activity cut short in mid-life; and we all picked us up some stick or flail or lath or thong; and all the men let down their shirts to their waists; the women for modesty's sake kept theirs on; and the children were not accounted sinners. But the friars, who had their hands full, commanded some lads to fall in behind them; and they gave these their girdle ropes to lash them with.

Hugh Cinqmort bowed almost to the ground and bared his head. He took off his shoes and upper garments, kicked them aside, and firmly grasped his loosed belt, which was of leather dyed scarlet, three inches wide, and set with cone-shape silver studs; and he stepped into the ranks of the men. The friars resumed the litany.

Now our tapers went out before we had taken many steps, in the breeze raised by our flogging. In our lips the chant grew louder and shriller. When our breath failed, our voices did not die down with it, but kept up a croaking roar to which no one could have borne listening who was not himself contributing. In this manner we tramped the whole, long way to the deserted excavations by the Wode bank. Here we humbled ourselves before the Lord God and implored His mercy.

Later we rested a little in the harsh yellow grass. Two of the women turned away and gave suck, first to their own infants and then to the orphaned babes. Although we were sore and feverish and cold, we felt as if out here we were safe for a while—perhaps because no carrion was to be seen, nor the pools of black, bloody vomit that defaced the town streets. How deeply sunk in wretchedness we must have been, to breathe so much more freely in boundless desolation! The disturbed earth gaped like the very jaws of death, the abandoned scaffolding rose from the crypt like gnawed and splintered bones. In many places the trenches had fallen in, and tools, timber and blocks of stone lay as they had been dropped by hands now lifeless.

"The Hand, I am thinking," one man thought aloud, "is the one thing holds our souls from perdition here and now. Pray St. Francis it may not loose Its hold." There was a murmur of assent, then silence again.

"When will it end? When will it all end?"

"It will be the end of us before it ends."

"It will end when the Lord God's just wrath is appeased," said the Prior, whose teeth were chattering, and whose very faintest movement wrung a choked gasp from him. He motioned in the direction of the children. "*He* surely means the world to go on, having taken least toll from among the innocent."

"White Hugh my brother was as innocent," said Dick Toolmaker.

All had spoken low and listless. Our hearts might well have stopped when one of the bereaved women began to shriek, "Nay, if it is not to be the end of the world altogether, if after all that we have lost we are to live on, then shall I call God cruel and curse Him, and call on the Devil to make an end of *Him*—" God be thanked, she exhausted herself soon. Had she gone on much longer, we must have strangled her or else be crazed ourselves.

Her cries had roused Hugh who lay stretched flat on his belly. Gingerly, with dazed eyes and sinews starting out about his throat, he raised himself. Between his ribs the taut skin fluttered. He gazed around; he was the lord; and in a voice that at first would not ring properly he proceeded to ask for whomsoever was absent.

"Your sons, Widow Shearer?"

"Dead, Hugh Cinqmort."

"Jacob! Are there no Tewsings left save yourself?"

"One other, Hugh. William's youngest—he whom Margaret is suckling over there."

"I see no Fowlers, no Merrimans—"

"Dead. All dead."

"The Smiths? The Wainwrights? Your daughter, Old Ned. Your big grandchildren, Gilbert?"

"Dead. Dead. Dead."

"God's will be done."

"Do you not ask after your sister, Mistress Trefeller?" Jeanne Widowson called, without turning round.

"She, too!"

"Not yet, Hugh Cinqmort. But John died the night before last, and she hopes to follow him any day now. All but two of the serving folk are dead. Excepting me, and little Alfred here, and your niece, Elizabeth."

"And Edwin your husband—when did he die?"

"I am not dead, Hugh," said Edwin, lifting his head from the weeds.

"It is not his doing if he is not," Jeanne said, in a shrewdish tone, that minded one of healthier days.

"Edwin has been foremost among the helping," a friar shook his head at her.

"He has been chasing death," Jeanne said as before. "One of these days death will let himself be caught."

"Oh, no!" said Edwin, as if bitterly. "Where is Brother Laurentius, Reverend Father? He was not ill two days ago when last I saw him."

"He and one other," said the Prior, struggling into the sleeves of his gown, "left Bedesford yesterday, to try and seek out the outcasts of the Beak—for their dying souls must not be left without comfort—since we are all of us rejected together. Those two, lord of Bedesford, and we three that you see here, and two brethren stayed behind in the town— we are the last of the friars in Bedesford. Brother Nicholas was the first of us to go. But he surely sits at God's feet now."

"I, too, am all alone," said Hugh. "I know not whether any of my kin be left alive elsewhere—"

"Do you know me, Hugh Cinqmort? I am from Thirchester. Sister Philippa that used to be Anne Cinqmort was alive a week since—her and two or three others they sent north, into Sweden. For the rest, the nunnery is empty, Hugh."

"They say that at Ellasea half-made ships and sea birds are the sole inhabitants."

"At Ovisham they have stopped burying each other."

"Have ye heard what befell at Friggsby?"

"No. What befell?"

"The people broke into the monastery and tried to force old Lord Benedetto to perform—you know what—the Mass of the Holy Spirit, the Mass that can bend God's will to his that sings it—"

"What sort of talk is this?" the Prior half rose.

"Well, that's what they wanted over in Friggsby. So he, the white-haired Abbot, was slain, and several monks that had not died before."

"What about Danesborough?" Hugh asked, after a while. "Are things as bad there as they are in Anglemere?"

"Hugh Cinqmort, new lord of Bedesford!" cried the Prior. "With your back bloodied in contrition, can you still cherish un-Christian thoughts?"

Hugh laughed joylessly. "You mistake me, good Prior. It was not spite made me ask. No. I but feared that, if Danesborough had escaped scatheless, this visitation might be the fault of—one of the other of us in Anglemere."

"Hugh Cinqmort," the Prior said again, "such vanity is worse almost than spite. The man must be demented with self-importance who can think himself sole cause of the Black Death. We all of us bear equal shares in this. Rest assured, Danesborough is suffering every whit as badly. I have had word from other places. All England lies adying now. France and Flanders were laid waste before us. And still the sickness is striding on, making graveyards of the northern lands where I was born, and the countries of the Mediterranean. Let no man aggravate God's anger with the wicked pride of a Samson destroyer."

Edwin Widowson jumped up in one bound. "Let us go, let us go back to Bedesford, where the sick are languishing for want of our aid. Let me help you up, Reverend Father. Here, Jeanne, take my hand. Go easy now."

Part Two
Juliana Trefeller
(1349-1351)

THE SURVIVORS

HUGH CINQMORT was born in the thirteenth year of his parents' marriage. They had prayed for a son so hard that there was no room in their hearts for joy in the daughters God had given them, and none in their thoughts for the reflection that He might be intending to spare rather than to deny them. Having tried to extort her desire from Heaven at great cost, Lord Gervase's lady, it was rumored, had finally resorted to the aid of other powers. So then they got Hugh; and his mother nursed him herself, and he wounded her breast ere ever he had a tooth. After him were born Gervase, Baldwin, Hubert, Anne, and Juliana, and he was a haughty and cruel brother to them all. When he was twelve years old, his mother came again to be with child.

"Is it not enough," Hugh railed at her, "that there are already nine of us to divide the inheritance? Have I not enough brothers, have I not surfeit of sisters?"

The birth pangs came upon the lady prematurely. She died, and Hugh's new brother died with her. Hugh was beside himself with destructive wickedness, after. Some said it was his way of sorrowing. Some said he had borne his mother uncommonly jealous love, but most of us thought this somewhat farfetched.

Lord Gervase forgave his heir, as the mother had on her deathbed, and continued loving him. Isabella, the thrice widowed, had returned to her father's manor, and she it was brought up the youngest children.

At sixteen, Hugh was given a wife.

The revenues of the quarries of Friggsby had always been shared equally between the Benedictine monastery, the lord of Bedesford, and the lord of Danesborough. Now, at the time of her husband's death the

Lady Agnes of Danesborough discovered a charter on which she based a claim that the Cinqmort's share should be added to hers. Abbot Benedetto tried to bring about an amicable settlement. But the Lady Agnes was anxious to show the world that no predatory hopes were to be founded on her weak-sexed rule, and she refused to temper her demand. Thereupon Lord Gervase also lost all inclination to arbitrate, and the great lawsuit was started.

When after seven years no settlement was in sight, both parties hearkened to Lord Benedetto's renewed proposals, and agreed to the marriage of Lady Agnes' only child and Lord Gervase's eldest son. Little Lady Agnes was eight years old, exceedingly gentle, and as pretty and fair in hue as her mother was mannish and swarthy. Lord Gervase took much delight in this daughter-in-law, and went to great expense to procure for her a woolly pony foal from some northern isle. We well remember her walking out with it. Being too timid to ride, she would lead the paunch-bellied little beast by a string of silk ribands twisted together, her other hand tightly clasping that of her nurse.

Before she had been married a year, Little Lady Agnes died.

The cause of her death was never clearly ascertained. The nurse, who might have confirmed or confounded certain ugly rumors, was sent out of the country. The family tomb in the parish church was opened and the funeral prepared with all speed. Yet before it could take place Lady Agnes, the mother, thundered into Bedesford with a train of armed men—no one knows how she could have learned the news so soon. Neither do we know what was said between the Danesborough lady and the Cinqmorts. But we can attest that she snatched an ax from the belt of one of her henchmen and hacked the metal-bound coffin to pieces to obtain sight of her daughter. A gruesome tug of war ensued, the mother catching hold of the little corpse at one end and Isabella Cinqmort striving to wrest it from her by the other. The henchmen of both houses came to grips, blood was shed, and the end of it was that Lady Agnes rode off with her dead child before her in the saddle, meaning to bury her in St. Peter's Cathedral at Damesbury. Again Lord Benedetto intervened, so that Hugh's wife was not taken across the frontier, but laid to rest in the chapel of Thirchester nunnery. The lawsuit was resumed.

The rumors spread to Danesborough; and although by all accounts the people had no great affection for their lady, they were so incensed that they took to hating the people of Anglemere as a whole for Hugh's sake. It is impossible not to return hatred, especially when it is reinforced by action.

With Hugh it was the same after his wife's death as after his mother's. Instead of abashed and repentant, he showed himself yet wilder and worse. We believe it was all this turned Lord Gervase so strange the last years of his life. For, soon after, he built the new bawn and, retiring thither for months on end, forsook the company of men for that of his cattle. Powerless to influence his best-beloved child, he must have sought solace in breeding wholesome creatures that were molded, for all that they were living flesh and blood, to his own carefully planned design.

Hugh went to the wars in France, taking with him a troop of well-armed men in good health and fettle. Of these, Jacob Tewsing was the only one to return.

Jacob and William were sprung from the Friggsby branch of the Tewsing stock, who for generations had lived in the closest connection with the quarries, just as Arthur's branch had with the wool trade. As a youngster, Jacob had accompanied his building master to Ely, whither England's best masons were called together to deliberate how the fallen central tower might best be replaced. Later on, Arthur persuaded his cousin to settle in Bedesford.

It was Jacob who eventually brought my lord's son home. Hugh was thought to be dying of a spear wound which had pierced his chest through and through. He lay sick in France for many weeks before they dared carry him on board ship, and remained bedridden for many months after. Hugh was prey to recurrent bouts of prostrate fever and coughing blood, yet he time and again recovered. Strange as it may sound, it has often seemed to us that God must have loved bad Hugh not a little, since He warned him so often and gave him chance after chance to mend his ways.

During the frightful privations of the winter and early spring of 1349 he labored unsparingly like the least and the best of us. Attended by one feeble old woman, he lived in the former gatehouse. All the other buildings of the manor had been shut up.

He was not the only one to live solitary in a husk of a house grown far too big. Only one homestead was there whose denizens had not all died and who yet left it to disintegration: that of the Widowsons. Edwin came to join Jeanne at Trefeller Court, bringing with him two half-grown children, a nephew and niece, the only other survivors of the tribe.

After John's death, Juliana had talked of nothing but her expectation of following him soon. She went back to his bed when he had been buried, and refused to get up again. The Black Death passed her by, and still she was confident, the more as it was discovered that she was with child again, and unable to keep down her food. Seeing that she had barely survived her first childbed, none looked to see her last out the nine months this time. And without Jeanne Widowson she would not have lived to see her son, nor he the light of day.

Jeanne never went through that despondent languor which it took the rest of us such efforts to throw off. There was for her no break and no difference between the time of sickness and its cessation. All through she had three helpless beings on her hands: Juliana, Elizabeth, and Alfred, to whose number Little Trefeller was finally added. Young as she was, and reared in a one-room hut, she accomplished the feat of keeping Trefeller Court more or less in order. In those days she acquired the vice of industry, as fatal in excess as its more common opposite.

God forgive our carping tongues: she encompassed even more. It is our belief that it was Jeanne who persuaded Juliana to help tide her fellow townfolk over the year of dearth. The preceding autumn John Trefeller had accepted four cartloads of mixed stores in settlement of a bad debt. In most parishes the people must cook nettles, tree bark, frogs, and puny worms, or were reduced to eating up what there was of seed corn, slaughtering also their livestock which they had no means of feeding until the spring.

John's posthumous son was born on the eve of the feast of his patron saint; and this time Juliana arose smaller, thinner, and more crooked than before, and she had to learn how to walk, even as her infant daughter was then learning. Juliana had cast off all thoughts of death. Before she could walk unaided she had inspected every corner of her property, and was full of complaints.

Jeanne at first could not think how to defend herself. She had not gained in beauty as Juliana had in ugliness. To save food, she had gone on suckling Elizabeth and Alfred until Little John replaced them at her breast. Stammering, she listed all she had had to do, ". . . and then there was yourself, Juliana, no more able to fend for yourself than the babes. . . ."

"If you deemed I was dying," said Juliana, "it was all the more reason to deal honorably and fairly by me. It is surely more base to let drifts of soot climb up the hall corners, and to have last year's rushes still on the floor, full of stinking morsels and fish bones that lacerate the feet.

Certainly it is worse to do this when the mistress is unable to watch and scold."

"Never were you unable to scold!" cried Jeanne, with tears in her eyes.

"Well I knew it," said Juliana sadly, "that my John was the only human soul who ever loved me. A heavy burden indeed is life without him. But I intend to bear it bravely. The rest of my life must be devoted to my husband's property and his children. I shall be a good steward. I shall not spare myself. Duty shall be my sole pleasure."

"It was not *my* duty to stay here and mother you and your child and do all the work of this big house. You should know better than to say it so often, and to me of all people, that none but John ever showed you true love!"

"Do you call this work now? Yet you knew of this house of mine when it held never less than half a hundred people!"

"You had half a hundred then to do the work. When you wanted more servants, John got them for you."

"And have you not had Geoffrey and Joan to help you? Have I not fed them, and you and your husband and son, and clothed and sheltered the lot? And do you talk to me of love?"

"It is not likely I shall do so again. Oh, Juliana! You do not know what you are saying! Try, just for one day, to see to all that needs doing here."

"Ay, taunt me for that I am a feeble cripple! I should ask nothing better than to be young and strong and able as you." Jeanne was a few months younger than her mistress, whose years still fell short of twenty. By this time she was crying so hard that Juliana also burst into tears, and drew her down that they might sit and weep together. "All my life they have mocked me, all that would not be alive now but for me and my bounty! Modest and womanly no doubt they would call it if now I walled myself up with John's children, like the blessed hermit, to starve naked! Do you know what I mean to do? This very autumn, as I live, I shall take John's wagons and travel in his ruts, all the length and breadth of this countryside."

"You cannot!" Jeanne gasped, dry eyed.

"I went with John everywhere, save to Ovisham. Think you I did not pay good heed to all he did? *He* used to call me shrewd!"

"John never went without a guard of well-armed men."

"The Black Death killed off the unrighteous with the good. There are fewer outlaws and highwaymen, too."

"Ay, and bolder wolves!"

"I shall take dogs, and travel not at night. There are two lads I have my eye on. I have not lain abed night and day these many months all idly. You must swear to me on your Alfred's head that you will tell no one till I give you leave."

Jeanne wept again, but with loving dread, as she would have, had Juliana announced her decision to swim across the sea or leap from a mountain top in hopes of flying.

As her preparations went forward, Juliana had to swear all in her house to secrecy. The companions she had in mind were Geoffrey, Richard Widowson's orphaned boy, and Jack Oxerd; these two were as eager as the Mistress herself. They were set to helping Edwin overhaul John's best wagon which had iron tires round solid wheels and separate axles, and a double roofing of hides and sailcloth. Juliana had only one pair of oxen now; these were put out to graze with the milch cows, and walked round the meadow thrice each night before returning to stable.

Edwin not nearly so overcome by Juliana's audacity as, for different reasons, they might have wished, disappointed both his wife and Juliana. No one but Hugh had the authority to stop her unwomanly venture, and without everyone else's active support he would still have lacked the power. So the worst she had to fear, if her plan leaked out, was dissuasion; and Juliana never shirked an argument.

She set out in searing heat at the beginning of autumn, and went on through showers, mud, and gales, and the foulness of decay everywhere, with only the one wagon and two half-grown lads. She neither disdained nor feared to visit the smallest of derelict hamlets or the poorest croft. She bought up rancid, maggoty pelts and new lambskins, lousy shearings, and well-dipped clipped fleece, and tried to garner some of the wool John had bought and paid for on the sheep's backs last year, nine tenths of which had rotted irrecoverably as the animals had died. She was not afraid to drive as hard a bargain as ever the flour and beans in her wagon and the famine made possible.

For days on end she was alone with the boys, the oxen, and the dogs. Many a night they spent in cold and darkness, surrounded by beasts of prey and sprites or under some lonely roof where more than a fire and the sign of the cross would have been needed to protect them. They went into the towns, too, and came out unharmed and with more than they had brought. They came back before Christmas, with a second wagon Juliana had bought at Cloudesley.

They brought what was more valuable still: two pairs of hands. Juliana had met James and Gillian Smith at Dameswood Ditch, near the border, and persuaded them to take service with her. They said they were not natives of Danesborough, having but passed through that country in common with many others from the devastated north, all pushing south in search of food and livelihood. We knew this was true; several like this pair had briefly rested at Bedesford; but they had admitted to being villeins in flight. James and Gillian told us unasked that they had legally obtained their freedom long before the Black Death, and they named York as their home shire, although the foreignness of their speech was no more marked than that of our Danesborough neighbors. Neither was James a smith by trade as his name had led us to hope. We had no skilled smith for miles around, excepting Dick Toolmaker.

Dick was the last to come out of a sloth of mourning. He sorrowed still for White Hugh, and that in such fashion as though he wished to make us feel ashamed because we had not died in his twin's stead. When some out of kindness asked him to stay at their houses, he replied he would be less lonely in the solitude of the Marsh; and during warm weather no one saw him.

But he did heed the friars' call for help to reinter the bones of the charnel house, which the snows and thaw of 1350 uncovered at the old churchyard. All the men went.

Jacob Tewsing came upon Edwin holding a jawless skull at arm's length while fingering his own face with the other hand. "It is so *small*," Edwin said to Jacob. "The friars say these were all grown men, yet my Alfred's head looks bigger. Look at this now, Jacob," and he made the other squat with him where on a smoothed patch of ground he had tried to arrange in order the many little bones of a hand. "I can see I have not got it quite right."

Jacob nodded and in his turn began to shift the delicate, clean fragments about. "The fingers are easy," he said with reverence. "To think that this is all we have with which to do our human best! You have never been to Ely. This is all we are given, and it makes things like Ely! Does it look better to you now?"

"Yes," Edwin answered, interchanging two more of the little knuckles. "But, Jacob, do you not marvel, that we should know, if not how they ought to go, at least how they ought not? For I asked James, and to him it looked neither right nor wrong. Nor did he think they were beautiful, these bones."

"We are craftsmen both," Jacob mused, his rough chin in his palms and elbows on his knees. "The law of all shape lives, a dumb tyrant, in our blood. And whence did that law grow? From things like these, the things that God first made out of nothing." He stood up.

Edwin followed more slowly. "Jacob," he said, "I have come to the end of woodwork."

Jacob showed no surprise. "I have known that to happen. Do you mean that your hand in its dexterity outdistances your thought and will not let you rein it?"

"Perhaps that is it. Jacob, are you very jealous of your secrets?"

Jacob glanced at him keenly. "There will be no building in stone for many a long day, Edwin."

"I know it. All the same . . ."

"There are no guilds now—ay, there are guilds, but no guildsmen." Jacob threw up his arms. "I will help you discipline your facile hand, if that is what you are after."

CHAPTER 2

THE BISHOP AT TREFELLER COURT

WHETHER the Black Death had exhausted our capacity of violent feeling, or whether their meager number inclined us to lenient judgment of our fellows early on in the months of Juliana's absence, censure was overlaid by anxiety for her and the boys. Their safe home-coming called forth hearty relief which grew into applause when the measure of her success could be taken. Folk forgot that they had been far from convinced by the young widow's argument that she and her children would starve if she stayed at home; and now ranked her wisdom and her position in the town almost as high as she did herself. So, when the Bishop's return from the papal court was advised, there was no question where he should be asked to stay, quite apart from the fact that Juliana had more servants than anybody else and that the manor was still shut up. Lord Jerome had left the country soon after the foundation laying, on a visit to Avignon, where at that time the scourge was thought to be slackening. Throughout its sway over England he was detained, but now he had come, on board the first French ship to land on our shores since 1348. Danesborough has no access to the sea, wherefore he must traverse Anglemere first, so that we looked forward to the visitation with doubled pleasure. Even before the feud, it had irked us all that the bishop's palace should stand in Damesbury town.

It was a yellow day wretched with cutting rain when he and two attendants came riding through the main street, a black bog that yet mirrored their forms, while the river Tew was like churned gruel and reflected neither Old Bede's Bridge nor the three horsemen who made its wood resound. They sat hunched, with dripping, flapping cloaks, and looked neither to left nor right.

"Hark!" the Bishop straightened, when angry barking greeted him at the gate of Trefeller Court. "Do you hear that? Dogs! Never have I felt so dulcetly welcomed. Help me down; these clothes are like a mountain upon me."

"Mon seigneur! Bien venu, mon seigneur! We have been watching out for you for these two days, and now that you have come we never heard you for the rain! I hope you suffered no mishap? Jeanne, take my lord's cloak. We have dry clothes in readiness, my lord, if you will deign to wear them while your own are drying. They were my husband's, of best Flanders cloth, as you will see—pray feel the nap—and scarcely worn. My men will see to your horses; let me show you to your chamber."

"Nay Mistress," said Lord Jerome warmly, extending his hand to her with his ring, "let me stay here in your hall a moment longer, let me feast my eyes on what they never dreamed to see again. It is all so clean, so warm, so bright—so furnished. I see friendly, frank faces that do not loathsomely deny that man was fashioned in God's image—women in seemly attire and modest attitudes." He sniffed luxuriously, "Wood smoke, dried herbs, lye, pulse porridge. Never, young Mistress, will I forget this day. You have my leave to remind me of it in the future, should there be need. Wherever and whenever and whatever it may be, I shall grant any favor you may ask, in grateful remembrance of this hour."

The next day the people of Bedesford—such as there were—came all together to wait on Lord Jerome, and he showed us the thank offering he had brought to bestow on St. Francis' Abbey: a crucifix of solid silver, gilded, with a domed window crystal in the center, beneath which reposed some shreds of the holy St. Francis' gown.

Trefeller Court became for all the world like a bishop's palace. Juliana and her dependents toiled and scurried from morn till night. Craftily they applied themselves to discovering the usages of the stately world to which the Bishop was accustomed, and assiduously tried to observe its domestic rites with a matter-of-course air. The main buildings rang with Latin; there was incessant going and coming. Juliana's house was the center not only of Bedesford, but of the diocese.

To the whole household consciousness of a great lord in residence communicated a vicarious self-satisfaction. One fine morning the Bishop sat jesting in the hall, waiting for his riding boots. Joan Widowson and Jack Oxerd came in with them, each bearing one. They fell on their knees, but instead of pulling on the boots set up a harangue which at first caused Lord Jerome to stop up his ears.

"Quiet, children! Quiet, I say! One at a time, or I'll have you out of here. Am I to be held to ransom over my boots?" Ready to turn it off into a joke, he grew full serious when he had heard them out.

"We want dispensation to marry, your Reverence," Jack said brazenly in his voice that changed from bass to treble. "We have a great love for each other, I and Joan. No one can say what the Fiend may not tempt us to do, if they do not let us marry."

"That is a fine way of imploring indulgence," the Bishop said in a tone of distaste which his French way of talking did a deal to emphasize. "It is yourself and this maiden whom you are threatening, my lad, and not me or the Lord God, when you contemplate throwing salvation away."

The chaplain, whose intercession the pair had been vainly soliciting, stepped forward and whispered in his master's ear.

"In what relationship do you stand?" the Bishop asked sternly.

"We never were related," Joan cried accusingly, "till Jeanne there married Edwin: everybody spoke against it, too. My father was Edwin's brother, and Jack is brother to Jeanne."

"We know," Jack broke in, "that there are many and many in like degree of kinship marry every day. Only we have no money to buy dispensation."

"So we thought," said Joan, her dark head bent coaxingly to one side, "you being a kind, good lord, and us having served you right well every day you have been here that you might give it to us, free."

"Go," shouted Lord Jerome, raising his arm in a great powerful sweep, "run, ere I give you what you deserve."

"But why are you so angry, Lord Jerome?" Joan piped. "For sure there can be no harm in asking!"

Lord Jerome with his own hand laid on till he had beaten them to flight. You may believe that they were made to repent, Jack and Joan, when Juliana heard what they had done. But God so ordered it that the Bishop remained with us yet awhile.

There were the usual visitors and messengers next day; all had gone when about vespers another two monks rode into the yard. We remembered having seen them before, notably the younger, whom Jeanne had poured the gravy over at the foundation feasting. The other was middle aged, short and bent and twisted of figure, with red-rimmed, lashless eyes from which water coursed at the slightest breath of wind or smoke. Brother William Goliard, the handsome young monk, had his habit split from hem to armpit on one side, wherefore he had borrowed a pair of huntsman's breeches showing, as the torn robe flew up, a faultless thigh that might cause one to regret his religious dedication.

Lord Jerome came out on the balcony to see what the commotion was about. In contrast to the dirty, stubble-visaged travelers his cheeks and chin gleamed like rose satin shot with blue, framed in the lappets of a tall cap trimmed with fur.

"Bad news from Friggsby, your Reverence," Brother William called up. Mud spatterings notwithstanding, he looked so fresh and sightly, with his strong round neck arched back, white teeth shining between parted red lips. As he announced it, you felt bad news was a thing to be welcomed, as the adversary's lance in manly contest. The Bishop sent his chaplain to fetch the monks upstairs.

"Friggsby is no more." Brother William stood erect before him, with sinewy hands folded and hanging straight down. From speaking Latin he fell into French. "That is to say, Friggsby monastery was burned down last Sunday. We set out immediately to let you know, Brother Oswin and I."

"But, unless memory deceives, the monastery was of stone?"

"Rubble, all rubble, my lord. We used to think it was of stone. Whoever built it deserved to he hanged. Whoever built it must have died a rich man."

"My lord, St. Benedict's-of-Friggsby was completed," Brother Oswin interposed in a reproachful singsong, "in the year of the war with Anjou. It was more than two centuries old. The art of building had not then reached its present heights. Building with rubble is customary in all regions where stone and waterways are scarce, my lord, and does not argue deceit, Brother William!"

"Seeing that our charter specifies the revenues to be derived from Friggsby quarries, I should not have imagined stone to have been so very scarce," Brother William continued with a smile. "Brother Oswin knows so little about architecture that his charity has not even been impaired by what we saw last Sunday. At St. Benedict's all the stone facing had obviously been deliberately constructed so as to give the impression it went all the way through. It poured forth like so much chaff. Once the roof had fallen in and one wall was breached, there was no holding the rest. In short, my lord, our monastery was not burned down. It fell down, it was blown down, like the heap of specious dust it was." He paused, breathing hard, then shook his head and laughed. "By Our Lord's blood, Bishop, those old bygone craftsmen put all our present lot to shame, though we may not share their views of design. Brother Oswin—"

"Knows nothing about architecture," said the Bishop, with a smile of fellowship at the older monk. "You really must not swear in my presence, Brother William. Neither," he had shifted his gaze to the younger, without relinquishing the smile, "should you address your bishop quite so unceremoniously."

"My lord." The young monk bowed low.

"I will take it that the zest of denunciation carried you away this once, my son. I gather, then, that, in contrast to Brother Oswin, you do know a certain amount about architecture?"

"I," Brother William turned with contrite affection to his companion, "know nothing whatever about books."

"So much I had also gathered," the Bishop said with a chuckle. "Your Latin is execrable. You are of French birth?"

"We had a captive French knight living with us at home, when I was young," Brother William answered modestly. "My kin came over with the Conqueror. But that is long ago."

"What is your name again? I believe I used to know a Goliard once, where was it—? When you were young, you say: how old are you now?"

"Twenty-six, my lord."

"You look less. Let me see. At your age I was Abbott at Hautechamps-Pompierry. Be seated, be seated, Brother—? Brother Oswin, to be sure. It makes me dizzy to watch you weaving to and fro on your feet. I hope you may find yourself able to continue your little nap sitting down. So. Wine, Brother William? Wine, Chaplain. Tell me, who has been ruling at Friggsby since the sainted Benedetto's martyrdom?"

If the Bishop had thought to abash the young monk by darting at him a sudden, flashing glance, he was disappointed. "If you can call it ruling . . ." Brother William said in smooth, oblique deprecation.

"Tell me," the Bishop relaxed and leaned forward. "No doubt you realized, Brother William, what led me to think the monastery might have been sacked. Your people murdered the old Abbot, did they not? They must be very savages. A more saintly monk I have never met. I never understood how it could have happened?"

The young monk sprang from his seat unbidden and began to pace the low-raftered chamber. "No doubt you never knew the full circumstances, Reverend Lord. The people of Friggsby did not have before their eyes, as we monks did, the daily example of Lord Benedetto's gentle virtues. What we knew to be unworldliness they came to feel as inhumanity. As you know, he was a scholar above all. But in one of the great famines of the early forties, the people of Friggsby took the image of St. Ursula from the parish church, stripped her of her vestments in the market place, daubed her with tar, and carried her round the streets in punitive procession. What can one expect of primitive minds? Worse outrages have been committed. Unfortunately this was just the sort of thing to rouse Lord Benedetto from his tomes. He saw to it that the severest penalties were inflicted. There cannot have been a single family did not lose someone at the headman's hands. We prayed and implored him, all of us—ay, we paid for it too," Brother William grinned in rueful reminiscence. "A death sentence was an assemblage of words to our mild Abbot, words made up of letters inked on parchment: good, just, lifeless words. Thenceforth they called him the Bloody Abbot, the people."

"What would you have done in his place?"

Brother William stood still, sat down. "I, my lord? We do not live this earthly life in the clouds, nor in books. What good did Father Benedetto's obduracy do to anybody? I say St. Ursula is not a heathen idol, to be honored with blood sacrifice. I believe she would have been better pleased with a new gown and, say, an annual fine in perpetuity. Whatever the manner of his death, Lord Benedetto would have gone straight up to Heaven. So I for one cannot account even his martyrdom a gain. I see nothing but loss all round. Now, perhaps, you will have me unfrocked."

The Bishop sighed and toyed with his seal. "My dear young friend, I cannot afford it." The young monk bent and kissed his hand. "Now waken your sleepy brother and go down, both of you, to see what they can scrape together for you in Mistress Trefeller's kitchen. Stay on for a day or two, we shall hold some more converse."

The Bishop made no secret of the quick liking he had taken to Brother William, nor any attempt to curb it. He amused himself luring the young man into further outspokenness, never catching him at a loss for an opinion, and again and again testing his graceful retreat and recovery whenever the Bishop saw fit abruptly to put him back in his place.

The Bishop probed Brother William's antecedents, the circumstances that had made a monk of him, and the nature and death of his vaunted architectural knowledge. The latter was mainly intuitive, acquired through love rather than careful instruction.

"Few men can love all the arts. For my part, I love only the one."

"You might put it another way. It may be the only one you are capable of understanding."

"It comes to the same thing, Reverend Lord."

"Do you care for nothing save eating and drinking besides—and talk, to be sure?"

"Eating and drinking and riding and sleeping—*living,* my lord."

"Yet you tell me you, the only son, ran away to Friggsby in opposition to your family."

"Ay. Where else but in a monastery can a man devote himself exclusively to living?"

"Your impudence takes my breath away." But the Bishop could not help chuckling. "Devil take me if I know why I bear with it."

"I amuse you. I have been content to be your buffoon because—"

"Content, forsooth!"

"And honored, my lord, because we all need cheering in these days, and because I know that you know I can be more seriously useful to you than that. Whatever my faults, I am not complacent enough to believe that you have allowed me to be with you so often just because you like me."

"Granted. Tell me then why you think I have spent so much time and breath on you. Hold, no!" Lord Jerome interrupted himself hastily. "Do not tell me, do not answer this question, not yet!" They looked at each other, and both laughed. "Tell me rather why you think I like you."

"Have I your lordship's permission to be frank? For one thing, then, because I understand the art of surprising by frankness without giving offense. For another, because—forgive the presumption—we are much alike, yet differing essentially. You and I take pleasure in all the same things. But I enjoy them for their own sake. Let me give an example: I enjoy imposing myself—my mood, my will—on people, but simply for pure joy of the thing. I entirely lack ambition. And I believe that you have realized this as well as I. Therefore do you like me; and therefore do you know I could be very useful to you. Shall I go on?"

"No!" Frowning and laughing at once, Lord Jerome waved both hands. "Upon my soul, you flatter me. I am not your equal, at least in penetration!"

At this, however, the young monk flushed crimson, and would not be persuaded to take the remark as anything but a rebuke. He recovered gradually, as the Bishop treated him, if anything, more graciously, drawing him in amongst the daily callers, and pushing him forward in conversation.

One day the Bishop suddenly asked to be taken to Cloudsway Waste. He applied to Juliana for a guide, and she named Edwin as the only member of her household who could be spared. Brother Oswin came to life. "If I might be so bold as to make a suggestion, Reverend Lord," he stammered with humble urgency. "Do not have the man sent for; deign to seek him out in his workshop; there is a sight worth seeing."

Immediately after her return Juliana had ordered Edwin to fetch the shutter panels which he had not touched since the Black Death, and to resume work on them. Edwin was most unwilling, but had to do as she asked; and had been given a shed to work in. He stopped and stood aside, confusion making him appear surly, before the invasion of Bishop and monks.

"He is shy," Brother Oswin said pleadingly to the Bishop.

"These look very fine carvings, my son," Lord Jerome addressed Edwin kindly. "You are the father of little Alfred, are you not? Your son is not too shy to bid me the time of day. Whenever he sees me he claims a ride on my foot! Will you not tell me about these panels?"

"They are bad," said Edwin, averting his face, as if it shamed him intolerably to see them look at his work.

"By no means," said Brother William encouragingly. "Is the design your own too? I think she"—he pointed at the figure, nearly life sized, occupying the center of the panel on which Edwin had been busy—"is exquisite. I like this sort of shallow relief work; I think it lends the figure an air of gradual, as it were self-generated growth. What are you going to do with the border? At present it is hard to tell."

"There will be a design of vines round three sides, and across the top there will be the letters spelling her name. Brother Oswin has made me the patterns for them."

"And what is her name?" the Bishop spoke as to a child.

"Chastity," Edwin replied, as gloomily as before. "She on the other panel represents Temperance."

"If I may explain, my lord," Brother Oswin put in. "Mistress Trefeller wants these for bed shutters, with Chastity and Temperance as guardians of her slumbers and her privacy."

Involuntarily Lord Jerome and Brother William exchanged glances, and both turned away to hide their smiles. But Edwin had observed them, and cried, "So you have seen it too, after all!"

"Is it that you want still more praise, Edwin?" Brother Oswin interposed again. "No doubt you have been going on too long, and need a rest from carving to restore the freshness of your vision and your hand. So take off your apron now and guide the Lord Bishop to Cloudsway Waste."

None of us had visited the abandoned site for a long time. The entire excavations formed one sweet, dazzling flower bed humming with insects. Every weed you can think of mingled its blossom with the trembling silk ears of purely iridescent grasses. Foxgloves and meadowsweet, poppies, cornflowers, chicory, ox eye, dandelion; sorrel; thistles of blue and of silver, wine-colored, and purple; irises, damply crumpled like newly born blue butterflies. Gorse, heather, and barcken had come back. The rust which had covered the old forsaken tools embellished their desolation with colors ranging from near scarlet to subtle ocher. On the idle stone, mosses had fastened, and other tiny, creeping plants. Against the sky the scaffolding trellis showed small dark clots here and there, of birds' nests; and all the little birds that had entrusted themselves to St. Francis flew up and beat the air with their wings; and our hearts moved in our breasts.

CHAPTER 3

THE RAPE OF THE HAND

EDWIN CHIPPED ABOUT on his shutters some days longer; then, nobody being by, he took his largest ax and destroyed them.

Some people, like Brother Oswin in his thorough innocence of heart, never could understand what to them appeared as an act of madness. But most of us had seen it in the end, or at least saw it after the event. Breathtaking as was their workmanship, the very beauty of the damsels labeled Chastity and Temperance, as well as the manner of their disposition in space, flamboyantly contradicted their names Nay, worse: they seemed to make use of the incongruity, more hotly to suffuse the beholder with a surge of lust. As Brother William had whispered to Lord Jerome: the shutters had been more suited to grace the couch of a king's whore than to make a fortress of a widow's bed.

Juliana was enraged beyond description; but the general stir was short lived, because of other events.

A lay messenger arrived for the Bishop, bearing letters from France, it was learned. Jacob Tewsing was sure he had met the man—there could be no two like him, he said somewhat acidly—fifteen years ago at Ely. Jacob recalled even the name: Stephen Colet.

However that might be, the man and the letters set going a whirl of privy activities among the Bishop's entourage; Prior Haakon and Lord Hugh were bidden to Trefeller Court and closeted with Lord Jerome and sundry others for many hours; and several times eavesdroppers caught muffled uproar.

We had not over long to wonder. The Bishop sent word to all the people that he would himself conduct a service at the manor chapel on the Sunday, and would afterward address us. Room was found for everybody; the friars came too, and all the Bishop's guests under Juliana's roof.

Bishop Jerome de Rocquefeuilles, in full regalia, proclaimed that he had arranged to take over from the friars the building site at Cloudsway Waste, and with it the wonder-working Hand. Whatever we might have expected, it was not this. The three Franciscans sat moveless, with bowed heads. They felt themselves to be so helpless that they would not even give us any lead; such was our impression.

The Gray Friar's position had always been difficult to assess: on the one hand they formed, as it were, the Pope's special, spiritual army; on the other, as far as we knew, most churchmen thought little of them, and many of the laity denounced them, for their mendicant greed and hoarding, and for their influence with the common people and women-folk in general—too often wielded for their order's material advantage. We ourselves had always praised *our* friars as exceptional.

Lord Jerome honored the assembly with declaration of his reasons. Firstly he said that the authors of the enterprise had lost everything in the interval and would lack the means of continuing for a long time to come. The Lord God, he said, in a dream had commanded him to build a cathedral here, before he had left France early this year, so that he had sold all his landed holdings, and was ready to devote his private fortune to the work. By way of his third argument Lord Jerome contrasted the glory of God with the vainglory of man: had the friars refused to yield, they would only have defrauded God of His new house and the service therein to be rendered Him. His fourth argument was blatantly seduc-tive: St. Peter's-of-Damesbury being in practice little more than a large parish church at present, Lord Jerome desired to make Bedesford his cathedral town. In passing he showed how resumed building activity could not but renew every aspect of life, trade, and traffic. His final argu-ment revealed that he was in possession of full Papal authority and patents royal.

What with the destruction of St. Benedict's-of-Friggsby and the terri-ble depletion of Anglemere's other monasteries, careful estimates sup-ported the founding of a new community at Cloudsway, in preference to refurbishing the old. This monastry should oversee the building work on behalf of the Bishop, with the well-born and pious Brother William Goliard as his vicar. And here was the noted Master Stephen Colet, late of the King's service, one of the greatest living experts on tower construction, whose advice now and in the future the Bishop had secured.

Under the Bishop's eye, Master Colet and Jacob Tewsing stiffly renewed old acquaintance at a second assembly Lord Jerome called together at the site, shortly before his departure. He went over it with them, to see what alterations in the ground plan the changed functions of the building might necessitate. Prior Haakon and his two friars hovered sadly on the flowered brink, while the Bishop, the future Abbot, and the two building masters waded through the cross-shaped wilder-ness below. The last-named couple scrambled further down into the crypt, where the lining of walls and floor and the thick rubble piers had been completed before the winter of 1348, albeit they were yet unconnected and roofless. The crypt was intact though waterlogged and teeming with frogs and water beetles.

Master Colet affected a square notebook with wooden covers; Jacob was content to gesticulate or draw his lines into the sand, when the whole party climbed out to confer on the bank. Both masons agreed that the long nave of the contemplated friars' church would do for the choir, so that the central crossing would be where the portal was to have stood. At first the Bishop demurred, calling the shape they had outlined something too long and thin; but the masons showed him where the rock bed ended, and where the root of a hill-swelling encroached, and he withdrew his objection. Listening to them, one of the friars, a simple, softhearted old man, was unable to stay his tears, although as a special boon the friars had received express assurance that they might retain their rights over the hospital.

Lord Jerome then spoke to us in a general way on the probable services required of the townfolk. Some of us gazed at Lord Hugh, and we did not like the look on his face. Hugh Cinqmort was very tall and but for his stoop would have been taller still; with his massive, harsh, violent face and sandy mane of hair he could look ravening brother to the lion blazoned on his shield.

The future Abbot of Cloudsway Waste did not know him as we did, and unsuspectingly allowed himself to be drawn into conversation. Very amiably the lord of Bedesford asked what sort of material the reverend lords were having in mind, since all the quarries were still idle?

Brother William threw himself into explaining with his usual enthusiasm. "This region is rich in rubble, flint, and ragstone. At a rough estimate it would seem that enough of these were collected before the Black Death for us to proceed with the arches and vaulting of the crypt without waiting until the weeds have been cleared and the new excavations added. Myself I would go so far as to say that there is plenty for at least the first course of the chancel walls, without further collections. We can have a neat inlay of trefoils in black flint along the first six courses, say—"

"All in all you will need a great deal of rubble and flint, then?"

"Well—Master Jacob, who has much experience in this mode of building, calculates that if we make the outer walls about seven feet thick we shall need—"

"Before you go on: has Jacob Tewsing also calculated the cost for you?" Round the two of them everybody had fallen silent, and as he grew aware of it Lord Hugh raised his voice the more loudly.

"Cost—?" said Brother William, with an uncomprehending smile. "It is not as if we had to send far and wide for skilled laborers—not, at any rate, in the beginning."

"That was not what I meant. I wondered whether you had realized that building with rubble alone will cost you twice as much as stone."

"How do you make that out?" The Bishop joined the pair.

"I will tell you. I take the price I have just this moment fixed on per hundredweight of rubble, or flint, as the case may be, and I multiply it by the quantities which I have roughly estimated you will need—" His voice, still falsely solicitous, was drowned in general tumult. He waited until it subsided, "For who dare dispute my rights over everything gathered off my lands? You, Reverend Lord—nay, do not try to silence me, it is well that the people should hear this—you have seen fit to dispute the very moderate ground rent with which, for the sake of my father's soul, I was prepared to content me—in spite of the fact that a cathedral is an entirely different matter from the simple preaching church for which the land was originally granted." He turned to us and shouted, "It has pleased Lord Jerome to inform me that researches he caused to be made in London revealed this area to have been waste common all along—so far I have only his word for it."

"You were shown the transcription of the Doomsday entry, confound you," Lord Jerome shouted back.

"Worse!" Lord Hugh laughed, flinging up his arm. "I have only Lord Jerome's *copyist's* word for it! Now let everyone take note. Lord Jerome holds that the discovery of the Hand stamped this wasteland church property. He has been bold enough to ask *me* to make restitution of all the friars' past payments. Thus *I* am to compensate the friars for the injury *he* is inflicting on them! But I shall be going down to London myself in a week or two. I shall fight for my rights so long as there remains the slenderest legal possibility of justice. In the meantime the Reverend Lords are more than welcome to clear my land of every crumb of rock and flint at present depreciating arable soil—at the lowest price I can afford to ask."

"Hugh Cinqmort, are you not afraid—!" the Bishop thundered.

"Afraid, my lord? What have I to fear, if *you* are not afraid? Despoiling these poor friars, and traducing the Lord God to give yourself authority! Little did I think a day would come when I would find myself their champion."

Prior Haakon agitatedly broke through our ranks. He was as tall as Hugh and even thinner, but between broad, square shoulders he carried a tiny old crumpled head without a hair left on it. "We want none of your championing, lord of Bedesford! Our sole regret is that none of us three is skilled enough to take any great part in building this new cathedral. But, my lord Bishop, you are welcome to such assistance as I for one can render with the timber monastery. And doubtless you have heard report of the great notebook, which was the pride of our house at Ovisham and was salvaged from the fire. If you will accept it, we shall fully gladly lend you that."

Thus was Lord Hugh made instrumental in reconciling the friars to their loss. Henceforward they entered into the project as wholeheartedly as the rest of us.

CHAPTER 4

OVISHAM FAIR

AUTUMN AND WINTER brought more and more wanderers to Bedesford for the term of the hungry season and perhaps for good. With them came the first rumors, confirmed after Christmas, that Ovisham town was making ready for a revival of its Easter fair. Business had not chanced, during his brief married life, to take John Trefeller round the country east of Bedesford; and so far Juliana on her own had merely retraced her travels with him. She was determined to go to the fair and this time did not trouble to conceal her preparations, openly offering to undertake small commissions for people. She took with her Geoffrey Widowson and Gilliam Smith and her three-year-old daughter.

Elizabeth, as she was called, was a fair and sturdy child, with rosy brown limbs whose firmness belied their dimples, her father's blue eyes, and soft straight yellow hair. She was dressed all in red, with a string of corals round her little neck. Yet she cried all the way to Ovisham, so that the company got scarcely any sleep. She only left off crying to be sick.

John's old shipmaster, whom Juliana had notified of her intentions early in the new year, came to meet the wagon at the town boundary, patently dismayed at the sight and squalling of the little girl. Juliana shook her even as she greeted him. "Master Lamb will hang you from the tall main mast of your father's ship for the sea gulls to peck and laugh at! She has been like this ever since she parted from her nurse at Bedesford. A bad, ugly, wicked girl is she, and I fear me takes after her Uncle Hugh."

"Whatever possessed—what made you bring her, Mistress?" the Captain asked, walking along beside the wagon.

"I deemed it would be a great boon for her to see the fair. I had no mind to be without both my children this time. You knew I have a son as well? He is too young to travel without grave necessity, albeit *he* cried to see us go. But this one here— She did not miss her mother either of the times I was away from Bedesford. My dog knew me again and rejoiced to have me back. My daughter turned from me with screeching and hid her face in her nurse's skirts. So now shall she forget Jeanne for a change!"

Master Lamb was not tall, but nigh as broad as he was long, especially at the shoulders. His neck and arms bulged with muscle, his fingers were like hammers. He walked as sailors do, swinging his paunch from side to side, and his cracked voice was so used to contending against storm and swell that he was incapable of lowering it.

"I have bespoken room for you and yours at the Cock and Bull, Mistress—the only inn that is open this year. Black Andrew—he's the host, though house and ground belong to the Cistercians—will grow so rich, this time next year he will be having his own tavern. Ever since the raid on Gannet Island he has been lucky. I was in it too, but the spoils did not make a wealthy man of me! Certainly I will tell you about that— later, for here we are. Look, Mistress. Yonder lies the sea. That is the lighthouse, over there, and that the harbor, horseshoe shaped. Right over there, at the northern tip, are John's warehouses, next door to where the royal flag is hoist. Turn this way now. That square tower with the four pointed turrets on top belongs to the lepers, or rather, the Knights of St. Lazarus. Theirs was the only church open at the time when I heard of John's death, so there it was I had a candle burned for him. Let me lift you down, Mistress."

Juliana had caused to be made over for herself most of John's clothes, save the very newest and finest, which were laid away in bay and rose leaves for his son. The heavy, boldly patterned cloth that had hung well upon John's burly frame, bunched round her in the most unsightly manner. Over a russet gown bordered with tails of marten, she wore a fleece-lined cloak, its enormous hood fastened with gold pins to her widow's bands. Amid all this her long little yellow face with its black eyes and snapping lips seemed to live independently, without a body. Howbeit she looked incontestably rich, so the captain comforted himself as he led her and Gillian with the child through the noisy taproom.

On two sides of the taproom, doorways opened into a number of narrow chambers with bedstraw on the floor.

Into one of these Master Lamb ushered the two women and the child and then helped the host carry in a settle and a brazier. He showed Gillian how to curtain the open door with cloaks, and fetched food and drink for them. Elizabeth fell asleep before she could be fed, and thankfully they laid her to rest on the bed. They made a hearty meal of porridge, stew of gannets, bread, and sweetened ale. Gillian soon joined the child. Juliana and Master Lamb sat on with the ale bowl between them and talked of old times.

"Gannet for sure makes vile eating," Juliana grimaced. "Pour me another cupful, Master Lamb, to take away the taste. Now tell me how you raided the Isle of Gannets. All we heard in Bedesford was that you made an end of the pirates' nest."

"Well, Mistress," said the Captain, warming the ladle again, "there is not much else to tell, really. We had all grown so tired here of moping through two successive winters. So we fittted up an empty ship that had been riding at anchor since the Black Death—every man belonging to her died in the Knights' lazaretto—all the lepers had broken out, you must know, and roamed dancing and drinking through the town. One or two of the ships out there have their crews and masters still on board. The Black Friars have been talking of rowing out to get the bones and giving them burial, but thus far—"

"Yes, yes, Master Lamb. We had the Black Death, too, in Bedesford."

"Well, so we took the Isle of Gannets by surprise. There were none too many of the pirates left, either. But not one got away."

"And the piratesses?"

"They fought like she-devils. Some killed their own children at the finish. There was one old woman, with gray hair loose and flying, pulled her two grown daughters back into the hut which was on fire, and barred the door on the inside."

"You killed them, too, the women?"

"What else? What do you think? Most of us were married men, and good Christians all. The Lord God was on our side. Only one of us was lost. All the rest recovered from our wounds. Look at mine"—he bared his huge arm to the shoulder, disclosing a deep furrow running its whole length. "I must show you my sword sometime—like an old toothcomb along the edges. I am keeping it so for the memory. It is on board your ship. You have never seen her, have you? Tomorrow you must look her over. We have kept her in good trim between us, I and Tom. What are you going to do about her, and about the half-finished craft John had building at Ellasea? You know John trusted me as I might have been his brother, and though I myself say it, like a trusty brother did I earn his trust. I mean to be as good a friend to you. Just you say the word, and Tom and I will get you a crew—if we have to go to Bedesford and fight the Cloudsway Abbot for a handful of men!"

"I have not heard of anyone save Lord William who contrives to get men to work for him at no more than the statutes allow. He grants land to anyone who will work it, on hundred-year leases, without mill dues. Hugh will not be able to do less when he returns. I long to see his face! For he needs serving folk even more than I do, having none. Did you know I was the first in Bedesford to get any strangers into my service? Ay, this Gillian and her man. Oh, listen to all the bells. Day in, day out we hear no bell, at home. We have a new parish priest, but none has set eyes on him yet."

It must have been long after midnight when they parted, and still the sounds of carousal in the main guest room went on. They sounded worse without the eye's interpretation, Juliana discovered the next day, when she too began to use the room. She and Gillian and the child met Geoffrey there and broke their fast together. There Master Lamb would daily call for and return her, himself having a standing arrangement with Black Andrew for his food all the year round, until such time as he resumed his proper employment. He was not ashamed to advance his growing debt to the innkeeper as a reason for urging Juliana to send him overseas, whereas his great longing for his element seemed to strike him as a thing it behoved him to hide.

There was very little loose behavior, much less sheer roistering, about the taproom. Staid and respectable folk outnumbered the young and feckless that commonly predominate at fair times. Everyone was here on business of one sort and another, even youth and shiftlessness steadied by tenacity of purpose.

Some others besides Master Lamb and his mate ate at the water-front tavern and there transacted a measure of business, although they had their beds elsewhere. The royal inspectors and excise men, the harbor master and the lighthouse keeper did so. Then there was a party whom he but pointed out to her, careful to sit with his back to them, and speaking out of the corner of his mouth.

"Nay, Mistress, those I cannot bring before you, nor you to them. I scarce know them to speak to. In trade you will come up against them soon enough. They are great merchants of the Staple, of London, and they have their own big yard here, and another at home, and a third at Antwerp itself. Ay, John knew them and—listen well—was worsted by them in his time. This brings me to a matter I have meant to broach all along. Mistress, have you thought of marrying again?"

"No!" said Juliana, cold and alert, raising her colorless eyebrows and pursing her mouth into an arrowhead.

"Do not look so at me that have naught but your weal at heart," the Captain pursued, undeterred. "In that case, have you looked about you for a business partner?"

"That I have not either; and I see no need of one."

"It will not be long before you do, Mistress. I should be unworthy of your husband's friendship if I let you stop me warning you. Ay, you have accomplished much and Anglemere is full of it. But now that things are beginning to settle and all the great men of commerce bestirring themselves again, think you they will let you keep the headway you have gained? Will they allow you, a woman, to join any guild?"

"Guilds! We have as many guilds as single craftsmen in Bedesford, Master Lamb! So can I call myself a guild too."

"You are wrong, Mistress Trefeller, and before you are many days older you will believe me. But it were better you did not wait to be convinced. They could find ways to stop your trading tomorrow, but they mean to teach you a lesson first, and it is like to be a costly one. If your wisdom is as good as its repute, you will empower some honest fellow to act for you ere you find yourself a great deal the poorer."

"I can see you have a partner in mind for me!"

"Yes. I will not deny it. Who else is there but myself? Unless, to be sure, you wished to hand over agency for your goods entirely to some other merchant. I should have spoken of this directly you arrived. Now you see why I could not immediately bring myself to it."

Juliana's face had softened, her eyes were half closed. If he thought this forecast agreement, he was wrong. "So they have been talking about me, have they, all and sundry? They shall have reason to talk more. You shall not lose by it if I win, Master Lamb. For it cannot be that they promised to fee you if you succeeded in frightening me off? Now must I say, 'Do not look so.' Did you not hear me? I said it could not be! But you have not told me who the third man is whom they have ever with them, those wicked two. I have seen so many go up to greet him, he cannot be mere servant of theirs?"

This person had attracted Juliana's attention from the first because of his strange, pleasing looks. He seemed young, and beside the color of his hair the Cinqmort sandiness paled to very ashes. It was the deep, dark red of the proudest feather in the cock's tail, and, trimmed evenly all round his head, it looked like a close-fitting cap of such glossy plumage. He was very well built and very well dressed, with a cheerful, square face and strongly marked features.

As by no flicker of contrition Juliana would concede him reason to feel wronged, Master Lamb found it outside his power to maintain an offended demeanor and withhold an answer. "He is a Fleming of Antwerp, and is lodging with them. He came over on one of their vessels laid up in Flanders during the scourge. A ship of his own, captained by a kinsman, left Antwerp for England just before. He has had no news of it since and is making inquiries at all likely ports. His crew and captain may be buried somewhere, and his goods in storage. Everyone that used to go to Antwerp every year knows him. He comes of a rich and astute family, and as he has not come to buy and sell on his own account, folk seem to think he can give them good advice. He denies it to none—so if you ask me it cannot be worth much."

Juliana soon had proof of Master Lamb's good faith. She knew, as John had known, that she had the gift for trading. She knew her chance was here and now, although as yet its nature eluded her. In the meantime she was made to feel intangible opposition. She could not strike one advantageous bargain. To show her mettle and boast of her resources, she let a fifth of her wool go at a loss before sitting back, so to speak, and holding on tightly to the remainder, with an air of unconcerned and indefinite patience.

One thing she counted vaguely as a gain was that she had come to be on speaking terms with the red-haired Fleming. Elizabeth had provided the occasion. Far from fretting any longer, the little girl had shown herself irrepressibly playful from her first morning at the inn. Gillian could not control her; her mother was often out. All the other grown folk delighted in her wildness and encouraged it until they themselves must regret it. At mealtimes Elizabeth could seldom be constrained to stay in her place on the bench. She would watch her opportunity to run round and pester her various acquaintances. Once Juliana, returning from the quayside, found her daughter sitting on the Fleming's shoulders as he ate, absorbedly stroking his hair with both her small ungentle hands. Another time, when they had been hunting high and low for Elizabeth, the Fleming retrieved her from the boat shed. He called himself Lucas, Son of Robin.

The only person whom the little girl's attentions had brought to serious harm was the innkeeper. She caramboled into him one evening as he came bearing a caldron of porridge just off the fire and, trying to save her, he scalded himself badly. Juliana punished her in spite of his intercession, and in spite of her private opinion that this same mishap might well have befallen without Elizabeth. For she had observed, as she knew others had also, that something of the kind was forever happening to the man. If he was not cutting or burning himself he would slip and hurt his knee or sprain his wrist, break his own spoons, spill or forget to stopper his own ale, and get his head bumped.

Overnight Elizabeth fell into a high fever. None could tell what ailed her. They fetched one of the Black Friars, whose church the visitors from Bedesford had been attending, and a leech wife from the ill-reputed east side, when the priest could not help. No remedy availed. The child lay insensible, now boiling to the touch, now cold as ice; now tossing and moaning, now limp and still. Matter seeped from her ears and nostrils and stuck down her eyelids, and she seemed to shrink visibly as her body was drained of all moisture.

Gillian, who had no children of her own, loved Elizabeth, although the child had given her scant return for her affection, and she tended her without rest. Juliana had never loved Elizabeth as she did Little John, even before she had him, but she did not want to lose her daughter. The guests all sent messages, suggestions, toys, and dainties. Master Lamb went about subdued by superstitious dread of a death in the house. When after five days Elizabeth showed no sign of mending, people began to accept it that there was no hope.

CHAPTER 5

SWAN YGERN

THEY PUT DOWN extra floor straw in the taproom and straw on the cobbles round the inn. Black Andrew lost some custom. The resident guests drank less to help them keep quiet, and went much earlier to rest.

Late in the evening of the fifth day, the innkeeper, Juliana, Geoffrey, and Master Lamb found themselves the only persons still awake and sitting up; others lay sleeping on the benches and the floor, or had retired to their rooms and alcoves. Gillian was with Elizabeth. Master Lamb rose at last and stretched, and offered to accompany Juliana to the midnight Mass at the Church of Christ-the-Infant. She shook her head and let it sink back on her arms, reposing crossed upon the table. Geoffrey said he would like to go with the Captain since he could not do any good here, and the two departed, shamefaced, with words of false hopefulness.

"Mistress Trefeller, all is not yet lost." Black Andrew got up and stood over her, leaning on his fists. "We have not yet tried everything. I have a woman living here that no one knows of, and she has great skill. Let me fetch her. But see that you do not waken any of these others meanwhile."

Juliana had sat up wearily and stared after him out of blank, red eyes.

He returned with a tall woman moving very quietly on long narrow, naked feet, dressed in a man's sleeveless kirtle of brown stuff with a belt of rope. Her slender arms were white but streaked with dirt. Round her head was tied a nettle-cloth kerchief which left bare her broad forehead and throat. She had great, sea-gray eyes. Juliana looked up at this woman in the same helpless, gaping way as before. The innkeeper motioned her to lead the way into the sick chamber. Gillian sat on the floor, one arm pillowing Elizabeth's head, her other hand chafing the small feet under the covers; her face was gray as wasps' nests. She whispered that there had been no change. She also was too tired to be curious.

The woman bent over the bed, nodded, and said that they must leave her alone with the child. She had a harsh, hard, foreigner's way of speaking, but that was only her voice, not her tone. The three of them returned to the barely glimmering hearth. Gillian fell asleep the instant she let herself.

Once the innkeeper rose and made as to tiptoe back to where a faint rim of light showed under the screen of cloaks. But he thought better of it halfway. Juliana looked at him, and, beyond asking questions, looked away again, at nothing. Afterward, she could not recall having heard any sound from the sickroom the entire time. Black Andrew fell to crossing himself and murmuring paternosters. Presently his eyes closed. The mother could not even pray.

She, too, must have fallen asleep. Suddenly the strange woman stood touching her shoulder and, as she started up, beckoned her to follow.

Juliana advanced hesitantly. She had to make more than one effort before she could bring herself to look at Elizabeth. The same two rushlights they had lit at dusk were still burning. It seemed to her that they were still the same length as when she had left the woman here. The child lay, pale and diminished enough, but with open, clear, and knowing eyes, her breathing regular and easy. When she saw her mother weep she looked frightened and began to struggle. The tall woman stepped between them and placed her long, supple fingers across the child's brow. Elizabeth's eye closed and she rolled over on her side, laid her cheek on her doubled fists, drew up her little knees, and slept. The woman helped Juliana to sit down.

"Is it true?" the mother asked weakly. "Have you made her well in this short time? The air is so clean and fresh in here on a sudden. Who are you? Are you a witch?"

"People that had no cause to love me have sometimes called me so," the woman said, in gentle rebuke.

"I did not mean to vex you. I hardly know what I am saying."

"Ay, you are tired out, body and soul, poor being. Come then, and I will refresh you." The woman drew Juliana onto her lap and rocked her slowly in her arms.

When she awakened, undressed and in bed, the woman was still there, in the light of dawn, squatting on her heels opposite the bed. The lights were burning even yet, and no lower. A few strands of hair with a little straw sticking in them had escaped from the woman's kerchief. Now one could see that her hair was as purest gold. We have never seen its like. Even matted and mixed with straw, it was unbelievably golden. The stray looked white against it and sheenless, and it made Elizabeth's fair head to look a dull, pale brown.

Juliana raised herself on one elbow. "So you were not a dream. Pray tell me who you are and how I may thank you."

"I am Swam Ygern, a princess and poor prisoner."

"Whose prisoner?" asked Juliana, beginning to guess.

The woman nodded, as much as to say she knew Juliana had guessed, and guessed aright. "Black Andrew brought me back by stealth from our ravaged island kingdom. I have lived, a bound prisoner, in an airless, lightless hole upstairs, ever since. I wonder if you can picture what that life has been like. Now at last he thinks he might let me go." She laughed a little, grimly.

"Where will you go?" she asked, trying to speak as if captive piratesses were encountered every day. "You cannot go back to your island."

"I know not whither I shall go. I did not mean he will let me go free. He will sell me. Thus my fate will be righted."

"How do you mean this?" Juliana said uneasily. But the woman only smiled, and never dropped or shifted her straight gaze, Juliana had a feeling that she was sunk in a deep slumber, yet being left aware, capable of enjoying the sensuous, healthful bliss of sleep. It was a revelation that such happiness could reside in so uneventful and impersonal a state. And even in the celestial thoughtlessness of the condition she recognized Elizabeth's savior for its source.

She did not think she had closed her eyes; but presently her eyes grew conscious of it that the woman in the room with her was Gillian, silently praying over Elizabeth. From the taproom came the noises of breakfast.

"Are you awake, Mistress? Is not this the fairest miracle?" Gillian smiled through her tears.

"Yes," Juliana said, absently. "You shall have a fine present for all your faithful watching. Help me to dress."

In the taproom everybody knew already, and rose to Juliana's entry with cheering and congratulations. Only Black Andrew did not come forward, but stayed among his barrels, avoiding even her glance.

"Did you know about this, about Master Andrew's captive?" she asked the Captain later on.

Master Lamb shrugged and averted his eyes. "Some of us suspected. Especially when all he touched began to turn out lucky for him at the first—and then when it seemed all the small, unliving things of this world began to persecute him. None actually saw him make off with her. But we did not find her among the dead, and we had noted her, some of us, during the battle, for her looks. I could wish your child might have been saved by other means."

"How do you know what means she employed?" Juliana flared up. "Elizabeth has not vanished since, when one made the sign of the cross over her, nor has any demon shrieked from inside her in response to prayer. Having killed all her friends and kin and laid waste her home, one might think at least you would incline to charity toward her, poor creature. A princess was she, so she told me—"

"They all called themselves kings and princes on that island." Master Lamb said contemptuously. "Our swineherds would deem themselves hardly used if they had to dwell in those kings' palaces! When you defend her so, do you keep in mind what she is? Not only did she live a heathen outlaw, to kill whom is not murder, but what do you think Black Andrew kept her locked up for? Not just to bring him luck, I'll warrant! You only have to look at her."

"For shame, Master Lamb! And I do not think she is so fair as all that."

"She *is* fair. Withal it is never unalloyed fairness which will take possession of men in the way Andrew has been obsessed. Maybe a woman would not know, nor be able to see it so."

"She is too tall."

"Ay, one wants to bring her low."

"—too calm and grave and proud—"

"Ay, it makes one want to break her."

"Master Lamb, how wicked you are and depraved!"

The Captain chuckled, "Nay, Mistress, I was but trying to explain. Any *man* would understand. Have you rewarded her? At all events, you must have no further truck with her, promise me that."

"I have hardly thanked, let alone rewarded, her, and so I cannot promise."

"She has lost no time in bewitching you," Master Lamb said angrily. "I will see to it that she does not trouble you further."

But he had not reckoned with the innkeeper's own designs, or those of the witch.

Still not overanxious to look her full in the face, Black Andrew sought speech with Mistress Trefeller and offered her his bondwoman for sale. "It is not only that she has such rare leech's skill. She is strong and most able besides, and good at keeping rats away and cattle in good health. They make good servants, her people, when once they have bound them to fidelity, so I have heard. They will do anything rather than break their sworn troth. I could get a better price for her from the Londoners. But if they had her to keep house for them here, I know I should lose by it in the end. Apart from that, Mistress, I wanted you to have the first refusal, that are of my own country."

"Why do you want to part with her?"

"I am a widower," Black Andrew replied virtuously. "I should soon have the priests on me. It is not always fair time at Ovisham. Most of the year I have few guests. Then there is not much work about the inn, and I go out with the others after fish."

"Ay, let me talk to her again."

She had noticed, and wondered whether other people had also, that no more accidents were happening to him.

"How can I be sure," she said to the bondwoman when they were alone, "that you will not deal by me as I believe you have by your present master, Swan? I cannot say the other."

"He is not my master," Swan Ygern said earnestly. "He does not own me. Can a thief own what does not belong to him?"

"Why do you want to belong to me? For I am right, am I not, and this is mostly your doing?"

The woman answered, "To tear your daughter from the arms of death already clasping her, I had in a sense to give birth to her anew. Thus you, her mother in the flesh, are become my kin by the subtlest, strongest ties. It is so that I am barren, yet it is ordained that I shall have a daughter. The first part of the prophecy has now come true. I must help fulfill the rest. Only in true bonding can freedom be restored to me: so the Powers spoke through the Priest-King's lips."

"What powers? Are you a baptized Christian? What is all this dark talk? You had better tell me your story."

"Had I that?" the woman smiled, and veiled her eyes with golden lashes. "Ay, we are Christians where I come from, but that our manner of worship, I am told, differs somewhat from yours. And the spirits of our royal ancestors dwell amongst us and speak through our priests that are also our kings. My father was the king. I was his only child and the Island's sacred virgin—as you on the mainland have nuns. Swan Ygern must walk round each new craft swelling our fleet, to bless it with cross and mead and torch of juniper. When a new house was built, Swan Ygern must sing safety into its foundations. On every new-forged blade, sword, or plowshare, she alone could confer virtue. I was our harvests, heaped with a tithe of spoils, earth wrung or sea won; I our mischances, punishment for which was not the least of my honor and glory."

"Then how could it be—"

"Wait. I was accounted very fair to look upon, among my people. One night, one of our warriors stole upon me where I slept in the sacred pine grove. He was big and strong, taller and stronger than I am, and he had his will of me ere I could summon magic to prevent him. I cried out, and the guards came, and killed him with their shields, so that I brought him death after all. But then what I deemed great injustice was done me. They punished *me* for that I was sacred virgin no more. My Father sat swaying over the sacred smoke and let the Powers speak through him. My life was to be spared, for our ancestors wanted me among their company in time, but I must retrieve what I had lost in lifelong bondage. But then I forgot Who it was spoke through the king, and I swore vengeance to all that upheld the judgment. I was given to a man of mean blood for his thrall and wife. So I wove my spells and brought disaster on my island and death to all that lived there."

"If you could do all that, and do what you did for my daughter, and make Black Andrew wish he had not got you, I should not have thought bonds and locked doors could have kept you prisoner."

"And you are right. It is not the jail has kept me so, nor the jailer. The powers I was born with are God given, like any other skill. It is only when we that hold them employ these powers for evil ends, that the Devil gains a part in them. Human weakness cannot always withstand the temptation of wreaking ill, when such is one's power. But, thus yielding, we not only give ourselves up to the Tempter. We also exchange strength for weakness. I have done wrong, I worked a great harm. Thus did some of the power go out of me. Before it can be replenished I must endure harm for the harm I did. I am not free. But it is not Black Andrew has my freedom under lock and key. Now if you buy me I shall belong to you. The life I want can only be founded in the luck of whomsoever owns me. You should never regret owning me. And it is ordained that you must buy me."

"But—"

"Soon I shall begin to think you are chaffering over the price of your child's life." The woman had risen, towering over Juliana, yet benign in severity. The sunlight was coming through the small window, its slanting stream cutting across and enveloping her, so that she seemed to be growing from, hovering in a fountain of it. Some of the sun's warmth brushed Juliana, who confusedly felt it to emanate from the other. The recollection of her sense of well-being in Swan Ygern's arms blended with other memories. She put up her arms, like a child, to have the embrace renewed.

"This is Swan, who saved Elizabeth," Juliana later made her known to Gillian. "She will stay with us. Bedesford shall see me return with yet another serving-woman. So maybe I will let you go, and James, as you have been desiring me to. We shall see."

Master Lamb was kept from hearing of the bargain till after it had been concluded. He was beside himself with ire and foreboding, which Juliana took as something droll. However, she did not at once resume going out to the mart with him, although her convalescent child could now be left in twofold charge. It was as if she had no further thought of wool and sales, content to have bought, content with her purchase. In after days Gillian told us she had found it far from pleasant to watch Julian's cooping herself up with this new toy, the witch. Sometimes Gillian feared the Mistress had forgotten her home and, like the knight in the lay whom the mountain folk lured underground, would never return among the truly living.

CHAPTER 6

LUCAS, SON OF ROBIN

"This Day You must come out with me, Mistress Trefeller," Master Lamb bustled up to her one morning. "The first Lombard ship came into port last night. They were delayed by storms, the pilot has been telling us. Little do they know they owe it to us, that they did not find pirates lying in wait for them, too! No good can come of having any truck with any of that breed, you heed my words, Mistress—"

"What breed? The Lombards?"

"You know well it was not them I meant, though it is also true few men have ever bested a Lombard merchant. You will not have seen all the sights if you do not see them. We might make inquiry, too, in a general way, as to what is doing in the southern lands they hail from. John and I once did well out of a cargo of figs, I mind. Come. Come out with me, dear Mistress. For a merchant not to have seen the Lombards is the same as—as for an Englishman never to have breathed sea air."

"It is true I need to buy a pair of shoes which I promised Gillian." Juliana pretended to consent grudgingly. But for once she got ready by herself, without dawdling under her new bondwoman's mothering.

Although the two were early, the mart already displayed its usual aspect, with the usual din. Horses stamped and neighed, crane ropes screeched up and down, handcarts and iron-hooped barrels striking sparks from the cobbles as they were rolled in and out of open warehouses. Everybody had hastened early to see the Lombards coming in. Master Goodrich and Master Mercer stood deep in talk with their Flemish friend and the harbor master.

"Ah, Mistress, look there!" The Captain suddenly nudged her.

The Lombards came striding with fragile aplomb, as different from the rest as Spanish horses are from Shire. Their eyes were like jewels, their locks like blue grapes, their complexions like finest parchment smoky with a cerise flame burning softly behind it. Their garments bloomed about them as full-blown rose leaves cluster on the stalk, puffing out the bodies, but emphasizing the lithe animation of thighs, calves, hands wriggling with what looked twice the right number of fingers, and slender, beard-furred throats. Compared with theirs, Hugh Cinqmort's wardrobe was dull and drab, even though in hue these silks and furs and velvets were so sober sad as almost to seem clerical. Pride sat upon them like contempt, as they forged through the crowds at the head of servingmen and carriers. Among the latter was a Moor and several men looking just like ordinary folk, piteously loaded.

Unexpectedly, Juliana turned right about, stamped her foot, and pulled hard at Master Lamb's sleeve. "Let us go. I *will* not stay here longer to honor them with our staring, those heathen peacocks! Well, do you stay. *I* will not." She was off, the crowd yielding and meeting again behind her. Master Lamb shrugged his lowering great shoulders and resumed his previous position.

Before long he was glad she had gone and so missed what happened, enabling him to bring her the news. He hurried so that he arrived at the inn out of breath and while the tap room was empty but for Black Andrew and a pauper crone who did most of the tavern's indoor work.

"What do you think, Mistress! Lucas of Antwerp, the red Fleming, got his news at last today. Ay, he asked the Lombards, as he has every new arrival since he first set foot in Ovisham. One of their Christian slaves came forward and swore on oath two of Lucas's crew had been in the batch of men among whom he himself had been driven to market. Ay, the pirates had got the lot. The rest had been drowned or slain or died of the bowel flux after, among the rats in the pirates' hold. Lucas questioned him till he must be satisfied. The man had the name of Lucas' ship all pat and described his cousin beyond doubt, it seems. Ay, the cousin was one of the pair."

"Poor Lucas."

"You do not know how poor, Mistress. I saw him with my own eyes, delving into his belt pouch, and drawing his hand out empty. In the end he ripped the big clasp out of his hat and gave it the man for harbinger's fee. And then you should have seen! When they parted, you should have seen folk move toward him apace from every corner of the mart. One would not have thought, to watch them all flock round him in the past as he might be a prince or sage, that they were his creditors, one and all!"

"But I thought you told me he was rich."

"I knew no better. Rich he used to be. But, you see, it is three years since the ship was lost, and the Black Death started earlier in Flanders and went on longer. I know not rightly how it was. There is Master Cyprian coming in now, he may know. Shall I go and invite him over in your name?"

The Master of the Royal Scales accepted with alacrity, and Andrew and his woman flew to serve him, to lose as little as possible of the talk.

The room had gradually filled; everyone was talking about the same thing. For sure, the company had never been waited on with like promptitude and assiduous hovering. Lucas himself was not there. The Master of the Royal Scales went on with his contribution, perforce addressed to Master Lamb. Juliana's eyes looked vacant, since all her mind was concentrated in her eyes, trying to listen in every direction.

"What will he do now?"

"He will have to take service."

"Does he mean to go back to Flanders right away, has he said?"

"If he does, he'll have to pledge his service to pay his fare!"

"Surely we are not such carrion crows, all of us? Surely the one or the other of us would give him free passage? Had I a ship, or even a cargo to be sent, I would offer to let him go with it."

"But how is he to live in the meantime?" Master Cyprian spoke up, brisk and strident. "He has a hankering to stay in England. Lucas' father came from these shores, knew you that? The mother was Flemish. They married two sisters, Jude and Robin. Alack, it is not a question of what he would most like to do, poor fellow. He will have to take whatever opportunity offers. And folk will scarcely vie to bid for his services, after today."

"His luck has turned," Master Lamb now seconded lugubriously. "He has lost too much. All his life he has had wealth behind him. He will be fortunate, poor Lucas, to get any employment at all."

Not until the Black Friars' bells tolled for nones did anyone get up to go. Juliana had meant to accompany the Crown official and Master Lamb to her warehouse, but she said she felt tired and begged them to excuse her. Gillian might avail herself of their escort. It was some time since she had had an outing; she and Geoffrey could go along to church.

The big room grew cold in untidy desertion. The fire was low, with a rustling, now and again, as of a mouse beneath the ashes. Juliana went in to Swan Ygern and Elizabeth, who were playing some impenetrable game of their joint invention. "Send her to sleep, Swan. I want to talk to you."

The witch in those early days was an odd mixture of trancendent sagacity and savage's artlessness. In all matters of nature, of the mind and heart, motive and feeling, her appraisal was inordinately quick and penetrating, her action or suggested action thereupon infallibly right. But her knowledge of the actual world was very small, confined to existence on the Isle of Gannets, and sea battles at secondhand. Battles for material ends, yet without material weapons, she had not then begun to understand. Life in Juliana's alcove, within sight and hearing of the taproom, was full of surprises for her. Juliana, whose wont it was otherwise to exaggerate her own part, underrating others', now in magnanimous infatuation attributed much of the work of her own brain to her possession of Swan Ygern. Now she wished to talk about Lucas with Swan Ygern.

In the evening, when all the company was again assembled, Lucas of Antwerp came also. Everybody raised a kindly outcry, asking where he had been and why he looked different. He spread out his arms to show off his changed attire; he had sold all his fine garments, gloves, and ornaments and all to have Mass said for his cousin and the crew. Several people jumped up and called him over to be their guest at this meal, Juliana among them. Howbeit, she went further and sent her little daughter scuffling through the litter to fetch him. This was the first time Elizabeth had appeared among the guests since her illness. A score of caressing hands were stretched out all along her path, amid blessings and fond apostrophe. It would only have surprised folk if the Fleming had failed to accept this of all invitations.

"You are very kind, Mistress," the Fleming said, with a little bow, accepting the cup from which she had drunk to him. But he said it as he might have done the night before, in courtly and by no means abject wise. He repeated the words when she expressed sorrow for his misfortune, but spoke only of the deaths, which he seemed to feel partly resting on his conscience.

"What will you do? Keep still, Elizabeth, else will I send you to bed."

"Nay, she is not troubling me, Mistress. I like to have her on my lap, such a sweet and comely little girl. Do? Oh, something—something new for preference."

"You have not struck any bargain yet, then?"

"No, not yet."

"Have you had many offers?"

"Not yet, either," Lucas laughed. "Nobody wants to be the first, I trow. Everyone wants to have another before him, to outbid."

"You may be wrong there," Juliana, lowering her voice, said gravely, with a flicker of a glance in the direction of the staplers who, sure enough, were looking their way, too. "Some may be trying to keep everybody else from making *any* offers. To get you cheaply, you understand."

"Oh, I understand right enough." The Fleming laughed again, and tickled Elizabeth, so that her squealing drowned the conversation for yards around. "And do I also understand aright, that you yourself wish to make me an offer, Mistress?"

"Might I not have been warning you out of pure kindness of heart?"

"That goes without saying. The more if my surmise is true, for you have let me know that you have mighty competitors."

"But will not this have set you against them?" Juliana let slip in perplexed simplicity. "There you go, laughing at me again! That I deem ill reward and ill manners." Even thus had John Trefeller used to laugh at his wife.

"Forgive me, Mistress. I must laugh all I can, these first few days, to keep from crying. Nay, if I wanted to close with them of whom we have been talking, why should this deter me? I know them well; folk do not grow so rich quite without cunning. I should merely be the more on my guard. But toward you now I find myself quite disarmed!"

Juliana suppressed the wish to bridle. "Do you mean you are willing to listen to me?"

"Every word you say makes me more willing," Lucas said, almost tenderly. "God help you, God help us both, Mistress. You need the protection of a man of business!"

CHAPTER 7

STRANGERS IN THE TOWN

THE TREFELLER WAGON arrived back in Bedesford about the middle of the third fallows plowing, so that folk were unable to welcome Juliana in form and flock to see at close quarters whom she had brought with her this time.

Juliana tapped her foot, not to find Jeanne ready at the gate, though the housekeeper came dashing out before ever the oxen were unharnessed.

"God be praised, Juliana, for your safe return—and Elizabeth, my darling," she cried, handed Little John to his mother, and went down on her knees in the black mud to greet her foster daughter. Elizabeth faced her unmoved. When Jeanne began to kiss her, the child jerked away, clasped the legs of Swan Ygern, and hid her face in her new nurse's dress. Still on her knees, empty arms still extended, Jeanne looked at the other woman whom thus far she had not spared a glance. Swan Ygern smiled down at her, and inclined her head, as much as to crave Jeanne's indulgence for a silly child. It was this, Jeanne said later, that pierced her to the heart, "If she had looked pleased as I know she was in her heart, I should not have felt worse than I already did. But that she, a stranger, should take it upon herself to ask *me* to pardon *my* Elizabeth. As if it were she and not I had given life to that child from the day of her birth and watched every hair grow on her head!"

"See, Jeanne," Juliana said genially, "behold the company I have brought back for us. No longer will you need to work so hard, faithful friend that you have been to me." Jeanne stared as if she had been struck. Juliana had never spoken to her thus: here was estrangement! "And there will be a man again at Trefeller Court, to keep those great lads in check that you ever complained you could not rule, and dealing with what Arthur used to see to—God rest his poor self-willed soul in purgatory. But it seems to me you are not looking very glad, Jeanne. They will not eat you, Swan here saved Elizabeth when everyone had given her up, and Lucas Robinson—though they used to be great folk, both, at one time, in their own countries. Oh, and there is Alfred. Come and let me see, child, how much you have grown. Elizabeth has shot up wondrously under Swan's care. Give me your hand, Alfred. No, no, the other one. Has your poor mother been too busy to teach you manners?"

Obediently, Alfred approached, looking faintly puzzled at the command to give her his right hand rather than his left. But at this his mother lunged forward and whisked him out of the way, behind her.

"Whatever ails you, Jeanne?" asked Juliana, handing her own son over to Swan Ygern.

"Leave him be," Jeanne said, in a choked voice. "Leave my son, my only lamb. I will not have him—measured."

Juliana shook her head and shrugged. "Well, need we wait out here in the cold until the others see fit to come and greet us? I should have thought at least they would be eager to unload, to see what gifts I have brought back for everybody."

"There is no one else," said Jeanne, leading the way, and pushing Alfred ahead of her. "You will find everything in a fit state to receive you, for all that I had nobody to help me. James and Edwin have been taking care of your fields, but they have scarce been near the house. Ay, here is some bad news. My brother Jack and Edwin's niece Joan ran off together the night after you had left."

"I grieve to hear it for their sakes," Juliana said with dignity. "I shall not feel their loss, not now. But I am sorry, too, for you and Edwin, that these young kinsfolk of yours should have committed their souls to eternal damnation. Here we are. Is not this pleasant? Ah, how I envy the lot of all women who may stay quietly at home, year in, year out. What do you say to my hall, Lucas? Is it not bigger than you expected? Wait till you see the rest of the buildings. You, too, Swan. I shall show you round in the morning. Now, perhaps, if Jeanne will let us have something to eat?"

Without a word to Swan Ygern, Jeanne had taken Little John from her and carried him to his cradle. Gillian followed her out into the kitchen, Swan Ygern making no such move. For once she did not even heed Elizabeth's tugging at her skirt. All she could do was gaze about intently, at the fine hangings and cushions everywhere, the well-wrought furniture, and the hearth that could accommodate an ox. "She looked like a new cat that wants to mark all the outways," so Jeanne described her. Lucas, Jeanne said further, bore himself like a guest, polite and approving. She could have given him a fair shaking. It is strange that these two did not take to each other. They had one thing in common which they shared with no one else: their aversion to Swan Ygern.

Jeanne and Gillian returned, bearing jugs and dishes, with little Alfred balancing a round loaf in one hand. He was no bigger than Elizabeth, but not as plump and rosy, and perhaps that was one reason why he looked older. He had fine hazel-brown hair which in time would darken to the color of his parents', and a clear-skinned, sun-tanned, happy little face. Jeanne, before sitting down, rearranged the bolsters behind Juliana's humped shoulders, and said she had sent Geoffrey to fetch James. But she jumped up constantly to see to the comfort of the others, and in any case would have had little chance to eat, glad to gratify Juliana's appetite for news.

"The fallow deer are growing to be a great plague again—worse than ever they were when Thomas was hayward. Folk are wishing Hugh would come back, that something may be done about it. But the upper Tew weir has been mended. The hop is coming along well but it looks as if there will not be many apples this year. Oh! and the lily Lord Jerome promised to have made, because of the flowers that grew on the building site, has come and is locked up in the crypt. It is made all of gold, except for the petals, which are of gems like purple glass."

She leaned forward on her elbows as she spoke. Meanwhile, her son bent over backward, reaching across behind Gillian for Elizabeth on Swan Ygern's lap. Mischievously, the little girl pretended not to see him, her blue eyes screwed up and her whole compact little body shaking with suppressed chuckles. Swan Ygern's eyes were still on other things. Alfred slipped off the bench and tiptoed round, and began very gently to pull at Swan Ygern's headcloth, a corner of which hung nearly to her waist. Elizabeth could hold off no longer and watched him with rewarding admiration.

"There is a swineherd again at last—one of the new people," Jeanne was saying, "and our parish priest is not yet come, but the friars have a new traveling altar and sing Mass each holy day out on the green—even at the Waste they sometimes do it, for all that the monks' dwellings are nearly finished. But what is the matter with me, witless woman? There is *real* news—you will never guess it, Juliana. Brother Laurentius is not dead after all. He is come back to us. You must send for him and hear his tales! He is the first to come back alive to tell them. Never have you heard the like, I promise—"

The head linen came off completely in Alfred's hand. Juliana looked up complacently as Jeanne exclaimed to see Swan Ygern's head shine suddenly like a lamp. Swan Ygern turned, smiling at Alfred, to retrieve the linen. Instead, she grasped the little wrist and looked at it closely. Jeanne leaped up.

"Let go my son's hand, you!"

Swan Ygern did not at once obey. "It might be that I could mend it," she said, placatingly. "You do not know. I am not unskilled in these things—"

"Let me look," Juliana cried, "I cannot see from here. What is wrong with your son's right hand, Jeanne?"

Jeanne was shaken by silent weeping. "Nothing, nothing is wrong with my fair little son. His right hand will grow and catch up with the left one yet, for sure. I took him to be blessed by the holy Hand the other day. St. Hand that has made whole many a true cripple. Already it has grown a little, little bigger than it was, I am certain."

"Come round here, Alfred, and show me," said Juliana. "How strange, Jeanne, I never noticed it before."

"It is because you used to see him every day, and now you have been away," Jeanne wept. "And the difference did seem to grow more marked only a few months back. I had managed to keep Edwin from knowing, till then. It is because of him I cannot bear it. Else for sure it were too trifling a thing to weep over. But he takes it so hard, Edwin does. Anything to do with Alfred—when Alfred falls and cuts his knee, Edwin seems to brood and sorrow over it and blame himself somehow!"

In vain Juliana tried to persuade her to let the stranger examine Alfred at leisure. Neither Jeanne nor Swan Ygern wished to hurt the child, yet neither would let him go.

The dogs barked outside and Geoffrey came in with Gillian's husband; and so Swan Ygern let Jeanne take Alfred away. Juliana asked the lad to bring a certain sack, and proceeded to distribute presents. Jeanne got a length of blue cloth for a holy-day dress and a little knife to be hung from her girdle, with a handle of carved narwhal bone. But Jeanne would not accept the latter. She seemed offended that it was tendered: such a gift could only cut asunder her and the Mistress' friendship.

Next day, Juliana took Lucas and Swan Ygern round Trefeller Court. She went to the trouble of unlocking every shed and storehouse, showing off everything there was. The big warehouse where all the wool was hoarded she left to the last. It was a lofty building, black—with tar on the outside and from sheer age within—and having two floors under a steeply pitched, finely ribbed roof. Here Swan Ygern began to lag behind, but Lucas displayed great animation, so that when the bondwoman did not follow them up the ladder into the loft, Juliana scarcely marked it.

"What is this?" he asked, as they had to wade through old, black wool loosely covering the gangways between stacked and suspended sacks.

"Oh, it is some old wool we found after the Black Death. I had it spread out like this after scalding, in the hope that the worst foulness might be driven out of it. I might have it worked up for our own use. I can hardly hope to sell it. See, the yolk is all gone out of it." She squatted down and ran her bony fingers through it, gathered some fistfuls and scattered them again.

"I have seen the merchants smell it," Lucas suggested.

"Yes!" Juliana laughed. "Would you say there was need to hold *this* close to your nose?"

"No! You see, so ignorant am I in these matters, I dare not consult my common sense." He, too, laughed and stepped out on to the rattling slats of the balcony, looking out over the yard and across at the houses and gardens beyond the Tew. Juliana joined him and stiffened, though she did not move away, when he took hold of her flowing sleeve. *"How much did you pay for this cloth?"*

The blood rushed back into Juliana's face and she twitched the sleeve away roughly. "Would you taunt me to my face, in my own country, Fleming? Do you think we do not know it here, what you are wont to say behind our backs in Flanders—that we are fools to let you sell us back our own wool at three times the price?"

Lucas' face grew red also. "I am no Fleming, you might remember, I have told you often enough. Ay, it crossed my mind what good sport it would be—and profitable—to silence that same old saying."

"How do you mean?" Juliana's blush faded but slowly, and her hand still trembled a little.

"The wool is here, and here is the most constant market for cloth. Why should there not be cloth made in England?"

"There is English cloth. Did you not know that? But it is quite unlike Flemish, and not as good."

"I meant Flemish cloth."

"But—but," Juliana stammered, still bewildered, yet taking fire, "such cloth can only be made in Flanders. Wool is grown in England, and Flemish cloth is woven in Flanders. It has always been so."

"There is no such thing as *always*. Time was when folk were *always* heathen, and the whole earth *always* unplowed wilderness. It is not the air and soil of Flanders make the quality of Flemish cloth, but the working secrets of her weavers. Secrets may be passed on—or found out. I have many good friends at home—I mean, in Flanders. At all events it is a thought to hold on to and turn over in one's mind of night—What say you? But do not speak of it, to anyone, no matter how well you may trust them," he added. "It is the kind of thought one must not even *think* too often, lest it take wings and roost in other heads."

"Juliana! Mistress, where are you?" they could hear Jeanne calling, up and down the yard. "Brother Laurentius is here."

At first glance the friar was not greatly altered. The wreath of hair round his head still contained as much ginger color as gray, his scalp and face and scrawny neck were still baked as red as Captain Lamb's. His hands were darker and showed some gout knots and callouses; but in all the years that we had known him his feet had surely been as scarred and black, the horn of the soles overflowing from under, as it were, with grit embedded in it as flies in amber.

Juliana asked for the friar's blessing and made him and Lucas known to one another. "Here is a countryman of yours. Strange, I have never met a Fleming who had not red hair. Yet this Lucas tells me they are not all so. Upon my soul, it is good to see you, Brother Laurentius. We all were sure you were with God. But no doubt everybody has been telling you so. It seemed such a long time since you had gone. Yet now that you stand before us, I cannot believe it was not yesterday!"

The friar nodded, all his wrinkles smiling. "It has seemed so to me, too. The years I was away have shrunk to the length of a night's dream and do not seem much more real, either. And now have I told my story so often, I begin to wonder whether I made it up in my head!"

"Oh, but you cannot have made it all up!" Juliana reassured him, so that he chuckled. "Tell us how you found your way to the outlaws in the first place."

"There was no difficulty. So many of them were sick that some had gone out to get help, even though it meant giving themselves up. Ay, you would be surprised to see how much brotherly kindness there is among them. Well, even so, we lost count of the time we spent wandering lost through the forest, Brother Hildebrandt and I, ere they came on us and took us prisoner. Many a night we spent up a tree and watched the wolves' eyes, alight, below. He died soon after we had been taken to the Beak, not of the sickness, just of the weariness and hardships. He was older than I and less strong; his soul is surely comforted. He knows, where I must still wonder, whether we did right."

"How so, Brother Laurentius?"

"Had they not come upon us, had we not gone out to them, they would have died at peace with God, duly executed, where now many live on, outlaws still. They were distrustful of us at the first. How could we have known there was sickness among them, they asked? Among them the sickness was different, more like the bowel flux, and not so many died of it. But when I could not save their chieftain, I thought for sure they would kill me. Howbeit, they did not hold his death against me. God guided their hearts so that they took a liking to me." He shrugged deprecatingly. "There was much to do. Not one of them, healthy or sick, had taken the sacrament in years."

"So they kept you with them?"

"In a manner of speaking." The friar smiled. "At first they did not like me to preach, but it grew on them. Then every child that had been born in outlawry I christened and instructed. Men and women came to me, begging to be joined in wedlock. Some would be married even as they lay dying. When the first year was out, as near as I could judge, I made ready to depart."

"Well, and then?"

"I must tell you that as soon as it seemed the sickness had passed, I had deemed it wrong to take further advantage of the dispensation I had to eat flesh meat—the more as it is mostly venison the outlaws subsist on. Thus do they sink more deeply into crime each day they eat and live. So I took to eating only mushrooms and berries, and sometimes a bird or a fishlet. So when I would have left they showed me a place where for months past they had been preserving berries and mushrooms and roots of all kinds—for my sole use, that I might be able to stay on without breach of vows. I am not ashamed to say that I wept tears. As time went on, I began to think God might give me grace to save them all yet, to persuade them to come out of the forest with me and be judged. But that was not granted me."

"And so you came back, good saint that you are."

"No! No! No!" cried the friar. "I could not redeem them because, in my pride, I was the most miserable sinner of them all. If people would but realize how with their praise they lacerate my soul! The outlaws themselves did so. And my eyes were opened at long last, and I saw that my staying had been no sacrifice, for I was happy with a vain and prideful joy: as the pope of the woods, thus did I see myself; and the Devil had all but got me. So when I showed them *my* salvation was now at stake, they let me go, and I pray God every day to reward them for it. Blindfold I must go, but they sent guides with me, and more food than I alone could have carried. Then they left me, after how many days I scarcely know, and melted away without a sound. When I tore the clout from my eyes, I found myself not far from Dick's clearing. And here I am as you see me."

Juliana took a deep breath. "You will not persuade many that you are not, what you will not have me call you. *I* think God sent you home that your skill may profit Cloudsway Cathedral." The friar did not answer, gazing down into his lap. "I forgot," Juliana said, apologetically. "Were you sad, to find that now it is to be the Bishop's cathedral?"

"God shall be served there, that is all we may care about," the friar said, low. "I hope I may be deemed worthy to contribute my mite of assistance. Ay, it will do me good to turn away from people for a time, made to work less malleable material, less easily deceived, less ready to praise and in turn deceive me. But now you must tell me something of your own doings, Mistress, that I have heard so much about from others."

Juliana needed not to be asked twice. But for some reason, unclear to herself, she did not go beyond the account of her travels about western Anglemere, compressing her most recent venture into one lame phrase: "And now I have just come back from Ovisham fair."

"So they tell me." The friar, having vainly waited for more, looked at her a little oddly. His glance shifted to Lucas, "You have left your wife and family behind in Flanders, Master? You mean to wait and see how things are here before you send for them? Or do you plan to rejoin them ere long? Whereabouts do you hail from? I was born at a hamlet just outside Mechlin."

Lucas had only answered the last question, when Juliana broke in over volubly.

"I have taken on Master Lucas as my steward, Brother Laurentius. Often did I hear my brothers say that when your horse has thrown you, there is only one thing to do against losing heart and valor, and that is, to remount straightway. Thus did I wish to raise up Master Lucas in his misfortune by burdening him with my confidence and responsibilities. He will not take it amiss that I say so openly to you that have been so unreserved with us. God sent me a sign that I needed no priest to interpret. When I heard that Lucas knows of a consignment of Caen stone—two whole shiploads it will amount to, he reckons—lying unclaimed at Antwerp, then I saw God had engineered our meeting. Do you see what it means? Lord William will be able to circumvent Hugh's trickery, and use finer stuff than rubble in the bargain! I left Master Lamb preparing the *Elizabeth* for a voyage this summer. Lucas will go with him, but first he must confer with the Abbot. The sooner he does so, the better. I thought perhaps you might take him to Cloudsway Waste on your way back today?"

The friar listened to her without comment, nodding slightly now and then.

"And where is the second stranger whom I hear you have brought back with you, Mistress Trefeller?"

"Swan? Where is she? Jeanne, have you seen her? She was with me and Lucas. Go out and find her, Jeanne."

At the suggestion that her new nurse might be lost, Elizabeth burst out crying.

"Swan? Is that her name?" The friar shook his head, with lips compressed. "There is talk that she comes of bare-shirt pirate stock, and about some right curious doings on her part. Ay, you know, Mistress, how fast rumor travels in Bedesford! Is it true? You must give me leave to interrogate her."

"She taught Elizabeth to say Hail Mary in Latin. So there cannot be much wrong with her. People will talk. Gillian was jealous of her from the first, and so I have no doubt is Jeanne."

Jeanne meanwhile was looking for the witch high and low. Not surprisingly the search took her some time. For Swan Ygern had started on a circuit of her new abode, and did not tarry to be found in any one spot. Quietly, albeit one could scarce say by stealth, she walked round every building, inside and out, touching doors, walls, hearths and chief gear, and greeted each with a soft chant of acquaintance. On the way she spoke also to such fowls and beasts as she encountered, addressed the grass, the trees, the well, and even the smoke from the chimneys. Jeanne said it turned her cold, to come upon the woman as she gave the oven fair words. She did not like to tell Brother Laurentius unasked. The friar averred it was grown too late for him to conduct examination now. He promised to take counsel with his prior about Swan Ygern, on whom, however, he conferred his benediction when she was led before him, and smiled, relieved, when she received this in the manner of all practiced Christians.

CHAPTER 8

AT THE SITE

THE FRIAR and Lucas set out for the site. At first there was silence between them, awkward in the extreme; and, no less awkwardly, both at last brought themselves to break it at one and the same time.

"Nay, proceed; you speak first—"

"Nay, what I would have asked can wait—"

Matters were not improved when it transpired each had thought to draw the other out a little, the friar about Swan Ygern and Lucas about Abbot William. Brother Laurentius was evasive—he could not trust himself to be just to the Abbot.

On the hill brow they stopped for breath. At that distance you saw less than you could hear of the work in progress. What showed up more distinctly than at close quarters was the scabrous indication of coming roads, graven by the to and fro of wagons, workmen, and visitors.

"It is in a vale, and not up on a hill!" Lucas exclaimed in astonishment.

"It is not much of a vale," the friar responded quickly, "the depth is no greater than the estimated height of the aisle walls. The towers will reach far above it, and will be visible for a great distance all round, except where Cloudsway Ridge bounds the view. The Ridge is the only real height for many miles. Today the haze hides most of it; but it stretches on to either side farther than sight can reach, the little Wode its ditch. In the west its foothills meet the London road. In future ages pilgrims will continually be seen coming along the skyline. A providential name, 'Cloudsway.' Does it not strike you so? I recall a time when people were fond of arguing about it. The crest being so like a road, some have it that it meant 'way-in-the-clouds.' Others said it meant 'where the clouds have *sway.*'"

The excavations were fully outlined, in the shape of a gigantic, prone cross with two bars. Closer, their shade lost its density and attained perspective. Movement, workmen and horses, became discernible, and you perceived the accidental castellation of structures varying in stage of growth. Yet no sooner were you right upon it all, than you ceased being able to fathom plan and outline, grasped only a moment before in their entirety. You stood confounded in the midst of a rugged maze. The way through to the apsidal end was imperiled by flying chips and falling tools, and holes and obstructions underfoot, screened by stone dust. The vaulting over the crypt was almost complete, its domes like rows of up-standing eggs, where the chancel floor was yet to come. On top of each egg two men had standing room. It took no little skill to work on this bed of globes which must be welded into level floor fabric.

The first bays of the procession path were under construction. Some piers were no taller than a man and as yet no more than rubble cores. Others, full-grown but for capitals, had already been united with the slendered shafts that embrace them in comely clusters. Two pairs stood firmly braced by their connecting arches, a third was in process of acquiring one. Between these two columns stood a great, solid piece of scaffolding, with slats and boles forming a stout semicircle at the top. This was used as a mold for the rubble and cement that in due time would harden and become the arc, from under which the wooden center, as we call it, could then be withdrawn, and used again elsewhere. It was the one method of Master Colet's introduction which Jacob Tew-sing found it in him to applaud.

"It's all very well," Jacob grumbled nevertheless. "For arcading it is pleasant and neat enough. But I took that man's measure years ago. If he could, he would make everything the same. An authority on towers, they call him. I tell you, if he had his way, all towers in Christendom would be as like as fingers. He is a man of memory, but not of vision. I have yet to hear him hum at his work, let alone sing. Materials are like brides. They want to be smiled on if they are comely; cajoled, consulted, and embellished if they are not."

Swan Ygern was duly examined by Prior Haakon, who pronounced himself in the main satisfied. He said that often certain practices, such as Jeanne had discovered her in, may be outlandish customs rather than nefariousness. "Folk are ready to denounce anything strange and new." Howbeit he remained in doubt as to the qualification of the pirate-king's chaplain, the validity of Swan Ygern's baptism, and the nature of her spiritual guidance hitherto, and advised a form of adult baptism as a safeguard. The woman submitted to his questions and rulings with a good grace. Juliana herself, although she could not quarrel with the upshot, was slow to forgive the interference, which meant that her indignation was visited on all who lived with her.

One day Jeanne Widowson arrived at the building site with a big bundle on her back and leading Alfred by the hand. Her face was swol-len with weeping. Some men took pity on her and fetched her husband.

Heedless of bundle, child, and onlookers alike, Jeanne flung her arms round him, weeping so that he could not make out what she was trying to tell him. So he resigned himself to asking the overseer monk for leave—thus losing all remuneration for the day's work, in spite of what he had already done. But if he were found idle, comforting his wife, he would be fined.

He took the bundle from her and picked up Alfred as well. At last she grew calmer, and he heard that she had left Trefeller Court for good. Edwin guessed she had cried so, chiefly because she was afraid what he might say. For now he must enlarge his hut, take on at least one field strip in addition to his garden plot, and obtain a cow or goat, probably poultry too, and a pig.

He said, "And is that all? Is not this all we have ever wanted, you and I, to live together? Are you so sorry to come to me that you weep? True, I can hardly think you will like it so well here, after what you have been used to these three years." You may imagine what Jeanne answered.

While his parents stopped in their walk, Alfred slid down and waded through the grass, which was cool and thick and very tall. He threw himself down into it, breast forward, and remained, absorbed in the tiny lives and tangled forestial depths of the sward, until Jeanne called him, and all three went slowly on, toward their home.

Smiling, Edwin watched his wife and son take possession of the hut. Alfred plunged into its disorder with the same self-sufficient rapture that had explored the world between the grass roots. Jeanne immediately attacked it. She appeared to him to dance as she worked: bending, sinking, rising on her knees, then suddenly erect, like a wind-swayed fountain in an instant's calm, whenever force of emotion compelled her bodily to underline her narrative.

". . . so she tore my hair again—Juliana. At least I can take comfort in the thought that I told her my whole mind! But oh, Edwin, that woman! Princess, she calls herself, thrall of thralls that she is! 'Ganna,' Elizabeth calls her, 'Ganna mine, Ganna here and Ganna there,' there is no end of it. 'Tell me another tale, my Ganna!' She has filled that poor, pretty little head to bursting with her heathen fictions, and the child believes every word, and will surely grow up without knowing lies from truth. Not that it's any of my concern. Let them see how they will get on without me, one and all. And another thing. Juliana will marry this foxy-haired Fleming. See if I am not right. Already he has all the keys. The countinghouse and all the papers in it are his to do with as he likes.

Every time she looks at him Juliana smiles and grins like one poisoned with brew of nightshade."

"And Geoffrey? How does he like having the Fleming set over him?"

"Oh, Geoffrey! He may not be a great woodworker, but he is *made* of wood. Juliana's dogs have more feeling than Geoffrey your nephew. It is all the same to him. I heard him whistling somewhere when I left today. It is not as if she owned me, is it, Edwin? You do not think she will wheedle the Abbot into forcing me back?"

Still on her knees, Jeanne had unconsciously adopted a pleading tone and attitude. Her head covering had long since fallen round her shoulders and her tresses had come loose. Her smooth cheeks glowed, her eyelids fluttered with a soft, mothlike beat.

"Where has Alfred got to?" Edwin asked suddenly, in a voice that she recognized, although she had not had the chance to hear it often lately.

She flushed, "Where—? Oh, over there. He had gone to sleep, poor weary lamb, on your unthreshed beans yonder. Truly it is time you had a woman here to see to things—"

"So was I thinking now," said Edwin. "A wise, considerate child is he, our son."

"No, Edwin," Jeanne whispered, with her long, broad eyelids tightly shut, yet unable to keep from smiling. "He may waken. Oh, Edwin, it is daylight still. It is not fitting. It is not like the times when we were young and could not be married. Someone may come, Edwin." Edwin made as if he did not hear her; and no one came.

But one evening not long after, Brother Laurentius visited Edwin and Jeanne at their hut, and sat down beside them on the bed, that nearly took up all the floor. Alfred lay on his back, close up to the wall, drowsily playing with some roots and pebbles.

"Yes, I have come to you, Edwin. Of all the people you, who in the old days used to come to me most often, have had least to say to me since my return."

"My father!"

"A father's feelings have I ever borne you, Edwin. Yet it was not you that told me you had taken a vow never to work in wood again. Perhaps they were wrong that said so? I have hoped they were."

"It is true, though," Edwin said in an aloof voice.

"Then have I never come across like folly," said the friar vigorously. "It cannot be acceptable to God—"

"So thought I at one time, and went back on it. I found out otherwise.

God *had* accepted it, and refused to guide my hand when I would have recanted. Those that told you about me, did they say nothing about Juliana's shutters, that I had to destroy? But that was not all. I tried to quibble next and told myself it was only fine carving I had given up, and undertook plain carpentry for the monks' chapter house. The very first day I nearly killed the man beside me. My ax slipped on a knot. *My* ax, on a *knot!* That showed me. It ought to show you."

The friar did some counting on his fingers. "You did not go on with the shutters until well after the Black Death. Oh, Edwin, I am so afraid that you vowed it from pride. That you valued your gift so highly you offered it up against the Black Death. I am not your confessor and I cannot make you tell me—" he waited, striving not to look hurt when Edwin refused him direct answer, and instead said defiantly, "Would you not say it is healthy and chastening for my pride, that my hands are great lumps of clumsiness at mason's work, to be given only the roughest tasks? Advise me. Maybe I ought even to desist from trying to get better at it?"

Jeanne, who thus far had sat quietly, patching the window cloth, spoke up, "I can advise you there. You have a wife and son to take care of. The sooner you improve your skill and your wage, the better God will like it. Ay, you may laugh, both of you. You know that I am right."

"Until quite lately Edwin's wife and child were well provided for," Brother Laurentius turned to her. "Now what possessed you to run off like that from Trefeller Court?"

"The work of that great house had long been too heavy for her!"

"So the moment she gets help, she leaves?"

"What is it to do with you?" Jeanne cried. "If Juliana has sent you to ask me to go back—"

"That she has not. Your going harmed none but yourself and this child here."

"Would you teach me how to love my son?" Jeanne's voice trembled with rage, and there was exasperation in Edwin's tone, too.

"Will not his soul thrive the better for my poverty?"

"These sneering questions do not come well from your lips, Edwin. Souls are not cabbages, that the same treatment profits all alike. I have seen more of your son than of you, since I came back. I can read all the signs, Edwin, though you may be blind to your own child's promise."

At this Edwin fairly shouted, "His hand, man! Do you forget his hand? What do you mean by coming to torment us?"

"Edwin!" Brother Laurentius whispered in dismay. "You know it is only because of the love I have for you and yours—"

"Have mercy, then, and love us less! Would you rescue a drowning man by a hook sunk in his vitals? Let me sink in peace, for Jesus Christ's sake!"

Alfred started up. Jeanne hugged his head to her breast and covered up his ears, rocking him.

Brother Laurentius got to his feet and settled the rope round his waist. Edwin sprang up, full of remorse. "Forgive me, Brother Laurentius. Forgive my unseemly shouting. It was because unwittingly you hurt me that I cried out."

"Most surely do I forgive you, my son. When there was a scant breath left in his battered body, Benedetto of Friggsby lifted up his aged voice that the murderers might hear him above the sound of their cudgels, as he forgave them."

"My father! Brother Laurentius!"

"Your father and your brother am I, in Christ, and I will take my leave now. One can see too much of one's relatives. I have been too much your father. It is no more than justice, that Heaven now should make me share the common lot of carnal fathers, in that the time comes for all when their sons forsake them." He made the sign of the cross over all in the hut, and departed in spite of everything they could say.

Jeanne put down the child and twined her arms round Edwin, pressing her cheek to his. "Do not fret now, my Edwin. You were right, even though he has made you feel in the wrong. Now shall we be safe from his prying for a while. At least I hope so! He is a very good man, no doubt, and no doubt loves you as he said. But I liked what you said, the way you put it, 'Love me less!'"

Part Three
The Witch
(1354-1357)

THE BROTHERS

HUGH CINQMORT had left Bedesford before Martinmas, but once he was in London time went by so quickly that he found himself well in the new year without as yet having made full inquiries after his kin. He had taken the oath to King Edward. He had seen and spoken to Baldwin, his next brother but one, but deferred a serious discussion until they might know for certain how many of the family were alive to share the inheritance.

The Black Death was at once too recent and too far away for information to be easily obtained. Public and private records were still in confusion, while personal recollections had begun to fade. Also, London had suffered a second visitation in 1349. He got conclusive proof that his sister Mary and her husband and children, of Essex, had all died. Gervase was said to have died about the same time; Hubert, the youngest of the brothers, had disappeared from the house of Master Jolybody (later Sir Bertrand Jolybody) the tailor, as early as 1347. Here Lord Hugh combined his researches with the acquisition of a new wardrobe.

He presented himself at Baldwin's lodgings—a small house rented of the butchers' guild—clad in a coat of clover-colored Flanders cloth with a little grape of silver bells hanging from the tip of each sleeve, a pale-blue silken shirt fastened with silver cord, a hooded cloak and train of matching blue with an inwoven pattern of marsh cinquefoil, and mole-skin lining, a silver-plated belt, soft mouse-gray gloves, and hose and shoes of finest archil-dyed leather, the toes being tied up to the ankles by little brass chains. The hood hung down his back, that he might display upon his crown a hat resembling a huge poppy. It had come from France.

Baldwin himself opened to his eldest brother's knocking, dressed in a long black gown edged with some dubious gray fur in an advanced state of dilapidation, so that it flew up about him like thistledown at every moment. He had the Cinqmort hair, albeit very thin and short, a high, straight forehead from which a short hooked nose sprang forward without indentation at the root, the same black eyes as Juliana, and a thin mouth whose lower lip protruded.

Lord Hugh motioned his hired porter to deposit the load of clothes sacks, shied a coin at him, entered, and closed the front door behind him, Baldwin backing rather helplessly. "Now my purse is empty," said Lord Hugh, dangling it aloft. "As I intend to take you back to live with me, brother, I deem it only fair that you should have me to live with you for the remainder of our stay in this leech pond of a city."

"But—" Baldwin stammered, horrified, yet smiling in spite of himself.

"The prices here are sinful," Hugh pursued serenely. "They bleed you for breathing their very air, clogged with stink as it is. I hope you will not think the family honor diminished because I have come unattended. With a couple of henchmen eating their heads off and drinking their legs away, I could not have stayed in London above a month."

"I eat and drink a vast amount myself, brother Hugh," Baldwin said wryly. "I fear me you cannot afford to drag me back to Bedesford."

"No sacrifice can be too great," Hugh grinned and clapped him on the shoulder so that the fur flew. "Meanwhile *I* would like to eat."

"I regret I have no servants either; I usually take my meals at the Hospitalers' across the way; so if you will deign to join me—"

"How soured you are, brother. You *need* my company to cheer you. If it be that you are still grieving for your wife, remember there are thousands of men would give anything to be widowed as you. If it is because you lost your post at the Treasury as I have heard, be equally thankful for your freedom from the cares of office. Cold beds are soon warmed, and spiced by variety; and it is more grateful work to administer property which is part your own than slave your eyes out for the glory of the Crown. What is their wine like, here?"

"Wine! And who is to pay?"

"Well, which of us is the host?" Hugh asked with raised eyebrows. "You saw my poor, empty purse."

"What about my poor, empty belly—tomorrow and the day after, and the day after that?"

"We need not stay here as long as that, and thenceforth you will be taken care of."

Baldwin sighed and for the present saved his breath.

"I know not how you can endure your present life," Hugh said, belching and pulling a face, on their way back through the frost-bound orchard. "Our Bishop is at the Treasury now, is he not? He has so little influence that he could not have saved your post for you?"

"It was his influence obtained the post for another," Baldwin answered dryly.

Hugh whistled. "Tell me what you know about him, brother. You must know a good deal."

"What sort of thing? And why?" Baldwin asked as they let themselves in by the back wicket.

"Stoke up the fire, it is cold in here," Hugh coughed, rubbing his hands above the pale, flameless glow in the hearth. "Well, for example, how does he come to be building a cathedral, at a time like this? And where is the money coming from?"

"Mainly out of his own pocket, just as he says. He really had the unique wit to convert all his holdings into gold immediately after the Black Death, before the devaluation of land had become universally apparent. His landed property in France was very considerable."

"He does not impress me as the kind of man," Hugh struck one palm with his fist thoughtfully, "who would be so clever just for God's sake. What does he want?"

"What do you think?" Baldwin shrugged. "What they all want, the high ecclesiastics. To be Chancellor of the Realm one day and Archbishop of Canterbury."

"What are his chances?"

"I should call them good, so long as he be granted health and life. He has many advantages, though as yet he has more and better connections at Avignon than in London."

"I am relieved to hear it. I was going to law against him."

"Brother, you are mad."

"This is no way to speak to the head of your house and prospective employer."

"Brother, brother, is not one unending lawsuit enough for you?"

"If a man have two fleas instead of one, shall he stop scratching? This case is much clearer than the other. Listen before you carp."

Baldwin, however, did not cease shaking his head when Hugh had told him all. "Until I look up the records myself I cannot tell how much of a case we may really have. But this much I can tell you now: you will never win it."

"That remains to be seen. I shall not win if I do not try. I should have thought you would be overjoyed at the thought of revenging yourself on him—in lawyer's fashion."

"What sort of revenge would it be that left me and mine in worse straits than he ever caused?"

"Can you think of nothing but money? Ay, you have worked at the Treasury too long to remember that the most priceless treasure is honor! I have used my ears and eyes this half year. England is no longer fit for a noble to live in. The King is not king here, and it is his own fault, valuing money above honor. If I were king, you would not see me groveling to Parliament for my taxes, bartering away rights and privileges by the handful against its vote! The King leads, and the whole country follows—to the dogs. Our father's power was as nothing compared with his ancestors'. And now behold me, undisputed master of less than half my father's dominions—"

"You are talking of what has been happening in the last three years, when, like most lords, you have had to lease out more and more land. But how else were you to have lived?"

"How does the bear live, lord of the forest, or the lion of our disgraced shield?" Passion carried Hugh into a fit of coughing. He would have fallen off the backless bench if Baldwin had not leaped to catch him. Baldwin was still holding him and drying his brother's lips with the sleeve of his own black gown, when Hugh continued, at first barely croaking. "Just because the Lord God weeded out their superfluity, are the villeins suddenly to hold themselves so precious? If I stamp out all rats save one in my barn, will that rat be suddenly ermine? I mean to put a stop to all this weak-kneed chaffering and villein petting where *I* rule. Perhaps then others, in high places, will be reminded by my example that honor does not change its nature through the ages. Howbeit before I can recover what has been lost, I must hold on to what is mine still. I shall not let go of my title to Cloudsway Waste. I shall not give up as long as I have breath, if it means that I die without roof to my head on a bed of leaves."

"Then it looks as if we shall all die homeless, all your kin."

Between coughs Hugh unexpectedly grinned, "I am glad you perceive at last that it is in your own interests to guard mine!"

"Brother, you are making yourself ill."

"Nay, brother," Hugh gasped, "abandon *that* hope. Though I am a sick man, be sure I shall outlive you. Just look at us. You look the elder by far, with your bald head. Ah, it's this London life. At Bedesford we shall make you young again."

"To be sure," Baldwin said resignedly, "you are in all essential ways unchanged. To be sure, I must go with you to help settle the inheritance. But after it has been divided—"

"After!" Hugh mocked. "Who knows when that will be? It does not do to look too far ahead."

Baldwin gazed at him speechlessly for a moment. "What are you scheming now?" he then said wearily.

"This: we know nothing of Hubert, one way or the other, and the same holds of our reverend sister the nun. There is no proof that Gervase is dead or that he left any descendants. While there are three, and possibly more heirs unaccounted for, nothing can be done about settling an estate. For that matter, I believe it is the same if there be but one heir missing?"

"If you are hoping starvation will kill off all the heirs save one, I must inform you the law does provide for the maintenance of claimants to an unsettled heritage."

"You are the only claimant who has so far come forward, and I have told you more than once I am fully prepared to maintain you. Indeed, Bedesford Manor claims you. I will say nothing of your duty, and that you should be eager to perform services our father had you trained for at great expense. Rather would I put it more winsomely in brotherly affection—"

But Baldwin would not let him do that, ashamed to feel that he had driven his own brother so far he would even violate his nature. "I see I must do what I can," he said hastily.

Baldwin had not seen his home since he was little more than a boy. He was dimly afraid of leaving his manhood behind in London, where also his young wife lay buried. Her death still seemed incredible, because the second visitation had caused it, just when they had felt so safe for having survived the first. He felt if he but visited her grave often enough, she might arise. But once the break was made, it was different.

Far from despising Bedesford after London, it induced in him that tenderness which the innocent and small is apt to call forth. Only the manor had lost none of its sinister magnitude in the eyes of one whom the first distant glimpse of the gate towers reduced to infanthood.

Baldwin grew insensible to time in the turret chambers. Alone, he climbed about the stacks of crude, old-fashioned chests, musty, mysterious bales, dismantled looms, and broken armature. He tore through sheets of cobwebs loaded with dust and shriveled crumbs of insects; more than one arrow slit he found blocked by birds' nests.

A fraying time began for Baldwin. The burden of responsibility upon him was rendered yet heavier by his lord's caprice. Although Lord Hugh had appealed to Baldwin's trained ability for succor, he seldom availed himself of it. Sometimes he would accept, or unpredictably reject, the fruit of Baldwin's toil and cogitations.

There was no money. No more flint and rubble had been garnered off Cinqmort's lands since the time Lord Hugh had gone to London on the payments for everything previously collected. Baldwin's few chattels had had to be sold to provide for the brothers' homeward journey. Lord Hugh still owed for his new clothes. Meanwhile they had to live through the spring and summer. Yet he absolutely declined to lease out any more of his land.

"You will not settle with Lady Agnes. You refuse to think better of suing Lord Jerome. You have no incomings from Friggsby or the slate and iron of Dameswood Ditch. Your rents this year will barely cover the stores we must get in for the winter. Say what you will now, but next year you will be compelled to lease out more, and compelled to make more concessions in the terms for having delayed so long. Why cannot you see it, Hugh?" Baldwin said in despair. "God help us, you are none so dull in other matters. You will have so little farm produce next year, and less and less in the years after, that you will have to pay more for food. To raise money you will have to lease out *all* your land in the end, and will then spend all you have raised on what you could have got for a third of the price had you not leased all your land. And so it will go on."

"If every time you said 'money' money came out of your mouth, we should have been drowned in gold by now. You would have me eat filth if that could get us money. And I had rather starve. Get me men, and I will show you how money is to be got, my way. Since I have had you with me, I have lost even such services as remained to me before, having had to make them over to the Benedictines for the summer. I cannot even gather in my outstanding revenues. Get me men, then perhaps I will listen to you next time. Forget everything else for the nonce and get me men; let that be your test as my steward."

"Would to God," Baldwin was roused to malevolence for once, "that you could get men yourself! Would that you could make me as your lowliest cotters. There is scarcely a woman under fifty hereabouts whom you have not debauched. There is not a child to call you father. Perhaps if you would be less mule headed, you might grow less mulish of loins." Then he, whom Hugh despised for the weaker, began to pity the lord, who stood quaking, stupefied with hurt and wrath. "Very well, Hugh. I will accept your challenge."

Baldwin had much of that cleverness which makes for power and advancement when coupled with self-interest. On market days bands of the wandering freemen were always to be found in the town square, to put themselves up for hire to the highest bidder or, if the bidding did not reach as high as they had hoped, pass on. Baldwin understood what it took us years to learn. The saying that every man has his price he knew to refer to quality, or kind, rather than quantity of remuneration.

He was quiet and retiring by preference and not from shyness. He thrust himself into the throng about the wanderers and raised his voice in rivalry against the spokesmen of townfolk and Benedictines. Baldwin alone was not blinded by the triteness of the truth that many people do not like work and will regard freedom as disability as soon as it is extended beyond the satisfaction of their appetites.

Baldwin made it clear that the manor offered idleness and freedom from responsibilities—though no wages were payable until the end of each year of service. All that would be required of my lord's henchmen was to eat, drink, play manly games to keep in good fettle, care each for his own mount, ride abroad, and, by way of maintaining order, follow merely the instinctive human bent for destruction. He took his examples from the fallow deer plague and the recent increase of sheep stealing: my lord's henchmen were to be *paid* to indulge in the royal pleasures of hunting and slaying. And he had tricked himself out so as to underline everything he said. He had ransacked lofts and armory for brightly colored garments and all that shone most in the way of accouterments, and strutted so that his sober-hued rivals lost the thread of their discourse with the wonder of watching him. At the first attempt he took home half a dozen men.

After this my lord declared himself ready to close with his sister Trefeller—graciously, as a favor to Baldwin, yet contriving at the same time to go against Baldwin's counsels. On their first meeting after the brothers' return, Juliana, through her steward, had proposed that Lord Hugh should let to her all his sheep runs west of Bedesford for a period of seven years. Against a reduction in rent and an option to purchase at the end of that period, Juliana offered to pay the entire seven years' rent in advance, in cash and in kind. When Baldwin essayed a warning, Lord Hugh said scornfully,

"There is no satisfying you. Now I am doing what you want, you want more: you want me to haggle. Craven hearted indeed must you be to fear a woman and cripple to boot."

"What is the good of talking in this way, Hugh?" Baldwin replied dispiritedly. "There is this steward, this Fleming of hers—"

"So long as a man's hair be only red enough, folk will respect him as a fox. But even if he were in truth the king of foxes—you do not think that stinging worm, our sister, will fail to quarrel with him long before the seven years are up, be it never so much against her interests?"

"Ay, you read her better than I, and you might be her twin," Baldwin said hopelessly.

CHAPTER 2
ALFRED

One Morning in summer Alfred Widowson woke before the time when his mother would usually rouse him. Warm and still limp with sleep, his little body was yet filled with a hum and tingling of excitement, as a hive bursting with imprisoned bees. For a moment he could not remember the cause.

He lifted his right arm, that the left hand might play with the pale, shrunken right: his unique, self-grown toy. It was marvelous how with the aid of light, shadow, some fold of bedding, and a little fancy the useless member could be made to represent anything he might like to imagine.

A year ago or so this hand, though small and withered looking, had still rendered such ordinary service as its strength was equal to. But as the rest of Alfred grew, it lagged behind. He had come to look upon it as a separate creature, which he cherished and sought to spare.

Everybody pitied him, he knew, and remembered him in their prayers. Because of him they pitied his parents, too, and this he found easier to understand, with a touch of guilty conscience.

Like all the resident laborers, Edwin had made himself a booth hut.

You do not see many such about nowadays, but at that time they were very common. With a framework of paired birch or spruce trees, walled with wattle, and thatched with broom or heather or whatever was to hand, they were quickly built, easily kept in repair, and soon enlarged. What was now the front bay had been added when Alfred and his mother had first joined Edwin. In the back bay, goat, ox, and chickens lived, and the floor was covered with dead bracken, while in front there was only bare earth save where rushes and straw lay banked up for the bed. In the center a hearth basin, lined with pebbles, had been fashioned, but this was used only in the worst weather. Usually the fire was lit on the cooking stones outside. The wattle door, fastened by latch pins on both sides, was kept unhinged in the daytime, except in deepest winter or during a storm. Behind the back wall was the midden, and Jeanne's garden.

Beyond the doorstep Alfred could see his mother's hens picking round the hot cooking stones, where the day's supply of corn had been dressed. Jeanne or Edwin must have gone to fetch the water before daybreak for they had finished their morning meal.

Behind an osier screen at the head of the bed, Jeanne was milking Brownstar and at the same time suckling her three weeks' old son Geoffrey—Jaffy, he came to be called. Alfred sighed; he felt he would be old and gray before the baby could give him companionship. And at this he remembered and leaped out of bed. "Mother! Mother, shall we not be late?"

"Wait, my son, careful," but a hidden egg had already cracked under Alfred's step. "Oh!" Jeanne said dispiritedly, "there today I really thought I had found them all! I am just finished. Come and take the baby for me, so I can bring in the bowl. Let me have a look at your face, in case it needs washing. I have saved a little water. And take off your smock. You must wear your Sunday kirtle this first day."

She set down the goat's milk, fastened her dress, and bound up her hair. Alfred, with the replete baby slung over breast and shoulder, arched backward over the bed and gently let his brother slide onto it. Then he went to stand between his mother's knees, hard put to it to keep still.

"Where is Father? Perhaps he has gone on ahead? What if we are too late, and they think we are not coming, and give my place to another? Oh, Mother, let us hurry."

Jeanne held him by the shoulders at arm's length to survey her work, then drew him close and kissed him. Alfred was so like Edwin it made you laugh, and withal so like Jeanne as she had used to be, it might well have made you cry. His little face, neck, and limbs were smoothly sunburned; his soft hair was almost as dark as Edwin's, and his gray eyes shone very comely in their setting.

"Give away your place, indeed! They should be thankful to get my Alfred! If they know what is right they will make you head of the bird scarers right away. If it had not been with you as it is, and if you had not so pestered us, your weak-willed parents, never, even had we been starving, should you have been sent to work beside fatherless vagrants (who had much better be motherless as well!). Be still. Your father is but gone to take the ox round to the Freemans at the west side. We are all of us going out together; it is my day for watering service. Listen. There he is now, and some others with him by the sound of it."

A paring of sun had emerged above the Easterwoods' skyline, where day was already bright. All at once life resounded as far as hearing could reach. The mists of dawn and dew were least transparent about the abrupt patterns of the growing cathedral, so that, where it ought to have loomed black against the background of gold-shot blue, it was instead softened with all manner of delicate shades. Alfred, who had been skipping and jumping high, tugging against his mother's hand, chattering and singing, fell silent as they approached their goal.

Edwin at first had walked by Alfred's other side. Presently he fell behind, the better to watch his son. Meanwhile, Jeanne was at pains to protest again to the others that Alfred's taking up employment did not signify his family was overneedy.

"Ay, his wage will pay for all his keep—half a loaf every week, a bowl of meat stew on holy days, and enough frieze for a frock without sleeves at Christmas. But at home and in the garden he is worth more than that to me. He had longed and longed so to be doing something for St. Hand's. There has been no keeping him away from the site this many a long day. I am thinking as a bird scarer he will soon have his fill of scrambling up and down walls and planks all day long. Nay, fear for his safety I have none. He is nimble as a tumbler or a cat. Ay, you, you changeling."

The trickles of people from several directions merged into a stream which dispersed again all over the jaggedly built-up regions, to the mortar pits and mounds of rubble, piles of stone hewn or yet rocky, the timber staples, and toward the Wode. Chains set up their clanking, ropes their creaking, trowels scraped, pails rattled, gangplanks thudded, and hammers and chisels resumed minting their flying largesse of sharp flakes and sound.

Alfred thought his good hand must become weak as its fellow, his mother's grip was so crushing. But he said not a word. He could tell she was feeling far from easy, for all that she had rejected as unbecoming to his dignity Edwin's offer to escort her and Alfred. She sighed with relief when Matt Feathers accosted them.

"You will be looking for Clement, Mistress Jeanne? So you are come at last to help us build St. Hand's, Alfred? Leave him with me, Mistress. I will take him to Clement, and Clement himself will lead him before today's Father Overseer directly the monks come out."

Jeanne thanked him in a faltering voice and went off to get her water buckets, without turning to give her son another glance.

For the first time he could look without envy upon the bird scarers' hurtling ubiquity. Already they were become to him boys like himself rather than shooting stars. He was going to be one of them, this very hour. He, too, would be clambering up and down the old stepped ledges of unfinished walls and half-reared arches, peering, sentinel-fashion, into the welter of crags and chasms, crawling on his belly like a lizard up hill and down dale about the vaulting. Clement took him in charge and left off working to make him formally acquainted with his duties.

You would be surprised at the speed and hardihood with which rats and moles, birds and weeds gained foothold all over the site. We could not be working everywhere at once. No sooner was one's back turned than grass would be sprouting along all rough ledges, tenacious creepers would claw round the ashlar with a network of underthrust roots, rubble fillings not yet fully encased would put forth tufts of moss and sprigs of bramble.

"Now, you understand that bird scarer is only a name, for brevity's sake. You are employed to wage war on weed and vermin also. Birds you are not to kill, for it seems they know whose house we are building here, and the craving to make their homes on St. Francis' bosom has proved stronger than their natural diffidence and fear of tumult. Neither will you destroy nests while there are eggs or young in them. Deserted nests you must spy out and remove, and do what you can without actually harming them to discourage newcomer birds. But for rats and voles and the like there is no clemency. Look here."

They had come to a halt before a small gallows, at a height within easy reach of a child, with a crowded array of furry corpses. Some had fallen down and bestrewn the ground with white fragments of tiny skulls and fragile bones. The whole stood in a cloud of seething flies and stench. Alfred caught his breath. His eyes watered and his hand shook as he pointed at a crucified mole.

But Clement forestalled him, "Ay, my Alfred, a bird scarer's life is not all joy. But there are plenty do not shun this part of the work. You will not be called upon to perform it. You see, it is needful to have some such display as this, as a warning to the live vermin."

In time, Alfred found that the workmen expected one further service of the bird scarer: that of signaling from his professional points of vantage the whereabouts and progress of Benedictine inspectors. Now and then the Abbot himself went the rounds.

Frequently it happened that Baldwin Cinqmort came out walking with him. The lawsuit contested only the ownership of Cloudsway Waste. The river Wode belonged to the Cinqmorts as indisputably as the Tew, and the monks must pay toll to Lord Hugh for fishing and transport on arrival. In all their perpetual negotiations these two were opposed, as, one would have thought, were their persons, habits, and positions. Yet each found in the other what he had so far missed in Bedesford: a peer in cultivated controversy; in a bracing, hostile sense, each was the other's only friend.

One day when they were thus taking the air together in heated dialectical sport and leisurely appreciation of the latest additions to the building, Alfred was dragged before the Abbot. Peter Franklin had caught him in the act of conveying a live mole over the palisade into the cloister garden. With one hand he was hauling Alfred by the ear, the other clutched the mole, head downward. The Abbot could not help laughing at the spectacle; even Baldwin had to smile. Peter did not see them until they had all but collided.

"I see," said the Abbot, with mock gravity, "that the malefactor has been found who uprooted the southwest chancel wall yestereve."

"Ah?" Peter wavered, wrath befogged. "Nay, have you not heard, Reverend Father, the wall but lost a course or two because it was not buttressed. Nay, but I have found out at last why we cannot get rid of the vermin. This boy was sneaking this mole in among your roses and vegetables!"

The suspended mole bucked slightly, opening and shutting its little pig snout, waving its four helpless pink hands. Alfred, who thus far had been passive in awe of the Abbot, at this began to squirm and cry out.

"Ay," the Abbot nodded down at him, "no doubt you expect to be

strung up next to your catch. But just this once leniency shall prevail."
Still chuckling, he and Baldwin sauntered on.

At that time the crypt had been given over to the painters. A fair
amount of light came down the entrance and through the grille beneath
which St. Hand's shrine was to be erected. For the present the Hand,
along with the Bishop's lily and other valuables, was locked away in
one of the deep storage niches of the north and south walls.

Humphrey Painter and his plasterer had staggered into Bedesford
half starved and half naked, although they had with them costly painting materials—like themselves unwanted anywhere. So Abbot William
had got them very cheaply. By now they had put on flesh, had two assistants in their power, and were well content.

Their work was easily injured, wherefore the bird scarers were strictly
forbidden access to the crypt, which in some measure became the rats'
and serpents' sanctuary.

Outcast that he felt himself to be, Alfred decided to transgress. Never
before had he been conscious of his disadvantage; the universal pity he
enjoyed had been meaningless, though often useful to him. Now he
could think of nothing but how to mend it. His mother had told him
that long ago he had been touched by the Hand, one Finding Day. The
treatment having failed, he reasoned that perhaps it was no good unless
the patient could pray for himself; he had been too young. It was worth
trying again. Finding Day would not come round for another half year.
His right arm was surely thin enough to be forced through the grating
of the niche in which the Hand reposed.

For one so small and swift and familiar with the building ground
it was no great feat to approach and descend into the crypt unnoticed.
Noiselessly, he hid behind some rubbish stacked on the shallow side
of the steps. He forgot what he had come for. Never had he seen anything so wondrous.

The crypt octagon was composed of seven equal walls and an eighth
which was much longer and ran parallel to the central wall that faced
due east. All round stood scaffolding standards, upholding transverse
planks three quarters of the way up. The bays between the massive piers
were filled with benches, and troughs and buckets of every sort; there
was an object something like an anvil and something like a butcher's
block, covered with grindstones, slates, mortars, and pestles, all stained
in different hues. The cobbled floor was whited as a dovecot from the
plastering work.

The long west wall, broken up by half pillars and recesses and the stairs, was bare. The other seven and several piers were fully coated with the plaster, showing traces of smoke stain only where the curve of the vault began. At first Alfred could not comprehend the designs outlined in charcoal and red chalk on the whiteness behind the scaffolding; then the large areas already filled in with color helped him interpret the rest. He had never seen painted images before.

Painters and plasterers at work on the east wall were making the most of the noonday light. Here St. Francis was depicted preaching to the birds and beasts of creation. His head began immediately below the vault, so that the aureole had had to be extended beyond the springer, while his feet met the ground. One hand pointed upward into a band of blue sky, the other was stretched out in benediction.

To the left of him the northeast wall was divided into broad, brownish strips: trees, crowned with interlaced twigs and green leaves and studded with birds. We mind the sweetest of these was the woodpecker, with his beak turned over his feathered shoulder toward the preacher. Lower down was more grass, and a deer, a hare, and a lion, of which latter only the hairy head showed. The southeast wall was likewise painted with trees, and a squirrel in the same attentive posture as the woodpecker opposite. Below there were the wolf, the bear, the fox, and other beasts of the wilderness. There was a wall of cattle and a wall of sheep and poultry. Next to them were the wave lines of water and reeds and frogs, and fish swimming in the direction of St. Francis; some fishes put their eyes and noses out above water. The north wall had a castle with a tower, some houses, and a church. The northwest wall as yet bore little more than a confusion of smudged outlines. Here bats, lizards, vampires, and a dragon were to be limned in a state of temporary virtue.

The plasterer had tied himself up in a hammock aloft and was gilding St. Francis' halo where it bent with the vault. The assistants stood one above the other on a ladder, laying on St. Francis' mantle. Humphrey himself, with a trayful of jars strapped to his waist, moved about below on his knees, painting flowers. Now he made a circle of minute white lines, dotting the middle with yellow, and there was a daisy; now he made a bigger blot with blue and added three tapering tails to it: and lo! there was a bluebell; he dipped into the pink pot and made a series of rapid passes at the wall: and there was clover for you, to the life.

Humphrey could outline, color, and shade everything you can think of in such wise that you recognized it directly, with only two exceptions.

His houses, even his towers and castles, he could never get to stand properly upright; and his horses vacillated between looking like oxen and looking like deer. Even then, it was clear the houses could not be anything but houses; and horses would be saddled, having no horns. His only real failure was the dragon which, the more ferocious he labored to make it, the more it appeared to be laughing.

He liked to talk as he worked. "Never leave the beholder to guess. Do not worry so much about how your object looks as what its looks will tell him. If an object be noteworthy, do not paint it small. If, on the other hand, it is low in degree of importance, do not give it unmerited size. If I had drawn those houses no bigger than thumbnails, we should still know what they are. Yet if I were to paint a fly at its actual size, no one would recognize—indeed, no one would see it! Therefore I must not be afraid to give a fly the size of a sparrow. Further. If St. Francis' left arm, raised heavenward, is shorter than that which performs the blessing, this clearly denotes that even while yet on earth he had not far to go to Heaven, while the length of the blessing arm shows the wide range of his intercession. The billowing of his cloak bespeaks his charity; the fact that his waist is so long means—"

This was the moment when Alfred coughed because of the smoke. He had tried to hold back the cough for a long time, and so its explosion shook him out of concealment.

At any other time Humphrey would probably have been enraged at the trespass, but just then he doubtless welcomed the diversion. For he asked kindly, "And what have we here? A little croak-frog spy? Did not your mother tell you how curiosity served the cat? You want to have a right good look at the holy St. Francis, do you?"

Alfred gazed at him as he would have at an angel of Paradise. Humphrey laughed, unstrapped his tray, and raised Alfred's chin in one cupped hand, so that the ghosts of daisies, bluebells, and clover came off on the soft child-skin. He picked Alfred up and carried him round the walls, pointing out all he judged to be of special interest to one of his age. Alfred took pains to keep his right hand out of Humphrey's sight, a thing it had never previously occurred to him to do, even before strangers.

CHAPTER 3

THE GREAT DEER HUNT

THE PLAGUE of the fallow deer had grown beyond all bounds. The first hay crop the deer had harvested; the second, by dint of constant vigilance we ourselves had reaped, but those gentle-eyed limbs of Satan ate up the ricks overnight. It was as if all the deer of the world had congregated in the Easterwoods and at the same time conceived a distaste for woodland diet—to be sure Dick said there was a sickness of lichens that year. They razed the sheep runs, nibbled the growing corn, trampled the garden plots, and ate the green fruit of the orchards. A time came when they let themselves be seen in daylight. We prayed God for an increase of wolves, since we must keep our dogs tied up.

Time and again spokesmen of the townsfolk went to the manor, to plead with my lord for permission to dig pits and set snares and loose our dogs. We tried to show him that already we had had to abandon this year's plans to extend the reclaiming of fertile land, modest enough since they had rested on the newcomers who must be slowly taught the ways and waywardnesses of local husbandry. Even if we succeeded in keeping the deer from eating any more, the labor of an unbroken chain of sentinels, men, women, and children was lost. We humbled ourselves and offered to pickle and otherwise preserve every carcass for the manor's larder, at our own expense, and likewise dress the hides.

This was my lord's answer. "Think you the lord of Bedesford hunts his noble cattle for the sake of meat and leather? Think you the privileges to which he was born are for sale?"

Lord William spoke for us, too (as against the friars' preaching Christian patience), but we could scarce expect his intercession to do aught but strengthen Lord Hugh's obstinacy. So the people of the old town and the new in their great need met together on the green one Sunday evening.

The friars saw us assembling and came, too. But there was nobody from the manor or the monastery. The friars' ranks had been replenished lately, by brethren sent to them from other parts of the country and the Continent, with all the zeal of men starting afresh. Prior Haakon had lent Brother Laurentius to the cathedral without reservation. The friar may not have been entirely serious when he told Juliana he meant to neglect men for a while in favor of stone. But meanwhile his intention had hardened, and he had begun to carry it out, deliberately blind, deaf, and dumb as regards everything save stonecutting. Therefore was it a surprise when he, rather than one of the others, broke into the people's blurred, "What to do? What to do?" with his easily victorious, trained preaching friar's voice. "There is naught you can do, my poor people, except bow under this new scourging. Remember the Black Death. I was not amongst you at its worst, yet do I recall how even at the start you all sighed and cried if only it would stop you would nevermore complain about anything. It may well be that the Lord God is testing that resolve. I lived nigh three years among folk would laugh at your present troubles, out in the wilderness, where the fallow deer come not once in a while, but live year in, year out."

A second voice, resonant as his, rose against him, and we looked at each other and rubbed our knuckles in our ears and wondered who it could be.

"It's the outlaws prey on the deer, not the deer on the outlaws, Friar, friends, do not believe them that tell you suffering is good. Ay, suffering that comes straight from God, turning your soul inside out, that's a different matter. But the suffering inflicted by man upon man, whether by deed or default, that can merely degrade us, smirch, cow, and extinguish the very spark God lit inside us in our mothers' wombs. God forbade our first parents to taste of the apple, but nowhere is it written that He forbade them to touch deer. If Danes or Normans were to fall on our shores again, this friar, who bids you lie down for the deer to trample on, would bless your arms and speed you into battle. If we may slay our fellow Christians when they seek to rob us, why should we not defend us against vermin? There is only one thing we can do. We must make war on the deer, or perish. So long as we all stand together, there is nothing to be afraid of. One man may be put to death. Two men may be put to death. But not every man in Bedesford. With every man dead, Lord Hugh would fare worse even than we shall if the deer go on having it all their own way."

"It is Clement Tare! It is Clement Tare!" the whisper went round.

Clement Tare, you must know, was the least skilled man of all who had come to the cathedral. He was willing enough, and ready to do anything, and was used for the roughest work. Generally speaking, there is a knack to even the roughest work, but Clement did not command any. He never said what trade he had followed in the past and it was an unwritten law not to ask newcomers too many questions. It was clear he was no husbandman either. Matthew Feathers, his inseparable companion, was unskilled, too; but he was full of knack. He was employed on similar tasks to Clement's and achieved three times more in a third of the time.

Both these men had the kind of features which made you think on first acquaintance, you have met them before, and which escape recognition in a crowd once you *have* got to know the person. Matt, on the one hand, gained consideration from being Clement's mate, and on the other averted from Clement's head the mistrust which oddity is apt to draw upon itself. Our regard for them stood in no relation to their short time in Bedesford or their lowly standing, so that even the surprise of Clement's sudden speech and commanding, as it were, practiced delivery did not impair its effect on us.

The other friars desisted from arguments soon, unable to make headway where Brother Laurentius had failed. Like a despairing old sheep dog he scurried from one group to another as we started dispersing, now darting north after those returning to Bedesford, now south in pursuit of the building workers.

"My brethren, my children—truly you are no better than children, no wiser than beasts in the fields! Can you not see who and what he is, this seducer? A foreigner, who presumes to tell you men of Bedesford what to do! I tell you he is an Occamite, a Lollard as they are rightly called, for that they are the weeds and tares of God's garden in England. Think! Tare is the name by which he brazenly introduced himself into our fold! Jacob! You surely know better. You will not let yourself be taken in? Edwin, Edwin Widowson, you at least kept quiet all through—now you tell these people what *you* think."

"I was thinking of other matters, that's why I was quiet," Edwin said, distantly. "I thought of my brother Thomas, and other matters."

The change in Edwin by this time was no longer debated but commonly accepted, and it had at last changed people's feelings toward him. At last it was understood and taken for granted that the smiling cast of his features was no longer more than a pattern stamped into the outer clay.

Brother Laurentius had only weakened his own cause. Everything we knew of Matt and Clement stood at variance with what every child knew about the Lollards: brutish idlers and blasphemers, with rosaries made of the fingers of priests and nuns.

Luke Robinson was another stayed outside the conspiracy, but as he was hardly one of us, while Juliana the widow would be held to account for any action of his, we deemed he did right. Stephen Colet told anyone that asked him the matter was no concern of his. So at first Jacob Tewsing was no doubt afraid of lowering his dignity if he joined in. Clement's appeals to his fraternal loyalty did not sway him in the least; Matthew's appeals to his failings snared him. First Matt, in his toothless hiss, spoke slightingly of Master Colet, "who was acting just as every-had had expected of him." Another time he let fall what a pity it was Dick Toolmaker should get sole credit for leadership owing to his woodward's lore—when all the while there was in our midst a scion of the ancient rulers of Anglemere. Finally, he talked Jacob into looking on, just once, at the moonlight archery practice. Now, Jacob was as proud of his exploits in France almost as of his descent, and more jealous of his skill with the crossbow than of his craft. The expert's pain in sight of fumbling incompetence proved decisive; and soon Jacob was foremost in all the arrangements.

Lord Hugh called the assizes unexpectedly. In spite of our belief that both friars and monks sided with us in their hearts and had been turning blind eyes and deaf ears to what was going forward, we feared he had been warned.

When we saw him, we understood my lord's preciptance. His face appeared smudged, so cavernous were its shadows. He coughed with a strained and delicate caution and the look in his eyes was searchingly envenomed—all signs that he was on the brink of another bout of sickness. He himself could not but know it, and must wish to settle what was urgent, besides seeking to vent the spite and cruelty which ever heralded outbreaks of the disease. There was a number of minor disputes, in deciding which he could work nothing worse than vexation for all concerned: questions as to fencing and paving duties, precedence to the bleaching meadows, the repair of Old Bede's Bridge and how the costs were to be shared out.

But there was entertainment for us, too. No less than four women were tried on charges of whoring, all newcome wanderers whom Juliana had engaged for the season. Three of them looked downcast, as well they might; the fourth bore herself with flaunting complacency. A certain amount of boastful dumb show told us that my lord himself must have lain with her sometime. Almost we could have found it in us to be sorry for her.

Newcomer that she was, she did not know that Lord Hugh invariably turned against the objects of his lust as soon as they had once submitted to it. Women are strange; no one ever accused him of using force, neither was it by gifts and bribery that he got his way. It was said, and we still believe it, that many women yielded to him the more readily for his reputed loathing of their predecessors, which they conceived as a challenge. In particular did this apply to decent young virgins who had most to lose.

Needless to say, it was this confident one whom my lord regarded with the most disgust, addressed the most harshly, and sentenced to the severest penalty, although her offense was in no wise greater than her companions'.

My lord did not rest at this. He said that he regretted there were others, actually responsible for whoredom in Bedesford, whom at present legal punishment could not reach, namely, those who attracted the worst scum into the town, and his gaze rested balefully on his sister's steward. The most he could do, my lord went on, was to prevent spread of the corruption.

"Therefore do I herewith forbid certain foreign usages which have been lately introduced and which are undesirable here. The very fact that my permission was not asked would render these practices unlawful. Whatever may be the custom in Flanders, in Anglemere, it is necessary to consult me before setting in motion any novel schemes. I know not how many of you townfolk have entered into private agreements with Trefeller Court to card, spin, and weave wool supplied by Mistress Juliana, in their own homes as well as under the supervision of certain guests of her steward's. I would advise these guests not to outstay their welcome. Henceforth, anyone found to be working more wool than their own sheep are likely to have yielded, and more than they can reasonably claim for the needs of their own households, will be fined in proportion to the hours of labor they will be reckoned to have lost, or rather, stolen. Subsequent offenses will be treated as theft proper, with the statutory scale of penalties affecting life and limb. The session is now closed."

He went off, leaning heavily on Baldwin's arm, with the henchmen swaggering noisily about them. Sure enough he had a fit of bleeding from the lungs in the evening. Our moment was come to strike at the deer.

First of all, the people clubbed together to burn a wax candle for Thomas Widowson. Then we made traps in the fields and pitfalls in the woods, and men and boys and dogs, and some women even, went forth, armed with stones and scythes, pitchforks and rude crossbows, and with firebrands. At the finish there were counted close on two hundred deer slain, apart from an uncertain number which, through their own obstinacy, had been burned to death in a ditch-ringed portion of the Marsh, and such as had been driven into the heart of the wilderness.

CHAPTER 4

THE WITCH AND THE LORD

Lord Hugh had been on the threshold of death so often, that none of us expected him to cross it this time, either. We did not relax any of our precautions against discovery, both of the hunt as such before it was well under way, and of the hunters' separate identities. The manor was in confusion, and nobody came out after us. When the hunt was over, Bedesford worked through the night, carting deer carcasses to Cinqmort Manor, until the dry moat was full up.

Baldwin and the henchmen went in terror lest my lord get knowledge of what had been done, and die of it. Now it was the henchmen's turn to work with ropes and planks and hurdles, to clear the moat before it filled the air with pestilence. And then they had to grapple with the sorting, salting, smoking, storing, burying, and burning. The stench of all this clung to them long after.

Meanwhile, Juliana also never thought but that her brother would recover, and hence obeyed his last decree, sending away Luke's friends, the Flemish weavers, whom it had been such a feat, and costly feat, to get.

Then Baldwin came to Trefeller Court and said that Hugh was dying, and implored her to lend them her bondwoman that had saved Elizabeth and already proved her skill in Bedesford, too.

"Sister! As you call yourself Christian—as you yourself hope to find mercy on the Last Day! He is your own brother and, good or bad, he is rightful lord over all of us. He is coughing day and night. The men say they cannot bear it much longer, for it sounds as if his insides are raked out of him with iron combs."

"He may be beyond her arts."

"Then at least your conscience will know you did not begrudge him in his extremity. Prior Haakon has not dared give him the sacrament, for that his strength may rally, before the end, enough to make full confession. Even the Benedictines sent a brother with a cask of colts-foot syrup, Juliana!"

Neither of the Cinqmort brothers had as yet seen Swan Ygern-Jane face to face. To hear a woman dubbed "leech" commonly suffices to render folk incurious as to her looks, and certain of her age. So Baldwin was taken aback when Juliana led her out to him, and found nary a word to say to the woman the whole way.

Since Hugh's illness he had known what had become of their mother's tapestries. They were hung round my lord's bedchamber, rather inexpertly put up, and rather out of keeping in their faded femininity.

All the bed gear was most fine, but had sadly suffered of late. There was a hearth, by which an old woman sat watching a caldron and some cooking bags. The sick man lay moveless under quilts and brocades; his breath soughed through the room.

The first thing Jane asked for was willow boughs, as green as might still be found, to set all round his bed. Then she stripped Lord Hugh and looked close at his French scar and felt his ribs, and laid her ear to his chest and back. She asked them to bring her a spear which did not belong to Lord Hugh; also a bellows, a frog, some birdlime, more water, more vessels, and a young cat with its eyes open, but yet living with its dam.

While search went on for all these things, Jane took a mortar and pounded linseed, which she mixed with the birdlime and some vinegar, and forced down Lord Hugh's throat, first of all to purge him. Waiting for this to take effect, she clipped his unbarbered beard, pared his nails, gathered up part of the floor straw into which his bloody spittle had soaked, and made sure of catching some of his water. All this she cooked together in a little stewpan. Next she gave Lord Hugh to eat of a paste compounded of red roses powdered and candied, and gillyflowers and pennyroyal treated in the same way, to clear his head that she might talk to him.

He opened his eyes on her whom he did not know, unsurprised.

"Listen to me, lord of Bedesford. I have come here to make you well. This is what I shall do. We must trick the sickness into leaving your lungs. You see this bullfrog? I shall make him swallow a decoction made of parts of you, boiling hot. This will make him croak for a time—a time during which you must preserve absolute silence, and choke sooner than cough, for the sickness is to mistake the frog's voice for yours and him for you. Meanwhile, I shall employ someone to work these bellows without cease close by your chest. This is to strengthen your lungs, even as the bellows are inexhaustible. But you must be quiet, no matter what it cost you. Do you understand? Do not speak. Raise your head and nod if you have understood me and are willing to do your best to help me. Shake it if you deem the sickness stronger than your will."

Lord Hugh was so weak that sweat streamed down his corpse-nosed face with the effort of nodding.

"Now I am going to give you a draught to help you be quiet. Close your eyes, lord of Bedesford, and I will seal them down with beeswax, after, when I kill the frog, to make it seem you have died. You must trust utterly in me whatever I may do. You will sleep and yet not sleep. You will hear and yet not hear. You will know and forget."

The frog croaked in Jane's hands, the bellows were worked by two men taking turns; and there was the sound of running water. Jane had set Baldwin to pouring water from one vessel into another continuously, to cool the sick man's burning blood. The kitten purred by the hearth.

Jane made as if she were tending the frog in her lap, speaking to him in a gentle voice steadily growing louder, "O my lord your coughing sounds most sorely. My lord, your skin is clammy. Your eyes are starting out of your head. Would that I could exchange you, O my lord that I am nursing in my lap, for yon man lying on the bed, whom nobody cares for, and whose lungs can be heard working away strong as bellows. But it is not possible. It is you whom the sickness fills entirely."

Stealthily she rose, still holding, bewailing, caressing the frog. Suddenly, with one leap, she gained the fire and dropped the frog where the flames were most dense—taking the sickness by surprise.

She staggered back and had to hold on to the bedpost. Her dress clung to her in dark, wet patches; strands of damp hair hung about her brow and temples.

"Keep the bellows working! Keep the water running!"

She took a short knife from its sheath in her belt and went back to the hearth. She lifted the kitten by the scruff of the neck and carried it, kicking and clawing, to the bed.

"Sit up, lord of Bedesford."

The man who for days had been unable to move without assistance, sat up. He seemed asleep.

"Open your mouth, lord of Bedesford. You are about to receive health and life to drink."

Holding the kitten above Lord Hugh's head, Jane cut its throat with a single stroke of her knife. The kitten's blood, steaming as it met the air, fell over Lord Hugh's quiet face like a dark, hot, wet cloth unwound off the bale. As much of it as poured into his mouth he swallowed. His face, his nostrils, his sealed eyelids did not even twitch.

> "One life of the cat
> I take for leech fee,
> For fee of execution.
>
> The second cat life
> Ends in its own death.
> Trouble us not, second life.
>
> Third life of the cat
> Goes to Lord Hugh.
> Likewise the fourth life.
>
> And the fifth and sixth,
> Seventh and eighth lives.
> Ninth life is Hel's, mother of darkness.
>
> Second and ninth lives, flee:
> Trouble us not.

Keep the bellows working. Keep the water running. Sleep, sleep, lord of Bedesford."

The sick man fell back and slept on. Jane took a cloth and washed the cat's blood off him. Once more she stoked up the fire and thrust the drained corpse down into it. At length she dropped her arms to her sides with a sigh, motioned to Baldwin and the attendants that they might rest, and said, "Now we may speak. He will not waken until cockcrow. Then if, striving to open his eyes, his lids break the wax, he will live. I have done my utmost. Now you must pray all you can."

"The spear you asked for, wise woman?"

"That I shall not use until we are certain the sickness was well and truly trapped in the frog and the fire. You must understand that what I have just done was to drive away his present sickness only. The spear is to heal the lingering hurt from his old wound. It is a pity we cannot have the spear that made the wound; but we can try. I shall bleed him a little and smear the blade with his blood. Therefore, see you, the spear must not be able to recognize him for its owner. Then shall I tend the blade, cooling it, anointing it, as if it were the wound itself. Many wounds have I healed in this fashion, but I never yet tried it with a weapon that was not truly the right one. Yet try it I will. Now it will be best if I rest me. Much power has gone out of me in these hours. And do you watch and pray. Pray for him and pray, if you will, also for me that have wrestled with Darkness and Death."

Jane stayed on in my lord's bedchamber without anyone else to help her, by her own request, save in the way of bringing and taking what was needed.

Nobody thought that there was danger to her chastity, and not only because my lord was still so weak. Mind you how Master Lamb had tried to convince Juliana of the bondwoman's effect on Black Andrew and indeed all full-blooded men? Well, either it required the sea air, just as the voluptuous flowers of the sea will fade without they are steeped in salt water, or men of the sea alone were prone to the sea-reared intoxication of the pirates, or else fresh baptism had changed the essence of her womanhood even as it had her name. We could see she was very fair, and stately, but the finest thing about her we deemed was her hair, which she wore covered up, showing solely in her eyebrows and eyelashes. It was inhuman, like strange jewelry, which one may admire but not long to kiss.

"I am awake," Lord Hugh called, in a voice still feeble but clear and dry. "Come and sit by me, woman. Talk to me."

Jane lifted the pot she had been stirring from its hook and placed it on the hearthstone. She fetched her spinning and sat down on the bed step. Her drab garments became one with the curtain dusk, the pale shapes of her feet, hands, and face alone showed up. Slowly the spindle sank and was tucked up again under her invisible arm; slowly the twirling thread emerged and grew.

"Talk to me. Tell me, how long have I to live now? How far will the cat last me? A cat's life is not very long."

Jane smiled. "So you are not satisfied, lord of Bedesford—you that a little while ago had only a few hours left of your own life?"

"There is a carp in my pond that lived there before my father's father's time and outlived the fish murrain before the Black Death. He has a silver ring through one gill. That is how we know him."

"And you would have had me bleed that carp into you? Fish blood is alien to man blood. And, as you cannot make bread without flour, so you cannot make a spell without what happens to be the ingredient proper to it."

"But why a cat?"

"Of all beasts the cat alone has nine lives. With any creature that has only one, life cannot be transferred, merely ended. Nine, which is three times three, is a sacred number, and therefore dangerous. Eight, which is four time two, each two being itself twice one, is like quicksilver and slips through your fingers. Seven is the most powerful number, and will not bend to any will. But six, a pair of threes, is fixed and limited and subject to control; lacking a third three, it is malleable. After all death debts are paid, six lives remain of the cat's nine. We reckon that its original nine lives total up to the span allotted to man. Barring accident, and discounting what amount of life you have already spent, the six hale, whole cat lives you have eaten should bring up your life again to three score and ten. But it is a life like any other, and is not proof against future disease or injury."

Lord Hugh lay still, thinking, for a while. "I was told that you call yourself a king's daughter. Never have I heard of kings' daughters being taught the crafts we leave to lesser folk."

"Ay, and so it took me to save you. Lesser folks' lesser craft availed you nothing."

"Yet should I have thought no king's daughter would willingly live enslaved. If it were I—they would have to keep me in chains. They would have to kill me before they could make me work." He stretched comfortably in his warm bed.

"It is easy to see you have never lain in chains."

"Do you think," Lord Hugh demanded suspiciously, "that now you have gained power over me?"

"Perhaps. If I troubled to use it."

"If anyone but you had answered me thus!"

"There you see it, already."

"What?"

"Anyone but me. I am excepted. It is my power." Jane laughed aloud rarely; she did so now. "Lie down, lie still. This is part of my cure, lord of Bedesford! I make you angry to make you well and strong, for to your soul anger is the elixir of life." After a moment Lord Hugh laughed with her. Such was her power.

Lord Hugh found the same as everyone that ever went to this witch for help. You felt it as a boon, rather than compulsion, that in private colloquy you would be moved to tell her everything about yourself, and more than you had previously known there was to tell.

"All my days, you must know, you Jane," Lord Hugh said to her another time, "I have been a lonely man."

"He that would rule utterly unruled must needs be lonely," Jane said, gazing only at her thread.

"No!" said Lord Hugh, after a pause. "It is not a master I have wanted, but a peer."

"You had a wife I am told, a noble lady—"

"My wife! None has dared mention her to me all these years. I have never willingly thought of it."

"Tell me, now," said Jane. Lord Hugh watched the light hurry in tiny spirals round her thread.

"It was not my fault. I did not ask to be married—to a puling little girl of eight. I was to sit her on my knee and feed her sweetmeats, to make her like me. I was twice her age. I sat, I should think, for an hour and more. On the one hand, she could not get enough; on the other, she must show off her dainty manners and turn each mouthful over and over on her silly little tongue before she could swallow. I thought I would have to sit with her until nightfall. When she lisped it for the hundredth time, 'Methinks now I should like another, dear Hugh,' I could not help myself. I crammed all that was left into her sticky little mouth."

"And she was choked?"

"No," Lord Hugh answered with a sigh. "This happened long before we were wed, on my first visit to Damesbury Castle. No, but she took a dislike to me. I thought the match might be broken off, but her mother only beat her when my Agnes said she would not have me because I had given her too many sweets. But she, my lady bride, behaved so wildly it was thought we had better take her nurse along, too. At the wedding everyone said how lucky I was, what a beauty she would grow up into. She was always crying. But the nurse was jolly. There was I, a married man, young and lusty and, I believe, not un-pleasing—she took pity on me, that is how she put it. I used to go and lie with her in the bed where she slept with my wife. Sometimes my wife would wake up and cry. Then we would have to hush her, with pillows and with sweetmeats. One night the nurse was not there when I crept in to join her. It was cold. I did not feel like waiting out of bed. Agnes was asleep. In her sleep she had moved so that she lay athwart the bed. I could not avoid touching her. Her little body was all slack, all warm and soft. I took up her hand which was flung right out to the edge, to make a little more room. Her hand was small and slack and soft. I bent the fingers and played with them; it was as if she had no bones at all. She was my wedded wife, the hardest thing about her my ring on her boneless, boneless finger. I did not know what I was doing till after it was done. You do not look at me."

"See. I am looking at you now," Jane said. "Tell on. Tell all of it, once and for all."

"She woke up and cried. I thought it was just her usual crying. I tried everything to stop her. The nurse came back and helped me. Then we noticed! I stole away. Nobody need ever have known. But the nurse lost her head. Agnes was dead by morning. My father—he said to me—My sister Isabella could not look at me without shuddering, for a long time after. Though they both stood by me when old Lady Agnes came. Oh, none can know what a time it was for me, after I was widowed. All thought only of the horror to the child. None, none considered what horror it all was for me. None has ever spared a thought for what this did to all my life that came after! I made atonement with much gold and penances, yet I have never been free of it."

"You were like a man would rather carry his foe on his back all his life, then wrestle with him face to face. No wonder you felt burdened."

"You do not shrink from me like everybody else?"

"From what I have heard, it seems to me the other way about, lord of Bedesford. They do not shrink from you, all the women whom you have tried, trying to kill as you did that once, again and again. Because they neither shrank nor died, *you* turned from them with loathing."

"What are you saying?" Lord Hugh whispered, amazed.

"What you yourself said. It was not your fault. It was you who were violated—just as I was. Someday I may tell you—violated and dragged down. I have also heard about you and your lady mother. It is said you reproached her from avarice. But to me it is clear those were merely words, the words clothing, concealing the spirit of your meaning as the flesh does us. In fact, young as you were, you were appalled to find her whom you loved so well still smirching herself in heat."

"Yes! Yes! How did you know, when I myself did not?"

"All your actions, as I have heard them recited, disprove meanness. All your life you have striven to cast off property, which is only another fetter tying the spirit down to earth. You have tried to rid yourself of all impure desires, little realizing that you only wasted time and substance, for you were not born with such desires at all."

"That is nothing to the substance I have wasted thinking that God must be set against me, to have allowed it all to happen so," Lord Hugh mocked, uneasily, as if he did not wish her judgment to be true after all, "when the contrary must be the case, since I am such a saint."

"Saint I did not call you," said the woman, with a little smile. "But if you do not feel strong enough in yourself to try for greatness honestly, and without the safeguarding excuse—in case you fail—that you could not contend against Omnipotence, why, then I cannot help you."

"You have helped me," Lord Hugh returned, shamefacedly. Whereupon he turned his face to the wall, for it hurt him to have been helped and to be forced to acknowledge it, graciously at that. For his life he did not feel indebted to her. Others, not he, had asked her to save him. Ay, there is no end to human vagaries.

So he tried to pay her back. He tried to deal by her as had ever been his way with women. This he found impossible. Her tacit, utter rejection of amorous congress was such that it not only debilitated his very attempt, but also began to make it credible that he, too, might be as she had said.

They went on as before some time longer. Then she said he was well and she must return to Trefeller Court. He could not dissuade and did not succeed in delaying her many days.

On the morning fixed for her departure, he stalked up and down the bedchamber, the while she collected her medicines and other belongings. "Are you ready now?"

She smiled. "Ay. And now it would seem you are in such haste to see the last of me, you have even forgotten to tender me a fee."

He did not smile, he did not frown, merely brusquely stretched out his hand, "It is not so. Come. I want to show you the fee I have in mind."

She hesitated, then followed. They met no one.

"You have not been through here, I think? Scarcely more than one room have you seen of my great manor. This is what they used to call the council chamber. It was built by Sir Baldwin the first, but the colored windows were added by Lord Gervase Lestrange, his son, that fell in Wild Wales. It has not been used, excepting for banqueting, in more than a hundred years. Here in this room my mother used to sit with her maidens and daughters. You see the light is good for all manner of women's crafts—two big windows. But look well at the ceiling. Sir Baldwin Redbeard started it, although it was not finished till Lord Hubert Dagger's time. This is the drinking room—the Little Hall we call it. High up on the wall there is Hugh-le-gros's mead horn that he got in Spain. No, we are not even halfway round. We are come to the inner tower, and I want you to climb to the top with me before I take you over the rest."

He unlocked a heavy, iron-bound door and led her through the lumber rooms and up the last stretch of narrow winding stair. Out on the top platform, an unsuspected wind made itself felt. Rooks scattered, cawing. "Look," said the lord. "Look below and look all round."

The woman did as he bade her. Hasty cloud shadows, unraveling at the edges, sped over the motley view, as if to guide her gaze and help the lord show off his dominions.

"Look," he repeated. "Look well and take your time. All that you see is mine, and is but a tenth part of what is mine. Look and see if you can guess what I would offer you for leech fee."

The woman wheeled to face him. The wind had torn off her kerchief and undone her hair, which fluttered about her like a mantle cut into fine shreds. Lord Hugh thrust his hands through it and clasped her by the shoulders.

"Yes," he said. "You have guessed aright You are a witch. You are a bondwoman. I know naught of your history—king's daughter that you say you were, among heathen savages without the law—while you have known me dishonored in weakness. Yet be my wife and lady."

For a moment she said nothing, gazing now at him, now at his fields, his woods, his river, and brave town. At last she closed her eyes and answered him, slowly.

"So, to reward me, you would try to bring me low, by foisting on me what I would not have, and should not, what would corrupt my nature and rob me of true life?"

"Jane, what could we not do together! Say yes, Jane! Perhaps I did wrong to tempt you in the way I did. What if I were to say you need have no truck with my goods and holdings, as free of property as you are with my sister, even as my wife? If it is bondage you need, I could buy you. What say you now, Jane?"

"Now I do thank you, gratefully, for that I know it came hard for you to say. But you cannot buy me, just as I cannot freely come to you. Your sister would not sell me. So it was ordained. Were I to escape, it would be at the cost of all my powers, and of my immortality. For without my powers, which are my soul and the nature of my nature, I should be less than a beast, and denied access to my ancestors' other world. *Your* Heaven and Hell are not for me."

"Nor for me! Nor are they for me!" Lord Hugh cried, as in sudden enlightenment. "Oh, Jane, my peerless peer! Cannot you take me with you at the least? Could we not be paired after all, in rarer manner, as would be right for such as you and me? Is there no way—of compact, of communion—"

"Belike there is," the witch said, and slowly gave him her hand. "Belike there is such a way for us, lord of Bedesford."

CHAPTER 5

THE FLOOD

ONCE THE HARVEST was safe and Lord Hugh's recovery assured, we began to give more thought to what he might do to us; amazed to recollect how lightly Clement had led us to dismiss the consequences. No doubt we should have done what we did anyway. But, the danger of famine having been averted, its bygone threat dwindled beside that which now hung over us all with all the multiplying terror of uncertainty.

Lord Hugh did, in fact, contemplate demanding the head of every tenth man in Bedesford, but Abbot William declined to lend him the support without which in these circumstances his vengeance was bound to fail, if only because all could, and would, claim sanctuary.

"Your brother should have given them his permission, and then the slaying of the deer would have been no crime," Lord William said to Baldwin, who had begged him to reconsider his answer. "If there were a law against the use of water, folk would still try to save burning houses."

"Granted that Hugh was in error to begin with," Baldwin said, doggedly, "still the law must be upheld. Folk will not stop at one law once they find it was broken with impunity. Once you allow them to think they have power, who can wonder, who can blame them if they use it?"

"Laws were made to uphold justice, not the other way about."

"If my reverend friend will allow me to say so, we are not talking about justice."

"I am talking about justice," said the Abbot, firmly.

About the middle of January the Abbot had it announced that, full five years after the Black Death, the special food concessions for building laborers must now come to an end. Observation of all important fast days had been reintroduced for some time, and none could have wished to say aught against that. But now the Abbot decreed that all Fridays were to be treated as days of fast. Furthermore, every resident workman was henceforth to regard himself as a kind of honorary lay brother and live on the meatless diet prescribed for monks. Some flesh meat every second day had formed part of the wages for which we had taken the oath. It was clear Lord Jerome had asked him to start economizing, now that we were to get stone from Friggsby again.

As yet we have said little as to the way the monks lived at Cloudsway Monastery. But the very fact that Lord William had so soon reconciled them to his rule and the comfortless condition of a new foundation will have indicated that he managed to make life pleasant for them. To him monastic law was no more rigid than temporal. Surely Lord William cannot have thought we did not know that most of the monks had themselves bled regularly so as to be accounted sick and allowed, accordingly, to eat well? If Lord William thought us deaf, he cannot well have thought us blind; and the stuff of food must be conveyed to the kitchens ere it can be consumed in the seclusion of refectory. Blind men, for that matter, could have told the monastery's daily fare: more savory odors, never rose from any chimney. It is hard to say which was the more hurt and surprised, Lord William when the Wasteside spokesmen called to remonstrate with him, or the workmen when Lord William called them ingrates and gluttons.

February brought severe frost and heavy snowfall. Even on our previous regimen it had been bitter hard to work in such weather. Those that owned shoes were loath to shred them on the ice crusts, those that had none did not like to bleed—there being no sick-bay pampering for us. Having got in the week's supplies, most of us laid down our tools and went home to bed and stayed there. In the end Brother Laurentius and two other friar masons alone continued at the site. Lord William swore next spring he would get him some men-at-arms.

The thaw set in overnight. People leaped from their beds and embraced, at the sound of rain. It stopped before dawn; the sun shone with all his might. About noon, sun and sky were hidden behind clouds that sagged low. And then there began such a rain as shamed the nocturnal burst into dribbling insignificance. Such a rain it must have been sent Noah scurrying for his ark. Upon the copious waters of the preceding twelve hours the rain begat so much water as you have never seen and, please God, never shall see.

It was not possible to light our fires. Outside trees without roots appeared to skate in mid-air, the pathways were bands of whorled water.

The friars that came splashing up to the huts said what was visible of Cloudsway Ridge was one infinite cascade. The Wode had quadrupled in width and was roaring along with tenfold speed; the Wode was assailing the cathedral.

The Abbot called upon all to come to the rescue and get further help—and God's curse upon us—we should have our meat. As the people slithered down the streaming hillside, many could not refrain from chuckling to themselves. It was so human in Abbot William to swear as any ordinary fellow would have done in like situation. Also, we at that moment had forgotten all about our grievances. Slyly we blessed the Abbot, that he had remembered for us.

The water reached up to the southern choir wall and was butting against the southeast transept. Our vanguard arrived on the spot just as the Abbot and monks were driven out of the chancel by the collapse of its two most southerly walls, complete with scaffolding and a window arch wanting little more than the keystone. One of the monks—it was Brother Oswin—scrambled back as soon as the echoes of the crash had subsided. He balanced on the rockery round which the rising waters eddied, and chanted the office for the dying. For some men, we heard, were trapped in the crypt. It had been the Abbot's first concern to have the entrance blocked. Not until this was done had the cries for help started up below; now the weight of the debris sealed the doom of their authors. Brother Oswin reported that part of the grille must have been smashed, but it was too high up for any down there to reach it.

There was no time to be lost. A few hundred yards to the west, the waters were yet a fair distance from the building ground and found to be reasonably shallow. Tied together with ropes, spades and mattocks strapped to their backs, half the men forded the river, and, arriving on the opposite side, fell to digging, in the hope of tempting the rampant Wode to diverge.

More and more people from the Old Town came to help; even Lord Hugh, and Baldwin, and the henchmen; even old men and pregnant women and some children.

They say wrong that will have it Hell is a place of flame. Nay, Hell is a place of wetness and inundation, the misery of which has not its like. Hell is a place where you have built and striven with everything that you have in you of love and bodily strength, only to witness inexorable progress of swift destruction. In Hell the damned forever rush to save what is yet standing, to be beaten off by its fall. And the waters mirror your handiwork, maliciously doubling what you are like to lose—what inch by inch you *are* losing. Thus do they go about breaking hearts in clammy Hell.

Apse and choir were one swirling lake. Here and there scaffolding still rose firm—with nothing to support. Elsewhere it sagged askew, or added driftwood to the swimming confusion. Wherever the eye lit on what still stood fast, the mind knew of the waters' undermining.

The northern walls and the choir's five courses of south wall and its aisle arcade were used as ramparts upon which we worked side by side in the hope of reinforcing them into bulwarks. Many children no older than Alfred were allowed to make themselves useful, but him we chased off time and again because of his hand. Time and again he returned.

Two men there were did nothing, though if moans and tears could have helped, for sure this pair would have propped up St. Hand's all by themselves. Regardless of his safety, Humphrey Painter rocked mourning atop the grave of his pictures and equipment, his assistant impotently tugging at the stolid rocks that formed the barrow. The next time he came back, Alfred tried his luck near them.

Suddenly there came a new uprush of water which swept the assistant off his feet and submerged Humphrey up to the armpits. Alfred was carried a few yards on the crest of the wave and flung to safety where tumbled stone and caked rubble were heaped highest. He realized that he must be near the grille of the crypt. Quite close to him, an arm of water was welling from below. Something was borne along with it, looking like the roof of some toyhouse. Presently, he recognized the calf binding of Humphrey's greatest treasure, his book of patterns, containing outlines and color charts of everything from leaves and birds to human likenesses in different attitudes, with notes of all symbols pertaining to age and degree of moral and mundane rank.

With a shout Alfred made a dive at it. His movement dislocated some ashlar, which grated to rest upon a block of stone slightly lower down, locking with it in such a way that Alfred's left-hand wrist was held fast between the two. He set his teeth and wrenched and tugged. He was determined not to cry out. He could tell that the trap would be easily sprung by simple upward leverage, although he might pull and thrust slantwise and laterally for evermore without success. It became the greatest of all necessities that he should perform this light rescue unaided.

The book floated out of his reach. His right hand was of no more use to him than a straw. But he would not cry out. Then, when he had to cock his head backward as far as it would go to keep his nose above water, he found he was no longer able to cry out. For now he *was* thoroughly affrighted, and his voice failed him.

Command of it returned the moment he was conscious of stronger hands freeing and lifting him up. He was wreathed in the strands of Humphrey's beard, snaky with water, as the painter clutched and kissed and thumped him. "Alfred! Nay, Alfred. Drowning without a word. Nay, you little fiend, I made sure you were gone from us! Ho, somebody! Get this child out of harm's way."

Alfred wriggled and lashed out with arms and legs. "The book!" he yelled. "Humphrey, your book! There it goes, over there! Catch it, catch it, quick!"

"My book!" Humphrey roared, but without letting go of the child he had saved. "Franklin—Frank—you there—good fellows—after my book, after my book! A picture of his mother in Heaven, for whomsoever saves my book! But for you, devil's spawn," he said to Alfred, "I could go after it myself! Keep still then, you that should by rights be dead."

"I'll save your book! Only make it a picture of my mother-in-law in Purgatory!" one of the men wading after it cried laughingly over his shoulder, for never was Humphrey so droll as when he was most serious. Also, the rain had stopped.

Some of the thick, splayed parchment leaves must have curled under, forming beneath outspread covers a little nest wherein air remained caught. The book swam on, faster than its stumbling pursuers. It passed out over the ruins, round by the easterly chancel walls, where the flood churned moatlike. There, on a sudden, without discernible impediment, it stuck. It stood, like a frog treading water, the currents making bubbles and a light froth about it. Gradually the covers moved closer together and rose: most weird it looked, said the man who was the first to reach it. He made to pick it up. It was as if stronger hands than his pulled against him from below. He thought of the men drowned in the crypt. He shuddered, and all but dropped the book again, when with a squelch and gurgle it yielded. By this time others had joined him, and they saw, where the book had been, a little funnel of a whirlpool.

Two of the incomplete chancel windows, though as yet without masonry to fill in the space between them, were still standing. After the southwest wall had fallen in, some months before, it had not been considered safe to connect them before the buttresses were all in place. One of these had not progressed beyond a deep hole dug for its foundation; its twin had grow a foot above ground before the flood demolished it. Debris and water covering both these vulnerable places, they had been entirely forgotten.

Jacob Tewsing swore that if these two holes had not been seen to in time, everything east of the first crossing must inevitably have gone. More than that, the whole site would have had to be abandoned, unsafe for years to come, and the whole work begun again from the first scratch into wildered ground, and the sacred Finding Place would never have been duly honored.

To be sure, Master Colet disputed Jacob's theory. But, in a matter which, when all is said and done, could never be either proved or disproved, even the monks seemed to prefer Jacob's view, which made a child and a book the instruments of God's saving purpose.

Next day the sun broke through again, and there was a rainbow. The flood was halted, the cathedral safe—albeit in lamentable state. The birds sang everywhere, enough to deafen you—and so did the people as they went on with the work; and the monks and the friars raised most noble incantation.

But when a water waste was made, of hollowed tree trunks, when the entrance to the crypt was cleared and the working parties descended among the faint, meaningless blottings that alone remained of the painters' labors, they found that the two green, bloated corpses were unknown, even as they had been unclaimed.

Yet what they had been and why they had come here could not have been clearer if it had been possible to make them talk. One bore the executioner's brand on cheek and forehead, the other had had his nostrils slashed years ago, and both had various other telltale scars. Both had been clad in whole wool fells, retaining the shape of the animal. They had not even troubled to remove the marks of the sheep's owners—Bedesford men. The locker grilles lay on the floor, cut and torn out of the wall with the stone in which they were embedded. The Hand was still in place, but the vessels were strewn about the flags next to tools and weapons and soggy torch stumps. The Bishop's lily had been wrenched from the slab of mosaic pavement.

Far from being a punishment for our unruliness and greed, as the Abbot maintained, the flood had been sent to prevent sacrilegious theft.

CHAPTER 6

THE VISIT

EDWIN'S WILFULLNESS had grown beyond all reason. For a long time folk had fruitlessly urged him to take Alfred to see Jane. Yet no sooner was everyone else satisfied of God's purpose in having made Alfred a cripple, than Edwin must needs fly in His face. He was as weak as he was stubborn in the wrong place. Apparently it was Alfred himself had badgered his father into this. So Edwin gave in to a child where he had held out against the counsels of his elders.

Luke was away on the *St. John's* maiden voyage. Between the trade seasons, Juliana had fallen into a state of restlessness. When word came of her sister, Philippa's return to Thirchester as the convent's new Mother Superior, Mistress Trefeller sallied in state, with two maids and Geoffrey to accompany her, to visit the tormentress of her childhood. Folk said she wished to triumph over Anne Addertongue, in her worldly greatness; but as Anne-Philippa was presumably at the goal of her own ambitions, like as not the sisters would agree henceforth.

Pride—and Jeanne—would have kept Edwin away from Trefeller Court, had not Juliana been away. Even so, nothing would persuade his wife to go, so that he himself must get leave of absence to take Alfred. And even so Jeanne murmured and muttered, packing up some small gifts for the leech woman.

Alfred knew he had been born in the town and that he had once lived there, but he did not remember it. All the way up the hill he kept on letting go of his father's hand to run ahead and come skipping back, his newly trimmed hair, fluffy after washing, flying out about his head.

Halfway across the green, Dick Toolmaker hailed them in passing. "Lord William has summoned me again—so courteously that I must not keep him waiting. The more as I shall only have to say him no again. See you on the way back, perhaps?"

"Father," asked Alfred, taking Edwin's hand, and walking more sedately, "what does Lord William want of Dick?"

"He wants him to come and live at the site."

"Why does he?"

"Oh, Alfred, you know very well. Because the flood ruined what it did not carry off in the way of tools. That's what the new forge house is for —as if you had not been worrying the builders every day with your questions! And there is new iron and stuff on the way from Groveshott. The Abbot thinks Dick would get the work done faster if he came to live amongst us and did nothing else."

"And would he?"

"I expect so."

"Then why won't he?"

"Because," Edwin sighed laughingly, "because he has a place of his own to look after, and he does not quite trust wolf and deer and bear to do it for him. And you know he is our woodward also."

"But couldn't he be both?"

"He cannot give equal time to both. Dick wants to do less toolmaking, and the Abbot wants him to do more."

"But doesn't Dick have to do as Lord William wants him?"

"Not Dick. Dick's a freeman, and nobody can make him do anything."

"Then I will be a freeman when I grow up. I shall be a toolmaker."

"Would you not rather be a building master, Alfred? If only you grow well, that is what I would have you be."

"I am going to carve wood and stone, like you," Alfred replied with decision. "Like Dick is toolmaker and woodward both, so shall I do a little toolmaking and a lot of carving."

"But carving is nothing, compared with what Jacob does, or Master Stephen," Edwin urged. "Carving is putting on little bits and pieces all over the main work, which could do without them."

"Oh, but it would not be beautiful, without," said Alfred surprised.

"That may or may not be. But which is the more important?"

"I had rather do what is beautiful than what is important."

"But if your salvation depended on it—if your father desired it so very much—" Edwin stopped at the child's uncomprehending gaze. He bent to hug him, "Like enough you will never need to decide, my poor son," he said bitterly, then tweaked Alfred's nose and ran. "See if you can catch your father, Alfred!"

Soon Edwin began to point out to him things and places. As nearly every able-bodied person in Bedesford had rushed to the aid of the cathedral, there had not been hands enough to save Old Bede's Bridge. There was a gangway of tree trunks and rope where the old bridge had stood. Beside this Bede's New Bridge was being built, entirely of stone. Lord William had let the townfolk have this stone at a very moderate charge, seeing that the structure was to test on a small scale Jacob's design for the central tower supports, which Master Colet heatedly opposed on grounds of impracticability.

Alfred had not met his kinsman Geoffrey's wife before. Meg was fat and fair, and made much of him, as she herself was expecting her first child. She fed him honeyed ginger from a jar in the kitchen, and then led father and son out to the back and beyond the farmyard.

By the orchard wall a number of servingmen were busy round the beehives; and a little farther on, in the middle of a meadow, there was a crowd of women. Jane, recognizable from afar, being the tallest by a full head at the least, stood by a pen set up at the entrance to a narrow passage between two thorn hurdles, down which sheep after sheep was being driven, leaving most of its wool behind. Edwin had heard of this practice, which Jane had persuaded Juliana to try out, and which in some cases was cheaper and easier than shearing. Albeit the moment of execution had to be well timed, as only at a certain period after the cold weather the wool would come off without hurt to the skin. One of the released sheep all but overthrew the visitors in its fright. This attracted the housekeeper's attention. Shading her eyes, she came away from the pen, two children running after her, a girl and a boy.

"Edwin Widowson, is it?" Jane said right pleasantly. "And your son; I remember him. Alfred, is not that your name? You can go back to the kitchen now, Meg. Elizabeth!" she stretched out one hand behind her, and the girl came round to her side.

She was big for her age, with her yellow hair welling thickly from under a cap embroidered with white flowers and blue. She smiled at Alfred.

"Elizabeth," Jane went on, "this boy is Alfred Widowson that used to be your playfellow and your milk brother. It is long since he visited you, and there are many new things here to show him."

Elizabeth beckoned to Alfred, saying, "We need not take Little John with us, need we, Ganna-Janna?" Little John, as big and fair and handsome a child as his sister, looked from one to the other silently.

"Little John is the host at Trefeller Court while your mother is away," Jane said. "If he does not go with you, it will be discourtesy to your guest."

Little John took Alfred's hand. It was the right hand, and its unexpected smallness and infirmity caused the younger boy to drop and stare at it, still without a word.

"You are not to take *that* hand," Elizabeth elbowed him aside and took it in hers.

"Why not?" Little John cried in an injured tone.

"You are not to, that is all," said Elizabeth. "That one is for me. You may take his left hand."

Scowling, Little John went and clasped Alfred's left hand. Alfred and Elizabeth exchanged the glances of amused seniors, and the three children ambled off. Jane turned back to Edwin, who stood looking in the opposite direction, seemingly engrossed in the men cleaning out the beehives.

"I sent them away because it will be best if he does not overhear us—your son. Unless I am wrong and you have not come to me because of him?"

"I did not think you would receive us so kindly—since we left it so late, coming to you!"

"Come with me into the hall where there is a fire. Better later than never, Edwin Widowson."

When they were settled by the hearth, Jane with some sewing, she said, "Now tell me."

"There is not very much to tell," Edwin gazed into the fire, and told her. He ended, "I dare not think what will become of him if he grows up like this. Better for him he too had been stillborn. Before he was born, I prayed only that his hand might be gifted—and my wife I made to go about with a piece of carved wood hung round her neck under her clothes."

"And now you do but pray that he may be able to use his hand one day?" Jane finished for him. Edwin did not answer, and she raised her eyes from her work, "You do *not* pray? Is this how you have come to me, for the Devil's aid?"

Edwin sat clasping and unclasping his hands. "I know not what to answer. It is true I know God will not listen to me. Forgive me if I have offended you—I—"

"*Now* you have begun to tell me the kind of thing I want to know," Jane said quietly. "Tell me why it is you think God smote the child's hand for your sake."

Edwin caught his breath. "I cannot tell you that."

"You mean you will not."

"No. I *cannot*. It is not for myself only."

"I should keep the secret whatever it be."

"God knows I believe you. God knows I should like nothing better than to tell. I have never seen you except from afar, yet you make me long to tell you," Edwin said, succumbing, like all the others, to the spell she ever wove of shadow, firelight, and unobtrusive employment. "Nor it is that I am *afraid* to tell. Day in and day out I live apart from my fellow men and outside communion with God. I do my work, not only without His aid, but against His curse. But if it should happen that my work please and become acceptable to Him in spite of me that performed it—then perhaps by the tip of one stone leaf—by one chip in one course of pier, I may yet be hoisted up into forgiveness, in the end. To no one have I ever said as much as this."

"How long has it been so for you?"

"Since before Alfred was born. Full seven years. Now you will see it was not slighting you—that we did not ask your help before. You see, soon after, what I may not tell you, all kinds of calamities befell here in Bedesford. Only I knew why. Instead of falling on me, they were heaped upon others, for I was held unworthy to be allowed to atone. I was glad when it came out there was something wrong with Alfred. At last, I thought, God had relented and was punishing me in myself."

"And now?" Jane asked when the pause grew too long.

"Now I have seen that he is no longer just my son, but a being unto himself. I must not wish to atone through him, either. O wise woman, if only you could help him—if you would cut off my hand for his I would gladly, gladly give it. You do not answer. Is it hopeless?"

"Nothing is hopeless, except there is death."

"I would be better dead."

"No one is better dead, and a craftsman least of all."

"That is not what the priests say."

"The priests do not always know what they are talking about. Nonetheless does it seem to me, Edwin, that you would be well advised to obtain some priestly guidance in your trouble. How do you know that what you think about it is correct? There is such a thing as pride of sin, exaggerating trifles. I cannot think what sin you can have committed, without anybody else's having come to know, that can be great enough to warrant such punishment as you talk of."

"Help my son if you can. No one can help me. The kindest thing you can do for me is to forget my blabbing."

Jane gazed at him steadily, then she nodded. "Very well, Edwin. It is forgotten. Ah, there are the children now."

Elizabeth and Alfred were still hand in hand. Little John followed a little way behind. "Alfred says you want to see him, Ganna-Janna," said Elizabeth.

"Ay, you want to look at my hand, don't you," Alfred said courteously, holding it out.

"Well," said Jane, taking it in hers, "if you say so. No pretty sight, is it?" She turned it about, bending the strengthless fingers. Edwin and Alfred both looked at her with wide, stricken eyes. "Well, it *is* right ugly, think you not?" she went on, fetching up Alfred's left hand to lay beside the right. "Like some blind, white, underwater creature. What! you would not cry for it? For such a worthless, unlovely thing, would you, a big boy like you, Alfred. Let it see you do not love it. Let it see you would rather have a fair and proper right hand, that you may be able to work wood and stone as your father's true son."

"But I cannot," said Alfred timidly.

"Oh, Ganna, he cannot!" Elizabeth cried reproachfully.

"Certainly he can," Jane said, her eyebrows raised. "He will be able to as soon as he is cured. And I shall cure him. There is nothing seriously wrong with his hand—hideous though it does look," she added again. "Between us, Alfred and I will get rid of it, for a better one. Shall we not, Alfred?"

"Yes!" said Alfred.

"You would not be mocking us?" the father said, having started to his feet.

"No. Why should I being doing that?" she said as though in wonder. "He must do as I say and come to me whenever I want him, that is all. It will take time, it will not be tomorrow or the day after that he is cured. My fee? We shall talk of that when it is due. Meanwhile take back your eggs and goat cheese to Jeanne with my greetings. Say to her for me it is not *my* wish that we should be unfriends. On second thought," she corrected herself with quick kindness, "let me keep the cheese. It will remind me of home."

CHAPTER 7

ALFRED AT TREFELLER COURT

WHEN FIRST he was up and about again, after his illness, my lord avoided the places of public congregation as far as he could. When he was seen, he wore an unrelaxed scowl and spoke to no one. It had become clear that the slaughtered deer were not going to be mentioned, let alone avenged. But after the flood, matters became easier. For one thing he had worked side by side with us to save the cathedral. And we wished to show him our gratitude, as well as our appreciation of his change for the better, since he had not resumed going after our women. As for Lord Hugh himself, he was in part appeased by satisfaction at the Abbot's defeat, similar to his own, at our hands.

Lord William, who had cursed and sworn at the laborers like a drayman while he was at odds with them, behaved as if nothing had happened, afterward. He had changed his opinion of us: he said as much to Baldwin, and it would influence him in the future. Meanwhile he nursed no grudge. The difference between his nature and my lord's had always been apparent in his dealings with women also. While scarcely less voracious, he developed a sort of fatherly affection for his paramours, whom he seldom cast off, merely adding new blood to their circle from time to time, and benevolently disporting himself among them all like a cheerful bumblebee among flowers. The number of his bastards was uncertain, as mostly their mothers were married women. He had formed a habit of making small christening presents in case of doubt. Soon, for decency's sake, he extended this to all infants born at the Wasteside.

On the birth of her second daughter, Margaret, Jeanne Widowson received half a pound of salt from the monastery, and at the same time was granted Alfred's temporary release. Jaffy and Martha she had borne easily, but with Margaret she was very sick. So the neighbors took Jaffy and Martha off Edwin's hands for a while, and the mother was at last persuaded to agree to Jane's suggestion and let her eldest son go to Trefeller Court for his cure.

When Juliana returned from Thirchester, there was Alfred earning his keep in her weaving rooms. She looked quite kindly into his upturned face, flushed with the exertion of moving about between the looms with his left arm tied behind his back, his feeble right hand set to plucking out the fluff that would collect in the cracks of the frames. With her own daughter she was not so kind.

A piglet without eyes had been born at Trefeller Court, and Elizabeth had adopted it as her pet, carrying it in her arms all the time, wrapped in a scrap of fleece, for a start. Then the piglet misbehaved when they all sat at table, and squealed in alarm, when it was thrown out, as if already stuck. So when it was the children's bedtime, Juliana kept her daughter up to beat her.

Alfred trembled in bed beside Little John—Jane was to sleep with Juliana this first night of the Mistress's homecoming. "Listen, listen, Little John," he nudged the other awake.

"Elizabeth is a bad girl," Little John murmured sleepily. "I—I am a good boy."

When Elizabeth came to join them, Alfred pretended to be asleep. He thought of running away in the night so that he need not face her in the morning. He awoke to find himself still there, paralyzed with shame and panic. He held his breath and tightly shut his eyes against Elizabeth's attempts at rousing him.

"Alfred, Alfred, time to get up. You are not asleep. Little John, come and tickle Alfred while I hold him." Little John obeyed till Alfred fell out on to the floor. He stood up panting and grinning, lost in loving admiration: she was just as usual.

"Now, Alfred," Elizabeth said, bustling round the boys. "Whatever is the matter with you? You haven't said your morning prayer for your hand. Did you remember to say your bedtime prayers, with me not there to watch over you?" Importantly she straightened the little bag he must wear next his skin day and night, containing a dried snake, for agility; fragments of ram and bull, for strength; oak chips, for hardihood; mouse's teeth, for tenacity; and a small bunch of assorted lichen, for rapid growth.

"Was it bad?" he asked diffidently.

"Oh, I told you things would be different when Mother came back," Elizabeth said matter of factly, and shoved Little John out of the door before them.

"Do you love her?"

"Who? Mother? Everybody loves his mother. Don't you love yours?"

"Yes," said Alfred, "but then she loves me."

"Everybody's mothers love them," said Elizabeth. "So do their fathers. I sometimes wish I had my father."

"You have Luke," Alfred suggested—Elizabeth had told him much about Luke.

"Yes." Elizabeth said a little dubiously, reflecting. "But I don't think it can be quite the same. I like your father, Alfred."

Alfred beamed. "Do you remember my mother?" he asked, eager for more.

"No," Elizabeth replied, too promptly. She knew Bedesford gossip had long ago decided that Elizabeth herself had been the real cause of Jeanne's quarrel with Juliana and her continued hostility to Jane. She added quickly, "Are you homesick for your mother today, Alfred. We could play at being with her, for a change, instead of going to Drofsedeb. Would you like that?"

From the day he came Elizabeth had drawn Alfred into an old game of hers and Jane's. Drofsedeb was the capital of Eremelgna, the underwater realm in the Straits of Gannets. Everything in terrestrial Anglemere had its replica in Eremelgna, reversed. Whatever they happened to be doing or seeing could be made to transport them to that land. An oxcart might rattle into the yard: all you had to do was to put the cart before the ox, and send them going in the opposite direction, and there you were in Drofsedeb. In Drofsedeb men sat at the looms, or rather hung upon them, upside down, and their work began with a finished web which they unraveled. Fish flew through the air and birds swam in the rivers. Huge flies were stabled in the byres, tormented by hosts of minute cows, and so forth. Little John could not be made to see the ox before the cart or the cow-beset flies, nor taught to add his own inventions. But Alfred had embraced the game with grateful zeal, seeing that it could enliven the weariest tasks.

Alfred was homesick at times, but not for his mother so much as for the building ground. He dared not allow anyone to guess this, knowing it would be thought wicked and ungrateful. It was not often that he asked Elizabeth to play that they were bird scarers of Cloudsway Waste, lest she divine his longings and feel hurt.

There was the tenderest affection between these two children. Elizabeth took after her father not only in looks. And just as her looks were not the *same* as John's, so other traits she had of him had undergone some change in being handed on. John, fair, robust, and shrewd even at his most generous had conceived a great love for one woman who was small, weak, and misshapen. Elizabeth, fair, finer-textured, and unbridled when it came to giving, loved every thing small, weak, and pitiful. Her heritage from Juliana added possessiveness to love and tenaciousness to loyalty. Although Alfred's deformity had helped arouse her love, his gradual improvement could not lessen it.

Jane smiled upon their friendship. As for Juliana, she concerned herself little with her daughter so long as the child observed a seemly reverence toward her mother and refrained from pressing rival claims on Jane's mothering and Luke's attention. Little John stood, as it were, between and a little way off from all. His mother was wont to say that every time she beat Elizabeth, Little John profited more than his sister. And this was quite true. Elizabeth might forget, and commit a given offense a second or third time; Little John took warning and never committed it at all.

Luke returned in the autumn. Just before that, one of the missing Cinqmorts had made his appearance at the manor, and after the slaughtering Trefeller Court prepared for a feast in his honor. Sent to help in the salting house, the children heard all about it.

The newcomer was Young Gervase, sole offspring of the late lord's second son. His entry into Bedesford had passed unremarked, as he came quietly and raggedly: another wanderer who might or might not stay. He brought with him proof of his father's death and his own legitimate birth. Proof of his identity was not needed: at fourteen or fifteen years of age he reached already to Lord Hugh's shoulder, and any stranger seeing uncle and nephew together assumed they were father and son.

After his father's death, when the sickness still raged through London, Young Gervase's mother had attached herself to a strolling scholar, with whom she had finally settled in Oxford. There the man's connections enabled the widow to make some provision for her son, entering him as a student at Merton College. We had not realized in Bedesford that these had been years of trouble and revolt everywhere, attaining their worst at Oxford. During the latest outbreak the townfolk had risen in a body against the colleges, set fire to them, bedaubed the bulls and charters with filth before tearing them up, and slaughtered every priest and every student they could get their hands on. Young Gervase was one of very few survivors. He had fled over the roofs to the tavern where his mother lodged, and she hid him, with the wallet containing his father's seal and documents, in the pit of the privy chamber. There, concealed under fouled straw, he waited until silence fell at last, to find the house aflame and the yard covered in the blood of the several resident secular clerks of whom his mother's paramour was one. And his mother he saw, too, among the dead, indecently composed by her murderers, and the words MONKYS HOR written upon her in mud. Now Lord Hugh had designated him as his heir.

To most Bedesford children, Lord Hugh was an ogre. To Elizabeth, Little John, and Alfred he was a buffon, regarded much as the Devil in certain fables, forever foiled and fooled by wily Christians, such as, let us say, Luke Robinson and Juliana Trefeller.

So when my lord entered on the day of the feast, the children burst from their ambush behind the hall door, with soot-blackened faces, and uteering blood-curdling shouts to startle and affright the Wicked Lord. Everyone jumped, except Lord Hugh. Gaunt and huge, attired in such splendor that the tapestries paled, he turned to survey the children who stood, not knowing what to do next.

"How thoughtful of you, Sister, to remember my favorite dish. These three are for my dinner? But hasten now and truss them for the spit. The hour is advanced and I am hungry. A little skinny, perhaps, but no matter," he had taken Elizabeth and Alfred each by one arm and was feeling them in a fearsomely realistic manner. Little John lay howling on his nose, having fallen over himself in timely flight. Alfred and Elizabeth struggled and protested with all their might.

The women brought in food and drink. Geoffrey and the Cinqmort henchmen came in, having seen to the horses. Meg whispered to Juliana that Jane would stay out with the children, and everyone sat down.

"Will you say grace, Nephew, learned as you are?" Juliana asked kindly.

Young Gervase's laughing face changed abruptly. He flushed as he said, "Nay, I am not learned, Aunt." Lord Hugh and Baldwin looked at him in surprise.

"Did they not teach you anything at the schools?" Juliana asked as before.

"Nay, but I have forgotten all my Latin," said Young Gervase, his flush deepening, and with a tremor as of defiance.

"But, Gervase—" Baldwin exclaimed.

"You have done well enough, so far, at home," said Lord Hugh. "You need not be bashful before your own aunt. He can read and write like a full-fledged priest," he turned, a little irritably to Juliana, "better than most priests, I should say. He has been reciting to us from all manner of books he knows by heart. What has got into you, boy?"

"Oh, very well," Young Gervase frowned, and his lip trembled slightly as he bowed his head, cleared his throat, and mumbled in such wise Little John could have said it better. By and by he grew easier. One of the maids, passing by him, choked back a surprised little yelp. When Baldwin, beside him, was not looking, Gervase stealthily removed the meat on his sober uncle's trencher, substituting for it the end of Baldwin's upper sleeve, so that Baldwin sawed a thick piece out of it with his eating knife before he noticed. Everybody was convulsed with laughter.

Luke Robinson sat looking at my lord in puzzled fashion. My lord was oddly likable today.

In the middle of asking his sister to forgive the children and have them sent for, Lord Hugh became aware of Luke's gaze. "I trust that it is not my presence, Master Fleming, has spoiled your appetite," he said affably. Luke, as was his wont when anything preoccupied him, had left his platter untouched, although Juliana herself had heaped it full of good things. "Is it the damage you have suffered at Friggsby? I have heard a rumor."

"Ay, my lord," Luke replied jauntily. "Some Danesborough villagers have now made me a full denizen of Anglemere. I am the latest victim in the feud. My Flemish friends that stayed with us here last year and whom I had settled at Friggsby had the house burned over their heads a few weeks ago, with almost a twelvemonth's work in it. Fortunately no lives were lost. My friends have taken refuge with the reverend lady, your sister of Thirchester."

"I hear you mean to travel west before Christmas," said my lord, grinning. "Are you going to spend the holy days setting fire to your rival's house in Danesborough, for the honor of Anglemere?"

"No, my lord. I am going to ask Lady Agnes for compensation."

Everyone stared, excepting Juliana who sat smug as if she had conceived this unheard-of plan, and as if it had already succeeded. My lord struck the board with the flat of his hand. "Then I know not whom to pity most, yourself or the lady of Danesborough!"

"Your lordship does me too much honor," Luke bowed, smiling. Everyone smiled. At that moment Jane came in with the children, washed and chastened. Luke made a grab for Elizabeth's pigtail, and added, "Pity *me*, if you will, my lord. See who is to travel with me!"

"Ah!" Lord Hugh kept his eyes unnaturally fixed on the little girl. "So your mother is sending you away for your Aunt Philippa to train up properly at her convent, Niece?"

"They are only going for Christmas," Juliana interrupted, looking suddenly put out. "Little John is going too. Alfred is going, to be page to my children, lucky boy that he is. And Philippa is in dire straits with the rats, besides which all her cows have udder sores. I promised her to send Jane, though I can ill spare her."

My lord jumped up and swung Elizabeth high in his arms. "I do not see how you can spare this one here, at Christmas of all seasons, Sister!"

"I might have known her unmannerliness would earn her *your* regard!" Juliana said sharply. "Her that did you an ill turn you hug and kiss, and my Jane, who nursed you through your sickness, you have not a word for. You are as bad as Luke."

Lord Hugh set down Elizabeth, who began to wipe her mouth and cheeks. He looked at Luke. Jane said, "I hope you are keeping well, my lord."

"Well enough, well enough." There was an end to my lord's lively pleasantries, no one knew why. He fell to brooding.

Gervase had got up to take hold of Elizabeth in his turn. She wriggled out of his grasp and for security climbed on Luke's knee. "Elizabeth!" said Juliana, in a voice not unlike her brother's at its worst.

"Let her be, Mistress. She is not troubling me."

Juliana took a deep breath, but Jane forestalled her. "Obey your mother, Elizabeth. You are too old now to sit on any man's lap."

Now Luke himself pushed Elizabeth off as if she was burning him. He turned his face aside to hide how red it had gone. His glance fell on Alfred, and he reached for him, "Alfred at least is not too old to sit on my knee, are you, Alfred?"

"Alfred is as old as Elizabeth," said Little John. Alfred hung his head and said nothing; but Luke kept him sitting on his lap.

Baldwin addressed Luke. "So you will not be going straight to Danesborough, Master? You will first deliver your charges at Thirchester, I suppose? Do you know the place at all? It has been as a second home to us Cinqmorts ever since the nunnery was first endowed by Queen Eleanor of blessed memory. Matilda Cinqmort was one of Her Majesty's ladies in waiting and a close friend. So the Queen made her the first Abbess of Thirchester. Generations of our daughters have received their education at the nunnery. My sisters used only to go for long visits, as the boys did too, when we were small. Has Juliana told you it was at Thirchester John Trefeller first set eyes on her? He had a standing agreement with the Sisters for their wool. They have never worked it themselves. In the midst of sheep, they have always imported flax and made linen."

"So I had been given to understand," Luke smiled. "But always does not mean forever. I am told Lady Philippa has found the affairs of the nunnery in grave disorder. Often need will launch new industries."

There was an awkward silence, everyone—save perhaps Young Gervase—having understood the underlying meaning of this passage. If Luke could persuade Lady Philippa to extend permanent protection to the Felmish weavers, avail herself of their guidance, and abandon linen in favor of cloth, his loss would beget untold gain. Baldwin had wished to let Luke see that he realized this, and that he did not believe Luke's story about going to see Lady Agnes. Luke, on the other hand, might as well have replied, "Quite right, my clever sir. Your brother has no jurisdiction over the demesne of Queen Eleanor's bounty and will be unable to thwart me as he did here in Bedesford. I trust he will not attempt to do so, for in her present straits Lady Philippa could do with her share under your father's will. If you leave her no alternative, you might find yourselves with yet another lawsuit on your hands."

CHAPTER 8

THIRCHESTER NUNNERY

LADY PHILIPPA was a most handsome woman, with a firm, smooth, oval face, its forehead enlarged by shaving, the eyebrows plucked out and replaced by thin arched lines drawn with sepia. Her voice was as a deep, slow bell; her skin shone with health and careful tending; and her garments exhaled a fragrance which made it a pleasure to breathe in her presence. Her smile was slow and measured as her speech and even more infrequent. Whatever she did, she did slowly and seldom. Most of her time she rested, sitting. Sometimes she was seen with a book, but it would send you to sleep, watching for the page to turn. Sometimes she did embroidery, gently drawing the longest of gold threads aloft through the hole her needle had pierced with the softest popping. When she ate, she was so dainty you could not observe that she chewed, till a brief tightening of her jaws and neckcloth told you she had swallowed her bite. Her jewelry was choice, and her chastity such that during her reign certain passages in a book the nuns owned, containing tales of the martyrs, were marked and not permitted to be read out aloud. At all times there was about her an air of quiet, imperturbable bliss.

"Why do you look so happy, Lady Aunt?" Elizabeth once asked.

"Because I lead a goodly life," Lady Philippa replied, after a thoughtful pause.

"Are you never dull, Aunt?"

"No," Lady Philippa replied, dreamily. "I am never, never dull."

"Do you never want to run? Do you never want to ride? Don't you ever want to stand at the loom yourself, or do pruning in the garden, or help a little lamb to be born?"

"No," said Lady Philippa.

"Are you taking cold, my aunt?" Elizabeth asked anxiously, observing a shiver within the folds of the Abbess' gown.

"No," said Lady Philippa. "I was laughing, Niece."

Juliana treated Jane as if bondage formed a tie more intimate than blood relationship, and the townfolk respected her. Without Juliana's example, the Abbess of Thirchester in all kindness received Jane as a valuable chattel pure and simple, and at once saw to it that she made herself useful. There were the rats, and the cows, the refurbishing of the workshops against the change-over from linen to wool, and the Christmas preparations for Jane to help with and prove Juliana's boasts. Luke had proceeded on his way the next day after their arrival. So the children were left to themselves, if one can call it that, with a cloisterful of pious women ready to instruct and play with them.

Little John was the favorite of the nuns, in his sturdy, pink-and-white chubbiness set off by thick fair hair and big blue eyes, firm and sound and solid as fruit. They vied for his favor with so much cosseting, that presently he would open his mouth to a proffered sugar plum only as a special favor to the giver. Before the season of Advent was out he had burst the seams of his best gown. A new one must be made for him at the last minute. The nuns fought for this task, the winners gladly sitting up through several nights. Not only was Little John's new holyday gown the finest ever seen upon one of his age and station, with drawn-thread work and inset embroidery, but he had a second one made for him by the jealous losers.

Alfred, despite his birth, was second choice, Elizabeth last. They were heavier and would not sit on the nuns' laps, and chattered and asked incessant questions which made the peaceful, simple women's heads ache. Nobody stopped them running about wherever they liked.

Alfred and Elizabeth had never guessed a convent could be otherwise, and exploring Thirchester gave them unending delight. They peered into the cells while the nuns were at Mass; tried the echoes of every vaulted passage; played hide-and-seek about the storehouses; offered various assistance to the lay sisters in the workshops and at the chapel oven where the wafers were baked; and ruined one plaster ceiling by stepping through it in the course of a battle with apples airing in the attic loft above. At mealtimes Alfred had to put on his new black frock with the silver button and stand behind Elizabeth's chair—and what torments they then suffered, with giggles that must be suppressed!

As he had promised, Luke returned in time for the festivities, but not alone. His companion caused a great flurry, being Lady Agnes of Danesborough. She had not set foot across the border for nearly twenty years. The children watched her arrival at the head of her men-at-arms, and at first thought she also was a man. Deep yet grating, loud without resonance, her voice was like a man's, and she wore a plumed steel hat over her silk headdress. The ground shook as she dismounted. She must have been nearing her fifties; her bushy eyebrows were snow white, but the hooked bristles round her lips were still quite black.

Luke made as to bring guests and hostess together, but a brusque gesture of Lady Agnes' dispensed with this. As simultaneously her grim features had softened at Lady Philippa's approach, it was manifest that henceforth she meant to deny the part which Luke had indubitably played in persuading her to come.

"I recollect you, Reverend Mother, as a tiny maid," she kissed the Abbess ring, "at my only child's lamented wedding. She would be your age now. Sometimes, when I have dreamed her to life, she looked as you do. My Agnes' little playmate was fated to become guardian to her grave. Will you grant hospitality to me and mine for the holy season?"

Lady Philippa took her in a graceful embrace and led her indoors. Later, she went to pray with Lady Agnes in the chapel at her daughter's tomb, which the elder Will Tewsing, Jacob's brother, had made. In the days that followed the ladies improved their acquaintance, but the visitor was not invited to the Abbess' cell until the morning of Christmas Eve. Lady Philippa was completing her toilet with the aid of the window-pane, which opened inwards, and reflected her face in miniature as many times as there were squares of lead-framed glass. At the same rate as the Abbess' breath clouded these, a plump elderly nun who was with her dived forward to polish them briskly, without pausing in what she had come to say.

"... and if we are to feed fifty poor, we shall need to use up everything in the west storehouse. The teal and pheasant from Damesbury will go in one repast, for the main board alone. Lady Agnes had brought some extra meat, but that is not much use to us now. Wine we have in plenty; we can lay down theirs. The weavers' Christmas offering will pay for candles. Lady Agnes' silver ewer I am inclined to advise you to sell, Reverend Mother, as we already have six such. The one thing nobody thought of bringing is salt. Our store will not last us beyond Twelfth-night. The woman Jane says she must have horn for combs. Wooden ones cannot be made fine enough without constantly breaking. And what am I to do about bedstraw for the holydays? It is not that I have left it too late, but that there are half a score more people than were expected. I dare not use bracken; we shall need that to make the fodder go further. Ah, you look like an alabaster angel now, Reverend Mother, but this brooch, perhaps, might go—yes, go! Sister Hilda is making her marchpane today. Shall I send in a sample, all hot and moist, for you and the Lady of Danesborough?"

Presently the guest's heavy footfall could be heard in the passage, dispersing a bevy of novices and maiden pupils, invariably to be found, despite repeated prohibition, outside Lady Philippa's door, in the hope that the Abbess might call one of them in and entrust her with some errand or other.

"She has permanent authority to deal with all household matters, has Mother Héloise," Lady Philippa sighed, as soon as the nun had withdrawn. "Yet will she come and ask me, whose spirit should be left to rarefied communion—"

"Who can blame her if she will not be debarred from communion with yourself, dear Reverend Mother?" A diffident smile threw Lady Agnes' face into disorder. Habituated to a grim expression, diffidence fairly set it trembling.

In Lady Philippa also an alteration was to be noted, albeit you had to know her very well to see it. The sameness of her mien and bearing, whilst anything but hard, was yet infinitely more inflexible than the virile mask of Lady Agnes. Now the delicate, healthy flush on her cheeks deepened and spread, the pearly sheen of her eyeballs attained to a diamond luster.

At first Lady Agnes held herself rigidly, afraid to exercise her bulk amid the dainty furnishing. By and by, the ladies came to business, and then it was Lady Philippa who displayed unwonted flutter. Both having been forced out of their accustomed demeanor, neither could recall an hour more pleasurably spent. It was settled that Lady Agnes would follow the Abbess' example and license home weaving under conditions such as Lord Hugh had forbidden in Bedesford. So far she had only half given her word to Luke, who had offered her commission on every bolt of cloth to leave Danesborough.

The evening of his arrival, Luke had exchanged only the barest of distant greetings with Elizabeth, so he went to look for her the morning after. Having sought her in vain all over the convent, he returned to the guesthouse and there found her, romping with the Damesbury henchmen. But she seemed equally glad to come out with him.

It was cold, but not windy. Holly and ilex, snow coated, resembled carvings in stone; the straw jackets of the fruit trees looked like ribbed white velvet; every thorn was delicately rounded; and from afar the square of the cloister buildings called to mind a jewel case, with the glitter of icicles under the eaves, the lid, as an overflow of the precious things inside. Transparent smoke rose straight up into a sky which was darker than the roof tops and the intricate enlacement of the trees.

"Where are we going?" Elizabeth asked. "Surely you did not mean to walk just nowhere? Shall I show you the pyre the village people have built on the green, for the Christmas bonfire? Greater you have never seen."

"Lovers take their lasses walking nowhere in particular," Luke said, with a smile that broadened as Elizabeth made a gesture of derogatory dismissal. "And if I want to have a little talk with you, is not that purpose enough?" Elizabeth pouted. "Ay, you know what is coming, I can see." Luke laughed, but then grew serious. "You know me. I am not given to faultfinding, am I? It is because I judge you to be a big girl now, of excellent understanding, that I address myself to you, instead of going to others about this. I looked everywhere for you this morning, and found you in the one spot where I would never have thought of looking. You are at once too young and too old now to keep such company, especially when there is fitter company at hand. Nor is it solely a question of what is fitting, but of what may be most profitable to yourself. Here at Thirchester you have great opportunities of amendment. No better pattern of womanly graces than your lady aunt could be found in the King's own household. All manner of gentle arts are consummately practiced by the nuns; and for the first time in your life you have the companionship of maidens of your own age bred up in the most courtly and learned manner. I had naturally looked to find you with them. At your age one learns quickly, and lastingly. If you take my advice, you will make the most of your remaining days here."

Elizabeth answered in a passion, "You know not what you are talking about, Luke. It is clear you know not what matters they are forever whispering and giggling about, these girls. Ay, all they could teach me I have long known, from Little John and from the hired women at home! As for what they *do,* that does not take much learning either. Let me show you. See, I, too, can talk through my nose; I can walk with my belly out like this; *I* could pretend at mealtime that I am not hungry and that my mouth is sewn up with thread—and go stuff myself in the kitchen beforehand, or in bed at night. Nonetheless could I well bear to stay a little longer. It is pleasant enough here, and better than at home! Why don't you ask my mother to let us stay here, me and Alfred? Everyone says you can talk her round in all things!"

"This is what comes of listening to the hired women!" She had never heard Luke speak so angrily—to her.

"It is not my fault that there is such talk," she said, defiantly. "It is everywhere, one cannot help hearing it. You talk of what is fittting and unfitting. If you know so much about that, why don't you marry my mother? *That's* what they are all asking! Now!"

She had been walking backward in front of him; now they stood still. Luke caught her looking at him with an air he knew: thus she would stand braving her mother. He took a hold on himself and said, courteously, "I did not know, though you are right and I should have. You were quite right to tell me. I am angry with the gossips, not with you. What do *you* think?"

Elizabeth was taken aback and hung her head. "What?" she faltered.

"How would you like it, if I were to marry your mother?" She looked at him dubiously, timidly; he could not help laughing. "Why would you not like it?"

"Oh, I know not—" Elizabeth said, puzzled. Then she giggled, as at the impossible. "That would make you my father!"

"Nay, that would never do, would it?" Luke cried, lifted her up and immediately set her down again.

Suddenly she bounded from his side. "You forget that there is more than one great lady here; whom I might learn from, Luke!" With legs wide apart and bent at the knees, she stumped so that chips of hard snow flew up at every step, every step seeming intent on crushing some creature underfoot. Her arms swung heavily at her sides, her neck was thrust forward, her face lowering: in imitation of Lady Agnes. "Bow-wow, I am a great lady, all womanly graces, bowwow; and your head will I bite right off—"

Luke laughed and shook her head. "No, Elizabeth, that is not kind. She cannot help her face, nor her build, which makes her walk thus. And people do not talk as she does unless they have weakness to hide. No, these people, that seem all crust, are far easier to handle than many a one that seems all softness. For once you pierce the crust in but one place, you have won, you have got inside, so the remaining crust is useless. Whereas the other kind are like down pillows. You may make an impression in one spot, but it will only rise up in another—I wonder whether I shall tell you a secret?"

Elizabeth skipped high, then composed herself to say fervently, "Oh, Luke, you know I shall not tell a soul."

"Well, I am thinking of getting a house of my own in Bedesford. That will stop their mouths! But I want no one else to know beforehand."

"Oh, Luke!" Elizabeth could not forbear jumping again. "Where will you have it? How big is it to be? Oh, you must tell me all and everything about it, now and all the time—and nobody will know but you and me!"

"I bought the bricks for it the last time I was over in Flanders and arranged for Lord William's tiles. Some people will have to know. You cannot build a house without anyone knowing. You know the place. It still goes by the name of Smithy Yard, in the Old Town, right by the market place."

"But that is an old house. I thought you were going to build a new one."

"You will see. It will be just like building a new one. Inside and out, I shall make it finer. I was thinking of talking it all over with you. No, I mean it," Luke said, catching her suspicious upward gaze. "Do you not think that will be a good game, all the better for not being a game entirely?"

"Oh, Luke! You must have red flag tiles in one room and glazed in another—and a wall fireplace, like they have in the parlor here—and an inside stairway—" suddenly Elizabeth stopped, as they heard the bell go. "Oh, I had forgotten about Alfred."

"What about Alfred?" Luke asked, testily.

"I must go to him. I promised. Ganna wanted him this morning. I was but whiling away the time, when you found me, waiting till he should be free."

"Why should he not wait for you now? Alfred and Jane, Jane and Alfred, those two are all you ever think of."

"Don't be angry with me, Luke. Tomorrow—could we not talk again tomorrow? We are to be sent to bed early today, so that we may stay up all through Holy Night, and here is half the day gone already. I must go to him. He will be looking for me everywhere. I will think up some more things for your house," she promised coaxingly, over her shoulder, already started on her way. "I had better run, so I will go on ahead," she flung back hurriedly, and was off.

Luke stood for a little while where she had left him, staring after the dwindling figure in its red cloak, slipping and falling two or three times, picking itself up, white with snow, and flying on. At length he followed briskly, albeit at an adult's pace.

Part Four
The Children
(1358-1361)

ALFRED AND THE MASTERS

THE MONASTERY was almost emptied of monks, since Abbot William had arranged a pig race in honor of Lord Jerome's father confessor and emissary, who was staying at Cloudsway Waste. Vague rattling of pots and pans in the kitchens came wafting through the air. The sound from the building ground were lost in the gentle, composite simmering all round. The heat was no more than pleasant, yet strong enough to render passing into the cool indoors equally a pleasure.

Brother Oswin was alone. He stood at his high desk, his cheek all but pillowed on the slanting top, where lay a sheet of vellum, already text-lettered, which he was embellishing. His paints, quills, brushes, and other delicate instruments were ranged over a bench at his right hand. Yet could he make drawings so minute it would have needed a fly's eye to appreciate their perfection to the full.

"Bother Oswin," said a young voice near him.

"Yes?" The monk did not look up until the line he had been drawing was complete. "Oh, it is you, Alfred. What is it, my son?" The flies drowsing all over his pate rose, disturbed at long last.

"May I stay and watch you for a little while? I have never dared before, for that there were always others with you."

Brother Oswin sighed. "Ay, nobody is afraid of *me!* Very well, if you promise not to jolt me and not to touch anything. Does not Humphrey want you today?"

"Humphrey has sent me," Alfred confessed, reluctantly, "for a pound of madder, and he wants to borrow the smaller pattern book. And he wants to know, have you any prepared white of egg?" Since the flood, all painting implements were kept in store at the monastery.

After a decent interval, Alfred asked respectfully, "What part of the holy St. Francis' life have you got to now, Brother Oswin?"

The monk answered with remorseful self-deprecation, "I had to cease midway, for I could not rightly succeed with the change in the Saint from a luxurious youth to a humble postulant. He must look the same, and yet he must look different. Do you understand? And no matter how often I tried, I either made him look too much the same, or else too different. So I have left him for the nonce and turned to St. Clara's blessed childhood. She too, has given me not a little trouble. See here. Here she is, as a little maid—my first attempt."

He selected one sheet and solicitously held it so close to Alfred's eyes that the boy must arch backward to be able to see it.

"Now here," Brother Oswin produced a second loose sheet, "you have the same little maid, done twice over, sad on one side and merry on the other day, that I may know how to do each when I come to it. Now look at the fair copy, in the book. See how I have fitted her into the frame of the initial letter—which is the letter C, my Alfred—in such a way that if you were to draw a straight line from each angle peak of her body, it would cross the contours of the C. For the cross, my boy, underlies all that is comely and orderly in Nature. Observing that principle in art, and devising opportunities for its application, is like praying, in a way, and always works out right. What? Those? Those are all failures which I discarded."

Alfred extracted one crumpled sheet from under the mixing slab. "Oh, here you gave her a little red cloak! Is she not just like Elizabeth Trefeller?"

"Nay, Alfred," Brother Oswin reproved him, "how can you liken the good saint to an ordinary little playmate of yours, even though she here be an unsuccessful attempt?? I suppose," he patted Alfred's cheek, "you long right sorely for Trefeller Court?"

"Not for Trefeller Court," said Alfred. "I never longed to live anywhere but close to the cathedral."

"I believe you are speaking the truth. No one can doubt God hath implanted a great love of craftsmanship in your heart. Did He, I wonder, implant a longing for the religious life to go with it?"

"I could not be a full priest," Alfred answered quickly, "because we are unfree, our family. That I know for I have heard it talked of. Before I was cured, Brother Laurentius thought my hand might get better if I were promised to the friars."

Brother Oswin took Alfred's hand, turning it this way and that. "So it is really cured? I must say, it looks like any other."

Alfred withdrew the hand and put it behind his back.

"And it is true, what folk say," the monk pursued inquisitively, "that she refused to let Edwin pay her?"

"Well," Alfred said uneasily, "Jane said I had done work to pay for my keep. As for the cure, she says it was easy. But I know that Father mislikes it. I know he is still pondering what he might do for her in return."

Brother Oswin grunted and wagged his head. "Oh, ay—that is the way, that is the way, to be sure. From what I hear, he is not the only one, Edwin, to feel bound in debt to her. One of these days she will foreclose, and then—" he broke off and changed his tone, repeating, "How is it with you, then, Alfred? Do you not feel drawn to life in the cloister, perchance helping to make books like this one here? I believe ways and means could be found—"

"Nay, but," Alfred interrupted, flushing, "I want to be married. I would like right well to be a monk, if only I could be married too."

Brother Oswin gazed at him speechless. Finally, he decided to laugh. "Ay, it is high time you thought of that! And may God bless and preserve the child's uncorrupted innocence," he added aside. "Well, at all events think over what I have said to you—and pray God to guide you, as I shall do also."

He patted Alfred's head, helped him collect what Humphrey required, and returned to his desk. About to leave, Alfred saw lying in his path the soiled picture of St. Clara in a red cloak. The draft had blown it down, it would be trodden on and lost. Brother Oswin had already relapsed into oblivion.

"In a moment, my son, in a moment," he muttered. "What is it you want now? Oh, there is not much art in it. It is too close to a would-be copy of Nature. Ay, take it—provided you think not too well of it, *and* provided you do not address prayers to it, for the saint was but an infant then, besides which this is not really she."

On the way back Alfred set down his load many times to make sure that the picture was in no danger of falling from inside his smock. He turned over in his mind all that Brother Oswin had been saying.

How often he and Elizabeth had put their heads together, marveling at grown folk's belief that they could render their talk unintelligible to younger ears simply by not calling things by name! How could he have failed to understand Brother Oswin's aside? As if Alfred, as if any child in Bedesford did not realize that clerical vows did not hinder fornication! But that Brother Oswin should not know the difference between that and marriage! Marriage was what warmed and lightened the harassed squalor of Jeanne and Edwin's hut. The other thing was what Little John forever spied after and Jane abhorred, so that Elizabeth and Alfred knew it must be ugly.

Whosoever had time in Bedesford Old Town and New would flock to view the latest growth and changes, undeterred by the hailstorm dangers. Many a time some comment or suggestion proved of value. Many a time someone's offer to lend a hand was acceptable. And folk came from all over the country to gaze on St. Hand's-in-the-making and talk to the makers, even when they had no special errand with the monks or the reliquary.

Two well-dressed strangers were with Brother Laurentius, exclaiming over his designs for the great Flood corbel. Alfred quickened his step in the short-lived hope that he would not be noticed. Brother Laurentius made such a point of favoring him as to make Alfred feel shamed and guilty before his equals in youth and insignificance.

"Alfred! Alfred, lad!" Brother Laurentius shouted, sure enough. "Come, take these strangers up to Humphrey. They wish to see the painting work. And show them around wherever else they would go. He is a bright lad," he turned to the strangers, while Alfred hung his head. "He knows every stone and hollow, and can explain what they are for." He winked and smiled at Alfred to indicate that he might look forward to a guide's feet. Alfred made as if he did not see.

The apse was all vaulted over, as were the center parts of the first crossing and its transepts, leaving only the aisles still unceilinged. The eight bays of the sanctuary were canopied in a shape we likened to a halved and hollowed pumpkin.

The eastern portions were the busiest. For, as soon as the sanctuary was fitted for worship, it would be consecrated and put to the Lord God's service.

We were building the Easter Sepulcher, with a frieze of crossbill birds cutting slantwise at one-foot intervals across continuous, undulating thorn—just as you see it today, only that the green, red, and golden paint work all over the carving now shrouds the secret of its joins. At the same time the rough recesses of the sedilia were being clothed with frontal columns and the pointed canopies that from afar look bordered with lace—lace which proximity resolves into fish, starlings, and tail-linked minivers. A flat world of color was growing round about where trowel and chisel were stilled for the nonce.

The side windows were boarded up; the big central one had a covering of sailcloth stretched on a frame which could be propped open so as to give the workmen light. Here moldings were still being made and set in place piecemeal, and so the wall was still caged in scaffolding, darkened and polished by ten years' use. A large, boxlike structure of wood protected the crypt grille from the dust which lay in great dunes all over the floor and permeated everything we wore.

The box was also used as a workbench, which Alfred's father shared with two other laborers. All four sedilia capitals were Edwin's work. The most easterly is made of squirrels, one starting out from each of the six convex sections. The second, which looks the simplest, was, in fact, the hardest to do, necessitating a deal of undercutting which has left the stone perforated as coral. It depicts butterflies and crickets between grasses. The third has the famous "thieving mouse"—one mouse only, at the center front, reared on its hind legs and clasping the stalk of a rich wheat ear. The fourth is the one he was employed on at the time of which we speak.

Alfred did not tell the strangers that this was his father. He was too proud of the fact; the glory was too great; it would be boastful. A throng of people pressed round Edwin, only just leaving him elbowroom, to watch the deft precision—yet looking almost flighty, it looked so easy—of hammer and chisel in his hands. You could never guess what he was going to do next, nor why. Yet the moment another chip was struck off and replaced by a flake of shadow, his action appeared inevitable, as did the result, however small and transitory.

On the bench before him rested two blocks of stone about the same size. One was already roughly hewn into the wedge shape prescribed by a third, almost finished piece, the other as yet merely marked with the measurements. The fluted column had a fourth section already in position upon the summit, showing how all the rest (like a tall, top-heavy cake sliced starwise) would ultimately come together into the one capital. The convex portion of each wedge was cunningly utilized to represent a tree trunk, each crossed by half a stag. Edwin was working on the leaves and acorns at the top.

"Who is that man?" one of the strangers asked Alfred.

"Edwin Widowson is his name," Alfred whispered back, airily.

"Oh," said the stranger, not much the wiser, and fell to dreaming of turning stonecutter first thing on the morrow.

First in the distance, then spreading near, the general hammering increased in speed and volume. The pig race must be over. The Abbot was coming down the path, nodding left and right and sketching benedictions, without interrupting his converse with the Bishop's confessor. Now and then they stopped, and the laborers bowed.

Edwin's audience thinned reverentially. Alfred's strangers gazed with joyous awe at the two men to whom the authorship of all this splendor was delegated.

"Show the Reverend Father how two sections will fit together so that a stag appears whole, Edwin," the Abbot commanded, jovially. "So, you perceive, my Father, the crowning subtlety of this invention, in that the pierce-work shadow cast by the almost detached foliage above confuses, breaks up, and thus illusorily erases any suggestion of a crack?"

The other mimed delight and amazement, and once more complimented both the Abbot and the absent Bishop upon their achievement.

"Well, Edwin?" The Abbott lingered affably in the fullness of his good humor. "Unless I am mistaken there will soon be another happy event at your hut. Is that right? Ask Jeanne what she would like this time for a christening gift, and let me know. Your fourth, will it be? To be sure, your fifth. Is this ready?" he asked, running two fingers round the rim of a millstone which Edwin had been given to shape, and which lay at the far end of the bench.

"No," Edwin answered, "not quite. The hole wants smoothing, and just there the edge still bulges—"

"It is not the edge will do the grinding," observed the Bishop's emissary with a smile.

Edwin inclined his head without a word. The Abbott said, "You do not know this Edwin, Father. Not very long ago he held us up for two whole days. Mind you the hare corbel, companion piece to the fox, on the south side of the crossing? Well, five ribs, meaning two and a half arches, were ready, waiting for the five-armed keystone, and the timber centers were badly wanted over at the choir. The corbel face was perfectly finished. But at the back there were some minute unevennesses. Would you believe it that this same Edwin here absolutely refused to let it go before he had ground the back to silk gloss?"

"Which no one will ever see?"

"God sees it," said Edwin.

The Abbot laughed. "That was not your argument at the time, Edwin! At the time, my father, he said that he did not wish to be shamed before the workmen of some future generation who may remove his handiwork in the course of possible repairs!" The Bishop's emissary joined in his laughter. "Well, Edwin, let me see it finished as soon as may be. I want Wode Mill to be in use this autumn."

"Full serious and stern are your workmen, Abbot!" the Bishop's emissary said, still chuckling, as they strolled on.

CHAPTER 2

ALFRED AND ELIZABETH

ELIZABETH AND ALFRED had been so certain in the belief that they would always live together, that they had never even thought of talking about it. Nobody had said anything in their hearing about his return to Cloudsway Waste until it was all settled. Then the news was sprung on them that he should leave Trefeller Court before the end of the week. They had sensed the others watching them, and so had not even dared exchange glances.

After Christmas Elizabeth had been given a bed of her own, apart from the boys, up in the carding room, with either Jane or one of the other women to keep her company. So that night she crept out without disturbing her bedfellow—Juliana had one of her bouts of headache and sleeplessness. Jane was with the Mistress. Without arousing her brother, Elizabeth wakened Alfred and, one finger at her lips, beckoned him to follow her. Their lithe, bare, knowing feet made no noise in the dark house.

They came to the rail-less balcony, below which the wagons were wont to be stood in the yard for loading up. A confusion of pulley ropes, slack and embroiled, rigged it like a resting ship. Elizabeth shivered and undid her plaits, that the hair might warm her naked arms and shoulders; Alfred, too, was only in his shift. He dragged some empty sacks into a heap, and they sat down side by side, twining each one arm about the other's narrow back, their hard, young, scab-crusted knees drawn up.

So long as they had been always together, they had not needed any tie. Now that they were to be separated, knowledge of a formal bond between them would leave them less lonely. And they felt that a bond was a bond anywhere, before God and before the powers of darkness in whose sight alike their secret doings were enacted—strengthening their fidelity and endurance, feeding their courage with half-magical ceremonial, hoping to snare the future fate they desired and making it wait for them to catch up with it. With vows and with oaths, with a few drops of blood they kissed drinking from each other's pricked thumbs, Elizabeth and Alfred pledged their troth.

They found them a secret bower, down by the Tew, shielded from sight by the old churchyard opposite, which everyone avoided all the year round except on All Souls' Day. On the north side the clay of the bank reared and descended in the overlapping slabs of some past land-slide, held firmly in place by a web of roots. Rushes and marsh grass formed an upstanding curtain in front of a series of shallow caves, their mouths overhung with swelling lips of moss and a suspended shower of brambles and creepers. Just beyond, where the tangle of alders with the scourge bundles of their shoots was at its densest, a tree grew that was really five, all springing from the same patch of soil.

"It is like a queer little house," cried Alfred, swinging himself up into one stalwart fork, where the ground floor would be narrowest and every succeeding story wider than the last—"

"Alfred!" Elizabeth interrupted, "why should it not *be* a house? The caves could be our outbuildings. We can play we are already married. It would be like practicing and forcing it to come true."

In time they reinforced the tree forks with osier and straw and such live pliant twigs as could be interlaced. They assembled stores, posses-sions, for which Elizabeth ransacked sheds and refuse heaps at home; and Alfred brought her some of the corroded ancient iron and shards continually unearthed at the site. She found a huge old iron key, which he laboriously cleaned of rust. This key was always hung on the same bough, and each time they came to their house, they played they must unlock it first, and lock up again behind them. Elizabeth had a sailcloth sack which was her dower chest. In it there were rags, shreds of fleece, odd lengths of moth-eaten fur lining, a skein of yarn, half a pair of shears, and a bodkin. She sewed herself an apron of sacking and some-thing she called a smock for Alfred—but this they had to rip down the middle before he could get into it. She kept beetles, grasshoppers, and snails in little boxes: these were her cattle. And though the curds she kneaded were only mud, she scoured all her dairy gear in full earnest. When it rained they would sit in the caves, sagely busy with their chores, and talking gravely of their breeding schemes, how the beans were coming on and the second grass crop, how many catches of fresh-water fish they might safely conceal to keep the tithe low.

Both went to the bower whenever they could get away, even if they could not always both contrive it at the same time. Elizabeth came almost every day. Her home was nearer, and teeming with manifold doings and to and fro of people, so that often you could not find those that were there, let alone miss the briefly absent.

But Alfred also had found he could come more often than they had dared hope. We regret to say he took advantage of the favor shown him by Brother Laurentius, Brother Oswin, and Humphrey Painter. All three were familiar with the idle drawings which he did in unoccupied moments—with a stick in the sand, or with flint, nail, or bone splinter on pieces of bark or yet unwhited walls. For days he would do the same object over and over—a head, laughing or crying, a bird in flight, but most often insects, greatly magnified, until he was either satisfied or wearied and selected something else for equal repetition. The monk and the friar spoke to Humphrey, who agreed to shut one eye, or both, when Alfred's services could be spared, that the boy might spend some of his time with the head scribe or at Brother Laurentius' tracing house. So when Alfred was not at the site Humphrey assumed he was with one of the others, and they did the same.

Juliana went away to a great christening ale at Clowes, where some distant kinsfolk of John Trefeller's had a mansion. Elizabeth was not sorry. The second haymaking had just begun, and at Trefeller Court they were not yet finished, as elsewhere, with the summer clip. The housekeeper was kept so busy—the more as the Mistress's journey had left the house shorthanded—that Elizabeth had more opportunities of flight than ever.

She was always before Alfred and would come forward to greet him with a leaf cup for his home coming drink, and over her shoulder bid her women make all ready for the master, "And be not so noisy about it!" for all round midges and flies muzzed tirelessly. "What have you brought home in your wallet today, my husband? A rabbit or a wild duck, perhaps, or a fish for our supper?"

She was taken aback when Alfred pulled a real object from his smock. It was a piece of parchment, neatly trimmed and nailed to a block of elm wood so that the nailheads formed a pattern framing the picture of a little man, outlined in ink and brightly colored, with red cheeks and lips, a long blue gown ending in a scrolled train, and pointed yellow shoes, and yellow hose and hair. She looked at him aghast, thinking he had stolen it—boys had been maimed and hung for less. When at length Alfred succeeded in convincing her that he himself had made it, for compliment's sake she pretended disbelief a little longer. Alfred explained how he had come by the parchment—part of the leaf depicting St. Clara.

"Now when I am away from you I have your picture to look at. I thought," Alfred said shyly, "that you might like to have such a picture of me."

Elizabeth put her arms round his neck and kissed him. Then she said thoughtfully, "But you have no such gown and hose, my husband."

"No. But you would not have me set myself down on *vellum* dressed as I am? When guests come to the house in the master's absence, you would not have them sneer at his raggedness?"

"That is true. But Alfred mine, your hair is not yellow."

"Ay," said Alfred, "that is something I learned out of Humphrey's pattern book. Humphrey says we paint angels with curls and waves in their hair to show the abundance and brightness of their affections, just as we curve their mouths so that it denotes the sweetness of their song, and straight noses their piety—"

"Why?"

"I know not, but so it is. It is the rule all painters must observe. So you see, I must make the hair yellow, else the curl lines would not show up, and my affection would not be in the picture. White hair I deemed would be *too* unlike. Humphrey has one black-haired angel in his book, but there the curls are picked out in gold. Brother Oswin keeps his gold leaf locked up."

Both started as there was a rustling and panting behind them. "Oh!" Elizabeth laughed. "Come and look. I have a surprise for you too." They tiptoed round to a shady little dell, where lay a big sun-browned boy infant. His fat little legs had kicked off all coverings, but now hung crookedly suspended as the babe gazed to see who was coming. His dark-blue pupils were so large that very little white showed. At the back and the sides of his head the hair was worn off, but above his round forehead it stood up, silky and black, and trembling gently in the breeze. He was Meg and Geoffrey Widowson's second-born son. Their first they had lost at the age of six months; both had been named Richard.

"Our son!" Elizabeth said before Alfred could utter a question. "Our own son, dear husband, whom we had put out to nurse these several months. Look how he has grown!"

"Oh, ay, our son," Alfred responded. "Indeed, he *has* grown. Which of us does he favor, do you think?"

"Both," said Elizabeth. "If you like you may pick him up and hold him. Now tell me what news there is."

Alfred settled himself comfortably, loosening his belt in token that he had eaten a large meal. "The biggest news is that my lord your uncle has lost his lawsuit against the Lord Bishop. That is what the chaplain came to see the Abbot about, only nobody knew it till now. It is said Lord Hugh will have to pay for the judgment, and a fine on top of it for that it went against him, and besides he must give to the monks what the friars paid him in rent. So people think your uncle Baldwin and the young lord are still away because they are trying to raise money."

"Is Prior Haakon's illness any better?" Elizabeth had composed her features in the judicious frown and pursed lips which she associated with grown-up converse.

"Ay, but he is still abed. The friars think there is no need to worry. It is only the fever he brought back from Rome in his youth, and it always comes back and goes away again."

"And how are my sisters-in-law?"

"Martha and Margaret are well, but Janet, the baby, has a rash."

"Babes will have rashes. Has Jeanne tried a cucumber in the bed, and the camomile wash?"

The next time Alfred came, Elizabeth was not there, nor the second and third days after. He thought she might be ill, but cautious inquiry set that fear at rest. He could not understand it. Then one day Jacob went to Bedesford, as he did once every week to look at the bridge, and a troop of laborers went with him in the wagon, but in the evening he returned alone. And then suddenly everyone knew all about Luke Robinson's house.

The first two cartloads of Flemish bricks, stored at Ovisham almost a year, it was related, had arrived in the market place and towered in great piles all over the grass-ringed cobbles of Smithy Yard. As the main concern at the site was the completion of the sanctuary, a number of unskilled workmen could be spared. Luke had got Lord William to lend him their services, by way of commission fee on the sanctuary tiles, which Lady Agnes had been persuaded to give to the cathedral. Jacob had taken a passing look over the derelict buildings and tendered friendly, free advice.

Luke, as it were, was giving Elizabeth his new house to play with. He took her all over Smithy Yard, leading her by the hand or letting her romp in and out the precarious old houses, just as it pleased her, and constantly made believe to consult her.

"I said," Jacob chuckled, "clearly you have no need of *me,* Master Luke. Oh, but he has, Jacob, says the maiden, I am only helping him decide *what* he wants done. Do you think Jacob, she asks, the workmen will take it amiss if I go out and join them for a little? Haply I can help them fill the hods. So off she rushes like the wind, and the next I saw of her, she was climbing all over the wheels, her frock all black with wagon grease, and really lending a hand, too, and everybody happy."

Alfred's heart was heavy in his breast. He wondered how long it would be before he saw her again. He knew Smithy Yard quite well. It was the sort of forbidden place that irresistibly attracts exploring youngsters, and had never been reported haunted. He was not angry with her, only dejected, putting himself in her place. To play, as Jacob put it, with a real house, required only half the pretense that their bower demanded. Then also, there was her peculiar capacity for pity which stopped short at nothing. Oh, he knew her! He knew she would be all afire with the thought that the old buildings were to be restored to honor and service. She would not love Alfred any less. But she would have no time for him, so long as Luke continued letting her help make amends to Smithy Yard for more than a decade of neglect.

CHAPTER 3

UNDER THE WEIRD OAK

Because the Work for everyone nearly doubled, Jane declared, the housefolk got double rations also of food and drink the while Juliana was away at Clowes, so that every night they slept like logs. Jane would be the last to go to rest. She did Geoffrey's round, loosed the dogs, saw that everything was locked, that no light had been forgotten in shed or stable, that clubs and battle-axes, fire hooks and water buckets were in their appointed places. Meg had asked for Elizabeth to sleep with her, since Geoffrey's empty place in bed had kept her sadly awake in the beginning. Jane granted this and had Elizabeth's bed to herself.

She undressed and washed the day's grime off her from head to foot. She combed out her hair and curried it with a balsam of crushed flowers and nut oil, tied it up in a fresh cloth, changed into another of her earth-brown habits—she would wear no other color—took her cloak, and the wallet and crook that she used for herb gathering, and stealthily left house and yard.

The stars were pale, the rounding moon as yet only a wraith. But the land was already fallen all into blackness, the shapes of tree tops, gables, and distant hills aping one another and distorted into menace. Jane turned her back on the two bridges and walked east along the northern bank of the Tew. The water mists rose and accompanied her, expunging her shadow.

Having reached the ford, which in pious remembrance had given the town its name, she kilted up her clothes and crossed, but went on along the bushy riverbank, as the manor overlooked the open road for a matter of some miles. Haphazardly she used her crook to gather in bunches of herbs, filled the wallet with them, and proceeded quickly. At a certain point, without slackening pace, she took a gnarled little something, shaped grotesquely like a man, from a canvas bag under her skirt, held it up straight before her, and addressed to it murmured invocation and commands.

The last steps she performed out in the open, and, halting on the brink of the moat, directly opposite the updrawn bridge, stood for a moment, erect and immobile, though her murmuring grew almost loud. Then with the aid of the crook and the chains of the bridge she pulled herself up to the gate. The manor hounds knew her well and did not bark. She manipulated the charm in semblance of human movement, saying, "Gateward, open the gate for me! Manorfolk, sleep and hear naught!"

The gateward imitated the movements of the charm and obeyed her, behaving as if it were day, and smiling at her woodenly as he held the great door for her to pass. He locked and bolted it behind her, turned stiffly on his heel, went back to sleep, and knew nothing of it all.

She pressed through narrow spaces between adjoining buildings, screened even in the daytime by deceptive shadows, and nettles, grown so tall their summer blossoms mingled with the buttercups and dandelions in the grass that bound the ruins of the old roofs. The maze was abruptly sealed by another wall with a lancet-shaped door, dank with moss and mildew, and heavily battened across. But the batten ends were fastened to the planks, not to the recessed stone, and opened inward to Jane's pressure.

Beyond the door you did not find yourself inside another building, but in a small open square, stone flagged. Yet to call it open is not quite right: in the center grew an ancient tree, its trunk so inordinately thick that it appeared squat, its twisted branches touching and in places grown through the surrounding walls, and its vast crown forming a domed plug of a roof, through which no light could filter, day or night, except for one nocturnal hour at midsummer, when the moonbeams were aimed through a gap in the upper boughs which did not otherwise become apparent. This was the true Weird Oak of Bedesford. None but the Cinqmort barons knew of it, and they had guarded its secret for generations. There was another great oak in the park which for a hundred years at least had masqueraded under the same name, equally proscribed, but sometimes nonetheless approached by the curious or the wicked or the desperate. Lord Hugh himself was always said to be fruit of that tree, garnered by his mother in unchristian wise. But this was untrue. It was to the secret, genuine Weird Oak her lord had taken the lady.

Here the witch and Lord Hugh would come together.

He rose at her approach in silent greeting. Side by side they walked forward and bowed and went in under trailing branches, where the man struck a light and touched into flame a small heap of dry twigs and aromatic moss built up on a hearth of white and black stones that the river had washed into smooth, flat ovals. Together they placed over it a little tripod of iron and a little iron pan with strange designs scratched in it on the inside, and therein the woman placed one by one ingredients for a decoction, of which, when it was done, she and my lord both partook. All the while Jane spoke her incantations, in a language which had remained unknown to him, and they breathed the vapor of the stew as it bubbled to her song.

The lord of Bedesford was the witch's acolyte and squire in those indescribable flights which followed—indescribable since these took them into a world where no words, no concepts, no material constituents of ours have counterpart or application or indeed meaning; disporting themselves inexpressibly in a life which they themselves called so only because there was no more approximate human term for it, an exercise of power equally unfathomable, with prize of pleasure and ful-

fillment no less impervious to earthly, waking grasp and communication. But none who has tasted of that can ever again be content
without it.

Thus Lord Hugh got the sense of might which he craved, as well
as the sense of union with his desired consort. He and his high priestess
both dissolved and so met, in the unbounded Elsewhere, which they
both namelessly suffused, thus intermingling far more completely, since
with every dispersed particle of their whole being, than men and
women can in carnal congress.

And yet more than once he repeated his plea that she join him also
in full view of Bedesford's everyday. The secrecy which was one condition of their flights irked him between whiles, partly because his hard-
won chastity—another condition—was approvingly misunderstood by
his subjects, and partly because it rounded off his dependence on her.
Withal he knew that it was hopeless. Withal he had to ask anew, as one
will explore a painful tooth again and again. Although he knew that
without her he had no access to those magic reaches, and although she
was so sure that he had been driven to lechery against his inmost desires,
sometimes it seemed to him it must be those same desires, unendingly
distilled, unspilled, dammed, and stored within, which formed the real
driving force of his transcendence. But therefore was he also proud of
his asceticism.

He never forgot, and was no less proud of it, that Jane had told him
he was equally contemptuous of property, for this lent a fine, grand
meaning to the manor's deterioration. So when she would have warned
and counseled him as regards his conduct in this world, he was ready
with twofold repudiation. He would be more strict than she in upholding the laws she expounded, and, since she would not accept the *right*
to advise him which he offered her, he would not cede her the occasional privilege.

But it was not only with her that my lord closed his mind to reason.
Baldwin frequently essayed like cautioning against the townfolk's
encroachments on the baron's power. My lord replied that he looked
upon Luke and his fellow councilors as benefactors, relieving him of
much tedious drudgery.

Anyone will point out to you the old council chamber, at the shoemaker's yard, which was, by Luke's suggestion, put roughly in repair
and so used. Ay, if you want to buy footgear or have it mended, you
must go to Honeycake Yard, before the Black Death a nest of rank
stews, but let to the first professional shoemaker in 1356. To keep body

and soul together and lay in a store of material, this man, a newcomer, additionally took on the vacant office of church steward, which in those days entailed little work. For the parish priest appointed in 1349 had never yet been seen; Masses were celebrated at the manor chapel only on the highest holy days, and Lord William had given us a written promise that the cathedral should serve parish purposes also, so long as we devoted to it the money and labor we had expected to contribute toward rebuilding our burned church.

Jane and Baldwin were not alone in misliking to see Luke stand so well amongst us. When Brother Laurentius, and the other friars on their mendicant rounds, started saying, why would not Luke be content with an earth floor, like everyone else, why must he try God with clinker tiling, hardly decent for a secular dwelling, they did not rouse much response. Most of us lauded this new enterprise of his as an expensive concession to seemliness, at the first opportunity when he could afford it. The married women, ever prone to solicitude toward bachelors, waxed positively tender of him, and shook their heads, as he was growing thin, and begged him to take better care of himself. For Luke, when an idea took hold of him, was incapable of troubling about anything else, until he had carried it out. At his slackest he would hurry over his food and care not what he ate. When nobody else was willing to finish the last crumbs of a barrel of spoiled fish or maggoty bacon, he saved the housekeeper the sin of throwing God's gifts on the dung heap. And he swallowed such dishes as indifferently as he would the choicest delicacies. At his busiest, he might forget to eat altogether, if he were not forcibly reminded.

But there was one thing people could not make out: whether or not Juliana knew about Smithy Yard. On the one hand, it was most unlikely that he should not have told her, on the other, it was unnatural for a woman to keep another's secret so strictly as Luke's had been kept until after her departure.

CHAPTER 4

HOME-COMING

JULIANA'S WAGONS ROLLED into the market place and the Mistress commanded a halt at the gates of Smithy Yard, that she might make inquiry as to the change and turmoil which there confronted her. The man she asked was one of the Flemings of the Wasteside tilery, who were making Luke's fireplaces and Dutch drains, the latter replicas of those lately installed in the crypt of St. Hand's. The slow-spoken Fleming was not halfway through his reply, when on the opposite side of the square the door of the council chamber opened, and Luke and his colleagues clattered down the ladder stair in Shoemaker Yard. He must have seen the party from the window and came straight across.

All signs of uncaring fatigue dropped off Juliana's maids and men, who sat up in the saddle like candles on their prickets. Luke took off his hat to wave to Juliana. The hat replaced, he casually linked arms with his companions on either side, and thus made them stroll up to her along with him. In unison they bade her welcome and asked had her stay at Clowes proved agreeable?

"Most agreeable," Juliana answered, in a tone she might have employed had the reverse been the case. "They are very great people my kinsfolk there. Their mansion is thrice the size of"—she gazed round as though at a loss for an example—"of Smithy Yard, not counting offices and walled grounds. They had minstrels playing to us when we sat at table."

"Look what *I* got for parting keepsake!" Little John had heaved himself to the fore, thrusting out his chest, on which reposed a large brooch.

"What do you think of this house of mine, Mistress?" Luke asked, as if there were no more natural question. "If you are not too weary, Mistress, may I show you over it?"

Juliana's train dismounted and stretched their legs. Groups had formed around some of the other councilors in the market place, to hear what had been decided at the session. Luke proffered his hand to Juliana and helped her down. Little John followed. They entered the yard, stepping between planks, troughs, and bricks, and men whistling at their work.

"Much have you accomplished in little time," said Juliana. "Be quiet,

Little John. Do not walk under the scaffolding. You were saying, Luke?"

"As you see, we have faced only the casements and door frames with Friggsby stone, but the roofs are going to be slated. Will not their color go well with the brick? For most of the doors I am merely having the old panels rebound and studded. All the stairways are inside and are going to have handrails. Down here all the floor is going to be tiled, up above there will be boles. Dick is making me some pretty locks. Look, Little John, see you that lad over there at the saw? He is Young Will, Jacob Tewsing's nephew, newly come from Clavis Green. He is of an age with you. Why not go and talk to him? He'll show you where there are some safe ropes to swing from. Tell him I sent you—"

Little John looked at his mother, who nodded.

In the large upper room, which ran the whole length of the center front, having four windows, Juliana exclaimed, "This is handsome!"

"God bless you for saying that," Luke squeezed her hand.

"Yes," Juliana said, faltering a little, "might you have let me know what you were planning—"

"I meant to surprise you," said Luke. "I wanted to have something to show you, before—" he broke off, as a volley of hammer blows announced that they were not alone.

The workman astride the window sill leaned inside and asked, "How did the session go, Luke?"

"None so badly," Luke answered, leading Juliana on. "You shall hear later." He said the same to her as she cleared her constricted throat to ask what the session had been all about. "There is one matter I have more at heart, and first of all I would talk to you of that. Come and see where I have been dwelling these last weeks like the outlaw in his cave, and where we shall be private," he added under his breath, for they had passed two more workmen fitting halved tree trunks for the floor.

"Luke's lair," as they had all called it, was in the north wing, whose upper story had needed least refashioning. Until the whole place was whitewashed, there was nothing further to be done to this small chamber. That was why Luke believed here they would be undisturbed.

In fact there were two before him.

Until the building work was ended and furnishing began, Smithy Yard held no more interest for Elizabeth. Today it had come to her to play that the next stage was reached, and she had spent the morning knocking nails into this sole inhabited room, sweeping the floor, and rearranging Luke's makeshift bed. She had cajoled one of the masons to help her shift the trunk chest, wherein all the plans were kept, so that it might be a window seat.

As she and the old man rested from the exertion, a familiar voice came from below. John was telling his story to Young Will.

Elizabeth and the old laborer looked at one another.

"Your mother is come," said the man. "Juliana is here."

Elizabeth continued mute. For once she was frozen through with a surpassing fear, whose cause she could not fathom. She was not doing anything wrong, and she was here by Luke's standing permission.

They came in, Juliana foremost. As soon as the doorway was free, the old workman took himself off. Juliana's face had worn an unusual expression: tense, yet soft and young. Now it was changed.

"What is *she* doing here?"

Elizabeth opened her mouth to welcome her mother, but could not speak.

"She does not even greet her mother," said Juliana.

"It is the surprise," Luke said cheerfully. "Elizabeth has been the greatest help to me. Her mother has all cause to be proud of her, young as she is, yet of such excellent understanding. She chose the tiles for this fireplace. I know not whether she guesses why it was I consulted her in all things. Perhaps you, her mother—"

"I have held my peace this far," said Juliana, "but now do I see it for certain that you must be mad. A wall fireplace! With colored tiles! Tiled floors, as in a church. Do you deem yourself a holy relic that you must encase you in a shrine? All this money spent! Whose money? Whose money, I ask? Mine, mine, without a doubt. Why else should you have been so secret about this—"

"Juliana, Juliana," Luke said, so softly that for an instant he did succeed in hushing her, and drew her aside. "I thought you must have guessed. Wait till you hear what treasure it is meant for, this shrine, as you call it. *I* can live in a hole in the ground as well as anyone, but you would not think this house too fine for your daughter?"

"My thanks for likening Trefeller Court to a hole in the ground," said Juliana. "Serpents do live in holes in the ground, so I suppose wherever they live becomes as a hole in the ground to them. So all you have had out of me already does not content you. You want to take away my only daughter and wait for my death to get half my property. Perhaps you have already thought out ways how to speed me under the sod? Oh, that my dear husband were alive—you would not have dared snatch his goods from under *his* nose."

"Juliana, stop this witless talk! Who has trebled your property?"

"Ay, boast!" said Juliana. "You are great at that, boastful red-haired Fleming that you are, for all that you call yourself English. Everyone laughs at it—behind your back, even as you have been going behind mine. Boasting how you charmed the Danesborough lady, boasting that in the end St. Hand's will be half your work. It is I, rather than you, has profited from our alliance, what in the name of all martyred saints made you enter into it?"

"You know well," Luke said angrily, taking her by the shoulders. "You know why, if no one else does. Because I preferred protecting the weak to preying on them! Because it tempted me to make a small merchant great!"

"But it is not beneath you to raise your hands against a woman and a widow and cripple! It is true I cannot contend with you if we are to argue with our fists! That would be something to boast of—that you worsted *me* in single combat!"

"Listen to me, Juliana," Luke said very quietly. "I know why you are so very wroth. I should have thought that you would be too proud to let all the world know it too."

"Had you counted on that? Ay, have you been too clever this once," said Juliana. On a sudden the tears were streaming from her eyes, yet her face and her voice were unchanged, unshaken. "In any case, I cannot tell what it may be you are boasting of now. If you are so wise and strong, and I so witless and so weak, let us see then, which of us will lose the most when our partnership is at an end—as I end it now. You will see it, you, a clown and a Fleming, will be nothing without me, a Cinqmort and Trefeller, to back you."

"Nay, Juliana," Luke said remorsefully, "let us talk reasonably now. I cannot let you do this, still less at this of all times."

"Now where is all your boasting?" Juliana, still crying, and still acting as if she did not know her own tears. "Now you come crawling and speaking sweetly, when the fear of ruin is upon you."

"If that is what you think—" Luke, began, but changed his mind. "And so, if I ask you for pity's sake not to do it, to spare me and forgive me?"

"I do forgive you as a Christian should," said Juliana, "but I will not be your partner longer. Thus must we hope that the headsman forgives the felon, and the felon him. Jesus Christ alone knows to which of the two I am likest at this moment! Elizabeth, come. Call your brother."

Elizabeth, who knew that it was not herself had caused her mother to look as she did, trembled with compassion for the poor hunchback whom Luke had reduced to tears.

"Are you tired, Mother?" she asked lovingly. "It will not be long now before you are home and seated at your own board in your own great hall, with everyone rejoicing that the mistress is back."

Juliana stirred, and looked at her daughter, in an old brown frock, somewhat outgrown and none too clean; so pretty, with her thin brown face that was yet soft and rounded everywhere, silky loops of hair escaping from the plaits framing the slender neck. Juliana shivered. Elizabeth adjusted the fur-lined cloak over her mother's knees.

Trefeller Court was all in a flurry, since Jane was not there to meet the Mistress. Gillian's little boy had upset a caldron of boiling grease over himself. He died of it that same night, in spite of all Jane could do. It had taken her years to help Gillian to her first living child. It can be imagined what their son meant to the parents. He was two years old, and they had ever encouraged his tiny headstrongness and romping violence by which they measured his vitality.

The housefolk could think of little else, at Juliana's board.

Juliana kept on watching Elizabeth, who smiled whenever their eyes met. Little John noticed it all. The suspense of watching Juliana watch Elizabeth dragged on until he lost all stomach to his food. When broiled lambs' tails were borne in, swimming in thick fat, he heaved and had to keep on swallowing dry throated. Yet he could not bring himself to go from the room.

The housefolk turned to those who had been away, with questions. "Have you heard about Luke?" Meg whispered to Geoffrey, just as there chanced to be a pause, so that her remark was audible to all.

"Elizabeth could not bear her mother's pitifully deepened pallor. "We have quarreled with Luke," she said in a clear voice, "because my dear mother would protect me from the fate of an old man's wife. So we do not ever want to hear his name again in this hall."

The silence went on and on. The housefolk could not find any more to say. Geoffrey jumped into the breach with tales of Clowes, but it was slow work and heavy going. Darkness had fallen and dishes and cups held only crumbs and dregs. At length the serving maids rose to clear away. Then Juliana asked about the weaving, which caused further delay. Presently, she turned to her daughter and asked how much she had spun.

Elizabeth flushed. It was not much, and everybody knew, so that she would not lie, though she could tell all wished that lie she might.

"Go bring me your thread for show," said Juliana. "You are grown so tall and womanly the while I have been away, I am sure you have mended your old careless ways and done all you could to improve your spinning."

Alas, when Elizabeth brought her work, it was all knots and rough raveling as ever. It was also matted with dust. A blind person could have told how long it had lain untouched. With trembling hands Juliana ruffled and tore the disgraced thread and flung it on the ground. "To hear you talk one would think you a grown maiden, and that you loved your mother as you ought, and as you pretend so hard," she said. "All your life you have not given me one hour's pleasure."

Without meaning to, Elizabeth flinched away from her mother's hand, so that she brushed her mother's porcelain drinking cup off the table. The rush strew did not save it.

Juliana closed her eyes for an instant. When she opened them again, they glowed. "That cup," she said, "was the most precious we had in the house. It was so rare it can never be replaced."

She did not say another word. Neither did Elizabeth speak again. One after the other the serving folk left. Only Little John, albeit feeling more and more sick, stayed on with mother and daughter in the darkening hall. Finally, his mother sent him out. So he sneaked round to where he knew of a peephole.

Jane returned after midnight. Disheveled and exhausted as she was, she went straight to Juliana's bedchamber.

Juliana was not abed. She was pacing the floor and wringing her hands, turning her head from side to side, and moaning under her breath.

"Oh, Jane! Oh, Jane!" She threw herself in the tall housekeeper's arms, and there wept and wept. Jane held and caressed her, uttering soft, meaningless words of comfort, and gradually undressed the Mistress, smoothed out and plaited her hair for the night, and put her to bed. By and by she heard all that was in the Mistress' mind.

"Oh, Jane! Why did you not work me a spell! Don't tell me you did not know. Everybody guessed, everybody knows! At Clowes I overheard roundabout talk of it! If it has gone so far afield, there must have been enough said in Bedesford to come to your ears."

"All people talked about was that you lived together in this house. I thought *you* knew that and cared not, knowing yourself sinless."

"Are you sure? Have they not been joking about me? Nay, you would not have suffered that, would you, my Jane? But he himself, he has guessed and he knows right enough. Oh, Jane, Jane! He taunted me with it!" and Juliana renewed her sobbing.

"I am sure you are mistaken, my poor, dearest Mistress. When we ourselves know a truth we would keep hidden from all others, we are ever like to read allusions to it everywhere."

"Oh, if I could believe that! But even then it would make little difference to my sorrow. The things I have done all these years, Jane, to win him, to earn him for my own! Oh, it is meet that I am punished— the chantry I gave for John, because everybody else was giving tiles. In honest truth I did so to make God give *him* to me, and also to make him love me. Oh, he *is* so fair and handsome, Jane. I know no man like him. And now, when I had such hopes! I have not told you about that. They held a great dancing on the green at Clowes, with peddlers and tumblers from many miles around. There was an Egyptian woman. She went round amongst the guests, and for every one had a word. To me she said that I had come to the christening from a funeral, to return home for a wedding, all in the same family. She said it queerly, and it rhymed, but that seemed to be the sense of it. The last event among the Trefeller kindred was John's death, you see. So I thought—"

"You must have forgotten Little John's christening, long after his father's death."

"There was no feasting then, Jane. Prior Haakon baptized him at the foot of my bed, for all thought neither he nor I would last out the night. She could not have counted that."

"But no wake was held for John either, was there?"

"I know. I am only telling you what were my thoughts. Jane, Jane, I am so ashamed. I gave her my shoe buckle, the one made of amber and silver. I was so *glad*. Then, when we drew into Bedesford—Folk looked at me so oddly, when I questioned the man at the gate. First I was angry that Luke had not said a word of it to me, his truest friend in all the world. Yet then, what with one thing and another, I began to think the Egyptian's prophecy was coming true sooner than I had expected. I felt like the youngest young maiden, Jane, close on thirty years old though I am. What shall I do? What shall I do?"

"Shall I brew you a draught of forgetfulness?"

Juliana lay back again, from long habit drawing the bedclothes up high to cover her meager, malformed body, and deliberated. Her tears ceased. "No," she said slowly, "I would not forget, either. Forget? Forget how he has injured me, and that I must pay him out? No."

"At least let me give you a brew to send you to sleep."

It was only an hour to sunrise when Jane closed Juliana's door behind her. She did not find Elizabeth in her bed nor—against all likelihood —in Little John's. Juliana had not given Jane any reason for beating Elizabeth, other than those she had given Elizabeth herself—most likely Juliana knew no other reasons. But Jane knew, and her lips were dry with dread.

She found Elizabeth still in the hall as Juliana had left her; but asleep and not dead, as at that ghostly hour even a witch could not but half expect. By the light of the dying fire she gathered Elizabeth into her strong arms and took her to bed. Now it was Elizabeth who had to do the comforting.

"It was unlucky I broke the cup. In any case, it is all over, so do not grieve me by looking so, Ganna-Janna. All *I* care about is that she did stand up for me against that man. Had anyone told me he was having such thoughts, I would have gone in great fear lest he get me, since Mother ever gave in to Luke. All the friendship I had for him is dead. So sly as he has been, too—getting me to tell him how I would like to see his house arranged, that he might turn round, after, and say it was all for me! Oh, I hate him now. Ganna! There is something I must tell you now—" and so she told of the compact between herself and Alfred.

Who can tell what the witch felt, what she thought then? Did she herself know, we must wonder? She may have hated Luke and been fond of the boy Alfred, but could she contemplate with aught but loathing *anyone's* possessing her Elizabeth? When she had smiled on these two children's friendship, because it gave her joy to see Elizabeth happy —so she must have asked herself—how could she have lost from sight the fact that children, too, grow older day by day? She must have felt her helplessness more sorely than anyone less accustomed to power and swift ease of decision. Events proved that she knew not what to do.

CHAPTER 5

THE BETROTHAL

LORD HUGH PRETENDED he alone did not know what Bedesford was full of—that he had lost the lawsuit against the Bishop. Soon enough, however, Baldwin returned to deliver the formal report. Gervase had been to London with him, for an opportunity of mingling with other well-born youths, learning to deport himself with ease at the royal court, and to be measured for a modish wardrobe. By all accounts the young man had made the most of his visit. His versatile frolics excused the last vestiges of scholastic manners. He had won in two of the poesy competitions arranged by the court ladies, had tricked Sir Bertrand Jolybody Taylor in the most amusing fashion, and rendered Baldwin's life a burden to him with constant pranks that made delightful hearing to all who had never themselves been their butt.

Baldwin went to see the Abbot several times. We thought any day to receive an intimation as to what Lord Hugh meant to do to raise money. There was a rumor that Lord Hugh had talked of demanding death fines for all those who had perished in 1348, but either it was untrue—although none but my lord could ever have thought of such a thing—or else the Abbot once more found means to dissuade him. Baldwin left Bedesford again before the next assizes, and still my lord made no special proclamation. It was known that the henchmen had not had their wages. They looked so down-at-heel and went so far out of their way to show they did not care that everybody guessed the manor must be in a very bad way indeed.

Lord William guessed that folk were sneering at the Cinqmorts, and all at once took it into his head he must lend them countenance. He asked Lord Hugh and Gervase to a feast. My lord would not go, but desired his nephew to accept, since Gervase's sportiveness, and display of recent sartorial spoils should surely douse this humiliating compassion. To his surprise, even when he had explained and given Gervase full permission to exercise his sense of humor upon the monks, Gervase was not to be persuaded.

Here is an odd thing: Gervase was fearless as his lord and uncle, save in respect of any member of the clergy, high or low. And this fear held no deference, but rather, resembled folk's recoil from contagious disease. It caused him to repudiate the slightest learning. In later years he would go so far as to deny ever having had so much as a smattering of Latin, and feign total ignorance of reading and writing.

Baldwin returned with evidence of a mysterious success. The manor got in bought winter stores by the cartload, the henchmen strutted, twiddling golden finger rings, and a musician, a barber, a cook, and a falconer swelled their number. Cleaning and repairs were set in motion. My lord and Gervase left Baldwin to supervise this work, while they rode abroad on a round of visits. Directly Bedesford had him back, my lord informed Mistress Trefeller that for kinship's sake he would not cancel her option on the Wodeside water meadows and grazing lands, but that she must make up her mind before the end of the year, as he had been offered more favorable terms in other quarters.

Juliana doubted the truth of this. It was unlike her brother not to set aside a previous agreement if such better offers had been made. But she could not afford to gamble on her doubt. She had hoped to get the option extended for an eighth year. She had never been in quite such straits. Another chantry payment was due, her fences needed renewing, and she was pledged to have her stretch of the North Ford Road paved by Michaelmas. She had more wool on her hands than her workshops could use or her two ships take across the sea. Like the man whose touch turned everything to gold, so she wallowed in wool. But they could not eat wool at Trefeller Court, though any day they might be reduced to burning it for fuel.

It has been said that Juliana's energy required obstacles, fully to unfold. The trouble was that in her present difficulties the fundamental obstacle was Luke. He was thriving more than ever, Lady Agnes of Danesborough having now entrusted him with the conduct of all her mercantile affairs. At long last, his good fortune was earning him envy among the people of both shires.

Now of all people it had to be Juliana who could not share this resentment—just when such a feeling would have helped her. She had come to realize that at the time of their quarrel Luke had already foreseen her predicament, and that he had honestly tried to save her, even allowing her to think he was pleading for mercy. In love pride meets its master. Juliana's decision to hate Luke henceforth had not worked the slightest change in her heart, so that she could not even help secretly glorifying in his prosperity.

Howbeit, as she must blame somebody, she took Jane to task. "All these years you have been saying that my welfare is your luck! Gillian you have made to conceive again, Walter Green's well that was dried up you have made to run anew, Andrew Freeman's purse that was stolen you brought to light, and Wall-eyed Kate has found a suitor. You cure everyone's ills except mine!"

She went on until Jane at last flung back the truth at her. "Ay, and I must not and cannot work against your own wishes! I have told you that, too, time and again. Your yearning and your inmost scheming all aim at becoming reconciled with him. *I* cannot make you want to bring him low, which is your only other way."

For the first time since she had owned her, Juliana struck Jane. She was repentant afterward, and also somewhat uneasy. But Jane bore it without retaliation for she still knew not what to do, herself.

During the next few weeks Juliana grew more and more irascible. Even Little John got a beating from his mother. Elizabeth, whose very caution caused her to break or spoil almost everything she touched, finally took to lying.

Not long before Christmas, she upset a kettle of tallow into the fire. Since after the smell had passed there was no trace of the loss, she decided to hope for the best and say nothing. Next day her mother sent for her.

"I want to know, Elizabeth, whose fault it is that we shall have to go without lights for the rest of these long winter evenings. I am asking you before anyone else, to give you the chance of being truthful. Think not I did not mark it, the many times you have lied of late, daughter. You know who is called Father of Lies, for good reason. The disasters I have seen to arise from quite small lies! For every single lie leads to countless others. You yourself have surely learned that by now, seeing that all our troubles at this present time are the outcome of a lie on your part."

Elizabeth stared at her mother, who had spoken in a reasoning, persuasive tone.

"Do not pretend you know not what I mean," Juliana went on, with her gentle chiding. "Love is a matter wherein none of us can help ourselves. My daughter must not be a coward. When Master Robinson asked for you last summer, you said you did not want him, and I took you at your word. Since then I have often gone over it all in my mind, and from various evidence I have concluded that you and Luke must have been in secret agreement—seeing that he let you decide everything about his house. Is it not so? Admit it now."

Elizabeth almost laughed aloud with the relief of conscious innocence. "No, Mother, truly and truly, I promise and swear, by your life and as I hope my father is in Heaven, there was nothing, nothing like that! Sooner than be Luke's wife I would—Oh, I hardly know what I would *not* prefer! You must believe me."

"I believe you." Juliana abruptly dismissed her, and Elizabeth was too pleased to escape paying for the tallow to wonder greatly what might be behind it all.

Luke Robinson sat in his countinghouse at Smithy Yard, going over the tallies with a hired man. The stableboy came in, and Luke looked up, "What is it, Jess?"

"Mistress Trefeller is here and asking for you."

Luke jumped up so that he overturned his stool. He pushed the men aside and made as to dash from the room, but then checked himself to step circumspectly. Juliana and her serving woman were still out in the yard, looking as though all round where they stood the ground were paved with raw eggs.

"You must think we have no manners here!" Luke called out from afar. "Is this what we have set aside a special parlor for—that visitors are left to stand out in the cold? Shame upon my servants, for bringing shame on their master! Nay, but this is a pleasure and an honor, Mistress Juliana—and Meg, too, looking doughty as ever. Pray come in, Mistress, and tell me what I may do for you. Smithy Yard is all at your service."

"You must not blame your man, Master," Juliana's voice shook, "for we would not enter till I knew how you would receive us."

"Could you have had any doubt?" Luke returned as in guileless wonderment. "Old friends that we are, you and I, and old comrades in many a joust. I will have fire fetched from the kitchen."

"Nay, do not trouble." Juliana had mastered her voice. "I should like to be taken round your house now that it is finished. It is so handsome on the outside, I should much like to view it within." She met his gaze squarely, but could not support it long and glanced away.

"Certainly," Luke replied cordially, "although you will not think much of it, being all bare and naked. Perhaps Meg would like to warm herself in the kitchen? Oh, Jess, Jess." He went back to the door to shout across the yard. "He will take you, Meg, and tell them to give you somewhat to warm you up inside, too."

Juliana had to keep on looking at Luke. Not having seen him since their separation, she noticed changes in him that had escaped her before. He did look wan and worn, just as people were saying, though he himself appeared quite unaware of it. Yet his hair was still so glossy and luxuriant as to suggest it got its strength at the expense of the rest of him. He was clad in an old gown of Trefeller Court weave, soiled, loose, and reaching far below his knees. It came to Juliana that the excellence of his build accounted for most of his handsome looks, not nearly so striking when the contours of his body were obscured. But her heart drew equal, dizzy gladness from what marred him as from the memory of him in other clothes.

As soon as they were alone, and out of earshot, Juliana stood still and turned to face him. "This is what I have come for, Luke. It is not easy to say. The day is nearly come round again of Our Lord's birth on earth to bring peace to all men. I should not be worthy to celebrate it were I to remain at odds with anyone. I have come to ask you to forget our differences, and let everything between us be again as it was before I went to Clowes."

"Say no more, dear Mistress, I beg of you. What are a few words spoken in heat between two such old friends!"

"I was wrong," Juliana said, again tremulously, "about your fire-places. This looks much more comfortable than the old-fashioned hearths," she motioned at the grate in which, however, no fire was burning. "Happy, I say happy the housewife who reigns where floors are tiled and washed easily, needing no litter—" There was a pause.

"Ay," Luke said, with studious lightness, "that is still the chief want of this house, and cause of its every other lack: a mistress. I fear me," he added, "things cannot be quite the same between us again after all. I shall have to go on living here now. Would you that I be your partner again?"

"Ay, it was a friendly, companionable arrangement," Juliana answered warily, hoping against hope that he might stipulate any conditions. "Though I must say I cannot complain. My business has in no way suffered."

"I am right glad to hear that," Luke said, heartily. "But then, forgive me, there can be no point in our disarranging all our affairs again, both of us, with another change, just when the disorders of the last have been smoothed away? But now you must sit down. You will tire yourself, standing."

"I came on foot." Juliana excused her yielding, and Luke's solicitous exclamations gave her time to harden herself for the final effort. "Now there is one further matter, Master Luke. Had I any closer male relatives at hand than a brother's son of my late John's grandfather—and he all the way out at Clowes—I need not deal with such matters myself.

I cannot count my brothers at the manor. I feel the lack of a near kins-man of sensible age more and more as time goes on and my children grow. I have never been strong in health, as you know."

"All the stronger of heart and spirit, Mistress." Luke said, bowing a little on the settle beside her.

"It is kind of you to say so. The last time we met, Master Luke, it seemed to me you were not disinclined to become kinsman of mine. I know not whether you are still of the same mind?"

"I am still of the same mind."

"My daughter," said Juliana, and stopped for breath. "My daughter Elizabeth has matured remarkably in these last months. I know not whether you guessed why I repulsed your offer so brusquely—you let fall some remarks, I remember, that I could not make head or tail of— but then, we both of us spoke in heat and confusion, did we not? She was not grown womanly then, you see, as she is now. She was a child. Though many are wed at her age and less, I took away a great horror of child bridals from what happened in my father's house when I was myself a child. No doubt you have heard tell something of the story of Hugh's marriage. I repulsed you without thinking, straight out of my feelings, you see—for could we not have held the handfasting, and fixed the wedding years ahead?"

"If you wished it, or she," Luke cried, in the fullness of his joy, "I would still agree to wait—so long as she was promised to me—"

"I do not wish that," Juliana said quickly, with a hint of pique.

"And certainly I do not. I but wanted to show you how pliant and pleasing a son-in-law you will get!" He did not see her wince, as he had taken both her hands and kissed them. "My dear, dearest Juliana, God will surely reward you for granting me such happiness."

They sat talking together a while longer before either of them felt the cold again. Luke would not allow the Mistress to make her way back on foot. He would have liked best to take her himself. But Juliana said he must not come near her house before the formal handfasting. After High Mass on Christmas Day, would that suit him? So he ordered Jess to walk a horse to Trefeller Court with Juliana in the saddle and Meg riding pillion.

Juliana and her household went to Mass at the manor chapel. Luke attended two services, one at the hospital and one at the Benedictine cloister. Then he rode straight to Trefeller Court, to the surprise of all that saw him pass, for as yet nothing was known of the impending alliance. Juliana's heart leaped when she saw him, dressed finely and to best advantage.

Elizabeth was clad in her mother's wedding gown, which Jane had altered for her. It was silken, and of a blue some shades deeper than her eyes, with white lilies embroidered around the neck and hem, and a bordering of ermine at the sleeves. Her hair was spread out down her back, and a fillet of red and white cords twisted together encircled her head.

Luke gasped a little when her mother pushed her forward into the light, "Whatever ails my Elizabeth?" for she was pale as one that has lain sick in a closet many months, her lips the color of bone, her eyes ringed in damp shadow.

"She has not been well," Juliana, Jane, and Little John said simultaneously.

"I have not been well," Elizabeth repeated after them, at a look from her mother. "I ate something—"

"My poor sweetheart—"

"She is better now," Juliana said, cheerfully. "Are you not, Elizabeth?"

"Yes," said Elizabeth.

"Yet your color is not such that you will take pleasure in this I have brought you, just yet," Luke said, regretfully, holding up a little net of gold thread containing some bunches of raisins. "But this, perhaps, may please you," and he placed a ring into her listless hand, of thick gold, with a ruby in the center, which was wreathed in tiny pearls and bracketed in the Virgin's monogram. "I may not put it on your finger today, not until we have the proper betrothal ale, but I wanted to see whether you like it. If you do not, I will get you another."

"Say it is a very beautiful ring—much too fine," Juliana prompted. "Little John can have the raisins, Luke."

"Yes," said Elizabeth.

Luke had brought presents for everyone in the house. After they had eaten and drunk, all the serving folk save Jane left the family to discuss the proposed match. Chests and wallets were opened and deed rolls compared, sticks cut and discarded in calculations. Elizabeth stood stiffly between her mother's chair and Luke's. Whenever Luke looked at Elizabeth, Juliana looked at her, too, and then Elizabeth smiled at Luke.

"You spoke truly," he said to the mother. "She has grown out of all recognition. My wild fidget has turned into a quiet, gracious maiden. The stomach upset is all of a piece with that, I reckon." He laughed. "Ladies must ail every once in a while."

They settled it so that the marriage was to take place at the conse-cration of the cathedral, lately postponed to St. Francis' Day,—"which will be most fitting," Juliana immediately agreed with Luke's first hint, "for we had her christened at the foundation laying. The Lord Bishop himself christened her, Luke, you must know, and I should like it well if the Lord Bishop could marry you two. I know he will, he will not say me no."

"Will you do without any betrothal feasting, then, Juliana?" Jane asked, in a compressed voice. "The time is so short, we shall scarce be able to make ready for the wedding, properly."

"We must do the best we can, and no one can ask more of us," Juliana answered sharply. "It is not every day we have a cathedral consecrated on our doorstep. There need not be a big betrothal feast, as the wedding will follow it so soon."

"But will they not think it strange, and indecently hasty?" Jane ven-tured again.

"Only the evil-minded will think it strange, and there is no way of pleasing them whatever we do."

"Come and sit on my knee just one minute, Elizabeth," Luke said tenderly, "just so I may know I am not dreaming and you are really promised to me now. What great joke is plaguing you so sorely?" he asked his prospective brother-in-law, who rocked choking with sup-pressed mirth. Encouraged at length, Little John spluttered out a very coarse remark. "That does not sound well from the lips of so young a lad as you are." Luke frowned, but he could not help smiling at the same time, and looked pleased and excited.

"He must have picked up this sort of thing at Clowes," Juliana apologized. She also looked excited, but none so pleased. "Ay, Luke, you can see it is as I told you—we need a grown man in the family."

"She is trembling, here on my lap," Luke said suddenly, in a low voice, as though speaking of a sacred matter. "Like a doe, like the tenderest little bird. The times that you have romped all over me, ever since I first knew you, a mere babe—many's the time that I found myself black and blue, after! And now she trembles, sweetly. Was there ever a man so happy as I?"

Elizabeth sat trembling, with downcast eyes, and did not utter a sound.

"That is enough for now," said Juliana. "Now you are a handfasted pair. Handfasted folk need to be even more discreet than others. And Elizabeth had best go and lie down for a while, as she wants to hear

Mass again tonight. Jane, you may go with her, lest she tear my gown, taking it off by herself. You may leave us, too, my son. Luke and I have much else to talk of."

CHAPTER 6

PREPARATIONS

THAT WINTER was exceptionally mild. God wished to give us all the help He could toward the sanctuary's timely completion. There had been some snow early in November, but nothing later. There were snow-drops and primroses by Childermas Day and a freakish flowering of yew and silver birch.

Most farmers at first hesitated to bank on so very early a spring and avail themselves of the unusual abundance of casual work people. James Smith was an exception and, long before anyone else did so, hired three newcomers who yet were not rightly foreigners. They were Jack Oxerd and Joan Widowson and their young son, and their return gave all the town much food for dubious talk.

Jeanne had not yet recovered from a miscarriage, and every hour Edwin could be spared from the site he must needs devote to her and their home. So he obtained leave for Alfred to represent him as the head of the Widowsons, and go to welcome Jack and Joan in the name of the family.

Alfred had always admired the legendary runaways, and was in a fever of delight at the prospect of knowing them at last. He had not seen Elizabeth since before Christmas, and knew she would be glad if he took her along to meet these two.

Approaching Trefeller Court from the rear, he distinguished Jane among a crowd of women in the meadow behind the kilns, and guessed Elizabeth would not be far off, so he did not trouble to go round by the houses. The women were shaking out tapestries and bed gear folded in storage for years, and baking the vermin out of others. Jane no sooner caught sight of him than she started toward him, saying in a loud voice, "Oh, there you are, Alfred!" as if he had been sent for, and,

"Come with me now, that I may give you the medicine for your mother." She took Alfred's hand and hurried him away to the laundry shed down by the strand.

"What is wrong?" Alfred asked, with a beating heart. "Has anything happened—to Elizabeth?"

Jane had bolted the door behind them, and now stood leaning against it. Deep lines were graven in her brow, deep hollows had appeared below her eyes and cheekbones. Her eyes flickered and shifted, her hands could not keep still.

"Are you ill, Ganna-Janna?"

"Well may you ask that, and well may I answer you yet to both questions. You must not come here any more. Never let Elizabeth see you, never let Juliana catch you. I am going to talk to you as to a grown man, and trust in you as Elizabeth's sworn friend."

"Then you know about us?"

"Ay, and so also does Juliana, mark you that! Elizabeth is to marry Luke this coming autumn. Be still, hear me out. When nothing else availed, she told her mother she could not, without mortal sin, because you and she had bound you to each other with eternal oaths. And then—! Oh, you cannot know, and you cannot picture it either, God be thanked. *I* could bear no more. *I* begged Elizabeth to give in, on my knees I begged her. And now her spirit is broken, too, at last."

"And he—he is content it should be so?" Alfred stood with clenched fists and teeth.

"Luke? There is little we cannot close our eyes and stupefy our minds to, if our heart's desire depends on blindness!"

"Yet can he hardly convince himself he is not an old man," Alfred said, scornfully.

Jane had to smile. "So old as all that he is not. A little over thirty, you young Alfred."

"Could not Elizabeth tell him, or you?"

"Juliana has thought of that, and she has threatened us with what she will do to Elizabeth, if we dare."

"What has become of your powers?" Alfred exclaimed, weeping.

"It has been fated so that I cannot use them in this."

"Could you not even make a fog behind us, her and me? I will save my Elizabeth and run away with her. We have often talked it over, when there was no such peril as now."

"Then never speak or think of it again. There are too many things you do not understand. Her fate, and yours, and mine are all part of an ordained design. That we may suffer while it is wrought out does not concern Them that planned it so for Their own great mystic purposes."

Alfred bowed his head. "May I not see her at all, even once? May we not even say good-by?"

"Yes, if you value your feelings above hers. No, Alfred. The best you can do for her now is to go away and keep away."

Perhaps she thought by then that she had found out what to do. Still, it is doubtful whether she knew altogether what she was doing. Certain it is Elizabeth was the only being whom that witch ever truly loved, and there is no pain like watching a loved one's pain. Yet must it have offended her that Elizabeth's revulsion and despair drew their violence, not from the threat of marriage in itself, but from marriage to Luke instead of Alfred.

At all events, she had succeeded in making Alfred feel there was no way out. You may imagine in what frame of mind and mien he arrived at the Smiths' place, where he and his father and grandsires had been born.

Gillian looked at him keenly, but spoke as if she marked nothing. "You have come to greet your relations, Alfred? They are out in the fields with James. I and Margery are just making ready some food and drink to take them. Will you wait and help us carry?" When they left the house, Gillian saw to it that she and Alfred lagged behind the serving woman. "What ails you, Alfred? I trust your mother is no worse?" she began her probing.

"No. She is mending."

"There would not be anything wrong at Trefeller Court, would there, Alfred? I saw you cross the bridge. Nobody has seen Elizabeth since Christmas, and then she did not look well. She is not ill, is she?"

"Oh, Gillian!" Alfred found he could not keep it to himself. "She is to be married, against her will. But you must not tell I told you. It is still a secret."

Gillian nodded, as one whose guess has been confirmed. "I see Master Robinson ride across almost every day. But I am no tattle mongerer, so I held by peace. It is he, is it not? And you, faithful little friend that you are, you grieve because she grieves? Well, let me tell you not to take that overseriously. Most like it is but coyness."

"Gillian," said Alfred, "it is not just that. It is not just that she does not love him, for she does not. You do not know. How can you? She loves me, Gillian, and I love her. We are betrothed. We swore great oaths, long since, that neither of us would ever take any other. Juliana

is forcing her into the sins of perjury and adultery, both. And my heart
will surely break."

"You must not talk so, Alfred." Gillian put one arm round his shoulders—he was as tall as she. "You are neither of you of age. Be sure the
Lord God will not hold you to oaths you took without your elders'
consent. Would Juliana ever give her consent for her daughter, my
lord's own niece, to marry one that is not even free? You Widowsons
have two vices. The one is pride, that, just because you are all craftsmen
born, you hold yourselves as good as *anybody*. The other is that you will
overvalue love. Hearts do not break so easily, my Alfred. Or else they
grow whole again endlessly. Nine times now my heart has been broken,
Alfred. Yes, every time I thought to have a son." She sighed, smiling at
him. Now her own, lashless eyes were wet. "There is no grief like
death, my Alfred. What, so she is to be married! Is that all?"

Alfred said nothing. Curiously, although her words could not please
him, they had comforted him a little.

James and a couple of his men were spreading a newly plowed field
with a mixture of dung, litter, and wood ash. Close by there was a
thicket, some of which they had cut down and burned for manure,
making also two large piles of faggots and twigs, one for firewood, the
other for the hurdles which the newcomers were busy constructing in
a patch of grass.

Jeanne's brother was not tall, but hard looking of body as though
fashioned of twisted iron, with pointed nose, chin, and ears from which
sprouted upsurging tufts of hair. His poll was black without sheen. He
had very small teeth, saw edged, like some children's. The hue of his
skin suggested that the sun had deeply encausted it with the dirt of
years before proceeding to tan it, and the same was true of his wife.
Their little son was no more fiercely browned than other children in
summer. All three were in rags, and those barely decent. Yet they looked
as sprightly as cubs come out to sport in a glade.

"Well, well," said his uncle to Alfred, straightening and stretching.
"So you are Jeanne's eldest, and almost a man! It is hard to believe. The
last time I saw you, you were not half the height of Frankie here, and
it seems only yesterday that Edwin hung about our hut, courting your
mother—of which you were the untimely result. Ay, time has flown, and
times are changed. Ay, and behold, now it is me, John Oxerd's son, is
a free man and able to come and go as I please, while your Widowson
father, I hear, is a churchland villein as ever, and poorer even than we
were at home when I was young."

After this Alfred felt a little awkward about discharging his message: "My father and mother send you their fond greetings and welcome to Bedesford. They bid you come and be feasted at our home as soon as Mother is herself again, and stay with us, if you have no better quarters, and meantime, if there is anything your kinsfolk can do for you—"

"Kindly spoken and kindly meant, I have no doubt, young Alfred," said his uncle, clapping him on the shoulder, "and you may take back our thanks to Jeanne and Edwin. They were not to know that we want no aid of any kind. All these years we have depended on no one. We have always managed to get our bread and meat and ale to go with it, you can tell them. Your good man, friend Gillian, has just asked us to stay on and hire ourselves to him for the year. But, if only in honor of our independence, we owe it to ourselves to reflect and consider well before we strike such a bargain."

"What did you come back to Bedesford for, if not to stay?" Gillian said, unkindly.

"How do we know how long it will pleasure us to stay? We must honor our freedom by setting it no limits. If it wishes to carry us forth again tomorrow, we must be able to obey."

"Now must I look my kinsman over, and kiss him," Joan came between them quickly, all smiles, "and so also must Frankie."

"Ay, you must love these your cousins well, young Alfred," her husband resumed, "for that they are kin to you twice over—by marriage as well as in their own right, as am I, too. For we take no shame in it, that we overcame the stumbling block your parents' imprudent marriage placed in the way of ours. The year we spent living in Nunscombe across the border, we did so well that we were able to buy us dispensation and were married in all form. In our wallet we still have part of the Pope's costly letter, and a certificate the mayor of Nunscombe wrote out for us, that all who wish may read how we became free. For Nunscombe town has a briefed charter, so that anyone residing there unclaimed for the space of one year becomes a freeman if so be his desire. It was our desire, and I changed my given name to Franklin. But as my father died an Oxerd, so will I—of Jacks there are many, whereas the Oxerds have died out but for me. You may make this known to your parents and anyone else in Bedesford. Albeit we plan to look up everyone we used to know, and show ourselves."

Alfred went away deep in thought. He saw what Gillian had meant by her contemptuous reference to these his relations, and they neither looked nor acted as he had expected. Nevertheless he could not agree that their runaway match had served them so ill. They themselves did not seem to think so. How, then, could anyone else?

Alfred was accustomed to it that no one ever mentioned his parents without in the same breath condemning their marriage. It had long ceased to have meaning for him—like a formula. But on the lips of the famous, incestuous runaways, disapproval of his parents' imprudence struck him as it never had before. For the first time he asked himself whether their marriage had turned out well or badly for them.

The loyal answer, that they still loved each other tenderly, could not disguise that they were anything but happy. One needed only to compare them with the Oxerds.

Jeanne, like every other laborer's wife at Cloudsway Waste, fell more and more behindhand with her householding, as she had to work daily at the site. It was this also which had caused her to miscarry—an illness that to her meant disgrace and bereavement in addition to pain and loss of time.

We who had not been daunted by the project of a whole cathedral when the Waste was yet nothing more than waste—we quailed before all that needed doing ere Lady Agnes' tiles could be laid down. Tidying the floor alone appeared beyond human achievement. The making of anything, even if it be a mountain, never looms so disheartening as the unmaking of chaos.

All the while the skilled workmen continued to ply their craft like woodpeckers. The whole carpenters' shop was engaged on a timber bell cot provisionally erected over the unroofed portion of the southeast side chapel. The laborers had at last decided on their consecration gift: a sandstone sundial, which was given to Edwin to make. It used to be accounted one of our cathedral's many wonders, for he made of it a representation of the Finding. The Hand stood out boldly in the center, while in place of numerals there were the figures of workmen and friars shaped in shallow relief.

At the chancel end of the choir the enormous Flood corbel, on which Brother Laurentius had been working since 1351, was in position. We recall when it was hoisted aloft, the unskilled hands ignorantly scattered in all directions, muffling their ears and eyes, because they would not believe the whole building could fail to collapse. In fact, of course, it was not till this corbel sat in place, supplying rather than requiring weight support, that the apse could dispense with its last center scaffolding.

The painting was all done, save where the masons still chipped and hammered, and where the last refuse must be cleared. Alfred was loaned to Brother Laurentius, to tint Noah's ark to the minute directions of the friar.

The forthcoming marriage had been made public on Finding Day. Luke was gone to fetch the bell the Abbot had commissioned through his agency, away in Germany, and which was bought with monies collected from the pilgrims over several years. He had taken both of Juliana's ships, and Juliana showed everyone her copy of the list wherein they had set out the purchases for Smithy Yard.

We all felt we had been misjudging Juliana, to think that she did not love her daughter. Even for such an advantageous match as this few mothers would have gone to so much trouble. She spent her days and half her nights at Smithy Yard. She spared not her ailing body nor her coffers. Luke had given her a free hand and set no limit to her spending of his money, yet in addition she pledged her hay crop for the year, to dower the bride most generously.

Elizabeth was to have brought Luke nothing but what comes to every house with a young wife. To make up for this, Juliana had set her seal to a most favorable division of the Trefeller estate after her death. Had she wished to adhere to the letter of their agreement, she could have sent off Elizabeth with no more than a thimble over and above her clothes and bedding. Instead, Juliana bought all kinds of gear that, strictly speaking, could be done without, although it must warm anybody's heart to have it; and only the best was good enough. For the wedding gown she bought new a green brocade figured with gold. Never had there been a maiden so fortunate as this Elizabeth.

As for Juliana's maltreating her daughter, which had been noised abroad by the Trefeller servants all her life, it was now seen to have been exaggerated as most such reports are wont to be. In view of her mealymouthed ingratitude before her mother's exertions, it would appear that indeed it was Elizabeth who had all along lacked in affection for Juliana, and not the other way about. And if it had been as Gillian told us under oath of secrecy, that Elizabeth was so very loath to marry, then you might be sure, we said, that Jane would have found means of helping her.

Jane merely talked to her foster daughter.

"I tell you it is true many a woman has found love, all unlooked for, in the marriage bed. For women form the better, nobler portion of God's subjects. To this day it is the same. Men grow crazed without women to ease themselves with. Whereas woman can lie content in a chaste bed, though some lesser women there are who cannot. But the least and worst of women is chaste compared with the best of men. So even if your husband should fail to make you love him, your power will be all the greater for this, as he will love you while your heart will remain your own. You will rule him, whose material power in Anglemere is second to none—"

"Power! What care I for that!"

"If power has chosen you, you cannot run away from it, in that it is like the plague. Think what I suffered and survived. Think of our linked fates. No one can love you as I do. You will always still have me. I have never asked anything of you. But now do I beg you to take pity on me, whose heart is scalded and blistered by every tear that merely wets your cheek. This is not the end of all days. Who knows what may yet happen? You fear this ill. It has not yet befallen you. When you need help in fact, be sure I shall be there to give it."

CHAPTER 7

CONSECRATION EVE

THE YEAR KEPT the promise of its January spring. There were no such May frosts and ruinous June deluges as many had predicted. It rained when it ought and the sun shone as it should. So abundant was the harvest, St. Hand's dispensed with a large number of laborers to help garner it. All remaining at the site agreed to abandon the restrictions of the resurgent guilds and turn their hands to whatever wanted doing.

For the space of two weeks the crypt was a fabulous kitchen, where candles were molded, incense compounded, wafers baked. Hardly had the decorations been put up and the floor cleared, when a falling hammer destroyed a tile in the procession path, one of a special set, of which none had been kept in reserve. So a dozen more had hurriedly to be made, as the shattered tile was an essential part of the pattern, to which its neighbor must conform.

The hammer was dropped from the central chancel window. Here we worked under the vociferous guidance of the plumbing master and a brace of Italian glaziers, who had brought the stained glass hither. It was the gift of a Lombard merchant who had been cured of ulcers in his throat on Finding Day, 1355, and departed with life-sized tracings of the huge window's moldings.

As the pieces were fitted together, we saw that the panes formed scenes from the life of St. Jerome, whereat there was great wondering. It was left to the Abbot to say that if, as seemed likely, the Lombard had forgotten which saint had helped him, it was fortunate he had hit on our Bishop's patron.

The glass was resplendently in place for Lord Jerome's arrival. He praised it warmly and stood for a long while, suffering its light to bathe and parti-color him. Altogether he was delighted. You must remember that the last time he was here, St. Francis-of-Cloudsway had been little more than a hole in the ground, while of the monastery not even that much had been in existence. He brought with him a brilliant company, also the altar cloth, made in France. Ten years older than on his last appearance, Lord Jerome had not grown any the less burly, nor had his massive features softened, so it must be the manner of his reception which made him to seem like a young bride.

The monastery was turned upside down to house him and his train. Brother Oswin and his under-limners were evicted from their workshop which, spattered with ink and paint, would not be the worse for addition of birdlime, and was given over to the Bishop's hawks. Brother Oswin borrowed Alfred to help him move the materials to his cell, where soon there was not room to stand.

Leaning on the boy, Brother Oswin ruefully surveyed the cell from the passage, saying, "I shall have to jump the distance from doorstep to paillasse of nights, God help me." Having vainly waited for Alfred to laugh, he added ingenuously, "Alfred! What has come over you of late? You have not said a word all morning."

Alfred started. "I have been thinking, Brother Oswin, of what you have always said to me, about turning monk. Lately I have felt a great longing to renounce the world."

Brother Oswin laughed aloud and rumpled his hair. "This is a sudden change of tune, indeed! Now, Alfred, enough of this hang-nose behavior at a happy time like this! I know well what ails you. Some come out in pimples, and others get the melancholia for their growing pains. There goes the bell! I did not dream it was so late! I must hurry. Off with you now into the fresh air!"

Alfred did not know where to turn. Brother Laurentius had no time for him either. Having spared himself the least of all his friars in making ready the hospital against the pilgrims, Prior Haakon was again fallen ill, retarding recovery with restless impatience. He had empowered Brother Laurentius to conduct the reception and overhauling of the Franciscan rood, which had been in store with the Cistercians of Ovisham since the pirate raid of 1346, and which was to be made over to St. Hand's.

It dawned on Alfred that God was justly putting him in his unimportant place. For years both Brother Oswin and Brother Laurentius had strengthened Alfred's self-esteem and his obstinacy with their attempts to win him for God's service. Now God would have nothing of his selfishness.

There was no one else to whom he could open his heart. His father always seemed in some way to blame himself for any hurt befalling Alfred, wherefore Alfred had long sought to keep anything like that from Edwin. As for his mother, he knew she could not be trusted to keep her mouth shut. He could hear her, publicly denouncing Juliana, and predicting a day when friars and monks alike would rue the lost chance of having her Alfred one of their number.

The Bishop had never seen a tile factory before, and Luke Robinson had never been introduced to the Bishop. To make good both deficiencies at one stroke, the Abbot arranged to take Lord Jerome among the Flemings' clay pits, and ovens, where Juliana with Luke was to meet them. The Abbot did not know enough about tilemaking, and the Flemings lacked adequate English, French, or Latin to expound in an entertaining manner, whereas Luke was equal to both.

"How would I not remember you, Mistress?" the Bishop said graciously, lifting up the little hunchback from her knees. "Indeed, I remember telling you I never should forget! I shall even forgive you making me feel old. Father William has spoken to me of your daughter's marriage, and when last I saw her she was scarcely weaned. And this is the son-in-law? I hear, young man, that I am not a little in your debt for this economical scheme," he made a gesture embracing the tiling enclosure. "But I see that the Lord God has already repaid you on my behalf. Such a wife as you are to get is worth ten fortunes. I stayed at her mother's house when hospitality must have presented well-nigh insurmountable difficulties, and never, before or since, have I found myself so well looked after!"

"*Mon seigneur est bien aimable,*" Juliana said, beatifically. "How I wish that on this great occasion, too, your reverend lordship might have honored my house! Your lordship may recollect that there is much more space than here at the monastery, and that all my rooms are a great deal loftier—"

"Yet, my daughter," said the Bishop, a little gravely, "is there something about these stunted timber cloisters puts the world's most splendid palaces to shame." His affectionate glance now rested on the Abbot, who received it with downcast eyes, in a reverent stance. Juliana felt deeply rebuked. When afterward she followed the Abbot to the cloister parlor to make final settlements connected with the marriage, she set her mark to more than she had intended.

Meanwhile Luke conducted the Bishop and his attendants around, from the shed where the tiles' shapes and patterns were devised on parchment and all past designs stored on rows of shelves, to the smithy and gravers' shop where the molds were made, the long benches and bins of different-colored clay which the workmen slapped and leveled and tagliated carefully into the brazen mold trays.

Hither had also come a deputation from the site, to inspect the replacement tiles for the procession path, just ready, for final coloring and measurements after shrinkage. Among them was a slim lad whose narrow shoulders and long legs betokened a recent spurt of growth, with thick dark hair so heavy the breeze could not stir its bird's-wing smoothness, and fine gray eyes. Strapped on his back was a wicker crate lined with moss, in which to carry the tiles if they proved satisfactory.

"That comely youth," the Bishop said to Luke, "reminds me of someone, though I mind not whom."

"It may be your lordship is thinking of his father, that lived in Mistress Trefeller's house before my time," Luke answered, beckoning to Alfred.

But Alfred made as if he heard someone calling him from the next room, whither he disappeared. The Bishop forgot him as the Flemings sent forward one of their master craftsmen to beg permission to make a set of tiles bearing the Rocquefeuilles arms, as their gift in commemoration of Lord Jerome's visit. In a high good humor Lord Jerome then left.

On the way to the account caster's office, where he had business, Luke ran into Alfred who did not see him until too late. As he made to dodge aside, Luke held him firmly by one crate strap.

"Now, Alfred, what is the matter with you, lad?" he asked, genially, shaking him a little. "What have you done, that you look so guilty?

I could tell you saw I meant to make you known to the Lord Bishop, which might have proved of great service to you."

"I do not look guilty," Alfred said passionately, "for I have no cause. And I was made known to the Lord Bishop long before you ever set foot into Bedesford. And there is no boon I would owe you. No, not if I were drowning, and you threw me a rope."

"What in Heaven's name has got into you, Alfred? We used to be good friends, you and I?"

"Ay, and I am not the only one you deceived into being friends with you!" Alfred cried, panting to get it all out in one rush. "If you must know, I hate you because you are wicked. You are forcing a pure, tender maiden—"

"Ah!" Luke nodded, as much as to say now he understood.

"Ah!" Alfred mocked furiously. "You are no better than a ravisher, without heart or honor, as all Flemings are. If no one dare tell you so it is right that I should, for it is me you are robbing as David, King of the Jews, did the knight Uriah—" He stopped, his ears ringing and nose and lip bleeding from Luke's blow.

"Next time you quote the friars' tales against anyone, see that at least you get them right, boy," Luke said, without raising his voice. "Go and ask and see if that same King David was not singled out to be grand-sire to Our Lord Himself—by that same wife who was Uriah's widow. Away out of my sight with you now."

As he watched Alfred retreat, slowly and with his head held very high, Luke somehow did not feel rightly pleased on his own account. It was not because he had struck Alfred, which the lad had unquestionably deserved.

Poor, young Alfred. He was jealous, in a laughable way it was rather sad. Yet it was not so very long ago that, in like and much more laughable manner, Luke had been the one to envy Alfred. Might there not come a day when, most laughable of all, an old husband should have cause to be jealous of a young gallant?

Luke's nature was full of kindliness. It would have been normal to him now to show some small kindness to a lad whom he had had to beat. The unnatural absence of any such wish made him feel that he had not, in fact, worsted Alfred. This must not be. And he must prove to himself, to Elizabeth, to Alfred, and to any who might have noticed Alfred come bleeding from an interview with Luke that he had naught but the most Christian friendship for his bride's former playmate.

On the eve of St. Francis' Day Luke paid the Abbot an unexpected call. He felt, he said, that his gift to the cathedral was insufficient. For he would have honored the consecration whether he were to be married or no, and if he were to have been married on any other day, he would still have made offering to God for his wedding. Full miserly would it be to take advantage of both days' coinciding. He spoke of Alfred, who at one time had been closer than a brother to his fair young bride, of Alfred's talents. He offered to buy Edwin's freedom and dower Alfred's entry into the Benedictine order.

The Abbot accepted with unconcealed pleasure, commending Luke's generosity and boldly bespeaking for him God's blessing and the whole town's approbation. At this Luke flushed, he did not know why, and he said, likewise without knowing why, "If you please, my lord, I would not have this made public."

"Oh?" said the Abbot, surprised. "Why the devil not?"

Hesitantly, gropingly, Luke answered, "I am doing this for God's sake and my bride's. I do not want profit or honor from it. Please me, and let this be a secret between us two. You can say it is the monastery's bounty." His heart still clamored that he had not given the true reason, but still refused to help him find it. And still he felt the dull-burning shame that had not left him since that talk with Alfred, and which ought now to have been replaced by the pleasing warmth of virtue satisfied.

The Abbot also shrugged, imperceptibly. He also could not credit Luke's stated reason, yet he could no more think of a better one. But he, too, was a practical man who valued his serenity above unprofitable research. He set himself a penance to combat his cynicism, and returned his thoughts to more interesting matters.

CHAPTER 8

THE WEDDING

A GOLDEN, GLORIOUS day was October the fourth of that year, 1361. But long before any could know this, last night's red sunset or no, folk were up and about at Trefeller Court. Next door to the hall, the bridal

gear was displayed, and some big chairs stood ranged in state. The
maids brought in fire and rushlights. Juliana, the Abbess of Thirchester,
Mistress Tryfellow of Clowes, and her plump sixteen-year-old daughter
Kate filed in and took their seats. Then Meg opened the door again, and
Jane and Gillian led in Elizabeth. The serving women were divided,
some looking after the remaining guests, some guarding the approaches
to the chamber, some waiting further orders.

A great barrel tub had been set up and left half full of water overnight, scented with powdered orris root, rose leaves, and extract of
camomile. The bath was now tempered with boiling water. Elizabeth
was in her linen shift, barefoot, her hair braided to make it wavy. She
looked half asleep and pale, but placid and in good health. There was
a perfume of Valerian on her breath. She did not even tremble, as most
brides will, although the early hour was chill, neither did she modestly
struggle when Jane took off the shift for her.

The ladies could not help smiling, the sight was such a pretty one.
Lady Philippa touched Elizabeth's bosom, which she could reach without rising or straining her arm, as Jane led the girl past. "Pretty as white
hind are you, Niece—only those will have to grow somewhat—" and
she gazed fleetingly down upon her own by way of comparison. Mistress Tryfellow laughed and exchanged glances with the others. "With
God's help that want will be remedied before the year is out!"

At this the brightness in Juliana's eyes leaped, and the red upon her
fleshless cheekbones deepened until it shone as though oiled. Unknowingly, she was all the while chewing her lips and kneading her fingers
together.

Between them Gillian and Jane lifted up Elizabeth and lowered her
into the bath. She did not gasp as she was immersed, but in a moment
her teeth began chattering. The women soaped and rubbed her all over
with flannels and wads of straw, so that on emerging she was warm.
They dried her with soft wool soaked in wine. They made her sit down,
and drew on a pair of fine linen hose, which they fastened with scarlet
garters, and the bridal shoes, of flowered Arras stuff worked over
wooden soles and heels, with blue laces ending in tiny silver bells. From
now on whenever Elizabeth stirred never so slightly, you could hear it.
She was made to stand up again and lift her arms over her head.

Just as Jane was about to throw the new, silk shift over the bride,
there was a commotion outside. It was learned that Little John had
enticed the sons of the squire of Clavis Green to join him at a peephole
and eavesdrop upon what no male creature was to have witnessed.

The brides women frowned and shook their heads, yet none too seriously. Elizabeth with startling suddenness burst into sobs. She was given a cup of hot wine and with a piece of white bread with butter and honey on it.

The tight brocade gown closed about her, the laying on of jewels began: Isabella Cinqmort's necklace, grandmother Elizabeth Trefeller's necklace, the brooch John had put into his daughter's cradle the first hour of her life. Then they hung a mantle of softest Flemish cloth about her, covered it with a sheet, and started on her hair. It came well out of the braiding, and was combed and brushed till it crackled. A woman came with a trough of white asters and late rosebuds, and these were fastened all over the long, outspread hair. That done, Jane and Gillian led her forward and helped her spin slowly before the ladies.

"That fold a little more to the left, Jane."

"Another flower, where the hair dips to the nape."

"The amethyst could go a little higher."

"Her mouth is sticky, and there are crumbs on her chin. Wipe them off, Gillian. Well, now."

"Beautiful. Oh, most comely."

"Nay, good sisters," said Lady Philippa, a little anxiously, "her hands are somewhat red, and her eyes. And her cheeks are a tr–rifle too white. Let me see. Get me some fresh bay leaves. Now close your eyes, Niece, like a good girl. So. Dip the leaves in the bath water, Jane, and plaster them well down over the child's eyes. Meanwhile, Elizabeth, put up your hands high again and do not let them down until I tell you. This is to drain the blood out of them and leave them white. Now you, Mistress Smith, and perhaps you, Kate, go and stand on either side of her and drum her cheeks with your fingers, that we may drive the blood into them. Go on. Go. I will tell you when to stop."

Elizabeth stood, for hours as it seemed to her, her hands up high, her eyelids sealed, strange fingers tattooing her face.

"May I drop my arms now, please?" she asked faintly. "May I have my eyes opened again? Oh, are not my cheeks red enough by this time?"

"Not yet, not yet," Lady Philippa said, yawning. "Patience, Niece."

"Before I forget it," said the Mistress of Clowes. "I advise you to have her fingernails trimmed. Where I come from, it is the general custom. And a wise one, I say. Many is the bridegroom I have seen to come down in the morning covered with streaks of gore. Though I will say your daughter seems meek and gentle. I see no point in risking your son-in-law's eyes, who is to be your mainstay in your old age, Cousin Juliana."

"I will pare them down myself, after," said Juliana.

The entire household was assembled in the hall to catch the first glimpse of the bride. The weaving women and plowmen that worked for Juliana only by the day had decided to wait and attach themselves to the bridal train, unlike the bulk of the people, who had been wandering up to Cloudsway Waste since the preceding evening, in the hope of securing good places. Apart from the wedding guests, there were many pilgrims to whom, like every other house in Bedesford, Trefeller Court had extened hospitality. Most of these also had stayed behind to swell Elizabeth's following, and acclaimed her loudly.

Someone brought a mirror to the bride. Elizabeth did not know herself. For the first time since she had been wakened, she began to feel warm—from the inside. She perceived a pulse of timid pleasure, which shocked her by its treachery, and, as she tried to suppress it, instantly doubled in strength and boldness.

They led her into the yard, with countless unseen hands constantly patting and pulling her, to steady the heavy finery against disarray by the wind. She felt dizzy, but not unpleasantly so. The last tether of reality snapped when her mother was escorted into the sunlight. For Juliana had had her gown made of the same brocade as Elizabeth's, with a mantle of the same Mary-blue Flemish stuff, and she, too, glittered with treasure. Now it was her mother whom Elizabeth did not recognize, and conscious thought recoiled out of reach at the question whether there were two brides or one, and, if one, which one.

She could not see Jane anywhere, Jane's rightful place in the cavalcade being far behind. The bride was mounted, the bride's mother seated in her litter. The hired fiddlers and hornblowers, those from Clowes procured at Juliana's behest, struck up; and they were off.

In the market place the train was complemented by everyone who had slept at the bridegroom's house. Luke was all in silver gray. The close embroidery on his gray doublet and at collar and wrists was silver, the fur edging of his short cloak costly squirrel, and he wore a cloud-hued silken cap that fitted tightly over his head, fastened under the chin. Since his hair was entirely covered, he, too, was a different person.

The crowds on Cloudsway were motley; the monks were garbed as one; and their identity, known to us each and every one by name and age, quirk and foible, was submerged in a unison of holiness, as they walked in measured procession round the whole of the cathedral. They

chanted in solemn harmony, and their tapers bedewed the somber ranks
with drops of bright burning that held their own against the sun. They
bore banners forked and shield shaped, and the great Franciscan rood
which was this day conducted to its home. The rock crystals of St.
Francis' reliquary cross wove its own aureole; the Hand was a core of
scaly glitter in Its ambulatory shrine.

The Hand of healing was as a scythe, for that where It passed all
were mown to their knees. The episcopal jewels shot forth long-armed
stars that winked in silent lightning or hovered in the haze of incense
and candle heat wherever consecration cross marked a station.

Then they passed inside God's new sanctum, and we, to whom it had
been intimate workshop until yesterday—we marveled that they found
the courage, consecrated ministers though they were. In the light from
the Lombard window the Bishop's regalia was momentarily quenched,
while Benedictine drabness flamed up in patches of deep blue, amber,
royal purple, ruby, yellow, and of green surpassing emeralds. A thousand
candles drove all shadows from the interior, so that the huge, white
piers were almost drained of solidity, yet fair, in their forestial heavenward trend, beyond description.

Women fainted and men wept with the lovely awe of the rood's
ascent into position. All at once the sedilia was in use, the stallless choir
in massed occupation. We did not understand all the goodly Latin sung
back and forth, for much of the liturgy was new, relating the Miracle of
Cloudsway Waste.

Next came the blessing of all beasts of Bedesford: the cows, and the
steers bemused with heavy chaplets, devout-eyed horses, and shabby
oxen, and the donkeys graced with the cross on their dun backs; cats
squirming in child arms, leashed hounds and free curs, falcons in cages,
chickens in baskets, also doves and geese; and ferrets swung to meet the
benediction in leather pouches with drawstrings—and sheep, a sea of
sheep, penned in a great fold made near the palisades; and some pigs,
very unruly in a smaller pen.

Later, the bride knelt beside the bridegroom. To herself she was no
more Elizabeth, he no more Luke, than the priestly Abbot had been
William Goliard, or the mitered magnificence before her a Lord Jerome
who long ago had let her ride cockhorse on his foot. She did not see, nor
even feel Alfred's faithful gaze.

The bride ale was held at Smithy Yard for convenience, and was
also a housewarming. The serving folk who had had to wait at home,
and those who had hastened to return ahead of the new-married pair,

stood shouting at the gate, which was wreathed in greenery and banners.

Thus far Elizabeth had remained in the company of her brides women, although on the way back Luke had ridden by her side. Here, now, she was abandoned, given up into Robinson hands. Luke leaped from his horse and held out his hands to help her down. It was as if now she woke up. She looking backward, to right and to left, with pleading eyes that met nothing but encouraging firm smiles and nods. She must let him take her hand, support her descending foot.

Holding on to her cold hand, Luke beckoned into the crowd.

"Here, Mistress, is your dog, that will guard your sweet sleep against stray comers, and here he that will protect your fowls from the fox— and here, Mistress," he picked up a something that was tangle-haired and had pins for teeth, the whole creature scarce bigger than a man's fist, "here is he that desires but to lounge in your lap and keep you from boredom, as long as there is none other to dispute that place." The guests roared their laughter; the little dog yelped; he had a collar around his neck with a metal plate in front, into which were graven the words, *"Amo domina."*

"Here, Mistress, is your own groom, and these two your women, to serve none but you alone. The rest you shall meet later." They looked decent, red-cheeked girls both. Neither hailed from hereabouts. "God and His gentle Mother send you luck and happiness, Mistress, you and your husband," the one said shyly.

Her husband! Elizabeth gaped at Luke, and again there was general laughter.

"Tomorrow, when I give you the keys, I shall show you over your house, Mistress," Luke said, lovingly, "though I myself scarce know it so well as you do! Now we part only once more, for a little while. Make haste, my darling, not to stretch it longer. For I hate every moment apart from you."

Elizabeth's two new maidservants came forward, with humble smiles, to attend her to the little rest parlor. Elizabeth braced her feet and cried backward into the medley of guests. "No, no! I want Ganna! Where is Ganna? Mother! Come *you* with me! Lady Aunt! Gillian!" She could see she was affronting Mistress Tryfellow and Kate, who were already at the parlor door, but she could not help herself.

The maidservant who had wished her luck said low into Elizabeth's ear, "Your mother is hostess at this feast, Mistress. She cannot come to you. And it is not fitting that your aunt the holy nun should be your tiring woman before all this company. And your nurse that I guess you cried for first, she is gone back with your mother's steward to your old home, because in all the flurry the wain with your goods was clean forgot. *I* shall be with you, you do not know me yet, but I mean to be the truest servant to you. Bess is my name, like yours."

The veil they had thrown over the bride to keep her neat and cover her before the Bishop was now removed, the mantle taken off, the shoes exchanged for heelless leather slippers, hair and jewelry readjusted.

The maid refreshed the bride's face with water and wine, then she had to hold her hands over a basin for them to be washed. As the towel was wrapped round to dry them, Elizabeth winced and shuddered. Her fingertips had not yet accustomed themselves to the cruelly shortened nails.

When they emerged, the missing wain from Trefeller Court was halfway unloaded. Jane, Geoffrey, and some others were arranging chests and furniture in a semicircle round two chairs, in one of which Luke was already seated. Juliana went to speak to him, and as if unnoticing sat down on the edge of the second—in her gown that was the replica of the bride's, except for the extra fullness about back and shoulders.

Accustomed to seeing her mother and Luke heading the table, at home, Elizabeth stopped where she thought she was supposed to take her stand, among the onlookers.

"Nay, darling, yonder is your place," whispered the eager Bess, pointing.

"The bride The bride!" the guests shouted again.

Juliana rose, unconsciously tossing her head, and gathered her trailing skirts close to her, as she withdrew behind the bride's chair. Her face was still rose hued, but her eyes and the skin surrounding them were beginning to show the strain of the last months.

"Nay, Mother," Elizabeth faltered, in a tone of beseeching apology, resisting the women who made to force her into her seat beside Luke, "*you* sit. Truly, I am not tired—"

"Fool," snapped her mother, her black eyes sparkling outright hatred. "Do as you are told."

Not many heard this, as they were taken up with the drollest elaborations on the bride's innocent statement. "Did you hear that, Luke? Heard you her challenge? She is not tired! God give you strength, man. It is plain you will need it!" and so on.

So Luke did not mark Juliana's hiss either. For years everyone had prophesied him ill health because he would not eat properly; now these gibes were all that was needed to send a craven chill into his heart. As had been said, so God-fearing a man was Luke, for all his easygoing jollity, that, with one or two exceptions he had almost forgotten, he had not sinned with women all his term in Anglemere. Asking himself whether he were equal to his guests' expectations, whether he had not forgotten man's natural skill, Luke in a moment was all doubt.

Elizabeth sat down, her lip quivering. Now she would have been grateful for another word of gay, kind reassurance from him, or the warm pressure of his hand. But now he did not even look at her.

The banquet was all hosts and guests could wish. Yet the closer day approached night, the more the good cheer waned from Juliana's face.

At last it was time to escort the couple upstairs. Everyone was handsomely drunken. Only the bride's mother had done more than justice to God's gifts, so that she lolled in drool-lipped dolor among the bolsters of her seat, unable to accompany her daughter. Luke had not drunk quite enough, and seemed something too conscious. The bride had not taken much food. The women had seen to it that what she did swallow was well spiced, to keep her thirsty. Now she felt only cold and hollow, stuffy mouthed, and so weary she thought she could neither stay awake nor sleep.

She was helped over to the bed, which was Flemish, carved and curtained, and had been blessed by two friars for good measure. She was quite calm. She was so very tired, and again everything was become unbelievable.

"This was the greatest day in your life, kinswoman," said Mistress Tryfellow, taking the browned flowers out of Elizabeth's hair, "so see that you impress it well upon your memory, that it may entertain you later when your days are dull." Kate sighed and turned up her eyes. "Nay, but you look like a plucked fowl now, without all this." Mistress Tryfellow pursed her lips, as she folded the bridal gown and laid it away.

"Is it that she is too thin, Mother?" Kate asked, hopefully.

"Ay. At all events she can keep her shift on," the mistress of Clowes nodded. "Would that it had sleeves! Now remember, child, whatever your husband will do is well done, no matter if you think it strange at first. More I dare not say before the reverend lady your aunt."

"I know," said Elizabeth, scornfully. "I know everything."

Mistress Tryfellow laughed and kissed her.

"Plucked you may look," Lady Philippa wept a little, bending over the head on the silken pillow, "but like a plucked angel, Niece, so take heart." She made the sign of the cross over Elizabeth and also kissed her. "The first daughter you bear shall be my godchild."

The men burst in, red and roaring. Nudged by Mistress Tryfellow, Elizabeth smiled politely at those of the jokes which were not quite so explicit that she must feign ignorance of their meaning. The men undressed Luke, and Elizabeth screwed up her eyes. More shouts and jests, laughter and blessings—and suddenly they were all gone, and only she and Luke and the bed remained.

Luke cleared his throat.

Elizabeth closed her eyes the more tightly. She opened them and stiffened as she felt his weight on the bed. There he was, in his long linen shirt, his old-familiar, freckled face, his lush red hair, about to get into bed beside her. Disbelief was no longer possible. It was done, it was true, she had been married to Luke, whom she had always known, and always known fully dressed. There is no horror like that of the familiar set slightly awry: a dragon is not so horrible as a calf with two heads.

Elizabeth started up in bed and opened her mouth, and screamed. She made no other movement, she merely went on screaming, as if hoping to beat him off with her voice alone. A hush fell on the dance and song in the rooms below, but was followed by the greatest uproar yet of laughter and cheers.

Now Luke was maddened by this. He had felt sorry for her when he came in. They had verily peeled him a child from those blazing bride wrappings. The poor thing could not but be frightened. Gentle tenderness filled him, aided, perhaps, by his late apprehensions. That she should take on so now angered him inexpressibly. He could have strangled her for it, carrying on as if he were a ravening wolf or a fiend—he, who had been her best friend all her life. Not only had the whole of Bedesford heard—the whole of Bedesford thought that deed already done, at which he was so fearful of failing.

"End your screeching, you screech owl," he said, "before they ring fire at Cloudsway—before they think out at Ovisham we're sticking pigs at this ungodly hour—before the burghers of Calais think the war is come to them again! By Heaven, but I will give you something to shout for—"

Down below, the witch lay shivering among the woolsacks where she had crawled to stop her ears. Everybody else was happy. Juliana was at least unconscious. Little John went from room to room, tickling the women that had fallen off the benches.

Part Five
Elizabeth
(1361-1366)

CHAPTER I

THE MISTRESS OF SMITHY YARD

MISTRESS ROBINSON of Smithy Yard did not rise until the sun was well up in the sky which, round about Candlemas time, was halfway through the morning. Now that it was certain she was with child, her husband had suffered her to divide the great bed of nights with bolsters banked down the middle. Every morning, directly he had left her, she would undo the barrier, draw the clothes over her head, and play by herself a game of Eremelgna.

When she had had enough of that, she would get up. She would not let her maids attend her in the mornings, because it amused her to make a slovenly toilet. Sometimes, when air and water were too cold, she would not even wash her eyes and finger tips. She put on whatever she had a fancy to, and if for many days together this happened to be the banqueting gown Luke had given her for the Christmas festivities—if its gold lacing became tarnished, the sleeve ends torn from being trodden on so often, the hem board stiff with stains, and the trimming of stone marten draggled—so much the worse for it.

She wore it the day Sir Bertrand Jolybody's son came to call, on his way to friends at Clavis Green. Luke was at Shoemaker Yard, and Asphodel Jolybody was shown into the visitors' parlor while word was sent to the Master. He sat there, fidgeting in his solitude, and looking closely at everything about him with a mixture of jealous curiosity and superciliousness. He jumped when suddenly he grew aware of a child regarding him with a sort of inquisitive detachment. He had not heard her come into the room because her bare feet made no noise on the tiles, marred now by bold muddy prints. Albeit not in his own house, the tailor's son thought he could not do amiss in shooing the creature from the room as you would a hen, amazed and aghast when she stood her ground. He stared at her and she stared at him, until he could endure it no longer and in a strangled voice bade her bring him something to drink. "Wait until you are offered a drink, forward guest," said the girl, and disappeared. He thought he could hear unholy laughter somewhere in the distance, after, and complained bitterly to Luke.

Although this was to him a very serious matter, Luke could not keep a wholly straight face, scolding Elizabeth, for she giggled so infectiously, and it was not often these days that they really laughed together.

"Well, you have told me so often that it is for the mistress to entertain guests in the master's absence, that I thought I must make a start. There is no pleasing you," Elizabeth said, with feigned sulking.

"Now you will make me really angry!"

"You would not think so highly of your fine guest, had you seen him as I did, picking his nose as he thought himself alone. Oh, you should have seen him start! Oh, dear, I dare think of it no more, lest I die of laughter!"

"You know well all this is beside the point. He thought you a servant, some beggar orphan employed in the poultry yard for charity."

"All the more dishonor to him, to demean himself and make great complaint!"

"—and so he deemed it needful to advise me, a Fleming, how to keep my English serving folk in check."

"Ay, that must have been galling!" Elizabeth sympathized maliciously. "What did you say?"

"What could I say? Should I have said, 'Oh, that ragged urchin as you called her, sir, that was my *wife*. My servants are all neat, hardworking folk that do their level best to make up for their mistress' negligence'? Is that what you would have had me say? I had to say my wife was on a visit with her mother, and discourteously refrain from pressing him to stay. What do you think I got me this great house for, I wonder?"

Elizabeth burst into tears. "I did not ask to be set over it. Everyone keeps on telling me how lucky I am, and listing all the gear we own as if I did not see it round me every day. I did not ask for any, any of it."

Luke could not bear to see her weeping. Besides, he told himself, it was bad for her just now. And so he finally gave in to her persistent demand that the woman Bess be sent from the house, for no better reason than that Elizabeth said she had taken an overmastering dislike to her.

After she had got her way, Elizabeth was even more unhappy. It was not true that she disliked Bess, who had shown her so much affection from the first, and her heart ached for the injustice of Bess's dismissal. But Bess's more serious love caused her concern for the young mistress's honor, so that she had long been the only one to reproach and implore Elizabeth to mend her ways.

Nobody realized—as how could they?—that Elizabeth did not enjoy acting in this manner. She herself could not understand that she did not enjoy it. The morning after her wedding she had promised herself that henceforth she would do as she liked in all things, no matter how inconsistent her caprice. Against her will they had made her the richest matron in Anglemere, so now she would take every advantage.

Juliana had taken to her bed for a spell after the wedding, and for the remainder of that year had never been quite well enough to leave Trefeller Court. At Christmas her daughter and son-in-law had gone to visit her. Now in February she at last announced she was coming to see them at Smithy Yard.

Elizabeth dressed with more care than usual and shamefacedly made a circuit of the house to see that all was as it should be. She went into the kitchen to consult with the women, who automatically cleared a corner of the dresser, where she was in the habit of swinging herself up to sit and chat. Today she remained at a distance, erect, with hands becomingly folded at waist height. She saw that they were all either smiling or hard put to it to suppress a smile. She felt utterly cast down by the humiliation that they should have penetrated her fear of her mother, and so she abandoned all her good intentions and with a haughty phrase left everything to them.

Juliana had Jane in attendance. Elizabeth was surprised, even taken aback. After the wedding Jane as a matter of course had pleaded to be allowed to stay at Smithy Yard for at least the first year—the first month —the first week of Elizabeth's married life. As a matter of course, Juliana had refused. Having given up the man she loved to her daughter, was she to throw in the one person on whom her peace and comfort were dependent? Yet their relationship was not what it had been up to the time of the betrothal. Jane's constant defense, that she could not have done anything against her mistress' inmost wishes, had gradually assured the widow that she had far greater power over Jane than she had ever previously thought possible. At the same time, she thought the less of Jane's powers. Jane had neither helped Juliana, nor extricated Elizabeth from an undesired fate. And Elizabeth herself thought much the same.

Juliana could have given no clearer proof of her feelings than by serenely leaving Jane and Elizabeth alone together when she asked Luke to take her to the countinghouse. She would have smiled to see the two of them sit in constrained silence for some little time.

"Well, my Elizabeth?" Jane asked in the end, with a sigh. "How goes it with you, child? I have heard so little about you—I suppose I must account that a good sign. If you had needed me, no doubt you would have found a way of letting me know. I take it that your marriage has turned out as I hardly dared hope. After all, you find yourself well contented with your husband?"

Elizabeth could no longer maintain her stiff, assumed indifference. "Cruel, cruel are you, Ganna, to say this to me. And you know that you are. You mean to be! You know my need right enough, and my misery. You did naught to avert it, and now you accuse me of the vilest unfaithfulness! Nay, it cannot be true after all, that you know what you are saying, else would you not break my heart, accusing me of contentment!"

Jane took her in her arms, kissing and trying to calm her. "Do you remember what I used to tell you? That you are my daughter, and will have to suffer even as I did ere we can be comforted, both of us?"

Elizabeth wrenched away and dried her tears with a vehement gesture. "I can never be comforted now. Alfred is lost to me, since they made him a monk."

"He is no monk as yet. It will be years before he can take final vows."

"Years! Am I to live like this for years? Rather would I die tomorrow."

Meanwhile, Luke and Juliana were conversing in the best of spirits. While he may not have admitted it to himself, Luke had missed talking with complete unreserve to someone who had his plans and schemes just as much at heart as he, and Juliana could not but sense his joy and relief.

"You see, Juliana, Lady Agnes had severed her last remaining connection with others, which means that if I were not an honest man I could now stop worrying about further improving the quality of Thirchester cloth. But I am not out for personal enrichment. What?"

Juliana had said nothing, merely glancing eloquently about her.

Luke threw up his hand. "If you do not believe me even now, how can I expect it of anyone else? All I want for myself are the means to carry on my struggle for the greatness and prosperity of this country. That is the truth. If it were not so, why would I trouble to go on improving our cloth? Now that we are of one family I don't mind telling you that I contrived to subsidize the weaving done at Trefeller Court so that you should not feel our working at a loss. You were, and still are, living on the wool trade in the main. As for me, agency for Damesbury Castle and Thirchester Nunnery, commissions on behalf of Cloudsway Waste, and above all provision of silks and spices and other overseas wares, have kept me going."

After a pause, Juliana asked what must be asked sometime. "Well, and how do you like life as a married man, son-in-law?"

Luke laughed a little, a little wryly. "I trow it takes some getting used to, like anything new. I am still learning."

"What? Have you come to regret it, so soon?" Juliana herself could not have said what answer she would liefest hear.

"No, no. I got the wife I wanted, and would have no other. She is still the fairest, sweetest, it is only that—to you, her mother, I may surely speak of it—shall I say she is something too pure, too chaste? And before we were made one flesh, there was between us a trust and openness and ease of understanding—all that is gone. Maybe it will come back one of these days." He ended on a note of inquiry.

"Has she *said* anything to you?"

"Oh, no, not a word, excepting that she asked me to let her alone now until our child is born, and that, I deemed, is not unreasonable."

"I remember," said Juliana, carefully, "when first I lived with my John, I was so fond of him, I thought it a degradation and a danger to be so fond of a man—so foolish are young women!—and so I said to him more than once, to protect my pride, you understand, that I had been *made* to marry him. Perhaps Elizabeth?"

"Nay, so fond of me as that she is not!" Luke grimaced ruefully. "But she will be one day, I hope and trust, when she comes to appreciate how lovingly I see to it that she gets her every wish. What did he say, your husband, when you spoke to him thus?" he asked, with sudden curiosity.

"Oh, he laughed, I think. He knew. He, too, was a great deal older than I. But I must tell you, from the first day I spent in his house, I was left in no doubt who was the master. Therein you may have failed a little, Luke."

Luke could not refrain from a little mockery. "He was a better man than I, your John, that is all I can say. He must have held a powerful secret."

Juliana smiled also. "Maybe so, Luke. Withal you are falsely modest. Mind you not how often I have let myself be ruled by you? With me you could always be stern when you thought it needful. Why not with her, your wife?"

"She is so young."

"If you wait until she is older, you will find it the more difficult to bend her to your will."

"Well, what am I to do? One thing, I will not have her upset."

"Then there is not much can be done, is there?"

"Perhaps," Luke said diffidently, "if it were not too much trouble, perhaps you would look in on her a little when I go away? It would be too much to ask you to come and live in my house during that time, I know, but it would make me feel so much easier about leaving."

He would never have guessed that he had transported Juliana into seventh heaven. "Luke, I will do it, though God knows my own house takes up enough of what little strength I have. On one condition, nay, two, I will do it. The one is that you will let me speak to my own daughter, for her own good, Luke, as well as yours. I promise not to lay a finger on her."

"And the other?" Luke smiled.

"The other is that you will listen to one more word of advice. You know you have no better friend than me, and none more zealous for your welfare—"

"Yes, I know that. If you call these conditions, I accept them both."

"Well then, Luke; you really must try to do something about your Flemings."

"What about *my* Flemings?"

"You see, you are already growing angry! Still, it is high time someone told you. If it were not for Lady Agnes, Luke, and for me—Philippa is right out of patience with them, as is everybody excepting only yourself that are familiar with their ways of old. Everything is better, where they come from. They must have bath houses, and wall fireplaces—"

"I thought you had changed your opinion about fireplaces! But what is wrong with the Flemings having them, and bath houses as well, since they build them for themselves in their spare time."

"So much industry is not natural, Luke. What with their everlasting boasts of all things Flemish, what are folk to think but that the Flemings work so hard in order to shame and scorn those that take their well-earned rest?"

"I have never heard anything so ill natured or farfetched."

"It is what folk are saying, Luke. And they are proud and haughty, the Flemings, there is no denying that. Look how they keep to themselves, south of the cathedral. They do not even sin with Bedesford wenches."

"Is that to be held against them? Since when were you an advocate of vice?"

"I am only repeating what I hear every day. Folk say that the Flemings shun fornication in reproach to all that do not. Where the very monks are frail, it is wickedly prideful to be so very continent."

"I cannot understand what you want me to do, Juliana, since it is clear whatever they do will be held against my poor friends. No doubt I myself fare no better."

"Oh, no, you are different. You are not as other Flemings. Folk still hold to that."

Luke sighed, pulled a face, shook his head and laughed, promising to think over what she had told him and see what he could do.

Before she went home, Juliana asked to speak with her daughter. Elizabeth, in her well-brushed dark gown and starched headdress, rose without a word and without the merest pretence of a smile. Luke gazed after them expectantly and made an effort to exchange a few words about the weather with Jane.

"Do you never do aught but glower?" Juliana asked her daughter, who stood stock still before her.

"I am not going to let you beat me!"

"I do not recall ever having needed your permission," Juliana returned, but not at all angrily. "But now I would not so dishonor your husband. He must be a saint, not to have beaten you himself, to be sure you can now shield you behind his unborn son. The way you deal by his property would be grave sin against God if Smithy Yard belonged to a heathen Saracen instead of your own Christian husband. If you have no love for him and no regard for your soul's future, do you care as little for the young life you have been blessed to bear? Have you not heard the friars preaching on how the parents' sins are visited on the children? Look what happened to me for my parents' sins! Every time your husband calls you fair, remember you have my virtue and your father's to thank for that! Not that *I* think you so very fair, but you are straight and healthy and clear witted. I should have liked to know my grandson assured of at least the same!"

Elizabeth was weeping bitterly, in a way she had never previously wept before her mother. It can be seen that Juliana, had not her own heart been torn in conflict, might easily have found other methods to make Elizabeth amenable to marriage than those that she had employed. And who knows, if she had done that, whether Elizabeth would not then have submitted truly, instead of holding on, with that part of her which no human hand could touch and no eye see, to that obstinacy which under torture acquires the title of integrity? And *then*, who knows—but it is bootless to speculate about what did not happen.

CHAPTER 2

NOVICE AND PRIOR

JULIANA HAD LESS faith in verbal argument than in blows. She had insisted on Luke's permission to talk to Elizabeth merely in order to reassert her parental claim on his wife. She was entranced in the prospect of becoming after all the real mistress of Smithy Yard, enjoying the confidences of its master and full power over his household. She felt so secure, that Jane could go to visit Elizabeth openly and by day.

"Are you alone? Are we likely to be disturbed? Where can we go to be safe from intrusion?" she asked, as soon as Elizabeth joined her in the little parlor. The listlessness of Elizabeth's greeting instantly changed into tense elation. They went up to the master bedroom.

From the folds of her cloak Jane unwrapped a small figure of wood, cracked and tinderish with antiquity, but stained with obviously recent color. "This is Saint Uncumber. Have you never heard of her?"

"Of her?" Elizabeth pointed at the bearded head of the image, clad squarely in its long wooden shift, and standing rigidly erect, with rigid outspread arms.

"Yes. In life she was a king's daughter, like me, who was forced into marriage, like you. She prayed to Our Lady for a beard to spoil her beauty and preserve her virginity. Her prayer was granted, the bridegroom turned from her with loathing, and thereupon her father put her to the sword, so that she went straight up to Heaven and a seat among the blessed. I will instruct you in her rites, that she may uncumber you of your husband. Receiving scant service in these days, the poor lady is apt to make the most of such honors as are paid her, and to take her time about acceding to the suppliant's request. Let her see you grudge her nothing, and be diligent in performance."

"Oh, Ganna!" Elizabeth was incoherent with gratitude, undampened by the hints of morose apprehension in Jane's rejoinder. And she could not get Jane to tell her where and how she had found the image.

Henceforth, without fail, Elizabeth prayed daily before St. Uncumber, morning and evening. She kept this from her confessor, telling herself that praying to a saint was no sin and therefore outside his province. So far from feeling unrighteous, her heart was lighter than it had been for a long time.

She went to church often, and this was the one thing in which she had valued the benefits of the married estate from the first. Her place was in the front rank among the housewives.

None that has not done without a parish church, as we had for thirteen years, can rightly estimate our delight in the cathedral opened to our worship. Abbot William had kept his word, and the lay congregation was allowed into both upper transepts and the unfinished part beyond the choir, and, provided we did not interrupt the work in progress, we had the freedom of the site for transacting the business of the town. Every soul in Bedesford waxed more and more assiduous in religious observances. Oh, we were good then, and goodness was no hardship, but the very breath of happiness in our lives.

When the Bishop had still been in Bedesford, immediately after the consecration, the central tower competition had been ceremonially judged. Besides Master Colet and Jacob, the competitors included Prior Haakon, Brother Laurentius, a Westminister man, and one or two other foreign building masters. Naturally, each of these had perfected his design over a period of months. However, for pious appearances' sake, each was immured on the appointed day in a separate Benedictine cell vacated for the occasion. The idea was that each would issue thence with direct inspiration. In fact, all that was left for them to do was spoil their drawings with finishing touches and pray hard.

The Bishop chose Jacob Tewsing's design, which had the advantage in that New Bede's Bridge was to some extent a model of it. But also it was very beautiful. We will attempt to describe it, for alas, go to view it you cannot, and the bridge is too small and crude in comparison, with totally different proportions.

It stood on four gigantic, pointed arches, each with another, inverted one poised upon its apex and rising to the support of the roof. The curvedly triangular spaces between the shoulders of the basal arcs were braced with circular tracery.

We were allowed to see the winning design—for that matter, the losers were more than willing to exhibit theirs—and although this great work could not but proceed very slowly indeed, you may imagine the breath-taking excitement of watching it take shape in bodily earnest. About Master Stephen's demeanor, the next few months, the less said, the better. The stranger competitors simply returned where they had come from; Brother Laurentius possessed himself with humility and said, with perfect truth, that after all he had never really been an architect. As for Prior Haakon, all of whose experience lay in timber structures, he was too selfless to care. Also, he was much too ill.

He was so ill he died at Easter. There was hardly anyone alive who remembered Anglemere without him. He had been Prior, first of all, at Ovisham, since 1335, and afterward had not stirred outside Bedesford for over fifteen years. We were fortunate to have known in him the pattern ideal of a good priest—unlike such good monks as Brother Oswin, and even Abbot William's successor, Prior Haakon had no earthly passion whatever to sidetrack his love of God and God's poor.

After the requiem Mass Elizabeth saw Alfred, but he did not look at her. At least she might weep freely, as everybody wept still for Prior Haakon.

Alfred was rarely seen at the cathedral now, mostly he had to attend Mass at the chapel behind the palisades. But at long intervals he was permitted to have visitors. His mother came, with her whole family, excepting Edwin.

The porter had got leave for them to await Alfred in the garden. Jeanne had sat down on a low stone bench between flower beds and currant bushes, with all her little ones closely about her. Alfred hesitated at the vine-wreathed gateway. It was so seldom that she could thus take her ease. In fact, he had never seen her, simply sitting, with her eyes closed and face turned up quietly toward the feeble sun, so that he was loath to disturb her. But the children saw him and called out.

Before they met she suddenly stopped still again, and, catching their mother's unexpected, deep shyness, the children stared and blushed openmouthed at Alfred in his cloister garb.

"Nay, Mother, you would not rise for *me*." cried Alfred, ushering them all back to the bench. "Nay, Janet, a big girl like you, would you cry on sight of your old brother Alfred? Oh, Martha, I know well you bite your thumb only in the face of strangers. It is only me, the same as ever!"

"That you are not," Jeanne said, with her shy smile. "Not so long ago you would not have thought of driving me back to sit! So courteous are you now and withal so easy, we cannot but become more bumpkin-like every moment, your brothers and sisters and I."

Accustomed to the Master of Novices' disciplinary sarcasm, Alfred flushed darkly, but then he realized his mother meant exactly what she said. In truth, to Jeanne he was not merely a few months older, without any change in appearance, but that his arms and legs were hid. He was an entirely different being. She looked up to this raw, floor-scrubbing, dung-carting novice with reverence and pride.

She questioned Alfred about his life and companions, felt his collarbones to see whether he had put on any flesh, and in turn bade him feel for the four teeth in his youngest brother's gums.

"Oh, but it is pleasant out here!" she said, with a sigh, moving her head from side to side, and breathing deliberately. "We are so happy in your good fortune, your father and I. To think that you may be a bishop one day. I have heard tell of popes of no higher birth than you. There were enough signs, had we but had the wit to understand them from the first. Your hand, that in my foolishness I used to rail at the Lord God for—and which was surely meant for a sort of badge, linking you with St. Hand, for when the miracle occurred I was pregnant of you, and thus you were marked."

"Mother!" Alfred tried several times to interrupt her; but the most he achieved was getting her to lower her voice somewhat.

"Why should I hush? I am speaking nothing but the truth. And then—think you your mother did not mark it?—you have been tried full hard before you have even reached manhood. None could have born it better than my son did."

"Father has not come with you?"

Jeanne did not answer at once, gazing round vaguely as though to make sure that Edwin was not with her. "No, Alfred. He is hard pressed with work, Alfred. They have put him on the diapered half columns for the Nazareth porch."

"I know. I have looked for him there several times lately."

"Children," said Jeanne, "look over there where the good monks have

planted Lord Jerome's mulberries. Just be careful how you step, and
don't touch anything. Sit you down beside me, Alfred. I do not think it
can be wrong to tell you this: that Edwin loves none of our children
more than he does you. I can see you wonder that he has not come to
see you. Your father is not as other men. To this day I do not know
the half of his thoughts. But it is my belief that he has never ceased
repenting our sin, of which you were the fruit. He is ever dreading that
some mishap may befall you. He wants to see you safe in God's good
books, that is why he is so glad you are to be a monk. But I want you
to understand that if he shuns you it is for your sake that he so denies
himself."

His mother's explanation seemed to fit in with occasional hints on
Edwin's part, yet it did not satisfy Alfred entirely. He thought this
might be merely because it had come, unexpectedly, from her. He could
not remember ever having heard her talk in such vein.

Jack Oxerd was now known as Franklin because he was a free man.
Franklin and Joan Oxerd and their son made no bones about culti-
vating one whom they expected one day to become an influential relative. They brought him a basket woven of split rushes and filled with
thrush eggs.

"Now we must make sure you will not forget your kin in your greatness, Alfred," said Franklin the elder. "It comes hard to a free man who
prizes his independence as I do, to make presents for a purpose and
not from simple fullness of heart. Your cousin Joan made this, and your
cousin Frank risked neck and limbs to gather these that we hope may
oil your throat and keep your strength up."

"Take heart, Uncle," Alfred said, laughing, "for your kind gift can
serve no purpose but kindness. First, can you believe it of me that I
would forget you? Second, I may not keep these eggs, but will have
to hand them straight in to the kitchens. Third, I must not sing above
a whisper these days, for, as you can hear, my voice has started whoop-
ing up and down. And lastly, I am the lowliest thing they have here."

"Who is to say," Franklin waved his hand, "that you will not be
abbot here one day, or something of the kind, all the same?"

"You are as bad as my mother, Uncle. If every novice became an
abbot, there would not be many ordinary monks. Not every novice
even gets to be a monk."

"Nay, but you will," Joan chimed in, stoutly.

"If you will pray God to accept me, Aunt, I should take it as great
kindness."

"Certainly we shall pray for you, all three of us," Franklin said, and he let it be seen he thought this a most crafty move on his part. "But you, right close to God's ear as you live here, do you then, pray for us in exchange!"

With the exception of Jeanne, the Oxerds had never been great workers, her one surviving brother the laziest of the lot. But James Smith had not the heart to part with him. The magniloquence constantly issuing from the little man never failed to cheer his master, who had entered Bedesford poorer than these Oxerds, and who could live content for days without uttering a word.

Everyone pitied in advance any man sent to succeed Prior Haakon, whose example it must be almost impossible to live up to. The new prior, for some years chantry priest to a great lord in Lancaster, reached Bedesford shortly before midsummer. It was soon seen that no one need be sorry for Prior Carlos Trinidad. If anybody deserved compassion, it was the Little Gray Brethren.

He was a short man, scarcely taller than Edwin, his skin yellow as oiled parchment, his chaplet of black hair mixed with gray; he had a knife-edge nose, long tapering hands; his voice sounded like a wooden screw forced home in haste; and he spoke English so badly it was as marvelous as his predecessor's proficiency in our language. When first he stood before his flock, addressing them, they were disconcerted by the clank of iron, stressing his abrupter movements. For soldered round his waist under the harsh gown he wore a chain. Before you were used to it, the thought of the sores it must girdle made your flesh crawl. He was so schooled to this mortification that he was able to control its sound, muting it entirely if he so desired, and deliberately using it to startle, overawe, and reproach.

His first interest was in the hospital's infirmary.

"*Multum parvum est,*" he said curtly, as they showed him over it. "*Quod ratione?*"

"Before the Black Death, Reverend Father, what is now the pilgrims' hall used to be the infirmary. But since then we have had more and more wanderers to accommodate, and fewer and fewer sick come to us. As most of them come but to stay overnight, meaning to seek healing of St. Hand, or else of Jane, we let the sick sleep with the hale, except they are dying, to be sure. So this closet more than suffices."

"*Cui 'Zhane'?*"

"A local leech wife, Reverend Father."

"I have read a copy of the collected accounts of the Hand's cures up to 1356. With so potent a healer at hand," the Prior punned, using an English interpolation, "what can anyone want with some superstitious old crone?"

"She is not very old—"

"Ah!"

"The people are poor, Reverend Father. This Jane more often than not refuses recompense. And there are so many minor ills that folk do not like to go troubling St. Hand with. And two things St. Hand cannot cure, it has been found. Leprosy is one, and any affliction of the hand another—"

"Have we any lepers here?" Prior Carlos broke in eagerly.

"No, Reverend Father. We never had a lazaretto charter in Bedesford. The nearest lazaretto is at Ovisham. We do very occasionally give shelter to passing lepers—in wintertime, when there are few wanderers."

"And this Zhane, will she see lepers?" the Prior asked, narrowing his eyes.

"Not so far as known. I doubt she would risk going so far against the law. You must know, Reverend Father, she lives in a great, teeming household that no leper would dare approach. And even if they feared neither law nor contagion, the Mistress and her son-in-law would never allow it." The friar explained the utilitarian charities of Trefeller Court which, weakening the position of the hospital, had for years fed the Franciscans' growing antipathy to Luke. Prior Carlos Trinidad grimly heard him out without any interruption.

He went on to question the friars as to every detail of local conditions. But we must say this for him, that he did not rest until he had supplemented their report with seeing for himself, until he was familiar with everything, from the lie of the land to the faces of people and their names and antecedents. The trouble was that, in loving remembrance of Prior Haakon, the people for the most part were prepared to resent the newcomer. And though none can deny that his ways made it easy to dislike him, we must also admit that the reception he met with was not calculated to soften his manner or his views.

His third Sunday in office, he called the friars together again after Vespers.

"My sons and brethren. Something will have to be done. Before God placed me amongst you, I was given to understand that nowhere was our order's influence so great as in this country of Anglemere, and particularly in Bedesford. Investigation has confirmed that indeed it used once to be so. Aged and ill as he was, the late Father Haakon's slackening the reins is perhaps not to be wondered at. Have any of you any suggestions? Yes, Brother Edmund?"

"You wrong the sainted Father Haakon, Reverend Father," the friar spoke up respectfully. "It is only since the cathedral was consecrated that we have preached to well-nigh empty meadowland. To be sure, in him we lost an incomparable preacher—"

"It is becoming and pleasing in you to speak up for your late superior. Your affection is a testimonial to my predecessor's character. Complete lack of discipline within this hospital and the absence of respect I have encountered outside, to say nothing of the groveling diplomacy that I find is expected of me on Benedictine territory—these, I fear, form incontrovertible proof of his practical failings. The irony of the whole situation, as well as the key to it, lies in the crypt of the cathedral, whose misappropriation is brazenly affirmed by its unchanged dedication."

"In truth, there was nothing we could do to prevent that, Reverend Father. Belike you do not know all the circumstances—"

"Pray credit me with a little common sense, Brother Wilfred. I am quite aware of how it all happened. But would you not call him fool and coward, in ordinary life, that failed to cry, 'thief!' and run in pursuit of the robber when the deed was done? What, then, would you call one who *did* run after the robber, but only to kiss his hand and beg to be allowed to carry the loot for him? Yes, Brother Laurentius?"

"I was going to ask, might one not call such a one a model Christian?"

"I will even concede you that, my son. One *might*. It requires a subtletry which I know well is all too rare, to decide correctly when to be meek and when militant. I am quite sure the late Father Haakon exercised such wit as he had conscientiously, and I am not recriminating. I but wish to inform you that I intend to pursue an altogether different course."

He paid his first formal visit to Lord William as the Bishop's vicar. In his capacity of Abbot, Lord William had so far evaded his Franciscan brother, having had him received by proxy. Each time the Prior had called, he had been made to state his business, which had then been referred to various monks in charge of appropriate offices.

For what seemed a long time Lord William sidetracked Prior Carlos with courteous questions as to what sort of journey he had had, what he thought of the weather and its prospects for the winter, and so on. The Prior clanked his chain in vain. Whether it was that the Abbot relented in the end or that he grew careless, at last the host asked what the newcomer thought of Bedesford. Quick as a swooping hawk, the Prior answered that it struck him as an uncommonly lawless parish.

"Ay, the Easterwoods are sore infested with outlaws," Lord William nodded sadly. "I have often thought it would be a most worthy and most useful enterprise for the preaching friars to undertake a serious apostolic mission, a sort of unarmed crusade, into this wilderness of ours."

Prior Carlos pretended to admire this as an inspired suggestion. "And I will most surely crave the Bishop's formal sanction of it—as soon as we have stamped out the lawlessness rife among the so-called law abiding, which must be our first concern. There is this man Robinson, for example. I taxed him with his malpractices. The knave pleads ignorance, which, of course, is no defense in law."

"What sort of crime? Smuggling, usury, tithe, or tax evasion?"

"I should not put any of these past him, but the offense I have in mind, which he carries on quite openly, is laying exclusive possession to the trading in certain commodities, as the statute puts it."

"If that is all, I fear we can do nothing. I fear if he were charged with that, we might find ourselves accused of high treason! His Grace of Lancaster, in company with the great Richard Lyon of London, is noted far and wide for that same practice, on an infinitely larger scale—"

"You can hardly compare Luke Robinson with the King's second son!"

"Neither," said the Abbot, gravely, "can you so compare their activities. Luke has never harmed anyone. Whereas those others already have two families to their credit."

"I see I am not to look for your support in combating crime."

"Say no more, lest you say too much, and find cause to regret it, my friend," the Abbot amiably cut him short. "If so be you came to me with 'crime' worthy of the name—"

"Would you say, then, that sorcery comes under that head? Very well, there is a flagrant case of it. A woman, without brief from any barbers' guild, or church license, doctoring all comers. I happen to come of a long line of physicians, at home in Castile, and myself confess to some trifling medical skill, so that I can judge of this woman's doings. I have tried my best, speaking to the people with kindness and helpful advice, but so firm is this evil woman's hold, that even the more respectable townfolk refuse to listen to me. Farmer Smith's wife even barred my approach to the cradle when in pure benevolence I bent to

see what her fat brat was squalling for. Do you mean to tell me that
you have heard nothing about her philters and spells and dancing under
the Weird Oak at the full moon?"

"Rumors. Shall priests of God lend ear to idle gossip? Have you any
proof, or witnesses?"

"One of these days," the Prior rose, whispering with fury, "I shall
bring you proof. I shall bring you witnesses."

"And you shall find me most ready to examine them," the Abbot
promised with an encouraging nod of dismissal.

The substance of this interview was common property by evening.

Prior Carlos went also to the manor. But in the presence of a mere
temporal lord he employed so overbearing a tone that he hardly got
beyond his opening phrases before Lord Hugh bade his men-at-arms
cast the Barefoot headfirst into the moat.

CHAPTER 3

THE TEMPTATIONS

LUKE WAS GONE and Juliana was coming, and would be in his place
of nights by Elizabeth's side. There was no time to be lost in taking
St. Uncumber out of the bedstraw. The maids were rushing all over
the house in diligent anticipation of Mistress Trefeller.

Between the Robinsons' farmyard and Walter Greene's meadow lay a
small wilderness where Luke meant one day to have a herbary and
pleasure garden. There stood what in the old days had been the least
and poorest of the dwelling workshops composing the yard of smiths.
Elizabeth had stumbled on it by accident when Luke had first acquired
the place.

Having pulled the wooden idol from the bed, Elizabeth dressed herself ready to go out, concealing St. Uncumber under her cloak. Sure
enough, before she could leave the room two serving women came panting in with fresh straw and festal coverings, and began at once to pull
the old bedding to pieces.

"We thought—it best, we thought—you—would—have it thus, Mistress," they ejaculated, between vigorous heaves, bestrewing the floor

with bolsters and flattened hay. "Your mother shall find naught to cavil at—at Smithy Yard. Are you thinking of going out? Mistress Trefeller will be here before noon."

"It is early yet. I have a mind to go to St. Hand's, as I feel low, and it will cheer me. You know I did not go last Sunday. I want no company. It is such a fine day, and dry."

Elizabeth managed to slip out of the house by a back way without encountering any more of her busy servants. Out of sight behind the farmyard buildings, she knew herself safe, let the hood slide down and raised her face, taking in the free air, the more delicious for that she breathed it all alone. Soon she had to take care and look where she was going, hold up her skirts and wrap them close that the undergrowth might not tear them or bring her to fall. Then she squeezed through between the young firs and slim leafless ash trees, that had reduced the walls once flanking a door to mounds of loose rubble. There had never been any windows; a little light filtered inside through the smoke vent and gaps in the roof and walls. The house was inhabited by brambles, nettles and bracken, shoulder high. Elizabeth laid the saint on a stone and looked about for a good place. Along one wall, under the weeds, she found an earth bank which doubtless had served as a bed. The edge was crumbling and soft enough for her to dig into the side with her hands. She made a hole which she lined with flat stones and shored up with a lattticework of sticks. There she hid St. Uncumber, pulled the downtrodden weeds together so as to screen the image, rubbed her hands clean and dusted her clothes, and hurried away, round by the fields, to avoid the main road. Her dress was in sad disarray, but none who met her beyond the green thought it unusual to see Mistress Robinson with headgear askew and withered leaves, burs, and thorny twigs clinging to her goodly gown.

At the site more people offered to detain her than she had looked for, on a weekday. At last she escaped to the cathedral, but as soon as she could, decently and without attracting attention, she left again and ran across to the monastry. And there, for a wonder, she did find Alfred this time.

He was in the garden, tending a bonfire. Its sweet pungent smoke had caused her to pull herself up on tiptoe and gaze over the paling. Alfred on the other side raised his eyes at the same moment. After a little Alfred dropped the stick with which he had been stirring the pyre and came over to her. On his side of the fence there was a large stone, enabling him to climb up and lean over on his elbows, so that she need not stretch.

Alfred had grown. His shoulders were broader, arms thicker, with muscles more prominent than the joints which had used to stand out most. His face was browner than ever, his shining eyes and thoughtful mouth and brow manlier than of old.

Hot after all her fast walking, Elizabeth had thrown back her cloak so that it hung down behind, without covering even the shoulders, and he saw without meaning to look her new-rounded breasts and rounding belly. He clenched his teeth.

He could not help himself. He whispered, "My Elizabeth." Had he not whispered it, it had been a groan.

"Alfred," she said, as though she must fetch up the name from the bottom of her heart. He put a hand over each of hers and pressed them, and then let go and withdrew his own quickly, and made the stake-tips prick hard into his palms. Now they neither of them knew what to say. They asked each other how they had been faring, and both answered, "Well." After a pause Elizabeth added, "And now it is so that I am with child, Alfred." Her eyes brightened, but did not overflow, with tears.

Alfred nodded. "And you are not glad?" Her tears began to fall. "You must not harm it with weeping," he remonstrated awkwardly.

Elizabeth swallowed and rubbed her eyes. At least this made her move her hands away so that the sight of their childlike, prisonerlike clutching no longer tore his heart in two. "No," she said, "I am loving it already, the times when I can believe in it." Now she laughed a little. "No, Alfred, but I am afraid, afraid for it. If only I could see it and watch over its growing! With none can I ease my heart as with you, Alfred. Alfred, I never feel sick, the way a woman ought."

"My mother was not sick every time, with hers. Surely, if you feel well and strong, it cannot but be of good health, too."

"So Ganna says also. Let me look at you, Alfred," she said, as if she had been doing anything else, and frowned as though she saw him far in the distance. "Today I want to look at you, for it, that it may grow like you to look at. Alfred, you will love him, won't you?" She had thought she might tell him she wanted the babe to resemble him not only for her soul's comfort, but also because it would be easier for them thus, when the time came that they might yet be man and wife. But she found she could not bring herself to say this.

"To be sure I shall. How could I not?"

"Alfred, now I want us to talk about you and me—"

"No! That is something we may not talk about, if we are to go on knowing each other, friends."

Elizabeth stared at him, as he might be a stranger, voicing unheard-of sentiments. Albeit he knew he was right and knew what it cost him, he felt guilty and ashamed. She made him feel that he was failing her, that he was no better than my lord when he used to cast off those that had trusted him with their love.

"So you want me to bear this burden all alone," she said, with a touch of scorn.

"This is a burden we may not share, though you know well you are not alone in bearing it," Alfred answered sorrowfully.

"Forgive me," Elizabeth said, after a pause, and sighed. "I must go soon. My mother is coming this morning." Alfred, too, looked round at the faintly rustling pyre. After that they were silent again and at a loss, yet loitering on, until it grew so late that finally they must part in haste, which meant, without renewed pain.

Alfred poked up the fire and fed it, then leaned on his stick and pensively watched the fresh jets of smoke. His gaze followed them to where they merged into one thick, wadded column, which unfurled, farther up, and melted into a misty likeness of Elizabeth, but an Elizabeth without a head or face. It was her body he saw, veiled not by decent, thick cloth, but in the flimsiest fluttering as of cobwebs or flowing water. It was the fruitlike breasts he saw and the curving beneath. His heart beat in his throat, and with the smoke's every sinuous writhing, waves of heat and cold succeeded each other down his spine. For sure the Devil must have stolen into his heart the while it stood unlocked, unguarded in Elizabeth's presence. "Away, avaunt!" he said under his breath, crossed himself and looked elsewhere—but the image of the smoke remained before his eyes like a bandage. So he shut his eyes. For an instant the smoke teased him once more, red and green now against the background of uncolored darkness. Then worse supplanted it.

He knew how children were got, but he had never pictured it. When he had felt his heart break, watching as Elizabeth and Luke were wedded, he had not asked himself why he should feel so. What had made him roam all over the building ground, wringing his hands and giving his feet leave to break his neck for him if they would, all through the night after the wedding? Only now did he know why: because it had been the wedding night, because Luke would possess Elizabeth—in that sense of his possession Elizabeth was indeed lost to Alfred. Now, with his eyes closed, he saw them getting the child she carried. And it was not only that thereupon he hated Luke with such a hatred that any previous feeling paled to a tolerant distaste. In his mind's eye there was pictured not only the slaying of Luke and the tearing him away from his wife, but there was also the leaping of Alfred into Luke's place.

He went through the rest of the day as in a dream. As in a dream, he suffered cuffs for his idle mooning, as in a dream lay on his knees in the chapel that night, took broom and pail in hand when the dawn came. If he were to be honest, he could not even call it a bad dream. For wrapped in it he experienced such delights—though the dream was a dream, the sense of delight was real.

As time went on, the dreaming was not dispelled. Wherever he went, whatever he was set to do, it held him, persecuted him with new variants. All things were food to it, fuel to the flame, manure to lurid proliferating flowers. He had no peace. In his sleep the dreams did not slacken, and he woke unrested.

To make matters worse, there was choice food for ribald talk just then.

The Abbot was shortly to embark on a round of inspection of all the religious houses of the See. Three times it had been postponed from year to year. Now, still prevented by pressure of affairs, Lord Jerome had written to empower Lord William in his stead.

Certain obstinate rumors made it necessary that Thirchester Nunnery be looked into. The nuns' close relations with the Flemish weavers, and Lady Agnes' frequent long visits, with her henchmen, had given rise to scandalous speculations.

"I myself doubt that there is anything in the rumor," Lord William said to Baldwin Cinqmort. "If there were, most likely no one would have heard anything of it. Usually, it is innocence comports itself so careless of appearances."

"For my sister's sake and the family honor, I hope that you are right."

"I feel sure of it, if only because I am acquainted with your sister. It amuses, though it can hardly surprise me as an old priest, that you, like most people, unhesitatingly assume the yet unproven charge is true."

"Then, even supposing you find nothing wrong, do you think the rumor will be silenced?"

"I think we can enforce penalties upon its repetition, of a sufficiently deterrent nature. With the poor nuns vindicated under the Bishop's seal,

I don't think that the punishment of libelers would provoke any sort of civic unrest?

Baldwin sighed. "Yet methinks I can hear folk saying it, that the clergy all hold together, anyway."

"What you mean is that folk will say *I* am hardly a trustworthy judge of the particular misdemeanor the nuns have been charged with. But I do not believe that many think as you do. For that matter, even you do not refuse the host at my hands, depraved though you evidently think me. As my priest's power cannot be impaired by my human failings, neither can descent of the Bishop's power on me be imperfect. On this journey I shall *be* the Bishop, and I am confident not only of acting accordingly, but also of being accordingly regarded." Baldwin looked abashed, but also a trifle astonished. The Abbot chose to see only the latter, and smote the table with his hand. "None can call me quick to take offense, but may I be damned if I expected you of all men to question my integrity! Nay, by God's blood, did you think I was going ajunketing to Thirchester?"

"No, no," Baldwin said, wretchedly. "I scarce know what was in my mind."

CHAPTER 4

THE FALL

Next Day the lesser fry of the monastery were marshaled to dig in the garden, and the Abbot made an unexpected appearance among them. He genially motioned to them to continue, and stayed to look on, exchanging a few words with the monk in charge.

"I wonder which of these could most easily be spared," the Abbot remarked, raising his voice, "to come to Thirchester with us. I find I am having to make a change."

"Need you take any of them, Reverend Father?" the monk, one of the small ascetic party, asked respectfully, expressing a fairly general opinion.

"I do not see why pious diligence should not occasionally meet reward on earth, nor why youth should necessarily be penalized. I should like to give one of these a treat. Whom would you suggest as most deserving?"

"They have all got their virtues, and all faults."

"That goes without saying," the Abbot laughed, also tapping his foot, however. "Alfred Widowson, come here."

"He is the youngest and least," the monk murmured, but not so that Alfred, springing to obey, failed to hear him.

"And is there no saying that the least shall be the first?" the Abbot tilted up Alfred's chin as if he were still a child. "How would you like joining the Bishop's train, Alfred?"

"He has been to Thirchester before," the monk interrupted nervously. "Many another has never been outside Bedesford."

"Why is it everyone constantly names Thirchester and never all the other houses in the diocese?" The Abbot frowned, forgetting that he himself had fallen into the same error at the outset of the conversation. "Your argument has no relevance. Have you any complaints of his behavior? If not, I think nothing further need be said."

Nevertheless there were some further attempts. The Master of Novices himself took the trouble to speak to Lord William, also Brother Oswin, whose concern had even less title. They soon realized that, had they said nothing, there might have been more hope of the Abbot's decision being revoked, or forgotten. He but grew so angry that it had in truth required more momentous cause for them to persevere.

None of this could remain secret at the monastery, and all and sundry speculated what induced Brother Oswin's wish thus to thwart his one-time darling. Some hinted it was jealous rivalry for Alfred's fond allegiance. But in the main the obvious explanation was accepted: that he feared for the lad at Thirchester.

Alfred himself was filled with sulky rage against his would-be protectors, whose endeavors rendered the promised boon even more desirable. He quoted to himself Lord William's reputed dictum: "Our Lord Himself needed to be tempted. Indeed, He needed to descend right into Hell. Without assault, there is no virtue."

The day of departure came at last. All the Abbot's train was mounted, Alfred sharing a horse with one of the men-at-arms who, behind the loaded sumpters, made up the rear. He had been given shoes and a clean gown. There was the first break in weeks of wet weather. The fresh air, making all colors look newly washed; the pale-glittering, wide sky, full of white and gray clouds that did not hide the sun; the sound of hoofs against stones and damp clay, and robustly cheerful voices; and the throb and movement of the horse, already stiffening his thighs in satisfying weariness; all combined to drive the sultriness and brooding from out of Alfred. Though he blushed when his saddle mate said he hoped for Alfred's sake that Lady Philippa's novices were pretty, it was no longer with that feeling of being unable to hold up his head.

In the field folk stopped toiling to salute the cortège. At the village of Cloudesley-St.-Veron's, their first halting place, all the people streamed forth to line the road and strew it with holly and spruce. The nunnery was next, its decorations fit for a king's tournament. Here as at Cloudesley, the inmates walked to meet Lord William, headed by Lady Philippa and the chaplain. The Abbess knelt to Lord William who leaped from his horse to raise her in his arms. In a clear voice she hailed him as the judge and defender of her house's honor. She and her flock were dressed in undyed, unsewn penitential robes, rope girdled, and with ashen stains upon their coifs. In the flagged refectory, however, bronze, silver, gold, and French and Venetian glass shone on whitest, figured linen, a relic of the days when Thirchester was famed for such manufacture, interspersed with roasting sucking pigs that had their ears cut into fringes and apples stuck in their mouths, red and white wine, and other sparkling delicacies. The Abbot decreed no business was to be transacted till the morrow. He and another member of Cloudsway chapter sat with Lady Philippa at the nuns' main table, the chaplain doing the honors at a separate one for the other monks; there was a third board, for lady sisters, postulants, and pensioners, and a fourth, set at right angles to the rest, for the henchmen.

"Lady Agnes' men," the Abbess thought needful to tell Lord William, "at all times fend for themselves in the largest guest house. We never see them save from afar, on arrival, and at Mass. They do not see us even then. As for the Fleming weavers, the Sister Portress and I are the only nuns to treat with them. They are never taken inside our workshops when the sisters are there. We do feast them on Christmas Day, when they sit where you see your servants today. Methinks it would be little to our honor to save our fame at the expense of openhanded courtesy—"

The Abbot waved his hand and diverted her with light and courtly talk.

At the monks' table, sedate merrymaking was slower to start. Food and drink also disappeared more slowly, as the guests could not keep their attention among themselves. The chaplain did his best to emulate Lord William's sociable fluency, but got less response. The many lights dazzled the eye with countless iridescent, intersecting aureoles. Sometimes one could hear wax sizzling or hitting the ground with small beady thuds. Alfred, at the bottom of the outside bench, had no one talking to him, watching without being drawn into frequent interchange of meaningful glances. He peeped at the novices, but distance and twinkling candle radiance rendered them all indistinct and alike.

Later they were conducted to the guest houses. Lord William shared the smallest and finest with the deacon and the scribe, each having a shuttered bed to himself. The monks were put in the largest building. They were not used to sleeping all together on two lines of unscreened benches facing each other along opposite walls. The sunken hearth fire, a cresset stone, and two torches stuck into iron holders near the door, provided friendly glow of warmth and of light. So it was a pleasant thing to yawn, chat, and stretch out communally. Alfred lay sleepless, and unregarded as before.

After matins the Bishop's deputy went around the nunnery, also looking into stores and accounts, with Lady Philippa at his elbow, although the chaplain made all the necessary explanations. The nuns had discarded yesterday's dress for their wonted habiliment. The Abbess, in a dark-blue gown and veil of soft nearblackness, was so fair as hardly to look human. The shining fleshliness which usually distinguished her beauty, like that which Little John Trefeller had inherited, had given way to a pale, transparent, otherworldly shimmer.

Lord William did not spare himself, not a cell was left uninspected. He had chairs arranged in the parlor, and a writing desk for his scribe, and asked that all the sisters be led before him one by one for interrogation and counseling. With him sat the deacon, one other monk, and the nuns' priest.

"Are you not going to call any of the lay folk round about, Reverend Lord," Lady Philippa asked, being the first to take the chair before the inquisitioners, "the farmers and villeins that have traduced us, and the Flemings that are our fellow victims?"

"No, for no formal accusation has been made. We are investigating a rumor, and that only incidentally. The Bishop does not wish to make it appear that we have taken heed of scandalmongering. After we have cleared you, we may take cognizance of what we shall then be able to denounce as baseless slander."

"You do not believe it, then?"

The Abbot grinned. "There is a note of—dare I call it disappointment, dear Mother?—in your question, which as far as I am concerned additionally disproves the charge. Nay, I entreat, do not frown. Justly proud as you are in the knowledge of the purity prevailing under your rule, you must surely agree with me that virtue can never shine so brightly abroad as when it has been called in question and has publicly defeated calumny. No. I have never believed it."

"May I ask why?"

"I have never yet heard of any nunnery, be its chaplain, its bedesmen never so decrepit or repulsive, where some rumor did not some time link them in unchastity. No neighboring nunnery and monastery but have been confidently accused of digging tunnels and secret cemeteries full of babes. Yet never have I come across an authentic account of such doings."

Lady Philippa inclined her head. "Ay—though I confess I hoped for reasons less—well, less general, my lord."

"Your personal qualities, Reverend Mother, which would render such licentious courses impossible even were they less improbable, cannot possibly require mention."

"That was a difficult moment," he said subsequently to his intimates. "Fair as she is, I swear she'd be safe in a camp of drunken soldiers, the Virgin bless her. I could not tell her that!"

He gave orders for the older, plainer, and reputedly most shrewish sisters to be brought before him first. Their testimony yielded all the evidence of petty spite, jealousies, and delight in talebearing he could have expected, also of sundry minor offenses, such as the concealed possession of pets, trinkets, pillows, and the like. But there was no hint as to anything less venial, which he was sure would have been beyond them to conceal.

For years nuns and lay sisters had seen no man save the chaplain face to face. Young novices were even more apt to be flustered. Each in turn found herself alone with a group of men, led by the bold, bad, suave, pontifically glittering Abbot of Cloudsway. His smile, his frown, his voice, vibrated now with reassurance, now with sternness; his affable asides, impulsive gestures and chuckles, all lent themselves, if not to dual interpretation, at least to involuntary flights of fancy.

Young Alfred restlessly prowled about the nunnery in the tracks of that earlier, happier visit, when no passage and no cranny had remained unknown to him and Elizabeth. He stumped up to the loft where they had pelted each other with apples until their feet strayed off the beams, so that they had broken through the plaster in between.

It was still used for storing apples, saturated with their scent which has the heady breath of decay in the mass. He grabbed an apple and took a bite, but it nauseated him and he flung it back on the rack. He stood angrily, aimlessly.

The door opened and someone burst inside, colliding with him. He had one glimpse of her face before she could compose it, before its expression became so much as startled. With her it was the same as with him. Anything else he noted not, knew nothing else. Like doe and stag they had rushed to the meeting, unbeknownst. He had put out his hands instinctively, to stop them both from falling. Their bodies felt each other acutely. They drew back. They put out their hands again to touch each other, shrank from the touch, advanced again. Their teeth showed; they might have been smiling. Suddenly they fell against each other, as they had first come together, and grappled in swooning greed. Now they were off the beam gangway, and the plaster broke softly, like immature eggshell, under their prone weight. They lay in a trough, a nest, half-sunk in the resilient latticework between floor and ceiling; their locked movements became languorous, as in underwater life, and the smell of apples covered them over. There was great sweetness in this; and, so spent were they, that together they dropped off into abrupt slumber. Alfred woke with a start which had been communicated to his body by that other with which it had rested intertwined.

They jerked apart callously and rose, all in silence. They had naught to say to one another, hardly had eyes, let alone thought for each other, engrossed in their own private, horrible aghastness. Alfred looked at the plaster. There was no pretending they could escape undetected. The very shape of the hole was a descriptive betrayal—or thus it seemed to him. His partner made a sound between sobbing and gasping, and in a whirl of draggled folds was gone. The door, not quite closed, swung slowly a few times.

He went out, fastening it with deliberation. His knees and hands, the muscles of his face were perfectly steady. He strode through the long, dome-ceilinged white passages. He must go to the Abbot himself, right away. Near the refectory he saw a little crowd of nuns, standing tranquilly, looking bright and cleansed.

In the parlor Lord William was laying his conclusions before the Abbess, in his most winning manner. The scribe was busy making a copy for her of all the investigator's rulings. "Now I would ask you this, Lady Philippa. Would you be willing, in future, to make any concessions to appearances?"

"I know not rightly how to answer this, my lord, till I know whether it be question, advice, or command."

The Abbot nodded, with a lurking smile. "Methought your cell looked something too bare, maybe that was because of sundry patches about its walls, showing that at some time in the past the Mother Superior's domicile was more fittingly endowed. And I noted sundry furniture of corresponding shapes in the treasury vault. There was a settle with gilded feet and fat bolsters, and some hangings with a pattern of *fleur-de-lys,* too short to go round any walls but those of a cell. There were some little vessels looked like salve pots, and certain smaller jewels meant to be worn."

For the first time Lady Philippa showed herself confused, dropped her gaze, and found no words.

When Lord William came out of the parlor, all smiles and benign nods, Alfred ran up to him and snatched at his robe in supplication. The Abbot ached in every limb from hours of sitting. He longed to relax and wittily discuss the day's work with a friend, but after one look at Alfred he did grant him a private hearing.

The silence went on so long that Alfred, prostrate at the Abbot's feet, dared look up—half thinking he had only dreamed the Abbot's presence, and that after all confession lay in fact still before him. The Abbot returned his gaze, and said listlessly, "Get up."

"What am I to do about this? What am I to do with you?" he asked after another pause, and waited as if for a helpful answer. "Ay, it is easily said, that I should send you back to your father, flayed and earless and unmanned. Others go about these exercises quietly, and the matter remains between them and their confessor and the Lord God. Such as you must needs see to it that the sin cries to Heaven so loudly all the world cannot but take note. And can you tell me what is to be done about *her*—whoever she may be, though I trow I could soon pick her out, if you cannot! Was she maid or woman? Know you not even that? The danger lies with her. The damaged plaster is easily explained. But will she run to her Abbess, as you have to me? Even if she waits to confess decently, in the proper place, her punishment will set all tongues wagging. You cannot teach me anything about women. A bitter blow is this for the Lady Philippa. What *is* to be done? Ay, ay, you need not say it again, that whatever I may see fit to do, you will accept as justice —how should you not? If only it were as simple as that! If it were only a question of justice, my boy, you should not be standing before me blithe and hale this moment!"

Alfred never knew what was done about her that had sinned with him. To the end of his life he prayed for her, asking also that her default should be added to the sum of his sins at the Last Judgment. But he never even knew whether or no Lord William had in the end spoken to Lady Philippa, although it was hard to see how else the matter could have been smoothed over. He himself was openly arraigned for the damage in the apple loft, so that everybody got to know this was not his first offense, and were thus duly impressed with the childishness of the trespass.

To begin with he was beaten as an apple thief, the severity of the sentence explained by his age and obligation to know better. The plasterers were called in as a matter of course and saw nothing suspicious in the hole. Then, in another private talk, Lord William imposed on Alfred certain further penalties, most of which he might undergo without anyone else being any the wiser.

Alfred could not help seeing that, his unfeigned wrath notwithstanding, Lord William thought more of him that had sinned as a man than he would have of a thiever of apples. At the same time he felt himself gradually being purged by atonement. As for the dreams, with which, waking and sleeping, the Devil had plagued him before, they had never once recurred. The memory of his mad initiation grew hourly less vivid. Though his ultimate fate was still uncertain, he was able to breathe freely and look everyone straight in the eye.

Not many weeks after they had been welcomed back to Cloudsway Waste, Alfred learned that he was to be sent away. Even though nobody would be told the reason, so that there was no official disgrace (indeed, he was not a little envied), the punishment was hard. And yet—and yet, he was not brokenhearted as he would have expected to be, had anyone foretold this.

CHAPTER 5

ST. UNCUMBER

ELIZABETH SAT SEWING in her own parlor, a small room on the ground floor of the east wing. It was narrow almost as a passage, but ran the whole depth of the building, so that it had a little triple window at each end. In each recess a cushioned chest formed a seat. Beside her on the chest stood an open coffer filled with baby clothes already finished. She laid her work aside to lift out one little garment, thrusting her fingers into the sleeves and moving them about, that she might make believe there were arms in them. Then she fitted a quilted cap over one fist and stroked it furtively.

Sensing the glance of her attendant, she abruptly let her hands sink into her lap. "I am weary, Madge. I will go and lie down on the bed for an hour." The woman nodded understandingly and only went with her as far as the stairs. Elizabeth made haste to put on shoes and wrap herself up, then she sneaked out of the house. Juliana, called their "Stepmistress" by the housefolk, was as usual safely busy somewhere else.

Inside the ruin, the ground was comparatively dry. Nonetheless Elizabeth unfastened her cloak and spread it out before she knelt to unearth St. Uncumber—her son's mother must not be allowed to take cold. She removed some withered flowers and added a new candle of pure wax to the store already collected at the back of the cavity in the earth bank. St. Uncumber knew that one day they would all be lit! There was no point in waiting for Jane, who sometimes joined her here, as Alfred had once used to do on the other side of the Tew.

"St. Uncumber! St. Uncumber! Hail, lady and champion of all that are oppressed in the marriage bed! St. Uncumber! St. Uncumber! When will you uncumber your servant Elizabeth? Have I not served you faithfully every day that I could these long, weary months? Oh, recall the fate you escaped and take pity at last on me that was trapped! St. Uncumber, hear me, pray for me, help me! Take away my husband, rid me of Luke Robinson. If you do not help me soon now, it will be too late—"

"Why so?" said a voice.

For a moment Elizabeth failed to take fright. She thought a miracle had happened—was she not praying for miracles?—and that St. Uncumber was speaking to her. A bearded she-saint might well talk in masculine strain. But in the same instant she realized that no saint would need to question her. She started with a wrench that tore through the whole of her and brought forth a shriek. She had fallen forward on her face and could not stop her body twitching and trembling, all at once drenched in sweat. The presence took hold of her and despite her struggling turned her over and helped her into a sitting position. He shook her and went on questioning her. Her mind knew that it was the Franciscan Prior, but for all the difference that made to her fit-stricken body he might as well have been a horned and bat-winged apparition. He relaxed his hold so that she fell backward against the bank, gathered something into his robe, and disappeared.

At Walter Greene's farmyard the whole family was engaged in repairing a leaky roof. One sat astride, another hugged it, with feet braced on the gutter. Some stood on ladders, others wallowed in broom and reeds or were bundling the thatch in preparation. It might have cost one or the other of them his neck when Prior Carlos Trinidad suddenly rushed amongst them so violently it appeared he had shot out of the ground, and without preamble demanded the instant loan of a horse. Gaping, the eldest daughter slouched over to the stable. The Prior tore the halter out of her hand, refusing to wait for a saddle, led the beast to a stone and after two attempts frustrated by impatience, swung himself on to its back. Kicking its inflated sides and striking now the neck, now the drear old rump with the flat of his hand, he managed to ride off, the Greenes all staring after him from their divers points of vantage.

The horse was senile and lackadaisical, the Prior on its back furiously pigging at thrice the rate of its trot. The sight created consternation all along his way back to the Waste, where he made for the monastery, not the hospital.

Never had he penetrated to the Abbot with so little delay. It was his hour. He was irresistible. The Abbot involuntarily rose as the Prior flew in, listened to him without interruption, and merely blinked in rhythm with the thumps the other dealt the table between them. Finally the aggressor snatched the image of St. Uncumber from his knotted sleeve and sent it crashing down before the Abbot, who could only nod agreement to the Prior's demands. He left the Waste triumphant, with a pair of henchmen.

Entering Bedesford in broad daylight, Luke, having walked on foot all through the night in the rain showed no trace in his gait and demeanor, merely in his appearance. He bandied merry words with the servants flocking round him, and greeted his mother-in-law with cordial pleasure, before calling for his wife. "Where is she? She is well, I trust? Where can she be, Juliana?"

"In her parlor, to be sure. She must have seen you from the window before any of us."

Luke gave her an amused glance and went quickly toward the east wing.

"Belike she is hiding," said Juliana in the empty parlor. "Truly, there is no end to her childishness."

Luke looked everywhere in vain, and began to be troubled and peremptory. He asked which of the women was supposed to be with the Mistress: it had been his parting order that she was never to be left unattended. At this Madge came forward and confessed Elizabeth might have gone out. "It chafed her so, never to be by herself. We have none of us had the heart to be her constant jailers. Ask the others, Luke."

"I will not waste time now with thanking you for your fidelity," Luke looked chillingly, "nor you, mother-in-law, for your discharge of trust. We must find her first of all. You all know how impetuous she is, and careless. Thanks to you, God alone knows how far afield she may have gone. It would seem that, but for me, the whole day might have gone by ere she was missed." He paused under the impact of increasingly unpalatable possibilities. "Someone must ride to Cloudsway Waste and see if she is at the cathedral. Ask at the monastery, too. Someone must go to Trefeller Court, and if Jane knows not where she is, bring *her* back here. We may need her, in case my wife has overtired herself or taken cold, or met with some accident. You and you go in opposite directions, asking at all the neighbors. This is no time to care what folk may think. Some of you must stay, as you may be needed, and so shall I, that any with news for me may know where I am to be found."

Elizabeth was discovered sooner than they had any of them expected, for she could no longer hold off screaming. A sobbing woman came running to tell them at the house, and everyone followed her out. Arrived at the tumbledown shrine, Luke thrust them all aside and stumbled in first. Only Elizabeth's eyes showed him that she was in full possession of her senses and that she knew him. He knelt and tried to take hold of her hand, scorching hot, slippery, and threshing. Helplessly he could think of naught to say but, "Speak to me, Elizabeth, speak to me, poor love."

"I am sorry, Luke," she gasped during a pause. "Forgive me, Luke. The new Prior—the Grayfrock—"

Presently the neighbor wives arrived, and Jane, who formed them into relays, there being so little room, and ordered the servants back to the house with instructions and errands. Elizabeth's mother did not come out, too frail to help, and without midwife's experience.

"Think you it will be long?" Luke asked.

The woman shrugged, not looking at him.

"Think you she will live? Can the child live?"

"God is merciful," said the woman, still not looking at him.

"Several times she has spoken the Prior's name. She may be confused in her mind—" He glanced inquiringly at Mistress Greene, who had uttered a smothered exclamation.

"I should not wonder, Luke, if he had something to do with this mischance." She moved over, and told him of Prior Carlos's strange behavior in her husband's yard. Another woman spoke up and described his ride through the town.

"Does anybody else know anything about this?" Luke raised his voice and stood up.

"Only that he has been hanging about this part of the town a deal," said one of the men.

"He has not called at Smithy Yard for a long time, though."

"Knew you, Master, that when first he came, he was forever calling and asking questions?"

"Ay, Luke. He used to come and sit in the kitchen or lean against the barn door, asking about the Mistress and how it was Jane brought her up from a babe, and whether she does not do strange things at times, Elizabeth—nay, you do not think he got anything out of your housefolk, do you?"

Luke set his jaw and clenched his fists.

There was a new spurt of sound and activity inside the ruin. One of the midwives called out shrilly. Outside, prayers and subdued talk were alike stilled, in the distance dogs were barking.

"My wife—" said Luke in a terrified whisper, and began to cry. He stood where he was and did not move.

Someone came out of the ruin, awkwardly holding something in a trough.

"Master Luke? Here. Your son was stillborn. We have brought him to show you. But your wife is hale and well. Please God you will have many other children."

"My son." Luke looked, and shivered. "My poor wife. May I go in to her now?"

Although air currents had all too free access to this birthing chamber, the atmosphere was laden with biting fumes, of herb incense and other medicines, mold and wood smoke, blood and sweat. The women filing out to let him in looked as they might after a day's field work at the height of summer. Jane sat on the ground, Elizabeth's head in her lap. The weeds and ferns were crushed and partly hidden beneath straw, hacking, and muddied blankets. Luke saw that Jane's feet and arms were stippled red with the sting of nettles.

"My Elizabeth," Luke knelt down and groped for her limp hand under the covers. "My best and only treasure, worth twenty sons to me. You shall have three gold rings, instead of the one I had planned to give you. Only smile—Can she smile?" he asked of Jane, foolishly.

Elizabeth stretched her lips in a smile, then her eyes shifted, dropped; she sighed. Luke bent and kissed her forehead, with the greatest care, but many times.

Outside, some of the housefolk dispensed warming drinks. Some brisker step became audible, accompanied by the clank of metal and the scrabbling gallop of dogs. There was confused interchange of words, a brief muted scuffle, and someone else entered brusquely. Elizabeth gasped; Luke was on his feet in one bound: there stood the Franciscan Prior. His skin gleamed like brass where protuberant ridges of bone stretched it taut. His habit was saturated by the rain and clung to him so that for once the clumsy links of his waist chain underneath were in evidence.

"The very man I want to see," said Luke. "But not in here. Not in here. Get out and wait outside. Be sure I will not delay in coming to you. Did you not hear me? Out, I said." He took a step toward the intruder, raising his fist, a sort of joy kindling in his eyes.

The Prior did not heed him, and asked, "Where is the child?" Jane and the others made desperate signs, shaking their heads and pointing at the childless young mother. The Prior nodded his head. "Dead? Ay. And the mother saw to it her child went straight to Hell. All the while she carried it beneath her black heart she made sure of that. There it is burning now in fires everlasting. Ah," he cried, whirling to face Luke who was going for his throat, "I know it is the custom in Anglemere to murder your priests! You will not do me aught but kindness, sending me before God's throne, a martyr—" Luke's hands sank.

There was silence outside as within. "Hold your peace till I have done," the Prior went on loudly, "and I trow you will thank me as your benefactor, Master Luke."

"It is not true," Elizabeth struggled up on her elbow.

The Prior peered as though so far he had not seen her. "What is not true, madam? I had not yet accused you. Here, Master Luke, look you well at this. Have you ever seen it before?" Once more he produced St. Uncumber. Jane stopped, and then resumed stroking Elizabeth's head.

"Ganna, it is not true, is it? What you told me is the truth, is it not, that though they cannot go to Heaven, unbaptized innocents go to a pleasant place?" Elizabeth was saying to Jane.

The Prior drew himself up. "Look at this now, Master Luke. Know you what it is?"

Elizabeth had not noticed before what he was about. "No, no!" she cried.

"This," said the Prior, "is an idol called St. Uncumber. Mayhap you have heard of its noxious rites? Wicked women forswear salvation, praying this idol to rid them of their husbands. That is what I caught your wife in the act of doing. I knew there was some such thing afoot, since she and her old nurse meet here so often. At last God has rewarded my patient vigilance—"

"Is this true, Elizabeth?" Luke asked.

Elizabeth did not answer and could not look at him.

"I see it is," Luke answered himself. He took a deep breath. "Nevertheless I do not think any purpose will be served by indicting her, Prior. Everyone knows women in her state are not themselves. It is a matter for her confessor, not for open court. I undertake to make rich gifts to the hospital on her behalf. You and I can settle about that at some more suitable time, Prior. No harm has come to anyone by reason of this—this—" he forced a laugh, at a loss for an extenuating term.

"You have myself and God's protection to thank for your safety, Master, and not the Devil's impotence," the Prior said. "Your wife is a sick woman for the nonce. I would not have her life on my conscience. Time enough to deal with her when she is better. But this chiefest sorceress here will I claim, and I have armed men with me, to arrest her. For your own sake and this sick woman's, witch, I advise that you come with us now without a struggle—"

CHAPTER 6

THE CAUSE OF JANE

JANE ASKED LEAVE only to hush Elizabeth first, and in full view of the company, without traceable resort to witchcraft, sent the exhausted girl into a kind of uncaring half slumber.

In silence we watched Jane go between the sword-rattling henchmen, with the Prior following at a strut. We thought, surely her meekness betokened some stratagem; out in the street, not a few people fell in behind. After a while some of us made bold to draw level with the Prior and ask what he meant to do for the growing procession was headed Tew-ward. But he would not speak to us, and only glowered haughtily and somewhat raised his voice in its recital of prayers of exorcism in the holy tongue.

In the daytime the manor drawbridge was scarcely ever up when Lord Hugh was in residence; the smaller door worked into one of the gate leaves commonly left ajar. Although, therefore, it swung inward with undesired ease under the Prior's knuckles, he went on knocking until the skin came off them and the gatekeeper, cursing, was forced to come out of his cubbyhole. One look at Jane, impassive between her guards, sent him off without further demur.

The gatekeeper returned with my lord and his brother and nephew, accompanied by henchmen, some still fastening the buckles of their sword belts and the neck pins of their tunics. Lord Hugh himself was attired in a long velvet gown, with the pile rubbed off in great patches, which was most lordly. Like the rest of us, he wore out his oldest clothes when at home without guests, but his least regarded rags were velvet.

It was one of the Prior's habits to thrust his face right into his interlocutor's, especially when in any way agitated. As he pounced on the three Cinqmorts now, Young Gervase pointedly bent to pluck a flower from between the cobblestones—it happened to be scentless dandelion—and with a flourish smelled it off and on. Thus offensively, he masked his shrinking recoil from the cleric's nearness.

Lord Hugh looked from Jane to the Prior and back again, and we held our breath. Although at their last encounter he had thrown Father Carlos into the moat, there was not the remotest chance of a repetition. The Prior held the ascendancy. You could have thrown him to the lions, yes, but taken no action to humiliate him. Even Gervase's waving dandelion failed to distract him in the slightest. We quailed for Jane. It was not likely that my lord would forego a turn of witch baiting just because years ago the same witch happened to have saved his life.

While the Prior outlined the case against Jane, Gervase flung his toy away, strolled up to the manacled prisoner, and walked round to view her from all sides, as she might be a carved post. The Prior concluded, "While in the recent past, my lord, you did not meet me with respect, let alone in a spirit of common zeal for justice, I have a greater faith in your honor, as a layman and noble lord of this town, than in the immoral vicar of the episcopal power at the Waste."

Truly, it was the Prior's day altogether. My lord could no more escape doing what he wished than the Abbot had been able.

My lord bade the henchmen take the woman down to the dungeon. "What if she fly away?" he then asked the Prior. "If she be all you say, surely stone will not prison her any more securely than the timber you mistrust?"

"As I tried to suggest, it is not only timber I mistrust. Howbeit stone is indeed safer than timber," the Prior replied.

We were very busy that day and far into the night, but not to recoup lost working time. Unasked, all Jane's debtors rallied to repay her, passing word of her peril wherever the news had not already penetrated, and deliberating how they should act. You perceive there was never any doubt that action must be taken on her behalf. It was said of us later that this was not all kindness on our part. It was said, and there may be some small truth in it, that we were also looking to our own skins. If she were found guilty, all of us would be guilty, too. Nevertheless, we hold this did not render our rush to protect Jane any the less sincere. Remember that she had brought to pass naught but good. Besides, she had never failed to achieve anything she attempted. Was it likely that of all people she would have failed Elizabeth?

Only Elizabeth at present knew that Jane had indeed failed her, and so she felt lost and bewildered, in a world all changed, with its denizens and its precepts, by that failure.

It was nearly dusk by the time they had settled her in the bedchamber. She had been washed all over with warm water and fine, gritless soap, and dressed in the soft, clean clothes prepared for her confinement. Her hair was tied back from her face, and pillows stuffed behind her, the smallest, topmost one covered in red silk and edged with foreign lace—just as though she had borne a living heir. There was a bright new fire, and a variety of bracing odors rising from as many little pots. A bowl of milk stood so that it would keep warm without curdling, and near it was the liddled silver wine beaker with matching cup, for visitors.

Waking to all this the next morning, Elizabeth began almost to believe that she had borne a child with mishap. But though her belly was unburdened, there was no trace of such a child; the cradle that they had in the room with them since Easter had been removed. Then, also, Jane was not by. It had been no dream, it was all true, even though they had not laid her among the rats on the bare floor in the cellar with a piece of old bread and a cup of rusty water—there stood the honey pot and a glass jar with candied pears within easy reach on the bed step.

Nobody else was in the room for the moment. The fire crackled now and then, and now and then raindrops hissed into it. The kettle bubbled. Folk were drawing water from the well. Brooms swished, pans clattered. She could distinguish all the different sounds of farmyard, warehouses, and countinghouse, and of the waxing traffic in the market place. Everything was just as usual.

She stiffened as there were steps at the door. It was only Mistress Greene with Nancy coming to see to her. Covertly scanning their faces, she found no severity, only the sort of strained, equable air folk will assume toward a child whose misdeeds are not their responsibility. Nancy stretched on her toes to add two tapers to the little lamp at the foot of the crucifix in its garlanded niche. Mistress Greene applied aromatic poultices to Elizabeth's breasts.

Elizabeth did not feel encouraged to talk. Trying with all her might to go to sleep, and pretending in the end with eyes tight shut, she grew more and more tensely wakeful. It was a long, dragging day.

Nothing distracted her from thinking about her firstborn. She thought of all the times she had burned herself in some tiny spot, how the pain of it had clamored above all other sensations. The flames of Hell not only envelop the whole body, they also suffuse and ragingly fill it; they are fire without end, that does not consume what it burns so. Jane had assured her it was not true, that the innocent babe must suffer this. But Jane might be wrong; she might have lied in kindness.

Elizabeth was anguished by her poor little son's loneliness—so new and tender and small as he was, knowing nobody down there, with no one to lead him by the hand or take him to nest in their arms. He would be like Thistle, the little dog Luke had given her on their wedding day, and whom therefore she had never liked. Too small and useless to join the dogs of the yard, unwanted in the Mistress's room, always humbly in the way, in the warm kitchen. Elizabeth was aghast at her own hard-heartedness. On Thistle's collar it said, *"Amo Domina,"* and she knew well the English for that. How could she expect God to be merciful toward her son, if she could treat so cruelly an innocent in *her* power?

"Are you awake, Elizabeth?" Nancy said from her seat by the fire. "Here. I have some nice porridge for you."

I am lonely, and I know one in this house is lonely, too. Elizabeth wanted to say. Bring him to me, let me have my own dog Thistle, in my bed and comfort him as I hope some kindly shadow soul will be comforting my poor babe.

"You feel lonely and dull, I trow, little Mistress," Nancy stroked Elizabeth's cheek. "Shall I fetch your little dog from the kitchen? Would you like to play with him a little?"

Elizabeth nodded vigorously, and held back her tears till the woman was out of the room. They brought no relief, being a hot, meager, reluctant trickle. Nobody had called her so, "little Mistress," since she had caused her maid Bess to be unjustly dismissed! Her sins and cruelties were crowding in upon her thick and fast. God was giving her a chance, here upon this barren, idle bed, to see herself in all her badness and amend her ways. Luke had never been anything but good to her. The one thing she could think of holding against him, the one thing in which he had indulged himself and not her—now that was also the only one extending hope to her. If she might but give life and love to many other children—then, and only then, she somehow felt sure, would the lost little stillborn soul be truly comforted.

Nancy came back with the dog under one arm. Elizabeth sat up and stretched out her arms for Thistle. He had been named so because his hair hung about him in feathery, pointed tassels like thistle bloom. His nose barely showed, and his round black eyes peeped timidly through a matted fringe. When Elizabeth groped for the accusing collar and pulled him toward her, he went rigid. She arranged him under the bedclothes, so that his tousled head just showed beside hers on the silken pillow. For a while he remained motionless, barely trusting himself to breathe. Presently, he heaved a sigh, put out his tongue for one warm lick at her palm, sighed again, closed his eyes, and slept, with a constant, piping little snore. Then Elizabeth slept also.

When she opened her eyes again, she thought it was nightfall. In fact, a new morn was dawning. Thistle was no longer in her arms. She craned and saw him, rolled up near the fire. "Why did you take Thistle from me?" she wailed. The dog, on hearing her voice, sprang to his feet and wagged his tail.

"I thought in your sleep you might crush him, or that his hair might smother you. Your nose was pressed right into it."

Elizabeth shrank back and pulled the bedclothes up to her chin. The person whom in the half-light she had taken for Mistress Greene or Nancy, was her husband.

"Here is some nice porridge that I have been watching for you," Luke went on. Silently, Elizabeth let him approach with bowl and spoon, climb the steps, sit down on the bed, and proceed to feed her. Silently, she opened and shut her mouth and even swallowed.

"Need I eat it all?" she asked after a while, diffidently.

"No, of course not," Luke said, surprised.

"I wondered that you did not come to see me."

"I wanted you to rest undisturbed."

"Luke!"

"Yes?"

"What are you going to do?"

"Do?" He shrugged and looked away. Finally, with decision, he turned back to her. "Perhaps it will be best if we talk about it, then. Only do not get a fever."

"If wondering and not knowing has not given me the fever—" Elizabeth said tremulously. "Luke, Luke, I did not mean it!"

"Did you not? Ay, perhaps you did not, quite, seeing that your ill prayers did not harm me, only my dog. He was drowned in a bog. I am glad you did not quite mean me to die that way."

"Luke," Elizabeth repeated desperately, dry eyed, "I never prayed for your death. Never once. How could I?"

"Then what was it you prayed for—to St. Uncumber?"

"I—I did not like the married state."

Luke grunted—almost it sounded like a curt laugh. She had heard it said that grief and worry will often age a man overnight. There was no thread of white in his gleaming hair, and he was carefully dressed, in good, stout garments, but his face did look older, and looked shabby, as it were, untidy in some way: disordered. He said, "Maybe I should have known it before, that you married me against your will. You should have told me the truth before it was too late."

"I never told you any lies, Luke."

"I suppose not." He sighed. "I suppose I set unreasonably great store by it, that we had always been such fast friends, you and I."

"Luke, what are you going to do?"

"This is the second time you have asked me that, my wife. I wonder at you. Do? What should I do? You are my wife and I am your husband. I will not say this has not hurt me. I am angry, too. God knows I am. But Our Lord enjoined us to forgive our enemies. I need only forgive my wife. Or are you still my enemy besides?"

Juliana was well aware that Elizabeth's outing had lost her mother any right to argue with Luke. Thus it was Elizabeth enjoyed the treatment of a blameless younger mother, and that Juliana was not allowed to see her until Luke thought it wise, and then only in his presence.

Beyond sending an eloquent glance round the room and smiling crookedly, Juliana made no special reference to what had happened, merely saying that Elizabeth looked well and would no doubt be up and about again shortly. The serving woman had left the room at a sign from the Master, who himself proceeded to offer his mother-in-law of all the dainties, still plentiful, there having been no visitors from outside.

Elizabeth braced herself and sat up. "Will you tell me, Mother and Luke, what has happened to Ganna?"

"She is in prison awaiting trial," Luke answered without gentleness.

"Trial! For what, if I'm not going to be tried?"

"Well may you ask!" Juliana could not contain herself. All the same, Elizabeth detected an inflextion of approval in her mother's tone.

"Would you like to see your own daughter in the dock with her?" Luke put in roughly.

"No, but neither do I *like* to see Jane endangered, particularly as it is my own daughter's fault!" Yet, wonder upon wonders, Juliana now actually smiled faintly at her daughter, as much as to confirm that they were allies. "But provided Luke will help us, Daughter, I think you may set your mind at rest. If we are to believe all he says, that your mind should be at rest is his foremost concern just now. Little does he know, if he thinks your mind can be at rest so long as Jane is liable to suffer on your behalf."

"Mother is right, Luke."

"She is, is she? Truly, you women are marvelous. I ought to feel flattered. You must think me a saint, and a giant that can overthrow mountains with the tip of his little finger. Well, I am neither. It has taxed me to the utmost of my paltry powers, humbling and grossly despoiling myself to bribe that hell priest of a Prior, running backward and forward between hospital and monastery, meeting people everywhere and having to talk to them as if it did not bother me that everybody knows my wife resorted to witchcraft to get rid of me. It is the last straw, that you should expect me to help Jane—"

"Think you that we, your nearest kin, do not know how good a man you are?" Juliana said, with the greatest sweetness. "Did you not yourself tell me how Elizabeth responded to your goodness? And you must not say that we *expect* your help. We but hope to persuade and remind you how very dear Jane has always been to us both."

"If she had cut my throat I trow she would be just as dear to you still —ay, and dearer, to Elizabeth!"

"Now, Luke, that was not kindly said. You told me you had scolded Elizabeth, and now the matter was to be forgotten. And you said you were satisfied she had failed to see her freedom meant your death. If you have forgiven Elizabeth, how can you persecute Jane? Indeed, as Brother Laurentius has deposed before the Abbot and before Hugh—"

"You do admit she is a witch!"

"Admit? Everyone has always known that, yourself included. It all depends on whether a witch works magic for good or for ill. But we know the law makes no allowances for that, and so we all pretended not to know for the benefit of the Prior. It is a wonder he did not indict St. Hand for sorcery! For he must be as jealous of Its many cures as he has been of Jane's."

"What was that you said, about Brother Laurentius, Mother?" Elizabeth cried, in great excitement.

"He has come forward as a voluntary witness in her defense. He has written out his testimony, and the Prior has not dared have him confined, because all the people are against him and with Laurentius, and are making one cause out of freeing Jane and getting the friar back for the cathedral. He has given it as his opinion that the image Jane gave you as St. Uncumber is no such thing, but an old-fashioned crucifix. In olden days, it seems, there was a rule that only thus might Our Saviour be depicted. It was held that having Him in crucified attitude was enough to remind worshipers of His sufferings, to show the cross as well would only make Him experience the torture over again. So that, whatever may have been Jane's intentions, no sorcery can, in fact, have taken place."

"Mother, Luke, has there been nothing further said about my baby, and whether it is in Hell or not?"

"To be sure there has. Many people think it was this finally decided

Brother Laurentius to defy his Prior. For he holds that as the babe never came to life at all it cannot even be accounted unbaptized. It died in the innocence of a babe unborn. There can be no question of Hell. The Abbot has taken up the point and proved it, and Prior Carlos has had to climb down and acknowledge that he spoke over hastily—"

"And nevertheless I have had to pay a goodly sum, that our first-born may be buried at the edge of consecrated ground."

"Luke, you do not grudge it?" Elizabeth cried.

"I do not grudge it for my son. But I cannot say the Abbot was justified in exacting it."

"Elizabeth, you will rejoice to hear this: how all and sundry have fairly streamed, uncalled, to testify on Jane's behalf, from the day she was arrested. Everyone that she has ever done anything for has gone to the Abbot, freely recording what boons they owe her, and swearing that she used no black arts."

"Forswearing themselves!"

"Now, Luke! You call the Prior hell priest, but talk just the same as he. Jane may command powers that are beyond other folk and yet be no sorceress. As soon might you call Edwin a warlock, for that he can do what no one else can. Seriously Luke, if you alone of all the people refuse to help, you will have Jane upon your conscience, you alone."

"Oh, Luke! We pray you!"

"You have turned this very cunningly, Juliana. But before I say you have won, you would perhaps tell me what manner of help you have in mind, that I'm to give?"

"There speaks our true Luke, Elizabeth! All you need do, my Luke, is withdraw your charge and testimony against her. After all, the Prior's charge rests solely on what he saw *Elizabeth* do. All you need do is go and tell them it was all a piece of childish play between your young wife and her old nurse, which no one in his right senses could take seriously. It is in your own interest. If folk were to go on believing that you believe your wife tried serious witchcraft against you, before long they'll begin to say you must have given her full serious cause."

"This final argument you might have spared me, Mother-in-law. Most men would rather be thought villains than fools. My trouble is that, villain or no, I shall look a fool in any case. I will do what you ask."

Lord Hugh did not commonly go down to visit any prisoners, having them brought up before him on the rare occasions when he wished to speak to them. However, a captive witch had best be left where she was secured.

So my lord's searching looks at the guards who lighted him down into the cellar vaults discovered no sign that they thought his behavior strange.

His footsteps raising a ghost following of echoes, the light gliding before him and huge shadows prancing at either side, he listened and headed for signs of life other than rats. A long-bearded man blinked gauntly up at him from the floor of a cavelike recess.

"Who are you?" Lord Hugh was taken aback.

"Harold," said the forgotten man, having to jog his throat with much coughing into remembrance of how to form voice into speech. "I am Harold. Harold is my name."

Lord Hugh opened his mouth for further questions, but stopped in time and abruptly removed himself and the light.

By contrast Jane was comfortably off. Her straw was new, dry and unflattened—no wonder, since my lord found her stretched out on the naked ground beside it. Her pitcher of water was three-quarters full, and most of her bread was uneaten. She sat up. Lord Hugh stuck the torch into a shackle ring let into the wall, and crouched down beside her.

"Why are you lying on the ground, my Jane? It cannot be to punish me? You know you should have had bearskins and silken damask to lie on, if I had my way. I could not come to see you sooner. You cannot conceive what a to-do there has been and, for that matter, still goes on. Or perhaps you do know?"

"No," said Jane, opening her eyes wide under brows drawing a little way together.

"It would do your heart good to see it. Everyone, everyone has flocked to your rescue. Work of all kinds has been at a standstill. I think now it is only a question of hours until I receive formal request to release you?"

"Release me!"

"Ay, for now at last the Fleming himself has joined the host of your defenders. Much of it has made me laugh quietly to myself. Withal it irks me, too. As lord of Bedesford I shall be lumped together with those who must yield you up to the people's clamor. For my own sake I could have wished they had all been baying for your blood. *Then* I should have done something for you in setting you free!"

"If it is true that you would do something for me, you will refuse to release me. Refuse to yield. Insist on it that I be tried and judged."

"What? Either you did not understand me aright, or else I have misheard you."

"Will you not do what I ask without explanation? You, that know if nobody else does how hard it is to speak in words of all that I am most concerned with? No. You will not. And I cannot compel you. It would be accounted self-slaughter. I must persuade you."

"You are not in your right mind."

"I am. See, I am speaking very calmly now. I have done wrong. I must be punished. By what I did I minished my powers."

"Then what the Prior says is true? I do not believe it. If you could bring death and disaster on all your people, how could you fail to kill one single man?"

"I did not boldly seek to work his death. I but placed the means in the hands of another. I placed another soul in jeopardy, and that of a woman with child, meaning two souls, and blood of Juliana, whose weal is the anchor of mine. So it was fated, for my ultimate redemption. Now if I suffer for it, I shall ascend to my ancestor's eternal life, full of the fullness of power, thus restored."

"You will never persuade me to this, Jane. Save your breath."

"Then I will not be the only one to regret it. You shall be among those must regret it, too!"

"Now you have threatened me. Now you have left me no other way but to act as *I* would, against your threat."

"I say again, you will regret it."

"And must I tell you again that I have never feared regrets any more than any other danger?"

CHAPTER 7

THE SELF-INJURED

WE DO NOT feel on altogether sure ground where Jane and my lord and Jane and Gervase are concerned. Firstly, as we have let you see, we only understand enough of those rarefied supernatural dealings to call them incomprehensible. Secondly, we learned about this portion of our story in circumstances which made it hard to disentangle cause and consequence, truth and untruth.

It appears that Gervase also went below to Jane. He offered to see her set free if she did his will.

Jane had long ago lost her rare, Viking beauty. Young Gervase had not come to live in Bedesford until after it had left her. Many others in like case had nevertheless fallen under its hearsay spell, as the rest of us never ceased being able to see her onetime fairness underneath her weatherbeaten fading, and spoke of her accordingly. Gervase was the exception, and this had made him curious about Jane in an itching fashion which she had never otherwise called forth in our town. Then also there was this obscure matter of Gervase's detestation of the clergy, springing from a fear of being regarded as one of them. Having amorous commerce with a witch, he would not only add to the Devil's horns, taste of the very essence of forbidden fruit, and prove his fearlessness, but also cut himself off forever from the victims of Oxford and his one twitching nerve of unreasoning cowardice.

As for Jane, she starved herself and lay on the bare wet ground in ardent courtship of the suffering which alone could bring her salvation. She had lost hope already, but cannot yet have resigned herself to despair. Here was another torture she could inflict on herself, without forfeiting her ancestral divinity by suicide.

On the other hand, love may have grown on her, all unforeseen, as it does on lesser women. All uncaring, Gervase taught her delight. She must exert herself to offer him interminably tempting returns, in order that he might go on consenting to delight her. It is an old, old story, of a woman's growing to love her seducer, until their roles become reversed and he would withdraw, she waxing more and more fierce in holding onto him, nay, in pursuit. She was older than he, whom at first she regarded as a puppy, later as the embodiment of youth. To retain her aloofness, she must be able to keep her young, gay swain. Thus the paradox. Thus the first weakening of her integral strength.

Slowly but surely she lost it all. To be strong, it would seem Jane must have needed to resist the pressure of other people's harry and besiegement, resist inwardly, that is, notwithstanding her perpetual outward responses to the demands made on her.

People had changed toward her.

Inexplicably, it was as if they had forgotten their own contention that no magic had ever been intended in the matter of St. Uncumber, directly this became the legal view. On a sudden, people expressed compassion with Luke and wonder at Jane's failure. Then Prior Carlos, bowed down by defeat and thus more likable, had a stroke of luck. An accident occurred at the site, requiring immediate assistance, so that the Prior's skill got its first notable opportunity. It must be said that he acquitted himself splendidly, not only saving the workman's life, but making good his promise that he should not be a cripple. There being no necessity for it, the Prior's importunity did not revive, and he did not run after them, more and more people went to him.

So when, sometime after Jane's release, Gervase called on his aunt, saying he desired Jane's advice about his health, Juliana was so pleased that she felt she must hide it.

"Oh, are you unwell, Nephew? You do not look it."

"That is the worst of some illnesses, Aunt."

We think that he did actually have some illness, and that Jane later on used it to dose him with philters.

Juliana was fond as ever of her bondwoman, albeit with some admixture of contempt. In the past she had lived enfolded in Jane's protection, now it was she took thought on shielding Jane.

Stripped gradually of her armor, Jane was hurt easily, and every hurt went deep. She and her foster daughter were estranged by the common knowledge no one else shared: that Jane really had disappointed Elizabeth's faith in her. Elizabeth did her best to act as though there were no rift, but that only made it worse.

Had her powers still been able to rise to complete supernatural withdrawal, she might have mended her self-sufficiency. But she had told Lord Hugh no more than the truth, and he experienced the proof. Unable fully to transport herself, how could she bestow on him the full satisfaction of their past meetings? Howbeit, the partial satisfaction he could still obtain through her, instead of weaning him, only sharpened his addicted thirst, with constantly renewed hope, constantly disappointed.

You must not think that the common people ceased applying to Jane altogether. Far from it. Those who could not afford alms to the hospital, and those particularly anxious to keep out of the way of Franciscan influence, remained faithful to her. And then there were others who desired what the Prior could not give them. By degrees the nature of her services changed also. Ay, she lent herself to the working of evil. Through her one could make one's neighbor come out in boils, sty, piles; one could make his cattle to abort, his wife's hens cease to lay, his sheep to grow bald. Her petty arts of earth-bound magic were unimpaired.

As apparently she still forbore from working evil on her own account, we could not be certain that she had anything to do with an outbreak of the scarlet fever in the year 1364. There was never any evidence against her. Yet should it have given us to think that the only families not to lose at least one child were the Robinsons and the Smiths—the latter still had only the one son whom they owed to Jane in the first place. Out of seven children (not counting Alfred away in Italy), Jeanne Widowson lost three, namely Martha, Dickon, and the baby, Laurence. Elizabeth by that time had three children living and kept them all.

Ten months after her first confinement she had borne Luke a daughter, christened Isabella. Then came two sons in successive years, Peter and Robin. At the time of the scarlet fever, she was again with child, of another boy, who received the name of John. Isabella, Peter, and Robin had been such big, strong babes from the first that, although their mother was still haunted by the memory of the stillborn, they had not caused her a moment's worry. With John it was otherwise. Not only was he puny and thin, but he gave trouble over his food from the beginning, and caught colds easily.

One such cold he did not seem able to throw off, retaining a cough which grew worse in the winter months. Elizabeth sent for Jane.

Jane had been asked to Smithy Yard many times during the past few years, but only as a friend and visitor, and she had never come. So that when she obeyed this call, she must have been struck by many changes.

Entering the yard, she found it full of horses and lavishly attired men all talking at once in the loud, jolly voices of the newly and safely arrived. Elizabeth, looking older and taller than she was, in sky-blue Thirchester weave with silver buttons and a plain Flemish lawn bonnet, had come out to receive the visitors and send off a messenger to find

Luke at the Town Chamber. Jane recognized Sir Asphodel Jolybody, and, recalling an old story, smiled at his solemn flourishes before the gentle self-possession of his hostess. But her mood changed again when she saw Elizabeth's maid Bess come out of the house with a kicking little boy under her arm, and speak a few words to the Mistress. She did not know Bess well and knew of nothing against her. But the very day of her release from prison had been spoiled, she remembered, by hearing of Elizabeth's request, while still abed, that Luke get back this maid for her. She had thought at the time, and still believed, that this had been Elizabeth's way of showing the world that henceforth she meant to repose her confidence in another.

Elizabeth greeted her lovingly, and asked the merchants to excuse her while Bess showed them into the hall and provided refreshments. The master of the house would not be many minutes. She plainly intended to honor and gratify Jane by acting so. Before going up she took Jane round by the farmyard, where the other children were playing.

"You have not rightly seen them, Ganna, since they were christened. This is my big girl Isabella, and this Robin, the second of the boys. They say Isabella is like me, but no two people have the same opinion as to whom Robin will favor."

"Has anyone told you he shows the Cinqmort blood? Well, I say so. I know the breed, and with their sharp, great noses they change a deal between infancy and manhood."

"You say it so grimly," Elizabeth laughed a little, and stroked the little boy's soft, rose-petal cheek. "There have been good Cinqmorts." She looked critically at Robin's nose, the merest button as yet, and shook her head, laughing again.

"A good many of them turn out handsome, too," Jane said, grudgingly. "I see you are going to have one more soon? Soon you will be old and worn like Jeanne, Elizabeth. Five children in six years!"

"I do not think I have too many," Elizabeth said, in a low voice. "If I were to have twenty children, I should still always be one short. Come with me to the sick babe now."

John slept with his parents for warmth. Without them, he looked lost, no bigger than a bead, upon their bed. Gazing down on him, Jane marveled that Elizabeth had lost time in bringing her to the bedside, and that she did not appear to be at all afraid. Jane examined the child, and felt more and more helpless, not knowing what to say to the mother.

All the appropriate remedies were displayed about the room. Elizabeth had picked up a great deal from Jane in childhood.

"Well, Ganna? Tell me why you think we cannot rid him of his nasty cough."

Jane wrung her hands, unknowingly. "It is the father's fault. The man grows thinner and more unhealthy looking day by day. How can he expect to get strong healthy children? And it's not as if he could not help himself. It is in his own hands, to eat more, and eat regularly. He thinks naught of it that he imperils your children, bequeathing them his habits—"

Elizabeth gazed at Jane in growing bewilderment. Finally, she became angry. "If you can think of no advice to give me about John, it would be more honest to say so, instead of fending me off with an attack on my husband. He is the best of husbands, and the best of fathers, too. John is not the first infant to be difficult of feeding."

"If you know better than I, why did you send for me?"

"I'll tell you. Because I have been wanting to amend our friendship. That is the truth. Because I had tried every bait save this, of asking your advice."

"Nay, you are above my advice now, are you not, Mistress Robinson? See, then, if you can save your child?"

"Oh, Ganna, Ganna, do not talk so to me. Have you quite forgotten—"

"Have I forgotten! You are the one that's fickle! Mistress Robinson of Smithy Yard has finer friends than her mother's old bondwoman. And think you I cannot see what has made you so fond of your husband? You prefer the bird in the hand to the one is flown to Italy. You do not know the meaning of fidelity. And you would turn round and accuse me of your fault?"

So they quarreled at last.

"We will give her spit the lie, you and I, Johnnie, shall we not?" Left alone, Elizabeth bent over her son. "Give your mother a smile, then! Catch my finger. You will not? Shall I find you some better toy?" She took out a little silver cup and made the light it reflected to wander round the room—another thing that was wont to please him. In rummaging for more she made a rustling noise that seemed to awaken his interest. Long ago she had cut Alfred's picture from its wooden mount, for easier secretion. It was the scrap of parchment which had rustled, so now she tried him with that, and he reached for it, crowing. She laughed and cooed and played with him, then, hearing a step, thrust the picture back into the box. The infant at once began to cry. Luke came up behind her. "Has Jane been?"

"Ay, and gone. There is nothing much wrong with the child. She could tell me nothing I do not know already. But you see," she smiled, "that it is enough for Jane to *look* at the sick. See how lively he is grown!"

She called for a woman to sit with the child, and accompanied Luke back to the hall. She was feeling full of affection toward him, because of Jane's attack, because of his kindness in deserting his guests to ask after the child, because he had not marked that she was flustered and that her manner remained somewhat overanimated throughout the meal, and because he encouraged her to take part in the general talk, though in the main it centered not on women's topics.

Fortunately, Sir Asphodel and his friends began to feel the effects of some days' travel fairly early, so that weariness did not overcome her before the guests had been lighted to bed. Yawning, she sent out the woman who had sat up with John and reported that he had slept most of the time. Luke tiptoed to look at the child and gently moved him further toward the wall, slipped out of his shoes and kirtle, and returned to his wife, embracing her persuasively. He had drawn her to the bed when Bess came in and saw them and, grinning, pretended to be much flustered. In tones of unctuous approval, she craved the Master's and Mistress's pardon, which Luke granted in like jocular manner, and said she had come to fetch John.

Elizabeth had never confessed it to anyone but Jane, that she misliked submitting to her husband in the presence of their young children, even though they be fast asleep and too young to understand in any case. So, when with many winks and other sly contortions Bess had carried off the child, Elizabeth felt obliged to refer again to John's marked improvement.

"Yes, I noticed." Luke let go of her and finished undressing. She lay down the while he still sat on the edge of the bed. "I noticed he was crying for a plaything you had whisked away. Neither was it the first time I have seen you toy with that. You always put it away when I come. I have often wondered what it is."

"Why did you not look in my box and find out?" Elizabeth asked, more sharply than she meant to, thinking he might have done so.

"Why, for that matter, have you never shown it to me—beyond letting me see you don't want me to see it?"

"You can look at it now. Bring me my coffer. Here."

"What in the name of heaven is it?"

"Have you no eyes? It is a picture."

Luke's eyebrows went up. "Yes, I can see that much. But surely it must signify something more than meets the eye—if you keep this childish scrawl hidden away among your jewels, and if you answer me so stridently." He waited.

"It is a picture of himself Alfred Widowson painted for me when we were children." Elizabeth held her breath. There was no sound from Luke for a long while. She sat up and put her hand on his shoulder, as he still sat with his back to her. "Luke, dearest husband. Let us speak of this openly once and for all. It is not your fault, but neither is it mine, that Alfred and I loved each other before ever you turned your mind to me. It is you who has been my husband; he has never had that." What she meant, shy of expressing it more clearly, was that Alfred had never enjoyed her *wifely* affection. But Luke thought it was enjoyment of her body, especially when she went on, "And if I have fallen short of pleasing you in any way, you must never think that it had anything to do with *you*. It is but that I am made that way. Some women love their duty and some hate it, just as folk differ in regard to meat and drink, and some would sell their souls for a dish some others abhor—"

"I did not realize that you abhorred it," Luke said by and by.

"Did you not?" she whispered—and on a sudden found her terror increased by the thought that what she had said was no longer true—not at this moment, at all events. Luke rose and put the casket away and blew out the light, and sat down again. She heard him pull the shirt over his head and drop it on the floor.

"No." He swung up his legs and lay down, pulling the coverings high over them both. "Of course I did not know. Need you have asked? What manner of man do you think I am?" He sounded vexed rather than wounded. Elizabeth, feeling the cold and missing the comfort of his encircling arms, was emboldened to move closer. But he held her off. "No, no, let us stay as we are now. What manner of man do you think me, that you believe I would still accept your sacrifice now that I have learned of it? I have never known that all these years we have lived together you have abhorred my love. I shall not trouble you with it again. No, do not weep. I will say to you what you said to me: it is not your fault. And I will try not to hold it against you."

"But, Luke, does not the Church forbid it?"

"It would be a droll thing if she did. No, most like you are thinking of full separation. We shall be living together as before. Chastity is never frowned on. No, you may rest easy."

"It comes hard, what I'm going to ask now: will not this drive you—into sin?"

"No." He sighed. It was her he wanted, otherwise he had ever found he could get along without women. "Go to sleep now, Elizabeth."

But that she could not do for a long time, and she doubted that he fell asleep before her, although neither of them stirred. In her heart she thanked God that at least she had another child on the way. Was it really to be her last? Her heart was torn with the pain of Luke's pain that she had inflicted, and also with her own longing for him from whom a bare few inches divided her, yet had he passed out of reach. Nothing had ever come between her and Alfred in their love and perfect understanding, though she had not seen him for years. It had been an honor for him to be sent away, and she herself had never hurt him. How could she feel compassion for him? How could she help thinking more about Luke than of him?

The baby died a few days later.

When the railing incredulity of the first grief had passed off, Elizabeth forced herself to go and see Alfred's parents at their hut. They were surprised, but tried not to show this, and answered her matronly questions about their eldest son as best they could—knowing little more than that he was alive.

Like herself, Jeanne was expecting another child, and Elizabeth asked her whether she would not let one of her brood be fostered at Smithy Yard. In that tiny hovel Jeanne had as many children living with her as Elizabeth had at Luke's great mansion. But Jeanne did not receive the offer as a favor." If you have lost one, I have lost three, Elizabeth. You will feel better, you will see, when you have got the new one. And you need not think you must do something for us because you did not come near us for so long, and because one of these days Alfred may return!"

There was nothing Elizabeth could say. She put a good face on it and determinedly waved away Edwin's apologies. She *would* not take offense.

Part Six
All the Destinies
(1368-1373)

THE YOUNG MONK

THE DAY WAS so hot it had better been becalmed. The languid sea breeze did not freshen it, but rather forced everywhere the smell of sea decay, harbor traffic, and order. Stone embankments scorched to flight folk that would have rested thereon. The stapled wool stewed in the bales. The spire of Notre Dame de Calais was all blanched away into the haze, the waterfront glare raddled even the newest of ships, and Count Philip's citadel minded one, not of defiance, but of defeat, a multitude of black shadows seemingly perforating it. Yet elsewhere many a genuine ruin still bore witness to the siege more than a score of years ago.

Therefore the young monk searchingly threading his way through the quayside crowds deemed it a strange thing that one should not be able to distinguish natives from Englishmen merely by their demeanor. Nowhere could he fasten on any noticeable, conqueror's blatany or an answering resentment. Such sullenness or arrogance as he discerned in faces here and there, were plain pointers to a man's heart or worldly degree, to be found equally amongst all nations. So he framed the question, which he put to all likely looking people, in the corrupt Latin commonly understood in all the great ports of the civilized world.

He was no taller than most men, of very upright carriage, yet without making one's neck ache with the vicarious strain too often conveyed by the stiffed-backed. His face was sunburned and his general appearance travel frayed, although he was shod: no wandering friar, but a Benedictine by his garb. His means and standing were hard to gauge, as, despite being lone, dusty, and ragged, he bore himself with easy, quiet confidence; also, he had a large wallet, plump as a farrowing sow, all over straps and cords and buckles, which he saved from being jarred with suggestive solicitude.

About to pass by a group of richly dressed staplers, he suddenly halted and addressed them, "Pardon, my masters, did I hear you speak in English?"

"Ay," said one, who, despite the heat, had a wine flask in one hand and the reeking cup in the other, "it is truly said only the Fiend is keener eared than monks." His companions laughed, for the noise all round did make the young monk's statement to sound like a boast.

"I was watching out to hear English," the young monk explained tranquilly. "I am bound for Anglemere in England, having arrived in Calais only this day, all the way from Italy—"

"Is the grape no longer sweet in southern lands? Are the rich Lombards grown tight fisted and their wanton daughters chaste?"

"As to that," the monk said, smiling, "you will have to seek information from others better fitted to give it than I. I am looking for one Master Lamb, Captain of the *St. John* in the harbor. Having been on the road this quarter year, I would rather go straight to Ovisham than—"

"Ay, your kind is not overfond of walking!"

"Neither would you be, were your feet all your horse and wains," one of the other merchants rebuked the first. Then, turning to the monk, "The heat, and the vagaries of business, are apt to make men surly without cause. I would say it were best you await Master Lamb at his vessel."

"The crew could not say when they are due to sail. If only I could get speech with him first, I might then go about sundry other business that I am come charged with."

"Try Grosse Margot's stew," said the first speaker with a guffaw, keeping his eye fixed on the monk, to watch him shrinking.

"Thank you, my son. Perhaps you will be good enough to tell me the way," the monk returned, disappointing him.

Still he had to stop and ask further directions many times, before some loafer, with an eye on the bulging wallet, offered finally to be his guide.

The place was so unmistakably a whore-house first and foremost, that when he asked was this Grosse Margot's *tavern,* a great silence of perplexity descended. One woman got off a man's lap; the rest stayed as they were, but made elaborate show of it that drinking was indeed their sole pastime. However, behind two rude partitions along both sides of the long room the sounds of splashing water and giggling, and of even more straightforward sport, did not cease.

The woman that must be Margot, for she was huge and unsightly beyond relief, recovered sufficiently to bare her monstrous red arms in a threatening manner and ask, "Hast come to preach, monk?"

"No," said he. "I am looking for a friend."

At this there were great shouts of laughter. The joke was against the monk, but he soon joined in the general mirth, which rekindled every time it seemed about to wane. It was like a storm, resolving tension. Even the whore mistress was transformed. The blubber jigging on her bones seemed more like honest fat than the gaseous inflation of decay. It turned out that Juliana's shipmaster had indeed been here, but had left earlier that day.

Outside, the monk was astonished to see dusk no more advanced. After the windowless tavern interior, the summer twilight dazzled. He found himself in a maze of close, twisting alleys, and reeled on looking up at the top-heavy roofs of houses, no two of which were alike in height and frontal structure.

He heard a noise behind, and turned quickly. A man obviously in pursuit of him had stumbled. Round a corner a short distance ahead a second man moved forward. There was no chance of flight here—not without wings. The men were upon him. Both had knives ready. One was his former guide. One held him, while the other cut the shoulder strap of the wallet, then slashing away at the fastenings. Involuntarily, the monk cried out to see all his earthly fortune so roughly handled.

The shabby leather in shreds, the robber squatted amid a heap of horn tubes and rolls of parchment which had tumbled out. Impatiently, he broke the string of one and began opening it out. It sprang back time and again; but what he glimpsed evidently would not let him rest. Without rising, he gathered up some loose-lying stones and, more carefully now, placed them on the corners and round the margins of the sheet, until it lay flat.

The second man unintentionally twisted the monk's arm, craning so hard over his captive's shoulder to see the picture on the ground. It nearly filled the page, in brilliant colors: green, softest blue, scarlet, jet black, pale brown, silver, and bright gold. There was to be seen St. George on his rearing steed, and aiming his gold lance at the monster worm. They were in a meadow that looked like a carpet woven of flowers. There was a brook with fish in it and pebbles, a patch of stony desert, and a wood behind. Behind that there was a castle, with tower and ramparts, drawbridge and moat, and a lily banner waving in the wind. And a maiden princess stood afar, wrinkling her brow, with interlaced fingers and long hair, waiting her rescue, her little dog crouched at her feet. The robbers called to each other whenever new features struck them. It seemed they would never look their fill.

"There are more pictures," said the monk, and they understood his tone of voice and movement of the head. "If you will but handle them with care—"

The second man let go of him. Presently the monk was helping them, prising the lids off the sheaths that held the more fragile drawings, and offering suggestions as to what might next be unrolled to advantage. There were sheets covered with initial letters framing intricately composed scenes, drawings of hands and precise-muscled limbs feathered with lifelike shadings, notes of church doors and window tracery, and one great double leaf depicting in penned outlines a building in process of erection, with scaffolding and tools laid out large and recognizable in the foreground, each with a mark, and then a text beneath. The robbers conscientiously helped in rolling up and putting aside what they had done with. The man who had torn the first string went so far as to retrieve and carefully knot the ends. They blew and brushed sand and dust off where the undersides had become soiled.

At last it was too dark to see well. The monk stood up and stretched, and let the robbers know it was time he went his way. He collected his belongings and as best he might tied the remnants of the wallet. Though this time the others did not assist, neither did they hinder him.

He was lucky in the end. Relying on his nose to lead him back to the harbor, he found the Captain overseeing the hurried store of water on board, for a favorable wind had recommended the *St. John's* departure earlier than intended. Master Lamb warmly clasped the monk's hand when he introduced himself.

"So you are Alfred, Edwin of Bedesford's son! I would not have known you. Nay, but I lie. Now that I've looked, I can see your father in your face and something of your mother, too. Faith, but they have done well by you in Italian lands! I shall be right glad to take you. You will bring us luck."

He was as good as his word, and his prediction regarding Alfred's lucky presence also came true.

"How long, did you say, since you left Anglemere? Seven years! That is a time."

"I expect a great deal has changed. Yet for me the strangest thing will be to find that Anglemere, Bedesford, Cloudsway, do really exist, on their own. All these years they have been with me as a fading, happy dream, such as lives only in the dreamer and dies when he does."

"Were you so happy there? Or is it that you have been wretched since? To be sure, the long ago always is a happy land."

"It is so. But in Italy, too, things went well with me. It would be churlish not to say so."

"Whereabout in Italy?"

"First I was sent to my order's house in Pisa, and after a year or so the brethren spoke to the abbot of a place near Florence, that I might complete my training there. And there I stayed most of the time. Sometimes their Brother Head Scribe took me away with him on short visits. I have seen much of the inside of monasteries, and their written, painted treasures. Of the land and its laity I saw little."

"Yet on your way to Calais you must have seen more than most men do in a lifetime, unless they be seamen, to be sure."

"Ay, then I saw many things. Many churches, some built as fortresses, and much artifice yet new to me, also plants and fruit I had not known before, many kinds of different countryside. Ay, inconceivably different, each from the other, if one has not seen them. And men and women, too. But they did not differ so greatly, much less so than their style of houses and the shape in which they bake their bread, though, again, all alike cut the sign of the cross into their loaves. I must tell you that only at Calais was I truly surprised."

"How was that?" the Captain asked, with a certain pride, for that he himself knew that surprising town of Calais so well.

"Folk were so strange. They seemed to go out of their way to offer me discourtesy. Elsewhere I have heard people talk and jest about *some* priests' failings. But I never met with a disrespect all ready and waiting to pounce on monk's habit and monk's pate as such."

"In Calais," Master Lamb reflected, "there is not so much monk rule."

"Then, surely, folk have fewer grounds for bitterness and complaint against us."

The Captain laughed. "Ah, but—where are your wits, young Brother? —folk also have less cause to fear you!"

"You may be right. What a task—what goodly work it would be, to root out all cause for such hateful fear, and thus also do away with this base counterpart of it!"

The Captain shook his bulky head, with a pitying smile. "I have heard of such talk ere this—ashore, in England. There are some folk, I am told, flit from shire to shire, and tell all who will listen that it needs only for the clergy to be poor, meek, and righteous, to make every living man, woman, and child true Christians in all their thoughts and dealings. I, that might be your grandsire, I tell you that none, none of these changes would change a fiber of men's hearts."

"Men's hearts change all the time, often from moment to moment. I am with you in thinking it needs more than a change of outside circumstances to change them. One should try and help change both, I think. One must find out what *are* the things *will* play upon the heart. I told you about those two robbers—"

"Ay, it was great pity you had no language in common. It might have made all the difference to their lives henceforth, could you have talked to them," Master Lamb said seriously.

"I am not so sure. We shall never know, of course, but this is what God led me to think at the time: that exhortation might have driven them into shamefaced truculence. They clearly were old hands at their sinister trade. They must long have abandoned fear of God, and the fact that they did not hesitate to attack me shows how much they think of priests. I did not even make the sign of the cross over them—not until my back was turned and they could not tell what I was about. It seemed to me that to have let them know I blessed them would have been like spitting on a vanquished foe."

Another time Master Lamb said out of the blue to the monk, "I am an old man, Brother Alfred, wifeless, and homeless but for this, Juliana's vessel." There being nothing for Alfred to do but look as much as to say: "I know it, but why do you say this now?" Master Lamb went on, "What you told me about those would-be thieves of yours made me wonder if you are not applying like treatment to me. You have never said a word about my going to such places as Grosse Margot's."

"What could I have said, that you are not telling yourself, Master?"

"Confound you, monk!" the Captain muttered, and stumped aft. But he did not like his passenger any the less, and by no means shunned him, the remainder of the voyage.

Alfred asked many questions about the cathedral, but there was not much Master Lamb could tell him, although it seemed a point of honor with him never to be caught out at a loss for an answer.

"The work goes on. You know how it is. It is the same in shipbuilding. There comes a point when so much has got done that you cease to note further additions till you are taken by surprise one day to find the work is finished. Work never seem to grow so fast as at the beginning, out of nothing. The less there remains to be done, the less you notice gradual achievement. Ah, well. Not that I've been near Bedesford at all recently. Howbeit, you may be sure I would have heard had there been anything untoward, holding up the work or spoiling it. So you can take it that the less I have to tell you, the better matters have been going! At all events, there have been enough deaths, and great marriages, too, to have paid for a lot that will be new to you?"

Abbot William had aged suddenly. Even so those that saw him every day had hardly noted the enlargement of his tonsure, not by any razor; the changed proportion of silver curls and black; the fact that his ruddy color was like a tattooing, independent of the flush and ebb of health. What they had remarked was his figure, always on the stout side, but trim and manly, giving way and turning flaccid, except for its recent paunch, which swelled out bold and taut. And in great despondency his friends marked in him traces of childishness. His love of pun and jest and mischief now fed on irresponsibility. His lusts, too, seemed to have lost the vigorous charm of evergreen maturity and matter-of-fact candor, and, without dignity or real impulse, to rely on the stimulus of snickering obscenity and a terror of impotence.

Alfred was struck at first only by the change in the Abbot's person, and by an indifference which had supplanted his erstwhile, plausible interest in whomsoever stood before him.

"Ah, ah, welcome, Brother, ah, Alessandro!" The Abbot's head stayed cocked, his pouchy eyes screwed up, as he continued trying to decipher the crabbed script of the Florentine letter of introduction.

"Alfredo, it says, here," Alfred corrected deferentially, "but—"

"Ah, Allegro, then. A strange name, but not unpleasing, Brother Allegro. Gay. Are you the gay sort, Brother Alessandro? I do not think you will find our regiment intolerably strict. You are, of course, expected to keep the chronicles, too, but you will not find a great deal to record at length, in these rural parts. Our old head scribe? Oh, yes, he is still alive. But he can no longer stir upon his bed, nor leave it. You say you would like to see him? Oh, very well, very well, my son, if you are quite sure you do not want to be shown to your cell first?"

Brother Oswin's tiny face was become, not more wrinkled, but split and cracked all over, and although he lay flat on his back, his limbs were frozen in the unnatural angles that crippled them, and stuck out weirdly, crablike. No one so far had recognized Alfred, but through Brother Oswin's frame there passed an instant movement, convulsive yet all but imperceptible, which managed to convey his intention of spreading his arms in welcome.

"Alfred! My little Alfred, grown so tall and strong! God bless you, God bless you! Come closer. I cannot lift my head. Nay, what a happy, blessed, blessed day!"

Alfred knelt by the straw pallet on the ground, his hands hovering, not daring to touch his old teacher's, their eyes smiling wetly into each other.

"Those must be specimens of your work, looking out of the wallet at your side," Brother Oswin said eagerly. "I cannot wait to see them. Pray show them to me, my dear son."

Holding each sheet so that the moveless man could examine it at leisure, Alfred kept his glance averted from that of the Abbot, who stood to all intents and purposes ignored. Lord William had not asked to see the drawings before accepting the newcomer for the post which the Florentine letter requested on his behalf. He understood others speaking Latin well enough, Alfred knew.

"Alfred," said Brother Oswin, weeping happy tears, "God has made you very great among us that practice this loveliest of crafts. He knows what I feel; I cannot find words to tell you. To think that He allowed me to guide your earliest, faltering steps! You see how sorely He has punished me for having loved Art before men, though He must know that I loved Him best of all. But because love is good even when it is misapplied, He has now rewarded it in these my last days. Look under the straw, where my head lies. Ay, it is my Life of St. Francis, holed and bound, albeit still incomplete. Hitherto, my unregenerate soul was racked, even as my body, by hopeless regret for this my most cherished undertaking, which I knew none but myself could truly complete. Now Our merciful Lord has vouchsafed me peace. I know you will do it. I know you can do it. Nay, more. I know it will be much the better for your work."

"Well!" the Abbot at last burst out, in English, "All along you were little Alfred Widowson of the withered hand, were you? Well! God's blood and Mary's milk! And you never told me, you rogue! Allowing me to treat you like a nobleman and a foreigner, a very prelate, forsooth! Alessandro, indeed! What? Ay, maybe so. As you say, Alfredo looks much like Alessandro in their Italian writing. Ay, maybe it was not your fault entirely. Come with me, that I may now judge if your specimen works bear out your repute, before instructing you as to your particular duties. Your Abbot's blessing, good Brother Oswin. This is the cell I had them clear for you, Brother Alfred. Had I known who you are, you could have shared it with one of its two previous inmates. For the time being we had better leave it as it is. We shall see."

The fractiousness of age had not made sufficient inroad into Lord William's temper for him to bear Alfred a grudge after the first irritation was past. Yet it seemed he could never quite correct the false start of their renewed acquaintance. By his manner he appeared ever uncertain whether Alfred was an Italian Brother Alessandro or the son of a former Bedesford churchland serf. Fairly soon Alfred got leave of absence to see his parents.

He had not had time thus far for a good look at the cathedral, the only building hereabout which had become bigger, and not remarkably the smaller for his own growth and absence and experience. Inside, it was no longer like a maze, its ruins-in-reverse recognizably coherent. Some of the outside portions, however, were less distinct of contour than they had been, beset with buttresses, standing two or three deep in several places, particularly in the open triangles between the apse and upper transepts, and linked with one another by curved bridges between serrated and cross-topped pinnacles.

"Now I know I really am come home!" he cried laughingly, arrived at the old booth hut, under whose roof he could not now stand upright. For there lay his mother with a new babe in her arms: Ruth, she had been christened, only a few days before. Edwin was in the act of rendering Jeanne some faithful midwife's service; a small boy sat on the bed, looking on, and two half-grown girls who had been dressing corn for the morrow on the out-of-doors cooking stones came crowding through the doorway behind the stranger. He knew they must have heard of his return, so that his appearance could not have startled his mother enough to do her harm. She sat up, rosy with excitement. It was Edwin who looked pale, and whose hands had started shaking.

"So you think you are become so great you may make fun of your poor mother!" Jeanne's scolding rang with fervent joy. "Look, Jack, this is he, your big brother, of whom you have heard tell so much. You remember Margaret and Janet, your sisters, Alfred? How handsome he is, my eldest son!" she appealed to the rest of the family as if they were not likewise kin to him. "But he is too thin, I see it now. You have done too much work and walking, and do not eat enough, I can see that. Please God it will be different for you at *our* monastery! Oh, Alfred, here you are, a real priest! Pity your youngest sister could not have wanted, to be baptized by you. And pity," her voice sank unsteadily, "that you could not have helped us bury the others. And then I had a son called Laurence, after Brother Laurentius. To think you did not know he had ever been born! Had it not been for Edwin—if I had not had your father to stand by me, I know not how I would have come out of that grief. You will pray for their little souls, I know. Do not be bashful, girls, go up to your brother, then, for his blessing! Edwin! What is there to feed our Alfred? Run next door, Margaret, and borrow some ale."

"Where is Jaffy?"

"Oh, Jaffy is well and thriving, with more flesh upon him than you have, my Alfred. He has been away at Friggsby quarries this last month, entrusted with errands for his father and for the lord Abbot himself, so see about the stone for Lady Agnes' waterspouts. Were you not told, at the monastery? Ay, the lady of Danesborough died not long ago. Guess how she willed away her property? Nearly all of it has gone to Lady Philippa—not to the nunnery, but to Lady Philippa herself. So the Cinqmort lawsuit is like to be ended before the Last Judgment after all. Of course the Lady Agnes left money for Masses to be said at St. Peter's, and at Thirchester, for herself and my lord's wife, her daughter. Yet she also bequeathed a large sum to St. Hand's, to be used, when the time comes, for gutters and waste heads; and what do you think? These are to represent sundry sins and vices, each in the likeness of someone she detested: Lord Hugh is one, think of that! and John Wycliffe another. Was it not sinful of her, and witty?" She lay back chuckling and shaking her head.

Alfred saw his father look at him a little worriedly: to see how the monk was taking Jeanne's chatter. "Do you find everyone much changed?" Edwin asked awkwardly on meeting his son's gaze.

"Not you and Mother. Brother Laurentius I would hardly have known, without any hair, nor teeth, either. It is those that were children when I left took me aback. I hear Jacob is dead?"

"Ay. That was the saddest thing happened in Bedesford since the child-dying. Still, it was as good a death as that of your grandfather's brother, Richard, and surely what Jacob would have wanted: to die of a fall at his work He was dead instantly, and providentially had taken the sacrament the preceding Sunday. But tell us about your past seven years, Alfred."

As at length they plunged into talks of crafts and workmanship, Alfred began to think that from their first constraint had flowered a new and equal interchange of fellow feeling and potential inspiration.

Jeanne listened with a placid pride that grew at the same rate as the talk ranged beyond her comprehension.

Then Edwin happened to touch his son. He had only placed his hand on Alfred's arm. But he started back, looking guilty, and that was the end of their pleasant, easy communion. Try as he would, Alfred could not renew it.

"Well, my son—who is not my son but everybody's brother—I do not suppose our paths will cross often in the future."

"Father!" Alfred tried to laugh. "We live but a stone's throw apart! In working hours we shall be even closer—"

"Yet shall we be living, by the very nature of our lives and business, as far apart as two men in two foreign countries. It was good of you to come and see us like this. You must not think that you need go on doing so. We understand—we shall understand," and Edwin looked at Jeanne, silencing her cry of protest unuttered.

Alfred knew well it was not that his father bore him no love. He deemed this an instance of poor-man's pride, which immediate argument and cajolery could only have stiffened, but which would surely consent to lower its defenses after a due time of unobtrusive wooing.

CHAPTER 2

THE WIDOW

On the Feast of St. Swithin, no one from Trefeller Court came to Mass in the morning, the whole household being fully occupied with the guests that had arrived the night before. Of the Smithy Yard folk Mistress Robinson was observed in her place with her maids and four children, but Luke was not among the men. After service the maids with Isabella and Robin went one way, Elizabeth another, taking only her eldest son and the youngest child, a daughter, namesake to Juliana.

Carrying the year-old babe on her shoulder and leading Peter by the hand, Elizabeth walked slowly, to enjoy the sun, across the fields to Bede's Ford, where the water had sunk so that the piled steppingstones were high and dry. Mother and son were singing together, the baby crowing, as they arrived at Trefeller Court. They were hot and disheveled, but the coif from under which some of her hair strayed was of silk, her loose gown girt tightly with a silver-gilt belt, and her countenance, even in self-forgetful gaiety, could never lose the underlying formal calm of the mistress of a great house. And Peter had already the long limbs, angular profile, and pale, sandy ruddiness one associated with Cinqmort lordship. So Juliana's guests saw at once whom they had to do with in her daughter and grandchildren, and saluted them accordingly.

Both the guests were women: Widow Susannah Naylor and her aunt. The widow, Elizabeth knew, was older than herself by a round ten years, but she looked yet older, and was quite inordinately plain. No feature in her face went rightly with the other. The single eye was well enough, but they were set too close together; each lip by itself was shapely, but for united repose the lower was too short and receded so that the chin must slope backward undented. The underchin was thrice the width of the upper, clean and rosy, but glistening like ham fat, and projected in a roll. She was not ugly: she was so repulsive that it took your breath away.

Her aunt could not be more than Elizabeth's age. Her face, rigorously coif enclosed, was pockmarked, but her figure was slenderly rounded, tall and high waisted, and she had comely hands. Her clothes were somber and threadbare, with her niece and mistress had everything of the best. Elizabeth could not remember ever having heard of a woman of twenty or so who was neither betrothed, wed, widowed, nor cloister-bound.

"What sweet children, Mistress!" the widow exclaimed. "Oh, you beauty, oh, you darling babe! What thick hair she has got, for her age: like flax, with a sheen. Oh, I would like to eat you," and she smacked her lips exaggeratedly; the baby laughed. "And this lad! How old is he: only six? The Lord God has surely blessed you, Mistress. I am told you have two more? I have no children of my own. I am rich. I have health, thank God, and land, and sheep beyond my own reckoning. My relations are not troublesome, and I can go my way in all things. I have everything save only children."

"Belike you lost some, Mistress?"

They were settling round the table, the widow snatching a place next to Peter. With her arm round his waist—albeit he wriggled—she went on talking to his mother, most earnestly.

"I never had a child. I never had the chance. You are Little John's elder sister, and a woman of note and great good sense, I can see, so that I have no doubt he holds your opinion in high esteem. I will tell you about myself, hoping that you may be moved to friendship toward me, and not set him against me."

Elizabeth looked at Juliana with a little smile but said nothing.

"I was married at the same age as you were, Mistress Elizabeth, and I have been widowed as many years as you have been a wife. My husband was ten years my junior: he was not yet eleven years old when he died, after six years of marriage. So you see my life has not been all honey and roses. You must not think I have had no offers since. But the first two were again young children, and I deemed I had had my fill of waiting a husband's maturity. Perchance they, too, would have died ere they were any good to me. The third was an old man, from whom the marrow had long since departed. And now I am too old. I could no longer afford to nurse me up a father for my children. If I marry next year, I can still get in a dozen children, perhaps more, if there be twins. I am rich enough to provide well for full two dozen, even if Little John had not wealth of his own. I do think he is the most well-favored young man in all England, your brother, Mistress. How proud you must be of him!"

Elizabeth inclined her head. Accustomed though she had been from childhood of hearing praise of Little John, it never failed to astound her. And she was sorry for this woman, humbling herself right and left to please her prospective kindred, when, had she but known it, Juliana was just as anxious not to let this alliance slip through her fingers. The widow misinterpreted Elizabeth's weak response.

"To be sure, he may yet repent him of the bargain. They are late, your husband and he. Think you he has run away to sea?" she said humorously, no doubt priding herself, poor thing, on acknowledging her plainness.

"Rest assured that the betrothal will take place!" Juliana caused Elizabeth to shiver for her mother's obtuseness. Her grim tone stated as clearly as words that Little John had no say in the matter either. But the widow actually received this with a grateful smile.

"I do not see why we should not be very happy?" she appealed again to the bridegroom's sister. "Disparity in ages is often a good thing, for one spouse will gain the restraint of wisdom and experience in return for the other's youthful zest. What is your opinion, Mistress Robinson?"

Mistress Robinson murmured a few noncommittal words.

"But you of all people must have an opinion," the widow insisted, "there being twice as many years between yourself and your husband as divide Little John and me."

Now Elizabeth felt angry with them all: with the widow for raising so personal a question in front of Luke's son, old enough to understand; with her mother for gazing at her with concentrated menace—as though Elizabeth were still a child to be cowed; and with Jane, who had come in a few minutes before, and stood with folded arms, also regarding her, in sardonic expectancy.

She said, "For my part, Mistress, I am always sorry for the older in such a marriage."

Jane in the background laughed so that the widow's aunt gave a start. Juliana broke in, stammering with wrath, "What is this you are saying? What have you to gain from preventing this advantageous match? So far as I can remember, it was always yourself you were sorriest for."

"Mother! and you too, Jane!" Elizabeth said in a quiet voice. "Bear in mind you speak before their children!" She turned to the bewildered widow, speaking slowly, to make sure she found the right words. "Ay, it is true, that was when I was young and silly. And it was that, more than anything, I had in mind, when I said what I did just now. A spouse ever bemoaning must be far from pleasant to live with."

There was a pause. Juliana was purple red in the face with the effort of holding her peace. She had remembered that there are times when it pays to sit mute and refrain from pressing a desired bargain.

Finally the widow said, faltering, "I know not rightly how to put my meaning. I do want my husband to be happy. But—but—even if he is not, I shall be content. I do not mind not being *happy*. There is only one way in which a husband can be satisfactory or unsatisfactory to me."

The mother of four living children bowed her head; she could not well say more.

Juliana, her voice trembling in relief and triumph, said without stopping to think, "You may rest assured on that score, too, daughter-to-be. He already has one bastard, at Wasteside Newtown." There was another crow of laughter from Jane. Peter, with the widow's arm still about him, had ceased his writhing, and listened openmouthed. Juliana herself looked out of countenance. Her words had not been like her usual, professed sentiments, and Little John's bastard might not after all strike the rich widow as an asset.

But it did so. The widow took a deep breath. "I quite understand a loving sister's reluctance to see her brother tied to so old and plain a woman as I am. Your daughter is yet young, Mistress Juliana, and the young can be cruel without meaning to be; whereas you and I, we understand each other. I swear to you both that neither he nor yourselves will ever have cause to regret this marriage—if so be God will grant me life to see it happen. I shall be the best of daughters and sisters to you. Do not fear that I am too habituated to rule. I am not yet so old that I cannot adopt new ways. I shall never preen myself with the wealth I brought with me. I will not fret and scold my dear young husband."

Luke and Little John came, and in their wake dogs and the servants with food, drink, and table gear. The visitors had not yet met Luke, and, shy of her young bridegroom, the widow at first did not take her eyes off the great man of the parish. The way he walked, the way his shoulders were set, proclaimed his position, as did the assurance behind his subdued and almost modest speech.

He went up to his wife and took her by the hand as if it were fragile and she a most honored stranger, then bowed to his mother-in-law, and only then to the guests—though this last bow was also the grandest and lowest. As he took off his hat and gloves he placed with them on the board a slate on which he and Little John had drafted a proposed marriage contract. Even though she deliberately set herself to see Little John as through the widow's eyes: all white and rose and gold, sap and strength, a pattern of young manhood, Elizabeth marveled that in her husband's presence anyone should continue to admire her brother. That the widow did so her simpering made plain, directly Little John came up to her.

He laughed and shook his curls, with an air of pleasure and conscious merit rather than amusement. His gaze steadfastly shied from traveling upward beyond the level of the widow's buxom chest, which caused her clumsily to make some play with it, in merciful misapprehension.

"This is my mother's youngest sister," the widow fluttered, pulling her aunt to the fore. "She has no other living kin but me, and goes with me everywhere. You will not mind it if she comes to live with us? She used to be most fair as a young girl, before the smallpox came on her. Just then I was widowed and wanted a friend to dwell with me. Now that I am about to marry again, I suppose I could dower her entry into one of the lesser sisterhoods, yet I do not feel that would be kind. Debarred from having children of her own, for sure she will find next-best happiness in looking after mine. And until then she can help me look after you. For you must know, Little John, that my possets and preserves are famous at Clowes and beyond. If your mother will lend me a nook in her kitchens, I will make you my pease-sweet tomorrow

—ay, it is a jolly confection, is it not, Aunt?—with open pods of march-pane and rows of marchpane peas, most pretty and lifelike, and quite heavenly to taste, though I myself say it."

CHAPTER 3

THE LADY OF THE MANOR

ALTHOUGH BOTH PARTIES wished for speedy marriage, it was not cele-brated until Finding Day the following year. This was not only in deference to the Trefeller custom of having their family events as far as possible coinciding with the cathedral's feasts. Mindful that she had promised complete submission after marriage, the Widow Naylor beforehand conscientiously examined and disputed every suggested set-tlement, until she deemed her future children to be in every wise safe-guarded.

By that time Young Gervase Cinqmort had already been married a full half-year. His wife was Griselda, daughter of Sir. Bertrand Joly-body and sister to Sir Asphodel, a maidenly looking weed of a lady, unremarkable of face and of reserved ways.

Since 1350 the Cinqmorts had made no attempt to pay off their large debt to the Jolybody workshops. Sir Bertrand in his lifetime had long written it off; Sir Asphodel nursed no hopes regarding it, but had neither forgotten nor forgiven. In Baldwin's memory it had not lapsed, either, and he it was first thought of canceling it through alliance by marriage. The Cinqmorts must first of all decide who was to sue for the maiden's hand. This was soon settled, despite Gervase's protests. Lord Hugh was unlikely to beget an heir, and Baldwin, farthest from the succession, would not be accounted a good match.

They proposed that the old debt was to stand the bride in lieu of portion. Needless to add, the Cinqmorts nevertheless hoped to derive financial benefit through her, on her brother's death, if not before.

Sir Asphodel agreed immediately. Such noble alliance was cheaply bought at the price of a debt his books no longer carried, and without expenditure on Griselda's dowry. The wedding was held at the tailor's mansion, and the bride borne off directly after, with all her wardrobe but without a single serving woman.

In fact she was eager to get away from home and all the ponderous familiar faces, and to start an entirely new life. Lord Hugh had assured her brother that the manor swarmed with maids. Even if he had not expressly said so, it would never have occurred to the Jolybodys to doubt that such was the case. My lord was intent on keeping down expenses, even to the extent of saving the cost of a serving wench's maintenance on the road. No respectable woman had stayed longer than a day at Bedesford Manor for the last twenty years.

In the course of the journey the Cinqmorts' true indifference to their new lady became more and more apparent. Gervase slept with her of nights and Baldwin helped her mount and dismount, and occasionally remembered to inquire whether she were weary or saddlesore. Beyond that they made few concessions to her presence. Unused though she was to being her own tiring woman, she kept herself neat, and rode trotting along behind them, singing to herself and thinking her own thoughts. As far as she was concerned, she saw no cause for complaint, until they came to Bedesford.

Then she was taken aback by what she found, or rather, all she failed to find and had ever tacitly regarded as indispensable to the most ordinary comfort. But first she enjoyed the reception accorded her by the townfolk, and waved, smiling her tight-lipped little smile, to the crowds lining her path, and at the manor gate drank to the henchmen out of Hugh-le-gros's enormous horn.

Her chests and sacks and coffers were borne into the hall, where she stood by her husband's side. Lord Hugh detached from his belt Griselda's keys which her brother had entrusted to him, mounted on to the table, and bade the henchmen open up the lady's luggage. Everyone, cooks, falconer, stable boys, and all thronged round. Griselda's astonished protest drowned unregarded. She was so small, most of the time they even lost sight of her.

"Look what we got with the tailor's daughter!" Lord Hugh shouted— in no unkindly jest, as he thought—before they quite forgot her. And in truth the tailor's daughter possessed a queenly wardrobe. There were mantles and cloaks and coats buttoned, buckled, laced; underkirtles that most people would have wept with joy to own for holiday top wear; festal gowns each of which might have been cut up to make two well-dizened bishop's copes; shifts of silk and lawn and silk woolen; head-cloths all lacework, or sheer and tight textured as glass; girdles of gold, silver, bronze, of woven beads, or many yards of broidered velvet; shoes and hose and gloves, fillets and ribands, enough to stock a fair; fine towels and pillow cases, and whatever else you can think of. She had enough to serve her own lifetime and thereafter enrich a dozen daughters' progeny—if they had but let her keep these possessions.

Lord Hugh acted on the assumption that all this had come to the manor in place of bride's dower. Presently everything she had lay spread in display all over the table, the benches, and draped over the open, empty chests, Lord Hugh making survey from where he stood, up high, with arms akimbo and legs wide apart. First of all he selected for himself two gowns, one with a long, detachable train, one fur-lined cloak, and one agate-studded belt. Then he picked out those henchmen who he deemed most deserved reward, and presented each with one of the gorgeous underkirtles.

Gervase forsook his lady wife ere all the best things should be gone, and righteously laid claim to the lion's share. Baldwin, who at the start had thought they were merely going to make an inventory, had his notebook smeared and crumpled as others reached across him to feel and hold up various garments, and he tried to remonstrate with the looters. In the end he was persuaded to accept part of the spoils, a vast-sleeved mourning dress of dark-brown cloth without ornament. But for all the good that did his conscience, he might as well have taken one with gold embroidery. Griselda was left with two gowns, one for every day and one for church going; against autumn and winter my lord promised her one of his mother's. All her shoes and stockings, and most of her headgear were likewise left to her, and some trinkets, salves, lotions, and sweetmeats.

Thus began her married life. Even Baldwin would have been indignant had any charged them with cruelty toward the friendless, helpless lady. For nobody ever gave her an unkind word, not even once did Gervase play a practical joke on her. They could truthfully claim that she never shed a tear in sight of anyone.

She had not lived in Bedesford a month when she began to ail. There was no disquiet, only jesting on this account, within the manor and without. But two months later she miscarried, for no reason. She was so ill that Jane had to be fetched to her bedside. Griselda required long and careful tending. Jane was glad and my lord was glad, albeit at cross purposes; Gervase perhaps was not so glad. Jane saved the lady's life, but did not restore complete health to her. Yet as soon as her husband was again admitted to her bed, she conceived anew.

For the first time one saw her agitated. Jane had to regale her with every story she knew of other young women that had started wedded life with miscarriages and yet lived to see large, healthy families.

And now they learned how they had mistaken this Griselda. For her own sake as well as that of the unborn, she demanded to take her place among the supplicants next Finding Day. My lord, and Baldwin, and Gervase most of all were set against it, but, gentle, bedridden, without anyone to support her, the lady got her way. They were made to see that she had an iron will if she chose to exert it. They saw that she had not so chosen hitherto, that all along her indifference to them had dwarfed their disregard of her. There was nothing left of which they might have stripped her, and as they desired the heir as much as she did, they could not starve or beat her into surrender.

One reason against Griselda's attending the anniversary ceremony was the leper test.

A handful of selected lepers had been brought hither specially from Ovisham, under the care of a knight of St. Lazarus. Up till then only isolated sufferers from this worst of sicknesses had from time to time approached the wonder-working relic, without success so far as was known. Prior Carlos had at length prevailed on St. Hand's guardians to subject It to properly conducted trial, that one might know with certainty once and for all whether or no the Hand prevailed against leprosy.

Prior Carlos was fortunate in the Abbot's indolence, against which he ever inveighed. Under someone like the late Lord Benedetto he would have been condemned as a heretic. For he boldly denied the accepted view that the Hand would not cure leprosy simply because this was no illness in the ordinary sense, but rather, the visible mark upon whom God hath rejected absolutely. The Prior held that, albeit token of the Lord God's particular disfavor, leprosy was still disease, and theoretically curable like sin itself. Since the relic had no effect on manual disorders, acknowledgedly because It was itself a hand, one could hardly expect It to heal its own old malady.

In truth the test cases were no sight for pregnant women. There were faces and limbs showing no more definition of form than raspberries— like raspberries not in color, but in the evenly blistered cushions of their surface. There were others with noses melting away and lichenlike scabs all over their cheeks. Some there were looked as yet but queerly swollen. We were told that you might stick pins into them without their remarking it. Most of them wore round their necks lead amulets dedicated to St. Giles.

The Trefeller wedding took place early, on the porch. In the interval before the main service people wandered all over the ground, exchanging comment on all that was new. Most notable was the completed rood screen, made to resemble a mesh of symmetrically interbraided thorn, with the symbols of the Saviour's passion worked into it wherever the eye desired weight and density for visual balance. Young Richard Widowson, not yet fifteen years old, had been allowed to cut his wood-wright's teeth, so to speak, on the screen, assistant in the carving and putting together.

Richard had shot up fast, nearly as tall as Little John Trefeller, though shorter in body and longer in the legs, with the true Widowson coloring as to hair and eyes, albeit with Meg's whiter complexion. Everybody liked the lad, as they had Edwin in his youth, yet differently, not for any special quality. Elizabeth Robinson had remained extraordinarily fond of him—considering that she had children of her own. And he had a particular friend in Brother Alfred.

Richard and Brother Alfred stood talking at the side door, where the chantry-school boys had just done singing. Mistress Robinson, walking with her eldest daughter, caught sight of them and changed her course.

"Brother Alfred! I have been waiting my chance to tell you how good it is to see you back amongst us, how well you are looking, and how proud it makes old childhood friends of yours to hear of your noble acquirements. I ought to chide you. You might have found the time, just once, to visit us at Smithy Yard!"

"You must forgive me, Mistress," Alfred stammered. She was at her very fairest that day of her brother's nuptials, dressed in a velvet gown of Luke's favorite dove gray, with white ermine around neck, arm-holes, and hips, and a thin gold chain lacing it crosswise down the front. She drew forward her daughter, so that Isabella came to stand between her and the monk, and bade them greet each other.

"She used to look like me when she was younger. But of late it has seemed to me that, strangely, she is favoring your family rather than mine or Luke's."

Alfred shook his head. He could not see it. Neither, be it said, could anyone else save the mother, who had so far confided it only to Bess. Isabella's eyes were gray, and her hair would probably grow darker than her mother's. That was as near as she approached likeness to Alfred. Whomsoever she took after, she was a lovely little maid.

Then the throng before them was cleft by Luke, leading Bess and another woman with the rest of the Robinson children.

"Ah, here you are, my wife," he said, over pleasantly, "and my eldest daughter also. So this is Brother Alfred, our old friend, of whose new doings we have heard so much. How goes it, Richard? You must do us the honor of a visit one of these days, Brother Alfred, and tell of Italy and seafaring. Elizabeth, it is nearly time. Come take your place for the Showing, my love. Brother Alfred, too, will wish to hasten choirward."

Elizabeth was angry and confused. Suddenly he pressed her hand and said quickly, in low tones, "Give over frowning for one moment, my love, and smile. Here is that hell priest whom we both detest. Pray smile at him with all your most punctilious grace." He himself doffed his hat and swept it to his breast, most scathingly.

The Franciscan Prior halted in his busy rush and raised his hand for benediction. It stopped in mid-performance. He seemed to stare at Luke and yet not at him, his eyes rather ludicrously traveling back and forth between two points beyond Luke's face at either side.

Disconcerted, Luke asked, "What is that you see over my shoulder, good Father—in broad daylight?"

"It is your own ears I am looking at, Master Robinson. Nothing could be more substantial. Will you be joining the file of the sick this day?"

Luke's hand left Elizabeth's and went up to his ear, then he rammed his fine hat well down upon his head. If there was anything could put Luke right out of humor, it was remarks as to his health, of which year in, year out he had had more than his fill.

"Nay let me look at them!" the Prior commanded.

"Another day, good Prior, when we have more time. Albeit I fear they will scarce repay your curiosity, my ears. They but got slightly frostbitten on the road last month. Come, Elizabeth. We must hurry now, children."

The Prior remained gazing after them, working his lips and wrinkled scalp, and thoughtfully tapping one muddy foot.

"Why did you not ask me to make you an ointment, husband?" Elizabeth asked reproachfully.

"I did not realize myself what must have happened until they began to feel tender. Now the soreness has gone out of them again. The last of the swelling will soon subside. So little as it was, you never even marked it. But that lynx-eyed leech in friar's clothing must needs see and make a song about it!"

Herself thinking it small wonder he was vexed, Elizabeth said no more.

The Hand worked its customary share of cures, but all the lepers remained leprous. The lady of the manor, however, found her health improved as she had hoped, God and St. Francis subsequently sustaining her so that she carried her child the full term.

CHAPTER 4

THE CHILDLESS

GRISELDA CINQMORT BORE a son, but he had eyes filmed blindly blue as a rabbit's are after boiling, and his little elbow joints were reversed, like the knees of the horse in the blest Brother Nicholas' vision. With reference to the well-known case of Alfred, the lady expressed hopes that Jane might mend this deformity, by magic and massage. Yet must there have been something lacking also in the baby brain, for the Cinqmort heir could not be taught to suck. Griselda and Jane had a few heart-breaking days, trying to force him. Through it all the babe cried unceasingly, with hunger. Hard lumps appeared in the young mother's breasts, and the unshed milk mounted to her head in fever, ere God had mercy on them and took back the little one, who had been baptized Hugh. Griselda lay sick for a long while, and Jane had to stay on, nursing her.

She stayed on after the lady was over the worst, for Griselda never regained her state of health before marriage. The lady's sole part in the manor's life was that of Gervase's bedfellow and object of Jane's service. Without passion or tenderness, propinquity and custom begat unending fruit on her awful fertility. For she conceived sometimes as often as thrice in one year. Mostly she miscarried, sometimes easily, in her sleep, sometimes in pain. Now and then she brought forth another nine months' infant, dead before it drew its first breath, or else deformed and deficient as her first. The longest-lived of these children died aged four weeks and a day.

That time Griselda had been unwise or feeble enough to allow the integrity of her indifference to be broken down by hope. One week—two weeks—three. It seemed to her the babe had survived years, and every day that saw it still alive seemed to decrease the danger of its dying. Poring over it every hour of its life, she could not perceive how it grew wizened and smaller, any more than she would have been able to observe its gradual filling out. As long as she held it tight in her arms, its wailing was stilled: another propitious sign. When the boy died, she would not believe it until he was stiff. Then she seemed resolved to weep herself to death. But the very tears died on her before she weakened herself mortally.

She was never strong enough to play her titular part, yet never faded quite away. She would lie for hours and weeks upon her bed, where Gervase nightly joined her, while in the daytime Jane attended to her needs. Sometimes Griselda would not exchange a word with either for days at a stretch; there was nothing between them for verbal communication. She lay and healed her fortitude with silence; in silence regained her removedness. People began to talk. First we marveled Jane could not do for Griselda what she had done for Gillian Smith and others. Next we concluded it was, rather, that she *would* not; and in the end we became convinced that Griselda's misfortune was altogether, actively, Jane's fault.

Occasionally she resumed her work and place at Trefeller Court. But soon enough Griselda's hour would strike again, one way or another, and Jane was recalled. She seemed to need periodical return under Juliana's wing, renewing her bounden allegiance and her contact with the material things composing Juliana's dominion.

However, Juliana did not seem to feel the want of Jane, neither in effect on her prosperity nor for her own happiness. It was most strange, after twenty years. In her place she had two housekeepers at her beck and call, new toys not only in their persons, but also in their position relative to herself. For in theory her son's wife was the real mistress of Trefeller Court; her daughter-in-law's aunt stood even higher, as a guest. In practice the Widow Naylor, as we went on calling her to the end of her days, was Juliana's abject thrall; and the unlucky aunt, her niece's slave, was doubly so.

A long time went by before Little John's wife complained even to Elizabeth whom, not without reason, she named her only friend, for all that they met comparatively seldom. One day, Juliana being present, Elizabeth asked her sister-in-law whether she would not like to make some contribution toward Margaret Widowson's marriage to their friend the Danesborough weaver.

Juliana answered for her, "Susannah gave away a silver ewer and basin only last week, and she is paying for the joists over the ringers' side chapel. God knows she will soon have given away everything she brought us, if we do not check her."

"It is my money after all!" the widow rebelled. "You shall not stand in my way. This may be just my chance. Our Lady will love me if I do this for a poor maiden. It is my own money, and my yearning."

"Mind you what you promised before you were married to my son? Before you had safely got him, you were willing enough to swear away pride, independence, and self-will. It is *not* your money now. It is his."

"There now you can see how your mother deals by me, Elizabeth!" the poor widow cried. "Thus it is every time I want to spend a farthing, or have my own way in the smallest trifle. A dog's life do I lead in this my own home, Elizabeth!"

"A dog's life, do you call it?" Juliana said threateningly. "However cruelly we may be dealing by her, Elizabeth, you may believe your mother that Susannah gets her own back on us! She is not the silent kind, you know that. And ever since your brother wed her, there has been no other topic in this house than Susannah's monthly courses. 'This time for sure I shall conceive. This time I know I have. My pulse is much faster. My heart beats so loud. I puked yester-even when I overate. I feel hot. I feel cold. My bowels are loose. My bowels will not move. My bosom is grown larger. I am thinner, for I nourish the unseen. I have an ache, an itch, a cramp.' Then will come the first herald throe, and she runs to tell me and persuade herself it is only a false token. Next we hear her chamber door slam, and weeping, and the beating of her head against the wall. After which the whole thing starts all over again. A dog's life, indeed!"

Juliana stopped, flushed and out of breath, unable to make herself heard any longer above her daughter-in-law's loud, broken-hearted crying.

"How can you be so unkind, Mother?" Elizabeth, helplessly stroking Susannah's head, said low.

"Unkind, am I? What about me, that wants a grandson to carry on my poor husband's name and house?"

"It is no fault of hers—"

"Luckily your brother has given twofold evidence that it is not his!"

There was little Elizabeth could do for Susannah, beyond inviting her to Smithy Yard more often, discreetly trying to talk patience and resignation into her, and letting her play with the children to her heart's content. The children liked and welcomed her whenever she came, although she could seldom bring them gifts.

"You are kind, Elizabeth, but neither you nor anyone can help me, save only God, with children of my own. What am I saying. Children! Mind you how I once reckoned on a dozen, not counting twins? Now I should be more than satisfied with a mere one."

"Nay, these things happen, you know that," Elizabeth said, averting her eyes in embarrassment.

"Oh, Elizabeth, it has come to this. I had rather have a child brought shame and grief on me, or a cripple or an idiot, a short-lived monster even, like the poor manor's lady than none at all, none at all."

A time came when it seemed the widow's wish was granted. Her courses ceased, she was sick of mornings, her bowels ceased to move, her skirts bellied. She sat in John Trefeller's bridal-gift chair all day long, not daring so much as to reach out for any thing. Baby weave was set up on her loom, and the aunt wove, cut out, and sewed from morning till night. The cradle was brought out of storage and its bedding renewed, and the names were fixed, Juliana Elizabeth or Francis John Giles. Then the pent-up matter went bad inside her and gave her a fever, and Elizabeth came and said a clyster would do no harm. The widow's abdomen went down. Bedesford laughed for a month.

The unlucky woman's obsession but went on growing, till it was not only at home that she could talk of naught else. You could tell part of her knew how laughable and bootless was her talk and tried to hold it back, yet out it would come. Because of the rumors anent Griselda Cinqmort, she would not appeal to Jane for counsel. For a long time she could not bring herself to consult Prior Carlos either. Finally he offered his advice unasked. He told her of the times most favorable to conception, as culled from the Scriptures of the ancient Jews. This only increased the poor wretch's difficulties.

"Oh, however am I to contrive it, Reverend Father? I have not breathed this to a soul: but it is so that my husband will not always— will not always—take me to his bosom. He says he knows it is useless. You can see for yourself I am not the fairest nor the youngest of wives."

She tried leaving him alone during those periods when the Prior deemed continence could be no loss, and then coaxing and tempting him on the right nights. She tried making him drunken. Once she even tried to overbear him with her weight. Often at the crucial date he was away from home altogether, at the instigation of his mother and Luke, paying court to his rich, aging Aunt Philippa at Thirchester.

He still let himself be ruled by them in all things, excepting fornication. Yet was it their influence alone saved him time and again from public penance. Since on his marriage he had come of age, he had taken his place at the Town Chamber on his own behalf and his mother's. This suited Luke well, as he could count on his brother-in-law's vote. The fact that he remained *Little* John although there was no elder John Trefeller, was not without significance. Only a legitimate son could have taken the "little" off him, as being the father of a family alone could have made him appear grown-up. Even his persistent adultery had not the grave appearance of full-blown sin. Neither did his example seem to corrupt other young men. Little John incited no more envy and emulation than a busy bull.

In the end the widow after all besought Jane.

"Thus and thus Prior Carlos has told me to act. But it has all come to naught, as Little John will hardly ever sleep in my arms any more. Ay, I know I could bring him before Abbot and Bishop for that. But I yet shrink from such a course. Therefore will I not let you go now, Jane, until you promise me a magic, a powder or potion or spell, to bring him to my bed at the right times."

"I do not command such magic," Jane replied. "I cannot compel love—"

"I ask for less than love!"

"It is unwise not to ask more than one hopes to get," said Jane. Yet the upshot was that she promised.

The widow's request came at such a moment that it acted as the final spark of anger to Jane's piled despair, we know now. Gervase had exhausted the variety of the witch's autumnal voraciousness. He had become immune to charms and philters such as the widow craved. Jane was maddened to be asked to help another where she could not help herself.

She waylaid Gervase and cornered him, still more incensed, if that were possible, by the having to act so. He had spoken out at last and told her that their commerce must be at an end. If she would not acquiesce and cease from coming after him, she should leave the manor, no matter whether his wife lived or died. She had so acquiesced, at least to remain near him. But now she told him she had changed her mind. Unless he

agreed to go on doing what she asked, she would impose on him the
Curse of the Little Things, that had staved off her the unwelcome lust,
long ago, of her captor at Ovisham, to force him in reverse.

Young Gervase laughed in her face.

CHAPTER 5

THE BETRAYAL

SIR ASPHODEL JOLYBODY had not troubled to come and see how his sister
fared since she had been married. But as in 1372 business brought him
again to Smithy Yard, he must needs pay a visit to the manor. Even
then he only brought her a chessboard and men—of which, it goes without saying, the Cinqmorts already possessed several sets. However, the
board was of tortoise shell and ivory. And the figurines came from
Cathay or India, subtly carved from an unknown gemlike stuff for
the white, the black of polished ebony. The set was so unlike anything
they had, that the Cinqmorts resumed a game they had not touched for
years, with a temporary enthusiasm that had actually twice partnered
Gervase with his wife—when neither of his uncles was at home. My lord
made Baldwin play him of an evening.

They sat in the big hall, Baldwin with open ledgers, charters, and
bills beside him, and a slate on which he jotted calculations between
moves, and Lord Hugh with a litter of elk pups in his lap and between
his feet. Griselda was on the other side of the blazing fire, warming her
latest pregnancy, her eyes closed and her hands stretched flat along the
wolf-head ends of the chair arms. Everywhere, round the thirty-foot
table, in the recesses, by windows, hearth, and doorway, henchmen
were dotted, performing household duties. Two were plucking fowls
and playing tug-of-war with the leg joints, one had a heap of bent iron
nails to hammer straight, others were sharpening tools, splicing rope,
mending saddle gear, polishing armor. The falconer was huddled in a
dark corner, carefully cutting the silken stitches with which a new
hawk's eyelids had been sewn down, a dead mouse on his knee for the
stoical bird's reward. In an alcove where the floor was paved, another

pair were busy laundering, with clouts and garments dripping from a line fastened behind them. Outside the rain was pouring down.

Gervase was pacing about the hall, humming to himself, scanning into the air with his fingers. His rhyming did not seem to be going well. The strings of his psaltery had snapped. He had kicked it away under the table. Next he tripped, and to steady himself put out his hand against one of the wooden pillars. He yelped, snatched it away with a huge splinter in his palm, slipped finally, all in one movement, and cut his hose and knee like any ten-year-old. With a somewhat comical sloth of caution, he went over to the chess players and stood watching over Lord Hugh's shoulder.

"Where is Jane?" Lord Hugh asked without looking up. Nobody answered.

The side door opened, and in came Jane with a truss of wool and her spindle. The henchmen she passed fell silent, paused in what they were doing, or else continued with haphazard haste. Griselda did not waken from her dream. Only Baldwin acknowledged the woman's entry in a natural manner, looking up and nodding. My lord forgot that it was still his move, froze with one elbow propped up, and stared straight before him. Gervase's versifying murmur started up again.

Jane did not sit down, and took up a stand enabling her to face all four Cinqmorts. She began to spin, silently. Gervase turned on his heel and went over to his wife's side of the hearth. Despite all precautions, his eyes met Jane's in passing. She smiled. She span.

An acrid stench came from where Gervase stood, and a yellowish upcurl of smoke. The end of his long sleeve had caught fire. With an oath he snatched it up and endeavored to choke its smoldering. An instant later one of the logs at his feet exploded into a fountain of sparks, one of which jumped into his eye, so that he snarled with the pain.

"In Devil's name, Nephew, what has got into you this evening, that you cannot take a breath without spreading unquiet?" Lord Hugh asked.

"I will tell you, Uncle," Gervase shouted, his fist still to his streaming eye, his face distorted. "This witch, this foul, hot crone has put a spell on me, to make me do her lecherous will. It is more than flesh and blood can stand. I never knew the meaning of remorse, till I had been foolish enough to lie with her. Ever since then she has given me no peace. The mere sight of her has long disgusted me. In God's name, Uncle, rid me of this pest!"

Lord Hugh had sprung up, and a puppy shrieked. But he spoke very composedly. "You lie. You are not the first to seek such vengeance. It is the other way about. You have tried in vain to win her, and so to vent your spite you accuse her. Is it not so, Jane? You see, I know her. I have known her a long time. Answer him, Jane. Answer me."

Jane stood stiff and straight as before; her spindle rose and sank, rose and sank.

"Jane, speak."

"Mind you," Jane said into the silence, "how I swore to make you regret? I never yet broke a promise, even if keeping it destroyed me, myself."

"You are right," my lord said after a long moment, during which no one had moved, all holding their breath, with him. "I was wrong not to give you what you asked, that time. I hope now it may come too late to do you any good. For now you shall have it: judgment and death. A hard death, Jane."

Everybody released their breath. Griselda had woken up and was trembling in every limb. The henchmen all stood like carved stone illustrations of domestic activities. Baldwin's mouth hung open. The years of dogged countertraining slipped off Gervase; he made the sign of the cross, slowly, amply, beautifully, as clerks are taught to do it.

Suddenly Lord Hugh spoke again, in quite different manner. The words tumbled over each other. "No, no, Jane! This must not be! How should I go on? Say it is not true. Only two words, that is all I ask, and you shall live. Just say, 'He lies.'"

Jane said not a word. Lord Hugh would have gone on, if one of the henchmen had not been before him. Such was the love Bad Hugh inspired in his wild men, that they risked what his own brother did not dare.

"Be a man, Hugh Cinqmort! Shame not your fearless warrior ancestors, that look down at you from these walls in the shape of the gear they bequeathed to you, even as they did blood, thews, and spirit! Whatever it may be that is between you and this witch—be a man, lord of Bedesford! When the snake stung you that time in the Big Forest, you did not hesitate to gouge out a whole wedge of your flesh. Have her arraigned once more, or, if you cannot trust yourself, be man enough to kill her out of hand!"

"Kill her, Hugh Cinqmort! Kill her! Kill!"

The henchmen had risen in a body, and in a body were converging upon the hearth. Each had armed him with what his task had laid to hand: ax and whetstone, greave and rope, hammer, strap-swung stirrup, knife and dagger, here and there a stool.

"Or shall we have to kill her for you?"

Lord Hugh turned back into his old self, as they knew him, and, roaring curses and threats at them, bade them take Jane off. She made no resistance, and was bundled out of the hall like an alien, stark larva carried off by ants envenomed.

Gervase sank down beside his wife's chair. Griselda took his hand and held it to her body, with the plain intention of dispelling evil magic with the holiest there is in earthly life. Lord Hugh took a few slow backward steps and sat down abruptly with his hands to his face.

But the following day he led a party to the court of the true Weird Oak, and had them look for evidence of Jane's sorcery, which was plentifully found. He had them pull down the walls, even though this meant also the collapse of some adjoining buildings. The first man to swing his ax against the oak trunk had it deflected into his own groin and died of the wound before sundown. So Lord Hugh had it set on fire and burned. It took two days and nights to burn, with men watching all the time, lest the fire spread, or go out.

CHAPTER 6

THE SACRIFICE

The Trial of Swan Ygern-Jane the witch of Bedesford was held in the unfinished part of the nave, which was decked with the parish banners, and flags and brilliant hangings from the manor. Four hurdles formed the prisoner's paddock, pieces of scaffolding served for bar and bench. Lord Hugh was transformed in the ermine vestments of justice. With him sat Baldwin, the Abbot, Prior Carlos, a number of monks and friars and, at right angles to them, the file of stiff-faced jurors. The people filled all standing room and perched all over window ledges and incomplete masonry. Manor and monastery henchmen guarded every gap; several of them were heralds, with betasseled trumpets. Jane was in chains, rope, and halter. Her face was pasty, like soap where there were wrinkles. Her hair was loosed in disorder. It still hung to her knees, but no longer showed golden. Had she looked to see, as she did not, she would not have met feeling in one countenance.

Baldwin read out the charge in Latin; but most of the proceedings must needs be conducted in language everybody understood. The Prior was marshal of witnesses. Young Gervase was called first. It must have pleased the Prior that so much of the testimony was necessarily also in the nature of public self-incrimination on the givers' part, to be followed in due course by punishment and penance. Perhaps we do him injustice —yet we do not think so.

After Gervase came some Cinqmort henchmen corroborating his evidence, some describing what had been found in the court of the Weird Oak and then swearing to the exhibits, and one, the gateward, telling how the Widow Naylor's—nay, the younger Mistress Trefeller's aunt—had come to inquire for Jane and a promised love philter. Thereupon the aunt and her niece must take the stand, and in a trice they were trapped into implicating Juliana. Juliana's name echoed through the aisles. Her kinsfolk looked dismayed and outraged. Luke made as to accompany her, but was harshly forbidden from the bench. The little hunchbacked beldame stepped forward unafraid, indeed, with the delight of battle in her Cinqmort eyes.

But she did not give battle on Jane's behalf. The whole interrogation was so conducted that she must defend herself, else, too, could she scarcely have held herself so confidently and unruffled. She, who was by nature and unrestricted habit so easily enraged, responded to my lord's mannered, vexatious inquiry with a belligerence calculated to give herself time to think, rather than rushing into the pitfalls of provocation.

Having had to satisfy the bench at length as to her identity, she was asked to give an account of her original purchase of Jane, which she did.

"You say, Mistress Trefeller, that, in need of hands to keep your children's property together, you did what anyone else would have done. How, then, was it that you had no rival bidders? Oh, she was a captive of whose existence few were aware? In that case we cannot suppose that she had had many opportunities of displaying her capabilities? You implied that the innkeeper was in fact anxious to get rid of her. This would not usually be taken as the right sort of testimonial? As far as we can see there are two alternative explanations. Either you bought her without knowing what she was—in which case she must have bewitched you into it for her own ends—or else you were perfectly aware of it, and hoped to profit thereby. Certainly your subsequent prosperity would point to the latter."

"My prosperity," Juliana said tartly, "is the result of my shrewdness and unsparing industry. If others were prepared to toil and worry as I, they would find there is no need of witchcraft, for good or ill. If I want to confound an enemy, I set my mind and strength to that task, just as I do in the cause of enrichment. If Jane has brought evil to pass, her magic merely brought into the open wickedness that existed under cover all along. Magic cannot call into being anything Our Lord left uncreated—as you should know, Father Carlos, that hangs whispering over the lord Justice's shoulder. It can only make use of and strengthen what is already there. She could not have bewitched you, nephew Gervase, had you not met her at the least halfway—"

"You are not here as prosecutor, nor to scold other witnesses," said Lord Hugh, and sent her back to her place amid ripples of suppressed laughter and congratulatory looks and nods.

Juliana believed that, as Jane had always proclaimed her luck dependent on furtherance of her mistress's welfare, the witch must have done her some secret injury, the results of which were yet to become manifest. And although in court she had spoken of the loss to herself as the bondwoman's owner, we knew she did not feel it as such. We knew, because everybody felt the same. We could none of us stomach the revelation of Jane's dealings with the Cinqmort heir. The very fact of carnal defection would have sufficed to offend us, in her. All the circumstances of her indecent pursuit of one so much younger, and so unwilling, had deprived her of any last remnant of compassion in the whole of Bedesford. Even if her doom had not been certain, we none of us wanted to see her again, after today. Elizabeth Robinson evidently did not feel equal to seeing her even this once more. She was not there with her relatives.

Another who had kept away was Brother Laurentius. He had declined so much as to listen to the talk about it all, beforehand. We could understand that he felt in some measure guilty, because last time his had been no small contribution to her deliverance. After her release from prison the first time, he had resumed carrying out his old plan, of flight from people and all matters of human moment, with far greater intensity and success than before.

Everything was made worse for Jane by the fact of everybody's previous intervention. Our Lollards were conscience fretted by their formal espousal of her cause as part and parcel of the people's struggle against oppression. Thus it was not enough for them to hold back, this time. They must find acceptable reasons in favor of her extermination. Jane was embodied evil, and her blood sacrifice would be pleasing to God, Who in olden days had decreed the casting-out of scapegoats burdened with the sum of people's sins. We might and we should cleanse ourselves through her.

But Edwin had spoken up in immediate support, Edwin, who for years had refused to open his mouth against anyone or to voice any opinions—so that his word weighed double, his vote decisively.

Edwin, like the rest of us, knew now that Jane was evil, no matter what she had been and done for us in the past. Like the rest of us, he must have realized that in the end no amount of repayment could ever raise out of her debt those whom Jane's arts had benefited. For no benefits she had bestowed but had begotten others, irrevocably multiplying. They were not such as could be thrown away again: health, wealth, children, and the like. Therefore it would be as well to have them purified by the bestower's expiatory death.

Also, Edwin at all times trembled for Alfred. He had tried hard to tear the love of Alfred out of his heart, fearing that where he loved, God would hate. Even if God found it impossible to hate Alfred—as well He might—He might yet devise further punishment of Edwin in his son. Though suffering only incidentally, Alfred would not thereby suffer less. The very healing of his hand had gone against the will of God. On the top of that, the witch had effected it. If the witch were made to atone for her crimes, that of healing Alfred was included, paid for, cancelled as far as Alfred was concerned. Thus he reasoned.

At a sign from the Prior the trumpets blew again and introduced a small procession of further witnesses, all women in unhemmed and ungirt shifts. They were all red of eye, and everyone knew them to be unchaste, except in some cases their husbands. These women stood arraigned for fornication and adultery (without mention of their partners), at the same time as they were here to bear witness against Jane. It had not required the Prior's researches to establish their offense; but he had wormed out of them full confession as to the means by which Jane had enabled them to carry on their vicious courses in safety. Some had had regular recourse to a brew of hers called the cuckold's potion, some to even more sinister charms.

The penitents had come in contritely enough. But as the Prior went through his private examination of them all over again before the whole of Bedesford, their remorse began to show less, as against a growing, vengeful self-pity. They were victims, implements of Jane's general, evil purpose, no more responsible for what they had done than were those very charms and potions.

This had a terrible effect on us. We all yielded to the same temptation. Preternaturally enlightened as to all the evil within ourselves, on a sudden, we saw and grasped our chance of laying it all at Jane's door. Oh, how we hated evil then—hated sorcery and the sorcery that had profited us—the more as still we could not find it in us sincerely to hate the profit, how we hated her! How we shouted our hatred!

We doubt that we succeeded in frightening Jane. Rather, it may be that the acid of contempt ate through her stolid containment from within and thus destroyed it. Or it may be that the evil she had made to emanate from herself had now enveloped her, the source, as well— the cuttlefish fuddled with its own cloudy liquor. They that talk a torrent of words know not what they mean, if they did not hear Jane at the close of her trial. Then our hatred did not stand up to her hate of us, but shrank and withered, and its heat was turned to icy terror. Her voice gathered unto it all the cathedral echoes. She admitted charges that had not been brought. And she cried out in regret of all the evil which it had been in her power to encompass, and which she had forborne from perpetrating, till now it was too late. But nay, she cried, it was not too late. She would come back, she promised to come back, she would see to it that she came back: and then beware, Bedesford!

"Have you nothing else to say, woman?" she was asked by the Justice.

"No, for if I did, it would be the better for you!" she called back, and we thought she had begun to rave.

For that was how she began to make sure of haunting us after her death: eluding all priestly attempts at helping her to repentance, by means of madness.

Brother Alfred entreated the Abbot to let him try. He also tried in vain. As he came out, spent, he met Prior Carlos on his way in, and said a few dejected words, wishing the other better success.

The Prior retorted, "That your suasion and exorcism rebound impotently cannot surprise me, monk. Is it not a fact that Jane bewitched your hand? By rights you ought not to be, indeed you cannot be a priest at all, for that cripples cannot be ordained. That right hand of yours which appears hale and unblemished is in fact nothing but Devil's mirage."

"If it were so, then surely it could never have withstood the sign of the cross. Every time I dipped it in consecrated water, the mirage glove would dissolve, would have dissolved beyond recall the first time I used it so. In any case, as everybody knows, Jane did nothing for it without pious incantations."

"Then there may never have been anything wrong with it at all—" the Prior said in a captious rush, immediately regretted.

Alfred, who before had tried to speak neither as wearily, nor yet as hotly as was his impulse, could now say with all the serenity of justified rebuke, "You cannot mean to suggest that prayer is powerless medicament, my Father? The while you held to it witchcraft had cured my hand, you never thought of doubting that it had been blighted!"

Thus the Prior in his cantankerous rashness had once again placed himself at a disadvantage; the day was not yet, when he would feel this most.

Brother Alfred repeated his endeavor several times, before he went to Smithy Yard and asked Elizabeth to help.

"Jane seems possessed—yet have I thought more than once that she herself had deliberately summoned the demons I would exorcise, and that she seeks to keep them out of range of holy water by means of an additional, conscious, simulated ferocity. That the demons inside her may not hear me, she keeps up such a screeching I cannot even hear myself, nor be sure that I say the words in the right order. You used to have power over her heart, more than anyone, ever. She may not be able to resist you. She may find it beyond her to repel *you* with such ghastliness. It is our last hope. Will you come?"

But Jane would not suffer Elizabeth to come close to her either. She threw herself about in wild contortions to keep the visitants at bay. And she raved, just as Alfred had described, with an unreal raving, as it were, on top of the real.

"Who took my bread, my bread and cast it upon the brackish waters, who took it and threw it and fished it up sodden rank to poison me with bait twice over? The sea? The sea? I have forgotten it. None they say, ever break faith with the sea. I have, even unto blind sight of it. Beach there is—wide, crazing desert, with stones upon it that were bread. For I was lured from it. Unfaithful? The words I thought were etched with fire, they are also gone. Within and within and within, even thus from out, daughter-mother-daughter withal. Thus it shall go, must be. Betrayed, betrayed. My curse upon the bait—in whom she loves, there let it roost and rust, corrupting, corroding. Thus, that it be as with me, late and defeated, without quenching, without slake. The powers have listened, they have heard. They have prepared the bed, that the curse may suit the unfaithfulness—suit and cap. Suit and cap, hose and shoe, and breech and smock, blouse and hood and mantle—" the witch fell to chanting, in a harsh, broad wailing singsong, like an infant told off to repeat its first lesson in the terms of apparel. This was worse than the spirant malignity with which she had uttered the preceding curses.

She made faces and clawed the air at Elizabeth. It cannot be more appalling to watch a loved one change into a toad. Alfred clutched Elizabeth so that the bruises showed for days after, and snatched her away from the obscene embroil.

In the morning the prison guards found the witch dead.

She sat, with legs stretched out straight before her, her arms, with clenched fists, extended rigid by her sides, her body arched and stiff, head pressing back against the wall. Her nostrils were blocked with earth dug up from the floor, her lips were drawn in and clamped shut between her teeth, her eyeballs protruding though the lids were down. She had achieved the supreme conquest of the nature of all living matter. Without implementing, other than her will and a little earth, she had done herself to death. She had done herself to death that she might haunt us.

Part Seven
Alfred of Bedesford
(1374-1377)

OUR LOSS

AFTER JANE'S REMAINS and medicine chests had been burned at the Marsh, we missed her. It was not that we wished her back, but that we were conscious of the gap where she had filled a place for over twenty years.

Brother Alfred had been deeply stirred in the course of her trial. Gratitude and childhood affection had been raked up in his heart, where they had lain buried under the scars of subsequent sorrows and the growths of later interests and obligations, harrowed by what had become of her. Each time he had visited her in prison, his desire to help her became more passionate; the memory of the last scene remained intolerable. He prayed God continually to guide her ghost his way, and bent much thought on how best to meet her then.

Everybody waited for her to reappear.

One person there was looked forward to that with a longing worse than thirst and hunger. My lord's hopes did not weaken with time, and he himself restlessly haunted all places likely to lure her, and fruitlessly dabbled in the ashes of the Weird Oak. For all the hand he took in the town's life the baron's place might also have fallen empty. As for Young Gervase, we could understand his evident reluctance to assume burdens which were not yet his, and which the present owner's indifference did not serve to render attractive. Yet he was clearly bored. It seemed he hardly knew what to do with himself. He even began to play his pranks on Lord Hugh, and that with impunity. Unbeknownst to all, my lord hated his heir so excessively that he could not bear to address him even by way of reprimand.

No more children were born at the manor. Gervase no longer slept

in his wife's bed, although he went to see her on occasion, which wa
more than her brother would do of his own accord. He and Luke were
now sole partners in a felt-hat manufacturing venture, and there wa
talk of Sir Asphodel's buying up the other's share. Luke was the only
merchant in Anglemere and Danesborough to have succeeded in run
ning the French blockade, and had several times accompanied his good
across the Channel. Some people held it against Elizabeth that she did
not display more anxiety during those periods.

The truth was that Elizabeth had not stopped thinking about Jane'
curse since Alfred had led her from the dungeon. She knew Luke wa
the one it threatened. The "she" of Jane's ravings could only mear
Elizabeth, she thought. It was in whom she loved that she was to be
cursed. That could not refer to her children. Jane meant the love tha
is between man and woman, for had she not alluded also to her owr
balked infatuation? And as soon as Elizabeth asked herself whethe
the beloved of her prophecy were Alfred or Luke, the answer had beer
instantly apparent. The prospect of a curse on Alfred worried her. The
very prospect of waiting, wondering what form such a curse might take
on Luke shook her through and through with ghastly fear. She wa
surprised only that it came as no more of a surprise.

But she felt certain that the wording of the curse made danger of
outright death unlikely. She need torment herself only with speculation
as to the nature and direction of the coming blow.

Luke's blockade-running was merely cocking a snook at the enemy
The few shiploads he got through could not prevent shortages from
making themselves felt, especially at the monastery. The Benedictine
revelries were not what they had been, in any sense. Jane's trial had
also created a dearth of adulteresses.

All this discontented the Abbot far more than it would have done
in his prime, when his appetites really had demanded satisfaction. Now
the dainties whose scarcity he deplored disagreed with him. But the less
stomach he had to his food, the richer the dishes he ordered, and the
greater his petulance when the wherewithal was lacking. The less he
desired amatory exertion, the more dogged and exhausting his endeavors
He was a very old man for his age. He was restless as if he could no
be either eating or demonstrating to himself in that other fashion that
he was still alive, still busy living.

While the time had not yet come for the gutters and gargoyles of
Lady Agnes' bequest to be put in hand, the seed of her notion for them
had borne fruit. The angel faces studding the arc over the Nazareth

orch had been molded in the likenesses of their makers—crudely
nough, but unmistakably once you knew. No one had told the Abbot;
nly because it had not chanced so, not because we thought he would
ake exception.

You must have watched masons at work in your time, so that there
s no need to tell you of the personal marks with which their work is
sually adorned under the whitewash. At St. Hand's the practice had
een frowned upon, but never stopped. Richard Widowson improved on
t. He had learned his letters at the chantry school, and had learned also
o see intrinsic beauty in them, no doubt under Brother Laurentius'
nfluence. So this youth, though not vain as youths go, had worked
laborations of the letters R and W into the skirting border of the
quire screen. The design was so intricate that the monogram did not
ormally show up. But when the Abbott came to see how the youngest
f the sworn woodworkers was acquitting himself, the sunlight and its
ttendant shadows happened to pick out the initials of the artificer's
ame. The Abbot rubbed his eyes, marveling that they should choose
o deceive him into seeing *letters*. He asked Richard about it, received
truthful answer, cut short further explanations and fell into a fit of
aging.

Young Richard's heart nearly stood still. Lord William himself must
ave awakened to the threat of apoplexy, for he suddenly turned and
vent away, staggering a little. Richard knew not whether to destroy his
arving, or for what punishments to hold himself prepared. The monks
urried home after their Abbot, to see that everything was done to
oothe and delight the remainder of his day.

The remainder of his day! That was what it turned out to be. He
tarted dying in the afternoon. He had had such attacks before: frightful
raps in his belly that made him roar and kick. They knew not what
o do with him, whether to lay him flat or prop him up kneeling be-
ween them like a woman in labor, whether to sustain him with food
nd drink or loosen his bowels and make him vomit. Prior Carlos was
way from Bedesford.

All over the Wasteside, mothers stuffed straw into their children's
ars and put them to bed with the covers over their heads. So sorely
id the Abbot scream. Yet he was serene as he had not been for some
ears. He received extreme unction, and cheerfully—this is, composedly,
onfidently—took leave of his spiritual sons, until they should all meet
gain, in Heaven. His pain was of the body only; in his heart there
vas peace, without a spasm of doubt. Now that death was nigh, he that

had clung to life with such impractical obstinacy was eager to get it over quickly. Before God, to Whom a thousand years are as one day, a twenty-four-hour death struggle must be short indeed. Yet the Abbot himself cannot have thought he had a quick death of it. His friends hoped that what he suffered would be taken off his term in purgatory. Lord William himself never gave a thought to purgatory at all.

The bereaved monks' grief would have been less bitter could they have felt as he of his soul's destination. Even the least devout were amazed by the innocence of the old sinner. Curiously, it was the most pious who found therein most hope of God's mercy on William Goliard's soul.

It was winter. They had time to send to Ovisham, where the Benedictines had a pair of renowned embalmers, and meanwhile make ready the Abbot's grave in the cathedral, the first within its walls. Richard Widowson prayed the chapter to let him make the Abbot's effigy, free of charge.

The chaper was almost continuously in session, not only to endow him whom they had lost with a semblance of life by exchanging recollections of him, but also to deal with a deluge of business arising out of the death.

"How many candles think you we shall need? Ought we to consult Master Robinson about it, or shall we just go ahead and have them cast? Where shall we apply for extra tallow? Widow Naylor would let us have as much as we wanted from her stock at Clowes. But it might be better to buy some off her mother-in-law, for she has not yet fixed her funeral gift."

"It is marvelously comforting, how quickly all these letters have arrived, in spite of the cold weather!"

It took them a whole day to spell out and translate each epistle.

"How beautifully the Lady Philippa writes on Lord William's memorable visit!"

"How generous her offer to provide for choir stalls and canopies in his memory!"

"Not a monastery in Anglemere has omitted to write and promise Masses."

"Oh, that Lord William were here to see it all!"

The Bishop's letter was not long in coming, either, but gave rise to other feelings over and above mournful complacency, although he, too, paid plentiful tribute to the dead man. Lord Jerome was all ready with His Holiness the Pope's own selection for the next deputy bishop.

In their Prior's absence the Franciscans had honored Lord William only with an informal delegation. Directly he returned, Prior Carlos Trinidad came to convey their official condolences. He, too, was several years older than Lord William had been, and therefore greatly shaken, despite a probable satisfaction at his old antagonist's removal and surmised reception Beyond.

"Now that I come to think of it, Prior," the Brother Cellarer said eventually, "you are a Spaniard, are you not? Mayhap you are acquainted with the apostolic choice for this our humble orphaned cloister. Where is the letter, brethren? Ah, yes, here. Don Jesús Rodrigo Gonzales, and some more names, but these seem to be the chief ones, inked in red."

At the beginning of this speech the Prior's face had assumed a certain weariness. No sooner had the presumptive abbot's name been pronounced, however, than his whole manner became extraordinarily animated.

"Yes, indeed, I know him well. The whole family is well known to me. He and I were at Oviedo together when we were novices. And I met him again later, when I had changed my order. You are very lucky to get him."

The chapter's first reaction was to smile, superseded by dawning caution. "Pray tell us about him, good Prior," they said with forced vivacity. "Is he—is he at all like our beloved Father William?"

"That he is not," the Prior answered with a smile, "but then, I feel sure you will welcome disparity. You will never get Lord William's equal. And then also, what Cloudsway Monastery needs now is a firm hand—someone that you can trust and lean on and look up to."

The monks looked at each other and silently encouraged him to go on.

"It is rather interesting." The Prior's gaze was far away in reminiscent musing. "Their family is an old and noble one, bred, one might almost say, to doing everything to excess. When they are wild and worldly, they are very firebrands. When they are devout, they are scourges incarnate. Jesús Rodrigo is a zealous, inventive, incorruptible disciplinarian. I have heard you complain of obstreperousness in some of your younger monks. Your troubles are at an end. If your accounts are not quite in order, if your finances leave anything to be desired, Jesús Rodrigo is the abbot you need. Dear me, how the time goes. I trust my next visit will mark a less melancholy occasion."

After the parting exchange of benedictions, the chapter for some little time remained dumb.

"It may be," the Master of Economy broke the silence, in a faltering manner totally unlike him, "that we had better go over the accounts again, quite soon."

"We had better—" said the Brother Cellarer, and did not go on, there being little need: each of the others was plainly engaged on completing the phrase in his own mind and with reference to his own department.

Another pause ensued.

At length the Brother Almoner's ruminations erupted, "The impudence, the blasphemous insolence, the hair-raising effrontery!"

The others cried in eager chorus, "What? What? Of what? Of whom?"

"Of having himself called by Our Saviour's name!" the Brother Almoner, squaring his shoulders and throwing out his plump chest, gallantly completed his ejaculation.

"Ay, that's just what I was thinking!"

"His Holiness' choice! Why does not His Holiness deign to take the trouble to inquire into local conditions and requirements before making these high-handed appointments!"

"Brothers, hold! Stay, brothers, we are echoing Clement and Stephen and Matt and their like—"

"Well, and what of it, anyway? I say it is no wonder, with such abuses of pontifical power, if the laity grumble!"

"Ay, one must be just and impartial!"

For a while they ceased being able to hear each other, so that in the end their shouts died down.

"Oh, brothers!" the younger deacon then said from his deepest heart, "Is not the future bleak? God help us, saints protect us. God forgive me, I wish I were dead and might lay me down to rest with our good Abbot in his sepulcher."

"Brother Anthony!" the Master of Economy thundered. Brother Anthony bowed his head to the heralded storm, and remained in that attitude although no storm followed. Holding their breath in the greatness of their dismay that what all had been thinking had been actually voiced, the monks got up one by one, avoiding each other's eyes and without any word or gesture closing their conference, dispersed.

CHAPTER 2

ELECTION

HEY DID NOT meet again until the communal repast in the refectory ext day. Just as the plenum of monks was about to rise, the Master of conomy announced that he would address the assembly. Only then as it noticed that he had eaten nothing.

"Dearly beloved brethren in Christ. Last night I had a dream, which feel it is incumbent on me to recount to you all. I dreamed I saw our ionastery wreathed in leaves and flowers and hung with banners as iough in welcome to a relic or great visitor. The visitor appeared, irne in procession. I wondered what he might be scowling at so ercely, till I realized that this was his habitual expression. He was ressed in a hair shirt with spiky belt, from which the stains of rust id blood, scarce distinguishable, spread up and downward. In his ght hand he wielded a great nine-ended whip with nails stuck in the raided leather and lead weights at the tips. With this whip he struck it to right and left at all who had turned out to greet him, and who iust bear it unflinching, on pain of worse punishment, the precise ature of which was not revealed to me. He went into the garden and e tramped down all the herbs and flowers, and with that whip of his— i, brothers!—he felled every one of our fruit trees, so laboriously, so nderly coaxed into maturity! Only then did he consent to come in- oors, where he set everyone to sweeping and scouring and casting ccounts, and to sleeping on nettles all the year round; and threw out ll our books and treasures, which he caused to be burned. And in the athedral all that the newcomer deemed superfluous ornamentation as lopped off with that whip, and he mistook some of the arched ranch work of the new buttresses for ornaments, so that portions of t. Hand's fell down, bereft of supports. Then I thought I saw St. rancis, dimly—the way you sometimes do, in dreams—and the misty diance that was he shed a celestial tear, and I understood him to say— cannot swear I actually *heard* him—that this was not what he had anted."

In the silence the Brother Almoner got up, brushing his brow with ie back of his hand, his genial countenance tensed, yet vacant. "Breth- n, this for sure is a most curious, most portentous thing. For I too as vouchsafed a dream last night. Mine was less clear, but Brother

Giles's dream explains it. I but saw a great unglad creature, somethin
like a raven, yet not unlike a bat, fall from the sky on to this, our hous
crushing it and stifling every breath of life therein. I woke in a swe
and to my own groans."

The Brother Cellarer and two deacons had risen simultaneously ar
for a few moments vied in offering each other precedence. It seeme
that they too had each received a nightmare, centered round serpen
scorpions, fire, brimstone, and desolation. The entire chapter ha
dreamed.

At the resulting chapter session, the monks at first experienced son
difficulty in meeting each other's gaze. But that passed, and they di
cussed what had to be done with incisive dispatch. They must ser
word to the Bishop immediately. The more they thought about this tas
the more delicate it appeared. Lord Jerome must have been expectin
Lord William's death for some time. Since at the present stage of th
cathedral the Cloudsway abbey was of nothing like so great moment
at its inception, there was the possibility that Lord Jerome had bartere
away his interest in the next appointment, against some more immedia
advantage in the game he played round about Westminster.

"Yes, but, brothers—"

"What now, Brother Anthony?"

"No doubt we shall convince the Bishop of St. Francis' antipath
But what if Lord Jerome's next choice, or the Pope's should turn ou
to be as—as—"

"I see your point. Yes, we might have to spend the rest of our liv
dreaming dreams."

"No such levity, I beg, Brother Arthur!" Brother Giles said warningl

"To proceed. Probably the best thing would be to submit our ow
nomination, with every deference, of course. It may well be that S
Francis will assist us with further signs and portents in favor of whor
we propose. It would be a pity and a waste if we had to pay into th
Treasury coffers what aspirant abbots usually have to furnish then
selves. Surely St. Francis would rather we conserved our money for th
cathedral's needs."

"All the same might a little gold prove useful wrapping to ou
missive."

"On the other hand, might not that detract from our dreams, makin
it look as if we ourselves did not fully trust in their authority?"

"Let us leave this tricky point for a moment. Supposing the choi
were ours. Whom would we suggest?"

They all thought.

By slow degrees a number of names was mentioned, all being re-
:cted on the grounds of unfamiliarity with local conditions, when they
/ere not disqualified by personal and moral deficiencies.

Had not each one been taken up with his own pondering, he might
.ave noted reflections of identical mental processes passing over all the
thers' features. To begin with each imagined himself abbot, and looked
ratified and condescending; next he remembered his particular unfit-
.ess, flinched, and looked self-denyingly adamant. Each looked up then
nd surveyed his companions, shook his head, sent his thoughts roam-
ng beyond this chamber, and shook his head again.

"No, brothers," the little Almoner said firmly. "No. It is one thing to
–accept St. Francis' help to prevent King, Bishop, or Pope from foisting
n us anyone patently unsuitable. But to propose anyone downright
inworthy—! No, no, no."

"There is one of our number who is without stain," said the Cellarer.

"Who? Who?" the Guardian said in honest inquiry, fixing one after
he other with a hopeful gaze, only to shake his head once more.

"Nay, to be sure he is not of the chapter. The late Brother Oswin's
uccessor. Brother Alfred Widowson."

"But he is *not* the only one. There are brothers Giacint and Paulus—"

"They fall into the *unsuitable* category," Brother Anthony said,
rinning.

"How do you mean?" asked the poor, puzzled Guardian.

"Brother Anthony means that there are other vows besides that of
hastity. Though the two you named have kept that one in exemplary
ashion, they have broken three others: namely, poverty, humility, and
bedience. Whereas Brother Alfred has never forgotten, and may, I think,
e trusted never to forget in future, his origins and what he owes to
hem and to his betters. He is engrossed in his work, too—almost as Friar
.aurentius. Do you mark my words and catch their meaning? I see
nost of you do. Neither should we need to be ashamed of him. His
ifts are an ornament to the institution. I really think St. Francis might
nake out a case for him."

"Brother Anthony, you have now said enough," the Master of Econ-
my rebuked him. "I charge you not to open your mouth again when
10w we talk the matter over to the end. One might say, you have made
our contribution."

CHAPTER 3

THE CURSE

ELIZABETH WAS IN the kitchen, surrounded by her maids, her two daugh
ters, and a number of women hired for the month. Winter was fa
outstaying his term, yet that had not delayed the ewes in dropping thei
lambs. Luke was out with the shepherds, as were most of Bedesford'
men. Occasionally one or the other of the people from the yard and
countinghouse put his head round the door with a question or message
One there was pushed the door so that it flew back against the wall, ir
his rush up to the Mistress—Frank Oxerd announcing an unexpected
caller from Danesborough. His stiff black hair, standing on end, added
to this youth's air of self-importance as an imposing hat might. It wa
two years since Luke had taken him to live at Smithy Yard as his
apprentice.

"The Master is not in, Mistress," he proclaimed, as if Elizabeth did
not know, "but he would be sorry to miss this man. I would counsel
you to ask him to stay and sup. I will tell him so from you, if you like
but he might be better pleased if you yourself entertained him in the
meantime."

"Ay, do you tell the Mistress what is fitting," Bess, who could no
abide him, said angrily. Elizabeth smilingly shook her head at the
woman and sent Frank back with the invitation he had proposed.

Next her sons came home with a neighbor's boy, their schoolfellow
all three boisterous and hungry. Elizabeth loved to watch her children
together, and to see them set off by friends. Each was different from
the other, and all of them so comely that almost she was sorry for other
mothers. Peter was the father's favorite, named as he had been after
Luke's long-lost cousin, and like him in looks, according to Luke. Robin
continued to testify to his Cinqmort heritage, but as yet none of the
Cinqmort faults, for which his mother was ostensibly looking out, had
materialized. In Isabella the parents' features had been so blended that
she resembled neither, except in that she promised to be a most hand
some woman. As for Lucy, no one so far had offered satisfactory sug
gestion as to whence she derived her angelic face and flaxen curls.

The two girls, up till then sedate assistants to the kitchen work, were
immediately infected by their brothers' noisy capering. Elizabeth and
the women called out in pretended scolding and held their greasy arm

high, out of the way, until it became seriously needful to stop the boys' swoop on all the food within reach.

"Boys, boys! Whatever is the matter with you, whatever has happened?"

"Nothing has happened, only that it has been settled the funeral will be a holiday for us—and today they have let us go early, because they are all so busy at the monastery, and everything topsy-turvy—"

"There was not really any school. Half the monks were at the cathedral, because it seems the clerestory will need shoring, and because there has to be final decision about Lord William's tomb—"

"Are they going to let Richard make the effigy?" Isabella broke in, and the boys, who took great pride in their grown-up friend, jubilantly told her yes. In the middle of this their grandmother appeared on the heels of the groom announcing her, Widow Naylor, and the aunt.

"They tried to make us wait in the parlor like visitors and strangers," Juliana interrupted her daughter's remonstrance to the same effect, "but I said I had not brought you up so that you will leave off working at the slightest excuse—"

"Did you tell them that?" Elizabeth's smile faded. "Nonetheless must you now allow me to act as I deem fitting in my own house, Mother. If you will please to follow me, Mother, Susannah, Aunt Anne. Ay, you come too, children, if you promise not to worry your aunt—"

Her sister-in-law protested that they did not trouble her in the least, even as the children fought for her hand. Juliana did what she could without outright commanding to draw their attention to herself. "Well, Isabella, has your spinning improved? At your age your mother was most proficient. Peter, I trow your freckles have trebled, and you must not strut so stiff necked, it looks unmannerly proud. Robin, when will you cease slouching like your mother's uncle Hugh. And there, if you have not a new rent in your frock, and right next to a darn, too! And where is my namesake granddaughter? You have not kissed me, Juliana."

The little girl strained away and piped that her name was Lucy.

"You know well your name is rightly Juliana, Lucy," Elizabeth said exasperatedly. "Whenever she comes, your grandmother can rightly say my children do not know how to behave. They are not always like this, Mother."

"So now that perhaps we may be able to hear ourselves talk—" Juliana began, when Frank Oxerd came running again, out of breath.

"There now, Mistress, the man is set on going after all! He says he cannot wait, that he has other business. I did the best I could. I do not think he has been bored, but maybe he does feel that he has been slighted. Come you out now and see him to the gate at least!"

Elizabeth groaned, half laughing. As she had expected, her mother did not let this pass without comment. "I see you train your serving folk no better than your children, daughter! Be off with you, Frank. A grown man, whoever he may be, can surely find his own way out. It is not yet dark. I have come to talk with you, Elizabeth, and talk to you I will now. What a picture this household is of the times we live in! The children are rude to the guests, and the servants chide the mistress."

"What has happened now, to discompose you, Mother?"

"I'll tell you what has happened. Alfred Widowson is to be the next Abbot at Cloudsway! In all my eventful life I never heard of such a thing. And you know who is most to blame? Your precious husband, Elizabeth!"

"How so?" Elizabeth could not help smiling at her mother's sudden disowning of Luke and handing him over to his wife, so to speak.

"Think of that!" Juliana turned to her companions. "He does not even confide in his wife. Has he never told you that it was he bought Edwin's freedom at the time of your marriage, without which Alfred could never have become what he is now?"

Elizabeth gazed at her speechlessly; the widow and her aunt sat in the stiff discomfort of conflicting loyalties and supernumerary parts; the children, not unused to altercations between mother and granddam, tried to become engrossed in some conversation of their own.

"We shall all be disgraced," Juliana pursued, "by our Abbot's low birth. It will be a fine thing, will it not, to have these Oxerds go about calling themselves his relations. As for that son of theirs, seeing how he bears him now, what will he be like after the investiture? Cloudsway Waste will become a byword for monks' unruliness."

"Cloudsway Monastery never was noted for excessive discipline," Elizabeth pointed out.

"At least Lord William could enforce his will when he wanted to. Oh, how it galls me to think that foolish Jeanne will be proved right— the way she was for ever prophesying her Alfred a bishopric! I had rather he were made a bishop, than our Abbot. Then at least I should not have him before my eyes! It is hard on a mother. Would that I had thought of giving Little John to the monks!"

"Oh, Mother!"

"Ay, you laugh. Foolish was I to look for any support here."

"What did you expect me to do?"

"Luke could do something to stop it yet, I dare say. We all of us could, if we rightly set ourselves against it, all together. That is the worst of it, that in the last resort I have only myself to blame, for bringing him here, to disrupt the town's whole state of being."

"Whom, Alfred?"

"No, no. That husband of yours, that I hauled up from the gutter, so that he might steal my rightful place in this country—sly, grasping, devil-haired Fleming that he is."

Elizabeth stood up. "You have greater cause than that to blame yourself, Mother. Had you not forced me to marry the man you now revile, Alfred would never have become a monk, let alone Abbot."

"I see you have heard the great news?" Luke, whose entry they had been too incensed to observe, smilingly made his presence known—his mouth smiled, but his eyes gazed coldly past the women. Even the children, who leaped toward him, overjoyed at what they considered the end of unpleasantness, obtained only a cursory pat or two. In a moment they wished the quarrel were still going on, instead of this flustered silence. Elizabeth, knowing that she had spoken in defense of him, knew also that he did not know this, and she was unable to master her confusion. "I gather the appointment does not please my mother-in-law?" Luke went on lightly. "But Elizabeth thinks it is a good one, I have no doubt."

"I do not see why it should not be," Elizabeth said with her back to him. "I do not think it can be condemned merely on the grounds of his birth. Who was Rogue Cinqmort, before he came to settle in Anglemere? Where were the Trefellers a hundred years ago?"

"To say nothing of the Robinsons. You must not leave them out, my wife."

"Will you take wine or ale, my husband? Sit down in your place by the fire."

Luke begged her not to trouble, and be seated. "I know you must be weary too. The servants know I am home and will soon bring all I want."

Juliana looked on for a while, then rose and said to her daughter-in-law, "Well, it looks as if we are quite forgotten, my Susannah. Maybe we have become invisible without our knowing it, eh, Aunt Anne? Well, well, we will not stay where we are not wanted, shall we, my dears. Well, well, well, here they come bringing the food. That settles it. I cannot see where there will be room for us three to sit and eat, do you, if these fine Robinsons are set on dining in the little parlor instead of in the hall, as they do when there are guests. Clearly we are not asked to be their guests. I can only suppose they want us to go. Come then, you two stand in daughter's place to me."

At the same moment as the others followed suit and timidly wrapped their cloaks about them, a servingman entered with a spare bench. Elizabeth had looked up, but said nothing. Having all but reached the doorstep, Juliana hesitated, but without word from her daughter could not well swallow her own. So the three women trooped out past the bench. They could be heard calling for a lantern, their man, and their horses out in the yard.

Elizabeth exhaled tremulously. "Do you start eating, Husband," she turned at last to Luke, who was doing as his children had done earlier, playing with them in pretense that the last few minutes had passed by him unnoticed. "Else everything will go cold."

Luke looked at her, and without shifting his thoughtful gaze started applying his knife to the roasted meat. Elizabeth could not interpret his look. "Are you angry with me, Luke, that I have quarreled with Mother?" Luke shook his head and went on looking at her. So Elizabeth turned her eyes on the children and addressed the boys with forced gaiety, "And you little knaves never said a word about the new Abbot!"

Robin and Peter looked at each other, faintly conscience stricken, for that they had forgotten this over other matters of greater importance to themselves. Seeing them exchange brief glances also with their elder sister, Elizabeth felt constrained to avert her eyes again. She had marked it before this, that her children did not care for Alfred in the way she had hoped. Meanwhile Luke had begun to speak.

"Are you surprised if I am just a trifle hurt—that you can find it in you still to speak against me in such wise, and *for* that other? Are you staring at me so because of the children? *You* took no trouble to save their ears! Do you think me so much of a holy saint as all that, that now you are as a pillar of salt with amaze at a mild rebuke?"

Little Lucy's face had gone as pale as her curls. She opened and shut her mouth, trying vainly to shriek, the while she pointed at her father. Noting at last that her gaze and Elizabeth's were directed in the same quarter, Luke looked down, and saw what it was horrified them so. Still sawing away at the meat, he had sliced off with it a piece of his palm, where it swelled to the base of the thumb. The lump lay on the table, and from the wound Luke's blood was streaming into the gravy. He himself was sickened, gulped, and tightly wrapped his left hand in his skirt. "It is nothing," he regained his hold over himself by commanding them. "Hush, Lucy, be still now. Bess, do you take the child outside. Surely, Elizabeth, you have seen worse than this in your time."

"It is not the wound. It is not the sight of it." Elizabeth gasped. She too collected herself and ringingly called for more maids to clear the table.

Luke after all was too shaken to do anything but what she demanded, and followed her up to their bedchamber. She made him sit down and got out her medicines, ripped off her coif and tore it into strips with the aid of her teeth, and tied up his wrist, before applying seasoned cobwebs to the wound and bandaging it. Next she took of his fell jerkin, and began to undo the lacing of his smock beneath, all smelling strongly of sheep.

"My poor husband! What have you got here?" For scattered over his chest were some unsightly boils and a number of scars denoting a previous crop. "No, keep still, do not act in this foolish way. Wait while I fetch an ointment."

Luke had flushed, so that his eyes grew moist. He clutched at the gaping smock, trying to wrest it out of her hands and cover himself up. "I never meant you to see this."

"Well, I have seen it now. How long have you been plagued with them?"

"What matters it? Now you may be content to see how God has punished me for marrying you against your will, so Jane said when I went to her with my affliction."

Elizabeth's hands sank into her lap; tonelessly she repeated the dead woman's name.

"But you need not fear that I will trade on my boils and sores, Elizabeth. I shall trouble you no more than I have hitherto. She gave me a salve, Jane, and taught me how to make it up myself, so you see—" His gaze had involuntarily traveled to where he kept the salve. Elizabeth jumped up and went to his clothes chest under the window. She lost no time over what was stored on top, but rummaged underneath, until she found what felt a likely receptacle: a ram's horn fitted with a metal lid. As she held it up, Luke's anxious movement to intercept her proved this was what she had been looking for. And so, quickly, she threw it into the fire.

"What are you doing?"

"Oh, Luke, Luke, my dearest husband," Elizabeth flung herself down where he sat, embraced his knees, and laid her head into his lap. "Why did you keep this from me? If only you had told me! It is a long, long time since first I started racking my mind how I might serve you, so as to make you turn to me again. Or is it too late? You have treated me so well in these years. You surely could not have, had you still loved me. You have slept beside me in this bed every night you were at home. If you still loved me, could you have kept to your side, never even putting out a hand toward me—never even in your sleep—never even when you were drunken? Many a night I have lain here weeping in the dark. Sometimes I hoped it was design, to help me know my own heart. But then I saw it again. It has been too long, no man would have kept to a plan such a long time. But at least you will let me tend you. When you said what you did, about this being a punishment on you— you cannot have been so cruel as to deem it the result of those ancient, childish dealings of mine with the false idol? You do not believe that, do you?"

Luke at first had tried to stop her, push her off, and pull her to her feet, but he had soon desisted. Retaining a listening expression, he bent forward when she, too, fell silent, and took her face in his hands. He gazed with a questing, simplehearted intensity that forced a sob from her, but her eyes did not falter. He shook his head and said in a high, gentle voice that went with his look, "But, if this is the truth, how came you to say what I overheard, to your mother?"

Elizabeth replied eagerly, her tears drying more swiftly than they had spurted forth. "She had angered me, reviling you. She holds you responsible for Alfred's appointment—she told me—I never knew, I had to learn it from her, about your generous deed at the time we were married."

"I wish I had never told her. Then, now that William Goliard is dead, none but I would know. I wish you need not have heard. It was not goodness made me do it. I know that now."

"Oh, Luke, do not talk so."

"I caused him to be made a monk because I was jealous and afraid."

"You cannot think me foolish enough to believe that? Lord William was a monk. All the Benedictines of Cloudsway are monks!"

"How strange. I did not think of it in that way." They chuckled together. "Why is it Juliana grudges him so?"

Elizabeth replied slowly. "I think it is because she knows Alfred and has known him from the time he and I were babes, and because Jeanne is said to have been so fair when she was young and Mother always was ill favored."

Luke could not resist her upraised lips, and the temptation of finding out what they tasted like, unresisting. He went on kissing her and pressed her to his sore breast, forgetfully, which was the proof of his yielding and belief.

"But tell me now, and tell me truly," he said after a while, "about your heart—and him, Alfred."

Elizabeth held his hand to her cheek. "Alfred and I were children together, and I still feel for him the tender affection of those days. I told you, we looked to be married, Alfred and I. But I tell you this: we never longed to share a bed—the way I have longed for you. There, I have said it. No, let me finish about Alfred. I want to say it straight out, that I think there could have been no wiser choice for the abbe. You will see. For may I not love you and still think well of him?"

Elizabeth wakened before Luke did, and there, in the place of the bolster that had so long divided them, was he. It was wrong to feel so very happy, for their new-found bliss rested on Jane's curse and her beloved was as sorely afflicted as man can be. Her lips brushed his worn and tired features, the slackly curled, bandaged hand, the poor martyred breast, and her love surpassed what she had thought the limits of emotion.

Oh, why had God singled out Luke in this cruel fashion? But it was *not* God Who had struck him down. If his illness was the result of sorcery—why, then the new crime which Elizabeth had already begun to plan, with her eyes open to its gravity, became, not only excusable, but a crime purely in the earthly sense, no crime at all in Heaven.

Master and Mistress appeared last, all the other inmates of the house being already assembled for Sunday breakfast. The housefolk nudged one another. Lucy clapped her hands and called to ask what made the parents look so mirthful. Elizabeth's headdress was awry. Luke had kissed her again, just outside the door.

"You look ten years younger, Master, for all that there are black rings round your eyes," Bess shouted. Isabella pretended she had dropped something and dived under the table, taking a long time to come up again. The other children laughed with the grownups, without knowing or greatly caring why they did so. "Here, Mistress, let me push some more cushions in behind your back! Look at her, look at the Mistress blushing! They have both blushed, both of them, look! So the bees swarm in winter, too, eh, Elizabeth?" for the Mistress's lips were noticeably swollen. The rest of the servants were not slow in seconding Bess and trying to outdo her. The hall echoed with forthright jocundity as at a wedding feast.

Elizabeth and Luke were startled, not so much because their nocturnal doings were thus paraded, but by the discovery that their long estrangement had been so well known. But they did not succeed in silencing the delighted acclamations, since they themselves could not keep their faces straight. They had to give up trying to eat and drink, as whenever they took a mouthful, some new sally was sure to make them choke. Then Luke threw dignity to the winds and accepted the part of a bridegroom, so that Elizabeth tried to hide her face behind a fold of her headcloth.

CHAPTER 4
THE FUNERAL

IF THE WEATHER took no account of the year's progress, the strangers streaming together for William Goliard's funeral took no account of the weather. It was nearly May, and still winter. Ecclesiastical dignitaries, squires and their ladies, with whom the deceased had hunted in his heyday, and many others came, from every corner of Anglemere and beyond. Lady Philippa was one of them. The Bishop was to have celebrated the requiem Mass but found himself unable to attend at the last minute, and sent his new chaplain.

Although there was no need for the effigy to be finished, and although indeed he could never have done it in the time, Richard Widowson hardly left off carving to sleep. Some of the eminent guests were brought to look on Lord William's face as knife and gouge had brought it forth at one end of the great log of oak wood. The body, with all insignia and mortuary properties, as yet was only roughly hewn out. So far only Edwin had stood over Richard, with counsel and directions. Richard had never made a figure in the round, and would never have pressed his services on the chapter without his elder kinsman's assured advice. Howbeit he had made a special journey to Friggsby, where many of the tombs wrought by a long line of Tewsings were still intact. Now the visiting critics debated the likeness, which Edwin had declared good. Most of them had not seen the late Abbot for years, and few showed themselves prepared to make allowances for the inevitable distinctions between effigy and subject. They all said the effigy promised to make excellent showing once it was colored with paint. On the whole Richard was not too disheartened, but once or twice he privately assured Edwin he too was going to give up woodwork after this, saying also that craftsmanship's sole protection against well-meaning destroyers lay in emulation of Brother Laurentius, forswearing all counterfeiting of actual objects.

Thousands of candles had been made and were distributed about the cathedral, the catafalque, and the funeral train. At the times when the monks were locked in their cells one could hear them practicing their choral parts. Everyone was pleased with the Abbot-elect for his decision to function for the last time in the choir during the funeral. The chapter tacitly congratulated itself on its perspicuity.

"I knew him a little boy—my niece's page, Mistress Robinson as she is now," Lady Philippa said in conversation with her brother Baldwin and the Bishop's chaplain. "I can hardly believe it—not that he is to be Abbot, but that he was that little boy."

"I suppose he does everything in his power, Reverend Mother, to deny his identity with that lowly youngster?" the chaplain stated rather than asked.

"Nay, one cannot say that," Lady Philippa hesitated, partly in groping for definition, partly from natural human reluctance to kill a promising interchange of censure. "I cannot say that he either crows or bears himself with uneasy ease. He does not seem to rank himself on a level with such as ourselves, nor affect to despise those that used to be his equals. My meaning is difficult to convey—"

"The good Reverend Lady has all the virtues of her gentle sex and holy calling," the chaplain continued to Baldwin afterward. "Forbearance, eager to turn into outright approval, becomes her well, where in persons of more complex avocations it would be stupid, not so say wrong."

"My particular friendship with the late Lord William," Baldwin said carefully, "makes it impossible for me to appreciate anyone else in his position, and thus in honor makes it equally impossible to condemn."

"In confidence, St. Francis' choice was a little inconsiderate toward the Lord Bishop. He had to go back on his pledges to His Holiness, and that after the Holy Father's counterpledge had already come into effect, if you take my meaning. I wish he had been able to come himself. I would like to hear his opinion of Father Alfred on personal acquaintance."

"Oh," said Baldwin wearily, "they are acquainted, good father. The Lord Bishop shares with the rest of our generation the privilege of having dandled Alfred Widowson on his knee. No wonder he can keep his countenance so well among us great folk."

The day before the funeral it began to snow. It went on snowing off and on until the following morning, when there was a longer interval. After nones those monks who were not needed for what little remained finally to be arranged inside the cathedral, went back to their pallets, that they might be at their best during the long nocturnal service. They awoke to a Wasteside covered so deeply in snow that they rubbed their eyes incredulously. The laborious trudge through waist-high drifts across to St. Hand's needs convinced them. Where the vaulting was yet naked, smooth white roofs had grown. All horizontal planes stood out, piercingly whited. Dusk came with December precipitancy.

We had to abandon all thought of attending the funeral even at a distance, that is, outside the cathedral, as planned. The flocks were in great danger. Bedesford had less than half a dozen professional shepherds. Old Town, Wasteside, and Flemingtown tileries each employed one, Luke and Juliana shared the services of a fourth, and James Smith, with some other new-come farmers, maintained the fifth. Now every man who could walk went out to help them.

We took makeshift sleighs and snow rafts, planks, tackle, poles, ladders, loads of straw, and gruel kept hot in leather bags and stone jars wrapped with blankets and sheepskins for swaddling frozen lambs. The women got ready cordial wines, medicines, and ointments against frostbite, stoked up the fires, cleared barns, threshing floors, and homesteads, while boys and old men took turns at keeping the snow away from doorways and gates.

From the manor, too, all were gone out sheep saving, except two that were to keep the fires going, and Griselda Cinqmort. The lady of the manor knew what was happening, but not because anyone had seen fit to tell her. The small, high-up window of her chamber showed her a domed oblong of snowstorm, and a corresponding shape of light, shiftingly mottled, lay stretched on the stone floor. On their way the henchmen had opened and ransacked every room for anything that might serve to warm men and sheep. They had rushed in on Griselda too, hardly looked at her before dragging the bearskin off the bed, and rushed out, leaving the door open. So she heard all the shouting through the passages and in the courtyard, where the snow muffled every other noise, save the clank and rattle of the portcullis.

Afterward, the quiet seemed palpable, more than a mere absence of sound. Griselda lay listening to it, oppression replacing the comforting weight of which her bed had been despoiled. She lay and stared until strain pricked a hundred needles through her eyeballs. The shadows of the snowflakes faded on the floor as the light grew dimmer. Hailstones spattered against the tiny windowpanes, more and more snow piling up in the angles of the lead frames. Her heart swelled and pressed against her chest like welling nausea and thrust up into her throat. She felt an overpowering need to weep, but there were no tears in her. So, tearless, she began to moan loudly, beastlike. The sound of it stopped her again. But her superhuman stolidity had deserted her, with the indomitable courage that was its product. Her loneliness was too terrible. Christ upon the cross had had companions. In His worst hour He had been the center of universal cataclysm. Her life had been useless and pointless, and would leave no trace. She would be happier dead. Even as a suicide debarred from Paradise she would be less unhappy. Hell fire was better than this. It beckoned like a hearth.

Thankful that neglect had forced her feet to keep somewhat in practice with the journeys between bed and bucket, she heaved herself up, and staggered to her chest for a pair of old shoes. Freezing too soon, her feet might fail to carry her the necessary distance. She pulled the remaining bedclothes round herself. Her knees quivered like an old man's chin, the legs seemed to be running away from her—running, like water. Yet they kept going. She was alarmed only because the effort drove sweat from her every pore, when it was cold she desired to be. Some of the wrappings trailed, then dropped off her shoulders. Then her tangled hair was whipped up into the air and swirled round, lashing her face, stinging as it grew heavy with saturation.

She opened her eyes. There was nothing to be seen but whirling snow. There was no visible ground beneath her feet nor sky overhead. She wept a little, that her last hour in the world should deny her other farewell glimpse than that of four walls which had bounded her sight for many long months. Bent double, she breasted the storm. The snowflakes dissolved on her lips and her tongue, which she put out to catch them, with a childish, panting glee. On her lashes and round the little hairs inside her nostrils they turned to ice.

Meanwhile we had reached the western pastures, fighting storm, hail, and snow not only for our sheep but for our very lives. We were only just in time to save one of the shepherds. He had crouched with his cloak tenting a ewe with twin lambs, frost lulled, and so covered with snow that only the dogs' yapping and scratching drew our attention to the seeming hummock. We fought; knee deep in snow, so that at every step we had to lift our legs high; our leaden ankles bruised by the harsh upper crust, which was shattered into grating particles like thick glass; with numbed faces and hands that ached violently as if crushed in the screws of inquisition; blinded and breathless, we fought. Oh, it was a battle!

We lost not one man, though one man lost a leg, after. We saved many sheep, though only about half, and less than that proportion of the lambs. The distance from the pastures to Old Bedesford was double that to the New Town, and so we made straight for the Wasteside. In sight of it at last, we were to a man illumined with the only thing to do.

Illumined, illuminated: the snow-befluttered beacon sheen of the cathedral alone kept us from losing our way at the last. They had placed torches in every aperture, the boards had been kindly torn from unglazed windows to make room for more. The snow was decreasing. Now it was mainly loose-drifting powder still swept through the air, leaving the ground hard enough to support us.

We were singled out to see with our bodily eyes a vision of the cathedral, all cathedrals, such as is usually granted only to the mind. In the midst of tempest darkness there is a light, and security. Man has a home, so we saw it. There before us rose the dim, vast, protective bulk, from which radiated the light of fires lit to save our souls without our bodies. Fragments of flame, seeming liquid, sprayed out in sheaves, and the white snow was laid with beautiful areas of ruby, amber, emerald, sapphire where the thousand candles shone through stained glass.

Clement Lollard started up a Kyrie, and everyone joined in. With joyful homesickness in our hearts we struggled the last of the way, hailing our God and home and haven with all that was left in us of breath and strength.

To the monks nearest the entrance it must have sounded like hoarse shouting—that is the only explanation of what they did. They, and the scoured and burnished henchmen, made an attempt to keep us out. We had forgotten about the funeral. By the time we remembered, we were right in the middle of it: panting wild snowmen, crying sheep, and dogs that barked, whined, and stank wetly.

They met us as invaders, and perhaps we should not have wondered and should not have allowed their angry resistance to make our inrush the more brutal. They were bearing William Goliard's coffin round the procession path and an edifice erected between choir and high altar, like a mountain of narrowing shelves, planted entirely with burning candles. It was warm inside, and bright as Heaven, although there were heaps of snow and shafts of wind where windows had been unbattened for the torches. Under the incomplete tower the central crossing was a snowfield, with footprints all over it, and opalescent reflections. The grave gaped black, banked with earth, rock, cobbles, and stacked tiles, and horse skulls.

Bleating for all they were worth, with humped rumps, jigging compressed, the flocks in a trice filled the cathedral. Presently some were to be seen, like mountain goats, inexplicably poised on isolated ledges to which there was no apparent access; and the lambs, carried in our bosoms and slung across our shoulders by their tied legs, responded with foolish vigor to the broad baas of triumph of perplexity on the part of those bold ones.

CHAPTER 5

THE NEW ABBOT

The New Abbot lay flat on his face, his arms stretched out in imitation of the cross. There was no other crucifix in his cell. William Goliard's image of Our Lord, made of silver and ivory, had been removed to the treasury. William Goliard's window glass, frame and all, had gone to replace the tattered haircloth blind in the pilgrims' chamber. William Goliard's inlaid Oriental chair was in the parlor, his bed had been presented to the friars' hospital, where at first it looked supremely out of place among rows of straw pallets, but in time became an accustomed fixture, sleeping up to six persons at the height of the pilgrim season. The tapestries, lectern, and carved chest were in the monastery storehouse. The Abbot's cell was as bare as the holy founder of the order could have desired. Or perhaps not quite: a settle had remained, but nobody could sit on it. The seat was filled with books, among them Brother Oswin's manuscript, which Alfred still had not been able to complete, and the scrolls and bound notes he had brought back from Italy.

He finished his devotions and rose, chafing the life back into his limbs. He stepped up to the settle, ran his hands caressingly over his treasures, but took up the Bishop's letter and studied it anew, not for the first time nor for the last. It did not go beyond the formulae, cold as corpses, hard as superannuated bread, of official gratulation, save in that it laid down in unwonted detail the course of action Alfred was to pursue. The first decade of his rule was to see at least the commencement of rebuilding the monastery in stone. The sale of water in which the Hand had been dipped should be carried on more intensively and more parsimoniously, and it was time Wode Mill were put in operation, to increase revenues and somewhat relieve Lord Jerome's purse. Partly to the same end—Alfred could not help thinking—maximum fines were to be exacted for every kind of offense under the Abbot's jurisdiction. Other penalties, affecting life and limb, should be used mainly to suppress all loose factions and opinions, incipient or rampant, which the Bishop lumped together under the heading of Lollardry. Alfred sighed, rolled up the letter and replaced it, and went to preside over today's chapter session.

In the passage he saw two novices leaning on their brooms and chatting animatedly. They looked up at his approach and smiled in a friendly way, without breaking off their conversation.

The chapter was in high spirits. Without the Abbot, the session had not formally begun, but they were already deep in discussion of what penalties were to be levied on Bedesford for the disturbance of the funeral. They had grown more and more hilarious, topping each other's proposals until they soared far beyond the bounds of the possible.

"Mind you how we had to race the sheep for the coffin, brothers?"

"Oh, oh, oh! God forgive us, yet I'll wager Lord William himself is laughing louder than anyone, Heaven bless him!"

By the time Alfred entered, they could no longer have stopped laughing with the best will in the world.

"Silence, I beg."

"Oh, oh, oh," the monks groaned and whinnied, some gazing straight at him in a helpless, beseeching manner, some going on as if he were not there.

"Silence! In the name of my holy office I command you to stop this unseemliness at once. Rise and greet your Abbot as you should." Astonishment as much as anything made them obey. The Abbot went to his chair and sat down. The chapter made as to do likewise. "Nay, you will remain standing, this time."

Nothing now could have been further from any of their minds than laughter. The face of the Master of Economy was no less convulsed than before, but with wrath, which he made no attempt to bridle. Some that might have been less daring were encouraged thereby, so that his voice rose against a general supporting murmur.

"If you think, Alfred Widowson, that we have forgotten who you are or are willing to let you forget it, you are in error. Who are you, to tell us to attend you standing? Stand before you, indeed!" Howbeit neither he nor his supporters had sat down. "Villein woodwright's son! Who placed you in yon seat you are so thoroughly at home in on a sudden?" At this the speaker cut himself short. The others also fell abruptly silent.

The Abbot paused before replying. "St. Francis, by all accounts," he said quietly. "As for my father's craft—I mind one Joseph plied it in Judaea, and his foster son after him."

Voice returned to the chapter. There were confused shouts.

"Silence," said the Abbot. "Listen to me, listen and understand. As previously it was my vowed duty to obey, so it is now incumbent upon me to rule. I see that the pleasure you expressed at my investiture had far other causes than I thought—and hoped. But I shall shed no tears over that, nor allow it to sway me. That I want you to know. My birth and my youth, those two things that you name as my chief faults, confer added obligation on me. Now, regarding the question of how Bedesford is to be fined—I think the cost of shoring the clerestory, to be borne by the entire parish, will amply meet the case."

Murmurs of protest arose again, but the difference of tone, even in the Master of Economy, was marked. The Abbot waited until, of their own accord this time, they subsided.

"I see I must make another speech, not because you are entitled to an explanation, but because once and for all I wish to ensure that you understand. Though I may ask your advice on occasion, decision is always mine. Let me remind you that monastic government bears no resemblance to public meetings such as the Wasteside laborers convene from time to time, nor to the similar conduct of municipal affairs. Abbots are not elected, any more than high pontiffs, though the external appearances of conclave may superficially mislead the unlearned and the thoughtless. The cardinals are immured, not as persons, but, you might say, as ballot counters. They are the channels through which the will of God may express itself beyond earthly misunderstanding. That is all. Whilst abbots are not normally so chosen, in this case God made use of you in the same way. Now I had better say at once that I do not count this in my favor. You cannot be more convinced of my unworthiness than I am. But whether I am worthy or unworthy is beside the point. I may turn out to be the worst of abbots. It may be that God chose me because His inscrutable design happened to require the worst of abbots at this place and time. However, the only fact concerning us is that it is God's design for me to rule in accordance with what my conscience conceives to be my sacred duty."

He paused, inquiringly, but no one spoke.

"You may advise me if I ask it. You may call my decisions in question, if your conscience so decrees. I, however, am under no obligation to heed either your advice or your strictures. If, in your opinion, I misconduct myself in any wise, you can appeal against me to the Bishop, if need be, to the Pope himself. But even while such an appeal may be pending, you will continue to owe me complete obedience until such time as I may be formally divested of my authority over you. So long as this is quite clear, I do not intend to cling to my rights rigidly, in soulless logic. Now, the regrettable disturbance of Lord William's funeral was due to the snowstorm, not to considered malice. So much for that. Now for a word about the future. I intend that our regimen shall return to the letter of our order's rules."

The monks looked at each other. It must have seemed to the Master of Economy that his brethren's glances constrained him to stand up to the Abbot just once more. For he cried, with a gulp and not at all resoundingly, "Why do you not tell us outright that you hold yourself a better man than your predecessor?"

"Because it would be untrue, for one thing. Nevertheless I would like to help shorten his term in purgatory. You that profess so much greater affection for him must surely share my desire. It is necessary to distinguish between the man and the Abbot. So do not level at the Abbot accusations aimed at Alfred Widowson. My brethren, my sons, do you imagine Alfred the man could regard undaunted the prospect of the years ahead? He could never even have accomplished this primary act of my accession."

"Reverend Father," the Brother Almoner said after a silence—and it was the first time any of them had thus addressed their new superior.

"Reverend Father, we can only hope that in bringing about the changes of which you have advised us, you may not be too hard on us if, with the best and most sincere intentions, we prove slow to learn, or backsliding. Granted that, as you imply, the act of assertion is painful to you—your inclinations and your habits are not such that you will have to deny yourself in the future, as we shall be called upon to do."

"I am not quite so fortunate as you think," Alfred for the first time betrayed impetuous warmth. "Cannot you guess what it means to me, having to put away all the work I want to do, and in which I had only just got fairly started? In all likelihood I shall be unable to resume it for years to come. Nonetheless I thank you for your reminder, and shall bear it well in mind."

Outside his own monastery, too, there was much for Alfred to contend with, much to be overcome. As Baldwin had pointed out, everybody, high and low, had known Alfred well from infancy. It worked not only so that it made him easy with them, but also, too much so, the other way about.

And Brother Laurentius chose once again to break his rule of seclusion, for the benefit of the new Abbot. He made certain amount of play with belongings to a different brotherhood, so that he did not owe Alfred any more obedience than was due to a deputy landlord. Whenever opportunity offered, he would accost the Abbot and importune him with the airs of an ex-officio confessor, warning him against pride, much in the manner of certain scriptural prophets, only that it was Alfred's conscience, not his deeds, which he took it upon himself to question.

Then there were his kindred. The first to seek audience with him were the Oxerds, with scrupulous ostentation attired in their everyday worst. Franklin, whose liking of his own voice had not decreased with the years, enumerated his cousin's powers and prospects as if these were obscure points which had so far escaped attention. Whenever he must needs pause for breath, Joan seconded him with amusing fragments of family history. Alfred braced himself against some extravagant request. At last it came. Like a pea, said Alfred later, poised on the top of a tower erected expressly for its support. Would Alfred use his authority to see that Luke Robinson increased Young Franklin's wages?

"Nay, you must see I cannot well do that," Alfred said, laughing.

"I can see nothing of the kind," Joan cried. "All I know is that you are powerful, and that blood is thicker than water."

"I may not use my power to benefit my kinsfolk, cousin Joan."

"Why so? Are you different from other churchmen?"

Alfred had to laugh again, but this only incensed Joan the more. "At all events Richard Widowson is no less related to you than our boy!"

"Instead of doing you a favor, I will ask one of you," said Alfred. "You must forget you ever had a cousin Alfred, or else remember him as one that has died. You see, before giving him the tomb screen to do—or rather, allowing him to share it with Will Tewsing—I had to forget that Richard is my cousin. Richard's gifts and industry—"

"What about Frank's? You Widowsons ever inclined to descrying gifts that do not take the form of craftsmanship. This precious Richard—"

"But see you not that Richard's employment at the cathedral is my affair, whereas Frank's at Smithy Yard is not? What would Master Robinson say if I offered to interfere?"

"Oh, we did not mean you to speak to Luke," Franklin expostulated reassuringly, as much as to say all difficulties were now solved, "but to Elizabeth. *She* will not say *you* no, and there is nothing *Luke* would deny *her*."

"Now you must not make me angry," Alfred said, swallowing an excess of wrath. "I have heard good report of your son, and Luke is renowned for fair dealing. He will reward Frank as is just."

Alfred could not tell to what extent the aura of deep grievance in which they departed might be real or assumed.

His parents did not come to him until he gave up sending them private messages through Brother Laurentius and had them formally bidden to attend him. Edwin behaved as he always did with the higher clergy, gazing down at his shuffling feet, so tongue tied he seemed surly. Alfred had to desist from trying to shatter this unnatural reserve, lest by contrast it make him appear hatefully condescending.

Jeanne, however, showed herself less impressed by her son's new greatness than when he had been a stripling postulant. "Just think, Alfred, your father says we must forget you now, or think of you as we do of your brothers and sisters that are dead! You heard that Margaret died in childbirth? Ay, and my first grandson died the day after her." She sighed. "I have lost nearly as many children as remain to me. I think I have suffered enough loss without mourning you too, while you are still alive!"

"Stop, Jeanne. Be silent, my Jeanne! Do not weary the Reverend Father in this fashion," Edwin implored her, in the failing voice of shame.

"Nay, I am not wearying him, Edwin. Am I, Alfred? Look at him,

Edwin, a blind man could see he takes a great interest in all these things, as indeed is only natural. We must remember even popes are got by mortal parents, even Our Redeemer made it look as if He were born in the ordinary way. I trow when His stepfather talked to Him of carpentry, He did not turn up His nose. You have no call to accuse our own Alfred of such wicked coldness."

"I did not mean it so," Edwin said under his breath. Alfred understood well enough that his father feared Jeanne's plaint might cause the Abbot to think they were asking his material assistance. So he was glad when his mother's train of thought swept her right on.

"Alfred, you look a little pale, Reverend Father. Every time I see you, you are grown thinner. I know I am only a woman and know nothing of theology, but I will not flinch from telling my own son that what I hear about the monastery fare these days does little credit to his rule. I wish I could come and oversee the kitchen, and stand over you at table, too, for just one week, and make you eat. There, look at him laughing at his poor old mother."

There were times when Alfred had to fight against regret that he had ever come back here. His return had been by no means inevitable. He had done everything, importuning, conducting himself irreproachably, winning friends that could speak for him and convincing them that granting his wish would be good, in order to promote it. In Italy he had formed certain views on monastery rule. He had not expected that he would find them endorsed in Anglemere, the country of idealized memories and longings.

The cathedral had called him most of all. It had held him thus from childhood. And now he did not feel that same wonderful, elating sense of being one with it and its growing. He thought he noticed it was so with others, too. The building work was no less part and background, purpose and, often, fateful director of everybody's lives than it had always been. But this was now taken for granted, as any fact is taken for granted and even happiness, when always with you.

CHAPTER 6

THE HAUNTING

THE MONTHS WENT by, and Luke did not leave Bedesford on his customary business travels. He went less and less often to the Town Chamber, and curtailed his periods in his countinghouse, taking all such work as could possibly be done in other surroundings and dealing with it in the hall, or wherever else his wife might also be. And they were so preoccupied with one another, they liked not over much to be with others. People began to talk about them once again, without the friendly jesting a truly new-wed pair would have occasioned.

Before long Elizabeth found herself with child. She said nothing of it to her husband until he noticed and took her in his arms and questioned her.

"Glad? Oh, glad is not the word for it, so long as you too, are pleased, Luke. I did not dare credit it, at first. It has been so very long. All my children are so big; our eldest is marriageable. He will be a lonely little fellow, this one."

"I dare say with God's help we will give him company before he is very old."

"I am no longer young. Soon I shall be thirty."

Luke laughed. "In that case I have one foot in the grave."

Elizabeth caught her breath, but answered quickly, "It is different with women, you know that."

"Are you afraid it will go harder with you this time?" he asked tenderly.

"No, no, though who can say? I was not thinking of that."

"But you are afraid of something? What is it, my love? Is it anything to do—with Jane? I see I have guessed it. I have never asked you before, have I, about the time you went to see her, just before she killed herself. Ay, you said she raved, but that might mean anything. Did she curse or threaten you in any way, that now you go in fear for the first child you have conceived since then?"

"It is something like that," Elizabeth said, with lowered eyes.

"We do not know for certain that Griselda would have borne healthy children without Jane. Your noble cousin's hapless lady never was strong, never did look like a grown woman made for bearing children. And she miscarried before ever Jane was called to her."

"I lost my first."

"I have not forgotten. But there was nothing wrong with the babe itself, so far as anyone could tell."

"You are right. It can do not good, and might work harm, to brood on possible mischance beforehand. We can but pray, and give to the cathedral. Poor Griselda. Luke, do you think she meant to make away with herself?"

"It is hard to see what else she could have wanted out in the manor grounds, in the worst of the snowstorm, when she had not set foot outside her own room for years. And then, everyone says the manor people were so very thankful when they found her, and even made thank offering to St. Hand's. It looks as if the Cinqmorts at least were convinced she sought death. God knows it as they do, that they gave her plentiful cause."

"I have sometimes wished I could *give* her a child to comfort her. What would you think of lending her, say, Isabella, to be her companion for a while? She is so sensible and gentle; Griselda is so much alone, and now at last they have got two serving women at the Manor—"

"You cannot be serious? I would not entrust anyone's daughter to that place, least of all my own. Even if things are different just now at the manor, as it is said, I would not dream of putting *her* to the test of it."

"No, it was just a thought. I know what put it in my mind, and I must talk to you about that. My Aunt Philippa is returning to Thirchester next week. You know Lucy has been at her grandmother's house the best part of every day. Lady Philippa wishes to take her back with her, for a few months or longer."

"And you want her to go?"

"If you meant what you said to *me,* when I was at Thirchester, surely you will like it too. Lady Philippa loves the child. It was you as much as Mother urged my brother to endear himself to her. Now, without any scheming on our part, it would seem our daughter has succeeded where Little John has obviously failed—which is curious by the bye, seeing that most women like him. You would not stand in Lucy's way?"

"No," Luke said slowly, "Lucy at Thirchester will be rather different from Isabella at her great-uncle Hugh's! To be sure, she might take to the religious life, but that is in God's hand and His Mother's. The danger of that, too, is rather different from taking like risk of both my sons."

For hardly a day had passed of late without her attempting to persuade him to let Peter and Robin become resident boarders, for a time, of the chantry school their grandmother had endowed. This institution had begun to bear witness to the new Abbot's rule before any other aspect of monastery life showed outward signs of internal changes. It stood to reason that more learning could be crammed into boys' heads when they were there all day, every day, and not merely two or three hours twice or thrice weekly.

Elizabeth told him it was not of learning alone she was thinking. Already a number of boys from other parts of Anglemere had been sent to the school, all descended from folk of substance, early intimacy with whom would stand Peter and Robin in good stead later in life. "Then they will not be troubled, as their father was, with the hard work of making friends of strangers everywhere."

"I trust as it is they will find friends ready made in many places, as sons of their father."

"Ay, but why not make life still easier for them, if it is in our power? Learning is a light burden, a little more of it will not weigh them down, and you never know how it may come in useful."

"Elizabeth, what is this?" Luke asked, half frowning, half laughing. "What are you trying to do? Why do you want to get rid of all our children on a sudden? You, that used to fret when they were not ever all about you at the same time!"

"I am thinking only of what is good for them."

But Luke would not yet commit himself.

Once he knew of the coming babe, she talked to him about it early and late. It was almost a reversion to the games of her youth. She would tell him stories of this child's babyhood, as if it were already older or else altogether a fiction. How should he have known that she did this to compensate herself beforehand, intending the child to spend its factual infancy away from her?

One day Jeanne came to see her. Elizabeth welcomed her with open arms—albeit she stopped herself in time from throwing them round her visitor. She still had trouble in remembering to avoid touching others as far as possible.

"Aye," Jeanne said with a rueful smile, "you had best hear what I have come for, ere you kiss me. And it is true I have never come until now that I want to ask a favor. Do not hold it against me, Elizabeth. No, we are all well. The truth is that it has become too much for me at last. I have seven children living with me; that makes nine of us in our hut, not counting the beasts. My son, the Reverend Lord Abbot, has reasoned with me till I have given in. More than once you offered to have some of my children to live with you. May I take you at your word? It is Ruth and Edmund I have in mind. What is it, my Elizabeth?" she asked, in a changed tone. "You are sorely troubled, I can see. What is it? You have changed your mind? Something has happened to make you change it? You cannot now make good your offer? Is that it? Nay, do not take it so to heart—"

For the first time since the night she and Luke had come together, Elizabeth wept. "I know not how to say this to you so that you will understand. You have guessed aright. It is so that I cannot take your children now. I cannot even tell you why. I know you will not speak of this to a soul, if I ask you. Promise me also not to ferret after me with the merest guessing in your own mind. Nothing, nothing has hurt me so much as this."

Jeanne showed her a cheerful face. "Do not weep, Elizabeth. You will allow me to do this much guessing: you would sooner have cut off your hand than refused me, were it not that you cannot help yourself. Do not weep on my account. It is worse, having to say no, than being denied. You can trust me that was mother to you in the first years of your life. Now I have forgotten every word that has been said and what errand brought me hither. Nay, *this* was my errand. I meant to tell you that I am going to let Gillian foster two of my children, that she has asked for time and again, her only son being now grown up. I used to think it would be lonely for them. Now I have come to think it will be a happy thing for them to live where their father and grandfather were born, and they themselves should have been, but for the Black Death and St. Hand's."

Even in Jane's lifetime people had begun to call on Mistress Robinson in matters that they did not wish to lay before Jane or the Prior because nothing more drastic than a friendly listener or advice was needed. In recent months she had wondered whether to close her Little Parlor to them, but had found no serviceable pretext, and instead made a rule that the room was not to be used for any other purpose, its tiled floor being washed a great deal more often than housefolk and neighbors deemed necessary.

Sometime before her child was born, she was fetched to a stranger in the Parlor—a country wife, Bess thought. The woman turned out to be Griselda Cinqmort, whose first words were, "You must not think I have come in these clothes to disguise myself. Albeit I confess I am not displeased no one has recognized me. While I have nothing to hide, I had rather not have the whole town attending on my affairs."

"You have been abroad so little, folk have forgotten what you look like, lady." Elizabeth apologized for her servants and dismissed the reference to Griselda's old and oddly assorted clothes. "I am doubly glad to welcome you as I see you well enough to walk, and walk out alone."

"Yes, I have been much better since that night I went out, fever-crazed, to help save the sheep. It must have been the turning point of the fever."

"Are the headaches gone, too?"

"Oh, no, but I am used to them now. So long as I can get about by myself a little. Mistress Elizabeth, it is not about my body's health that I would talk to you. No doubt you are surprised. If through all these years I had not been bedridden, I hope we should have got to know each other as well as I would like us to assume we have, today. I always liked the look and general report of you, Elizabeth, Cousin."

Elizabeth wished she could have returned this handsome speech, but found herself unable to do such violence to her astonishment. As Griselda intimated, there had been little opportunity for Elizabeth to revise the impression invariably created by the lady's name and her treatment at Cinqmort hands. She stammered, floundered. Griselda smiled a little—only one corner of her mouth curved up, the other turned down—and made haste to end the pause.

"I will not pander to false shame and pretend to think you have heard no tales of my life at Bedesford Manor. Much of what you will have heard was true. But it is different now. My husband and his uncles came so near to losing me, and had such hard work of bringing me back to life, that they must have grown fond of me. They have been very good to me since. These clothes—I have no doubt that, had they but thought of it or had I remembered to ask them, they would have bought me fair and decent apparel. I know not what has become of my wardrobe. You know how it is in a house where the mistress is confined in sickness. I did not think of calling on you till this morning, and then I did not want to put it off, so long as I could find some sort of coverings."

Elizabeth kept her countenance. Affection superseded embarrassed surprise, on Griselda's inconsistent glossing over the fate of all her possessions years ago—a tale which all Anglemere knew and was not likely to forget.

"Now my husband and uncles have begged me to name what I most desire, and if it is in their power they will see that I get it. Ay, it gives one a strange feeling. But it is not love, that feeling. I cannot love them now. It is not that I hate them. Only, there is nothing in me now that could attain to love of them. Can you understand? There is no one I love, nothing, not even myself. And that is my one great wish. I want to acquire someone to love. It is of no importance to me to be loved in turn. I want to do the loving. Therefore I have thought of adopting a child—only for a time, and not by law, because of the succession. You, I thought, are the most likely person to know of a suitable infant and advise me. Then, when all is prepared, I can go to Gervase, and my lord and say, '*This* is what you can do to please me.' I think I can pledge myself, and pledge them to it, that the little guest will get the best of treatment in all ways."

Elizabeth pressed her folded hands to her breast. This was a heaven-sent chance for the babe she was carrying. Yet should she not, must she not suggest one of Jeanne's? If only to prove that her faith in God's mercy was strong enough to deserve and earn His help, she ought to plead the cause of Ruth or Edmund Widowson. But her faith was not strong enough. She was weak, she could feel herself trembling at the mere thought of relying on Mercy only. Surely God would never be deceived by a gesture merely shamming faith?

She took a deep breath and answered Griselda.

We might have known that Jane's spirit would wait to manifest itself until we had got out of the way of expecting it.

A certain little boy of Bedesford was moved to lose his way about the Marsh fringe of the Easterwoods, and found in the charred depression left by Jane's pyre the first landmark to guide him homeward. A few days later he was struck down by a quinsy of peculiar virulence. Before the life was choken out of him the disease had fastened on a number of others. For sure there is no worse death to watch your children die of. And very few indeed recovered. Only a few grown or half-grown folk fell sick. Isabella Robinson was one.

So Elizabeth at last obtained Luke's consent to sending the other children away before they should catch the sickness from their eldest sister. The youngest and weakest, Little Luke, was in particular danger. Him they would send to a place where there were no other children at all that might have carried the infection. The manor was such a place, and a two-weeks-old suckling would hardly have his morals corrupted by my lord and his ribald men! Fortunately Elizabeth had bespoken a nurse long before the sickness was thought of. And now Peter and Robin were not the only Bedesford sons to be packed off to the monastery. All parents who had sons of the right age and thought of it in time, before the chantry school was filled up, did the same.

In spite of everything Jane can never have lost some vestige of tenderness for her foster daughter. She had stayed her hand until after Little Luke was born and ready to be sent away. Elizabeth got up on the fifth day after her confinement to nurse Isabella. She would not have left this even to Bess, not to a hundred Besses. She even neglected Luke. What is more, Isabella mended and lived, and once again Elizabeth suffered no loss, but rather, gained in more ways than one. She had got her children away, and with regard to Isabella she gained time and a natural spell of separation between her daughter and Richard Widowson.

In the days when Elizabeth had worked her hardest to make Luke amenable to the dispersal of the children, and when she had been casting about for justification to lend the expected babe to Griselda Cinqmort, Isabella had taken her completely by surprise, craving the mother's support for her betrothal to Richard.

"What is your hurry?" Elizabeth asked, with a stab of suspicion. "Why has not Richard dared to come with you? And why do you insist on locking yourself in with me like this? You are not usually afraid of your father."

"Oh, Father's mood is so strange. He has not come out of it for months now. He does not see one. He does not listen. He smiles, he does not want to listen. When you are with him, *you* do not want to listen, too. But he listens to you. That is why I told Richard to wait till I had spoken to you. You can prepare Father, and then you and Richard and I can go to him, together."

"What makes you so certain I shall be with you?" Elizabeth intertwined her fingers till they ached. She felt like nothing so much as letting herself sink to the ground and crying out against the weight of her burdens. "I did not even know that you and Richard were especially fast friends. I suppose I must not charge you with secretive dealings until I see how much is due to my own failure to keep my eyes open."

"Oh, Mother," Isabella said, laughing, "you know well he and I have been friends ever since I can remember. And indeed I do think you might have foreseen this, for who is there would not admit that he is the finest young man in the whole parish? Not only is he handsome and liked by all, but clearly he is headed for great renown. And though he is not rich, nor free born, he is near relative to the Cloudsway Abbot, your own great friend."

"What do you mean by that?"

Isabella looked at her mother wonderingly. Elizabeth forced herself to speak evenly. "Well, well, we must talk about this again some other time. I am afraid, my Isabella, that it happens you did not choose your moment at all well—through no fault of your own. It so happens that just now your father and I both have certain weighty matters, unsettled, on our hands. You have given me no reason why you cannot wait, and so—"

"I cannot see what could be weightier or more pressing on you than my future and my happiness."

Now it was Elizabeth stared at her daughter. Could this be she, always so good, so placid? From the moment that, herself little more than a child, she had felt new life stir within her for the first time, she had vowed to rear her offspring without the fear that had overshadowed her own youth. Ay, it seemed she had carried that out, all too well! "You are too young, I dare say, to conceive of it otherwise. Yet am I surprised you cannot think of anything that might be even more important. I cannot go into these matters with you. You will have to take my word for it that there *is* something more important, that the lives and happiness of many more than one are at stake—"

"Ay, that is what the older folk always tell us. 'You don't understand,' when they can't think of a good reason to give us. Give me one good reason why we should not settle this here and now, between ourselves at least! What other lives and happiness can there be in question, that I have not heard of? I am no longer a child. Is it that you have forgotten to note? Before you saw that I am a woman, I should be old, too old. Secrets—often and often have I heard yourself say it, that there are no secrets in Bedesford. You may think that there are secrets that I do not know, but I could list a dozen straight off. I know that Egbert, Fillipin's eldest son is really the late Lord William's, and so are Arthur Newcome and Halt Ned at the Waste; and my Uncle John has sons and daughters aplenty; and Master Colet's wife ran away from him years ago at Ely, with a piper; and my lord murdered his wife, and I know how too; and Grandmother—"

"Preening yourself with such ugly knowledge still does not prove that there are no things unknown to you, my child. As for giving you one good reason why we should make haste slowly in so serious a decision—why, I could give you fifty. Nay, do not interrupt me. Of course

I have nothing against Richard himself. As you have said, he has been almost like one of my own, and I have always had the greatest friendship for the family to which he belongs. But for one thing you are both of you too young—"

"At my age you were already married!"

"True, and I was married far too young. I swore no daughter of mine ever should be."

"But this is different, as I myself want it. You were married against your will."

"What makes you think that?"

"Everybody says so."

"Do they so? Well, that just goes to show that you should take less heed of what folk say, and try and look about you more and train your own judgment. You are not ripe to be the mistress of a household. I was married too young to know my own heart and what I really wanted. You may be as mistaken in thinking that you want Richard, as I was, thinking I did not want your father. My mistake, happily, could be righted easily. The other way about, it could never be corrected. Don't you see? Then also, Richard as yet earns very little."

"Edwin and Jeanne married on less than he has got. They married on less than nothing, being in debt."

"I should be a bad mother indeed to let that stand in recommendation. Have you never looked at Jeanne and thought what kind of life has been hers? She who was the fairest maiden in Anglemere—"

"As soon as women grow old, it is ever said of them they used to be the fairest of the fair, once upon a time," Isabella mocked, tossing her head. "So I have marked, since you want me to use my own judgment, Mother! Besides, why need my life turn out like hers? The circumstances are quite different. We should live at Smithy Yard the first few years."

Elizabeth all but laughed at this: as she strove to empty the house, Isabella strove to fill it! "Isabella, you surely know yourself this is no way to speak to your parents and dispose of them. Go, and I promise to think about your wishes and your welfare."

"No, Mother, I shall not go without you give me your answer one way or the other—"

"Will you not?" Before she knew she was doing it, Elizabeth had struck her daughter. They stared at each other, both aghast. Elizabeth asked herself whether, then, she had been wrong and her mother right and wise. Isabella had staggered under the blow, it would be easy, and was tempting, to subdue her by main force. Isabella's attitude, at bay, made it clear that was what she expected. "Well, if you will not go from the room, I see I must," she said, and without looking back left her daughter.

It was only a short time until the birth of Little Luke. Afterward Isabella had seemed sorry, and, without reference to what had passed, had done all she could to ease her mother's days. Then came the sickness, and during her convalescence Isabella clung to her mother as though all other love had been swept from her heart.

Little Luke was everything one could have hoped. Even the menfolk likened him to an angel the very first week of his life. His skin was not mottled, but clear white and rose; the hair upon his head long, thick, and silky golden. His mother hardly dared so much as look at him after the first showing, in the knowledge that she meant to part with him.

She did not step outside to greet Gervase when he came in person to fetch Griselda's foster son with his nurse and fatherless milk brother (who was rumored to be his true cousin, of Little John's getting). Bess made the Mistress's excuses and repaired to the sickroom with report of the meeting between Little Luke and the future lord.

"For a start it is a good sign that he came himself, I'd say. To be sure, he could have done no less. Ay, he did not like his errand any too well, one could tell—before he *saw* our treasure. Alison made him take the babe in his arms for a moment. Then, Mistress, he *had* to smile, for the babe grinned full broadly at him, so forward as he is in all baby ways, our youngest. Now why do you weep, Elizabeth?"

"Do not scold me, Bess," Elizabeth said weakly, wiping her eyes. "I was thinking it very hard on such a little creature that he is, sent out to win himself affection, instead of biding where it comes to him without effort on his part."

"Now you do talk foolishly. It is no effort for him to be winsome, as he is so by nature. No babe need be wept for, I think, if taken in state to the manor, where he will be brought up like its heir, yet without losing him his real parents."

"You must go and visit Alison full soon, Bess, soon and often," said the mother, her throat sore with quelled weeping, "that we may keep watch over him even from afar."

Whatever may have been her apprehensions, they were not borne out. The infant won the love of all the manor folk. My lord alone took no notice of him, but that in itself was a great thing—seeing that even perfect infants will be noisy.

Bess made Alison tell every smallest circumstance of the reception, and meticulously passed it all on to Elizabeth. All the henchmen had turned out behind Griselda, who stood leaning on Baldwin's arm, and although some nudged each other and smiled sneeringly—at least they were all smiling, one way or another. Griselda, pale, dropped Baldwin's arm to take her borrowed son and press him to her shallow bosom, and laid her face against his fragrant cheek. Then unaided she swung him high for all the men to see, whereupon they crowded round with those cries that are wont to rise wherever a new babe is first displayed, but which sounded most strange in this company. Gervase stood by, striving to look unconcerned.

"Dull witted as she is, that Alison," said Bess, "you could have found no better nurse for him, Elizabeth. She loves him ten times better than her own son. True, she never wanted *him*. She was beaming all over, telling me no one had eyes for Botho on her back. She said she herself forgot all about him!"

The whole day Little Luke was on view in the big hall, everybody constantly returning for another look. Whatever this babe did—doing the same as all others at his age—it was commended. Admiringly the henchmen called each other to witness that he cried, and, later, with gross snorting pulled strongly at the nipple, and now, pausing, gurgled loud and long, fore and aft, and then sprinkled the attentive spectators with his water, trained in so dear, so trim a little arc (they cried), the while his heavenly blue eyes gazed gravely into unseen distances—oh, there had never been such wonders!

Elizabeth must rejoice that the thing was done so promptly, and could not then very well be undone. For shortly after it appeared that a childless house was not necessarily a safe one. Two of the grown folk that died had had no children living with them. Susannah Trefeller's aunt was the one, and Gillian Smith the other. Gillian was one of those about whom nobody thinks a great deal while they are yet with us, but when they die, we feel outraged by what seems like betrayal on their part. James, her husband, was not alone in feeling that the quiet, nimble, colorless woman had deserted.

Only Jeanne Widowson did not care. Jeanne had lost two children, the same Ruth and Edmund whom Gillian had agreed to foster—only that week after week Jeanne had found fresh excuses to postpone actually handing them over. There is no telling whether she so much as grasped the news of Gillian's death. She cried and talked of her own loss day and night, till folk feared for her reason. When they would comfort her, saying even so she had more children living than most people, she would fly into wild rage.

"Children are not eggs that you can count, that, if one falls and breaks, you do not know which one it was. Oh, give me back my two angels, give them back to me!"

The neighbors were so worried, they looked in whenever they could, with kind words that invariably made her worse. The Lord Abbot came to her, but his mother turned against him—as if she resented his being of the family and yet not of it.

One evening Clement and Matt came, without Stephen. Edwin was at home, and so were his big sons, Jaffy and Jack. For once it was men predominated in that hut. Heaven knows how they found room to sit.

"Folk think," Jeanne broke off her wailing to answer their solicitude with the hostility of pain, "that if they all flock around me, it must help. And I tell you if every soul living in this world came to me, it would not help a whit, since God hath forsaken me."

"And that, you think, makes it right for you to forsake the living who still belong to you and depend on their mother and wife?" Clement asked. "What makes you think God has forsaken you? It is no more possible that He should do so than that the air should forsake your lungs while you live. The tie cannot be severed that links you with your Creator, Who bought your salvation with His blood, Who knew you ere you grew inside your mother—thus did David son of Jesse sing when the Lord God tried *him* in his child—"

"Who is he?" Jeanne growled, as much as to say, "How dare you liken anybody else's trouble to mine?"

"Nay, but you are an ignorant woman, Jeanne Widowson," said Matt. "King David was Our Lord's great-grandfather on the father's side—only, the family fell into poverty—"

"He did not say *'King David,'*" Jeanne said angrily. "And what is poverty?"

"Matt did not mean that poverty was the sore trial the Lord God inflicted on King David, Jeanne," Clement said in his quiet voice. "No. King David's dearest son did not simply die, though he did die in the end, by no means in a state of innocence and certain bliss, like your two children. No, his most dearly beloved son made war on David his own father and sought his life, because he coveted the crown. Your children love you, Jeanne, one and all. What would you say if they hated you, Jeanne, and plotted to rob and kill you?"

"I—I would say," Jeanne faltered, "that I had rather they were alive and hated me, than loving me and dead."

"Then would you not be a good mother, if for the sake of having them in this world but a short while longer, you would have them consign themselves to eternal damnation. King David, too, at first said thoughtlessly, as you have done: My God, my God, why hast Thou forsaken me? Why art Thou so far from helping me, and deaf to my sore cry? And then he remembered, and went on: But our fathers trusted in Thee, they trusted, and Thou didst deliver them; they cried unto Thee as I do, and were not confounded. Oh, I am poured out like water, my heart is like wax with the burning sorrow, it is melted in the midst of my bowels. My strength is all dried up, and my tongue cleaves to my jaws, and I am brought into the dust, the dust of death—"

"Yes, yes!" Jeanne wept, no longer only for herself.

"I have called upon Thee and I know Thou wilt hear me, O God, said David. Shew Thy marvelous loving kindness, O Thou that healest. Keep me and fold me in the shadow of Thy wings. So now have you prayed with King David, Jeanne. And now listen to what the Lord God answers to those that have cried unto Him in their grievous distress. For a small moment, saith the Lord Our Redeemer, I hid My face from thee, but with mercies great and everlasting will I comfort thee. And thus you shall go out once again with joy, and be led forth in security. The mountains and the hills shall break forth before you into singing. All the trees of the fields shall clap their hands. Instead of thorn shall come up the oak tree, and instead of the briar the fair birch tree, and their gentle shade, my Jeanne, shall never be cut off."

Jeanne held her face in her hands. Edwin's hand lay still on her gray head. They were all silent. Then Edwin sighed and thanked Clement.

"And you must know it is all his own Englishing, from the Latin books!" Matt burst out eagerly.

"Books?" said Edwin. "What books are they?"

"They are the Holy Scriptures of Our Lord. They are goodly comfort, are they not? That was how he saved me, Clement, the year after the Black Death it was, when we met together, in a ditch where I had fallen, sick after roaming wild as the Fiend rode me, with pricks of bitter memories and evil thoughts."

"God would have found your soul without, you know that," Clement interposed.

"It does seem strange," Jaffy Widowson said suddenly, "that those who are safer against sorrow than we out in the world—that monks and priests, and not we, should have access to the comfort of the Lord's word."

Clement put a hand on the young man's shoulder. "That is what I think too, my Geoffrey. I go further. I call it cruelty and wrong. I say that withholding God's word from the people is worse than rendering them blind, deaf, and dumb."

"Talk not of matters you don't understand," Edwin said to his son. Jaffy had ever been the most tractable and least troublesome of all the Widowson children. Perhaps it is with children as with goods, and folk do not value what they have not had to pay for, in suffering and anxiety if not in money. "And surely you are wrong, you must be," Edwin turned to Clement with equal vehemence. "God's purpose needs wickedness and sinners here on earth, as surely as He allows the Devil to live."

CHAPTER 7
THE ERRING

MUCH HAD CHANGED since those early days when Brother Laurentius accused Matt and Clement of what they were, and our ignorance laughed him to scorn. Abstruse as the Master of Balliol's dissertations were reputed to be, their gist had become commonplace, confidently discussed in simple laborers' huts.

In the years before he became a Lollard, we had marveled—or at least said we marveled, meaning that in fact it did not in the least surprise us —that no relatives or friends of Stephen Colet's ever visited him in Bedesford. But as soon as he had joined the promoters of the Great Society, other emissaries (so we came to realize) were constantly coming to see and briefly bide with him and Matt and Clement, whom he had taken into his house.

We speak of the Great Society without ultimate knowledge. There were rumors and there have been rumors ever since, and nothing more definite than rumors. It was and is said that those whom one loosely called Lollards were trying to bring the people of all England together into one sworn brotherhood, to overthrow the wicked and the mighty and the corrupters of the Faith in order that the people might millennially reign.

At all events, a new kind of wanderer had begun to appear: men who sought neither work nor charity, merely the chance of talking to all whom they could get to listen. They did not preach, like the friars; they but involved you in conversation, having none of the stranger's wonted shyness, nor being daunted in the slightest degree by the obstacles of divergent regional speech. They bore tales of happenings over the rest of the country, and they both asked and tried to mold your opinions on the condition of the people in the land and the teachings of Wycliffe, Ball, and Occam. Albeit strangers are one's sole source of news and these harbingers made few material demands, we did not always take to them kindly.

For it became a very dangerous thing. The Master of Balliol himself had the friendship of princes and his wide renown as a great scholar to uphold him in his unfearing boldness, even after Pope Gregory XI had issued the edict against him and his followers. The obscure followers had no such protection, and against them the papal will was enforced.

Not a few of the stories they retailed in Bedesford now concerned comrades of theirs, hunted, imprisoned, tried, or slain without trial, in other parts. We marveled they did not deny their fellowship at least by silence (thinking of Gervase), and for a time felt most uneasy at being seen in company with a stranger.

But it is a curious fact that danger will also attract. About this time Dick Toolmaker first named himself a Lollard, also Will Tewsing who had lived with him ever since his uncle's death. We think it was they two went afield on behalf of the Bedesford offshoot of the Great Society. Dick, as a free man and woodward, could frequently absent himself for weeks at a stretch, and Will had long been helping him with the forest duties.

So you can see in Bedesford their calling was not quite so precarious as in most other places. We were not likely to haul them to justice. My lord was still awaiting the return of Jane in solitary roaming and inexpert necromancy. Prior Carlos was powerless against the Cloudsway Abbot's obstinate blindness to the presence of Lollards on his territory.

Lord Alfred stood in correspondence with Bishop Jerome, who was aware of the monastery reforms, if hardly of the Abbot's leniency in regard to the hunting of heretics, imposition of fines, conduct of Wode

Mill, and his dilatoriness in rebuilding the cloister. In all the years since the foundation, nothing could have induced Lord Jerome's chaplains to miss their annual stay as Lord William's guests. The second year of Alfred's rule, the then chaplain contrived to represent other business as more urgent, the third he pleaded illness, so that after the first year there were not even any more proxy visitations.

Alfred sent regular account of St. Hand's progress, and the Bishop received the revenues punctually, without requests for additional funds. It would seem that he trusted Alfred; it would almost seem that for the time being the cathedral had become a matter of less compelling urgency for him, too. No doubt he had other irons in the fire, quicker of taking form than a work aimed into eternity.

No complaints reached him. There were no valid grounds on which complaints could have been made. Although it was William Goliard, Alfred had succeeded, and although under him life was hard and often tedious, the monks had become more than resigned. They were not proud of him as they had been of his predecessor, but they felt security in him. William had ever figured in the foreground. Alfred was one with the general fabric of the monastery's life, so much so that in the end they forgot he was responsible for those aspects of the life which they did not relish. And they came to dislike them less. Have you never known that feeling, of unpleasant work well performed, and thus doubly satisfying for its unpleasantness? This is not to say that all hostility to him had disappeared, nor that there was no more grumbling. But as Alfred was not to be swayed by consideration of his friends any more than of his opponents, he was not afraid to risk affection and peace over and over again. As his purpose was unassailable, these undercurrents were, again, part of the general life, rather than disruptive of it.

What, we sound as if in our eyes Alfred could do no wrong? Far from it. In his treatment of youngsters, novices, and lay schoolboys we always considered he went astray. He omitted to provide express relief from the boys' studies and labors. No doubt it did profit their growing souls. But it meant—at least we think it was the consequence—that the worst of his domestic troubles arose from the lads' dormitories and the chantry school.

The boys were greedy of every excuse for wild excitement. When the cat first appeared in the cloister garden, you might have thought it was a comet, instead of a small, misbehaving beast that destroyed the young lettuce and scratched up seedling plants and rare herbs and flowers, in pursuit of easement. To be sure, it never ruined what was not valuable. When it took to catching birds and poultry, it killed only those that the monks could least afford to lose. When it made a noise of nights, it was invariably under the window of a sickroom. And then it attacked an unsuspecting young postulant in the currant bushes. At this it was thought the cat must be a mother with kittens, and the boys hunted all over the garden (thereby creating much further damage) for her lair, in vain. The cat was seen only when it suited her, and that never once outside the monastery grounds.

Further the new broom that had swept the monastery clean had raised understandable hopes among the building workers. We still got the wages fixed twenty-five years ago, and a penny did not buy what it had done in 1350, for all that in many ways times were better. It was no sudden light that showed us we could not make ends meet. It had merely failed to strike us before that this might be remedied, that the dwindling penny might be, not stayed, but supplemented. Then also, there came to us report of the new young King Richard's building activities, which raised the value of building workers everywhere.

When we heard that the Abbot had at long last gone back to his and Brother Oswin's book—meaning that the work of reform was done in so far as he need no longer take constant active part in it—we deemed it the right time to approach him. Our chance came with his next visit of inspection round the cathedral.

He had hardly appeared in public since his investiture, and everyone thronged to get a good look at him. He looked tired. Well might his mother exclaim he was thin! Yet this only aged, dignified, refined him. A stranger would have sworn our Abbot was of noble blood. Yet we suddenly found ourselves too shy to speak to him. In the end Abbot Alfred noticed that wherever he passed there was a halfhearted surge toward him, then a nudging, and sidling retreat. So he asked, and our spokesmen stepped forward.

They told him—and, engrossed as he had been, it might reasonably be assumed he did not know—of the King's men that were hunting and seducing and impressing building workers throughout the country, offering, not only higher wages and better living than anywhere else, but also greater opportunities for craftsmen. They reminded him how, in the old King's days, certain masons had once banded together and escaped from Cloudsway Waste, intending to meet the royal train on the road to Norwich and putting themselves in the way of being carried off to Westminster. Lord William had had them caught and punished, since then no one else had tried—and no one *wanted* to try again

now. We only mentioned it—so said our spokesmen—to back our plea
that wages be raised and certain disabilities removed. We were yet too
modest to ask the same privileges as obtained in the King's household.

We could tell at once the Abbot was displeased. His expression grew
haughty, his mouth had a wryness as of disgust, which cut us to the
heart. What we thought giving him information, he chose to interpret
as insolent sarcasm.

"I never looked to hear myself so addressed by you. Where I have
shown sternness, I have reaped gratitude. You, whom I have treated
only with kindness, see therein only weakness. Weak was I, you think,
in the funeral fine; weak when at this last child-dying I advised you to
make smaller gifts to the cathedral than your then grief caused you
ruinously to proffer; weak and weak, to let free speech prevail. I would
not care what you thought, were it not that you see fit to act upon it.
You see fit to call me to account, and wait to do so until I have returned
to my own dearest craft. You think impatience will not let me say you
no! You think because I have striven to purify my house, that I am one
of you, and against its inmates—a wasp worm set to destroy it from
within. What was that word your every phrase contained? Justice? Ay.
On your lips it would seem to apply only on behalf of the subject,
against his superiors. Justice works both ways, all ways. I should defend
you against injustice with my life, no matter against whom, but likewise do I stand, a shield, between you and the monastery, the cathedral,
ay, Bishop and Pope, if so be you threaten injustice to them. Let now
your greed and sloth reflect on the difference between your lives and
ours. You want your hours of work shortened. How many hours of *rest*
are the monks'? No sooner is he sunk on his bed, than he must rise
again, in darkness and cold, to pray. Holy days to you are days of rest
and feasting, for the priest they mean increase of sacred duties. You
clamor for better quarters—which could only be at the expense of St.
Hand's house, while we decline to take advantage of the Bishop's
liberal injunction to rebuild ours."

When he had finished, his face was calm and again kindly. We
waited. Though we wished ourselves far away, our feet dared not yet
move. Edwin had been invited to be one of our spokesman but, as we
had known he would, refused. But he had drawn near all the same,
some of us thought to mortify himself before his son by giving a false
impression of accord with his fellows.

Alfred hailed his father and brothers, and stopped to say a few words
to them. He moved on through the crowd with the same natural and

pleasant informality, so much as if nothing had happened, that we began to doubt anything had. At the edge of the crowd he noticed Clement —the confessed Lollards had decided to remain in the background, not from timidity, but so as not to prejudice our cause. Clement bowed reverently, awaiting the Abbot's address.

"Well, Clement, you that were my taskmaster not so very long ago, do you hold me to be a very harsh overlord?"

Clement looked at him a moment longer before replying. He shook his head and sighed heavily, "God help me, I cannot but see your point of view, even though you will not understand ours—for I must tell you that you misjudged our reasoning. God help us, indeed you are the worst kind of Abbot! One good, honest, pious man like you that strives to make the best of a bad way of government and to rule justly and gently, and spares not himself, does more to hold back a change for the better than a hundred bloody tyrants."

The Abbot was taken aback. He smiled uneasily and, his gaze wavering past Clement's grave, steady eyes, nodded farewell and went on. With his arms crossed and a brooding stare, Brother Laurentius had taken up an isolated stand, trying to make it impossible for the Abbot to miss him out. Bent on making his way home now without more delay, Alfred defied him with another affable nod in passing.

But there was no escaping Brother Laurentius in the long run. Inexorably he tackled the Abbot's conscience another day.

"Have you ever asked yourself, Alfred Widowson, why you indulge in Lollard-coddling? Have you persuaded yourself you are impelled by mercy, or the desire to turn the other cheek?"

For once the Abbot cannot have been wholly displeased to be forced to reveal his mind.

"If you must know it, then, it is true that at heart I am in agreement with much of the Lollard teaching. How could I answer Clement when I knew there was some truth in what he said? Yet mine is not the kind of heart can school itself to ignore the minor ills of the present day, in order to further the major weal of the future."

They had chanced to meet on the green, and there they went on standing, heedless as in the darkest privacy of the confessional.

"Alfred, my son. Alfred, Abbot at Cloudsway. That God may give me grace to pierce your ear and touch your heart, through that armature of ice and stone with which your all too active reasoning encloses it! What have you to do with mundane logic? In Heaven mercy is the keystone; it is in Hell they talk of justice! Earthly justice is not your

rovince. And were it so, then you would have acted wrongly the other
day, when you refused the Wasteside's request with arguments that
were beside the point, swaying the emotions under pretext of appealing
to reason. What I feared for you all along has come to pass. You claim
authority absolute over all that are under you, yet you deny and set at
naught any authority whatsoever above yourself!"

"Excepting God's."

"And what makes you think that you know God's mind better than
those whom in His wisdom He placed above you? Who are you to
treat direct with Him? Who but God Himself ordained the hierarchy
of mediators? In the beginning it may not have been pride led you the
road of Lucifer. It was but that you were determined to serve too many
masters at once—Your conscience and your art and, *lastly,* God. Cast
off the others, Alfred. Men and men's lives are not your concern. Also
leave it to others to imitate His creations with graven imagery! God
alone is your master; in His service alone lies your work. Would you
barter with Him, offering Him painted books in lieu of mystic sacrifice
of your whole self?"

"You are wrong. *He* demands more than that of me—"

"There is no more."

"Now who is measuring immeasurables? I did not mean more in the
sense of greater value. I was placed where I am in order to rule. That is
a practical task. As for men's lives, which you say do not concern me:
if it is pious to give to the needy, why is it impious, wishing to see an
end of all need? And if it is to the glory of God to carve stone and
build churches, surely the making of fine books can be no less so."

"But," the friar cried, with tears in his voice, "you will come to grief,
between art and administration, Lollard convictions and adherence to
things as they are, speeding the building work and trying to salve your
conscience of oppression, the service of man, and service of God!"

"Leave me to try."

"Leave you—ay, henceforth I will leave you, as I have long left all
others and all else! You have as good as said I stand accused with you,
that I work at ornamenting St. Hand's. What you fail to understand
is that I am laboring to find a way in which that sort of work, too, may
become solely mystic communion with God, abstracted, purified of all
human concepts! Whereas you work for the human eyes, that more and
more things may become intelligible to it, instead of widening, perfect-
ing transcendental means of divine communication beyond language
and very thought!"

Alfred continued to pray at his every orison that he might be given grace to help save Jane, and he watched and waited. The quinsy was only an act, not an appearance.

One night he dreamed of her. He saw her, and she opened her mouth to speak, but he could not hear her. The darkness about her was full of unearthly din. She tried again and again. He could see her lips move, but he could not read them and her voice was drowned. He awoke, but the noises did not vanish along with the apparition. The Abbot rose and made for the cell nearest his own, when hasty, naked footsteps approached, and a small lamp, which chased the shadows before it like a swarm of routed bats.

"Reverend Father!" cried the Master of Novices, in whose hand the lamp was none too steadily upheld—in the other he clutched his skirt wet with night dew. "It is the boys—they are after the cat. For days, it appears, they have schemed and planned for this—do with me what you will—it *ought* to have come to my ears in time! If we cannot stop them, God only knows how little will be left of our gardens. What shall I do? What can one do? Shall I rally the brethren? O dear saints! Just you listen, Reverend Father!"

In truth it sounded as if all Hell were riding loose.

The lamp had gone out. A spray of moonlight fell through the open door of the Abbot's cell. He made an abrupt movement and plunged back. Before the Master of Novices could voice another question, the Abbot had returned and, pulling the other along by the arm, hurried him out into the grounds.

The moonlight, knowing only black and white of all the hues, had created a strange landscape out of the familiar plots, playing with depths here conjuring false chasms into innocent plains, there bridging hollows and erasing stumbling blocks. It was like a fantastic guessing game set for all comers with black roses, bright silver cabbage leaves, soft-edged gray boughs and pitchy foliage, with hard white sparks over all, like holes in a window screen, of the dew that outshone the stars which it reflected. Clad as in colorless motley by an angular patchwork of light and shade, the jumble of cat hunters was freed alike of solidity and the danger of individual recognition.

The Master of Novices was submerged in the turmoil. Alfred could not make himself heard. By this time all the other monks had come out, inaudibly mouthing and gesticulating, like Jane in his interrupted dream.

Alfred began to pray aloud. God would hear him, as would a ghost

if there were any such about. He withdrew a small, pale something
from his girdle and waved it before him. He stood alone, casting a long
shadow. Then suddenly he stood alone no longer. Confronting him was
a small, humped shape, accompanied by its shadow as was he.

Silence fell until one could make out the distant whispering of
snapped twigs and stalks still echoing the tread that had broken them.
A deep, compressed circle of boys and men formed round the Abbot
and the cat.

Alfred spoke to her, low. After a moment the cat answered, with a
short, throaty twitter, and her folded ears stood up and swiveled. Then
she gave a start and raised one paw, meditatively held it at right angles,
shook it as if to disembarrass it of a sleeve, bent her head and began to
wash the limb devotedly. Again Alfred spoke to her. Now she made as
if she did not hear, sat down, and applied her tongue to a hinder leg.
Somebody uttered a nervous titter. Alfred motioned the onlookers to
stay quiet and still. Cautiously he advanced upon the cat, with the small,
pale, waving object outstretched. The cat ceased from smoothing her
fur and lifted her head to him. All could see the glow of her eyes. Alfred
stroked her. He turned, and she followed him indoors, busily. Monks
and boys stayed behind, staring, though there was nothing left to watch.

Alfred burned the charm with which he had lured the cat to him.
It was Brother Oswin's picture of Elizabeth, that had been intended for
the infant St. Clara.

Part Eight
Rebellions
(1378-1381)

ISABELLA

Not Many Eyes at Smithy Yard had closed during the night, so that by the first drowsy bird's trill everyone was out of bed. Waiting the sunrise, the air, though chill, had a close, perfumed heaviness which, whilst pimpling the skin with shivers, yet left the lungs gasping for sufficiency. The sons of the house were leaving it this morning.

Breakfast was over. Cocks began to crow. The courtyard came to a reluctant life with the clip-clop of horses across the cobbles to the gate. From every door people emerged. The young men, schoolfellows and friends of the Robinson lads, came out of the barn where they had lain down briefly after the feasting. Peter and Robin tried to behave as if they too were but onlookers, and to lose themselves out of the way of handclasps and fond glances.

Master and Mistress appeared, with the two foreign ship's captains who were to carry off the boys, and whose servants alone stood apart and at ease, chatting callously, yawning, by the horses. One was a Flemish spice merchant and owner of a small fleet; Peter, the heir, was placed in his charge. The other, heavy-boned, bronzed, with bare, hairy arms and legs, hard, curly black hair growing deep into his forehead and a beard of the same concealing half his face, had his home in Iceland. He was no merchant, but an accomplished navigator with his own ship which he loved like wife, mother, daughter, and priceless steed rolled into one, and which from time to time took other people's cargoes. That Robin, taller than any of his family, albeit still narrow in the shoulders and too long of leg, was to fellow this piratical-visaged captain, the lad's own raw Cinqmort looks made to seem appropriate. The Norseman's scars and gory tales bore witness to so many dangers overcome,

355

that almost they were tokens of security, instead of leading one to tremble for the youngster. His mother trembled, to be sure. The good-byes began.

The boys looked dazed; whosoever failed to grasp their hands clapped them on the shoulder, smote their backs, patted their heads. Bess embarrassed them with tight hugs and loud kisses that brooked no evasion. To make matters worse she took their baby sisters from the nurse's arms and thrust their little nodding faces close up to the boys', talking all the while in valedictory baby language, and sending further, smacking kisses into the air on the babes' behalf. Sobs became audible and the first tears fell.

In a moment it was all over. The foreigners and their charges and servitors had mounted, and, pursued by well-wishing shouts, clattered out of sight behind the outer wall. The women held coifs and aprons to their eyes, the lads and young men, and Isabella, rushed to the gate to keep the cavalcade in view as long as might be. They returned at a slow, shambling pace. Everybody stood about a little longer, vacant, drowsy.

Elizabeth took her hand out of Luke's and smoothed back her hair, which the other women took as a signal that henceforward this day must be dealt with like any other. Isabella took her hand out of Richard's. Elizabeth told her to take the young people back to the hall and see that they got another warm drink and be their hostess. "Wait for me, Luke," she turned to her husband, "I would like to walk with you in my garden."

Bess and the nurse brought her eighteen-months-old Margaret, and Alicia, who was not quite yet one year. Margaret had been weakly and ailing from birth, but her younger sister was fat, healthy, and full of unruly vigor. These infants of Smithy Yard led a life apart, so that folk held it against the parents, saying that their later children were to them no more than accidental fruits of their unbecoming, belated heat. Elizabeth still found time to see people in her Little Parlor. She thought more of benefiting strangers, folk said, and thus spreading abroad her name and fame, than of caring for her own.

There were few kind words spoken of the Robinsons in those days. Largely, we think, this was because of their secluded life. They were at once too old and too young for such retirement. Depending on which way one looked at it, it was either indecent or reprehensibly lax. Here was Luke, still under fifty, playing the stay-at-home invalid: yet had he not always said that, the worse he looked, the better was his health?

And he was not too frail to beget a new child every year! Nearly all his traveling was done for him by Young Frank Oxerd—who thus grew more and more insufferable—and who, moreover, not infrequently received callers in the Master's stead. It was not right for Luke to rest his buttocks in his countinghouse—when he was not cooing and cuddling with his wife—seeing that he controlled so large a share in the life of the town and two shires. At least they might have given notable feasts several times a year, as John Trefeller had always done, and as even his aging widow valiantly went on doing.

Now, too, in the broad light of morning, when it behooves all children of Adam to be at their busiest, these two took each other by the hand, like any knight and his lady fair in a minstrel's lay, and tripped out of duty's way to wander behind screens of hawthorn.

In honor of her sons, Elizabeth had put on a wine-hued silk dress which clung to shoulders and arms, but fell voluminously in fluted folds from her breast and the point of her shoe. There was no color in her face except for fading crescent streaks of sun-brown on her cheekbones. But, against the spotless white of her headgear, at least her pallor looked alive. Not so Luke's which gave an impression of brittle surface, framed in the rich, bloomy texture of a golden red velvet cowl, which he had taken to wearing all day long, indoors and out, because his wife coaxed, "it so became him!" now that his hair had thinned and come all over gray. His suit of clothes was of his favorite gray, down to hose and soft leather ankle boots, so nicely fitted that his spare figure still looked well setup, although he moved with a deliberate caution that never relaxed its stiffening check. So people accused him of haughty demeanor, and Elizabeth had to be thankful for their mistake.

Before she knew it, she had sighed. Luke passed his arm round her middle. "Now you must take a hold on yourself, my wife. Cease from regarding our boys as all but dead lest—" in spite of his jesting tone he crossed himself "—lest thereby you conjure death upon them. Before this you were eager to send all your children away—"

"Oh, Luke! This time it is different, you know well. We do not send grown folk off to sea with an easy heart, let alone two such young children. I could wish that at least you had let them go with your own ship or my mother's. Oh, I know, you have told me why, for their own good, you would not have it so. But it seems hard."

"You really talk as if they were the merest infants. At Robin's age you were a wedded wife, at Peter's already a mother. The trouble is that you have never been to sea. Therefore your mind is all beset with fears and fancies. How often have I been away from you, and returned safely?"

"But, Luke, two years! Two years—that is to say, three or four—if we ever see them again! But you are right, I must stop this. What I really wanted to talk to you about was Isabella."

"What about Isabella?"

"You say I was married at Robin's age. She is older than he by three years. And it is two years ago that she first came to me about wanting to marry Richard."

"And what did you say? And why did you not tell me?"

"I said I would put in a good word for them with you, in my own time. I wanted to see how firmly they loved each other. And then I wanted courage to speak to you."

"My cunning wife! So you would compel me to chivalry? Can you seriously tell me what you were afraid of?"

"I was afraid you might say no, and then feel obliged to abide by your word ever after. Many's a time you have reveled in her loveliness and talked of marrying her off to great advantage."

"You cannot say I have been in a hurry about it. You cannot wrong me so much as to think that I might place the glory of our house above her happiness. The question is only how is one to know, beforehand, ever? Look at us two. But did I let myself be blinded by the general terms on which Sir Asphodel desired to have her for his son—who will not come of age for another six years? Did I jump at Master Goodrich's offer to treat for her with those wealthy cousins of the great Richard Lyon in London? Few men in my position would have let that chance go by. I never told you that your mother has been pressing for an alliance with the Tryfellows of Clowes—whom I know you dislike, though I never knew why. I agreed with you from the start, not to let her be married too young. Do you know—ay, no doubt you do!—what has been at the back of my mind? I always hoped that in her the wrong that was done you might be prettily repaired, and that she might get a husband of her own finding."

"If she finds happiness half as great as mine, I shall praise her luck and ours. But you see how we have failed. We should not have kept this at the *back* of our minds! Surely no parents of daughters ever acted as we have, as if we were kinless hermits, instead of seeing to it that she got out among people! It seems to me we have been lucky that, left to her own devices, she did not make worse choice."

"I must say, my love, Richard is not so bad a match as all that. He is unfree. But so was your friend, the Abbot, to whom Richard is cousin. If it has to be said: if I could free the one, I can do the same again. This time it need not cost me quite so dear, for why should not his parents remain as they are? Though I may not often talk about it, do you think I have forgotten of what sort of stock I have come myself? My father was less than a villein, for that he was a runaway. And it is no pleasant thought that somewhere in English lands, if he but knew it, there lives someone could claim legal right to impound me and my descendants, and all our property! So it does not become us to be so very proud. After all, it is not as if we were not blessed with daughters in plenty, whom we may yet send out after earls and dukes one of these days! If those two children love each other—. We know him, we like him, everybody likes him. We shall not have to get used to calling a stranger, son. He is a Widowson, with the Widowson hand. There is work enough for ten like him at the cathedral, enough to outlast ten lifetimes. He may grow renowned far beyond our frontiers, and found a great house, before he is very old. I should not mind to see my fair eldest daughter mother of future Widowsons—and neither ought you, that once aspired to like place!"

He paused, stood still, and looked at his wife with narrowed eyes and mouth. Her eyelashes came down, her lips had hard work to keep straight. "Well! Cunning, I called you, and did not see *how* cunning! You attacked him, that I might defend, and break all my own weapons one by one before ever using them! I ought to have asked you why, then, having known all about it these two years, you made no attempt to oust Richard from Isabella's heart—if it were true you misliked the thought of their union! You have never found me hard to persuade, have you? I would have thrown open my house for feasting, and sent the two of you to be feasted in return—had you but asked me. But you wanted her to have her Richard, did you not? Too seldom do I bear it in mind, that I took to wife one was reared by a witch!"

"Oh, Luke!" Elizabeth protested demurely, though not as yet entirely sure of him. "What may I tell our poor, patient child?"

"I suppose," said Luke, walking on with her, "that really I ought to thank you, since you did it for me, acting the part of the harsh parent, and bade them wait and prove their affection! Tell her to send her swain to me."

"Oh, Luke! No, you yourself shall tell her that, and see her face."

There can be little wonder that the childhood love between Mistress Robinson and the Cloudsway Abbot, and consequent scandalous whis-

perings of a later day, had ever remained one of the staple tales of
Bedesford. Luke naturally knew of this, and with advancing years it
irked him no less. Howbeit, it gave him dual reason to send Elizabeth
to negotiate about Richard. On the one hand, he so seldom left Smithy
Yard that if he himself were to wait on the Abbot, folk might think he
did not trust his wife. On the other hand, an abbot was an abbot,
whether his name be William or Alfred, who as a matter of course
would seek to overcharge, so that playing on his memories might result
in a better bargain.

Young Frank escorted the Mistress, trying to make it appear that she
merely accompanied him on an errand of which in truth he was as ignorant as Luke wished everybody to remain for the present. In one
way Elizabeth was well pleased to go in place of Luke, as she did not
want him to meet the Franciscan Prior, whom on most days one was
certain to encounter at the site. But she too knew of the ancient rumors,
and wondered whether Alfred would be embarrassed.

Once upon a time she would have been more sure of Alfred's thoughts
than of her own. Strangers now, they were doubly strangers for having
once been such fast friends. What could either she or little Alfred
Widowson have in common with the Abbot?

She had heard that he looked older than he should, and almost found
herself resenting—because of Luke—that yet he looked so healthy. Or
could it be for Alfred's own sake she deplored it? To see him weighed
down by his powers and duties into sickness and decline might have
warmed her heart toward him. Whereas now, without enmity, it was
as cold as unshaped stone. This made it hard for her to be more than
polite, and she worried lest he falsely deduce excess emotion clumsily
concealed.

He waited for her to begin in amiable calm, and she could not find a
way to begin. Suddenly a shadow fell on the flags between them,
soundlessly changing—so it seemed—into the body which had previously
cast it, from the window ledge. A small, gray-golden cat stood there
and looked the visitor over. The Abbot bent forward. "Chatte!" he
called softly. The cat waved the tip of her tail but did not turn her
intent head.

"I have heard of her," said Elizabeth with a smile. "She follows you
everywhere, and has to be locked up when you go to say Mass. I would
like to have one of her kittens next time, if there is one looks like her.
She is a beauty right enough."

"She has never kittened all the time I have had her," the Abbot responded animatedly, and then looked, Elizabeth thought uncomprehendingly, as if he wished he had not told her this. "She is offended with me because I would not suffer her to come into the parlor with me—though as you see she has come all the same. It is I, Chatte, has cause to be offended!" The cat kept its back to him and reared up against Elizabeth purring, and pushed its nose into her caressing hand. "Usually she will have naught to do with strangers!"

Elizabeth fought down her chuckles. That the sage ruler of Cloudsway should not himself see the joke of his parental interest in this pet! How attentively he watched them now! All at once she found she could meet him like any other human being, and laid before him Luke's wishes for Richard Widowson and Isabella.

As she, if not her husband, had expected, Alfred was eager to smooth their path. She found herself telling him more than the bare facts.

Richard's parents had been bidden to Smithy Yard with their son to talk about the marriage, and had been unable to decide whether to be more glad or afraid—afraid of Juliana.

"But what can she do," asked the Abbot, "so long as I have nothing against it?"

"It is not what she can do, Reverend Father, but what she might *say!* I thought their dread most flattering to an old dame like Mother!"

"And what did she say?"

"Oh, she is very angry. You see, Luke pointed out to Meg and Geoffrey that any purchase money must come out of Isabella's portion, so that it will profit her husband if his parents remain unfree. They said they did not wish to be freed—what should they do with themselves, free? I think they hoped this would appease Mother. But apparently she storms and says that for years she had been paying the monastery for Meg and Geoffrey's service. If they were free, she would be the gainer by that sum, as Richard's parents at their times of life would undoubtedly stay on with her against their board and lodging—which is all they have had in effect all along!"

"Still, it must make up to them for all Juliana's tongue-lashing—that their son is the luckiest young man in Bedesford."

"Yes." Elizabeth felt uneasy again, interpreting this as an allusion to her and Alfred's lesser luck, once, in the same situation. "Though it is early yet to speak of luck," she said, looking at his cat, not at himself. "Sometimes our greatest happiness comes of our being thwarted. Have you never found it so, Reverend Father?"

"Ay," said the Abbot, and rose, ending the interview. "But it does not follow that getting one's heart's desire necessarily turns out ill. So I will call those two children lucky until the event proves me wrong—which I am sure God will not suffer. It shall not be for want of my earnest prayers, nor for want of their mothers' prayers, I know."

"If you mean—if you think I begrudge my sweet child—" Elizabeth started up. But the Abbot made as if he did not hear, blessed her, and, his cat at his heels, was crossing the doorstep before she had completed her sentence.

She went over to his chair and heavily sat down on it, not caring that someone might come and wonder and turn her out. She had been about to flaunt her happiness at him. Now it came over her again, in what depths of misery this happiness was rooted.

CHAPTER 2

"PEOPLE SAY . . ."

SEVEN YEARS AFTER Margaret Widowson's death, her Fleming married her sister Janet. The wedding feast was held at Edwin's hut, that is to say, rather more than less in the open air. There was scarcely fewer guests than were wont to attend the greater bridals, and no dearth of the greater folk themselves, excepting such that otherwise would come from other parts of the country. But then here there were the groom's countrymen from the tileries, in full strength. Boards and benches had been set up before the bride's home and outside the neighbors' huts, and the wedding gifts were mostly contributions to the banquet. The day was not fair, but nothing short of a snowstorm would have daunted the guests.

There was no shortage of good ale; no doubt it was because of the fresh air that conversation continued staid and decent well after dusk.

Then, suddenly, Richard Widowson and Young Will Tewsing came to blows. They caught us unprepared, so that none stepped between them in time. For these two were supposed to be a model pair of friends, having shared in the greatest amity the work on the canopied screen of

William Goliard's effigy, and likewise the railings around Baldwin Cinqmort's tomb.

Will had come to be regarded as one of those rare beings, a confirmed bachelor and woman-hater, for that he had lived, man and boy, with wifeless men, and had never been known to go awooing, though nearly the same age as Mistress Robinson and Abbot Alfred.

Will kneeled on Richard's chest, thumped his foe's head on the ground by the ears, and bellowed, "—none but an earl, or a Hanseate merchant, I thought, would be allowed to come near her—my fair one, whom I have watched from afar every day of my life since she grew up to maidenhood! But you must come, you, and deny all decency and send forth the Abbot, your cousin, to press your suit with his leman, her mother—and he lets you go, when St. Hand's needs as many men bound to it as ever it can get—when I held back modestly, though my heart bleed never so much. I that am a Tewsing—"

They rolled over and over, now one was uppermost and now the other, and blood flowed from their mouths and noses.

Dick and Edwin succeeded at last in dragging them apart before they killed each other, or infected the whole company by their lusty example. We did our best to pretend that we had not heard a word.

But that afterward the town talked of little else you will readily believe. One consequence was that Juliana got her son to take her before the Abbot, in hopes of persuading him to forbid her granddaughter's marriage to his cousin, or at least withdraw his consent to Richard's manumission. This proving fruitless, she decided to make the first move toward a full reconciliation between Trefeller Court and Smithy Yard.

The Robinsons had merely been awaiting a favorable moment to do the same. Whether it was solely that they had had so little truck with each other for so long, or that, herself due to become a grandmother in the next year or two, Elizabeth had mellowed. Juliana in the meantime had acquired at Smithy Yard the standing of an ancestress with endearing foibles. One need only think of Richard Duckleg, or Rogue Cinqmort whom, for example, his descendants owned with smiling pride, though he cannot have been anything but burdensome to know in his lifetime.

"Now that we are friends again, my children, let me talk to you as a mother should. Had you not lacked mother's counsel this foolishness would never have gone so far. I scarce believed my ears when first I heard of this proposed match. It is not your fault alone. It is a sign of the degenerate times. Look at our Abbot! What did I tell you when Alfred Widowson was raised so high. A pig will not be content save in a pigsty. I quail to think what foreign visitors say about that tattered monastery. At least in the lamented Lord William's day there was stateliness and cultivated living inside those beggarly walls. Whereas now—! You should hear Alfred's own mother on the subject. I happen to know he is disobeying the Lord Bishop's express commands. I told him I would let the Bishop know. He said . . . But you must not sidetrack me. If nothing else, Luke and Elizabeth, ay, and you too, Isabella, that bear my noble sister's name—your great-aunt, that stood me in mother's stead—if nothing else, there is a principle at stake. You do not want to go down in God's ledgers among the gravediggers of England's greatness, do you? My mother, and my mother's mother, and myself, and, God be thanked that I can say so, my daughter (and do you not also thank God and your mother for this, Elizabeth?)—we were none of us consulted when it came to marrying us. Marry by mutual agreement, forsooth, like any cotter's brat! Why, then, go to the trouble of true marriage at all? I cannot think why Hugh has issued no legal restraint.'"

It was decided Luke himself must go formally to bid the manor folk to the wedding of his eldest daughter. Then he fell ill with boils behind his ears, and as they had best not leave it much later, Elizabeth once more went in his stead.

Frank, who made to follow her and Gervase into the hall, was told to wait in the henchmen's house. Until that day he had never been inside the manor. The henchmen and he had waged their war of gibes on meeting in street or market place, where they were the interlopers. There he had taken it upon himself to bear him toward them as the living expression of the townfolk's sentiments, and in like manner they concentrated upon his cocksure person all their contempt for the newcome settlers, that fellowship from which they themselves had sprung and diverged.

Relegated to join them now on ground peculiarly their own, Frank tried to keep his end up by swaggering all the more. Years-long cohabitation had taught the henchmen to communicate among themselves mysteriously as beasts and ants. By tacit consent none glanced up at his entrance. Frank with nasal arrogance gave them the time of day, eliciting no response; and found himself confined to a dumb show of superciliousness, still unregarded. The henchmen went on converging in undertones. By slow degrees they raised their voices.

"Is it not a sad thing, brother, to watch one's rapid downfall after a steep climb? Here is this fine young man, that but lately had risen to such eminence, among the clodhoppers—all of a sudden naught but a lackey dog, creeping at his mistress's heel. Let it give us pause for sobering reflection."

"It might not be a fall, brother. It may be lackeydom always was the highest pinnacle of his aspiring?"

"There is a third possibility. Whose word have we for it that he was in fact the Judas head's grand steward, but his own bragging?"

"If so be you are talking about me"—Frank could not contain himself—"let me tell you that I *am* Luke Robinson's steward and mainstay, as my taking his place by the side of his wife today merely goes to prove. For this day, you must know, Elizabeth is come not just to visit her son, but on an errand of great family concern. Luke meant to come himself. Being detained, he sends me."

"Oh, are *you* here, Frank Oxerd? 'Tis shame, the way they treat the most important man of Smithy Yard, setting him to kick his heels amongst the likes of us. Doubtless Luke lets you take his place beside his wife at other times, too—seeing he is so weak he could not undertake the journey to Bedesford Manor. Or maybe he too would have waited meekly among the servants, the while his wife parleyed with her great kinsfolk?"

The baiting went on. Frank must have felt indeed like a beast with darts thrust into him from every side, not knowing where to turn first in impotent defense and counterattack. Maddened, he grew the more earnest, the more hilarious the henchmen waxed in extravagant fancy. He argued, almost pleaded, where they teased. He cited instance after instance in proof of his assertions, which they only used as springboards for very somersaults of absurdity.

"Ay, ay, of a certainty, Master Frank. And we have heard you will give the bride away at the forthcoming wedding? No? Now whatever can be the reason for that?"

Frank folded his arms, and at last wisely contented himself with a portentous mien. Exuberant in the satisfaction of his tormentors' curiosity and consequent loss of advantage, he finally answered their pestering. "If you really want to know, it is because Luke dare not strain my loyalty so far. Ay, for he deliberately misled me. Many a time he sat and talked of her future with me, and I advised him as I thought good and right and proper. It was all settled that Isabella would be married so as to further the greatness of the house. He knew my feelings for her. 'Frank,' he would say, 'though you are young in years, there is none I know possessed of better sense and more cordial concern for my daughter's welfare.' What is more, he must have marked, even as I did, that the maiden was by no means indifferent to me. So I, like an honorable simpleton, kept out of her way. Who knows what would have happened otherwise? With every modesty I say, I know, full well."

"Ho, ho!" roared the henchmen. "Well, well! Like mother, like daughter! Wait until she is married, this Isabella! Then shall we hear of some right merry doings!—seeing that in her bashful maidenhood she has been playing such games with all of three low-born swains!"

The tale was too good to keep to themselves. If Will's words had spread quickly, Frank's boast was everywhere in no time at all. The henchman who told Lord Hugh was in bed for a week. If he were surprised at my lord's thus acknowledging, in no uncertain terms, Isabella as his kinswoman, the maiden herself proved that she was so. She flew in a truly Cinqmort passion. The news of Will's long, silent attachment and public fight with her betrothed had not appeared to agitate her. We could not see, therefore, why Frank's prattle, which in any case only the ill-natured even pretended to take seriously, should send her clean out of her senses. If it was suggested that she should set foot outside Smithy Yard she threw herself on the floor in a fit of fury and shame and sobbing refusal.

"Your locking yourself away at home will not stop folk thinking this and saying that about you, daughter. It is high time you learn folk will think and talk no matter what you will or won't do," Elizabeth tried to reason with her; and Luke added, "Besides which it is not at all certain that they have nothing more serious than yourself to talk about in these grave times."

But this only made the girl carry on worse than ever; she had made up her mind that she wanted her father to dismiss Frank and force him to make public recantation. "If you will not punish him for injuring my fair repute," she wept and stamped her foot, "the world must think that what he said is true! If you love me, if you do not hate me, you must do this, Father!"

"She is overwrought, what with the wedding preparations and the bygone years of waiting," Elizabeth said apologetically.

"In sooth the girl must think there has never been such a thing as a wedding before! Cannot you see, Isabella, that if I did as you ask, *then* folk would think, not only that there was some truth in Frank's story, but that there is a good deal more behind it? I tell you it would be said everywhere that you lay with all three lads—Nay, Elizabeth, it is time for some plain speaking. Her grandmother is right, and Juliana's ways with headstrong maidens are wanted in this house. Ay, Elizabeth, I must say it—"

"Do you see how you cause discord between your father and me? You would deserve it if we broke off this match in which we have indulged you as surely parents never did."

"Ay," Isabella stormed, "send me to be a nun, then, since you prefer that wicked braggart to me!"

"How should I not prefer him that has never proved undutiful to me, where his obligations as my servant are far smaller than yours as my daughter? That he is a braggart I and everyone have known since long before he grew to manhood. To punish him for that would be like punishing you for the color of the hair upon your head. You want him to be publicly disgraced for a word, admittedly false and annoying, he let fall in private—a word that cannot injure either you or me. I should be punishing myself most of all if I were to dismiss him. Now let there be an end of this."

Isabella bided quietly until the next time Richard came to see them.

Richard was an upright and good-looking young man, much the tallest among the Widowsons of his day, and lighter of complexion, his wholesome features rendered doubly pleasing by his frank and unassuming mien. His handclasp was strong without playful crushing, warm yet unsweating. We have said little about him because—well, because we never could find much to say about him. But that is not saying anything against him. If we have said more about Isabella's love than about his, this is only natural, as in itself his love entailed no conflict. Once he had wooed and won her, there was nothing further for him to do but wait until she was given to him.

Be that as it may we will relate how Isabella challenged him to support her against her father. "For it is so, that I cannot live if Frank is to stay under the same roof as I. You may have thought I had forgotten, Father; but you see I am not a child whose mind is different from day to day."

"But mine is so," Luke replied. "I often change my mind. If it were not that I have grown to like this young man right well, and if it were not that I fairly yearn for the day that will make you a woman, Isabella —as God is my witness, I might even go to the trouble of calling off the marriage. So changeable am I that today, as you perceive, I cannot even find it in me to be very angry. Boredom is wonderfully calming.

Now I will say my last word in this matter. Our trade across the border is such that it will pay us to have a second countinghouse and offices at Damesbury, and it has long been talked of between myself and Frank that he is to move there eventually. Now I *could* send him thither sooner than I had intended—not as yet for good, mind you, but in preparation."

Isabella clapped her hands and started up to kiss her father. He lifted a restraining finger.

"Wait. It will go hard against my grain to do this. Doubtless it is because you are your father's daughter, that you care so much about what others may think. But I, I would rather have it said of me that I ran away in fear of some person, than that I had driven someone from his house and home. I had rather be called coward than cruel. Which would you rather they said of your father?"

This was a masterstroke. Isabella sat mute, haggard with indecision. "Richard!" she appealed again.

"Ay, what does Richard say?" Luke inquired, interested.

"I say," Richard said slowly, "that if Frank leaves, Isabella, it will go to show that you have no faith in your husband. I pray you will not think me ungrateful for all your goodness toward me, Master Luke, but what with my living at Smithy Yard after the wedding as it has been agreed, I shall look a poor fellow indeed if my wife continues to look to her father's power to protect her."

Isabella looked more harrowed than ever.

"You see, daughter," Luke chuckled, "that you have to choose between pining away, and being talked about as the daughter of a cruel man and wife of a weak."

So Isabella had to give in after all.

CHAPTER 3

THE FUGITIVES

LUKE CONSENTED to his second daughter's postulancy some little time before Lady Philippa's death, which occurred in the year 1378. So the Abbess' last will made plain her assumption that Juliana Robinson would one day succeed her at Thirchester. Her personal property, most of which had been derived from the elder Lady Agnes' bequests, was to be equally divided between Lucy, the nunnery, and Masses in perpetuity for the testatrix and both the Ladies Agnes.

Two other deaths had thinned the Cinqmort race. Baldwin's heart had failed him in his sleep one night, and at last recognition of his faithful stewardship was wrung from Lord Hugh, in the shape of an effigy worthy of its position directly opposite that of Abbot William, on the north side of St. Hand's nave. So the two unequal friends slept in close symmetry. Albeit it is studious Baldwin lies equipped with the great of baronial descent, while the Abbot is depicted as a toyless, austere monk.

Griselda Jolybody also lay at rest in the cathedral, but she had only an engraved slab of stone. As before her demise there had been no talk of fetching Little Luke back to his parents' house, Elizabeth could not well refuse her sister-in-law, who went down on her knees that the child might be lent to her for a time.

Little Luke was a cheerful young soul. At their parting Gervase had tears in his eyes, while the child waved, smiling, until they were out of sight. When his mother came to see him, at the Manor or at Trefeller Court, he was enraptured, yet when she said good-by he would simply return his attention to his everyday companions. Of his brothers and sisters he was well acquainted only with Isabella, who took to visiting a good deal when first she enjoyed the married estate. His namesake father was to him little more than a myth, but his younger sisters at home hardly knew old Luke any better. Once she had extracted from Elizabeth a promise of annual payment for Little Luke's food and clothing—for the principle of the thing, said the grandmother—Juliana admitted that he gave less trouble than any child she had ever known, including Little John. As for the Widow Susannah, some of her latter-day oddities did in fact disappear after she had had the care of the child for a while.

Nothing of great note sped or tainted the flowing continuity of lives in Bedesford during this period which, as now we know, was yet one of growing, gravest moment of us all. Looking back, only the cattle murrain of 1380 stands out. But it was a strange disease that took off steers, oxen and bull calves, sparing females. In the end James Smith's lean shaggy bull remained sole hope of our herds' future. Few of us cared to go farther afield with our cows, because of the expense, for those were the days when increased taxation, the rights and wrongs of which have never ceased being debated, began to be seriously felt. One subsequent explanation is that the young King needed money, not only for the wars, but also for building and kindred good works to adorn England and glorify her name among nations.

Even if the King had gone round in person with his explanations, the people would have been no less discontented. It has also been said, after the event, that the smaller local lords reimbursed themselves for the trouble of collecting what the treasury decreed, gathering in something extra for their own coffers. We did not know about that then and do not know it now. All we know is that great want and desperation fell on many shires.

As in the years after the Black Death, our country of Anglemere was in slightly better case. We had St. Hand's, and Luke's crosscountry and overseas trading. We had mild Alfred Widowson for Abbot and careless Hugh Cinqmort for overlord. Here is an odd thing for you. In the very days when almost everywhere else their harshness and rapacity caused the lords to be more and more violently hated, we disliked and feared ours rather less, neither his nature nor his government being much in evidence.

We recalled a time when the Lollards had astonished us by linking in the same breath matters spiritual and animally quotidian. Now the whole of England was doing so, and the cause of the new poll tax was made one with that of transubstantiation. John Wycliffe, it was said, had put up so devastating a fight when brought to trial at Westminster Abbey that bishops had drawn corporeal swords against the purely verbal attack with which he conducted his defense. How could the weakness and ulterior motives of their claims have been more clearly proven? The poll tax assessment struck the people as an act of defiance on the same bad rulers' part, a bid to renew their power, which now stood identified with the theological assertion that consecrated bread and wine change factually into God's flesh and blood, as against symbolical interpretation. For those vampires sneered that the poll tax ought to please Wycliffe and Wycliffites, who had ever preached all men's equality in the sight of God, for that the assessment made no distinction between rich and poor—which was in fact what constituted its ruinous injustice. Think what it meant to poor men with large families, each member of which was priced at the same rate as those of the wealthiest and of the least prolific!

News came to us always through the same channels. The passing visitors of Dick and Stephen, and, lately, a fresh tide of wanderers from various parts of the south. For in the south desperate deeds were beginning to be committed by hard-pressed communities to keep from being bled white, and by way of preventive measure men were gibbeted for a word or a frown. All these new wanderers were fugitives. None of them asked leave to stay, except one batch Dick and Young Will led into town one day in winter.

There were four of them. Two were little more than youths, and it was the tallest, though not the eldest, whom the other three seemed to look up to with something very like meek obedience. He had a lean face with prominent cheekbones from which thick, flaccid skin drooped into folds flanking the mouth and a long wedge of chin. His eyes were small and black as currants and, like the little tufts in currants, the pupils appeared to project from the eyeballs. His head was entirely bald. Nevertheless he looked younger than the gray-haired fourth, although they told us it was only recent grief had bleached the latter so.

They came from near Reading, Dick and Will informed us. The bald one and one of the youngsters had been used to catch and train hawks for their livelihood; the other two were charcoal burners, so that none of them was skilled in husbandry or mason's work. Dick might have been somewhat overconfident in promising them work and bread, but he rightly trusted their stories to elicit Christian compassion at the site. Their stories are of no importance. They were very sad.

The Count-roller, a pious and upright Wasteside man whose own father thirty years before had adopted the surname of Newcome, enrolled the four unfortunates among the unskilled laborers without more than mentioning it to the monks afterward. He was not mistaken in assuming that the Abbot would have agreed none ought to condemn these poor men to outlaw life, which inevitably must make Devil's vassals out of the most innocent victims in the end. In fact the Abbot was not asked. As far as possible he was left undisturbed to the completion of the *Life of St. Francis,* in which he was immersed. Though we hardly ever saw him, we could visualize his beatific oblivion. Edwin had reached a similar stage.

Edwin was then working on the image which has become known as "St. Francis on the Shelf," and which he had started years ago, his own private, uncommissioned offering to St. Hand's cathedral. We had always known it would be his masterpiece, and one could tell he himself thought more of it than of his other works, although he always protested that, compared to such things as the grasshopper-and-butterfly capital, this full-rounded figure was child's play. He thought he would be able to finish it this time. But that was not to be.

The central tower of Jacob Tewsing's design had risen to the height of its first story, and there for the present it rested. Or rather, all other labor and ambition was suspended, in order that the tower might be left to rest. Bede's New Bridge, you may remember, was a model of it. Master Colet had always said that the lateral emphasis upon a bridge unfitted it to serve as a pattern for an edifice whose meaning—not to speak of weight—lay in its being perpendicular. Jacob had proved to the satisfaction of Abbot William and Bishop Jerome that stress and counterthrust were fundamentally unaffected by any mere shifting of proportions, which would beget its own readjustments. Indeed there is, at Wells, we think it is, a not dissimilar structure. But at Cloudsway we began to doubt that it would work.

Not until long after the inventor's death had the tower grown sufficiently to reveal weaknesses which caused it to lean over heavily upon surrounding masonry, so that neighboring walls cracked and showed a tendency to outward yielding. Stephen Colet, who joked very rarely indeed, said at least the faulty tower had taught him more than he had previously realized remained for him to learn. At one time there had been hopes of saving it without sacrificing the purity of the central design, by adding to the buttresses wherever new signs of peril appeared, and at the same rate. Soon it was seen that if this were continued, a higgledy-piggledy forest of buttresses would result, completely enshrouding the core of the actual building, so that none but birds and angels could ever see it. The only other way was to shore up the tower from within, round about central crossing, yet without allowing ties and struts to appear too blatantly for what they were.

This was a problem which peculiarly lent itself to Brother Laurentius' solving. He hit on many a device to conceal from the eye the true nature of various, seemingly superficial decorations. But in the main he only planned the methods of disguising these afterthought supports, Edwin being ordered to shape prototype patterns which the lesser masons then repeated many times and fitted together into vast continuous bands. We, or at least the experienced masters among us, should have seen even then how Jacob's grand concept was being spoiled and fretted by these ingenuities—as an untaught woman may smother her loveliness with a surfeit of ribbons and brooches, or draw attention to the very blemishes she wishes thus to hide. The truth is that to the last we refused to acknowledge what our eyes surely told us. We were not accustomed to seeing any building schemes go wrong here at St. Hand's. In the face of every difficulty and need of accidental resource, the cathedral had gone from strength to strength, beauty to beauty, ever since it had been begun. Yet everyone of us that had ever made so much as a stool or spindle knew it in his heart of hearts that there is no correcting mistakes by means of lavish ornamentation. More than that, we were all initiated in the craftsman's truth that the temptation to apply such meaningless flourishes is in itself a warning to stop, consider and, probably, reject and start afresh.

Now it happened that a kind of border had been decided on, to go around the tower's four sides halfway up the first story. The riddle here was how to prevent this band from creating a break in the wall's longitudinal moldings, which rejoiced the upward gaze and drew it on into infinity. Edwin was hoping to carve the frieze segments into corresponding, rounded, vertical fissures, to stress rather than interrupt the soaring trend. He had not only to determine the happiest mixture of contrast and similitude, but must also bear in mind that other hands than his were going to execute the majority of identical segments. So he tried out different sorts of stone, against samples of the main fabric.

At his desire another load of assorted blocks was conveyed to him on the back of one of the falconers from Reading. Edwin had not seen much of them. Low in the order of laborers, they naturally consorted mostly with their own kind. Once he had seen them settled, even Dick took very little notice of them.

The hodman staggered under the excessive burden. His legs and hands shook after he had put it down.

"Stay a moment and rest, friend," Edwin said. "You will find a ladle hooked to the rim of that butt. You can do with a drink to put new heart into you."

"Thanks, Edwin of Bedesford," said the other—rather loudly, so Edwin's assistant thought. He looked up on hearing a curious little choking sound, and started forward, but the bald hodman was before him and caught Edwin in his arms. But the dizziness seemed to leave the little man as swiftly as it had come; and Edwin struggled to free himself. The assistant could not hear what Edwin said, as the hodman outtalked him.

"Poor old man, you have been worked too hard. Rather than think of others in your kindness of heart, you should look to your own health, as clearly it is time you did. For wherever I go and wherever I look and ask, 'Who made this?' they answer me, 'Edwin Widowson, onetime woodworker,' so that on the first day I begged them to point you out to me. Ay, they said, he yonder is our present Lord Abbot's humble father, and I marveled and praised Our Lord God for that there are still such things as good fortune and virtue's reward in this vale of tears. How proud you must be of your son in his greatness!"

Edwin had succeeded in thrusting the hodman aside. The assistant wondered at the brusqueness of one who usually took pains to bear him courteously toward folk he might have had a right to account his inferiors. "Why should I be proud? His greatness, as you call it, has nothing to do with me. His greatness of heart, ay, that is another matter —but that has nothing to do with me either. Whilst for his sake I must rejoice in his position, it would be no grief to me were he to lose it. And neither, I know well, would it hurt him. Good man that he is, and marvelously gifted—"

"There is not much can hurt such a one," the hodman agreed obsequiously, "save perhaps the loss of his father. Particularly if such loss were incurred under certain circumstances—" he broke off and slapped himself across the mouth. "You must forgive me, good Master Edwin. My mind still runs on the kind of thing I have so recently escaped. I am older than I look, you know. I find it slow work, to become accustomed to this new and better way of life. You that have made sure of salvation by helping this great church ever since the friars started it—good and kindly as you are, I know you feel right glad every time some poor sinner like myself is given the same opportunity, even if it be somewhat late in the day, sometimes. Another thing I find as I grow older. My memory is dimmer every day. Is it the same with yours?"

"No," said Edwin, "it is not. Do you talk of salvation? I will tell you this. To have seen and watched all that I have, to have been able to build, help guard, this fair monument to Faith and Divine Mercy, is—I mean it would be—well worth eternal damnation."

"None could say fairer than that, Master Edwin," said the hodman with a smile, and went his way.

"Did you know him, Edwin?" the assistant asked.

"No."

"Are you not feeling well this day, Master Edwin? Belike you are sickening for something?"

"No. I am as well as usual."

With that the younger man had to be content.

CHAPTER 4

THE ROYAL OFFER

ISABELLA DID NOT allow her grandmother to forget that she was a mere artisan's wife. She made a point of dressing accordingly, and with a severe, nunlike modesty such as few nuns inflict on themselves. After the manner of the newly wed, she also did everything she could without impropriety to make herself look older.

Richard, it must be said, conducted himself admirably as Luke's son-in-law and lodger. He had lost nothing of his unruffled candor, daily walked the long way to and from Cloudsway Waste, although Smithy Yard could well have spared a horse for his use, and toward Luke as well as everybody else behaved with the same ingenuous freedom as before. Few could have maintained it so, particularly at Juliana's house, where his mother and father were among the serving folk. Many a man would have either cringed or swaggered, if not before the mistress, at least before the humble parents themselves.

At the end of Bedesford's great Whitsuntide fair of 1381, of which Smithy Yard had borne the brunt as regards the housing of visiting merchants, Juliana bade the whole family to a feast, that they too might know it had been a holiday season. Bess came with Elizabeth, whose youngest son, named Jude, after Luke's father's brother, was a babe in arms; sickly Margaret, too, needed watching, especially at mealtimes.

"Margaret looks bile green as usual," the grandmother remarked, according to her fixed habit of addressing a word to each of her descendants on arrival. Bess patted the child, her sense of justice outraged so that it overcame her everlasting distaste of Margaret's clammy skin and death's-head eyes and nostrils.

"Margaret," said Elizabeth, smiling at the child, "will outlive all her generation. She will be as the cracked pot. Will you not, my daughter?" Margaret answered, "Yes," with listless gravity.

"You should have suckled her yourself, as you did your elder children and this my sensible newest grandson that would not be fobbed off with nurse's milk, nor cow's, nor ewe's. None of the others was so fat and handsome at his age, Elizabeth. Even though you would not have him christened Gervase or Hugh, but chose to commemorate some low-born Fleming nobody has every heard of."

"I did not feed Peter, nor Little Luke, nor Alicia," Elizabeth pointed out, with an odd, fearful side glance at the praised infant. "On the other hand, I did nurse John that died."

Juliana was diverted to ask after her two eldest grandsons; Robin fared still with the Icelander, but Peter had left the sea to follow some German merchant burgher of one of the big northern free cities.

"He made up his mind to this all by himself," Luke said proudly, "and alone he went to parley with his new master and arranged everything, which included also parting from Master van Straaten without ill feeling. God keep and preserve and prosper both our sons out in the world. Ay, thank God we hear from them as oft as can well be expected. Last year we had tidings from Robin on three separate occasions, and this year already we have had a letter from each. I am glad we sent them to school, after all. It is pleasanter by far to get letters which you know their own hands wrote. Hired scribes like to write different words from those that are dictated, so that the screed might come from any one, and the script cannot reassure you that the authors are truly in good health as they claim to be. I meant to bring them along to show you, mother-in-law."

"There is another letter I would give a great deal to see," Juliana said after a pause.

"Oh?"

"Yes. Unless it is not true, this new rumor Young Frank has set going about you. If it be a lie, it is my duty to let you know; if it be true it is I to whom information is owing."

"Well, what is it?" Luke asked, smiling a little.

"They say that the King, through Lord Jerome, has offered to borrow money from you, Luke. They say that you have refused. They say you would have been made a noble, had you accepted. But you would not have refused—I can hear myself how impossible it sounds. I beg your pardon, Luke. I should have known better than to waver in my disbelief."

Luke's smiled had broadened. "It is true all the same. You do not think Frank would gossip *against* my interests? He has not spread this behind my back, either. Though I have refused, I confess I deemed it useful for the fact of such an offer to become known," he laughed.

"Let me make sure I understand. Do you mean to tell me you really declined such an honor—the double honor of being put in the way of serving your King, and of becoming one of his nobles—and thus restoring to the family I founded what it lost because of whom I wedded?"

So great was Juliana's agitation that she even vented it in detraction of John Trefeller.

"I deemed the honor too expensive, Juliana. Firstly, I should not wonder if the offer of nobility were to have stood me in lieu of interest. Secondly, placed as I am, with so many sons to start in life and daughters to dower, not to mention those whom God may yet send us, with shares in so many ventures over and above the overseas wool trade and inland cloth manufacture—placed as I am, and knowing what I know, I should be worse than a fool to let myself be flattered, tempted, or even scolded into this."

"What, then, do you know that nobody else knows?" Juliana drummed the table with her knuckles.

"The evidence is there for all to see, though all may not have the wit to add it up. This King that we have now, Juliana, is none so safe upon his throne. God knows whether by this time next year we shall not have another sitting there. He needs money all too badly—else would he not risk his crown with this poll tax. You know as well as I that to lend to the overneedy is unsound business dealing. If one wants to do that, I say, then one ought to give away all one has and divide it among the poor. Admittedly that would be pious. Yet I mind you did not act so yourself, when you had children to provide for. To lend to the great, and lose, is folly without saving grace. Since time out of mind the goldsmiths of London and the merchants of the staple have been the moneylenders of the Crown. The King would not turn to such as me if the old source were not running dry. And this means that goldsmiths and staplers have reason to believe a new loan will not save him, so that they would cut their losses rather than increase them. In which case it is probable they already have another king in view. So I might lose my life as well as my money. No, no, Juliana."

Juliana glared at him. "If all other forsake him, that surely is all the more reason to stand by him—poor young King! You have sons of about his age. Take care that others may not deal by them as their father does by his anointed sovereign. What do you say, Little John? See, Little John says the same as I. So does Susannah. Every right-thinking person will. I never heard such heartless, unmanly, miserly talk. Talk of losing your life, at least you might leave a baronetcy to your heir!"

"Be quiet, Mother," Elizabeth interposed, "and you too, Luke. He talks like that to tease you, and also because he is such a modest man. He has made himself what he is. He does not need to be ennobled. He is too proud to want it—he cannot want anything that one must kneel to accept. For his father's sake, too, a poor runaway—"

Little John guffawed, "If I know anything of people, his father would be happier than anyone to see his son with spurs and a coat of arms! Look at Jeanne and her Abbot son, and Meg and Geoffrey with their Richard!"

Luke stopped shaking his head at Elizabeth and turned to his brother-in-law. "You might be right, were he alive today—God rest him. But he died thirty-five years ago. He died in state of grace. Added to which, I have had so many Masses said for him, he is almost certainly out of purgatory by now. So he will by now be wiser, purer, better than any mortal man. I know that he will think as I do in this matter. I know he will understand that his son means to honor him."

"We cannot disprove that any more than you can prove it," Juliana sneered. "All I can say is, I shall never again dare to look Lord Jerome in the face—the way my son-in-law received his kindness."

"In bringing me to the King's notice, Lord Jerome hoped to be kind to none but himself. Have you ever thought how serious and how frequent the troubles in the south must be, for us to hear them all the time? There are many men like me among the would-be rebels, and this is part of an attempt to buy us off. We all know how much Anglemere owes to Lord Jerome's ambitions! And now, just when it looked as if they were about to be realized, the state of the country and the King's coffers made them pass him over at the last moment and appoint Sudbury Archbishop and Chancellor. Archbishops can be deposed the same as kings. I was to have been a pawn in Lord Jerome's game against Sudbury. Now tell me that it is uncharitable of me, to decline to be used in such a manner!"

"And so it is uncharitable," Juliana said stoutly.

Luke said to Elizabeth in bed that night, "You know, it will not surprise me if your mother is turning over in her mind some scheme of writing to Lord Jerome and proposing to take my place, on similar terms. I doubt if I got it into her head that it is not purely a question of moneylending."

"But, Luke, how can you be so sure that you are right? No one has told you so. You have only worked it out like this in your own mind. While you may be right, you may just as likely be wrong, it seems to me. So tangled a web of double-dealing as you lay at Lord Jerome's door, I marvel that an honest man like you can think out such things, let alone be so confident that they are true!"

"If I could not, there would not be such merit in my being honest," Luke yawned. "You will see. One way or the other events will prove me right."

"Ay, because you will explain it to us, how they have proved you right! One way or the other, indeed! You do not give yourself niggardly margin!"

"Wait and see, wait and see, my love."

"About Frank, Luke, he is still to go this week?"

"Certainly. Why do you ask?"

"Mother said something—that my lord is set on stopping him. She said they had words at the fair. Did you know about that?"

"Yes, I know. Frank behaved foolishly. Faithful and shrewd as he is, I shall not be sorry when he is out of the way for a while. There are times when I too find him trying. But let us go to sleep."

Luke could have told his wife more about Frank's clash with my lord. For one thing he did not wish to distress her, for another he feared she might try to persuade him to keep Frank at Bedesford after all. And he was not at all sure that the firmness of his resolve was not mere obstinacy, so that he shrank from exposing it to further attack. True, his decision was backed by the best of reasons, but he had lived long enough to have encountered all too many instances of even such good reasons merely nourishing what had sprung from more obscure roots, beyond reasoning. And obstinacy, he had ever been wont to declare, is the sham strength of the weak.

For thirty years he had laughed at people predicting his decline. Now he had begun to think the prophets would have the last laugh after all. He had begun to feel as he looked. Though he did not feel exactly sick, he felt his strength on the wane, his health namelessly failing. He put it down to approaching senescence, and determined to give it the lie and thus stave it off. He had a nagging suspicion that his firmness, in regard to both the royal offer and the disposal of Frank, was such a means of counterfeiting vigor, or even another herald of crabbed old age.

Strange to relate, that year's Whitsun fair, signal for riot, bloodshed, and conflagration in so many English towns and villages, was a particularly happy one in Bedesford. The sun shone brightly in a blue sky faintly veined with white, and the still-young verdure everywhere glistened as though varnished. There had not been such a multitude of booths, peddlers, musicians, and tumblers since the consecration, no doubt because unrest was said to be brewing throughout Norfolk, and

many who had meant to attend the fairs there had spread over Angle
mere instead. The market place and commons were thronged; and the
monks, the friars, and the parish guilds had turned out in splendid
processions with untold banners, several of them new. We were delighted when there came a fourth procession from the manor, with yet
more banners, flags, and pennants, and horses plumed with may and
birch leaves. My lord himself, decked in lambent violet and emerald
and lime greens that combined with a hat of flaming orange into a
wonder of brilliance, seemed in most affable humor. Gervase was away;
perhaps that accounted for it. In any event, even Lord Hugh's heart
must have been warmed by the townfolk's unaffected, unexpectedly glad
welcome on this his first public appearance for a long time.

You must understand that the bandying of jeers between henchmen
and townfolk was a long-established convention of manners, not necessarily charged with special malice. Our greetings that day took the usual
form, and were returned in kind. But Frank must have said something
rather more pointed and cutting. He was in a state of high elation because of his impending departure. Luke hastened after his steward, but
was too late to hear Frank's actual words: he and the henchmen were
already embroiled in right serious vituperation. The din was so great
that nobody besides the contestants heard precisely what was said. By
the time Luke reached them, my lord had joined in, and Frank was
answering him back.

"Master Robinson!" My lord turned to him, his face strained and
voice twanging as if someone were shaking him by the shoulders, "For
the sake of the kinship between us I will warn and appeal to you before
I take action. This young man here tells me he is about to remove to
Danesborough, in your service. I cannot recall that my permission was
asked, nor that I waived my right to a removal fine. Frank Oxerd is
bound to me as the son of his parents. That I was lenient on their re-
appearance here and forbore to mark them for life as runaways, by no
means signified that I relinquished my claim to them. You are no doubt
aware that there is a law forbidding the apprenticing of villeins' children
to any trades. Perhaps, because I made no demur against your taking
him into your countinghouse, you thought that *I* was unaware of it?
Perhaps it happened to suit me at the time to put nothing in the way
of his training, since I realized that my brother Baldwin could not live
forever. To be sure, there can no longer be any question of Frank's
succeeding to the stewardship of Cinqmort Manor. But neither can I
allow the impression to prevail that I am content to have my rights and

power flouted. I must command you, Luke Robinson, to find some other man, freeborn, to set over your Damesbury house."

Both Frank and Luke had been trying to interrupt him, the former with passionate reiteration of his parents' enfrancisement. Now his master made the point for him, and added that it was impossible to send anyone but Frank.

"Impossible, do you call it?" Lord Hugh cried, at white heat. "Impossible, is it? All the world knows why. Because in this manner you have bound yourself to stop the mouth of your daughter's low-born paramour that debauched her before she was out of her nonage—like mother, like daughter—since you yourself did not mind taking our present fine Lord Abbot's leavings when you married. Ay, and it is only Jane you had to thank for it that your wife did not succeed in putting you under the sod twenty years ago. No wife of mine should have tried the like and lived. Ay, they tell me, at home you are not so manful as out here in the market place—"

Nobody, ever, had had the courage or unkindness to refer to the story of St. Uncumber in any of the Robinsons' hearing.

"Your wife," said Luke into the awful pause, "did not need to do anything at all to be murdered by him that was her protector before God and men. You can no more sway me with insults than with threats. God be thanked, the ways are past when you and your like could override or pervert the law of the land and get your every desire without more effort than a word or two requires. I would advise you, lord of Bedesford, to shout less loudly about your power, lest the echo tell you how much it has dwindled."

Lord Hugh struggled in grim silence against several of his men who were risking their lives for his, stopping his upraised sword. For him to have slain an unarmed townsman of Luke's standing in the midst of outnumbering crowds, would have meant death, not long delayed by the manor folks' superior weapons. Luke faced him for a moment. Then, without bowing, turned and went off with his steward. But he was very wroth with Frank too and did not speak a word to him all that day.

He thought it wise to tell his wife that he had been there, as she was bound to hear of that. His hope that nobody would have the heart to tell her more was not betrayed.

Neither did his reading of Juliana's mind prove too inaccurate. However, it had not occurred to him that instead of writing she would herself go all the way to London. Nor would he or anyone else have thought it possible for her to complete all preparations and make off before any hint of this reached Smithy Yard.

Juliana said to Geoffrey Widowson, when they were well on the London road, "How surprised they will be, my daughter and her husband! He knows me well, none better since Jane left us, but he did not know me when first we went traveling together, you and I, eh, my Geoffrey?"

"No, Mistress," her gray-haired steward said, smiling from ear to ear. "Indeed it is just like old times. I could fancy myself young."

"I am young again!" Juliana cried. "Would that they could see me! Oh, would that I could see them! Ah, now they will be grieved and anxious!"

As to this she was perfectly right.

"Poor Mother, she must have gone out of her mind. We shall never see her again, my heart tells me! And she never even gave us the chance of saying, Godspeed and bless you!"

"It makes my blood run cold, to think of her out on the roads," Luke agreed, pushing his fingers into his hair under the hood, "in the midst of these latest upheavals."

"Kent, methinks, is on the other side of London?" Little John ventured. "For Suffolk at least should by now lie well behind her."

"Ay, but all Cambridge and Hertfordshire are up in arms as well," Luke said impatiently. "I wonder you dare open your mouth at all, brother-in-law, since it was in your hands to prevent her going, or at least to let us know! There is no excuse whatsoever for your witlessness and greed. She at least wants the honors for you, not for herself!"

"You talk as though you did not know Mother!" Little John defended himself, not without justice. "In the past, whenever you have wanted me to do or not do anything, have you not always relied on her making me? And I had it all again. All she did soon after the Black Death, ere ever she had you or Jane to help her. Travel, she says, was much more unsafe in those days than it can be now. She said, if none outraged her then, they will not do so now that she is an old woman, and it sounded reasonable to me—"

"You and she both, you never think beyond rape and such like! Hunchbacked as she is, she never thinks men might slay her for other treasure!"

"But she said surely I could not think her such a fool that she would take the money with her—"

"She said! Nonetheless the gold is gone, and it was only when you could not find it that you came bleating at last to us, is it not so? Any other man would have gone after her first—"

"Why don't you go after her, then?"

"Because it is too late now. Had I no family, I would still try it just the same."

"I have Susannah to look after!" Little John shouted, much aggrieved.

At this the others had to laugh, and the more enraged Little John showed himself, the more they must laugh, until, ceasing exhaustedly, they were incapable of resumed severity.

"Mother ever kept her guardian angels busy," Elizabeth said, drying her mirth-bedewed eyes. "I trow they will enjoy being back in harness! I trow they will do their best. We have been talking as my uncle might, at the manor, likening farmers and artisans, people like ourselves and all our friends, to brute rabble and wild beasts! Had matters gone that way here in Bedesford, would not you have been among the rebels, Luke? Mother is small and weak and white of hair, and she has no charters to be wrested from her. Once in London—yes, I trust her to make her way through fire and flood, if she is set on it—she will have none less than the Bishop to protect her."

"And who will protect the bishops, pray?"

"Their holy office, surely. The Lord God."

"Neither protected Benedetto of Friggsby, who by all accounts was an honest man. St. Thomas of Canterbury, too, was, I would say, a holier archbishop than Sudbury, who happens to be responsible for the poll tax."

"In that case I hope it is true, what you were forever telling us, that Lord Jerome himself wanted to be archbishop, so that people will not count him among the Lord Sudbury's friends."

"The Devil argue with a woman!" Luke said, for honor's sake. It was plain his wife had more or less convinced him. "Be sure to remember all these arguments, Elizabeth, when Isabella comes to hear of the peril her Richard's parents stand in!"

CHAPTER 5

JULIANA IN LONDON

NOBODY EXCEPTING LUKE in the heat of the moment, evinced surprise that Little John had kept his mother's secret. She had him and his hapless wife so firmly under her thumb that, directly she was gone, they missed the pressure, and instead of enjoying their freedom, were in a constant flutter of indecision.

For making all ready in practice Meg and Geoffrey had been responsible, their task encumbered by the need to keep the other housefolk out of it. These two Widowsons had become more and more abjectly subservient to the Mistress ever since the marriage of their son to her granddaughter. It seems their guilty conscience was persuaded that in strictly carrying out this dubious behest of hers they were given the chance of repairing the hurt which kinship with Richard had dealt the house of Trefeller. Albeit the rest of the household could not but realize something out of the ordinary was afoot, Juliana's servants were not accustomed to question her or run to get outside advice on her doings.

Juliana left Anglemere before dawn, the day which saw the first rioting at Dartford. Her son and daughter-in-law continued to obey her injunctions, giving out that she was sick and they and Meg nursing her, until the evening the seventh, when Bedesford learned of the wildfire events. To be sure, by then a variety of rumors sought to account for Geoffrey's disappearance, and the housefolk of Trefeller Court wondered whether Juliana were dead and what gain her son expected to derive from postponing the announcement. And by then the Suffolk risings, if they had not engulfed her company, made a barrier for her against pursuing relatives.

On the sixth day of June John Ball was freed by main force from the Archbishop's prison in Canterbury, and Rochester Castle was sacked. Some say it was on the seventh, some the ninth or tenth, that the hundred thousand Kentishmen gathered round Wat Tyler of Essex and John Hales of Malling.

You may well ask how the news reached us so speedily. Everybody marveled at it then, and the question has never been answered to this day. If we could not penetrate the means and ways of the Great Society, nobody ever will. They may have used beacons of a sort, or communicated through a standing chain of spies all over the country. Afterward every attempt was made to find out about this and perchance explain the terrifying sumultaneity of the rebellion. Either none ever betrayed it, or else the inquisitioners judged it wisest to suppress what they discovered.

Geoffrey was not so well-versed in driving horses as in directing ox teams. Howbeit he got in good practice before ever the wagon, with his wife and mistress inside, was held up in districts of vociferous assembly. Naught worse befell them than occasional, cursory search and general harangue. Later on they sometimes passed or cut across long trains of men of all ranks, singing, shouting, armed with clubs and scythes and pitchforks, with longbows, and even with swords. But they had a sufficiency of their own food with them, dependent on roadside hamlets only for water, and Juliana wished neither to turn back nor to delay and so purposely refrained from making inquiries.

Bear in mind that we, like the Widowsons, are being wise and knowing a long time after these events. Caught up therein, how could the party from Bedesford fully appreciate just what was happening, and on what a scale? A man struggling to keep his head above drowning waves little knows how large or small an area they may cover. Juliana reached London by afternoon on the Tuesday, June the eleventh, just ahead of the Essex men who marched upon the city on one side of the winding river Thames, while the men of Kent advanced along the other. She had heard a great deal about the multitudinous seething of London town, its slow torrents of traffic and trades, so that she accepted the turmoil calmly. Her steward and his wife by long-standing habit lived encased within their mistress's mood as in a cradling glass shell interposed between them and external circumstances. Her calm made them impervious to affright, just as her wrath would have made them tremble in paradisiacal peace. Now, too, language difficulties supervened. They never even realized until much later that the gates and bridges of London were all closed behind them only a few minutes after their entry, unchallenged, in a turbulent sweep of crowd and chaos which, innocents that they were and country cousins resolved not to be astonished, they failed to recognize.

"How they shout! It is a wonder they can understand each other! How they throng and jostle and battle for right of way! It is a miracle they ever get anywhere, any of them," Juliana, peeping through the cart hood, said to Meg in a censorious tone. "Still, no doubt they are used to it. When we look at an ant heap, we cannot tell how its milling to and fro is ordered. Geoffrey, halt in the nearest spot where there is room. It were foolish to go on another step without asking the way."

They did not find it at all easy to arrest attention, and thereafter to make themselves understood. Even then the name of Rocquefeuilles was received blankly. At length Juliana thought of mentioning that the Bishop of Anglemere also held office at the Treasury, whereupon they got a surfeit of directions, inasmuch as they did not know except by name any one of the numerous, world-famous landmarks their informants took for granted.

Can you wonder that they thought less and less of the upheaval round about, whose extent they had not means of gauging, all taken up with the profuse grandeur of London and its diversity of fine buildings, gardens, streets, trades, filth, unheard-of water conduits, and innumerable shapely churches? Have you ever been to London? It is said to be like nothing else on earth.

The Treasury was likewise in an uproar, whether the place were being got ready for a siege or whether its vaults were being emptied of their contents for safekeeping. Lord Jerome was not there. Eventually someone offered to guide them to the Bishop's palace, at exorbitant recompense. It was not far. The shameless guide grinned openly.

Rocquefeuilles Palace was exceedingly large and handsome. Another surprise, since it looked like an emperor's court rather than the abode of a man scarce anyone seemed ever to have heard of. Surely so great a building must be known to all Londoners at least by name? The guide chuckled when Juliana asked him. Apparently the palace was indeed well known, but under an old name, Mandeville House, which had already weathered and resisted a number of successive occupants. Apparently the efforts of Lord Jerome and his retainers to substitute Rocquefeuilles for Mandeville were a standing joke about the neighborhood. Twenty years they had lived here, and were still trying. At the massive, ornamented entrance the liveried robber left the party to its own devices and the distrustful courtesies of the Bishop's doorkeeper and guards.

So their troubles as yet were by no means at an end. It took Juliana a deal of sharp talking before the major-domo was induced to come out and do the honors of the house. He called for servants to unload what he took to be Juliana's gifts to the Bishop, but she asked that the wagon be left as it was for the present, in the inner courtyard, asking only that the horses be seen to. Although the courtyard was teeming with people, no one had made a move toward the horses, a breach of manners unique in Juliana's experience.

The hall floor was covered in patterned tiles, and the benches round the walls were of carved stone. The major-domo offered them refreshments, but Juliana deemed it bad enough to be left awaiting the Bishop in the public hall, without eating and drinking on what at home would be styled the beggars' benches.

They sat in a row, she and Meg and Geoffrey, the marble cold gradually diffused throughout their bodies. They moved nothing save their eyes, darting glances of would-be haughty suspicion at the occupants of other benches. But those others moved often; they were not waiting, merely taking brief spells of rest and consultation: monks and squires and minions of all kinds, frequently rejoining the ceaseless back and forth between the arched doorways.

At long last there was heightened commotion at the main entrance, and Lord Jerome strode in, his head swiveling from side to side as different messengers importuned his ear without staying his progress or dispersing his retinue, composed of chaplain, scribe, page, and three henchmen heavily armed. Juliana precipitated herself off the bench and was mollified by his recognizing her and irately roaring for the chamberlain.

"I commend your seeking refuge with me, Mistress," he said, extending his ring finger for her kiss. "I am glad you thought of it betimes, ere my palace be filled with others having less claim on my protection. Much as I should like to, I cannot now attend to you myself. But I will bid them make ready one of the guest chambers. Now if you will pardon me—"

But Juliana would not let him pass. "Reverend Lord, be so gracious as to listen to me. I do not think that we shall need to put you to any inconvenience. If I might speak to you privily, without delay."

The Bishop frowned, but no doubt he thought that to speak to him with such assurance, she too must be a harbinger of grave and urgent, perhaps secret news. Stranger instruments had been employed. "Come you with me then, Mistress Trefeller. Nonetheless must you allow me to have all made ready for you and yours—where else would you go at this hour? We are having early curfew."

"That is what I want to tell you," Juliana replied as soon as they were alone in a small, bare, vaulted antechamber. "I want you to take me to the royal palace straightway, Reverend Lord, for it will do the poor

King good to hear that I have expressly hastened hither with the loan which my graceless son-in-law refused to furnish."

"My dear Mistress," the Bishop said after a pause. "What are you thinking of? You cannot be serious? Money is the last and least of the King's thoughts this eventide. You cannot mean to tell me that it is this errand has brought you all the way to London? And that you have come all this way entirely unscathed? I can only say St. Hand has wrought another miracle. The whole south is in revolt. London is like an ant heap one has thrust a stick into—"

"That is what I likened it to, myself!" Juliana said with fleeting pleasure. "And that is why I think I come out timely with my homage and my offering to the poor young King. I shall gladden his heart, showing that there are some rally to the cause of Christian order. I shall gladden his eyes with full cheering sight!" Before he could prevent her, she was at the great oak door, dragging it open with all her strength, and called for Meg and Geoffrey to bring in one of the woolsacks. "To say money, as you do, with easy contempt, and to *see* what I have got here, are two different things," she panted, slashing at the bale with Geoffrey's knife. "Look, Lord Jerome! Look, and tell me again that the sight would not rejoice and hearten the King!"

The hoard of hard, bright gold coins, shining from out the masses of raw gray wool, in truth looked wonderfully rich and fair. "There are five more bales like this one in the cart!"

Some of the Bishop's people, who had pressed in behind the Widow-son pair and formed a living wedge in the door, uttered gasps of respect. The Bishop crossed himself, with eloquent looks at Juliana and her treasure, sickened by visions of the risk she had run. He drove them all out again, excepting Juliana who still stood regarding him triumphantly over the glinting, disemboweled bale.

Lord Jerome pushed his skull cap askew, scratching his head, and one by one twirled the rings on his fingers. He paced up and down. "How can I make you understand—" he broke off short, no doubt awakening to the absurdity of the situation. It was not for him to recognize any demands upon him on the part of this inconsiderable old lay woman. It was preposterous that he should reason with her. But then, it was no more preposterous than that he should have given in to her in the first place, closeting himself with her as if she were a man and person of consequence, at her request, at such a time as this! There it was; he had allowed it to happen. How to retrieve the rightful balance between them? That he should ask himself this question was the greatest absurdity yet. Juliana would have been amazed to know that the Bishop was identifying her with the forces of insurgency and attributing his false position to their headway everywhere.

Why did it not occur to him to subdue her by sheer superiority of vocal power, by threat of excommunication or bodily expulsion from his house, or by merely leaving the room? We say, he felt constrained to argue, because he was uneasy and ashamed in the consciousness of his own motives which had suggested the loan. Since Juliana would not be shifted from regarding the loan as the prime issue, he must convince her that it was no longer even relevant.

"It is too late, Mistress—"

"How can it be too late? Has the King withdrawn the poll tax? Then he still needs money. And unless a man be dead, money never comes out of season."

"In other words, you care not whether the King wants your money or not. You want something for yourself. It is not that you want to help him. If so small a sum could make or break him, think you I would have sent to Anglemere?"

"Then why did you?" Juliana swallowed the insult to her riches.

The Bishop sighed. This was worse than ever. He had achieved anything but what he had intended. How was he to tell her of his plan to lead the way in sapping the growth of revolt by bribing the great commoners into self-interested loyalty? Yet had he told her just that she would in all probability have been satisfied. She would have seen no need to probe any deeper. Again, it was his knowledge of what lay behind that scheme made him fearful of further questions.

Had he succeeded, he would surely have been called on to supplant Sudbury who would almost certainly be deposed. Credited with the invention of the poll tax, Archbishop and Chancellor, Sudbury was the target of the nation's hatred, which would be appeased by his fall. If he were to stay in office, the poll tax could not be rescinded without grave humiliation to the Crown. On the other hand, if he were punished for being its author, it might even have been possible to let it stand.

"Look here, Mistress Trefeller. There is murder, pillage, and burning at Gravesend. Maidstone is in the hands of a ferocious mob. In Essex several great manors have been leveled to the ground. London is besieged, do you understand? There has not been such trouble in the land since—oh, since the Normans came across the sea—"

"I am not afraid. It cannot be worse than the Black Death. You were not in England then."

"You misunderstand me. God's blood, madam, all I am trying to show you is that the King, and all the rest of us, have our minds and hands full to overflowing. How can I make you see?"

"That is just it. You cannot, Lord Jerome." Though fairly launched, and quivering with impatience, Juliana bowed, to correct any impression of irreverence. "My son-in-law warned me that I might never see my money again. If this could not restrain me from leaving Bedesford, think you now that I am here anything can sway me? Mind you how in the year 1350 you told me most solemnly if ever I wanted a favor of you, to remind you of your stay in my house, and you would grant it, whatever it might be? I might have asked a greater thing than merely to be allowed to show myself and my golden woolsacks before the King. Will you stand by your word, Lord Jerome, given thirty years ago?"

The Bishop realized at last that nothing short of splitting her skull and bodily taking hold of her brain would enable him to move it. Her mind was closed to whatever might be said. No matter how long they might go on, they would continue talking of two different things. Now that she had claimed the sanctuary of his honor, he had no weapons against her. He sat down, letting his hands fall on his knees.

He must count himself fortunate that it was in his power to take her to the royal palace. The King might not be there, might already have gone to the Tower. Yet, everything was in such a state of disorder, to bring about such a meeting might not be so outrageous after all. If no purpose could be served, at least no harm could come of it either. Who was the King? A boy fourteen years of age. It was not he making the decisions. And yet again, boys grow up. The young King might be charmed by the unusual interlude, and be profitably reminded, in a few years' time, who had procured him such entertainment in his hour of trial, if they all came through it safe and sound.

At last it was grown so late Juliana could not do other than submit without demur to waiting until the next day.

She did not sleep, and was up and dressed before dawn, but the Bishop had not even been to bed. He was ready for her, and did not gainsay her contention that if they went as early as was decent, they would be sure to find the King at home—albeit he had to smile to hear her, had the Bishop. It reassured him to find he could still smile, and still smile at Juliana. She for her part was gratified that he would join her in her hooded cart.

"Better seat would not be yours, Reverend Lord, if you were Chancellor of the Realm," she jested, pointing at the woolsacks on which they were sitting. She did not notice him start and glare; she had no eyes for anything outside her, anything but her anticipating visions. By Lord Jerome's order the sailcloth cover was kept tightly laced up. On his passage through the streets of London he had no desire to be seen, nor to see. Juliana did not even ask his reasons, and the fearful, self-explanatory noises ever and anon seemed to make no impression on her.

Alighting at Westminster, she peered about her brightly, but the Bishop was sure she would not have recognized any part of the royal residence had she come again the next day. His own men brought the woolsacks after them. Once more Juliana was forced to sit and wait in a public hall, howbeit there was no room for her on any bench this time. She sat on her bale and did not know for how long, unseeingly smiling, tense, and deaf to all and everything around.

At length Lord Jerome came back to her, escorted by some tabarded pages, and the misshapen, weirdly attired widow of Bedesford was led through the rooms and passages of that greatest castle unto a small, richly furnished solar with two doors. The woolsacks were deposited at her feet. Then she was left alone to await the Majesty of England.

So that is all anyone but Juliana could relate of the audience.

"I was not afraid, though I did feel I was in a fairy tale, and I knew the King would too, directly I opened my sacks. They came in—the King's mother was with us just at first—and I said my say and did my good-fairy deed. I remember thinking, having lived to do this, now I shall not mind dying. Then we talked. She, the King's mother, thinks as I do, and says the lords' terror is not only ignoble, but unnecessary. She, like me, met some of the rabble on her way from Canterbury, and like me, met with no affront. A stalwart and gracious lady she is right enough, as one would look to find our splendid Prince Edward's widow; but where they had their eyes, the many men said to have wooed her, and those that have named her "the Fair," I cannot conceive. Fat and gross she is like Martin, my father's bailiff in my youth, and she is old—about as old as I that have grandsons of an age with her child the King! Ay, we are both of us old wives, and I never held the title of Fair Maid of Anglemere (maid, forsooth! how many husbands has she buried? Three, or is it four?)—but I tell you I am thankful to have been small and nimble all my days. It is all she can do to walk, the Lady Joan, and when she sits, she cannot rise without the help of two strong pages. Presently she left us together, the young King and me. I spoke French with him, once or twice. He is the dearest, neatest, daintiest young Majesty. Those that call him weakly are much mistaken. A man needs not to weigh three tons to be a perfect knight. It was David slew Goliath, not the other way about. And he is bright and quick of mind, and not above listening to his elders' advice, be he never so much greater than they. He is as good as promised to reward me, when the time comes, in the person of my son. He said only that his guardian council must consent to it. Your Majesty, said I, don't take it amiss in a subject old woman to advise you. I've got grandsons older than you, Your Majesty, I said. Get rid of your guardians and tutors now, else they will be with you when you yourself are a grandfather. They will be dead by then, says he. Oh, witty youth! He said, My father on his deathbed made me swear ever to honor Simon and Wishart—"

"Guichard, Mistress Juliana—"

"*Wishart,* I distinctly heard His Majesty, you will pardon me. Where was I? Yes. So I explained that he might honor his old tutors without continuing in leading strings to them. If at your time of life I had allowed myself to be ruled and overborne by legal guardians, I told him, where would I and my children have been? Indeed, one might ask, what would have become of Bedesford? For I brought Luke to Angle-mere. And who knows, if I had not found the means of maintaining my house, the Bishop would not have been able to stay long enough to conceive the plan of the cathedral. See to what pass your guardians have brought you, King Richard, I said. If you take my advice, you will dispense with theirs in ending these troubles that are now upon you. He let me kiss his hand. There was no room at the palace for me and Meg and Geoffrey, but if all I hear is true, about the royal guest dormitories, I shall be better off continuing with you, Reverend Lord. Did I tell you the Princess Mother came back, with some knights and lords, and came between us with some affairs of state? Ay. Then I deemed it the most mannerly course to say adieu."

We in Bedesford heard the same account many times, albeit in somewhat less ebullient rendering, and without the immoderately sanguine digressions into the future to which Lord Jerome had to listen. Belike he did not listen. The noise in the streets was now infernal, and progress was so slow as again and again to appear at an end. Every now and then one or the other of the Bishop's men would put his head inside the wagon to report to his master.

The portals of Mandeville House, or Rocquefeuilles Palace, were guarded by a double file of men-at-arms. Outside there was a crowd, as yet doing no more than shouting threats and hurling muck at the smooth white walls, and unsuspicious of a church dignitary's presence in a jolting bucolic cart. In the palace court another crowd lay in wait, of friends, messengers, retainers, and Lord Jerome barely allowed the cart to halt before plunging among them. Juliana was left to stand until he remembered to call for a page to help her find the chamber assigned to her party—she had not been here long enough to know her way. With Meg and Geoffrey, she began all over again, and they made more rewarding listeners.

She had not nearly come to end when Lord Jerome, followed by his chaplain and some lay servitors, burst in upon her.

"Tell your servants to pack up all your goods and stow them down in the wagon. Take off your festal dress, or at least cover it up well. We are leaving London. The people are opening the gates. So at least there is a possibility of our getting out. We must at least try it. Yes, I am coming with you. After all it would seem you were sent by Providence."

His tone and set face, and the faces of chaplain and henchmen, all at once stabbed her to the heart with fear. She rose up in instant obedience, without a sound, shaking in every limb. Had not obedience meant activity, she must have fainted. The Widowsons crossed themselves and called on the Trinity, but set to work sensibly and rapidly. Soon the guest chamber was cleared of their belongings. Below in the courtyard, the Bishop's servants were hurriedly thrusting a few sacks and coffers into the Trefeller wagon, between a medley of horses, adding their neigh to the hubbub of shouts and hoof clatter, running feet and wheels and barking dogs. Four horses of the palace stables were joined to Juliana's two. She was lifted in under the hood, Meg, Geoffrey, and the Bishop scrambling after. One henchman swung himself up on to the leading cart horse, the rest, already in the saddle, cruelly reined in their dancing mounts, waiting for the cavalcade to start. All the men wore their own clothes, unblazoned.

They made their sortie and succeeded in creating a passageway for the wool cart, guarding its rear with light skirmishing, enough only to delay and confuse the yet undecided mob. The last of the train barred the great gates behind them. The mansion was left empty. All of whom the Bishop could or would not take, had been told off to seek shelter elsewhere.

Juliana sat huddled, immobile in herself, yet all giving up to the cart's constant jogging. Her fear was still growing; she noticed that the Bishop had changed his finger rings. The episcopal stone was no longer among them. A drab cowl and mantle wrapped him round.

"If any stop us," he said, "we are man and wife, you and I, and all these our housefolk. I am a merchant—a clothier. Our house at South-wark has gone up in flames, it caught fire by accident. I am told the whole district is burning. We are fleeing because we are old and de-fenseless. We have no relations nearer than York—"

He kept on at this, adding detail to detail, first trying to rehearse her, then persuading himself that her dazed condition would be even more serviceable corroboration than any supporting statement on her part.

As she lolled ever more numb and dumb, his loquacity mounted. No chink in the canvas afforded glimpses of the tumultuous streets. His men had orders not to consult or inform him of what was going for-ward. It were best folk thought the wagon contained only goods. And if the worst came to the worst, he would know it soon enough. But many times he took hold of Juliana by arm or shoulders and shook her, to extort some semblance of response, of human companionship.

"Clearly this great upheaval has not come about by purely natural means. There is the overwhelming, sudden concert of it. Either God, for our sins, is taking direct hand in it, or else the rabble have wise, evil men to lead them, that conjured the powers of Hell to their aid. Lam-beth Palace is already in their hands. The King and the Archbishop have gone by boat to the Tower. Some traitors opened up London Bridge. My man Guy saw the vanguard Kentishmen streaming across, with his own eyes, so I know it is all true."

Part Nine
The Year of Deaths
(1381)

CHAPTER I

YOUNG FRANK

It Is Difficult to keep the dates straight in one's head, but if Mistress Trefeller and the Bishop of Anglemere got out of London, as they must have done, before King Richard's first attempted parley with the rebels at Greenwich, the storming of the Tower in his absence followed by the execution of Archbishop Sudbury must have occurred before the Friday of that bloody week. So the great day of the King's meeting with Wat Tyler, and Wat's death, and the granting of the people's charters at Mile End, must have been the Saturday or Sunday. It took six days for the news of the King's subsequent treachery to reach Norwich, thence Ovisham received and passed it on to Bedesford in the course of the next day. Now we know where we are. It was only two days before this that Bedesford learned the full extent of the risings. That means, the nineteenth of June. We have got it right now, for Frank Oxerd had planned his departure so that the end of the week would find him fairly settled and hearing Mass at St. Peter's-of-Damesbury on the Sunday.

The town was all agog with the tidings of London, of Highbury, Cambridge, and Bury St. Edmunds, Ely, St. Albans, and neighboring Norfolk. In London the King had made himself leader of the oppressed, stepping into murdered Wat's place, and was issuing writs freeing everyone from serfdom. John of Gaunt's manors everywhere had been seized and destroyed, but no pillage was permitted in the people's armies. This extenuating, sanctifying rule was broken solely where a former priest, of Beccles, led the rising in Suffolk. But there is some excuse, in that it was the secreted hoards of wicked Richard Lyon and fiendish Justice Cavendish which were plundered. In Norwich and Yarmouth, under Bacon of Baconthorpe and Good Geoffrey Lytster of Falmingham, all government passed into the hands of the people, with courts of the people's justice conducted in orderly fashion at castle and cathedral. And it all befell within the same very short period of time, encompassing no more than two weeks from start to finish. But everybody knows all this.

We were proud of our neighbors, but proud also of ourselves, since we had won, by means more or less peaceable and painless, much of what these others were having to wage war to attain. True, the oppressive charters held by manor and monastery had been neither annulled nor destroyed, but the worst of them had gradually fallen into abeyance.

In a way the rebellion then seemed more remote, less credible than it does now, although times have passed and changed. We could not then follow it through causes and development, as one does in glib survey of the past, nor feel it so seriously.

Franklin and Joan could even profess themselves disgruntled, saying these events distracted folk's attention from their son's leave-taking feast, thereby trying to make out that greater ceremony would have surrounded it otherwise. In truth, they had every reason to be pleased. Luke shared the cost with them, and many townfolk and Wastesiders flocked to the gathering, for the sake of the Robinsons and Edwin and Jeanne, where they would not have felt obliged to honor an Oxerd. Of Frank's own friends only Little James was missing. On Juliana's recommendation he had gone to see the Tryfellows of Clowes, who had a bull for sale. The Smiths' old bull was worn out at last. There was no sign from my lord. Those were the days when lords kept quiet, with the drawbridge up.

Frank took only one man of Luke's with him, intending to hire others in Danesborough. Both rode beside the great oxcart that had Luke's goods in it, accompanied by two of his big dogs, a parting present. They had not gone many miles beyond the town boundary when the dogs stopped, faced about, and growled and bristled, presently barking mightily. All round there was only pastureland; no other human beings were by. But behind, a swift-thundering host approached, whom there was no outdistancing. It was my lord and his men, and without parley they fell upon Frank and his companion and pulled them from the saddle. Both had swords of a sort, but had not thought of drawing them in time. Two henchmen busied themselves with Frank's companion by the wayside. A second pair forcibly stood Frank up before Lord

Hugh; the rest, having helped to overcome and bind him hand and foot, proceeded to make merry havoc of the cart.

Lord Hugh, high upon his black horse, raised his whip. "Now you and I will hold converse, Frank Oxerd."

Helpless, and sore afraid as he must have been, Frank answered with true dignity, "I cannot hold converse with you, my lord, until you drop that," nodding at the whip.

"Would you make conditions, even yet?" cried Lord Hugh, and slashed the whip across Frank's face. A henchman laughed.

Frank had had time so to nerve and brace himself that he managed not to flinch, albeit some moments passed before he could speak. Lord Hugh was silent also. "Great is your valor, knight of Crécy," said Frank then.

"You are trying to goad me into making an end of you quickly," Lord Hugh said through his teeth, and broke his whip across. "But that shall not be. You are coming back to Bedesford with me, and there in sight of all I will make an example of you, and raise up the law again, dealing by you as it is the law for runaway serfs. The Cinqmort name will shine again as in my father's day, and give courage to the craven nobles of the land."

The man who had come with Frank was three-quarters dead by this time, so they left him beside the hamstrung oxen, setting fire to the plundered wagon ere they went.

With wild and jarring clamor they rode back into the town, through the main street and across the market place. Frank was fettered in such wise that, half-suspended between two henchmen's horses, he had to try and keep up with them. The streets were fairly empty, but the market place, and especially the entrance to Smithy Yard, were thronged, it being rightly supposed that some men who had come to see Luke had brought further news. Lord Hugh halted his train and shouted.

"Look and see whom I have here, good people of Bedesford! Hold your questions, you know the answer full well. Yet, if so be you want to learn more, come to the manor, come to my manor after me!" With that they galloped off, horribly dragging Frank.

We sent all the women and children home, forbidding them with gravest threats to follow us. Except Frank's mother. Her we could not deny.

We men, young and old, armed ourselves. Some went to spread the word throughout the town and its rural environs. We waited till we were a crowd, steadily growing, and proceeded to the manor in heavy unison of tread, but scarcely speaking. We did not need to speak. On the way another troop of horsemen overtook us—Gervase and the henchmen who had been out with him. They looked hot and anxious. Later we heard that one of the men Lord Hugh had left behind had gone off on his own to fetch the heir away from a feast at Clavis Green. They had to let the drawbridge down for Gervase. We saw this from afar, and heard the creak and clanging when it was raised again behind him. We still had the better part of a mile to go. They were afraid of us. Well might they be afraid. We fetched up at the moat. More and more of us arrived and stood. We had not realized we should be so many, thus assembled. We waited.

We went on waiting. Dusk fell. We piled fuel for bonfires and lit torches. All the time still more of us came. We ourselves could judge the powerful volume of our voices, still pitched quite low. Then word went round that we would shout, all together. We called Frank's name. We called for Frank. Our voice was as a roll of drums, the drums of the armies of Heaven or Hell.

Two torchlights appeared on the roof of the gatehouse, between the battlemented towers. Two henchmen bore them up, illuminating my lord in warrior's garb. We fell silent, that we might hear him. Lord Hugh spoke to us. He told us justice had been done. They had branded Frank, cut one ear off him, and slashed his nostrils for good measure. They were holding him a while longer to make sure he learned his lesson. "Tomorrow he shall be returned to you. So go home to your beds now, good people."

We had hurdles and carts, ladders and beams of timber. We had fire, and we were all armed. We all stayed. The muffled hum swelled again. Someone climbed up on the pillory platform and hushed us once more. Torches were raised to light him like my lord. The man was Dick. With him were Will Tewsing and some Wasteside laborers, and about a score of others whom nobody knew.

"Hear *me* now, my people of Bedesford!" Dick began, with a wondrous resound to his voice. "We are all of one mind, and it is meet that I shall be the one to cry it out aloud for all to hear at one and the same time. We mean to avenge this unlawful outrage against a decent and law-abiding, free young man, and avenge him we shall, and get him out, or never hold up our heads again. I have waited many years for an hour such as this. You all know me. You do not know me. He whom you have known as Dick the Toolmaker and Dick the Woodward is your rightful leader in this enterprise, for he and none other is the rightful Cinqmort lord. I have bided my time, for I wanted my rights and not a bootless martyrdom. I dared not reveal myself to more than a few of you before the time was ripe. Only the green men of the Easterwoods have been my sworn vassals since I and my sainted twin were lads. I have sworn to issue a free pardon for every outlaw that has been my man. I swear to you now that I shall make good any losses any of you may have incurred at their hands. They had to keep alive somehow, to serve me through the years of bitter namelessness. Ranged here beside me you behold them that have ventured from out wilderness' shelter to my aid. See also those who came to Cloudsway Waste at my bidding, to ensconce them near at hand. See them and greet them anew and trust them, for my sake! My henchmen I will not call them till I can house and pay them at this manor of mine. Oh, friends!" he cried, and spread out his thick, muscular arms as if to fold the whole multitude to his breast, "if only poor White Hugh could have been spared to see this day! Whether I win or lose, it has been so fine, at last to be telling you! You shall hear the whole story in due time. Now I will only say that I and White Hugh are the sons of Old Lord Gervase, got many years before he sired Hugh and the rest, or ever saw their mother. Our mother was not of noble blood, but he wedded her in secret when she went with child of us. The record perished with our old church, and so, I think, did she. Mind you the Hermit? No wonder the Black Death came and the Cinqmort luck went from bad to worse! Are you with me, people of Bedesford? I swear it before God that my first act in my rightful place shall be to redress all Cinqmort wrongs and to grant you such rights, exemptions, charters as the world has not seen before! Have you not known me, all my life, as a man of my word? Up, up, and after me, my people of Bedesford, and let our war cry be, 'Young Frank! And Right over Might!' "

Thereafter all shouted at once, and it mattered not that we could hear each other no more. Did we believe him? Of course we believed him. It was even as if we had always known and helped him lead and conceal his secret life. The firelight leaped about the churning mass of us like the visible lightning of our fervor. Our huge crowd voice was our best battering ram. But hurdles, ladders, beams, and very carts were thrown across the moat, and over the tangle of such bridging we threw ourselves, our whole embodied, vital fury against the mere stone of Cinqmort Manor walls.

CHAPTER 2

CLOUDSWAY NOISE

LORD JEROME NEVER inquired precisely how the wagon's escape from London had been encompassed. It was too likely that one or more of his henchmen had known the Rebel password or had friends among the new guardians of gates and bridgeheads. That was one of the most paralyzing, lingering terrors about the rebellion and its aftermath. There was no telling who was of it or, indeed, who was not. The more of the facts behind it were brought to light, the more far-reaching its allegiances and entanglements appeared to have been.

The whole pattern of life had been disturbed and, disintegrated, danced in a constant, hectic change of constellation, so that the very air seemed strange material, and nothing, however objective, visible or wonted, appeared as what it was. You did strange things and felt strange feelings, as any beings would, enchanted—themselves intrinsically unaltered—into a world so unknown one might have been transported to the moon or among the prodigies of the realms beneath the seas.

Lord Jerome owed his men a great debt of gratitude, and he discharged it by means of the same unawareness, feverishly manufactured, from which throughout the flight he extracted would-be security—just as unseeing travel in the close, lightless confinement of the wagon allowed him to fancy himself invisible and invulnerable. The men were his sworn vassals and owed him fidelity. Undoubtedly they themselves conceived of it thus, for he was not a man like Hugh Cinqmort who of himself inspired love in such as them.

They had slipped out of the warring city in the night, and hid for a day in Middlesex Forest, also to slay them additional proviant. Then the passengers came out of the wagon—Juliana having to be carried— and the Bishop made the effort of leading a thanksgiving prayer, afterward wandering in circles about the thicket with, ostensibly, his breviary.

Meg had to tend Juliana like a child, a torporous dead weight of a child. One of the Mistress' eyes was closed, and though Meg tried, she could not lift the stiff lid with her fingers. The other eye stood open, unwinking. It was impossible to say whether Juliana were asleep all the time or uninterruptedly awake.

It was no light matter to manage the vehicle through woodland and over marsh and heath and fields. The henchmen were not skilled in this, and Geoffrey knew nothing of this region. Wearily meandering, they but kept a general northerly course. Most days had sunshine, and the moon was out, of nights, with the clouds passing through its surrounding haze in a semblance of smoke exhalation, for in the darkness there were always fires to be seen, charting the land and measuring out its distances. Mostly they traveled at night, and spent the daytime resting in concealment. To find safe cropping for the horses was one of their gravest, most nerve-racking necessities.

In the comforting gloom under the hood, wedged in with Meg and Juliana and the baggage, stiff in every joint but inexhaustible of monologous musings, the Bishop underwent successive changes of spirit and temper.

Soon after they had made good their escape from the areas of immediate battle, he began to speculate as to whether after all he himself were not among those rejected of God. He sat up straight and smote his forehead with the joyful notion that God's saving hand might be descried in what at the time had indeed seemed like a miracle, if an ill one. Namely, the fact that he had been passed over when archbishopric and chancellorship fell vacant. As it had turned out, had he not every reason to praise his Lord Creator for that?

His next line of thought and discourse took the form of defense against any possible charge of cowardice. By and by he stopped proving that he had not run away to save his life; and in a third stage declared his mounting anger. So far from continuing to embrace at least a metaphysical part of the responsibility for the rebellion, he dropped all allusion to God's design or the Devil's aid in it. Instead he began to rail, in a straightforward, revivifying manner, against the rebels as such and the feeble, intimated opposition.

The nightly sheen of burning manors grew dimmer and less frequent. But then the provisions began to give out and they to suffer hunger. Nobody knew how much longer they had to go on. Only Juliana gave no sign of caring. At last Geoffrey proclaimed his certitude, on evidence scarce less inexplicable to himself than to the others, that they were drawing near their destination. Another day and a half, and he announced he recognized the country, pointing out landmarks which to the other appeared no different from the features of ground over which they had previously passed. Now they dared travel by day again. At the point where the path up Cloudsway Ridge and the highways to Thirchester and Danesborough branch off the London road, Lord

Jerome decided it were best to make another short detour, to rest and obtain food at Cloudesley-St.-Veron's.

The surrounding villages were quiet. It was extraordinary. People were plowing the fallows, with an unmoved leisureliness that to these travelers seemed inane, not to say demented. By no means all of them straightened to gaze after the wagon and its escort.

Cloudesley Monastery appeared deserted. Its gates were closed and not a dog barked in the courtyard.

"No smoke from the chimneys!" Lord Jerome said hungrily.

One of the men clambered up the outer wall and looked over. Through the glass panes of the porter's lodge he saw a wizened little monk eying him with terrified menace and brandishing a crucifix. Thereupon the party raised such a shouting and din of arms struck together, that some monks came out on the roof between the gables, hauling pails from which arose steam and smell of pitch. Plainly they believed massacre now to be upon them, and plainly they were all ready for it. The Bishop hammered at his brow with both fists, but just when they had all despaired of making the monks comprehend, there were gestures of relief and joy aloft, and, pails still in hand, the would-be defense toiled out of sight behind a chimney stack. It was like a fairy tale. All at once gusts of divers sound blew in lively crosscurrents from the monastery, and a stream of monks spilled all over the courtyard and threw itself at the gates to open them, then scampering round the Bishop with hosannas.

The cold buildings grew warm and rang with activity. Everywhere monks scurried with arms full of all sorts of loads and mien manfully tautened.

As soon as Lord Jerome had eaten and drunk his fill, he proceeded to inquire into the state of affairs that had confronted him. The monks defended themselves: their foundation was very isolated; there was no manor, no great house of any description, nearer than Bedesford, no one but villein farmers about them. "And we are all of us old men, Reverend Lord."

"All the more reason that you should not cling to what remains to you of life to the exclusion of all dignity, ay, and trust in God! A sorry example have you given to the people whom your mode of living should serve as continual instruction! Know you not that nothing so incites pursuit as timorous withdrawal? The harshest tyranny will not so certainly make rebels of subject folk. What lambs they must be, these your villeins here, not to have fallen upon you though you so clearly showed them you expected it! Seeing that God in His mercy set you to herd so spiritless a flock, the smallest spark of enterprise would have inspired you to spread abroad the impression that in your case the serfs had actually made themselves their venerable overlords' protectors! Oh, is there aught so galling as the sight of shining opportunities cast away? You might have planted here the germ of antirevolt, which might have spread peace and submission as fast and as wide as unrest has spawned elsewhere."

"But, your lordship, they had not looked at us at all kindly of late. When we called on them for the June hay, they muttered and murmured and hintingly spoke of the changes in the land, about to reverse their position and ours! They *refused* to pay the mill dues!"

"No wonder, if to frighten you all they had to do was look and hint and mutter! I am too wroth to laugh as one should. Words fail me, to vent my contempt. Tomorrow you must have them called together on the green, that I may address them and undo the damage of your holy meekness."

"But, Your Reverence, what if they ask you too about the remissions at your own seat? What will you answer them?"

"What seat? What remissions?"

"Is not Cloudsway Waste destined to be your residence one day? Is it not already called so? And is not every Wasteside laborer permitted free use of his own querns, although Wode Mill has been working several years? Even the Flemings of the tileries may choose between their own mills and Lord Alfred's."

"I know nothing of this," said the Bishop after a pause, in a quieter tone. "I *am* not sure that I understand. Pray explain. Tell me more. Take your time, my sons."

Happiness and good-fellowship after all suffused the candle-lit, food-scented refectory as the monks sat entertaining their Bishop far into the night. Again and again the call went out for more wine, for ale, for new meat courses, savory and sweet. The kitchen hands sang jubilate at their heated work. The Bishop's gorge rose after his enforced fast, but the spiritual satisfaction of perfect wrath and a concrete object for it, maintained harmony in his maw and kept his eyes open and ears alert. He had no scribe with him and called for tablet and stylus to make notes. He laughed and joked with the chattering old men and helped their memories and beguiled their scruples with judicious flattery and confidential intonations.

Tottering with fatigue, he had himself supported to rest by the assiduous Chapter, likewise a trifle unsteady of leg, and enjoyed refreshing sleep. His men had long since sunk into the straw of the stables. Juliana and her servants had not stirred from the pilgrims' hall.

The next day there was the gathering of the people on the green. And then two kinds of news arrived together: of the doings of fighting Henry Spencer, Bishop of Norwich; and of nocturnal conflagration where Bedesford lay.

Lord Jerome leaped among his dozing men like a lion and stirred them with foot and hand and sonorous phrase. Before nightfall they were on their way along the foot of the Ridge.

The weather had turned cold again. The wintry air, particularly in the early morning, combined with the June light and the June look of all things green and growing, the perfumes of summer and the summer sounds of birds, into an atmosphere of rarefied, burgeoning tranquillity. At the cathedral, the Abbot was celebrating Mass, not before the high altar, but in the Lady Chapel, which also still served as a ringers' room.

We believe that Lord Alfred had chosen the side chapel because it was small and we could not follow him there, for he had found the Wasteside dwellers before him. With the exception of those now revealed as Dick's spies, Dick himself and his lieutenant Will, and Carlos Trinidad with a handful of friars, nobody had left the site for so much as a look at the scene of the disturbances at the Old Town, not even Matt, Clement, or Master Stephen. These three were as irresolute as the rest of us. You perceive, the instantaneous, transporting ardor in Bedesford had not sent its spark across to the New Town. Here we were merely soberly concerned with what it might be right or wrong for us to do, or not to do. The people of the New Town belonged to the monastery and had no quarrel with it. Yet, was that the whole truth of the situation? And is a half-truth ever any better than a lie? If it were true, that man's conscience is his inborn guide to right, did not our idle, safe repudiation of our brothers' troubles put us in the wrong? Whatever the outcome, should we ever be able to forgive ourselves? Would those our brothers ever forget?

The Abbot made his way through the waiting crowds—nobody save Brother Laurentius had taken up his tools—without a word, without even letting folk see that he saw them. The acolytes did as he did. It appeared there was to be no quorum of monks. The people took it that the Abbot also wanted guidance, and so for a start followed his lead in worship, going down on their knees everywhere, although the service was invisible to most. But our thoughts would not be collected and submerged in prayer.

Many of us rose and prepared after all to find some occupation for our hands. Brother Laurentius had fairly hurtled upon his work. Frantic hammering echoed from the corner between western door and wall, where he was finishing some panels. People avoided looking in his direction as strenuously as he held himself aloof, averted. But it was not that his diligence shamed us. It was not that which made one wish to bar him out of ken. There was something about his avid, tranced conduct made one shudder in a nasty dread. Somehow, despite the insistent evidence of his corporeal presence, he contrived to make it appear that, rather than ignoring us, he was inexorably removing himself, dwindled out of being with us.

He had traveled a long way since the days when he loved and was beloved, when concern for all Christians had driven him into that hellish moil where immaculate mystic laws are parisitized and soiled by principia of earthly justice and injustice, and from which he had extricated himself only at the cost of all human relationship. In like manner his art had retreated from imitation of earthly shapes, until in the end it overshot that goal which he had set himself, of expressing and conveying feeling purified of sensual distraction. But it, his art, had soared utterly beyond comprehension. Uncomprehending, feeling could no longer follow and grasp his creations, so that their forms became senseless also to the eye. Bereft even of decorative meaning, his works had attained a soullessness, from the point of view of the beholder, which was the opposite of what he had aimed at. . . .

Yet the incessant ring of his tools also assailed our conscience with the shame we denied just now. Edwin, for one, tried to emulate him, and went so far as to lift the shrouding sacks from his image of St. Francis, but his hand told him at once that anything he touched today would irreparably suffer. Furtively he looked about him. Near the Lady Chapel he saw his son Jack, equally at a loss, knife and gouge aimlessly in hand, surveying a piece of carving in the door which he and Richard Widowson were making together. Richard was not there. Edwin's impulse was to go and ask whether Richard, then, had not come back to the site this morning, but he stopped halfway. What was the good of finding out?

Jaffy had gone a week ago to attend the christening of his sister Janet's Fleming babe. Now Edwin wished he himself had gone to Danesborough as his daughter had prayed him. He wished he could have been anywhere but here. Several people made as to approach him. He ducked back into his own workshop and pretended to be busy.

The redoubled force of every echo only stressed the unusual quiescence.

Suddenly a monk hurried through the door on the monastery side, stood still, as to find his bearings, and made for the Lady Chapel. There, afraid to disturb Lord Alfred, he went on tiptoe and gesticulated to attract the others' attention, finally speaking to them in the sign language which was the monks' means of communication during ordained periods of silence. But its stock of word symbols was too limited for what he had to say, so that he whispered, "Our Reverend Lord Bishop is come. He is here. He is at the monastery. He is coming hither!" Nobody seemed to heed him. He whispered his cry again and again.

The Bishop entered, not by any side door, but by way of the great western portal. At his heels came a troop of men-at-arms. Ay, they were still armed, to the teeth. The Bishop himself scattered iron echoes at every step—and they were angry, long, pounding steps that he took. One might not have known him. He wore no distinctive vestments under his cloak which billowed, dusty and torn, in the wake of his irreverent stride. Mud had splashed, not only all the way up his boots and thighs and the open skirts of his gown, but up to his face, where in places it had dried caked as potter's clay among the gray beard stubble. He had a steel cap on his head, so that one could not even see he had a tonsure.

The workmen, skilled and low alike, backed out of his path. Edwin stood up in his enclosure. Only Brother Laurentius did not falter in his hammering. The Rocquefeuille henchmen had a glow about their faces, like reflections of the Bishop's purple flush, yet with a slight difference, likewise discernible in the quality of their footfall. The Bishop was obeying his impulses, and he was as much at home in any cathedral as housewives are even in alien kitchens. But for all that they lived and acted under the protection of their oath of fealty, his men were uneasy in modeling their behavior on his. They were fevered and thrilled through with a mixture of guilt and adventure.

"Abbot, where are you? Answer, as you are a man! Where is he, bad vicar of my office?" cried the Bishop.

At this there was a forward movement among the workmen. From the hindermost ranks came the first murmuring, "Hush!" "Be still!" "Do not go outside, take off your arms in the churchyard like Christians!" Voices grew louder, raised now also in the forefront.

The Bishop stamped his mailed foot and again shouted for Alfred, by his full name. The syllables collided and merged into each other, rolling unrecognizably, like growl of thunder, about the vault compartments overhead.

"Be still! Be still! Take off your hats of steel and shirts of mail!" All round the cry was taken up—such chorus the house of St. Hand's had not heard before. "Divest you of your arms, you heathen! Step quietly, stop, bend the knee to the Host of God's body!"

The monk who had given warning of the Bishop's arrival came back from the transept with arms outspread, "God's service is proceeding in the Lady Chapel—hold—"

Lord Jerome charged on as if he meant to go straight through the monk, albeit at the last he swerved a little, merely brushing him aside.

But on the threshold of the chapel, the Bishop did halt. Many candles burned and fused their radiance with the sunlight entering by way of the sanctus bell cot. Their sweet warm breath had lured a few bees inside, that gleamed golden as they floated, sinking, drugged, through the haze of incense. Sweat stood out on all the bony parts of the Abbot's face, but that only made his face shine as in a glory (we deemed). There were gold flecks even in his black hair. He was as far away as Brother Laurentius, but away on our behalf, not coldheartedly fleeing from us.

"What do you think you are about, Alfred Widowson?" the Bishop shouted into the sacred, murmuring peace. "Rebellion has fallen on your parish, murder and pillage and rapine and fire, right under your nose, and here you act as if you knew it not! Such pretence will not deceive God, nor even men. You have waxed too secure, and stupid, in your craftiness! You have forgotten who and what you are, vice abbot of Cloudsway! You are not pope. It is for you to do as your Bishop orders. I order you to stop this mockery of a service, stop your impious misuse of wine and wafer for immunity. Stop, answer me, I say! It is you bears responsibility for what is happening in the Old Town. What has been happening here, at the New, insidiously, is no less your work. Rebel! Traitor! Murderer! Incendiary by proxy. Parricide, leveler of the might and authority of your Mother Church! The Fiend alone knows what you have been doing with the sacred funds entrusted to you! Of all the noble abbots in my See, it would be you alone dared to act counter to my mill edict! But I have full list of all your other seditious doings! Wycliffe is a white angel compared with you!"

The Abbot was on the point of raising the host.

"Mayhap this will cause you to attend. The rebellion is over, in London as in Norwich!"

The ciborium in Alfred's hands shot forth a bright untrembling beam of light.

"—as soon as they have established order in the town, my men shall go from house to house, destroying private millstones—"

The Bishop fell silent, as much with exquisite, self-intoxicated rage, all the more exultant for towering yet pent-up, as with lack of breath. He looked backward and saw his men stand close and stiff in artificial staunchness, and behind them the growing mass of gaping lay folk. He drew his sword and flourished it, so that it glinted in the eyes of all who clogged the mouth of the transept, and started toward the Abbot, and struck at him. Jack leaped forward when the Bishop did, to ward off the blow from his brother, and cut the palm of his hand open against the sliding edge of the sharp blade. The Bishop but jarred the ministrant. The host was tumbled on the flag tiles, and Jack's blood poured down over it.

"Murder! Sacrilege! Sacrilege! Kill! Kill!"

Jack led the outcry, and the monks took it up, and the people throughout the body of the church. "Kill! Kill! Kill!" rang the blast that had subdued London town itself.

The bell, which had told folk as far as sound would carry that Mass was about to be consummated, hardly paused before changing over to the Chime of Distress—the signal summoning the people to the defense against flood, fire, or sudden war. The young monk who gave it tongue hung himself into the rope pull with the abandon of some possessed dancer, swooping all but to his knees and shooting up again to strained erectitude, on and on, the sweat streaming down his contracted face and the veins swelling on his blistered hands. The tocsin reverberated through the cathedral so that floor and walls seemed to throb. The glass and window boarding rattled and tinkled, and men's clenched teeth of their own accord hummed and clicked to its thrum.

"Kill! Kill!"

The Bishop's men drew their swords.

"Kill! Kill!"

The Abbot had thrown himself upon the Bishop, gripping his sword arm and staying it, stretched aloft. They stood tussling, swaying, uttering no sound beyond their heavy breathing. At last the sword fell, clattering, and the Bishop threw his arms about the younger, slighter man, in an ursine hug rendered the more formidable by the weight and hardness of his armor, and belabored and felled him, but then was up in one bound to confront the howling inrush of people. Alfred lay insensible, with face all bloodied.

"The Bishop has slain Lord Alfred before Our Lady's altar!"

"Kill! Kill! Kill! Kill!"

The henchmen, bemusing uncertainty fallen off them, darted hither and thither and laid about them with their swords. The Bishop, after several thwarted plunges, had at last retrieved his weapon and was holding the press of monks and building workers at bay. His mouth was wet and open. For all his bulk and ire one remembered he was an old man. But that, there and then, only augmented fatal detestation.

Bishop and henchmen fought their way out into the transept and, inch by inch, toward the central crossing. Jack Widowson, who strove in vain in the direction of his brother, was wrenched backward. He found a sack and wound it round his disabled hand, presently to use it as a shield from which a spray of blood flew out at every sudden movement, while with his left he whirled a heavy wooden mallet.

The whole nave was now a battlefield. Another band of the Bishop's men had arrived from the monastery, at the same time as the vanguard of Flemish tilers obeyed the summons of the bell, which still went on tolling. Neither force knew what it came for until caught up in the thick of the fight.

Those workmen whose tools were little use as weapons swarmed up the scaffolding, so close on one another's heels they looked enchained. They clambered about the triforial embrasures, shouting, distorted of face and heaving muscles, dislodging, prying loose, hurling down into the fray anything they could lay hands on, planks and mortar buckets full and empty, stones from the fabric of the gallery and its approaches. A good many Flemings, having come unarmed, made haste to follow and outclimb, out-do them in destructive resourcefulness. Ladders and poles tipped and crashed into the medley below, so that the whole web of scaffolding creaked and trembled, sagged here and there, its uprights slanting, quill-like, in suspense. There was one fellow crouched propped in the angle of a cornice, who dexterously swung the plumb line, so that the lead struck whomsoever he wished, on the ground, until friends and foes were indistinguishably intermingled, and he desisted. Higher up and higher still about the raw-edged ledges and promontories round the airy base of the central tower, tugging figures clung, their foothold mere wrinkles in the rind of the cathedral. The men fell to their death, sprawling, with screams. By and by the rest gave up and one by one descended.

Jack Widowson, toppling on hand and knees, also crawled out of the battle. Some of the others, waiting to get their breath and allay the quivering of their calves and arms, carried him to safety.

He heard that his father and several others were gone from the cathedral. A number of the Bishop's men who had been left at the monastery had launched an attack on the Wasteside huts. There was some indecision among his rescuers whether to go or stay—until they were deprived of choice. As another wave of war overflowed toward them, shouts of wrath and lamentation made it known that Brother Laurentius had been killed.

All alone in the side chapel but for him that had tolled the alarm and had been cut down, Lord Alfred was reviving from his swoon. At the first he could not distinguish between the droning in his head and the noise outside it. Then his eyes took in the pools of bloody desecration, and he levered himself up. He reeled a little, but soon regained full control of his body. He took the crucifix from the altar and walked out into the transept.

CHAPTER 3

THE DESPOILING

ALL THROUGH the night the battle of Cinqmort Manor had gone on. When the attack on moat and gates began, Dick sent his outlaws with some of the people for guides, back to Bede's Bridge where some rowing boats were anchored. They were to make for the junction of Tew and Wode, and attempt to enter the park by way of the mill wheel and a tottering birch-stave bridgelet, and, if they ever got as far as that, fall upon the manor from the back. At the worst this would distract and deplete the defense of the gate walls. He had it all thought out. No doubt he had thought it out untold years ago.

The moat was spanned, the gate assaulted partly under cover of the drawbridge, which helped obstruct the arrows from above. Dick had told us not to make overserious efforts to scale the wall in other places, but to see to it that the henchmen were kept engaged and spread out over as wide an area as possible. We used some lighter, overturned carts for shields, from under which we raised the ladders and grapple hooks. Like cumbrous unsteady beetles we must have looked, with wavering, horrid feelers. No scalding caldrons were brought into the fight against us. The manor folk had either forgotten or disdained them. When they did think of hurling down flambeaux, it was the bridge that caught the burning missiles, while the great oak doors groaned and shrieked under the blows of our timber beams, bound and reinforced with iron drag chains.

My lord's henchmen were not trained soldiers. Ay, we have pointed it out many times that they had started out from the same ranks as had replenished our husbandmen and building laborers, wherefore these erstwhile brethren hated each other as Cain and Abel. How many of all those Franklins, Freemans, Smiths, and Newcomes had risen to be more than farm hands, more than unskilled masons of the lowest order, in the thirty-odd years since the Black Death? Not a great many. And on the whole those whom Baldwin's descriptions of a lawless, easy life had tempted into my lord's service had not been the best, nor the cleverest, of the wanderers. Neither had they been put in the way of acquiring special warrior's skill. They had practiced their archery, to be sure, and played the more violent ball games in the tourney hall, and perchance improved their horsemanship. But beyond that no greater strategy and martial art had been demanded of them than sufficed for the slaughter of game in the woods and the beating and harrying of my lord's subjects. They knew no more of siege warfare than would come to anyone when he finds himself in fact besieged. In a way they must have felt relieved when their chance came for single combat, where strength and superior arms and individual ferocity count for something.

On the other hand, the people of Bedesford far outnumbered them, and the people of Bedesford were beside themselves with rage that had good cause. If you have no cause to defend, the stoutest defense work will not keep out fear, which will act for the assailants as another, invisible great weapon. No one at the manor, excepting only Lord Hugh himself, felt that Young Frank had been dealt with lawfully. True, not a henchman had hung back from pursuit of Frank, or held off plundering Luke's wagon. Not one had spoken against taking Frank to prison, but deliberately maiming him for life as if he were in truth a criminal was quite another matter. They had had no qualms in regard to Luke's servant whose body had fared rather worse at their hands when all is said and done—because no legal rigmarole had attended their illegal savagery. In any case it is absurd to suppose that any of them would have openly dissented from Lord Hugh. Howbeit, as we have seen, the men whom he had left behind at the manor had been sufficiently uneasy, even at the start, for one of their number to go out after Gervase.

Further, Gervase had endorsed their vague alarm. To the last moment he had tried to dissuade his uncle from the deed of mutilation. After it was done, of course, there was nothing else for it but that he must stand by Lord Hugh in every sense and uphold the justice of his rash act against his own convictions, if necessary even at the cost of his own blood. Yet we cannot believe that under the circumstances he risked his life ungrudgingly and fought as furiously, recklessly as we did. For Lord Hugh, too, now that he had once more bethought himself of the requirements of earthly power, it was important to remain alive.

Having said so much, we deem it scarcely needful to recount step by step how the attack progressed, how many fell on the way, nor how they got their death wounds. The siege, properly speaking, was over early in the small hours. Not a henchman had the wit to lurk in our rear once we had broken through and scoured the hollows in the wall for cornered survivors. The bulk of them retreated into the main buildings. It now became a matter of besieging room after room, house after house. We cannot say that they did not fight bravely. It was only that complete neglect of forethought or adaptive planning doomed their struggles from the outset. Had it been a question of playing for time to allow rescuers to reach them, their unvarying, concentrated defense and wholesale abandoning of successive positions might have been honored with the name of tactics. But they had not sent out any messengers—for whence, they thought, could aid come to them, as everywhere the same was presumably happening? Only Prior Carlos was obstinately unimaginative enough to have despatched two friars with tidings of our war, unknown to us and to the manor forces.

No watchmen had been posted in the park, and no archers manned the battlements rising sheer out of the Tew waters, so that our boating party circumnavigated them unhindered. Soon after dawn this party arrived formally to occupy the warren of lesser buildings. Hand-to-hand fighting had ceased. We held the great hall with all adjoining apartments, and Lord Hugh and Gervase and their men were barricaded in the lumber tower.

So there in the first lull, Dick made another speech: Young Frank, and possession of the manor were our prime objectives; we held the manor folk as good as imprisoned, and thus for the nonce might leave them, to be dealt with at our leisure, as soon as all other demands on our time and strength had been met. Unwilling guards were posted round the tower, from which issued no retort, of sound or projectile, to their threats and jeering. Nothing but arrows could have been shot from slits, and the top platform remained stubbornly deserted.

Even when daylight had fully brightened, our rallying points, the huge bonfires, were kept burning. Indeed, a fresh one was started in the courtyard. We needed torches to penetrate into the dungeon. Young Frank was soon discovered, and with him one henchman who fell on his knees, holding up empty hands in supplication. His sword lay on the ground before him, with the hilt humbly pointing at the enemy, and he implored our mercy. He had been left behind with orders to kill Frank in the event of our success, and behold, he had spared him. But, though the coals in the brazier had expired, the branding irons were still in evidence, and while Frank's warder proffered his sword in such piteous display, he had overlooked the scourges lying near. So he was dragged up into the light of day, and soon ceased begging for his life, begging only to be killed outright.

Gently, gently, four townsmen carried Frank. He was not capable of showing any great joy or gratitude. He was laid to rest with his head in his mother's lap, in an open, side porch to the great hall, where he would be sheltered, yet visible to all without encroachment. Prior Carlos forsook his station on the flat roof of the gatehouse, the two friars still with him coming after with caskets of medicines and cordials.

He had been up with us all night and undergone his most gruelling trial yet. Again and again he had fruitlessly attempted to impede us with preaching, forced, rather like the defense, to leave one point of vantage after another, as our advance caught up with him. Had he spread-eagled himself as a living bolt across gates and doorways, the people, we dare swear, would have stormed on even over his body. He himself must have realized that, for, to give him his due, he lacked neither courage nor determination, and if he had thought his death would attain his object would have done naught to save himself. As it was, he did what he must do to the limits of his voice and remarkable staying power, and ministered to the fallen as soon as he could extract them from the fray. He and the other two, who could barely keep in step with him, saw to Frank's roughly bandaged injuries and yet untended back. No one obstructed or took the slightest notice of them.

But when my lord's lone, much more distant figure appeared high above on the tower platform, everyone took note immediately. Fists flew up, and cudgels and pitchforks and axes were raised and shaken in a frenzy, also the flaming torches, so that the black smoke swirled up, and the scythes flashed, singing in their sockets. A great, terrible uproar of hatred sent the air atremble, so that one would scarce have marveled to see the whole tall stone fastness shiver into pieces.

My lord gazed round and round, over all that the tower surveyed. Lastly he looked down on the roaring, gnomishly foreshortened multitude. He turned his back and looked up into the sky, and then, descending, disappeared again. Men ran up against the tower, below, as if hoping to shatter it with their bodies. It took a few moments to distract their rage back into its main and proper channels.

My lord returned to the vent holes, where Gervase and the men were spying on the scene of destruction. Frank's guard was still alive, and still there were people clamoring to take their turn at tormenting him. My lord, too, gazed on for an instant. He stepped back and motioned to the others also to come away and attend to him.

"I will not die here. Nay, even if an honorable and a quick death were promised me—no, I say, no and no! We have no food up here, nor water. We have not many arms left between us. All we have is lumber. If there were no other way, we could hurl down ourselves, as a last throw. But there is a secret passage comes out by the fishpond. Whither would I go? Not far, none so very far. I want but to creep to earth in the wilderness and die there in my own peace—if I have to do myself to death in the manner of Jane. We have had our day. Now there is an end. Now *they* will rule the world as masters. There is naught to salvage and take with us, and thus it seems to me there will be no burden of ignominy to our flight—if you will flee with me, Nephew, and you, men? With luck we shall cross the river junction by the mill, and thence it will not be such a long way to the marsh, and nearly all under cover. Come with me. Yet if you will not, I shall go, myself."

We had forgotten them again. Even so it was the same as if we had known we now had the manor to ourselves. All the furnishings and the great chests were borne out onto the cobbles, the banqueting hall was stripped of the ancestral treasures of the Cinqmort race. Some found time to make mock of these. One man balanced Baldwin Redbeard's shield on his head like an overgrown comical hat, another pretended to stagger, overcome by the centuries-old reek of Sir Hugh-le-gros's big silver-mounted drinking horn. Others again decked themselves with arras and bedspreads, mincing potbellied in caricature of noble ladies' stance, and lisping oaths in queer falsetto voices when they tripped over the huge trailing folds. Bolsters were slashed and the feathers given up to the wind, or wool and straw stuffing thrown on the bonfires. Many an old chair or bench, stoutly wrought door and split window shutter went the same way. Men began to empty the plate coffers, deliberately treading delicate bowls and flagons of silver into unrecognizable twists.

"Men! Men! Friends! Fellow townfolk!" Dick yelled, and jumped to prevent further damage. Then he had to rush at another group and beg them to desist from further needless demolition of doors and windows that had previously been forced. After that he dashed inside, to try and stem the hunt for other movables, next having to look on at lusty ax blows cutting the charter trunks in pieces. He could do nothing against the first onslaught on the documents. The axes were flung aside, and, shouting with laughter and triumph and venom, folk dived in and threw up armfuls of rolled parchment and sewn books, trampling them in the mire as they fell, adding them to the fire, tearing them up with a sound most satisfying, or spitting and urinating on them. "Men! Men! Friends! Fellow townfolk! Brothers!" Dick wailed. In the end he had to get hold of Luke Robinson and James Smith to help him get a hearing and create some order.

Luke probably understood what was happening: Dick's slavering, bulge-eyed anxiety to preserve what he claimed for his own had begun to annoy us, our lifelong respect for our toolmaker and woodward fast yielding to ridicule. His prancing and bleating like a crazed old goat was too laughable. Last night we had gladly ceded him redoubled authority, if only because it was good and heartening, and useful, too, to have a leader. Now he seemed to have forgotten all about Frank and vengeance. But Luke could see beyond the paroxysm of the moment, and on his intervention we remembered again that Dick had not been so careful with his life as of his presumptive property, having fought in the forefront of the battering.

So Luke's son-in-law, Richard, was posted opposite two men who handed him the charters ready unrolled, and two others took up a stand on either side of him. Richard read out the writing (and he did this right creditably, stumbling only over very ancient letters), and translated them as best and as briefly as he could. Those which made naught of the rights of the people, those which meant grievous wrong, were consigned to Richard's left-hand comrade, who passed them on to the fires. But any that briefed the ruling Cinqmort's right to the manor and lands, and certain reasonable privileges, Richard handed to the right, where they were carefully laid in a special casket. Dick sat down to recuperate near Joan Oxerd and her son.

When they had started out, the leader of the water party had been Will Tewsing. By the time they had traversed the park it was he no longer. Although he knew the way and the other did not, Will by imperceptible degrees had lost his place to one of Dick's outlaw friends—the one with the black eyes and long chin and bald head, who had sought speech with Edwin in the guise of a fugitive falconer. He retained his captaincy even when they had rejoined the main body under Dick's command; and somehow the two forces continued, if not divided, at least distinct. Even Will himself looked to the greenwoodman for orders.

This former water party, then, was busy ransacking the chests and halberd racks which had been removed from the armory. All of a sudden that outlaw leader swung himself up on the nearest ledge, sill to a tall window whose frame, panes, and shutters had gone in the assault, leaving jagged edges as the wall was part timber and daub work. He stood poised with predatory grace in the peaked hole which served his figure like a niche. His men stopped wrangling over the arms of state—axes with gold and silver inlay, daggers shaped like undulating tongues of flame, swords with engraved inscriptions in the blood groves—and looked up at him attentively.

He opened his mouth wide and laughed, long and loud and purposefully. "What, Priest? What?" his fellows roared.

"Strange and ludicrous doings are these!" the one they called Priest laughed again and slapped his leathern thigh.

"What, Priest? What? What? What?"

"For sure nothing like this has befallen through the length and breadth of risen England!" Every now and then he went on laughing, most evilly, ho! ho! "Nowhere else, for sure, are the people risking life and salvation, sacking a manor house, not to raze it to the ground for all time, but merely to drive out one lord and put in another! Even if we had proof, and not just Dick's word for it, that he is a Cinqmort and rightful head of the accursed tribe—still I would say: a lord is a lord, whatever his name; and a shackled lion that, as soon as freed, hastens to the nearest ox yoke—why, he *is* a castrate ox and deserves to be whipped and goaded and, at the last, eaten up entirely! Wait till the people of London and Norwich hear of this! They will split their sides laughing. All the castles and manors that are yet standing will be blown down by that mighty laughter which shall shake the land from end to end. And when freedom and happiness are sole rulers in England, the name of Bedesford will be a byword everywhere for folly and slavishness, to the end of time. If it did not make me laugh so hard, I would sit me down on a stone and weep. Fools! Fools! Fools and foolish slaves! Even if Dick be truly minded to keep the promises he made last night, dare you trust in those that will come after him, whoever they may be? And what surety have we that even Dick himself will be faithful? What did Dick do when it chanced that one of us was caught at the marsh? Did Dick strive to defend our friend and his, or try helping him escape? Nay! He forswore himself to his vassal's doom. Because he trembled for his own skin. A fine liege lord to swear fealty to, upon my soul! Think well before you bind yourselves anew. Ay, listen well too, you men of Bedesford! Let us save our friend Dick from temptation—the temptation to err as is human upon having tasted power and wealth. Every stone, every crumb of mortar, every lath and bole of this old stronghold stands for a drop of bloody sweat, a sigh, a tear, and unjust profit wrung from the lives of the weak. Let us level it to the ground, this monument of cruelty, lest it stand, a perpetual encouragement to would-be tyrants! Give me a brand from the fire. Who is with me? Burn, then, burn, break, and tear asunder, lest it be said of us that we wished to enrich ourselves by pillage, lest the purity of the people's judgment be called in doubt, lest Dick get some of it back! Would you have pity on unfeeling stone and tapestries, where those that owned them knew no pity, ever, on the flesh and blood of their own kind? After me, after me, make sacrifice as in days of old to the God of justice! Burn! Burn! Burn!"

And, "Burn! Burn," the people chanted the response, even as their brethren were howling, "Kill!" over at Cloudsway Waste.

The outlaw whom they called Priest flung a flaring pine branch into the hall behind him, where the floor was still covered with straw and rushes. He leaped down and relit a dead torch, and ran indoors, and more and more followed his example, running and singing, with sparks and smoke whirling behind them, touching off rotten wood, draperies, and beds, even carrying whole shovels of red embers inside the manor houses.

It looked as if Dick must surely go out of his mind. He screamed like a mother whose babe is roasted. When the first tall flames waved upward through the openings of the great hall, he ran halfway in with arms extended, as if to choke them out with his bare hands. Then he scurried hither and thither, trying to stop folk from taking away pieces of the bonfire, trying to stop their wild incendiary gambol round the buildings, cursing, imploring till he was hoarse. But the Priest's devilish, "Ho! Ho!" remained constantly audible, like a fanfare.

Joan Oxerd tried to shift her son away from the timbered porch. He was heavy. He groaned heartrendingly when with clenched teeth she hardened herself to tug at him, so that after all she found it impossible to persevere. The heat was growing. She called for help to carry her son to safety. Name after name did she call, in mounting desperation, as those that owned them swept past with yet more flares and brands. Not one so much as looked round at her. The tears ran down into her open, toothless mouth; she wrung her spindly hands and ran back and forth, to left and to right, only a few paces, for she could not stand still and dared not leave Frank. Her own husband and Frank's father neither heard nor saw nor thought of them.

Prior Carlos had rallied once more to stop this new outrage, with no more success than Dick. He stood by, a weary, weary old man who could not understand, in natural terms, what enabled them still to go on as they were. The people, shouting and leaping and glorying in destruction, without rest or any more solid sustenance than an occasional drink of water from the well. Water. He roused his friars and made for the kitchen, where the three of them gathered up buckets and soot-covered pots and pans, and stumbled to fill them at the well, and went on running backward and forward, uselessly throwing water on the steaming walls. Then at last did they attract attention: people laughed at them.

Then the Franciscans grew aware that the old chapel had caught fire, and they turned and ran to save the rood and sacred vessels. Herein they failed also. The rood was already burning, a black, diminishing skeleton cross, but thickened and seeming to twist where one knew the Saviour's figure hung, against a crackling, cruciform glare. The altar and Widowson chest were shut off by an unbroken screen of flame. One friar was struck by a falling quoin. Without a sound he sank sideways, so that the flames closed over him. It was all the other two could do to get out again, scorched, blinded, and coughing, with little fingers of fire scrabbling all over their gowns. Again some of the people paused, to help them quench these.

And as we paused, we began to think. And as soon as we allowed ourselves consciousness, we began to become frightened. It transpired that some of our number were missing and not to be found among the dead and disabled. They would not have run off. They must have got lost, with their torches, in the maze of the older buildings, whence also black and slate-blue smoke was pouring in thick, opaque coils that had a livid yellow sheen across their roots, most ugly to see against the sunlight. Where the fires had had longer to mature, the sky looked as though the sun were already setting again. The red haze was alive with rotating black smuts. Everyone was coughing, all eyes smarted and overflowed. One's hair began to flutter, one's clothes to smell baked and singed. The flames grew higher than the lookout tower, and the heat became unbearable. God, God, we thought, only then not before: what must it be like *inside?* There was flesh and blood like ours trapped in fiery furnace. They did not sing, or try to, as the hermit had. Perhaps it was only that naught could be heard above the voice of the fire. But then we heard, no less unbearably, the screams of forgotten horses and cattle. Not a few of us vomited, wishing to die. There was a reverberating crash as some invisible building fell in and a huge sheaf of smoke and sparks gushed up high above the fire peaks. Streams, armies, peoples of rats fled starwise from the burning as if we stood not in their way—so that *we* yielded.

Nay, Joan and Frank were not forgotten. Luke had seen them, under the oaken lintel festooned with winking chains of flame pennants. Luke took hold of Frank under the arms and Joan took his feet, and thus they shifted him. Mercifully Frank was short and slight. All the same the going was very slow, the more as the poor young man moaned most dreadfully, jolted in all his maltreated body.

Slowly, giving the buildings a wide berth, they rounded the last corner out into the broad court that extended all the way to the gatehouse and outer walls. All the people were there, dazed and sickened. Prior Carlos, no longer a gray friar but a black, stood on the broken wall, where tumbled stones made a stepped mound. Now he could make himself heard; no one was talking. But his cracked and tired voice did not carry far. Moreover, we were all listening to voices inside us.

When folk saw Luke and Joan with the man whom we had been avenging all night and all day, there was general movement toward them. Franklin the elder won the race by many heads. But the victim could not yet be laid down. The ground was littered with the slain, and dismembered fragments and jelled blood, and stained, discarded weapons. Luke said something to Joan and Franklin, and they followed as he backed and swerved sideways.

The Prior saw it first and gave a loud cry.

Luke's back was one smoldering mass, with charred, glow-rimmed holes eating into the layer of clothes reduced to coal. The worst thing was to see that the man himself had no inkling of this.

For a moment everyone lost the power of speech. Then someone dashed at Luke with a steel cap dipped in the horse trough, and threw the water over his back. It sizzled so that we all began to retch again, and small jets of white steam flew up curling.

"What is it? What is the matter?" Luke tried to look over his shoulder. "Here, Franklin, you take him. Let me get my hands free."

"Behold what the Lord God hath done!" intoned the Prior—and you may be sure every syllable of his went straight to our hearts now. "Behold the miracle, the miracle of His wrath! Lo, and He took one and singled him out in the sight of the people, one man whose overweening pride peculiarly fitted him to be the scapegoat, and the ire of the Lord fell into his flesh like lightning. Behold and see, he burns and feeleth it not. See the snowy ulcers where his shirt is torn open. See his swollen features, rigid as those of a waterspout. See his ears, thick and waxen as a boiled pig's—see how he is become a leper for his sins and yours! As this man's body, so are all your souls—leprous! leprous! Fall upon your faces, then, and beat your breasts and cry, 'Unclean!'"

Many of us did fall on our faces. The rebellion was over in the Old Town of Bedesford, defeated in victory.

"Let go! Let go of my son!" Joan shrieked. "Oh, I *pray* you, Master Luke, let go my poor son!"

The rest of us backed right away until, against the battered wall, we could go no farther, although none but the three Oxerds had been close enough to Luke to fear contamination.

Ay, we know it now, as you do. It was not thus at one stroke that the worst sickness had fallen upon the foremost man of our town. But at the time we knew it not. We had seen so little of him in the last few years, and during the last twenty-four hours we had had other things to do than take a good look at one another. It ofttimes happens that you *suddenly* see what is *suddenly* pointed out to you. Thus we saw all at once that beyond the shadow of doubt Luke was a leper. And, accustomed as we were to miracles in Bedesford, we never thought but that the Prior was God's true interpreter.

CHAPTER 4

BATTLE'S END

LORD JEROME HAD set such a pace that he had lost two horses on the road from Cloudesley to St. Hand's, and three henchmen: one had broken an arm when his mount fell on top of him, and someone had to stay with him until help might be sent; and the third was too burly a man to ride pillion. The others had begun by pitying the big man who was left to make his lone way after them on foot. Before they reached their goal, they envied him. They were ready to drop from the saddle and go to sleep as they struck ground. Lord Jerome had driven them on with oaths and gibes, telling them many times that he was nigh twice the age of the oldest among them. But they had not the same surpassing rage coursing through their veins like wine or elixir.

Like their master, however, they were enraged by their reception at the monastery. The porridge, to which the cooks had hurriedly added, was at once thin and lumpy, burned and half raw, while the insipid ale and stale whey were insult upon injury. Cursing, they had followed Lord Jerome's lead and emptied their iron ration of sack on an all but empty stomach. Drowsiness fled before that curious superawakeness which sometimes comes of a light head. A vying garrulity went with it, and soon they had talked and drunk themselves into a boundless truculence, such as the Bishop would have welcomed in them earlier. We are speaking, you must understand, not of them that he forthwith took with him to St. Hand's, but of the majority, who were to sit and await further orders. For two or three of these that was more than they could endure. They started splashing the despised ale over the walls, emptied the whey butt and slid, like children in winter, over the inundated tiles, threw the pewter ale jugs out the window and the wooden bowls on the fire, and bombarded their comrades, who sought to quiet them, with the porridge. Then they upset the benches so that whosoever had remained sitting rolled in the mess on the floor, and with denunciations of the timid presently stormed out. On the way to the Wasteside one of them fell over his own feet and immediately started snoring; so only two of them were left.

Howbeit this pair did a sufficiency of damage. The Bishop had told his men how he meant to have order restored and his edicts enforced as soon as might be, and they desired to do it now.

They were sobered a little when they heard the bell ring at the cathedral for Corpus Christi. And after the alarm signal had been rung for some time, it began to penetrate their skulls that something was perhaps amiss. Thereupon they turned and went straight back.

When Edwin and the others reached the huts, they could not be blamed for thinking an army had passed. Particularly at the outskirts of the New Town, they were met by women wailing under roofs that hung crooked and partially torn down, and before doors forced from the hinges and split into their component planks. Garden plots had been trampled flat, chaff and floor strew dragged out-of-doors and split, all over the paths; there were fruit trees despoiled and cut down, bedding and other household gear pulled out into the mud, with milk poured out and eggs trodden into it. One cow and some goats had been mutilated, and a pig killed and mangled beyond recovery for food. And everywhere there were fragments of the shattered, rude, small private millstones, lying amid the grain scattered round and about. The loose fowls and beasts were feeding on it, jostling the women and children who tried on their hands and knees to salvage some from between geese and hens and rooting pigs.

Edwin's hut was farther up the slope. Plodding on as fast as his legs and lungs would let him, he began to hope that perhaps the invaders had not got as far as this. There was increasingly less evidence of the raid. From a distance his dwelling looked no more unkempt than usual. There was no one to be seen outside the door. "Jeanne! Jeanne!" he called. A woman came out, but it was not Jeanne. She was wringing her hands, with smears of blood up to the bared elbows, her face damp with tears and sweat.

"God be thanked that you have come, Edwin. Come in quickly now to your wife. My son has run to the hospital to try and get a priest to her. Your little boys are next door at my house. I must go back and see what all those children are doing. Make haste. Go in to your wife's bedside."

Without so much as a word of thanks Edwin ducked through under the lintel. The hut was in disorder right enough, but had he looked he would have seen their little set of millstones perfectly intact. Jeanne lay on the bed with the clothes heaped over her anyhow. Jeanne on the bed —blood—hurry—a priest: into Edwin's mind there flashed the horrible old story of the death of Little Lady Agnes. Older women than that child had been known to die of rape. Thus, then, the drunken soldiers had brought his Jeanne to her death. On seeing him she looked so glad that he could have cried out with the pain of it. She bade him come to her, quickly.

"What have they done to you, my poor sweetheart and beloved," he said, over and over. "Do not talk of dying, my Jeanne. Now I am here. Edwin is with you. I will make you well."

At last she understood what he thought had happened to her. To his amazement she laughed; but it hurt her and she clutched her middle. "Edwin, as long as we have known each other, you have let me see you deemed me childish of wit. But it is you has less wit than a child. Have you no power of reckoning, have you no eyes to see? Look at me, man! Reckon up my age. I lack but three years to the half hundred. Yes, I counted them up, my years, full often these last few days, therefore have I them so pat. And to look at me most men would guess I had passed the threescore. Look at me, look at me, for once! Much gold would you need to offer the most godless soldier before you could get him to outrage me. We have spent nearly the whole of our lives together, and I know you have not looked at me, not looked to *see,* ever since you became my husband."

"If you mean that for me you have always been the fairest of the fair—if it is that you complain of—"

"Ay, it *is* that!" Jeanne cried so that again she winced, but she would not be silenced. "And most bitterly do I complain of it! How would you like it if one told you that to him you had always seemed the tallest of men. I am *not* fair, Edwin my husband, it is years since I had more than two front teeth, since my hair was long and thick, since it had any color. Of the rest I will not speak. You were never at any pains to hide from me that you thought my eyes stupid for being unable to read and understand your works—that is the reason, I know, why you have ever regarded me as a child in mind. But to me it seems worse, to be as you are. To see things only as they are *not,* that you may live in your craftsman's world alone, turned away from the real world around you. You have not lived *with* me—you have long forgotten, long ceased to think of me— for all that you were ever good and faithful. Often have I envied other women their worse husbands! For at least they bear their burdens together."

"I do not think I understand, my Jeanne," said Edwin, but he was lying. "None can say we have lacked troubles in our life together."

Jeanne looked him straight in the eye. "You talk of those troubles that might have been anybody's—nay, that *were* everybody's at the same time. Poverty, you mean, and the deaths of our children. Your real burden, your very own, you have always kept to yourself. You would never let me share it. You tried to deny it before me as if I too were only a stranger."

"What are you talking about? Rest still, you are tiring yourself, I can see—"

"It is no fault of mine if I know not what I am talking about. It has been your secret, that burden of yours. Ay, and your pride, Edwin. You did what you could to keep it from me, and then you looked askance at me because I could not guess! Every now and then you threw out little hints and dark sayings and watched me from the corner of your eye to see what I would make of them. All I could make out is that you *have* a burden. You saw to that. And when you had satisfied yourself that it was no clearer to me than that—then you smiled. You smiled at me that was too childish and dull to follow you through a door you kept locked and barred."

"The load was mine to carry alone. What manner of man would I be, to shift the weight on to my wife's shoulder—her whom I promised God to cherish and protect?"

"Ay, this is not the first time you have hinted, in your dark sayings, that in some wise the burden has to do with me, that you first took it up for my sake or because of me. That was far worse than letting me share what you had to bear, for you condemned me instead to bearing burden of my own unaided. I have borne it as long as I could. Either it is that, a poor, harassed woman, I am the weaker of us two! or else—or else, my Edwin, your burden cannot have been as heavy as mine! Will you not tell me, now that I am dying, what it is that I have done, or that you think I did, for which we were punished in our children?"

"Punished in our children?" Edwin repeated, sincerely uncomprehending.

"Do not fob me off with pretense any more, Edwin, lest I find no peace even in my grave. None of the children I bore you has been or done what you wished. You have never forgiven our Alfred for that he did not turn his heart and hand to building work. And our other sons you never loved as you did him from the start, because they never even gave you cause to hope that they desired to be building masters. In our first years together I went on rejoicing, whenever I knew I was to bear another child, in spite of the fears that never left me, on account of the way it went with our first-born. But later on, Edwin, I lost the strength rightly to rejoice. I lost heart, Edwin, since it was clear I could not bear you children to your liking."

"Oh, Jeanne!" Edwin groaned. "As I live—as I hope to be saved yet —it never entered my heart to blame *you!*"

"Then it *is* true, and none of them fulfilled your hopes! Why, Edwin, why? What son could have achieved more than our Alfred? Wherein can he have failed? He is a great lord and a great craftsman, and as great in goodness of heart and deed! He knows it too, just as I do. I mind I asked him, long ago, how it could be he was not bashful and tongue tied, mingling with the great ones. He smiled—a sad smile, I deemed it. He said he owed that to you, for that in your eyes he had never done rightly well. Since his father did not think it such a great thing for Alfred to have become our Abbot, or that the work of his once-crippled hand should be famous even in Italy—his success could be no very great thing to himself. Thus, he said, he had no trepidations in being great—seeing that sort of greatness does not count with you, and therefore cannot count for himself. I have not told it well, but maybe I have given you the drift of it. Our other children, too, Edwin. They have all been dear, good children, well favored one and all, and not ungifted. One of them even carries on the age-old Widowson craft. Why would you not be satisfied?"

"I had some foolish thought," Edwin whispered, hiding his face from her, "that if one of the sons whom I gave to God just as He gave them to me—if one of them raised Him up a house, it might be reckoned as intercession for me."

"But you are all of you alike helping raise up St. Hand's," Jeanne said in wonder.

"You know not how grievously I have sinned. No one knows it. The greater the sin, the greater, surely, must be the work of atonement? Jeanne? Jeanne, what are you thinking?"

Jeanne had been lying back, her blue eyelids closed. Without opening them, she weakly shook her head so that the straw rustled. "I know not. Now my thoughts no longer let me catch them. Forgive me, my dear husband. Now after all it seems to me I am no less childish than you have thought me, and that I was wrong to accuse you—accuse you. Forgive me for speaking to you as I did—when I should be grateful that I can have you beside me while I die. And I have never loved you less than when we first came together, never, never, and I know you too have gone on loving me. I thought I could do what Jane used to. I made stealthy inquiry as to how she would set to work. But—"

Edwin harshly asked her what she meant, and gradually got it out of her. She had found that, all unexpectedly, so late in life, she was once more with child, and the Fiend had persuaded her that she could not bear it. She could not start all over again with new babes—particularly as they would not give Edwin what, unfathomably, he wanted. So she had tried to make away with the unborn. Ay, the day before yesterday it had started. Until today it had overcome her so that she had to get help.

Edwin took a hold on himself and did what he could to ease her. But he soon saw that in truth there was not a great deal he could do. They were both too wise in matters of childbirth for him to dare contradict her. When a woman bled like this, there was no saving her, without a miracle.

Edwin knew there would be no miracle. If only the priest would come! He kept on pausing in his ministrations to go to the door and look out. He did not know whether to tell her, and rob her dying hour of its pale, feeble peace, or whether to leave her in unrepentant ignorance. She did not seem to realize what she had done and how it would be regarded in Heaven. Her death would be accounted suicide, on the top of child murder. Without absolution she was condemned to Hell everlastingly. For this reason he finally kept silent about it. If God denied her a priest, time enough for her to find out when she was in Hell.

This was a test. If Jeanne could be shriven, it meant that God was relenting and for the first time striking at Edwin himself. He would be deprived of Jeanne, but with Jeanne it would be well. It would be a sign that God meant after all to let him expiate for his sin and crime, that salvation, however distant, was yet to come within his reach someday. Whereas if Jeanne were damned. . . .

Great as the sin had been when he committed it, enormous as it had grown with all the times he had gone to communion, it was now increased to such dimensions as the thought of man could not even grasp. For he had committed it so that he might be her guardian and protector. Her end proved how totally he had failed her. O Lord God, he who had not addressed the Deity for thirty years prayed, it is enough, more than enough to take her from me. Make your peace with this innocent whom *I* have brought to this, and I promise I will not ask to be saved, myself, any more.

He was at the door again. "Edwin," Jeanne's voice came plaintively. "Need you be so anxious, is my sin so great, that you cannot let me die

with my hand in yours?" He came back at once and squatted beside
her again and took her hand in his and looked into her eyes. "Edwin!"
she said with a little smile, giving his hand the faintest shake. "I gave
birth to the best man ever bred in Bedesford and the best of good, holy
monks, whose intercession has benefited every soul in this parish. Do
you not think that will weigh in my favor? And he will pray and say
Mass for me, his mother, so long as he lives. We know that. You need
not fear for me so greatly. I shall be out of purgatory in no time, you
will see." Edwin laid his face on her hand and kissed it—that for a little
he might not have to look at her.

She had not thought beyond purgatory, had she? As for the credit
she took in her Abbot son—ah, God had at least granted her one mercy,
she had not heard what had befallen at the Cathedral. For Edwin there
could be no doubt that the clash between the Bishop's sacrosanct person
and his people must be Alfred's fault, the fault of misrule with which
the Bishop had reproached him. Was not Alfred Edwin's son, and so
did it not stand to reason that in causing Alfred to become Abbot God
had pursued His same old punitive design? Besides, Alfred was probably dead, cut off in sacrilegious wrath.

Raising his head again, he surprised a watchful frown on Jeanne's
wrinkled forehead. "Edwin," she began almost playfully, but was in
mortal earnest before she had done. "You think it is Hell for me, do
you, my Edwin? I should not mind burning unredeemed in all eternity, if only I might look forward to your joining me. So you see, I
know your love is better than mine. You would never ask such a thing
of me, but I am not strong enough not to ask it. If it is so, that I must go
to Hell, promise that you will come after me, Edwin. If you love me
truly, Edwin, then you would not be happy in Heaven without me in
any case. I know I had rather be in Hell with you, than in Heaven
without you."

Edwin promised her, gladly, and also sadly, for he knew his destination without need to promise.

At the cathedral the Abbot had given up trying to make himself
heard. His head had cleared. He made a movement to take off his stiff
vestments, but thought better of it. It was necessary that he should
catch the eye and convey his identity at a distance. He placed the crucifix safely in a corner on the floor, and began to ascend the scaffolding.

He had not climbed anything more infirm and irregular than a ladder
since he had been a bird scarer. It gave his hands a certain joy to clasp

raw splintery wood and seek out their next point of grasp unaided by intended railings. He kicked off his sandals before he had gone many yards, for his soles and toes, too, had to recapture an old, sentient agility. The heavy gold-embroidered garments hung steeply down behind, pulling at him. Every now and then his feet were snared in a fold. He trod on the stole, which, scorching the skin off the back of his neck, was pulled away and fell. Now and again he gazed down between his flexed arms and knees, savoring the sense of increasing height and space.

Presently he ceased to enjoy his boyish pride and prowess. He hung, engrossed in looking at certain lines and angles which surely were not as they should be—even if he discounted any distortion due to his unwonted view.

He had nearly reached the gangway round the base of the open tower, level with the vaults of nave and transepts. He was alone in these heights, face to face with stone ribs that he had been accustomed to think almost fragile, they looked so graceful, and here now they were so solid as almost to seem uncouth. Struts and planks that looked like threads and slender stalks from below did not even vibrate to his weight and movement, for all their precarious extensions. He could no longer distinguish the shadows of the vaulting, being swallowed up in their somberness. But, feeling himself to be so small that it astonished him, he felt only an access of greater courage. The ant at the breast of a mighty oak cannot but trust in its security.

He climbed down again, as far as the clerestory. A structure of poles and runways that had used to be the workmen's path from the embrasure to the tower had been disarranged, so that he had to risk a jump, unless he wanted to go right down to the ground. Only for an instant his daring wavered. A few feet to the left of him hung the plumb line which one of the workmen had so gleefully wielded. It seemed to hang in contradiction of its whole nature and purpose: aslant, stiffly, monstrously aslant, thus for the first time producing in Alfred the tingling sensation of falling. But he overcame it, and landed safely.

He leaned over the balustrade, shouting, and the echoes lent him most rousing aid. The clash of weapons stopped and everybody gazed up. The pale faces looked like leaves turned over by a wind. A few fell on their knees. "The Lord Abbot! He hath risen from the dead!" But Alfred felt certain that they said this because, like himself, they wished to end the fight. The rest, on both sides, likewise guessed his intention, and opposed it with confused cries before he had a chance to express it.

However, only voices were raised. Once the sword arms had been made
to pause, their impetus would not so easily be recaptured.

The din abated. Alfred hollowed his hands before his mouth. Once
he was started, curiosity maintained silence for him.

"I will not enter into any dispute now. There is no time, hear me, you
people, all of you, *there is no time!* Stop, I say stop accusing each the
other and excusing himself. There can be naught for anyone down there
to say—that have been shedding Christian blood in God's consecrated
House. Ay, and consecrated priests among you! Think you His forbearance without end? Look—look whither I am pointing! I am no
building master. Most of you down there know more about building
than I. Follow the timber standards upward with your eyes—there, on
the north side, where the tower wall begins—does the looming stone
look perpendicular to you? To me it does not." Already the crowd immediately under it was thinning. The Abbot began to move sideways
toward the west. "Away! Away! Retreat while yet you may to safety!
Throw down your blasphemous arms, and fly!"

There is no telling whether Alfred really thought the tower might
fall down at any moment, or whether he but deemed the suggestion a
good ruse. Nor can we say how many of us then believed the one or
the other. But do you try it sometime: go and stand, *without* having
committed any special misdeed, right under a great lofty tower, and
but tell yourself that there always is a possibility of its collapse. We dare
swear you will not stay there long. How many notable cathedrals can
you call to mind whose central towers did not some time fall—not once,
not twice, but half a dozen times? Even without such a threatening
departure from the vertical as Alfred could point to, we think—we
know, we would have taken fright. Picture yourself gazing, gazing,
with your head thrown right back between the shoulders, up into a
vast funnel of perspectives, sunlight glittering into your eyes and its
companion shadows seeming to get into them like smuts or moths. Of
itself your vision begins to weave and wheel in circles, incline, close in.
Add to that a slayer's and blasphemer's conscience and the smell of
blood and the lingering tang of sparks struck from cold iron—ah, not a
few *ran,* away from the central crossing! Again there was a ringing of
swords and tools—but it was the flags resounded under their discard-
ment. Instinctively opponents had disentangled and were retreating in
different directions.

The Bishop not only stayed, but deliberately stepped farther into the
center. He shook his blade, now at the Abbot, now at his men, now at

the people, nearly rending himself asunder in abusing them all. Howbeit you could not hear much. The echo that had helped the Abbot's down-trained voice rebuffed upward cries. But something that he shouted reached his henchmen, "Would you leave behind the wounded? Even if your craven hearts accept without test this hell-priest's trickery. Would you leave your wounded comrades to be crushed? Oh, shame, shame, and my potent curse upon you—!"

Some were shamed, and started forward.

Jeanne was dead. No priest had come. Numb and tired out, Edwin stepped out of his doorway for a breath of fresh air. Vacantly staring, he noted that the wind had changed, as it did out here so often, at the same time as it had increased in force. It was blowing north from the Ridge. He went on staring nowhere in particular, for that his eyes burned unbearably when he shut them. Suddenly he saw a sight which he did not believe. The massive great stump of Jacob's tower, for so long an easterly landmark, crumpled and disappeared. There was no sound. An instant later a tremor came through the ground beneath his feet, and faded away.

But the crash was heard at the manor, above the roaring of the flames and the tolling of "What have we done?" within our breasts.

CHAPTER 5

THE SCAPEGOATS

In Fear Is a dull amity of the flesh, forgetful alike of rancor and affections. There is no living calmly in spaciousness without a comfortable faith in the morrow. Bedesford town was become too big for those that must wait news from the battleground. They had all flocked together at Luke's house, the only one with stone walls all around it. There they stood and sat and rubbed shoulders, and looked and listened not to one another, their eyes and ears strained in unison, but apart.

As more and more kept on coming, Elizabeth tried to make room, begging them to take turns, resting indoors. But although the house

was ample and inviting, few could bear to stay long within, feeling
shut off, and preferring the overcrowded courtyard. Elizabeth could not
even keep her own family and serving folk inside. Little Luke was also
in the throng, brought hither by his foster mother and his uncle. The
latter kept on mumbling, unheeded, about his aches. He alone had gone
home when the attack began, bent double by what he said were colic
pains. By this time it appeared he had pains everywhere.

Quite late in the day—after the crash that had dried the last spring
of courage in even the most sanguine breast—Elizabeth's mother and
Jaffy Widowson arrived with Meg and Geoffrey in the Trefeller wagon.
He had found them at Cloudesley-St.-Veron's—so he told Isabella, as he
gave the old woman into her granddaughter's charge—whither he had
been sent with letters from Damesbury cloisters and from Thirchester,
and she had insisted that he take her home. Juliana's head was nodding
and her lips dribbled, but both her eyes again worked together. She hastened as for refuge into Isabella's arms. Isabella took her along through
the crowds in search of Elizabeth. The Mistress patted her mother's head
in almost absent fashion, preoccupied by what she saw in her own
daughter's face.

"You must try and cease from thinking about Richard, love," she
said gently. "Put your grandmother to bed and tend her."

Isabella willingly put her arm round Juliana again, with a deliberate,
protective tenderness which in truth must have cost her great conscious
effort. Yet she could not forbear from asking, "How can I? Can you
keep from thinking about father?"

"Every now and then I can," Elizabeth answered with a sigh and a
gesture round. Isabella gave her mother a look of earnest contrition,
squared her shoulders, and turned the old woman toward the house.

Elizabeth raised herself on tiptoe and beckoned to one of her maids
whom she spied, elbowing herself across the yard, obviously looking for
the Mistress. "Here I am, Madge. Come to the kitchen with me." After
a closer look at the girl, who had not answered, she added, "No, send
me one of the others. You need to rest."

"Mistress," the girl stammered. She was as blanched as Isabella, and
her teeth were chattering. "The Master is home. He wants you to go
and have a word with him in private. He is waiting in the little shed
by the old flax plot. You are not to let anyone know. I am not to tell
anyone else, either. He said—bring medicines. Oh, Mistress—" and she
fell to weeping with uncontrollable cries and, shaking all over, would
have sunk to the ground had not Elizabeth helped her over to the wall,

sat her down against it with her head between her knees and the Mistress's cold hand on the back of her neck. People hardly glanced up. In more than twenty-four hours' waiting this was not the first occurrence of its kind. When the cries ebbed to a shuddering whimper, Elizabeth left the girl and hurried into the house.

Having gone up to the bedchamber and collecting what she needed, she stole out by a back door. Although she had waited for this many years, she did not find that waiting had fortified her.

The door of the old shed stood half open. At her approach it moved till only just ajar.

"Luke!"

"Come a little closer so I need not shout—but not too close. There, stop where you are now. Do you not hear me? Stay where you are, I tell you—"

But she went on and, leaning her whole weight against the door, tried to force it open. His voice, when again he cried out for her to stop, was such that she desisted, waiting until he himself had told her that he had learned he was a leper.

"Then you may safely let me in after all," she said. "It is a long time since I knew this, and slept in your arms just the same."

Thinking, because of her calm voice, that either he or she had gone mad, Luke made her repeat it. "Oh, Luke," she said, less calmly, "let me in, and do not flee from me now that you can comfort me for all the long years that I bore this knowledge quite alone. When all the time I had to scheme and watch, to keep you from finding out, and keep you apart from the rest of the world."

The door swung open, and Luke stood facing her, with hanging arms and a curious, peering look, as though to see in his wife's eyes a sudden, terrible change in himself. These mirrors failed him. "My Luke," she said, with tears in her eyes at the very sameness of his appearance, though dirty, soot-stained, and in rags, and his appalled, gingerly stance. He pointed at his breast, made as to touch his ears, then shrinking from contact with himself.

"Is that—" he asked haltingly, "is that what it was all along, that was wrong with me? And you say you read the signs?"

She nodded. "Now, what did you tell Madge? She was badly frightened. Does anybody else know? How came you to find out?" She spoke resolutely, and drew him down to sit with her on a heap of old sacks. "We have not much time to think out what to do." She stopped, for she had seen his back: "Turn a little more," she said in a gruff, low voice.

"I must have light to see. Does this hurt? This? No? Good, that makes it easier. Keep still." She went on working in silence. He too held his peace. The burns looked much worse than they were, because of the charred fur, cloth, and leather, which had in fact protected the man. Finally she asked, "This is how you found out?"

"Yes, and others found out before me. It was shouted from the house-tops well and truly." He told her, and added, "But now, my wife, must tell me why you deceived me and disregarded the commandments of God and the Church, and suffered me to imperil everyone—yourself and our children before any. It was not—not honorable. You are laughing!"

"I could not help it. It was your talking of honor. I was not thinking much on honor, in these years, my Luke! And if you think back, you will see that I did all I could to keep the children and everyone else out of your way."

She felt his arm grow rigid under her hand. "Was that why—?" he blurted, and stopped.

"No. I did not pretend to love you so as to protect our children. If you but think for a moment, you will see there had been easier ways. I need not have schemed to keep you. Why did I 'deceive' you? I knew this had come upon us, not because God hated you, but Jane did. She had cursed you, she told me so herself, that last time I went to her. Oh, that was not the least of it—waiting and watching for her curse to declare itself! For she did not tell me what it was to be. See you not? It is a *false* leprosy that fell on you, because Jane conjured it. But why should I make long apology? Had I not every right to keep you with me and among the living if I could?"

Luke could think of many arguments against, but what was the use of settling to a nicety the principle of what was past?

"Now, Luke, it is for us to put our heads together and devise a way out. You know not what it means to me to be talking about it, to have someone to help *me* plan! Two heads are better than one, even if yours were not the sharpest in the land. There always is a way, we need but find it. So let us think."

"Elizabeth, sweetheart. There is no way out of this."

She was silent. He got up and moved away, "We may as well make a start. Though God be praised, that He did not allow you to take any harm up till now, there is no sense in tempting Providence at the last moment. For it seems to me, now that I myself know, the danger of me may well be stronger than it was before in my ignorance. If that sounds witless to you, humor me still." He paused, to let her understand, without having to say it, that he must now be regarded as a man upon his deathbed. Her head sank still lower on to her breast, but she made no sound. "I shall live here for the next few days, and you must have food and drink placed no nearer than that stone over there. And send some blankets. My back? You have seen to it once. It will heal. And if not— Ay, send some blankets for me, too. When I am gone, you must promise to have this hut burned to the ground. You must not call me cruel, for speaking of all this now. There is a great deal must be said. Listen carefully. For you and the children, Elizabeth, this has happened for the best—in the best way, if it had to happen. The battle is over, and our side has lost. Whatever form retribution may take, at least my heirs are safe in the possession of my goods—for that as soon as my condition was discovered, I became as a dead man legally, and my property passed unto them. There may be attempts at confiscating it nevertheless, but you stand a good chance in contesting them. At all events you should be able to retain a fair portion."

Elizabeth shook her head. "I verily believe you are enjoying this."

"Enjoying?" Luke's voice rose, as much as to say that even if he were, she ought not to begrudge him any enjoyment. Then he smiled, "And why not? I shall not have many more opportunities to exercise my worldly wit. Now, at this moment, you think you would not care if our children were beggared. Once you had to watch them starve, you would care."

"Maybe so." Elizabeth spoke as though dispassionately. "It is true, I shall have little heart to fight for possessions which, as you yourself say, we should certainly forfeit were we able to keep you with us. You talk of starving. People do not starve to death. Unless there be famine. And then we should not be able to eat your gold and cloth, either."

"There are many stations of wretchedness between hunger and death from starvation. You would not like to see your children come to live like rats—watching them fight the swine in the mire for their meals, having no clothes to put on their backs, and no fires to keep them warm."

"You know well it would never come to that. There is my mother. And after all, we are kin to the Cinqmorts."

"I did not spare myself in building up what we have. And I did not work so that my wife and children should one day be paupers or pensioners, or cuckoo carrion crows. I expect you to scheme and strive and fight your hardest. I believe you will sorrow for me. I believe that you will miss me. How much better, then, to have no time to think on it! I shall not be so lucky, myself."

"One thing you must do for me," Elizabeth said in the same, quiet tones as before. "You must not reckon your fate worse than mine. It will be worst for me. It is ever worse for the mourners. And you will not be really dead. *I* had rather be dead and in purgatory, Luke, than face what is to come."

"Now it is time for you to go back," Luke said sometime after. "People will be coming back from the manor, with all the tidings. Be hostess to them still, all of them. They will need it."

Elizabeth went obediently.

She also did not look very different from what she had, an hour or two before.

At the cathedral the silence prickled in Alfred's ears, so that from time to time he shook his head. The air was swarming with particles and laden with a strong smell of dust that grated in his nostrils and seemed to collect, befogging, behind his forehead. He was not aware of wringing his hands under cover of the wide sleeves wherein he thought them quietly confined. It was night again. He was still in his vestments. Dimmed by the dust, they still glittered. The moonlight had full ingress where previously the tower had dammed it, and blatantly it made the most of the great screes of heaped stone all about the central crossing. At some points it was impossible to skirt the ruin, and the Abbot had to climb across on hands and knees, which were soon scratched raw. He welcomed their smarting, as it helped him pierce through the stupor of singing silence and congested dust in his head.

Nay, the cathedral was not empty, nor was he alone; it was but that he was the only living soul in it tonight. He was coming to where bodies lay uncovered, having died beyond the reach of the tower avalanche. "Who are you, friend?" he asked, bending over one.

There on his back was Matthew Feathers, with flexed legs looking insubstantial, and a mass of entrails that had slid out of him: but at least even the blood had no color in the night. Not far from him was Alfred's brother Jack, less than twenty years old, his soft-bearded face faded into expressionlessness. Two monks lay crumpled together, their robes spread wet about them, so stiffly interlocked that when Alfred sought to turn one over, the other body came with the first. Here was a Newcome, there a Franklin, one of the Bishop's henchmen and one of the monastery's; and some whom Alfred had no means of recognizing. There was no living wounded.

"Can no one answer me? Was Bishop Jerome right? Did I pave the way for this in all the time I governed here? Am I a murderer and, worse, sneaking murderer by proxy? Where does God's will begin, where does it end, when we have to make our decisions? If He were sole, true, heartless author of our errors, why should He have placed that tireless voice of conscience in our breasts? Then had there been no need for commandments; then beatitude and damnation, both, were frightful arbitrariness. Good and virtue would be vaporous figments, evil the only ruling fundamental truth. Now do I begin to understand in what beliefs Jane worked out her life. No, no. Better to believe that I have sinned. So trying to do right is also self-indulgence? Yes, when the result is this. I own my sin. Yet do I rightly *know* it? Let it suffice that I will own it. Oh, ay—and it is ever hard to keep from also loving that which one is owning. There is a duty for me somewhere. But where? What is it? I do not know that either."

His back was to the mounds of broken stone. Straight ahead opened the aperture of the western portals, clean cut between the jutting bases of future twin towers. Here there was nothing to show that St. Hand's had suffered any injury. He drew level with the enclosures of the building masters, untidily screened with hides and stakes, and the workshops, merely roped off, belonging to Edwin and Brother Laurentius.

The Abbot slipped through under a rope into his father's bay, for the solace of that disorder which he loved, of benches and tools, rude shelves and dirty scrolls, and, above all, stone refuse. He stooped for a chip on the ground that caught the pale light. It was not quite as big as his thumb. No ordinary chip, but a bird's wing, carved perfectly and tenderly. For some reason Edwin had held it unworthy of its place at the foot of his statue of St. Francis. It could not have been struck off by accident. The raw surface at the shoulder end was too broad to have broken away under anything but repeated and deliberate strokes. Ah, such was litter here. There were gems underfoot, that only the supreme unselfishness of the craftsman could persuade a man to discard—sweepings more precious than pearls and rubies, because of their birth at the human hand.

Alfred held his breath. For once the truth had escaped its guard. He felt greater love, and greater awe before the works of man than before those of God's creation, just as he had placed the welfare of men's bodies before that of their souls.

He could atone for his sins by going away. Yes, that was what he must do. Here, where his heart was tied to so much stone, he could never be sure that it repented sincerely—since detachment is half the nature of sincerity.

But, to exaggerate one's fault is the worst falseness embracing an untrue charge so as to mask, excuse, and in the end deny the real crime. Thus even humility and self-distrust have their place in the Devil's arsenal. It was a lie of Devil's prompting, that he did not value souls— for did he not love men? "Ay, more than I love Christ!" There it was again, that perilous hypocrisy of exaggeration. Wait, though—perhaps it *would* be true to say that he bore human beings a more devoted kind of love? For they needed it so much more. And was that wrong, necessarily? Was it not, rather, truly following in the footsteps of the Saviour? "Here am I back where I started. Clement, who makes no bones about loving men the most, ever held that I loved them too well—in the material sense. Brother Laurentius, too. No. *He* said it is myself I love. That I seek to deal by men justly and kindly and spare myself pain. How can I know? How am I to get my bearings in this ambush-ridden wilderness of my soul? Is it in action, in the very wish to act, that I err?"

A little way on, the friar's bay was a fantastic orchard of trial arches, waist-high pattern blocks for springers and vault ribbage, all standing upright, curving various ways, spaced like trees. "Where are you, Brother Laurentius? Or have they removed you alone?" At length he came upon the corpse he looked for. Brother Laurentius had been crushed to death between the door, tall as a house, of seasoned ship's oak, bound and thickly studded with iron, and the wall, where three oblong stone panels, already in position though wanting the last polish, framed an offertory niche. Alfred had been told of his death; now he saw it illustrated.

Brother Laurentius had lived up to the logical conclusion of his flight from human beings. He had not budged when the door swung back on him. He had refused to take cognizance of any conflict. He had gone on with his work. Alfred knelt beside what was left of him. Praying, he gazed up at the smooth contours of pattern on the friar's last panels, suggesting nothing in the living world. He tried to see them as through the dead man's eyes and grasp their abstracted standards of pure design and form, but even he could not so much as tell whether they were good or bad. He had a vision of Brother Laurentius, dissolved into realms of inarticulateness, pouring his disembodied spirit into the vast, unimaginable deep from which God Himself had had to wrest primordial conceptions, among them very time and space. His head spun, and in his stomach all went dry and sour.

"Here you lie, dear Brother Laurentius. I miss your accuser's voice this night. Most honest were you in striving to rid your own soul of its inborn vices of vanity and pride, which tinged your every breath with taste of aloe, and which you were ever quick to smell out in others. Honest and sorely tried, for that the more you labored to frustrate them, the greater the pride you needs took in so doing. Should it be called pride, then, that bade you go on with your work till you died? Or was it God's selecting you to point a moral lesson for the rest of us? Now at least do I see this, that I acted even as you, ignoring life and its realities in favor of some abstract ideal, or ideal abstraction, I know not which to call it—only that you paid the penalty yourself, with your own life, whereas I've paid in stolen coin: the lives of others. Tell me, should I seek death, to get out of debt? I'm proving your old charge, am I not, by my very question! So your answer to that is no. Then what am I to do, Brother Laurentius? The manner of your life and death surely is another indication that the time of monastery rule is drawing to a close, though I doubt you would have it so. The doctrine whereunder it flourished is being revealed for a perversion of the pure truth. Was it not purity of truth you too sought, in your own way? Though the Lollards have classed me among those who would delay the resurgence, the victory of that older truth—delay for sure is the worst we can cause, I and the other, harsher guardians of corrupted dogma. But, having at last accepted the charge and pleaded guilty, I should be despicable if I continued as I am. Help me, Brother Laurentius. I need no assistance, you say? My duty is clear, and I know it? Ay, I dare say I knew it twenty years ago in Italy, where the power and the glory, which here were then already in decay, still stand as the rock of St. Peter. Do you call the work which I have loved so dearly a mere shield against the arrows of compelling truth? Very well then. I must go and become as Clement and Matt. There is little doubt I would have imitated them long since had there been no St. Hand's in Bedesford. Without St. Hand's, I might never have returned. But there is also this, Brother Laurentius: the Widowson hand. In its blessing there lies also a curse: for he that owns it can be good at nothing if he be debarred from exercising his gift. Totally unhappy men are seldom good. You too came back from among the outlaws, Brother Laurentius, for out in the wildness your craftsman's hand had to be idle. With such as ourselves the human quality resides in the cunning hand, so that if we deny it, we become as animals. And since we were created men, we thus fall below the level of the beast which lacks the means of turning traitor to its nature. If you admit that much, Brother Laurentius, see you not that the particular gift of my hand can only be employed inside a cloister? Perhaps—is that what you advise—it would be meet for me to abdicate and end my days in obscure industry, like Brother Oswin, here or elsewhere, far away for preference. No, no, that *would* be treachery. Escape into the pleasances of conscious virtue, escape from the distractions of responsibilities. Ay, that in fact is what you did, yourself. It may be that, ever alert as you were against vanity and pride, you overlooked the fault of self deceit? And yet, how else, save by thus cutting yourself off, could you have penetrated so far ahead of the rest of us—who, when we try to follow your gaze, can see only that your vision tells us naught, *as yet?* The long view and the short. Perhaps God hath made you to speak to me after all. Perhaps He wanted you to show me that the long view far ahead into the future, though right and good, may yet lead to error. No, I could not bear, for the sake of taking the long view, to desert my people here and now, that they may be brought to greater suffering for my absence, unto that despair which shall spur final liberation. I cannot believe God would rather I did my utmost to aid future generations, than that I tried to soften present hardship. *He* placed me in this position. Even if I were sure that I am going against His will, I should still have to obey the conscience He implanted in me. And then it must be His purpose, to have me go against Him. So I would bank on His forgiveness. Ay, true enough, dear Brother Laurentius. I have in fact decided to follow my own inclinations, no less than you did. But you cannot call me self deceived in this, nor self righteous. I shall not spare, nor pander to myself. You demand an earnest? What is there left for me to give up?—Chatte!"

The cat had never before entered the cathedral, although she had followed him much farther afield.

"Well, Jane!" the Abbot, expelling pent-up breath, said out loud. Others beside her heard him. Sometime ago a party of monks had preceded her, coming to find him, but held back by the sight and intermittent sound of his lonely wrestling. They had stayed, huddled, afraid, palsied with guilt, shame and compassion, just beyond the south-side porch, in the shadows under the triforium, where even their glances and gestures of questioning communication were mutually sensed rather than seen. "Well," the Abbot spoke with saddest gentleness, "so it is you

I am to give up, is it? No harder thing was asked of Abraham. Almost it would seem to me easier to slaughter your own son upon an altar, than to sacrifice the last chance of saving from perdition an old friend and creditor. Ingratitude comes harder than desertion. Ah, is this it, that after seven years with me you are still so fast in the infernal service, that you would tempt me to fly from Bedesford after all? I did not fly from here to keep another. I will not fly even to keep you—even if it mean that you shall not be saved, never."

They saw his hands move, as if to stroke the small beast at a distance. Chatte gleamed slenderly in the open doorway between the towers to be, her pelt blooming with a bronze sheen, alone in all the gray and blackness. As she cocked her head slightly, her eyes, hitherto invisible, suddenly showed up, blindly luminous emeralds—in daylight they were gray and had sharp slashes of pupil. Her tail, which had shot upright on Alfred's address, waved at the tip as his voice went on. "Just when you came into God's church of your own free will," Alfred murmured, "and at an hour when I need not chase you hence for fear others might see—" The church looked ever more immense, the cat more diminutive, one against the other.

Having crossed into the aisle, the cat with neat inconsequential haste sat down and began to wash, and as unexpectedly walked on again. It seemed as if she was carefully keeping the Abbot in sidelong sight, carefully pretending other interests—or, more subtle and more sinister, pursuing her real interest under cover of pretense. Her tail hung low and, as she changed direction, appeared to have her sliding black shadow attached to it. She crouched, went on almost crawling, circuitously approached the central crossing, almost disappearing on the way, so noiseless and so little as she was, from the strained observers' eyes. She made for one of the dead men. One could see her clearly again, as her legs stretched and back arched. She was pushing her face against the dead hand resting on the dead breast, demanding a caress. Monks and Abbot watched, as stone. Suddenly the dead arm was dislodged and fell to the ground. There was a snarl they could all hear. The cat had leaped into the air and vanished from sight. But not even Alfred thought that this was sorcery. He never thought but that a frightened cat had hidden. Jane had gone out of her. And he might keep her.

He remembered Abbot William's saying that complete self-denial will not make a good man—not if living with his fellow men is part of his vowed lot. Ridding himself of all failing or impropriety, he would in fact only take unto himself a new one: stopping up the channels of sympathy and forswearing that reserve of humility essential to the ruling. To remain brother to his brethren, he might keep a pet against a statute—almost he might say he was obliged to keep her. Like Abraham, he had been tried. Passing the test, the patriarch had been provided with a ram, and Alfred had received a cat. Jane's pacified soul was flown, to rest. (And indeed henceforward Chatte behaved more as an ordinary feline, attached to the cloister kitchen rather than the Abbot, and admitted suitors, and had kittens thrice a year, until she died.)

The monks nudged one another and made concerted noise with their feet, to simulate arrival; so that the Abbot might come forward unembarrassedly to meet them.

CHAPTER 6

DEATH TO THE DEAD

"I WAS AT Crécy." Thus Lord Hugh's refrain, as he hymned his own dying, on a bed of leaves. About him the leaves and dead twigs crackled, under him they but rustled damply for he shifted all the time, without changing position.

"I was at Crécy."

They all knew it. Of late years my lord had taken to speaking a great deal of the French adventure and his part in it, and recounted the same incidents over and over, in time using always the same words and phrases, which the others had come to know by heart. Gervase had frequently made mock of his uncle's latter-day failing. Now, if he could have undone that, he would gladly have paid with any sacrifice.

Because he used it incessantly, my lord's voice was grown toneless; and still he would go on. "All men know, and no one names Crécy without the remembrance that its horrors far surpassed anything in war since wars began. I had rather face Crécy again, ten times over, than even go on remembering this battle, the petty battle of my manor. I cannot get it out of my mind's eye. I cannot get the feel of it out of my marrow. What can I do, to rid myself of it? Waking and sleeping, I have it

with me. Help me against it. Batter my head in if naught else can
erase the memory!"

The henchmen's coarse faces were besmeared with tears. None was
able to keep still for long. The ground of their hideout was strewn with
broken sticks, with tree bark plucked to shreds and crumbled into
tinder, and handfuls of grass, moss, and weeds torn up with earth about
their roots. Not a beetle or spider they saw but was killed vindictively,
for ambling about in busy unconcern, for having its health and full use
of its limbs and knowing naught of hatred and despair.

"I went through all the worst of it," Lord Hugh gabbled on in his
strengthless, grating whisper, "in a ditch below King Edward's wind-
mill, and all that went before, all the misery that half the army perished from. And daily hope dwindled, as did all recollection of a sane
life and a dry. And then the shambles, and the dread fear, your bowels
turning traitor. The howling bowmen from Genoa, while the voices
were frozen in our throats. And we had to stand fast. Give me Crécy
over again—"

Contrary to what happens in most dying men, Lord Hugh appeared
to grow larger. Perhaps it was because his bony frame lay stretched at
full length, while the others were squatting round him, shadow dappled.
His huge, fleshless shoulders and flat broad chest might have belonged
to a bygone age of giants and dragons. The blood from his lungs which
had made his clothes look over gay when first it had saturated them,
had long dried to a hue of mourning. The stubble on his face had
grown so that it was a short white beard, not unbecoming.

"Their faces, their eyes," my lord groaned, turning his head from
side to side. "Beasts look not so. The swart southern bowmen, the raging Germans did not *know* us. Here I knew each face, and knew its
normal look. They all know me and know my manor, in whose shade
they have lived all their lives. I remember when my sister Juliana was
small, and she saw her first rat. Mice she knew, but a rat she had never
seen. It jumped out at her from her nurse's trunk where she had gone
to steal a pear. She took it for a mouse—only an unnatural mouse, hor-
ridly overgrown. *Thus,* see you, see you? Thus were their faces, their
looks of hate. None may call me coward. I was not afraid. I am not
now afraid. It is but the horror of it," he said, as though pleadingly.

Sometimes his mind wandered on to other matters. This was especially at night, in the cold, wet June nights. Then fever freed his fancy
so that it might comfort him. He thought himself with Jane, borne up
into their onetime other-world.

We have said it before, that God must have been most partial to this rank sinner, Lord Hugh. Few good men are granted such friends as abided with my lord in those his wretched last days. They bore the rain with him and the storm, against which the trees were no protection, and they did not flee when he surrounded them with conjuring madness in the dead of night. And every time a twig cracked or an acorn dropped, they thought themselves discovered. Every owl's hoot sounded artificial to them, as the watchword of pursuers about to seize them. Without my lord they would long have been away. They could even have dragged him along somewhat farther. But they would not shorten his life by one hour, nor increase his discomfort and minish the hardly bought dignity of his end. The worst of it was that he coughed less, so that they thought with a bed and fires and a roof over his head he might yet once more have been nursed back on his feet.

"Why was it, how came it to be? In my lord Gervase's day it would not have happened. I mind when Thomas Widowson was put to death—and he a serious man whom all held in respect, unlike this Oxerd-lad—there was much moaning and petitioning; but—! Times are different, you say? Then how came they to change? The guilt is mine. It must be; I let the power go, the fair edifice of order to decay—but how, *how* did I do so? Was I not stern enough? Did I not guard my rights, the law, with great severity throughout my term? Yet the fault must be mine, by act or omission—for never would God have destroyed an ordered world, merely because I am a sinner!"

He was not hungry, but demanded constantly to drink. They devised contraptions to catch the rain and dew, for the nearest brook was far enough away to make the journey dangerous. Howbeit the rest of them must eat. It was not easy to get meat, without dogs, and nothing but a few swords and daggers between them. They rigged up some snares, with little success; and once a woodcock was brought down with a stone. They ate white mushrooms and brown, chewed unripe berries and pine seed.

Then he turned against his nephew and heir. So at least they thought, from all of whom he had concealed his hatred for seven whole years. He would not suffer Gervase *near him* where he could see his face. He slapped aside the hand that would give him water, if he discovered it belonged to Gervase. He called him robber and deadly foe, and cursed him with incomprehensible gibberish. Gervase wept unashamed, sometimes aloud, like a woman, when his dying lord showed him such unkindness.

From the beginning one thing weighed heavily on all their minds, and at last there came an hour when they might give words to the thought and talk over how it had best be put into action: Lord Hugh must have a priest. "No matter what it cost us. So far as he is concerned, it will scarce matter if *they* do catch us now—if only we can get him ghostly aid. For even *they* would not dare keep God's solace from a man so nearly dead."

"The best thing were each one of us went in different direction—some priest there must be, somewhere, alive and brave."

"And leave *him* without attendance and defense?"

"Well then, one of us must try and get into Cloudsway Waste."

"Which one of us? Who?"

The sick man was slumbering. Slowly they raised themselves on their knees and glared at each other in the gloomy silence of the wood. Then each knew how much he longed to be moving—he and all the rest—even if it meant running into their enemies' arms. And so they might not vie for the perilous honor as they would have done, for that it was also a boon. It lacked little and they would have drawn their knives against each other. Gervase claimed the errand, being now their lord in all but legal name. Oh, but how their red-rimmed eyes flashed then, as they set themselves against his decision *because* he was their master! So lots were cast, and the two men who won—only they called it losing—went off like Christians in antiquity to the arena.

The spell of waiting proved their worst time yet. The spirit of even the least fanciful fell victim to the most gruesome anticipations. Also they were in terror lest Lord Hugh die precipitately. They took turns in warming him with their bodies, one on each side, one pillowing my lord's head in his lap, and one chafing his feet.

They lost count of time, for all that light and darkness succeeded each other, as ever. Their yesterdays all intermingled. At times they quarreled over their estimates, all at variance. When first they heard approaching footfall, they persuaded themselves it was birds, hares, wind—as it had been, so often before. Nonetheless they froze tautly. But then—but then there came a sound neither birds, beasts, nor breath of air alone could have produced: thin tinkling of silver bell. As one man they jumped to their feet. The sick lord blinked and coughed, awakening.

"Where are you, brothers, where are you? We cannot find your lair!" the returning shouted powerfully, and their fellows broke cover and also let their voices ring.

Prior Carlos came through the bushes, which the two that had fetched him parted for his advance. With a firm imperious tread he came, quick but unflurried, as he might be visiting my lord on business at his manor —so that one forgot he had scarce been on visiting terms with Lord Hugh in Bedesford. His worn gray habit looked sumptuously whole and clean to the fugitives; quite without rust, monstrance and bell seemed of a novel metal.

My lord's eyes were clear and conscious. "So you hold me to be dying!" he said to the two with the priest, as much as to accuse them of the vilest treason. "To be sure I am," he then added. "I have been dreaming, and I had forgotten. It is high time I died. There is no place for such as me on earth. The sooner we all lay us down to die, we nobles, the better for ourselves. Die, Gervase, die! Would you had died seven years ago! What would you live for now? Since God wills it, let now the beast in human likeness reign. Have you come to confess me, Spaniard? What would you have me say? For sure my sins are common public property. Not one will I disown. Will that content you?"

The Prior knelt beside the welter of leaf mold and human decay. "Content, my lord? Indeed I am most heartily content to have found you in time. We all thought you were burned to death, you and yours. God will requite you these last martyred days, I make bold to promise. I have come to take you home, that you may die in a good bed. We have got horses, tethered in a clearing. You shall return to your own town over the bodies of the rebels. Ay," he cried, in triumph and deep, wrathful pity, "they shall be made to pay homage most fully, most fully, to your last hours of earthly life! Your manor shall be raised up to new strength and splendor. Rest assured there is enough grieving and fearful suspense in Bedesford to make up for all you have suffered here in the wilderness—"

But Lord Hugh would not believe him.

The Prior tried to tell him that all over the land the rebellion had been put down, as swiftly and devastatingly as it had started. Less obstinate men, unbefogged by fever, found it hard to credit. In vain he tried to convince the dying lord that armed help had followed the call of Franciscan messengers, from Norfolk, Danesborough, and even other parts of Anglemere—though not until he, Prior Carlos Trinidad, with some assistance from the Abbot at Cloudsway, had restored the peace of Bedesford. "Everything is as it was before the fourth of June. The King is cutting up the charters he was forced to sign, with the sword—with the headsman's ax. The King's knights and soldiers, justices and headsmen, are marching through England, and with blood they are expunging the black chronicles of the two black weeks."

Lord Hugh only laughed scornfully. "I am not a child afraid of darkness. Think you to make my dying easier with your pretty lies?"

The Prior had to stop, my lord grew so enraged. So they had to humor him ere he could be anointed and fed the heavenly sustenance. And so he died out there, refusing to return.

CHAPTER 7

DEATH TO THE QUICK

ONCE AGAIN THERE was great assembly at Smithy Yard. The Mistress and her women had their hands full and scarcely a moment to rest their feet, which was a great blessing to them. Without time to think, they could not pause to feel. Thus thoughtless and unfeeling, Bess was heard to grumble, " 'Tis *worse* than a wake, this; more work than a wedding."

"I did not realize my husband had so many friends," Elizabeth said, welcoming yet another distant acquaintance, some workman from Cloudsway.

"Mistress," the man answered, "if Prior Carlos spoke truth and God smote Luke on our behalf, what dearer friend have we on earth, even those of us but knew him by sight?"

"From his funeral," another interjected, "we might have stayed away, just sending our prayers from afar. As it is we owe him the one loving service it is in our power to render: to let his mortal eye see we are not afraid of him—and let him be comforted by our numbers."

"Afraid? Why should you be?" Isabella, at her mother's side, said savagely. "Are not most of you doomed as he is? As well may a drowning man be afraid of the shark." They bore with her in silence, mildly averting their eyes: for Richard her husband was one of those for whom room had been found in the Wasteside jail, and who thus had not even the illusion of the unconfined, of hope.

"Afraid or unafraid," Elizabeth rebuked her—yet might she have been speaking on some trivial household matter, "all these good people might have stayed at home, were it not that their hearts are full of noble kindness, for which Christ will surely reward them—and my prayers shall mind Him of it day and night." Mother and daughter passed on. "Have you marked it," Elizabeth asked with a smile, "that from me they do recede away? It is harder to keep from shunning sorrow, than to confront that other curse." She sighed, but in a moment hospitable duties had caught them up again.

A wave of silence flooded the courtyard from the gate, and a lane opened for the priest and a Knight of St. Lazarus, preceded by St. Hand's rood, come down from its lofty home for this. A monk and a friar bore it between them, updrawn hoods falling forward round their faces so that they were obscure. The Knight was clad in armor, though his steel cap was unvisored, with a long sword at his side, and a voluminous cloak marked with the cross. At first folk were too busy looking him over, taking the priestly vestments beside him too much for granted, to note particularly who it was bore them. Presently nudging and whispering deflected all attention on the priest: for the Cloudsway Abbot himself had taken on this sad service.

Calm and steady of bearing as before, Elizabeth made a sign to her serving folk, whereupon they went from guest to guest, distributing tapers, and bringing after a basin of coals, to light them. Then she went to meet the priest with obeisance and seemly words, placed herself at the head of the small solemn train, and led the way to the shed where Luke had lived ever since he knew what ailed him.

A few paces from the door they halted, near a collection of empty dishes and cups. "Lucas, Son of Robin," called the priest, his voice compressed and strange, but unfaltering, and audible to all the company behind, "is this your house, and are you at home?"

Response did not come immediately, so that when it did, the audience shuddered, as they would have before speaking tomb. "Here am I," and the leper came out into the doorway, facing his obsequies. Elizabeth alone gasped; the rest were so quiet that one and all heard her. Without her tending, without any employment save inactive brooding, Luke had changed unbelievably since the last time he had been seen in public. Almost it convinced even his wife that the Prior's assertion was true, and that God had smitten Luke only on that day of war. For here stood an unmistakable leper, with bulging eye sockets, cheekbones, lips, and ears; eyebrows that had gone bald, and lids, lashless. He kept his face in full view, without expression, and spoke blurredly: his very lips shrank from touching each other.

"Lucas, Son of Robin," said the priest, "by reason of this grievous affliction which it hath pleased our Lord God to send down upon you, it is our lawful duty now to lead you from this your earthly home. Fix your eyes, my poor and beloved son, on that other home, with Him, which assuredly awaits you. This your bodily infirmity will strengthen your hope of salvation and bliss, so long as you keep mindful of your manly valor and your Christian condition, and bless and praise God without cease, without rancor, and without belittling your own sins. Fortify your courage with the thought that it is not only whom He loves that God tries the most, but also of whose strength to stand trial He is certain. Remember at all times the torments He suffered, hanging nailed and bleeding on the cross, willingly burdened, at the same time, with all the sins of the world—ay, yours and mine among them, and Eve's, and Cain's—and so you will not dare bemoan you for your own sufferings, only for the share that you yourself have added to His burden and agony. Remember Job, of whom He likewise made example. You are about to join a great and noble company: saints and kings have been of that fellowship, and queens have been proud to humble themselves at their feet. St. Francis was shown the way by a hand as yours, on which we in Bedesford have built our cathedral. Praise the Lord for that He hath vouchsafed you this chance, which is not given to many that choose the worldly life, of freedom from other duties and pursuits that you may devote the remainder of your days to preparation for your meeting with your Maker. Be consoled, my son and dearest brother, by the prayers and the love we shall everlastingly send out after you. Come." And he went up to the man in the low doorway, sprinkled him with holy water, took him by the hand, and drew him forth, with a few whispered words as to his immediate conduct.

The procession reformed, first the cross, then the priest, then the sick man, and after him the Knight of St. Lazarus. They were allowed to proceed a few yards, and then the sick man's family and friends formed into ranks of three and followed, all that hemmed their path gradually falling in behind. Elizabeth walked between Bess and Isabella. Folded over one arm she carried a heavy length of the best cloth, dyed black; over the other hung some poor, new, rust-colored garments; in one hand she bore a lighted candle, like everybody else; in the other a bowl, small and deep, carved out of wood. Her eldest daughter held a stout staff, and Bess had a parcel tied with cord. Thus began the long march up to the Waste and the cathedral. Most of the way we could hear the funeral bell. The soldiers that guarded Bedesford like a very wall, mercifully kept out of sight. At St. Hand's more people were assembled, among them Juliana, borne hither in a litter.

In the nave, the priest halted the procession and withdrew with the sick man, to confess him. The congregation took its wonted places. The high altar and the side chapels east of the central crossing were not yet in use again; nor were they to be seen for the towering ruins, although clearance work had been continuous. There was no dearth of willing hands. For many this would be the last assistance they could render the cathedral. To all it was a means of distraction. Now, in Luke's honor, they left off.

The friars cannot have started out from the hospital until the funeral bell ceased, being the last to arrive, with a number of the charity boarders, for their edification. Many people gazed curiously at the Prior, but his face was as expressionless as Luke's. Something about his gait was different. Later we learned that he had had his waist chain struck off him. One can only guess what had decided him, what other mortification had replaced the chain and rendered it superfluous, and your guess is as good as ours.

Leading the sick man by the hand, the priest reappeared, and cried, "Let the trestles be brought!"

Two men came forward with a pair of trestles, roughly knocked together in the carpenters' shop, and set them up a certain distance apart under the direction of the priest and the Knight. These two men were Edwin and his son Jaffy.

"If so be," the priest called again, "that a black piece of stuff is at hand, let it now be brought!"

Elizabeth stepped forward and held out her length of fine cloth, which Edwin and Jaffy took from her, opened out, and hung carefully over the trestles, so that it formed what looked at once bier and tent.

"Come, Lucas, Son of Robin," said the priest, holding up a fold of cloth and motioning him in underneath between the trestles, where he must kneel. When the cloth fell back in position all you could see of Luke was his knees and his feet. He cannot have known this; and his feet occasionally moved, betraying him as he would not have allowed his face or hands to betray him. "Let earth be brought in readiness," said the priest in a low voice. James Smith brought it.

Everybody waited. Abbot Alfred stood with bowed head for a moment. He raised it at last and fixed his gaze on the eyes of Elizabeth, and she, looking like a sleepwalker, let him hold them thus.

"Let now this man, having the appearance of one dead, although by the gift of God he still lives in body and spirit, let him now devoutly hear the Mass."

There followed the burial service over Luke Robinson. So that, this being finished and the holy water having been sprinkled, when Luke was bidden to come out from under the black cloth, he was a dead man. He stood where the priest told him, and suffered earth to be cast on both his feet by the priest, who said, "Be dead to the world, Luke Robinson, be dead to the world and again living to God."

Now was the time for all the people to turn to the widow and condole with her. This they did, but happily none could put any heart into it here, so that their murmurs, and her replies, were forms, as in a game. Nevertheless, some women had to be removed. The dead man's family, however, were given grace to comport themselves very decently.

The priest then bade the dead man go outside the church. All by himself Luke had to go, and stand before the porch, awaiting what came next in the ritual. The priest with the Knight of St. Lazarus followed measuredly to the door. The congregation faced about and dispersed by other exits, arranging itself in less ceremonial groups, some farther away, some closer, under the open sky. The single bell started up again.

"Have the dead man's kinsfolk brought all that is needful?" the Abbot asked. Elizabeth made as to bring the tunic, hood, and skin gloves and buskins she had ready, but the Knight interposed and made her throw these things at Luke's feet, also the carven, shiny new beggar's bowl. The things flew askew and only a short distance, so that the Knight had to pick them up and hand them to Luke. Isabella had to throw the leper's staff, Bess pitched her parcel. The dead man unwrapped it, and as soon as it was free, the object inside emitted a sound that made everyone instinctively start as to flee: it was the clapper. Perhaps before this it had not quite come home to us—the difference, to us, between this leper whom we knew, and others, who appeared before us solely as the unclean, accursed scarecrows of God's ire. True, his poor body was not yet become an abomination. Nevertheless we could not believe that it would ever seem right and good and just to us to pelt him with stones, filth, and convulsive abuse. At his worst, the man caged inside his dreadful flesh prison would only need to signal to us, "I am he you knew," and we would remember the real he, as we would any prisoner behind mere stone and iron bars.

The priest again took the dead man by the hand. "I commend your soul, Luke Robinson, to all these assembled people, that they may aid

you with their prayers, so you shall know, wherever you may be, you
are not walking unaccompanied. You shall know yourself surrounded
at all times by the thoughtful love of your fellows, in addition to God's
love, which you will not yet have learned to value the most. I pray
that its precious reality may be revealed to you soon, to be your mainstay. And now we must take you to the open fields."

Some, but not all of the people followed on behind, straggling, no
longer in austerely ordered train. Arrived at the town boundary, the
Abbot formally handed the dead man over to the Knight, and once
more addressed him.

"I forbid thee that was Luke Robinson to enter at any time any
churches, except under the special direction of your guardians. I forbid
thee to enter the market place, the mill, the bakehouse, or any assembly
of the people. I forbid thee ever to wash thy hands or any other necessary things in springs or any running waters. And if you want to drink,
you must draw the water in your own cup. I forbid thee to go abroad
without thy leper clothes by which thou mayst be known by everybody,
and thou art not to go barefoot.

"I forbid thee to speak to folk except in a whisper and against the
wind, that thy breath may not offend the charitable." These were the
only words at which Luke suddenly looked up, sought his widow's
eyes, and showed an emotion. "And thou are not to walk along any
narrow path, lest thou meet another. Also thou are not to touch children
or any young people. Thou are forbidden intercourse with women, and
to eat or drink or sit in company except with lepers. Also I urge thee to
remember that every faithful Christian is bound to say every day Pater-
noster, Ave Maria, and the Credo, to fortify himself with the sign of
the cross, and with a frequent saying of, 'Bless ye.' Worship God, and
give Him thanks, have patience, and the Lord will be with thee. Amen.
Farewell."

With that he turned his back on the dead man and the Knight, who
turned theirs on him and the people, and they walked away from each
other. Once, a little while after, the widow turned round again, yet
shutting out the sight of her eyes with grinding knuckles, and thinly
shouted, "Good-by, Luke. Good-by, my Luke!" But the dead man did
not answer her. The Abbot himself supported and conducted her on.
He seemed to have run out of comforting words, and stayed her but
with silence.

CHAPTER 8

THE REVEALING

EVERYONE WAS BACK at work save Edwin. His shrouded statue of St. Francis leaned in the same corner, secure between wall and pier, where he had stowed it when fighting began at St. Hand's. Although it had reached that stage of near completion when work becomes as running downhill, and at a time when everybody else sought refuge in employment, he was unable to summon enough interest in it so much as to lift the sacks. Yet he loitered on about the cathedral; go back to the hut he would not. He was even leaving it to Jaffy to negotiate with the monastery regarding Jeanne's burial. "Edwin Widowson is idle," folk said, and could not believe it, any more than that Juliana was fallen into helplessness, Lord Hugh into the grave, Luke into banishment, and the whole parish under threat of extinction.

Edwin talked to himself and to his dead wife a good deal. "See, Jeanne, now you are gone from me, the work has ceased to come between us! You see? For all that it seemed to you to shut me off from you, I needed you to make me want to work." When he thought someone might have overheard him, he would hunch his shoulders as one guilty of a baseness, and move away. We left him alone, delicately. We half expected him to pine away or grow benighted—in which, it was felt, he would be luckier than most. But no such luck came to him.

He could not die, being sound in body and not having taken part in the fighting. He could not go on living as heretofore, since the purpose of his life and of that ancient enormity, its crime, was gone, unfulfilled.

The conviction grew on him more and more strongly that in Bedesford he would never find the salvation of direct atonement, of suffering punishment in his own person. The selection and general acceptance of Luke for Bedesford's scapegoat was the ultimate torture, beyond which God *could* not mean Edwin to suffer by proxy. Not that he had any right to expect the saving curse of leprosy in his own flesh. He had realized the presumption of such a hope when he listened to Alfred's solacing the victim. The urgent prompting of his heart, articulate, no mere vague unhappy churning, was surely a message of God's, the first vouchsafed him since the night he had set himself apart from the Christian community. His heart most vehemently desired him to follow the leper—surprisingly, we say, because no traditional precedent suggested such a course, and because in thirty years Edwin and Luke had exchanged few words beyond the common courtesies.

Luke was so lonely. Edwin thought he had never fully understood the meaning of loneliness till the hour Luke stood being declared dead and cast out from the world of living men. So terribly alone as he had looked, Luke had become nearer and dearer to Edwin than any other creature now on earth. Jeanne was dead, Brother Laurentius was dead, most of his old friends must be accounted dying. The Abbot of Cloudsway was son to him in no way save the accident of blood. While for none of his other children had he ever cared with anything more than unreasoning parental love. The cathedral, for which he had to tremble all the time his tainted hand helped its growth along, would be safer for Edwin's removal. His statue of St. Francis called him no longer. The only image to make his heart beat faster and his fingers twitch was of a leper—The Leper—standing alone. Oh, that he might have thought of such a memorial to St. Francis' guide before this! Now he would never get permission for it. Everyone would think with the authorities that it was a pretext to commemorate Luke, who, weighted with the sum of the community's sins, might deserve its gratitude and pity, yet could not but pollute its sacred center by his presence, even in stone.

Poor Luke, the poorer for having been so rich in all things—He *must* have someone to go with him into exile!

So far Edwin got before it struck him that he at all events could not follow the outcast. The one man who knew Edwin's crime, who had it in his power to destroy the cathedral and everything it stood for, and who would not hesitate to do so if this suited his black heart—this threat embodied was among the prisoners without bail.

Abbot Alfred had vowed to make a picture Bible for the peace of his mother. But for the nonce he had locked his books, quills, and brushes away. With the King's men perforce lodged under his roof he nursed a gentle, aloof, courtly relationship befitting host and guests. He did not talk to them about the matters which engrossed both them and him, partly to discredit Prior Carlos' insinuations, and partly to reserve his intercession to the last and thereby give it greater force. Prior Carlos was forever visiting Bedesford's dead guests—when he was not calling on Lord Gervase, who with his men enjoyed the hospitality of Trefeller Court.

There was a succession of funerals, as in a time of plague, to which the general suspended motion of life in Bedesford indeed bore manifold resemblance. In arranging for these, many questions of abstruse nicety could be raised, and Prior Carlos put himself forward to make sure that raised they were. This relieved the Abbot in more senses than one. He had had reason to fear the other might try to forestall him with the prisoners doomed under the fatal title of "ringleaders." From the start the Prior had expressed anxiety on their account, lest their term of salubrious waiting were not utilized to install in them sincere repentance. The Abbot questioned both the kindness and efficacy of the Prior's way with sinners *in extremis.*

With the worst will in the world no more than three grown men could be compressed into the lockup. Three men could stand and just about sit there simultaneously, but only one at a time could stretch out to sleep. So the fifth and sixth "ringleaders" had been placed in the dark cell for unruly monks.

Alfred went first to the lockup, where there were Clement, Stephen Colet, and Richard Widowson, all rendered unfamiliar, their differences in age obliterated by full-grown beards. The light coming through a small, dense grating was scant; of air there was little, or pure air there was none. It was very hot, the floor a noisome quagmire. He spoke a blessing upon entering, and they apologized that they could not kneel. He in turn asked their forgiveness for adding to the congestion, and asked them how they had fared thus far.

This simple and, one might perhaps have thought, lame question set all three talking at once, breaking constraint. Their meals had been good all along, they were eager to tell him. Isabella had permission to bring food for her husband, which meant that she made sure of bringing enough for his fellow prisoners. And although they could not get sufficient water and their gorges were set against whey and ale in here, baskets of freshly gathered cherries and early currants were frequently admitted. "Our guards are merciful. But they will not tell us any of the news."

So the Abbot told them all he knew of everyday happenings. As to their fate, they asked no questions, and he deemed his equal silence intelligence enough. Before their animation could subside, he left, promising to come again soon.

Into the dark cell he took a lamp with him. Dick and his outlaw friend had their feet shackled in great iron rings and chains, but their hands they had free.

"You have brought us a light to look at!" Dick exclaimed gratefully as soon as he had learned to see again. This appeared to vex his comrade, who growled, showing his teeth, "Must you lisp and simper like a child or idiot, man?" But Dick was not shamed, and shed a tear, so placidly withal that the Abbot wondered whether there might be some truth in the outlaw's words. The old man looked changed, too, and it could not be merely the shadows, or that his face was still screwed up against the light, for his face had fewer rather than more wrinkles. "You are looking at me, young Alfred?" Dick continued, with a patriarchal serenity. "Ay, I am a changed man, I know it. Strange, but so it is. It feels as if a part of my twin had been returned to me now to carry within me. Did you know White Hugh? Nay, you were too small to have remembered. You cannot have been many months old when the Black Death tore him from me. He liked Edwin your father, did White Hugh. There were not many people whom he took to. Mayhap if he had lived—Ah, no, I mind when he still lived I used to tell myself it was more for him than for myself that I conspired in self-destroying hatred. And after he had died, it was for his sake still—so I told myself. To avenge him, you understand, on those who had remained alive. A man's heart is an odd thing, young Alfred. As for his Reason, the less said of it, the better. Nay. Had I stormed the manor openly or forthrightly attacked its lord even in the secret wood—only then would I have been as I am now, ere this. It's the conspiring made me what I was. To see the manor go up in flames has been like an exorcism or bloodletting. Do you know, I feel pure and good and weak. It is fine and happy to feel weak and good. Women feel so, I am told, after birthing."

"Give over, give over," broke in the outlaw. "You need not be a woman to feel so. You need but to bring forth your dung after long incasement."

"Do not disturb my talk with the Abbot," Dick said, almost with indifference. "It is good to be telling someone, Alfred. Strange, is it not, that a man cannot even fully savor pleasure without he shares and communicates it to another. Secrecy, in good things as in bad, is the root of all sin. Mark you that down in the book, Abbot. I tried to share with *him*, but he would not let me. You see what he is like. He is all bad. He has never so much as loved anything good. I have. I loved my innocent brother. So God sent him back to me just when I would have damned my soul forever, and here I am, saved." And he broke into smiles.

"He is feigning madness," the outlaw said to the Abbot. "If ever there was a coward's trick—!"

"You see how it is with him?" said Dick. "For a man to be happy, he must be either mad or shamming—that is all *he* knows!"

"Yet are you too doing him, injustice," said the Abbot. "Even if only by hating him—for hate, Dick, like joy, needs to be shared, and if he seems to hate you, it is but proof that you hate him. Relinquish the last bitterness, be a truly good man, Dick, before you must die! Moreover, he, that you say is all bad, has done at least one good deed that I know of, and one that it was hard to do and will cost him very dear. He alone of all the wild wolves whom *you* loosed upon Bedesford, and who were not slain, he alone did not escape. There was time enough, Dick, for any unbound by family or goods, to save themselves before the ring of swords was closed. There was nothing but his own will to prevent him. He chose to die beside you."

"Oh, very shrewd!" the outlaw applauded. "I am glad someone at last has seen that I was caught because I so intended. But you are too ingenious, Abbot, and too simple at the same time. I cannot blame you. You do not know me. This whining old woman here beside me does. But then, I cannot blame him either for not knowing what nobody knows, only two men in all the world. One of those two is me. The other is—not with us here. I will tell you. It was to make known this unknown matter that I let myself be caught. Will you confess me, Abbot? Dick's presence will not embarrass me. Indeed, your credulity may require a witness. And although he does not know so far, he will know the truth when he hears it."

"Wait," said the Abbot. "Be reminded that there is no absolution in a mere revealing of your secrets, whatever their nature. You must repent. You do not bear yourself repentantly."

"One strange thing about this confession I am about to make," said the outlaw, with his head on one side, "is that it calls for greater repentance in another."

"You know it is not for you to confess another's sin."

"I am not *obliged* to implicate another," the outlaw corrected him amusedly. "Yet if my sin and another's are inextricably intertwined—surely I *may*? Surely, I must! You make me wonder, Abbot, if I have mistaken you after all. It is not often I misappraise a man. Can it be that I was wrong to say there are but two men living know what I am about to confess? Is there a third, and are you he?"

Dick sat up, and cried suddenly, "*These* are the ramblings of a crazed mind! Do not listen to him, Alfred!"

"Ah, do you begin to see already?" the outlaw asked in tones of ominous approval. "Well, Abbot, whether you know or not, hear it all from me you shall, with a witness for it that you have been told. Once upon a time, Alfred Widowson, there was a youth, a woodworker, who had got a certain maid with child. And once upon a time there was an outlaw chieftain, whom the pirates abducted and held to ransom. Now, on a certain day in the spring before the Black Death, a piece of statuary, made of gold, was dug up from a certain waste common."

The small, pointed flame inside the lantern burned on with scarcely a flicker, there being no outside movement to impel it. The outlaw talked without gestures. The Abbot leaned back against the door with arms folded and head inclined in the practiced self-effacing quiescence of the confessional. Dick had given up all hope of interrupting, and crouched so that his face was hid.

"Now I wonder, Abbot, whether you, that are a widely traveled man, ever heard of a thing called the Thieves' Candle? No? Yet I tell you, you have, in a way. Mind you the pickled cats' paws your witch made for some adulteresses? Those were offshoots, you might call them, from a main stem of magic, that used to be well known at one time in the district where I come from. I was pushed into the cloister before I was ten years old, you must know, because there was a famine. At the best of times the country was barren and poor, so that not only outlaws lived by robbery—and robbers, conversely, were not always outlawed. Well, you take the hand of one executed as a felon, paying the corpse by means of burial with certain rites. You put this hand in pickle for a certain number of days, chanting over it as prescribed. When it is ready, you set light to the fingers, and, holding this pickled candelabrum before you, will go about your thieving errand in enchanted safety. For the Thieves' Candle renders them that are to be robbed blind, deaf, and insensible. If the night be stormy and you cannot wait, you are excused lighting flames that could not maintain themselves, provided you sacrifice a portion of the spoils to the hand's ghost afterward—which, if you omit, circumstances will seem to conspire to see you caught out and hanged. I have known cases. You can imagine that such Candles are very rare and valuable. Usually it is difficult to get hold of a felon's hands the while they are still fresh. Unlawfully burying his body is even harder and more dangerous. Then the pickling takes time; and then, of course, the fingers are burned down and the hand is used up in but a few expeditions. So we could hardly believe our luck when Thomas Widowson was hung at the marsh, with his hands ready severed. Dick was in on all this part of it. We could never have done any of it without his help. How dismayed he was when his dear friend's brother appeared and started asking questions! I have often wondered, Dick, what you thought, after. There were only two ways by which we could ensure us against betrayal on his part. We could either kill, or else entangle him in complicity. Having seen him depart with us, were you not even surprised when later he reappeared, alive, with money in his pocket? When Thomas' hand was found in the place of the golden one, can it be you did not know it again?"

"I never saw it, not till after it was all jeweled. For that matter, I never saw what you had made of it in my backyard. I never saw it again after we had taken Thomas off the tree." Dick's voice came muffled. He raised his head from his arms and addressed the Abbot, "The thought never entered my mind, that it might be Thomas' hand —since everyone said the gold hand had turned into leprous flesh—how *could* I have thought—?"

"Had you not suspected, had you not been afraid to think and therefore deliberately stunned thought altogether, you would have known," the outlaw said with decision. "Why, you did know! You have known all along! Only you did not let yourself think on it that you knew. Just as you let us take your old friend's body and make Devil's work of it—you did not let your thoughts roam much about the matter of that, either!"

"I did," Dick said disconsolately. "I reasoned that all out. I deemed Thomas would be glad to lend his hand—against the manor. It was because he transgressed against its law before, that he was condemned. I had to help you, did I not? I felt that Thomas understood and consented."

"Yet you did not tell your confessor, did you?"

"I did that, too."

The outlaw whistled. "Who was your confessor in those days?" he asked eagerly. "Not Brother Laurentius? I knew, I knew it!"

"You are wrong. It was Brother Nicholas. And I know what you are thinking now, malice incarnate! But I did not go to confession until long after the first commotion had died down, about the miracle."

"The miracle, he calls it still! Do you see it, Abbot, how this miracle becomes as a key to the true nature of everyone concerned in it? Brother Nicholas could not bear to lose his visionary's repute. He preferred to die. I dare say he fasted himself to death. The times I have had to listen to the tale of his saintly wasting away! He was not to know there would come the Black Death, and might have saved him hunger pangs and trouble! But no doubt you are impatient to hear about your father's part. You must forgive me these digressions. Well, we had to get him to go across to the pit, for he knew the place, we should never have found it in the dark, there were not enough of us to risk a fight— we did not know how many guards there might be. So that is how you came to be born in wedlock, Abbot! It was your father stole the hand of gold and left in its place that of his brother. The times I have laughed at that till I ached—and still the jest never palls!"

"It is the Fiend himself you have locked me up with," Dick said, low, with a shiver. The Abbot spoke simultaneously.

"You will never convince me, villain," he said to the outlaw.

"I think otherwise," the outlaw returned placidly. "I am not saying he knew what he was doing at the time—except that he was stealing the gold, he knew that, right enough. But you see the manor had slain his brother, for what all thought a good deed. And the manor stood between him and your mother. Everybody knew the manor would claim the find. It was not over hard, to work upon his feelings—though to say so may be false modesty on my part. He was young and despairing. The risk and the crime were not so very great. There would be no jest, had he known what sort of charm it was we pressed on him—or had he intended dropping it. No. Then he had been a man after my own heart, and one whom I must bow to. For, since I am making confession, I must admit I had not planned that, either. Perhaps I wronged Dick a little while ago, since even I drew no inference from the fact that both treasure and charm were in the shape of a hand." He shook his head in benevolent deprecation.

"He had it in a sack, you see. He did not know where he had dropped it, when he came back to us. It was only then we found he had it no longer. We melted it down there and then, the gold. Poor Edwin felt very bitter. His coffer that he'd been so proud of he offered for fuel. A full third of the gold we gave for Thomas' soul. Jed went with Edwin to Ovisham, to make the rest into money—Edwin would not have known how to set about that. He got what he needed, and we had what was left—and none too soon for our chief," the outlaw said with momentary gentleness. "So far, so good, Abbot—or at all events not so very bad. But as soon as he returned to Bedesford, he must have understood how it had all happened, just as I did when I heard. And he kept silent, your father. He has kept silence for more than thirty years. How large an edifice has been builded upon that precarious foundation, his silence! How long I have looked forward to bringing it down!"

"Then what," the Abbot asked quietly, "made you wait until now?"

"If you had the choice between drawing one letter finely and embellishing a whole book, which would you take? If a man be bent on destroying, will not he fulfill himself best, holding his hand till there may be something worthy of the tearing down, something whose collapse will echo far and wide like thunder, instead of giving out one brief eggshell crack?"

"You might have died. You must be quite an old man."

"I do not look my age, do I? My Lord the Devil promised to reward my patience, and kept my body from decay. I could not venture before Abbot, Bishop, or baron, could I, to prove my declaration, without forfeiting liberty and life? I was not yet wearied of either. I wanted to see friend Dick's game played out, too. And my lord the Devil had assured me that I should have my full span. I have passed it now," he said with a transient, as it were artless regret. And then, quite unexpectedly, he himself was shaken by a shudder.

"Yet why, why did you ever long so to destroy? What caused you to make your pact with the Devil? Why do you hate us so—my father, and Dick, and me, and all the faithful souls whom the denying this old miracle would imperil?"

"No good ever came my way, that I noticed, but that I had to fight hard for it with fair means and foul. The best and finest man I ever knew got the worst fate. I learned at last the only good is Evil. The only lord for upright men is Satan, whom your God did out of what was his. The Devil is my lord."

"What are you going to do, Alfred?" Dick whispered after a silence.

"What can he do?" said the outlaw with his former derisive glee. "If he takes no steps to announce it, I shall, when I come up before the judges, which will be so much the worse for him and everyone else—"

"I will tell you what I am going to do," Alfred answered Dick. "First of all I will give thanks to God that He let me hear it *now*, and neither earlier nor later—at a time when there can be no wavering as to the right course. And then I shall see to it that my father's sacrifice of every chance of happiness and peace of soul shall not be rendered vain, as this man's design and that of the Devil have been rendered vain. You, outlaw, you that feasted all these years upon the knowledge of your malignity and the insight it gave you into what is evil in others—you failed to see something else. The while my poor father robbed the pit, *God and St. Francis sent Brother Nicholas a vision*. God and St. Francis outthieved the Devil and appropriated his design, rearing upon it a bastion of faith. They brought Thomas' desecrated hand to honor, and through it healed the sick. And when the time was ripe, as it has lately ripened, They bade me prepare for some sacrifice, the nature of which They would not then reveal. And then They made it so that you have yielded to the temptation of confounding me, rather than waiting till you stood safely before the King's justices. Tell me, did they teach you to write, at the cloister, in your youth? They did? I am glad of that, more than I can say."

"Why?"

"Because that means it would not be enough, to rob you of speech. Though murder is the greater sin, I had rather commit that than cut out your tongue. Will you be shriven, outlaw? Will you repent and repudiate the Deceiver whom you have called lord?"

"I have been too much for him. I have driven him out of his mind," the outlaw faltered.

"Will you not be shriven, outlaw? I am not mad, else would I hardly make this offer."

"No, he is not mad," the outlaw said in perplexity, then went on firmly. "But you are not the man I thought you, Abbot. I cannot recall such another misjudgment. It serves me right, for crediting what they all said: that you were a good man. *I* must have been mad! No, I will not take the sacrament at your hands. God, who sees you even in this dark hole, will forgive me that I seem to spurn His food. Thus my Lord hath ensured that I must keep our compact."

"Alfred," Dick tugged at the Abbot's sleeve. "Alfred, do you confess and absolve *me*. Then let *me* be his executioner. I am doomed to die anyway. What would anyone think, when they found him slain beside me, but that I did it? I shall always swear that it was I. You may as well let me be the one to do it. White Hugh inside me tells me that it will be part atonement. Whereas you would load yourself with needless sin."

"Crime and sin it must remain whichever of us does it. Whichever of us does it, we shall both be murderers." Howbeit Alfred hesitated.

"Hey, ho, help, murder, murder, help, ho." The outlaw suddenly sprang up and beat with his hands upon the door, stamping his feet to make the shackles rattle.

Alfred, the younger and stronger of the other two, with full freedom of movement, went for the outlaw's throat to stop his mouth.

But he agreed to let Dick take the guilt upon himself.

CHAPTER 9

THE MARTYRS

THE OPEN ROAD stretched wide and long across the flat land. Far away, to east and west, there were some cloudy humps of forest. Closer-to only isolated groups of trees and hedges marked the meadowed plain. Behind, the turnpike had vanished below the northern horizon, and in front no sign of the next hamlet was as yet growing into sight. Larks and grasshoppers sang all round. Luke walked slowly. There was no hurry for him, no more, nevermore.

Some leverets hopped out of the high grass ahead and into the road, looked at the wanderer, hopped back, and out again, and at last across into the turf bank opposite, all with a comical simultaneity of performance. Luke would have smiled, had not the lifting of his mouth proved an unexpected effort, in which he could not trouble to persist. A little later he discerned another movement in the distance. Someone emerging from a clump of bushes to stand in the middle of the road.

Luke had not seen another human being for what seemed a lifetime, and although so far he had counted himself lucky for this, tears now started into his eyes. He did not realize that his arm had gone up in the habitual gesture of greeting, until the clapper in that hand did its work unbidden. Thereupon he fell to wielding it deliberately. This was the first time he had had to use it.

The other did not stir. Luke stood still and rattled the clapper even more violently. The other man moved; he began to advance. Luke shook his staff in one hand and the clapper in the other, and in addition shouted as he had been taught.

"Unclean! Unclean! Away, stranger! Unclean!"

The other quickened his pace. It occurred to Luke the man might be deaf, so that it might be best to let him get a little nearer and make sure he saw the leper's uniform—for blind he was not. He too had started waving.

"Luke Luke! It is I, Edwin!"

Luke only thought of dodging up the bank into the meadow. Do it he could not, and stood, mechanically continuing to sound the clapper.

"Away! Stop! Madman! Oh, what are you doing?" he said dully, Edwin's arms already clasping him, while the clapper gave one last unheeded rattle. His legs yielded at the knees. Edwin sat down with him, right there upon the hardened ruts in the middle of the road. "Where have you sprung from so suddenly, Edwin?" he asked, his swimming head in his hands. "To be sure—you may take short cuts and pathways too narrow for me—"

"Now I am a leper too," said Edwin, smiling. "I have trod those pathways for the last time. And I had my fill of them in this rush to catch you up before you got to the crossroads—since no one knew whither you would be sent."

"No one has seen you touch me. None will ever know. Unless the worst has happened. Yet so brief contact should hardly suffice—" Luke sighed, shaking his head slowly. "I never thought to see anyone from home again. I know not whether to thank or berate you. The leper's powerful blessing on you. Now go. Go."

And now it was for Edwin to tell Luke of his wish and persuade him to grant it. The leper could not believe his ears; that was why he failed in immediate response. He gaped and stammered and shook his head with giddy vehemence, breaking off his arguments every so often, again and again to make sure that his incredulity was mistaken. Neither was he capable of arguing with the requisite heat and cogency.

Edwin, on the other hand, found himself endowed with an overriding volubility, almost lighthearted. He pointed out that Luke could not prevent him—once he had missed the opportunity of convincing Edwin that his company as such was repugnant, at which Luke must give a helpless growl of a laugh. Edwin spoke, albeit darkly, of the motive springs of his desire, yet not so that his yearning for his own peace and salvation, or his surpassing pity, could wound the leper.

Luke could not resist Edwin's pictures of their future comradeship. Yet he was horrified at his own weakness in this. Had the rot already eaten through his flesh into his very soul? No matter how he tried to down it, the weakness was stronger than himself. To every objection Edwin had an answer. And Edwin argued with honest ardor, from his heart, where Luke was but struggling in honorable retreat.

To be sure, the Luke that had crawled out from beneath the trestle under the pall was not the same man as he who had gone in. How could he have been? At one stroke he no longer was what he had always been: a particle of the community, but a being totally apart. If all the world had died and he had been the sole survivor, his loneliness would not have been a whit more real or more stark. And since all that exists does so in relation to everything around it, the inner man was changed under the altered impact of all things external; and as his nature was different, so was the nature of all things.

Already he had fallen into the way of some of those little rules and habits which make up any condition, carrying their own pride. He would no sooner have thought of scooping drinking water with the hollowed hand, than in his previous life he would have forgotten to lace up his clothes. He was not even quite bereft of duties, nor of a worldly purpose: it was his responsibility to protect others from physical contact with himself. The Knight of St. Lazarus had business in Danes-borough, and on the parting of their roads had without a qualm instructed Luke in finding his own way. So modest, so altered were Luke's demands and expectations of life, that the Knight's trust in him *as* a leper had warmed him to glowing.

The life to which Edwin was so set on condemning himself was the same as Luke's own. Therefore he could not view the prospect with the horror of a clean man legally alive. To be sure, as we have said, he had not yet encountered healthy people that knew him not.

Thus it was that Luke and Edwin went out of Anglemere together.

Nobody dreamed of doubting Dick's confession, that he had quarreled with the outlaw known as Priest, when the body was found. Nobody any longer thought of Dick as one of us. The very revelation of his lifelong, lurking duplicity had set him apart from all other rebels, who had risen to a cause, where he had waited, like a spider, for a cause to rise. For him to have choked to death his companion in arms and doom was the ultimate baseness which lost him all compassion. Alone of all the condemned rebels in England Dick had none to grieve for him. Dick found this easier to bear than did the Abbot.

(Therefore also did Jesus Christ descend to sacrifice Himself for the whole of mankind once and for all: that no mortal might be tempted to put himself in the way of dying for his people. Only to God's greatness may men or women make themselves blood witnesses. You can see it by the chain of crimes Thomas Widowson had begun, unselfishly: unselfishly, each crime his crime begot led to a worse one; martyrdom for Bedesford's sake became one with guilt; from martyr to martyr damnation was bandied on, like a ball—only that this ball must ever adhere to some person; it could never be dropped, left to roll loose.)

Edwin's disappearance was the gentlest of Alfred's sorrows. Truth to tell, he was glad not to have to face his father now, with bloodguilt on his hands and unholy knowledge ever present to his consciousness. Most people were uplifted rather than downcast by the loss of Edwin. There was a fine, calming, spiritual satisfaction to it. The disapproval with which folk had never quite ceased to regard Edwin and Jeanne had ended directly the story of their love became past history, that is, with her death. The story was no longer a cautionary tale, but as pretty as any fiction. That Edwin could not bear to stay where he had lived with his beloved gave the conclusion its rightness and beauty. The stranger soldiers guarding Bedesford too had heard the story, and, knowing that there was no charge against the venerable lover, they had let him pass out of the town. Nobody thought of blaming him for deserting his family, who had a natural protector in the Abbot.

And then, it was such a short time before the trial that Edwin thus tracelessly removed himself.

Wherever the tide of rebellion had flowed, men were being put to the sword, hanged, disemboweled, quartered, flayed. You heard of fresh examples every day. Nobody questioned that in Bedesford, too, executions would follow the trial. There was no hope, no doubt, save in regard to the manner of death and the disposal of the bodies. Between watches, the stranger soldiers were knocking up a scaffold on the green. Not until the eve of the trial did Abbot Alfred call together a council of the representatives of law and vengeance.

It would seem that Prior Carlos had spoiled his own case. So used was he to having to pit himself against authority, that he forgot to adapt his manner to the knowledge that this time authority was on his side. He employed circumambulatory suasion where he could and should have stated facts and outspoken opinion. He should have rammed his points home with clean blows, instead of causing irritation as with gnat bites and pinpricks.

The Abbot by contrast acted without subtlety and spoke baldly, had the temerity to invoke mercy by its name, and put forward certain practical considerations in its favor, such as the numerical inferiority of the soldiers and the inspiriting effect of desperation driven to the limit of endurance. He called Lord Hugh's action against Frank illegal, and Lord Jerome's armed attack before the altar sacrilege, which there was no gainsaying. As he avoided the almost irresistible mistake of asking too much, his intercession was successful. All the condemned were to be simply beheaded. Dick alone was to be drawn and quartered, but that only after strangulation. All, including even Dick, were to be granted burial. Thus it was settled before the trial. And thus folk went to the trial in a quieter state of mind than they had enjoyed since the rising.

All morning the armed messengers of the justices and of Lord Gervase went from house to house, rounding up defendants. The rest, and women and children, went after them, to Cloudsway Waste. For form's sake the Cinqmort lord was on the bench beside the Londoners, along with the Abbot and the Prior. It was not a lengthy trial.

One hundred and twelve men were sentenced to death, with banishment of their families in seven cases (all Newcomes and Franklins), additional fines in fifty-nine, and only eleven forfeitures of all property. However, the town as a whole was to defray the cost of rebuilding the manor and St. Hand's central tower, so that the judgment could not be called mild, besides which one must expect a certain amount of burning and pillage at the hands of the soldiery after the executions.

Bishop Jerome's body, or parts of it, had been dug up, placed in a London coffin, and arrayed in state near the scaffold. Mangled out of human semblance, black, and by now odorless, it was not so very terrible. It was to witness the executions. Some prisoners were used to open up a tomb in the cathedral where the Bishop might afterward be laid to rest. Lord Hugh was there already, as yet without monument.

The prisoners were herded in a fold made on the green, in sight of both the scaffold and the cathedral. The night being their last, it was not thought worth while to give them pallets and the like. Few would be able, few would want to sleep. Also, they were allowed to receive visitors. The families of most stayed out there the night through. But about midnight the guards complained of weariness, and as no relays could be spared for rest so long as visitors had to be searched, admitted, supervised, there was an end of the visiting.

Friars preached to the watchers, also leading choral prayers to St. Joseph, intercessor for an easy death. The priests started on their round of the condemned. Abbot Alfred was among them. The Prior did his share, preaching.

All this is halt and dry. We wish it to be so. We can have no wish to bring that night back to life. The same holds for the next day.

As he had vowed, the Abbot did not spare himself. He stood up in front of the scaffold the whole time, with a monk on each side supporting his arms, which held up to the sight of the dying a cross and St. Hand Itself. Dick did not once fix his eyes on the latter, although they left him to be the last to die. But it must have comforted him too, for that It gave consolation to all the others. When the executioners approached Franklin Oxerd, Joan his wife called to him from out the onlooking crowd, and plunged a knife into her throat, that he might still know in this life that she was departing it with him.

Part Ten
Completion
(1386-1400)

TIDINGS

FRANK OXERD, who had not been seen in Bedesford since he left the town soon after the death of his parents, came over from Danesborough in May, 1386, to render his accounts to Mistress Robinson. He was still her steward, although he had so prospered that the affairs of Smithy Yard, which had set him up at Damesbury, had ceased to be his main concern.

He had called into being an overland carters' service, Danesborough being a country somewhat backward in respect of roads and safe traffic. It had started with his attainment of the Danesborough agency for the bishopric, when at first he had followed Luke's example and undertaken errands and commissions free of charge.

Previously the Robinsons had been the Bishop's agents; but Elizabeth had decided gradually to disembarrass Smithy Yard of its superfluity of interests and therefore declined to apply for renewal. Also, her brother wanted the appointment. That in the end Frank had got it against Little John's rivalry and despite the manner of his parents' end, was in part explained by his marriage. People were most curious to see what manner of woman she was, his wife, daughter of a goldsmith with London alliances.

She was as sightly and proper as anything belonging to Frank's train. He brought just the right number of servants, all dressed impeccably according to their offices. His wagons and oxen, his horse and his demeanor, all were exactly what they ought to be. His wife was quiet, sound, and comely, and mother of twin sons and a baby girl, and it was clear she thought her husband the finest and wisest of men. Well and good: she loved him. Still one could see no reason why her father had accepted such a suitor.

Frank himself enlightened his hostess. "I know full well what everyone is thinking. Folk are wondering whether my good wife had been dishonored before I came to woo her, since they can find no visible blemish in her on account for our match! You must know, Elizabeth, I never was quite so foolish as I may have made out, in my youth," he said, with a rueful twinkle which in truth took her by surprise. "Now I am my own master, my condition speaks for itself and indeed for me. I do not need to talk. You are laughing at me, and I deserve it!" and he also smiled.

"But you *are* changed, Frank! And I beg you will go on talking!"

"To be sure, I am not quite the same. Who would be?" Frank motioned with his mutilated head. "At first it was not easy, I admit, to know how to bear myself, with my nose as Lord Hugh left it, and only one ear. At first I could not decide whether I had liefest slink about in the shadows with a mask before my face or whether to thrust it at other people, as in challenge. I had to make myself a new manner, to go with it, see you? Now I am so used to it as if I had been born thus—after all, some are born worse disfigured. It has been harder for you and everybody else in Bedesford to meet and look me in the face, than for me to be looked at, or even to watch your uneasiness. You will find you soon get over it."

"Frank, you are a man."

"Ay, that is another thing—one grows older. But I must give my father-in-law his due. If I took heart, it was largely his doing. We met in the way of business, and I was able to discharge some errands to his liking and profit. From the start he judged me on my merits, as your husband—God comfort him, did also, and not by my unjust scars or my birth. As for my parents' resting in unconsecrated ground—to you I can tell it, that my wife's father was on the side of the rebels and aided them with money and rede if not deed. He lost friends and cousins by the headsman's ax, down in the south. So, though no offense could be brought home to him when the King's judges went the rounds, he was already tainted by association, and need not shrink cautiously from kinship with Joan and Franklin Oxerd. May God reward him."

"May God give him *full* credit for his goodness!" Elizabeth laughed, with a little grimace.

"What would be the sense of blinding myself, in gratitude?" Frank countered, seriously. "That would defeat the very thing for which I am indebted to him and make me out the merest abject butt of his charity."

"Upon my soul, Frank, it is good to hear you!"

"It is good to see you, Elizabeth. The more as you look better by far than—than I feared to find you." Elizabeth protested with a gesture. "I do not mean that you have not grown older—"

"Now that is more like the old Frank!" she laughed again.

"—but you look—happier—than I dared to hope." Frank remained serious. "Just as it irks me when strangers would pretend that my face is like any other, I would not insult you with silence on your sorrows."

"You are right," Elizabeth responded in the same vein. "My sorrows have not weighed me down. God be praised, for that He rained sorrows upon me right after Luke went—else might I not have been able to bear *that*."

"I heard you lost several children, one after the other, ere I had long been gone," Frank said, after all somewhat awkwardly.

For she must know it, that there had been not a little talk. First Margaret had died—looking, it was said, very much as Luke had, about the face, when he became a leper, and the mother had not allowed anyone to see the child's body. Still, Margaret had been sickly all her short life. But Margaret had scarce been buried when the youngest babe, Jude, was found stifled in the cradle, on his face. It was not very likely that he had turned himself right over, at his age. Still, if God wills it, anything is possible. Alicia had not begun to ail until two years after she had lost her father. She was too old for her mother to do anything but tend her. She had taken a twelvemonth to die. Again Elizabeth had so contrived it that no outsider set eyes on the little girl during her illness, and in her coffin she had been half veiled by bandages. Everyone knows that children are most prone to that infection.

But more explicitly than this folk had not spoken, even among themselves. The word leprosy had never been uttered in context with these deaths, nor the suggestion of crime. Elizabeth had had so much to bear, with a newly widowed daughter also on her hands through it all, it was felt this matter must be left as solely between her and the Lord God. Time was when it would not have been thus slurred over, such a woman's great trials notwithstanding, when leprosy had been regarded as God's curse pure and simple, and never in the light of mere disease. But Bedesford had honored St. Francis' leper for nearly two score years; and God had crucified Luke with leprosy, not for his sins alone, but mostly for ours.

"It was not an easy time I had," Elizabeth agreed steadily. "It was no easy time for anybody here. We had the soldiers quartered on us. It was a year and more before the last of them left. My cousin Gervase himself went to London to beg that they be recalled. You can still see the traces of their sojourn everywhere in Bedesford. The town has never had the means to mend all the damage. We have each patched our own, piece by piece, as best we could. But few orchards have been replanted. Perhaps they never will be. There is more grazing land, and people have stocked up their folds instead. For my brother's sake I must be glad of that. The extra wool goes to his yard as of its own accord. I betray no secret. You know and everybody knows that neither of my parents' children take after them in merchants' acumen and drive."

"His case and yours are rather different," Frank said with a hint of scorn.

"You must not talk like that, Frank. We must be just to Little John. It is not his fault, but our mother's. He was older than you are now before he was allowed his first decision. Until her strength failed so suddenly, Mother decided everything. She brooked no advice save Luke's, and would trust none but him to be her deputy in anything, ever. You know that. My brother was trained up to be guided, not to lead. Happily the Trefeller business needs no leading. It is like a good, old horse that knows its way, you can sit and nod in the saddle. Yet I do not mean to blame Mother, either. It is hard to see how else she could have acted. Pity you could not have come to her funeral. It was a goodly one. It was the first big funeral in Bedesford celebrating a natural death—"

"Your children—" Frank contradicted before he had time to think. "When young children die it hardly seems so natural."

"What about your other children?" Frank said quickly. "Give me the news of them."

"Isabella you have already seen. She is more like my sister than my daughter. Sometimes I must say she is as a mother to me," Elizabeth shook her head and uttered that little laugh which he had marked before, sad but tranquil. "She will not remarry, she says. And now I have come to believe she never will. It seems I shall have no grandchildren by my daughters. That I do regret. A strange woman's child cannot be the same, I am thinking, even if its father be one's son. Lucy —did you not call to see Lucy at Thirchester? She is well, and continues well content." She laughed again. "If Isabella mothers me, Lucy is like my aunt—my aunt Philippa, of blessed memory. Whether it be because they dwelt in such close friendship, or whether they took to each other because they were so like from the start—who can tell? Peter and Robin have been home several times, though not once did it fall out that they came both at the same time. No, they are neither of them married. I am hoping to see them both together this year, or early in the next. Perhaps, if I send you word, you could arrange to join them here? You see, I want to settle the future. Peter is to take over Smithy Yard, but I want to wait until Little Luke is fifteen years old before I yield up the rule of this house entirely. I want to see him grown up, and sure of his way and his inclinations. I am hoping that he and Peter will be partners. At present his heart—Little Luke's—is all in sheep, and he has such a way with them. Ours all know him and hearken to him, as they might be dogs. He can do with them what even Jane could not. Well, I want to talk it all over with all of them, and with your assistance. I also hope that you will go on acting on our behalf another five years. Little Luke is ten now. Robin has told me many times that he will not forsake the sea. You ought to see him! He wears a beard—a red beard, though his hair is nigh as dark as yours. He is brown as a nut, and his teeth are nut-white. I fear me he has been no monk in his bachelor manhood. Little Luke is out at school, you will see him later. He is so good and gentle. That is one reason why I want to be sure of his welfare before I cease being the mistress here."

"He should be safe enough with his own brothers."

"It is not that I do not trust them. But you must have come across his kind, yourself. There are people make it impossible for others not to take advantage of them. I must make sure. Also, I want to settle everything for Isabella—"

"You talk as if you thought of dying, Mistress."

"We none of us know how long we have got. Howbeit I do not feel like dying just yet. I have other plans. There is Isabella with your wife and sister-in-law. Have you been shown over the house, ladies? Come to the fire and rest, the ale is hot."

Isabella truly looked younger sister to her mother: her maiden sister, much more nunlike than her late great-aunt or Lucy in their splendid, healthy sleekness. She looked faded and drawn, with a mien of such all-embracing kindliness as comes only from a heart irreparably broken and kept alive in purest resignation. With Frank she behaved as though she had forgotten all about her old hostility, but for which Luke might never have seriously contemplated establishing him at Damesbury. Frank himself had not forgotten, but had lost the cause from view, so that, whilst growing more reserved for her presence, he showed no uneasiness at seeing her already on whispering terms with his wife. The sister-in-law was much like the young Mistress Oxerd, having the same bright, candid look and bearing. Behind them came two nurses with Frank's three children: as plump and clean as two cows with their calves at the Whitsun fair.

"I pray you will not let us interrupt you, Mistress," Frank's wife said winningly. "My husband has been so eager to hear all about his old friends. Though my sister and I may not catch all your references, be sure we shall not disturb you with questions in between. So pray tell on."

Elizabeth smiled at her, considered, then threw up her hands. "God help me, now I cannot think of anything to tell. What else has happened, Isabella?"

"I know not what you have already told him, Mother," Isabella said with an indulgent smile. "Does he know that James Smith has three sons? Otherwise James is not doing too well. Some of his land has gone bad on him. Oh, have you told that at Trefeller Court there is now a lawful heir to my uncle John?"

"No!" cried Frank, laughing and slapping his thigh.

"It is not quite as you think," Elizabeth broke in, trying hard not to laugh also. "My nephew is no son of poor Susannah's. No, you tell it, Isabella."

"You will tell it far better than I," said her withered daughter, but without any hint of reproach such as Elizabeth seemed guiltily to expect for her access of mirth.

When Juliana handed over the keys of Trefeller Court and took to her bed, this time not to rise from it again, she had imposed two conditions on her successors. Firstly, Little John was on no account to press the King for repayment of her loan, even after she was out of the way. Thus she calculated, the King's conscience would make the more certain that he kept his promise. But this would be of little value without a son of Little John's to carry on the noble name. Furthermore, Lord Gervase had no children, and without a Trefeller heir to dispute it, the manor might fall to Elizabeth's descendants, or, worse still, be willed away to the Jolybody stock. Sir Asphodel, who had equipped some soldiers for Gervase in autumn, 1381, was clamoring for reimbursement. So Juliana stipulated that Little John procure a son by adoption.

The widow, poor soul, by that time had started going a little queer in the head, as women ofttimes will at a certain age. Nevertheless Elizabeth had cherished a hope that the choice might fall on Little Luke, of whom the Trefellers and the Cinqmorts were alike so fond. The widow herself wanted him well and truly for her own at last. But Juliana was set against this, seeing that there was a plentitude of Little John's own flesh and blood.

So what was surely a unique gathering had been called together at Trefeller Court, of all the bastards of Little John's getting. A few did not accept the invitation, being the sons of married women. Three or four were impostors, notably one, a great hulking swineherd in the tileries' employ, and the image, albeit stupid looking, of Abbot William Goliard. In the main they were genuine, of all ages between a few months and seventeen years. There must have been nearly a score, and then there were the mothers accompanying the infants, and other witnesses to speak for some of the others. Two hapless women had brought girl children and were shown the door at once.

Little John sat in a chair, between his mother and his wife. He alone looked sheepish and baffled. Everybody else had sharp eyes and flushed cheeks. He acknowledged every claimant. He could not make up his mind which one to favor.

Poor Susannah's wits became confused in the midst of such abundance. Seeing all the children she and her husband might have had together, it seems that for odd, benighted moments she thought them hers, and exultantly called Juliana to witness her pride. She was no use in helping the decision.

"It would be only right if we kept them all! Look at this one! Look at his dear, round legs and burnished John's hair! Nay, but this one— his limbs are like sticks, and he is all spots and sores. For sure the Blessed Virgin would want us to take and cosset *him!* Oh, oh, look at this sprightly sprig! a feather in his hat and all. Ay, lad, the girls already know you for your father's son, I'll warrant! Ah, that one has wet the floor: it means he feels at home here, for sure it is a Sign! And oh, the babes, the little ones! Nay, Juliana. Nay, my husband. We shall have to take one of *them,* that he may grow up knowing no other parents. But which one, which one? They are so alike. They are alike darling angels. It will be company for them to have each other, in this house full of old folk. Oh, very well. I know whatever I may say is wrong. But I think we must have these two—no, the three of them. And yet, when I gaze round and see *him* again, and him, and that one—"

"Sit down, Susannah, and hold your tongue," Juliana at length put her down, with something of her old manner.

The children were called up for inspection, one by one, and subjected to various tests to show up their natures. Juliana waved away the smallest, because there was no means of telling how they might turn out. In the end a lad of about Little Luke's age was selected, a sturdy, fair-haired bird scarer of Cloudsway, whose mother had died at his birth, and who had answered the question, what would he do if given a penny, with the cautious yet smiling reply, "Why, thank ye right heartily!" This, Juliana deemed, showed he had his wits about him, without making him out a skulking fox. After the others had been dismissed, the widow grew well pleased with the winner, whose name was also John. From that hour onward she had no more eyes for Little Luke. This, then, was how Elizabeth had got him back, to live for the first time at his real home.

But the King, you must know, lost his throne before he made any move to ennoble Juliana's son.

The following Sunday the Oxerds went to Mass in great state. Afterward Frank paid his respects to his cousin the Abbot, and presented his family. Then he had himself shown over the cathedral, where the repairs were nearly finished, the new tower about to be started, and saw the Bishop's tomb, also Juliana's, eventually to be graced with an effigy of John Trefeller, though his bones reposed inextricably in the plague pit at the old churchyard. So much Frank saw under monks' guidance. But when he went to speak to his humbler kinsmen, Jaffy, Jacob, and James, they led him out into the new growth of the cloister walk, and there, with fingers to their lips, silently indicated the first corbels.

Each corbel in the cloister walk, stranger, bears a face, which is meant to represent someone lost his life when the Rebellion was put down. They are not all good portraits, for that we must be able to call them this saint and that on inquiry—all except Dick and the outlaw, Priest, whom we call Belial and Beelzebub, and Joan Oxerd, who is A Lost Soul. But those who knew could recognize them. The saints, we trow, forgave us. After all, some image makers use mortal daughters of Eve as models for Christ's Holy Mother.

Outside, many people lingered about St. Francis' Churchyard and the Wasteside green. Frank placed himself at the head of his train, gave a hand to each of the goldsmith's daughters, and made for the mounting stones by the railing where the horses were tied up. Thus he came face to face with Lord Gervase, who had just swung himself into the saddle, waiting for his henchmen to follow suit.

For a moment one thought their physical positions favored the Cinq-mort lord. Looking down, from his high dapple-gray, upon Frank who, yet unmounted, had to raise his face and thus display his mutilated nose most crassly. Yet behind Frank there stood enough dependents to people a small village, all well fed, well clad, clean, and shod. Behind the lord of Bedesford came a single pair of rather unkempt men with dented breastplates and tarnished sword belts.

"Well met, Frank Oxerd. Have you come back for a sniff of Bedesford air?" My lord hailed the other first, loudly and jauntily. Some of us bit our lips and closed our eyes. The reference to sniffing, an action of the nose, was undoubtedly anything but accidental. "Have you come to get an *earful* of Bedesford news?" Yet Young Gervase had done everything in his power to dissuade Lord Hugh from his unlawful action against Frank! It does not require much thought to understand what prompted him now. Hugh's wretched end, his own shabbiness, and Frank's prosperity made it a pious duty to be brazen.

"Ay, my lord," Frank replied easily. "Allow me to present my wife, my wife's sister, my children. I trust I see your lordship well?" It had been most difficult for him, you will agree, to hit on just the right way of receiving and returning my lord's salutation. And how easily his show of equanimity might have appeared groveling! Instead, he managed to suggest that the permanent results of their last encounter were a matter of serene indifference to him, while in regard to the injustice of the outrage forgiveness was but living up to Christian precepts.

This put Lord Gervase at an immediate disadvantage, also making it impossible for him, in dignity, abruptly to break off a chat which he had been the one to start. So for him it went from bad to worse. At the other end of the conversational seesaw, Frank could hardly help rising to increasing heights of condescension, at the same rate as my lord willy-nilly fell into defensiveness.

"I am glad to see you so free from rancor," Lord Gervase at length tried to re-establish supremacy.

"What's done is done, and what is bygone, gone," Frank said with a shrug. "Nor would it become a man to hold another answerable for the misdeeds of a third. I am thankful to say that I have no complaints."

"That is plain," my lord smiled with his lips.

"Ay," Frank nodded curtly. "So I would even say this, my lord. I should be right happy to see you our guest at Damesbury one of these days. I make bold to promise your lordship entertainment that will do honor both to you and to ourselves. What do you say, wife?"

Will it astonish you to hear that in course of time Lord Gervase followed the invitation? Whether it be that he thought Frank had not extended it seriously, and thought to embarrass the newly high and mighty; whether it were boredom drove him; or whether, craving change of scene, he had no wish to descend in his poverty upon his equals, we cannot say. The manor was not yet rebuilt. But after Juliana's funeral he had left Trefeller Court and moved into the gatehouse chamber, where Lord Hugh had resided during the Black Death, preferring its squalor to the cramping, specious comforts of kinfolks' hospitality.

Yet, when one comes to think on it, he had ever led a guest's life. Albeit Lord Hugh had designated Gervase as his heir, he had not allowed the young man to forget who owned the manor while his uncle was alive. Perhaps, after leaving the shelter of Juliana's roof, the combination of discomfort and responsibility, alike unaccustomed, proved too much for him, regardless of pride. To be an heir had suited him; dependent, yet ornamental rather than hireling.

The difference between ornament and pet is not great. At Danesborough they may have made much of him, to begin with, for the satisfaction of his host. But soon enough the commoners' gratification of having a noble lord in their midst would have asserted itself, if not in Frank, assuredly in the goldsmith and his daughters—to say nothing of the neighbors. One month became two, then half a year. In the end it came as a surprise to none, that my lord suffered himself to be married to the young, wholesome sister-in-law.

The goldsmith had no other children. He could have well have afforded to let the pair dwell and rule in Bedesford. But somehow that did not come to pass. The whole family went on living together in the mansion under the Oxerd sign. The Trefellers and the Robinsons severally stayed there on occasion, and pieced together their reports.

In a sense Lord Gervase was the center of the household, round whom everything revolved—everything, that is to say, in respect of the comfort and fineness of the home. His wife pampered him, the housefolk sang his poems and helped spread them through the shire and beyond. His father-in-law, and even Frank Oxerd, upheld *his* judgment in all matters of taste. But when all is said and done, these were not the main concern of the house. The very women knew about what was doing in the way of business—but they told Gervase, when perchance he asked (from sheer politeness), not to worry his head with such humdrum affairs. His children were brought up outside his power, though taught to give him every affection and reverence. But when aught troubled her, his wife confided in her sister.

All agreed that, honored and humored at all times, Lord Gervase enjoyed the life. Nonetheless it would seem that at heart he apprehended it as clearly as the visitors who summed it up. For although he had at least two children living at the time of his demise (in the year of the truce with France, when the King rid himself of his guardians, and the timber of Cloudsway Monastery began at last to be replaced with stone), it was found that he had willed the manor lands away from them. He bequeathed these to his young cousin, Luke Robinson the Younger.

Now, his widow could have contested the will, but, with the consent of her kin, she decided to rest content with the titular lordship of Bedesford for her descendants. Needless to say, such a division of land and title did not long endure. Today Bedesford is a municipality not unlike London, with only squires at the manor. And there are well-to-do commoners in Danesborough by the name of Cinqmort, while the earls of Danesborough have a pair of horns and a goad among their quarterings. We have two squires. The second is Big John Trefeller, Little John's adopted heir, for Little John had been Lord Gervase's acting steward, and was minded to go to law against his nephew, Little Luke. In the end repeated citation of past example persuaded him to settle out of court and agree to an unequal partition of the Cinqmort property between the two houses that had sprung from it.

CHAPTER 2

THE LEPERS

THE COCK CROWED. The moon had set and all was in darkness. When the church bell, less than a hundred yards away, began tolling, it was sound, and not light, which helped one place the window. The window was of fair size, two foot square, with leaded glass panes in hinged frames. The whole little house of one room was well and stoutly built, and kept warm by sharing each of its side walls with another exactly like it. The door had a grating at eye level, with a shutter that could be lifted from outside, and no bolt or key. The furniture consisted of two pallets, one stool, one large leather jug, two staffs, two bowls, and two clappers. One of the occupants stirred and wakened, and lay, listening a while longer. Now their own bell no longer knelled alone. It was well worth listening to, the song of the innumerable bells, intricately swelling and abating, when the breeze was right, from Canterbury.

Now the Knights were trooping across the churchyard. Now the darkness grayed, the first birds began to chirp, babies to cry stutteringly, children emit shrill matutinal chatter. Adult murmurs came, too, and coughing, and an animal wheezing, cackling, and grunting. Only when the real farmyard noises resounded from the stalls and enclosures between the houses and the Black Prince's spring, did one realize that the former wheeze and grunt and cackle was of human origin.

He had had plenty of time to get used to it, yet every day the realization smote Edwin afresh. He could not stop himself waking in time to overhear the whole sequence, every single morning, year in, year out. Luke as unfailingly would sleep through it.

It was not yet time to rouse him. Edwin got up, careful to make no noise. By the first light of dawn he inspected himself, surveyed his face in a bowlful of water, unwound the bandages covering his arms and neck and looked at what was beneath, shook his head, and tied the filthy rags about him again. It was a matter of form: he did not really expect the marks of leprosy. His hair and beard, every strand a differently-hued shade of grime and senile fading, were long and wild, and he had scarcely washed himself since the day he joined Luke. The dirt upon him must be hardened in several layers. He had nigh as many skins as an onion. That, and his hairiness and ancient bandages, was all the disguise he had—all that he needed. If he had to wash before others, enough layers of dirt remained under what came off, and new bandages waxed as bad as the old very quickly. He was an abomination to himself. He daily saw innocent children in all stages of rotting alive. His own spare old ill-used body remained healthy.

He tiptoed over to the other pallet.

"I am awake, Edwin," the creature thereon spoke. "Were you thinking I might have died in the night? Alas, I can feel life strong within me yet. Oh, I shall live to make your life more loathsome to you day by day. For years I shall go on, I trow. We never thought, either of us, that corruption could be so unendingly inventive, did we? Why do you stay with me?"

"Because I would miss this your every morning chant, I verily believe," Edwin replied. "Come, let yourself be washed, dear brother. Did you sleep well?"

"Ay. Very well. I dreamed."

Edwin having helped Luke to get up and complete his toilet, they both went down on their knees for the prescribed prayers. All round these prayers were being said. You could hear the spring bubbling, and the footfall of the Knights returning from the church. A scent of burning porridge called to breakfast.

Edwin pulled Luke up on to his feet, handed him his bowl, and took his own, as well as staff and clapper, which Luke was no longer able to use. Very slowly, because Luke could not go any faster, they went out into the barely sun-touched court and joined the stream of their fellows, all making for the kitchen wicket.

Here indeed that exuberant inventiveness of decay, defying the art of God and man, boastfully gloried in superabundance. No two men, women, or desecrated children were as like each other as are the most divers, hale members of the race. They jostled and pushed, bade each other the time of day, and exchanged such gossip as the night had either interrupted or developed. There were crosscurrents of venom and jealousy and of overeffusion. A number of lepers were not on speaking terms; and love, so far from uniting them all in suffering fraternity, was more often but a strategic demonstration.

Today a third Knight came up to stand beside the two that dealt out the gruel, and intently scanned the passing file. A remark of his was overheard and passed on backward to those still waiting their turn. There were some highborn pilgrim ladies coming, and the Knight was to select two deserving cases for their ministrations.

The courtyard buzzed like a garbage heap. For this meant that the pair who had lately served for such occasions must have died or fallen out of favor. Everyone looked round to see whether they were present. If there had been a death, it must have occurred during the night.

"Do none of you know? To be sure, these are the first visitors this year. The pilgrim season has only just started."

"It may be that Gerry and Tump can no longer move."

"In that case they could still be carried to the parlor."

"But they might no longer be deemed sweet enough for the noble ladies," someone cackled, and a chorus of loud guffaws went up.

Show lepers were supposed to be determined by their age and the length of their stay in the community. People began to ask whether at any time in the past such seniors had been withdrawn when advanced disease made them too appalling. But none had been here long enough to answer with any authority.

"Mark my word, Tump forgot himself and spoke to a Knight in the way he did to us," a female leper said, vindictively hopeful.

"I always marveled the Knights were deceived by the honeyed cringing of those two."

"Too long did they strut amongst us as if they owned the lazaretto."

"It isn't as if folk could take any credit in having been born, and sent here, ahead of others."

"If the choice fell on me, none would mark any difference in *my* bearing. Not that I desire it."

"Nay, *you* don't desire it, do you. That's why you have been crawling round Sir George this many a day, with flattery and firewood and loud-mouthed meekness!"

"Can I help it if I've been here seven years?"

"You lie. It is not even six."

"At all events I was before *you*."

"I marvel God does not strike you dead on the spot. Hey, Joan, you will bear me out—"

"What would be the good of it for the ladies' souls to wash and kiss either of you? Look at you both! You don't look as if there were much wrong with you," she to whom they had appealed said, with only relative truth.

"Ay, it would serve them best to get *you*, walking cesspit that you are—"

The quarreling lost all restraint and swiftly embroiled everybody. In the middle of it the excitement felled one leper in a fit of contortions and foaming. At once the rest ceased reviling each other and sought to do what they could for him, as tenderly as their decrepit limbs allowed. The Knight who had been about to come and restore order, stepped back into his place.

"You two," said the other Knight, when Luke and Edwin had their bowls filled. "Eat up here and now, and come with me."

Luke, trembling, could not swallow, every mouthful went the wrong way, spilling the front of his tunic or rending him with coughs, so that presently he gave it up and begged Edwin to have his share. Following the Knight all the way back past those yet unfed, Edwin and Luke tried to look modest and unconcerned.

In the parlor there was a wall fireplace with logs laid ready to be lit, two long, narrow tables with benches, two chairs, a stoop, a crucifix, a painted image of the Blessed Virgin, and the escutcheon of the knightly order. The floor was covered in Dutch tiles, the walls were white-

washed, with three windows piercing each of the two longer ones. This
building stood by itself, at the entrance to the quadrangle. Edwin and
Luke were told to sit down in the big chairs and wait. They were left
alone.

Suddenly Luke said, "Strange, is it not, my Edwin. Here we are, glad
and proud to have been chosen. Yet I mind it well, what I felt when
first we got here and learned of this custom. It seemed to me the worst
—the very worst that can befall a leper. To be sat down here, an object
of the greatest horror, and therefore of the greatest charitable piety—
the hardest trial, set for other souls to redeem themselves by and prove
their worth before God. I mind how I shuddered inwardly and thanked
the Lord that yet I was a long way from being suitable. I remember it,
Edwin. Yet I feel it not. I feel—God forgive me, and my poor wife too—
I feel much as I did on my wedding morn."

"I," Edwin nodded, "feel as I did the first time Brother Laurentius
praised handiwork of mine. Strange."

They sat in silent meditation until the Knight came with the ladies
and their servants, the latter carrying clothes bags, basins, towels, ewers,
and jars of perfumed oils and salves. The Knight made a few explana-
tory and commending remarks about the show lepers, pointing out that
Edwin, though not so ravaged as Luke, should be honored for his great
goodness and patience toward his brother in misfortune. There was a
noticeable edging, on the ladies' part, in Edwin's direction. Then the
Knight told the lepers a little about the ladies. The least of them was
more highly born than any Luke or Edwin had ever met when yet
they were accounted living men. Some wore pilgrim's hats tied over
their silken headdresses, or hooded cloaks of velvet with much fur. The
mud crusts over their shoes displayed the heavy excrescences of underlying jewels, and their fingers shone with gold, their breathing bosoms
tinkling with it. Their hands and faces were smooth, apart from some
wrinkles and veins in the more elderly—but those one did not count,
here. Their eyes were bright, and no mere fissures in swellings of unfathomable structure. They smelled of ambergris and of good, honest,
healthy sweat. As the servants, under the Knight's direction, made
everything ready, the ladies chatted in subdued but celestially clear and
flexible voices.

"Oh, I am stiff! These roads! These hired mules!"

"It is much pleasanter here than I imagined. For most of these people,
these must be far better houses than they were used to before."

"Not all lazarettos are like this one. It is one of the finest in England, perhaps in all the world. Prince Edward, you must know, endowed it richly, having found relief at the spring. Is this your first time of leper washing, Lady? I have been here twice before. And I dare swear there are not many foundations in the country which I have not visited. They are not all so conveniently situated and easy of access as this one, so close to Canterbury town, and by the pilgrim road. You look a trifle pale, Lady. Be assured the first few moments are the worst. You may take it from me that has done this times out of number. There is nothing like for making one feel purified and holy, soul safe and contented afterward. There, there, sit down a moment; it is nearly time to start."

"I think it is only because of the other ones, outside," the new initiate whispered, "that waved and gibbered at us and thrust at us with hands without fingers. I think it was that they *did* so still makes me feel faint —not that they *were* so— Our two here are—are *quiet*."

The fire was lit and all the necessary gear in position. The ladies kilted up their skirts and pinned back their sleeves, and finally were arranged in two groups before the lepers. There were two to each foot. Kneeling, they stripped Luke's feet and Edwin's of buskins and bandages. One of each pair took the basin in her lap and placed a foot in it, her partner pouring over it the water from the ewer. Edwin twitched once or twice; Luke felt nothing. The servants stood behind their mistresses, handing over soap and scent and the like when required.

"Is there no merit, then, in doing this only once?" the young pilgrim and her veteran protectress continued their conversation over one of Luke's feet.

"Oh, yes, there is," the other said reassuringly. "Except that to my mind there must surely be greater virtue in a repetition—when you already know what it is like. But if today you have fulfilled a vow, there is no reason to worry and think you have not. Nay, it is but that I myself seem to have come to need the exercise the way some must regularly journey to certain invigorating baths." She smiled, lifting the foot and signing to her companion to take the basin away and spread a towel over her lap. "Nay, do not throw out the water. It will still be needed. Now the nard, and the babes' water ointment. So. You are doing very well, my dear. Nay, it is by no means usual," she went on, not without complacency, "for folk to go the rounds of all the lazarettos— for lay folk, at all events. I cannot call to mind having met more than one other person who did so, in all my journeyings. Ay, another woman. Just an ordinary woman, too, not a great lady. Rich, to be sure, she must be. The expense mounts up, what with essences and perfumes, and sets of brand new shoes and stockings every time, over and above the cost of traveling. I met her last; where was it? At Norwich in Norfolk. She had already been to London, and this settlement here was the first she had ever gone to, she told me. She only started a few years ago, when her family no longer needed her. Among the lower orders, my dear, it is only widows and grandmothers can go on pilgrimages every year! Once every year she goes, this woman, timing it so that her visit falls on a certain date, which is that of her marriage—it has stuck in my mind because she put it somewhat oddly. She called it the date of her second marriage to the same husband. I meant to ask her about that, but we got talking, and it slipped my mind. You see, she was not a real widow. Her husband had been put away as a leper after the Eighty-one. (Did I tickle you, my brother-in-Christ? Hold still, then; I will take better care.) Of course she had not been told to what lazaretto he was sent. It was her great wish and hope to find him and be given grace to wash his feet. She did not think it likely he had died meanwhile, as he was not greatly diseased at the time of his going, and would not be sixty years old now. Of course, you never can tell with leprosy. Sometimes they live for years, and sometimes they die in a month. I promised to pray for her, that she might find him, poor soul." The lady jumped, as the leper unexpectedly spoke.

"Most like she would not know him if she did find him."

There was a pause, then the lady strove to answer in a natural tone. "Oh, but *she* will not be so changed. See you. He would know her and make himself known."

"It depends what manner of man he is," the second, lesser leper said softly.

"If he loves her as it seems she loves him," said the worst leper again, "he would never, never tell."

"Is he weeping?" the elder pilgrim asked the supervising Knight over her shoulder, with an expression of ghastly terror. "Weeping *tears?*"

The younger, previously more squeamish one, had already risen to her feet and, unbidden, was wiping Luke's cheeks of the teardrops, pure and crystalline as anybody's, which besprinkled them.

"What was her name, that other woman's?" asked Edwin, "that my brother and I may also pray for her?"

"Widow Smith, was it? Franklin? Robinson? Brown? Some such name. Of Bedesford—that I do remember, because the Anglemere relic lives there too. Dare I hope," said the lady, a little acidly, "that you will pray for us, too, that have tended you this day?"

"We will pray for you with all our hearts," said Edwin. Luke only nodded.

"The Lord saith: what ye have done unto these, ye have done unto Me," said the Knight.

The ladies finished dressing the lepers in the fine footgear they had brought them, then kissed the shoes, rinsed their hands in the washing water, and in humble formula begged for the lepers' blessing.

When they had gone, leaving offerings for a wax candle apiece, the Knight told Luke and Edwin to take off the new hose and shoes and put on their old ones again. These pious gifts were usually too brave for lepers. They were collected in a special storehouse, and taken away annually to be sold in London, the proceeds contributing to the upkeep of the lazaretto.

CHAPTER 3

THE SETTING FREE

IN THE BEGINNING leprosy produces unwanted additions to the mortal casing it afflicts, later to make it dwindle. The more Luke's body was eaten away, the more the prison crumbled—the more impenetrable it became. The core of life within it in truth was terribly strong. The means of movement left him; his voice strings, tongue, and onetime lips became useless. He was unable to help himself or to make known his thoughts or wishes. Inside, beyond all communication, yet with undiminished powers of hearing, there lived on and on the same person that had inhabited this body ever since God clad a soul in budding flesh, in his mother's womb.

Edwin had to do everything for him. A baby is less helpless than was Luke. No mother could have been more devoted. Unanswered, he had to go on talking to the prisoner, too. Nevertheless he dreaded the day that would leave him without Luke. And nevertheless he prayed God constantly to release Luke.

At last the day came and Luke's spirit, by nature lively and cheerful, broke from the wreck that had bound it so long.

Edwin longed for a breath of fresh air, and of freedom, too. He looked about him and suddenly could no longer comprehend how he had been able to exist in such confinement. For an age, it seemed, he had not even spent more time out of doors than it took to fetch food for them both. It was long since the office of show lepers had gone to another pair. They had had no visitors since the last rites were performed over the mute rudiment. Edwin had *not* made anything with his hands since leaving Bedesford. He felt now he could not stay at the lazaretto another instant.

He could not bear to wait for any third person to find them together. He would only be praised again, and confidently assured of heavenly reward. Now he knew that his urge to accompany Luke had drawn some of its substance from a well-masked cunning. Punished by proxy all his life, he had confusedly hoped to atone, through Luke, by proxy. And all along there had been the promise of Luke's deathbed. When Luke lay dying, Edwin had imagined, he would relieve his heart and recite the story of his crime, put into words for the first time. He had hoped to be selfish beyond belief. Why wait until Luke lay dying, unless he had cherished a sneaking wish to make use of Luke as a messenger sure of God's ear? But then before Luke died in actual fact he had needed talk of happy things—robbing him of his faith in a sanctified leper's hand was impossible. It seems curious, perhaps, for Edwin never reflected that his own faith, after all, had not been shaken by his knowledge, for he never doubted any of the Cloudsway miracles (which none could have witnessed and doubted), realizing that in them God had at once set to naught and made good use of Edwin's crime.

God not having granted him leprosy, it was his duty now to escape from the lazaretto and seek atonement along other paths. The settlement was guarded, and he had no clothes but his leper's uniform. Washing off his carefully accumulated counterfeit leprosy presented the hardest task of all. Only his bandages were simply discarded. Luke had died in the small hours, time of most deaths. Very quietly Edwin opened the door and edged along the row of houses that formed one front. They looked bigger and statelier in the solitude, the church on its hillock bulked like a cathedral; black and solid yet distant, against the bare, quiet stretches of moonlit ground. By cautious stages he crept across to the churchyard. He had not been afraid of night and its demons since the Cloudsway robbery. If the powers of darkness had not pounced on him then they never would—not, at least, until the parting of his soul and body.

Creeping from shadow to shadow, grave to grave, he at length gained shelter behind the church and made for the surrounding wall of loosely piled stone slabs. He had to wade through a field of nettles, and then clamber up and across. Canterbury was less than three miles away, and at either side of the pilgrim road there were only open fields. He walked, blissfully alone, with cool, earth-scented air all about him.

He hid in a ditch, near the town wall but off the road. There he stayed without food, drink, or covering—and it rained most of the time —all day. Once a dog nosed him out and stayed, barking fiercely, for a long while, but at length grew bored and went away. When dusk came round again, Edwin stiffly slipped cover and made for the gates, just before they were closed. There was such a turmoil of late carts, pilgrims, and other that, as he had hoped, he got through crawling along under a heavily loaded wagon. The only really difficult part was getting out from between the shrieking wheels before they worked up speed again, without being seen by driver and watchmen. But he managed that, too. If his heart beat at all faster, it was with the exertion knowing that God meant him to act as he was doing; his confidence never faltered.

Once inside the town, hiding was easy. The odors of evening meals all round were less easy to endure. He drank some rain water that had collected in a potsherd. He waited until after curfew had been rung, then at the back of some poor tavern found what he was looking for— a confusion of narrow alleys and crowded, jumbled houses, a fence, and a large festering mound of refuse. Dogs started baying as soon as gingerly he set about climbing the fence. He made the sign of the cross and joined his voice to theirs, shouting, bellowing, took a deep breath and closed his eyes and pinched his nose shut with his fingers, and immersed himself in the midden. He wallowed in it, covered his hair, his beard, his face with it, all the while crying hoarsely now, for help. He tried to breathe through his mouth only. The unseen dogs were in a frenzy. He could hear doors and windows opening and voices clamoring. When he had racked his wits for a way of escape, God had sent him a memory of Young Gervase, and how he had come to be spared at Oxford.

Presently he was surrounded by people, some with lanterns, and creating such a hubbub that none would ever recollect what they had or had not heard. Edwin tried to struggle out toward them, but without pretense now had hard work of it, falling and splashing backward. A dozen helpful hands were extended, but at first plainly could not bring themselves actually to grab hold of him. It was the women in the crowd who gave the lead in final, effective resolution.

Edwin stammered out some fragments of the tale he had prepared. He was a pilgrim of the poorer sort, whose gray hair and lean purse had not protected him from being set upon when slightly tipsy and stumbling in search of the privy, robbed, beaten, and on the top of that thrown into the muck, after which his assailant had run off jeering. He counted on it that every kind of hostelry was crammed at this season, and that everyone might assume he had already been inside this particular one. The color of his hair he mentioned because no one could tell whether he be young or old. A young man in his present straits would have met with nothing but derision. As it was, the irresistible humor of the situation was softened by indignant sympathy; even though they were shouting with laughter, people hastened him indoors and purposefully went to work on him. On all sides, slow-dying giggles notwithstanding, condemnation of the invented villains was loud and earnest. Sure enough, more than one of the guests remembered having sat next to an old man that must have been Edwin, and even to have seen him on the road, just as many had heard the robbers' receding footfall.

His unexaminable clothes were pitched back on the midden. Naked, and unaffectedly shaking from head to foot, Edwin was stood in a tub and doused with buckets of hot water. All the neighborhood collected round him in the kitchen of the inn, and several women dashed back to their houses for free gifts of soap. Edwin thought the skin would surely be shredded off him; folk took it in turns to scrub him down with straw and rags. The innkeeper brought him a pair of old breeches. One of the women fetched a patched frock of her own, which there and then she cut to the right length for a kirtle. Someone else offered him a hat. Then they sat him down in the taproom and fed him till, dizzy with creature joy, he thought he would surely burst. He longed to know what he looked like. His hair and beard being smoothly wet and beautifully combed, the clean wanness of his face overspread by a flush, there must have been a childlike appeal about this small old fellow. They all vied in doing him kindness, and left him to sleep until midday.

Having supped so late and well, he was hungrier for his morning meal than he had been throughout yesterday's complete fast. But the innkeeper and his wife were sober, and busy with the concerns of a new day. While Edwin was told to forget his night's debt, they advised him to seek further aid at the nearest Franciscan hostel.

Edwin did not know the town, but even if he had it would have baffled him. For a little he wandered about without asking the way, trying to get to know again what life was like and how it was lived, what innumerable objects and usages went into it and had to be taken for granted. Thus must infants learn—only that for them the lesson is long drawn out, not concentrated in awareness, and that their uncertainty will not create around them the hostilities of mistrust. The one useful habit which had stayed with Edwin was that of secretive reticence. He knew there was not even any need to fear that he might talk in his sleep. So far was he from betraying himself, when at the hostel he found everyone agog with the news of a runaway leper who might at any moment appear in their midst, that it did not occur to him to be afraid. Nobody could have taken him for a leper. Apart from his voice and ways, none at the lazaretto would have recognized him.

A little sadly he took his place among the mendicant pilgrims. Charity looked more goodly from the giving end. At the lazaretto, doing voluntary penance, he had never felt himself to be its object. There were only a few here elderly or old, very few sick, and but two crippled. The rest were able-bodied, and none too likable of countenance. Edwin gazed longingly at others, who were paying for their lodging, journeyman artisans they seemed for the most part to be. He looked about the cellar hall in hopes of lighting on something in need of mending, so that he might repay roof, straw, and broth.

He was still looking when he became conscious of two of the envied ones conducting a studiedly loud dialogue, somewhat stilted for the parties' complete agreement and clearly offensive intention. They were marveling that all sturdy beggars had not long since died out—of shame.

"Shame," Edwin impulsively broke into their discourse, "is a penance like nettles and whips—ay, very like. And it is not the bitterest part of this discipline of begging pilgrimage, either. Giving up work in itself is much the worst. Life without work is worse than death, for it is a living death, just like leprosy."

There was a pause, then one of the pair cleared his throat and asked awkwardly, "Is it so—have you made a vow to beg, grandfather? You must not think that we were aiming at such as you—"

"Yes. I made such a vow," said Edwin, and in his heart he vowed it then.

But in the night he suddenly awoke, to an odor of scorching. Hunting round for it, to make sure some lingering dream had not deceived his senses, he discovered that the bottom of the brazier had burned through—on the top, ash and cinders were cold and black—and allowed glowing embers to roll under the floor straw. Much of it was smoldering. He gave the alarm, and the hospital—and presumably the whole quarter where it stood—was saved. So when Edwin departed with the other beggars, the friar who saw them to the door blessed him warmly, saying that instead of receiving at their hands, Edwin left them his grateful debtors.

And thus it went on, the Divine persecution, all Edwin's pilgrim days. He was not permitted to endure the chastisement of charity.

Back and forth he trampled across the countries of England, to all the shrines he knew or heard of, be they great and splendid or obscure, the most and the least frequented. The band to which he had attached himself at Canterbury changed gradually, Edwin remaining its sole constant member. Sometimes the ailing, seeking cure, predominated, sometimes the sick of heart, or confessed sinners carrying out a vow; sham cripples, tumblers, and other parasites of the more holy resorts; students; or the same sort of vagrants that had composed it at his entry.

He came to overlook the times when the mumpers' traditional thanksgiving on departure was as true for him as for the others, and the nights when he slept in a ditch. The other times recurred so often, and so impressively. In order not to let him earn forgiveness, God contrived for him to earn his keep.

There was another occasion, on some farm in the Cotswolds, when Edwin gave the fire alarm in the nick of time. He refused to accept anything in token of the farm people's gratitude, but weeks later found in his knapsack a ring which only they could have secreted there. He made offering of it the next time they sought shelter at a religious house, which meant that he not only paid for bed and board, far more than it was worth, but that the whole band was detained for questioning until he succeeded in convincing the monks that the tale of how he had got it was true—one of the young beggars, the strongest and most shifty visaged of the lot, was even subjected to torture. But not Edwin himself, not he!

Once, in some townhouse, the hostess's spindle broke, and Edwin, without thinking, took up a knife and mended it for her—and the heavens did not fall down, his hand did not wither, though he had carved wood for the first time since he had destroyed Juliana's shutters.

At a wayside hovel in Wiltshire he delivered a reluctant oversized babe, no other experienced midwife being available.

Another time his practiced eye caused him to warn folk about a great tie beam which, when inspected, proved to be all but rotted through.

He had himself badly mauled, protecting a young boy against an angry boar.

How often folk cut him to the heart, saying, "You are not like the others. If only there were more like you, they would not have such a bad name, nor be likened to rats, locusts, and soldiers. You have nothing to thank us for, bless you." They were to know how cruelly they were hammering home, again and again and again, what he knew only too well.

Wherever he went he would feast and punish his eyes, looking at the carving work in the churches. Almost everywhere masons and wood-wrights were at work, if only on repairs, in odd corners. He realized that on a great cathedral work can never end; he thought of the Wandering Judas and wished God might have devised a similar punishment for himself. If he was to know no peace, could it not have been given him to wander from church to church through the centuries, rendering some small service to each, with hammer and chisel and stone saw?

And then there were temptations. Hardly a great church where he watched and chatted with the workmen, but had lost its central tower at some stage. In some it was said to have fallen down more than once; in one case—where was it? Salisbury? Exeter?—it had been rebuilt eight times. Perhaps, then, there was nothing so especially terrible or personal in the collapse of St. Hand's finger. In the south there was not a hamlet had failed to play its part in the great rebellion. Everywhere children and cattle had died of sweeping murrains from time to time. As for the Black Death, memories of it were fresh all over the country as in Bedesford; and in many places there were legends, obstinately defended, attributing the scourge to unique local wickedness. How foolish and vainglorious they sounded in their variety and mutual disregard! Thus, by goading his vanity into recoil from like conceited folly, the Fiend was trying to lure Edwin into disowning the full measure of his sin.

A time came when he went on with his pilgrimage only because he knew not where to go or what precisely he was making for. He hoped, with waning conviction, for some sort of sign.

One night, at Lincoln it was, he threw himself between two of his ruffianly comrades who had started quarreling on the hospital threshing floor and were snatching up flails against each other. The first blow struck the mediator across the head. As he sank to the ground, in the fraction of a moment before his senses left him, Edwin marked that they stood, aghast and pacified; and so he thought that he died happily, for them.

But alas, he wakened back to life, though there was hell raging in his head, and its bloody sparks and fiery stars kept the darkness from soothing his eyes. Round him the ground was sticky. He groped about feebly, found a flail, an overturned cup, a lump of bread: all the company had vanished, as if the earth had swallowed them. Thinking him dead, they had run away. He tried to cry for help but the attempt cut even through the hellfire in his head as with barbed knives, so he had to wait until he was found. And when the householders did come and find him, he gathered that it was broad day. For him it was still bloodshot night. He had been blinded. The first sign, and sign of God's relenting, had come to pass. He had at last sustained hurt in his own body.

There was no doubt as to the charitable treatment he now enjoyed. Even when the headache and biliousness began to abate and the wound to stop suppurating, Edwin was too weak not to submit to his hosts' decision that he must stay in their care until a batch of trustworthy pilgrims could take him with them. In any case, being blind and unversed in the ways of blindness, he could not hope to take matters into his own hands.

Meanwhile everything was done to nurse him back to full health. Not only did he have a good bed and, later, a well-cushioned seat in the chimney corner, not only did they feed him on strengthening broths and the thickest of blood-making ale, but they saw to it that there was always someone to sit with him, if it were only the younger children, sent to him to be kept quiet and out of mischief, when no one else had time to watch. An old grandfather had recently died, so that without any effort on either side Edwin slipped into his place.

To be sure, his experiences provided them with more entertainment than could have come their way in all their previous life. But neither the most inflated vanity nor the most groveling humility could have made out that thereby he was repaying their great loving kindness.

And yet Edwin could not remember placid contentment such as he now felt. He could remember but not recapture the old gnawing unquiet, even though he was no less awake to its cause and understood that his journeys were by no means ended. Apart from the relief of the sacrifice, he was curiously comfortable in the loss of his eyesight. He had pledged himself not to work, ever again; now keeping his vow could not entail any more struggle. The visible world was rich in beauties, but in his memory they were unfadingly stored. Never again could a chance view of tools give him pain, neither could he deliberately inflict pain on himself by going to see carved stone and wood. In his darkness he might finger gauge, knife, or shape and surface wrought of them, with a gentle melancholy, but there would be no more aching, hungering, thirsting after any of that. And he joyed so warmly in folk's goodness—it was not that he merely appreciated the benefits to himself. His hosts knew by christened name every member of his kindred, ancestors, and children, and discussed them with him as they might old friends. He had never told them his surname, or where he had been born, and they also respected the secrecy of the quest that had sent him wandering.

So really it was only a question of time when they should ask why his nameless search had never led him to the famous shrine of Bedesford in Anglemere—for he had listed more than once all the holy places he had seen, and his benefactors had the names of these as pat as those of his family. In a way it was strange that this happened no earlier than it did. Edwin saw another sign in the coincidence.

A small company of respectable pilgrims came and craved a night's shelter, and told of a great Easter celebration which was to be held at St. Hand's-of-Cloudsway, partly in honor of that cathedral's completion. They themselves were aiming to attend it.

Then Edwin knew that he, too, was permitted, indeed meant to go, for he could not see the completed Cathedral. The pilgrims were willing to take him. None of them were over young or strong, so that they had allowed themselves ample time. A man who, though blind, was in full command of his feet, would not greatly delay them, nor prove much of a burden.

Thus it fell out that his hosts did not oppose his going as he had dreaded. Had he not been so eager of himself, they might even have urged him on, confident that whatever it was he desired would be granted at the one great shrine his wanderings had thus far missed out. There was no likelihood that they would ever meet again in this life. He could not so much as express his gratitude adequately. Angels' tongues and eloquence would not have sufficed, he felt.

Nonetheless their parting was not harrowing, but took place in quiet and cordial good cheer.

CHAPTER 4

SAINT HAND

THE QUALITY of his youth seemed to have returned to him, which had inclined everyone to be his friend. The other pilgrims, whom one might have thought preoccupied with their own ailments, defaults, and hopes, took Edwin to their hearts and were at unceasing pains to consider his ease and pleasure. When they branched off the London road, where the winding path ascends Cloudsway Ridge to run along its crest until level with the cathedral, they began to describe for his benefit all that could be seen.

"You can tell we have now passed into the district of the wonder-working Hand. The little river below shines gold and glass. The pasture lands are green and succulent. The bare brown plow-broken earth looks so rich—it is like filling your belly with good heavy pudding to gaze on it. Beyond this hillside that we are on, the land spreads mostly flat for miles. Ay, there are forests too, but the fertile plain has the upper hand. There are many, many roads—at least two that are fit for wagons, so far as one can judge from up here. Oh, there are some wagons creeping round a bend, like beetles they look—far ahead—now they have gone. Ay, we can see some tiny horsemen now, their spears bravely glinting— without these we might not have marked their movement. We can see no one working. Anyone going on foot will long since have outdistanced us. There are some houses here and there, but nothing that looks like a hostelry. So it cannot be far now. Half a day's walk from here, they told us at the turnpike, remember. So maybe we shall get to Cloudsway Waste before nightfall."

But this they did not accomplish, aged and footsore as they all were. When dusk drew near they took shelter in a hut made of boulders, within a square enclosure of more boulders and heaped thorn, and propped between some crooked ash trees to one side of the Cloudsway path. The hut had earth banks along both sides for beds, a stone-lined hearth, and an ancient cheese box containing a half cheese scarcely younger. There was plenty of brushwood all round, and a trickle of spring water near by, so that any pilgrims having miscalculated their distance, or overtaken by bad weather, were perfectly safe here for a night or so. They talked little, each thinking ahead, envisaging the festival.

Before the darkness was very old or they had settled down to sleep there were footsteps and barking outside, and a man with two dogs and a pine torch came in. He was one of the valley cotters, he said, whose duty it was to look after the hut. They had been seen from below, and he had come up with additional refreshments and a warning. He guessed they had become confused with the dates. This was Saturday night and Easter Sunday was tomorrow.

Thus the pilgrims' strength was revived into fever of haste. Their very thanks were stammered hurriedly.

The timely herald sounded middle-age of voice. Edwin made no move to retreat from the area of warmth which told him his face was well in the light of hearth and torch, wondering whether a man settled so close to Bedesford would recognize him whom he was almost certain to have known by sight in the old days.

But he would not have known himself. His hair was all white. The beard which before his pilgrimage he had never sported, was straight as goat's wool, only thicker and softer, matted and food soiled in patches, else it, too, had been white as snow. You could not see his mouth until he opened it. His eyebrows were still dark, but the creased twitching skin of the eyelids was darker. In the last few months the constant use of a staff had bent and bowed him until now he was no longer able to straighten his back. A small man all his life, now he appeared tiny, and most frail. "Blind Edwin," they called him. There were many men called Edwin in the world. How many were still alive that would have recognized the mark of the Finding up his right forearm?

So they went on, admonishing each other all the while to control their forward straining and step circumspectly, lest they stumble and fall or tire themselves out and be late all the same. There was half a moon and neither rain nor wind. The cold, happily, was not freezing, and acted merely as a spur.

Thus it was given them to see the sun rise from the Easterwoods, and tell Edwin about it. Cloudsway Waste, with Bedesford and Flemington to either side of it, lay in plain view, composed of soft slate-colored shadings. The cathedral spires were the first objects to catch and appropriate the light. The pilgrims were in incoherent disagreement as to how to describe this to Edwin: if gold were white, or whiteness golden, then they would say that was what it was made of, the holy Hand of Anglemere. Ay, and that was just exactly what it minded one of, they cried, a great fair hand at once poised in benediction and pointing up, upward.

Edwin's heart beat so hard and loud as he had not thought an old man's could. Not in this manner had it beaten when he feared it might burst under the effort of climbing. He asked whether there were three towers or but two. Of course there were three! Someone shook him in affectionately feigned impatience: how could the great church have looked like a hand otherwise?

The throbbing inside him melted, flowed out, merged with a vast surrounding palpitation: the bells of Cloudsway Waste had set up a majestic tolling, calling, hailing, drawing them nigh.

The pilgrims went down on their stiff, night-palsied knees and rendered up thanks to God and St. Francis for having brought them safely hither. They rose and prepared to descend what were called the Pilgrims' Steps, down to the Wode bank, where, Edwin learned, there was a bridge leading straight across to St. Francis' churchyard. Down they went, stumbling and slithering and attempting to be each other's brakes, sending before them cataracts of sand and rubble, calling to each other in breathless mutual encouragement.

"Now it is sunny day, Blind Edwin. All the people in their brightest finery are flocking inside. We shall be just in time, only that we will not get good places, but what matter. Oh, would that you could see it all. The red-gold sun is behind the cathedral now, so that it stands in a blazing halo. And where the river flows close to it, near the western end, its glories are doubled, shining also in the water—"

The bells had stopped. Edwin felt cold again. Without needing to be told, he knew that they had stepped into the shadow of the cathedral. Never, he thought, would he be able to thank God enough for the new perceptions come to him in blindness. The infinite blackness of his sight and the depths of coolness in which he was thus suddenly steeped gave every fiber of him knowledge of a magnificence to which working eyes had been too limited and object fettered to do justice. Into the silence now burst angelic singing of monks. There was no time to walk the circuit of the cathedral, praying, thrice over, as they had meant to do. God would forgive their impatience to be with Him. Again they knelt, in the porch, and kissed St. Francis' doorstep.

"Look," they whispered, crossing themselves, upon rising. "See the cherub faces, like a row of beads worked in the arch of the doorway— and the deer heads where the arc starts and ends—why deer, think you? —oh, and there—"

In this wise step by step Edwin came to hear of much that he had never seen or imagined. By and by they began to name things that were known to him. Then he did suffer a few pangs of hopeless, longing curiosity. Still it was not like a home-coming to old places peopled by ghosts. Where he was, as he was, he missed no Jeanne, no healthy Luke, no Brother Laurentius, and no officiating abbot. His sense of well-being, as in a blithe but uneventful dream, was undisturbed. Had he been able to see, the splendidly irradiated high altar and the Easter Sepulcher under bolsters and garlands of all the spring flowers would have been too far away for him. As it was, he could even make believe that he smelled the flower fragrance through the incense and honeyed melting of wax.

They were sidling along the west wall, following the contours of the front tower's inner supporting piers, pointing, whispering, crossing themselves, and holding fast to one another all the while. Edwin could tell that the kneeling congregation left only the narrowest of lanes for them to pass along. Presently some turned and remonstrated with angry hissing. Someone rose and came up to them.

"Are ye Turks that ye know not how to bear yourselves in God's House during Holy Mass?"

"We cannot see anything—we are old and sick, each one of us. We have wandered for many weeks without resting," Edwin's companions whispered in confused simultaneous appeal. "All through the night we walked, hoping to get here in time—"

The others appeared to reflect and take pity on them.

"Step very quietly, then. There is no pushing you farther to the front or center, but I know a little place whence you will be able to see the Hand when it comes to the showing. Look, here you can kneel right under the holy St. Francis on the Shelf, the Unfinished, where he rests on his clouds of birds in the recess hollowed out of yonder pier. Now keep very quiet and disturb nothing—hush!"

All sound save the celebrant's voice and its tidal echoes had become stilled. Edwin's friends again knelt cumbrously, plucking at his sleeve to make him do likewise. But he edged a little farther first. He must touch at least the foot of his St. Francis' shelf. His useless eyes had filled with tears, he felt so moved and honored by that appellation, "The Unfinished." There was a smell of whitewash and paint, and he was pleased because he liked that, but thought nothing of it otherwise. He was not to know that their guide had accompanied his last words with a warning gesture at a medley of ladders and dismantled planks which leaned, slanting up toward the gallery, in the corner beside the niche-bearing pier.

Slight as he was, and for all the hesitant delicacy of his groping, the little blind man upset the tangle of workmen's leavings when he ran into it.

A gasp went up from the congregation in his vicinity. Edwin could tell what was happening, but not in which direction to flee or how to protect himself. He stumbled back into the close-packed, kneeling bodies, and in the very act of falling received upon his head the blow of a scaffolding standard.

Nobody else was hurt, the long piece of timber rolled off Edwin, stayed by a dozen warding hands. He was groaning in unconsciousness. There was no room to lay him flat nor light to see. A call for a priest was passed along. Meanwhile some men bore Edwin into the center aisle.

Edwin awoke to a renewed, voluminous, and lovely swell of music, which somewhat muted the pain roaring once again through his head. His head was pillowed in somebody's lap. Many others were grouped round him, dimly familiar, yet unknown.

"Wake up, make yourself right awake, Edwin," said the voice of one of his pilgrim companions. "God is near you, in the hands of His priest. You are dying, Edwin. You are to receive the sacrament."

"Edwin," said another, bending very close. "Your name is Edwin Widowson, is not, my son—my father? You are blind, they tell me. Do you know my voice? My dear father, I am Alfred."

"But are you then no longer Abbot, Alfred, that you can be here with me?" Edwin asked weakly.

"Ay, but the Lord Bishop himself is celebrating today's Mass. They said—an old wayfarer—so I came myself from the choir. God be thanked. God be thanked that I may see your face this once more."

"I can see you too," Edwin said in the same feeble, dreamy voice. "You have grown old too. You too have gone gray, my Alfred—my son and my father, as you say." It was only after a moment that he added, wonderingly, "I am blind no more. I can see. I can see the great forest of everlasting stone trees. I can see it all."

"Now I will confess you," Alfred said gently. "There may not be a great deal of time, Edwin Widowson."

"I cannot confess," said Edwin.

"I should have said I will absolve you," said the Abbot close to his father's ear. "For what you will not confess is known to me. Do you hear. I stand surety Our Lord will forgive you. Nay, He *hath* forgiven you, if it be truly so, that your eyes have shed their late veiling. Look,

look about you and *understand* that He hath most surely forgiven you."

"But I must not be saved," Edwin said as before. "I promised, I promised your poor mother. I sinned so greatly to make her my wife and so as to be answerable to God for her soul. And then when it came to the end she died, damned. I promised. I promised to join her in Hell. She is waiting for me, trustfully. I will not be sneaked through the crack in the door of Paradise—with Jeanne waiting and waiting in the flames, through all eternity."

"Our Lord will forgive and redeem you both, I trow, despite yourselves," said the priest in a trembling voice. "What

For Edwin was struggling to raise himself a li coming out of his nostrils and ears, and he did choke and spit just now. Alfred helped him adj new angle, Edwin's gaze was drawn straight u partly rendered indistinct by taut-strung skein tral crossing. "This is not Jacob's tower," Edw uneasily.

"But do you not remember—" the Abbot be

In the middle of the lowest tower story, falling light, a square of darkness opened, thought. And therein became disclosed an not for this wicked sinner Edwin Widowso the same. He had long golden hair, the a curving white wings. His face was no bi he was still so far off, but it was brightest lo down upon the dying flesh so kindly. In thing that glittered. The chanting rose melody. And right down, dipping towa censer which the angel swung by a long, fine, lustrou ing it fly to and fro the whole length of the nave, and bring and leave clouds of pearly mist and heavenly spices.

Thus Edwin Widowson of Bedesford died happy in the certitude of forgiveness and all-healing Good, the while—so vast is St. Hand's—the service went on to its conclusion undisturbed.

But the angel did not wait to come down until the Resurrection was proclaimed, for he was young and full curious as to the nature of the irregular, pigmy commotion he had witnessed from his lofty distance. He had not even spared time to take off the white robes from over his novice's garb, albeit they had become stained and musty in the narrow tower chamber. One wing he held clamped under his arm, the other, somewhat askew, was still fastened to his shoulder, and the golden wig showed his own hair through its disarray. Perhaps it was not entirely without design that, thus distinguished and recognizable, he thrust himself through the crowds, whose Easter he had helped make memorable. The pleasing, unaware modesty of his mien broke up in agitation on sight of the Abbot kneeling beside a dead beggarman, whose hand he held clasped between his own.

"Oh, Reverend Father!" he whispered, for his youth was in no wise inured as yet to the thought and the spectacle of death, and he also sank down upon the pavement.

"I bless you," said the Abbot, "for that this poor old man thought you were what you portrayed. Look," he said, and showed the lad Edwin's hand, which was still warm and still flexible. "See this hand, so old, so worn, so calloused and gnarled and beautiful. Small and weak is it not? Especially here, with stone towering all around us. It is with hands like this one that we make cathedrals great as mountains, and move Heaven and Earth."

He kissed the hand and placed it on Edwin's breast, where its fellow was already reposed.

There, it is dawning. God be with you and with us, Pilgrim.